THE BLACK HALO

Iain Crichton Smith was born in Glasgow in 1928 and raised by his widowed mother on the Isle of Lewis before going to Aberdeen to attend university. As a sensitive and complex poet in both English and Gaelic, he published more than twenty-five books of verse, from *The Long River* in 1955 to *A Country for Old Men*, posthumously published in 2000. In his 1986 collection, *A Life*, the poet looked back over his time in Lewis and Aberdeen, recalling a spell of National Service in the fifties, and then his years as an English teacher, working first in Clydebank and Dumbarton and then at Oban High School, where he taught until his retirement in 1977. Shortly afterwards he married, and lived contentedly with his wife, Donalda, in Taynuilt until his death in 1998. Crichton Smith was the recipient of many literary prizes, including Saltire and Scottish Arts Council Awards and fellowships, the Queen's Jubilee Medal and, in 1980, an OBE.

As well as a number of plays and stories in Gaelic, Iain Crichton Smith published several novels, including *Consider the Lilies* (1968), *In the Middle of the Wood* (1987) and *An Honourable Death* (1992). In total, he produced ten collections of stories, all of which feature in this two-volume collection, except the Murdo stories, which appear in a separate volume, *Murdo: The Life and Works* (2001).

Kevin MacNeil was born and raised on the Isle of Lewis and educated at the Nicolson Institute and the University of Edinburgh. A widely published writer of poetry, prose and drama, his Gaelic and English works have been translated into eleven languages. His books include *Love and Zen in the Outer Hebrides* (which won the prestigious Tivoli Europa Giovani International Poetry Prize), *Be Wise Be Otherwise*, *Wish I Was Here* and *Baile Beag Gun Chrìochan*. He was the first recipient of the Iain Crichton Smith Writing Fellowship (1999–2002).

Iain Crichton Smith

THE BLACK HALO

The Complete English Short Stories

1977–98

EDITED BY

KEVIN MACNEIL

Birlinn

First published in Great Britain in 2001 by
Birlinn Ltd
West Newington House
10 Newington Road
Edinburgh EH9 1QS

www.birlinn.co.uk

The publishers acknowledge subsidy from the
Scottish Arts Council
towards the publication of this volume

ISBN 1 84158 171 2

British Library Cataloguing-in-Publication Data
A catalogue record for this book is available on
request from the British Library

Typeset by Antony Gray
Printed and bound by Omnia Books Ltd, Bishopbriggs

Contents

MR TRILL IN HADES

SELECTED STORIES

UNCOLLECTED STORIES

Editor's Acknowledgements

First of all, I would like to thank Donalda Smith, whose support during my period of tenure as inaugural Iain Crichton Smith Writing Fellow has given me some idea as to why she was such an inspiration to her late husband.

I want to express my most sincere thanks to the following for their many, many efforts on behalf of this book: Neville Moir, Stewart Conn, Helen Templeton, Andrew Simmons, Hugh Andrew, Gavin Wallace, David Linton, David McClymont and Morna Maclaren.

Grant F. Wilson's *A Bibliography of Iain Crichton Smith* has been indispensable.

I must also thank the staff of the National Museum of Scotland (Edinburgh), the Mitchell Library (Glasgow), and the Scottish Poetry Library (Edinburgh) for their helpfulness.

Every effort has been made to track down all of Iain Crichton Smith's English-language stories, but, given how phenomenally prolific Iain was, I must accept the possibility that these volumes are not quite complete. If any reader knows of a story by Iain Crichton Smith that is not included in these volumes (other than those stories in Stewart Conn's recent edition of *Murdo: the Life and Works*) I would be most grateful if they would get in touch with me via the publisher, in order that any such story might be included in future editions.

Finally, I want to acknowledge that working on these volumes has been a genuine labour of love and I wish to dedicate my own efforts to the late Iain Crichton Smith.

from
THE HERMIT
and other stories

For Donalda
with love

The Hermit

One day a hermit came to live in or rather on the edge of our village. The first we knew about it was when we saw the smoke rising from one of the huts that the RAF had left there after the war. (There is a cluster of them just outside the village, tin corrugated huts that had never been pulled down, though the war was long over and their inhabitants had returned to their ordinary lives in England and other parts of Scotland.)

Shortly afterwards, Dougie who owns the only shop in the village told me about the hermit. The shop of course is the usual kind that you'll find in any village in the Highlands and sells anything from paraffin to bread, from newspapers to cheese. Dougie is one of the few people in the village that I visit. He served in Italy in the last war and has strange stories about the Italians and the time when he was riding about in tanks. He's married but drinks quite a lot: he doesn't have a car but goes to town every Saturday night and enjoys himself in his own way. However, he has a cheerful nature and his shop is always full: one might say it is the centre of gossip in the village.

'He's an odd looking fellow,' he told me. 'He wears a long coat which is almost black and there's a belt of rope around him. You'd think in this warm weather that he'd be wearing something lighter. And he rides a bicycle. He sits very upright on his bicycle. His coat comes down practically to his feet. He's got a very long nose and very bright blue eyes. Well, he came into the shop and of course I was at the counter but he didn't ask for his messages at all. He gave me a piece of paper with the message written on it. I thought at first he was dumb – sometimes you get dumb people though I've never seen one in the village – but he wasn't at all dumb for I heard him speaking to himself. But he didn't speak to me. He just gave me the paper with the messages written on it. Cheese, bread, jam and so on but no newspapers. And when he got the messages and paid me he took them and put them in a bag and then he put the bag over the handlebars and he went away again. Just like that. It was very funny.

'At first I was offended – why, after all, shouldn't he speak to me? – but then I thought about it and I considered, Well, as long as he can pay for the messages why shouldn't I give them to him? After all he's not a Russian spy or a German.' He laughed. 'Though for all he said he might as well be. But I don't think he is. He wasn't at all aggressive or anything like that. In fact I would say he looked a very mild gentle sort of man. The other people in the shop thought he was a bit funny. But I must say that after you have travelled you see all sorts of people and you're not surprised. Still, it was funny him giving me the paper. He wore this long coat almost down to his feet and a piece of rope for a belt. I don't know whether his coat was dirty or not. He looked a very contented sort of man. He didn't ask for a newspaper at all, or whisky. Some people who are alone are always asking for whisky but he didn't ask for any. All he wanted was the food. He had a purse too and he took the money out of the purse and he gave it to me. And all this time he didn't say anything at all. That has never happened to me before but I wasn't surprised. No, I'm telling a lie. I was surprised but I wasn't angry. They say he's living in one of the RAF huts and he doesn't bother anybody. But it's strange really. No one knows where he's come from. And when he had got his messages he got on to this old bicycle and he went away again. He sits very upright on his bicycle and he rides along very slowly. I never saw anyone like him before. It's as if he doesn't want to speak. No, it's as if he's too tired or too uninterested to speak. Most people in the shop speak all the time – especially the women – but he wasn't like that at all. Still if he can pay for his messages he can be a Russian for all I care.' And he laughed again. 'There are some people in the village who don't pay for their messages but I can't say that about him. He paid on the nail. And after all, in my opinion, people talk too much anyway.'

2

That evening, a warm, fine evening, I was out at a moorland loch with my fishing rod, pretending to fish. I do this quite often, I mean I pretend to fish, so that I can get away from the village which I often find claustrophobic. I don't really like killing things, and all I do is hold the rod in my hand and leave it lying in the water while I think of other things and enjoy the evening. Out on the moor it is very quiet and there is a fragrance of plants whose names I do not know. I might mention here that I was once the local headmaster till I retired from school a few years ago, and I live alone since my wife died.

I was born and brought up in the village but in spite of that I sometimes find it, as I have said, claustrophobic and I like to get away from it and fishing is the pretext I use. When people see you sitting down dangling a rod in the water they think you are quite respectable and sensible whereas if you sat there and simply thought and brooded they would think you eccentric. It's amazing the difference a long piece of wood makes to your reputation among your fellow-men. After all if I never catch anything they merely think I am a poor fisherman and this is more acceptable than to think me silly.

So I sit there by the loch with the rod dangling from my hand and I watch the sun go down and I smell the fragrance of the plants and flowers and I watch the circles the fish make in the water as they plop about the loch. Sometimes if there are midges I am rather uncomfortable but one can't have every-thing and quite a lot of the time there are no midges. And I really do like to see the sun setting, as the mountains ahead of me become blue and then purple and then quite dark. The sunsets are quite spectacular and probably I am the only person in the village who ever notices them.

So I was sitting by the lochside when I saw the hermit at a good distance away sitting by himself. I knew it was the hermit since there was no loch where he was and no other person from the village would sit by himself on the moor staring at nothing as the hermit was doing. He was exactly like a statue – perhaps like Rodin's 'Thinker' – and as Dougie had said he looked quite happy. I nearly went over to talk to him but for some reason I didn't do so. If it had been anyone from the village I would have felt obliged to do so but as I didn't know the hermit I felt it would be all right if I stayed where I was. Sometimes I watched him and sometimes I didn't. But I noticed that he held the same pose all the time, that statue-like pose of which I have just spoken. I myself tend to be a little restless after a while. Sometimes I will get up from the lochside and walk about, and sometimes I will take out a cigarette and light it (especially if there are midges), but I don't have the ability to stay perfectly still for a long period as he obviously had. I envied him for that. And I wondered about him. Perhaps he was some kind of monk or religious person. Perhaps he had made a vow of silence which he was strictly adhering to. But at the same time I didn't think that that was the case.

At any rate I sat there looking at him and sometimes at the loch which bubbled with the rings made by the fish, and I felt about him a queer sense of destiny. It was as if he had always been sitting where he was sitting now, as if he was rooted to the moor like one of the Standing Stones behind him whose purpose no one knew and which had been there forever. (There are in fact Standing Stones on the moor though no one knows what they signify or where they came from. In the summer time you see tourists standing among them with cameras but it was too late in the evening to see any there now.) I thought of what Dougie had said, that the hermit was not in the habit of buying whisky, and I considered this a perceptive observation. After all, lonely people do drink a lot and the fact that he didn't drink showed that he was exceptional in his own way. It might also of course show that he didn't have much money. Perhaps he was not a monk at all, but a new kind of man who was able to live happily on his own without speaking to anyone at all. Like a god, or an animal.

All the time that I had been looking at him he hadn't moved. And behind him the sun was setting, large and red. Soon the stars would come out and the pale moon. I wondered how long he would stay there. The night certainly was mild enough and he could probably stay out there all night if he wished to. And as he obviously didn't care for other people's opinions he might very well do that. I on the other hand wasn't like that. Before I could leave the village and sit out by myself I had to have a fishing rod even though I didn't fish. And people in the village knew very well that I didn't fish, or at least that I never brought any fish home with me. Still, the charade between me and the villagers had to be played out, a charade that he was clearly too inferior or superior to care about. In any case there were no new events happening in the village apart from his arrival there and therefore I thought about him a lot. It was almost as if I knew him already though I hadn't spoken to him. It was as if he were a figment of my imagination that had taken shape in front of me. I even felt emotions about him, a mixture of love and hate. I felt these even though I had only seen him once. Which was very odd as I had always thought myself above such petty feelings.

Sometimes I thought that I would take a book out with me and read it in the clear evening light, but that too would have made me appear odd. Fishing didn't matter but reading books did, so I had never done that. The hermit wasn't reading a book but I knew that if he had thought about it and were a book reader he would have taken his book out with him and not cared what people thought of him. He wasn't a prisoner of convention. I on the other hand had been a headmaster here and I could only do what I thought they expected of me. So I could dangle a rod uselessly in the water – which I thought absurd – and I couldn't read a book among that fragrance, which was what would have suited me better. After a while – the hermit still sitting throughout without moving – I rose, took my rod, and made my way home across the moor which was red with heather.

When I arrived back at the house Murdo Murray was as usual sitting on a big stone beside the house he was building. He has been building this house for five years and all that he has finished is one wall. Day after day he goes out with his barrow to the moor and gathers big solid stones which he lays down beside the partially finished house. As usual too he was wearing his yellow canvas jersey.

'Did you catch anything?' he asked and smiled fatly.

'No,' I said, 'nothing.'

He smiled again. Sometimes I dislike intensely his big red fat face and despise him for his idleness. How could a man start on a project like building a house and take such a long time to do it and not even care what people thought of him or what they were saying about him? Did he have no idea what excellence and efficiency were? But no, he lived in a dream of idleness and large stones, that was his whole life. Most of the time he sat on a stone and watched the world go by. He would say, 'One day there will be a bathroom here and a bedroom there,' and he would point lazily at spaces above the ground around him. Then he would sigh, 'My wife and daughters are always after me, but I can't do more than it is possible for me to do, isn't that right?'

After a while he would repeat, 'No man can do more than it is possible for him to do.'

As a matter of fact, we often wondered what he would do with himself if he ever finished the house. It looked as if he didn't want to finish it. The children of the village would often gather round him, and help him, and he would tell them stories as he sat on a big stone, large and fat. No, he would never finish the house, that was clear, and for some reason that bothered me. I hated to see these big useless stones lying about, as if they were the remnants of some gigantic purpose of the past.

'It's a fine evening,' he said.

'Yes,' I said, 'and there are no midges. Why don't you go out fishing yourself?' I added.

'Me?' he said and laughed. 'I've got enough to do without going fishing.' And he probably believed that too, I thought. He probably believed that he was a very busy man with not a minute to himself, living in the middle of a world of demanding stones.

'If you want any help at any time,' I would say to him, but he would answer, 'No, I'll do fine as I am. If I don't finish the house someone will finish it.' And he lived on in that belief. He shifted his big buttocks about on the stone and said, 'I used to go fishing in a boat as you know but I never fished in the lochs.

And that was a long time ago. Myself and Donald Macleod. We used to go in the boat but I never fished the lochs.'

I felt a tired peace creeping over me and I didn't want to speak. Sometimes it's impossible to summon up enough energy to talk to people, and I had been growing more and more like that recently. I was growing impatient of those long silences when two people would sit beside each other and think their own thought and then finally like a fish surfacing someone would speak, as he was doing now, words without meaning or coherence. Why was it necessary to speak at all?

He was clearly finished for the day, sitting there surrounded by his stones. Perhaps he didn't want to go into the house in case his wife would nag him for not making quicker progress. Or perhaps he was sitting there inert as a mirror on which pictures print themselves. In the late light I thought of him as a man sitting in a cemetery with rough unengraved headstones around him. Perhaps that was what our world was like, a world of rough unengraved headstones, lacking the finished marble quality of the world of the Greeks.

Big rough stones on a moor.

I left him there and went back to my own house.

When I entered I felt as I usually did the emptiness and the order. The TV set, the radio and the bookcases were in their places. The mirrors and ornaments and furniture had their own quiet world which I sometimes had the eerie feeling excluded me altogether. When my wife was alive the furniture seemed less remote than it seemed to be now. Even the pictures on the walls had withdrawn into a world of their own. I often had the crazy feeling that while I was out my furniture was conducting a private life of its own which froze immediately I went in the door and that sometimes I would half catch tables and chairs returning hastily to their usual places in the room. It was all very odd, very disquieting.

I went to the cupboard and poured myself a whisky and then I sat down in my chair after switching on the fire and picking up a book from the bookcase. It was a copy of Browning's poems. Since I retired I had far more time to read books unconnected with my job but I didn't read as much as I thought

I would have done and what I did read was mostly poetry. I would find myself falling asleep in the middle of the day and at other times I would pace about the house restlessly as if I were in a cage which I myself had built.

In the chair opposite me my wife used to sit and she would tell me stories which I hardly ever listened to. 'Kirsty's daughter's gone away to London again. They say that she's walking the streets, did you know?' And I would raise my head and nod without speaking. And she would go on to something else. But most of the time I wouldn't say anything. It didn't occur to me that my wife's remarks required an answer and for a lot of the time I couldn't think of anything to say anyway. Her voice was like a background of flowing water, a natural phenomenon which I had grown accustomed to. Now there was no voice at all in the house except that of the radio or the TV and the only order was that which I imposed on it.

I sipped my whisky slowly and read my Browning. I drank much more now since my wife had died. Not that I actually loved her, at least I didn't think I did. It had never been a large glowing affair, much more a quieter, more continuous fire. We were companions but we weren't lovers. But in those days I didn't drink as much as I do now. I think loneliness and drink must go together, as Dougie said. Browning however is another matter. His poetry has a cheerful tone and apparently he was in love with his wife, or at least so we must believe after that dramatic elopement. I wondered what people would say of me when one day I died in this house as was inevitable. They might perhaps say, 'Well, he was a good headmaster. He was interested in the children,' and then dig a hole and leave me there. On a cold rainy day perhaps. And then they would go back to their homes. But they wouldn't say that I had done much for the village. I hadn't, of course. I had always been a stranger in the village. Just as much as the hermit was. Though I had been born and brought up in it. My thoughts had never been the villagers' thoughts, they aspired to be higher and more permanent than the business of the seasons.

It was strange how quiet I felt the house was, as if I missed that monotonous conversation, as if even yet I could see someone sitting in that chair opposite me. But of course there was no one. Mary was rotting away somewhere else, in the damp ground. In spite of Browning. In spite of the illusion of warmth which the whisky momentarily gave me.

3

The following day I met Kirsty who was on her way to Murdo's house with a cup in her hand. An evil Christian woman. She never misses a sermon or Communion, going about in her dark clothes, with her thin bitter face and the nose from which there is a continual drip like the drip from a tap which needs a washer and which makes an irritating sound in the sink night and day. She has a daughter who appears periodically from London and then goes away again after a stormy period at home. It is said that she works in the streets in Soho but this may be malice since anyone as bitterly Christian as Kirsty is must be brought down to the level of common humanity and given at least one cross to bear in this fallen world.

It wasn't long before she spoke about the hermit.

'It shouldn't be allowed,' she said.

'What shouldn't?' I asked.

'That man living in that hut. Why, he might be a murderer or a thief or a gangster. The police might be after him. I wonder if anyone's thought of that.'

'Oh, I shouldn't think he is any of these things,' I said. 'I'm told he looks very gentle.'

'So do lots of murderers,' she said sharply.

I didn't want to be talking to her. I was listening to the music of the sea which one can hear clearly on a fine summer's day, as this one was. Sometimes when I hear it I don't want to be talking to people at all. What would we do without this ancient unalterable music which lies below our daily concerns and which at the deepest moments of our lives we hear eternally present, with its salty echo?

'And the children,' she said, 'go to school past that hut. He might . . . why, he might . . . '

'He might what?' I asked.

'Well, you see things like that in the newspapers. People like that. Strangers, lonely people. He might give them sweets and . . . '

'I don't think you need to worry about that,' I said. In the old days I wouldn't be talking to her at all but now I would talk to anyone. That was the extent of my downfall, of my hunger. Would it not be better for me to be like the hermit if I had the strength?

After a while she said, 'Some people say that it's love that sent him here.'

'Love?' I asked.

'Yes, the women say that. That he was disappointed in love. That is why they say he won't speak to anyone.'

I nearly laughed out loud. Why should this woman be talking to anyone about love? This bitter salty woman addicted to Christianity? Why, her greatest love was to shake hands with the minister.

'It's possible,' I said. 'It's possible.'

'Well, why else would he not speak to anyone? Aren't we good enough for him? I don't suppose he even goes to church. He has never been, so far. And perhaps where he came from he never went to church either. I think the minister should go and speak to him. If he was led into the ways of God he might improve.'

The music of the sea was growing louder and louder. Why don't you drown her, I pleaded with it. Why don't you extend your salt waters as far as her skinny body and drown her? Why do you allow her to exist to spoil the harmony of your ancient world? She is the thorn in our side. Her confidence, her silly confidence, is the thorn in our side. Her invincible vanity is obscene.

'What does the minister say to that?' I asked her.

'No one has spoken to him about it,' she said.

'Well, then, perhaps you should do that,' I said. 'Perhaps that is your destiny. To bring his soul to God.'

'More than him need to be brought to God,' she said with a wicked sidelong glance. I knew she was getting at me, because I never go to church myself.

'Oh,' I said, 'I'm not a hermit. And how's your daughter?'

'What do you mean?' she asked.

'Oh, I was thinking about the hermit,' I said. I had slid the knife into her for a moment and I was pleased with myself. She had thought I was talking about her daughter haunting the streets of Soho in her hunting leathers, though I couldn't imagine that large gross body exposing itself in a nightclub or walking the yellow streets of London. I almost laughed out loud again.

'Well,' she said, 'I think something must be done about him. What does he do with himself anyway? He may be plotting something. For all we know he may be a spy. And the children should be protected.'

'From what?' I said.

'I told you already from what. But you don't care. Maybe you're a friend of his. I don't know why else you're standing up for him.'

'I'm not standing up for him,' I said. 'I'm only saying that he hasn't bothered anyone.'

'Mm, well, he may do it some day.' And she closed her bitter lips like a trap. 'It's not natural for a man to be going about not speaking to anyone. If a stranger comes to the village he should act like the other people in the village. And anyway he's dirty. Everybody says that. He wears a piece of rope for a belt. And his coat is dirty.'

I nearly said that we are all dirty but I didn't. I just wanted her to go away and leave me alone, to leave this day with its flowers growing wild around us and the sun so warm in the sky. She disfigured the day in her black clothes. And she disfigured the music of the sea. And anyway it was said that when her own daughter was home there was nothing but quarrels between them, and their own house was dirty with half empty coffee cups lying about and her daughter getting up at noon and sometimes later. And sometimes the house was not cleaned for days and weeks. Still one couldn't say these things to her. I wondered how the hermit might have handled her. Perhaps his muteness might have reduced her to an equivalent silence. The triviality of her mind confounded me. And all the time I wished to listen to the music of the sea.

She twisted the cup in her hands and said finally, 'Well, anyway, that's what I say, and remember that I said it when what will happen happens. Things that aren't natural will cause trouble, you mark my words. I'm surprised that you, a professional man, should be standing up for him.'

A few years ago she wouldn't have said that to me. She wouldn't have dared to talk to me in that way. Of course a few years ago I wouldn't have talked to her at all. But now she knew I had no power and no position and she thought she could say what she liked to me. Before my retirement she would have been bowing and scraping and speaking only when she was spoken to and she would have thought it a great honour that I spoke to her at all.

'Anyway,' she said, 'I've got to go to Murdo's house. I've got to borrow a cup of sugar.'

'And you certainly need it,' I said to myself as she walked away. 'I know of no one who needs sugar more than you do.'

Still, one couldn't live on the music of the sea. That was certain. I couldn't understand why she was going on about the hermit. She didn't truly understand as I did the spiritual threat he represented. She was only saying what she did because she had to have something to talk about and it was the same with the other women of the village who had concocted a story of disappointment in love as the reason for the hermit's appearance among us. Naturally when confronted by an inexplicable silence they had to explain that silence in their own way, and in a way flattering to themselves. It was funny that they should not have thought of him as a monk sworn to silence, they had thought of him as a man condemned to silence by love. What vanity, what enormous vanity! As if only women could be responsible for that final silence! Why, I could think of a thousand other things that might have condemned him to silence. He might for instance be a poet or physicist whose world had failed him. It seemed to me highly unlikely that his silence came from a failure in love, except perhaps from a failure of love as far as people in general were concerned, and not exclusively women. Soon, however, a myth would grow up about him that he had left the world he had lived in simply because he had been jilted and that this had perhaps driven him 'beyond the seas' and so on. What a trivial explanation! Only I, I was convinced, knew the meaning of his silence for I partially shared silence with him. Only I knew the depth of the question that he posed. Only I knew the threat his silence was to us.

4

I was born and brought up in this village and there is nothing about it that I do not know. For me it is a processional play with continually changing actors. Some are playing at one time sad parts and then happy ones. There is the tragedy of the Disappearing Daughter, the comedy of the Appearing Son. The young man for some reason puts on the disguise of the middle-aged man and the middle-aged man in turn the guise of the old man. The earth flowers with corn and then becomes bare again. The sky at moments is close and then as far away as eternity. I have seen the people, as if they belonged to the Old Testament, bring water from the well, and later sit down in front of television. I have sat in a small dark desk in the school and then I have sat in the headmaster's study. I have taught the little children about the thunder and the lightning and the autumn moon.

When I was seventeen years old I left the village to go to bare beautiful Edinburgh where I attended university in the large shadow of its history. There I read many books and studied many subjects. There, I, with others of my generation, wondered what the world means and what its destiny is. I have walked down Princes Street among taxis black as hearses and been entranced by the theatrical appearance of the castle where the drama of history repeats itself nightly. That lighting told nothing: it was merely a fairy lighting. In youth one devours everything indiscriminately and ideas arrive like revelations. I have walked among the leaves of autumn tormented by desire and nostalgia as if for a world once known that would never return. I have read and debated there, but the skies had no answer to give, only the bloody answer of past history. As I listen to the sound of the sea here so I listened to the sound of the traffic there and found it senseless. I read whole libraries driven on by my merciless mind and at night I went to plays and to the cinema. One night I met a boy from our village staggering drunkenly about the street but he did not know me. The city is a terrible place of stone and mad music, of white-faced clocks and massive buildings. The city has no meaning at all, and its plays are not real plays, they are sensational potboilers.

There one day in the library I met Mary. I took her to the cinema and then back to her house where in the shadow of her garden her face shone with a greenish light, as if she had caught some demonic plague. Later she was to become my wife. In those days she used to play the violin and she told me she used to ride on horseback down the leafy avenues of Edinburgh. Together we explored the city; much later we married and I brought her to the village. She had no Gaelic and couldn't understand what people were saying unless they spoke English which some of them couldn't do very well. She did not love the seas and moors as I did. We never returned to Edinburgh, mainly because of her. At the time I did not understand that her reason for not returning there was not that she didn't love it but rather that she loved it too much and she couldn't bear having to be parted from it a second time. How self-satisfied I was! She stopped playing the violin. The two of us would sit in the evenings in our respective chairs staring at TV or at each other after I had finished my schoolwork. My schoolwork was my whole life. The little children came to me in all their freshness and were taught. Their sorrows and joys and tendernesses were my own. The secret innermost recesses of their minds were open to me. Life flooded from them to me and daily I was renewed. My life had purpose and meaning and desire. But my wife sat alone in the house in a village which she did not understand – not its secret linguistic recesses, its private clannish corners – and I did not think of her or if I did I put the thought away from me as if it were an unbearable wound. I did not wish to think of the life she led, of the life that she didn't lead. No concerts, theatre, cinemas. She did not have her orchestra as I had, she didn't understand the changing drama, closed to her because she could not speak Gaelic. She was an unwilling bored spectator all her days in this village. I condemned her to imprisonment. She was as much a prisoner as if I had passed sentence on her like a judge.

One day I arrived home unexpectedly from school and found her in the kitchen with the violin in her hand. As soon as she saw me she rushed out of the room with it and put it away again in the room from which she had taken it. I couldn't make out whether in fact she played it when I was away at school or not. She could have been a great violinist, they had said that, and I believed it. But she had given it up for me. And what had she seen in me after all? Perhaps the fatal attraction of the exotic. What is your island like, she would ask me. And I would say, The people are so pleasant and friendly. And then of course there is the sea and the moor. It is always beautiful and always changing. And she had found it boring and uncaring. What was the sea to her? Merely a meaningless mass of water. Then later she was seized by cancer, that terrible disease without music or mercy. Maybe I had condemned her to it. Some nights she would scream with pain and I could do nothing. The violin lay unused in the unused room. Bare loved Edinburgh with its resounding streets was far away. My wife's hair had become grey and hung in wisps from her head. She had nothing to say to me at all and I nothing to her. She would drink whisky and cradle the bottle absently in her arms as if it were a silent violin. And the village went on with its own concerns. What had I done to her? What did life mean after all? Was this what it meant, all it meant? All the books and philosophies, was this what they all came down to after all? All those nights of blazing discussion and debate, was this the end of them? Truly, it was. Truly it was a possible ending that had happened.

5

The following day I talked to the postman. He had brought me an airmail letter from my brother in New Zealand and a catalogue from Athena. Athena is a firm which sells reproductions of paintings by post and I already had quite a lot of these, some by Van Gogh, some by Dali and some by Breughel. My favourite painters are in fact Vermeer and Breughel: I admire Vermeer for the cold mathematical clarity of his paintings and Breughel for the strange spawning fertility of his. Sometimes I myself try to paint but the paintings I have done are vicious and aggressive and inhabited by small murderous animals in an atmosphere of intense silence as of a desert.

The postman is called Hunchbacked John and he takes his time delivering the mail, sometimes stopping here and there for a cup of tea and telling everybody who he's got letters for. He knows of course when there is a letter from the Income Tax people but he is also adept at knowing all other official notifications even when there are no clues on the outside of the envelope. Season after season: spring, summer, autumn, and winter, Hunchbacked John whose gaze is not much above the level of the ground drives fiercely forward on his errands.

I accepted the thin blue letter from him and the catalogue and then asked him if he ever delivered any letters to the hermit.

'Not at all,' he said, 'he never gets any letters. None. From anywhere.'

'That's odd,' I said. Had he seen him?

'Saw him once,' he said. 'He was sitting in front of the door mending an old coat.'

'How had he looked?'

'He looked very contented. He didn't speak to me. I said, "Hello, it's a fine day", but he didn't answer. He just carried on sewing his coat. I think he must have been mending it or putting on a button.'

'And he never got any letters?'

'No, none at all. He doesn't expect any. I can tell. I can tell the ones who get letters. Some people in this village never get any letters, others get a lot of letters. Some people don't expect any letters. The hermit doesn't. You can see by his eyes.'

'By his eyes?'

'Yes, by his eyes. He's a man who has given up expecting any letters.'

For some reason the words so baldly spoken depressed me. What must it be like to expect nothing, not even letters? I myself looked out for the mail every day. Sometimes I would stand at the window watching Hunchbacked John making his way along the road and wondering if he was going to come up the path to my house. Other times I would stand at the door of the kitchen and look down the lobby. I would wait for the letter box to click and then I would watch the white letter drifting on to the mat, like manna from heaven. I would walk down the lobby watching the letter which might after all be an agent for a complete transformation of my life, the letter innocent and packed with joy, or menace. Every day, once a day, I am like a small child waiting to see what Santa Claus has placed for him on the Christmas Tree. Maybe somewhere in the vast world a being known or unknown has decided to write to me, to me alone, with news of the greatest importance. This letter has perhaps travelled the whole world by boat or plane and then finally arrived on this mat in this particular lobby. What magic has taken place? What news lies inside that white square? How could one exist without that opening to the universe? How could one live without that possibility of renewal or resurrection?

I said to him, 'Why don't you . . . '

'Why don't I what?'

'Why don't you pretend you have a letter for him and then you could . . . '

'Why should I do that?' he interrupted bluntly before I had finished.

'Well, you could go to the door and you could see inside his house and see what he does with himself.'

'Oh, I couldn't do that, I couldn't do that.' And then for good measure, 'Oh, I couldn't do that.'

His literal mind repeated the phrases as if he were an old rusty bell.

'Of course not,' I sighed. 'But think . . . '

'No, I couldn't do that.' And he slowly raised his eyes towards me like a gun being swivelled upwards and a light of intelligence dawned in his eyes as if he were to say, 'Yes, I know you. I understand you completely.' But he didn't say anything except, 'I know the ones who will never get letters. The hermit will never get a letter. He has given up. He has given everything up.' What a desolate phrase. I wondered if Hunchbacked John himself ever got any letters, trudging on as he did through all the seasons of the year delivering other people's mail. Looking down at the ground he would see the stones and the changing seasons but he would never receive a letter of his own. It would be like a bank teller perpetually counting other people's money.

How strange the world is and how many different kinds of people there are! Before him we had a postman who rode a bicycle. He was a young boy and he was so careless that if no one was at home he would place the letter under a stone at the door. Another time, because he hadn't closed his bag properly, about twenty letters were blown away on the wind, some of them never recovered. Another time we had a very religious postman but the less said about him the better.

'Well,' he said at last, 'I must be on my way.' I hadn't offered him tea though perhaps that was what he wanted. Not that I particularly wanted to read my brother's letter which was usually nothing more than a statement that he was still alive: he never had any news of the slightest interest to me.

'Well, cheerio just now then,' I said and watched him steadily plodding away with his sturdy limited literal mind and his crooked body. No, of course he wouldn't have the imagination or the daring to do what I had suggested. And yet it would have been interesting. If I had been the postman I would have done it. Such a little white lie. But then much might have been discovered.

Perhaps for instance the hermit's house was full of books like my own. Or perhaps there was nothing at all there, not even furniture. Just the fire and perhaps one table and one chair like those in a meagre painting of Van Gogh's. He too had been a kind of hermit. That was why I liked his work so much, though not as well as I liked Breughel's or Vermeer's. The truth was that I too was like the hermit but without his extreme daring. At least I spoke a language and he didn't. Even that night on the moor I was conscious of the language of the birds which they speak among themselves. Perhaps he wasn't even conscious of that. For everything and everyone has a language except perhaps for the stones which Murdo brings home on his wheelbarrow. Even the sea has a language. Even a violin. Everything has a language but only human beings have learned to hide and not reveal their world with their language. But to have a language and choose not to use it, what a terrible decision that must be! What a terrible burden that must be, to act like a stone and be a human being! What bitter strength it must take to sustain that. What power or immense disgust. Or perhaps what holiness, as if one were talking to God and human language was seen as a slimy repulsiveness, like an old fish quivering in one's hand, like a rotten old jellyfish, phosphorescent and rotting.

6

There is in the village a girl called Janet. She is about eighteen years old, with long black hair, a diamond-pale face, and a marvellous bum. Every morning, cool in her morning suit, she passes my house on her way to the school where she is some sort of clerk though her spelling, according to the new headmaster, is not so good. But what does she need to be a good speller for, with that cool infuriating body, those legs, that bum?

It was a day of steady rain, drip drip, the hole appeared in the ground. The minister was speaking into the high wind, his cloak flapping about him. I could hear carried on the wind, but vaguely, as if they were the last gasps from a dying mouth, words like 'resurrection' and 'eternity'; but I was watching the coffin. We approached after a while that deep narrow hole and each took a tassel and lowered the coffin, hexagonal like a bee's hive, into the earth, into the hole. We lowered it slowly. The wreaths, few and small, were laid near the hole.

And coming home the first person I saw was Janet, her lovely alive body, eel of the day. And it was then that that sickness struck me, ridiculous object of sixty years old. The young girl was a banner, unconscious and engraved, against the stupidity of death. In bed at night I thought of her and I dreamed of that hole in the ground and above it, flourishing like a young tree with buds in its branches, Janet's young body, potent with fruit and blossom.

Every morning she passes my house in the early dew, some-times wearing her yellow dress with its yellow collar, trim and young and cool. Who cares if she can spell or is educated? I create a picture of an Einsteinean mind being put to rout by the movement of a girl's leg or foot, by the motion of her bum. It is a plague that I suffer from, O I know it, I'm old enough to know that, but I'm not old enough to cure myself of it. Where is the remedy for it after all? Mary was never as beautiful as Janet, not even in her youth. Her face always had a serious expression as if she were concerned with some deep problem that she could never solve. Janet's face has no deep problem imprinted on it. It has grown like a blossom, it is itself, it is not concerned with the meaning of the universe, it is as natural as a leaf in the sky. Its coolness is that of the diamond, its perfection its own. I know that I am speaking words without meaning but I cannot stop myself. Language is running away with me because lan-guage cannot explain what I feel, because a young girl's perfection is beyond language, because her perfume uncon-scious and fertile is what language cannot embrace. There are mornings so perfect that language cannot express their perfec-tion since the mornings are so new and our language is so corrupted by evil and distortion and double meanings and used ancient stained blasphemies. To know these mornings is to be young again. O if only I could . . . just once . . . in my youth . . . those legs, those eyes . . . that face. The sickness is delirious and intolerable. It can have no cure. It must only be endured. I have often thought of this. Life and mathematics are different from each other. Problems in mathematics are soluble since mathematics is only a game after all. Problems are insoluble in life since life is more than a game. One can often find no solution to them. The reason why we look for solutions is because we confuse mathematics with life. And that is the worst of all confusions. It is also the confusion that when a problem is spoken it is halfway to being solved. Hermit, wherever you are just now, have you solved your problems because you refuse to speak them? No, all you have done is to take all these problems on your back, since you know there is no solution. Your silence perhaps is the most honourable stance of all. You at least are not a ridiculous old man writing his silly lyrics to a young girl. At least you have saved yourself from that.

7

The day I came home unexpectedly from school and she was cradling the violin on her breast like a child ... That is the image I shall always keep with me. For she couldn't speak Gaelic. And people would sometimes come to the house and speak Gaelic and she couldn't understand them. And her English sounded foreign among all these people. An alien with a violin which she couldn't bring herself to play and which remained silent in that room since no one could appreciate her music. Once a man from the village came to the house and asked if she would play the violin at a local dance. He thought he was doing her a favour bringing her into the middle of things. Her violin – at a village dance. I nearly laughed out loud. The meeting of two worlds in absurdity. Naturally she wouldn't play. She was too shy to. And so the whirligig of time brings in its revenges, its mockeries, its echoes. She had no language at all to speak to them, not even the language of music. For they were used to the melodeon glittering in the moonlight in the open air at the end of the road not in fact far from the hermit's home. Their music was not the music of excellence and rigour, it was the music of abandoned gaiety, amateurish music. But she had been trained in a harder tougher more silent school, where the music was squeezed out of the soul and was not an emanation of the body. And often at night as the sun goes down I hear her voice crying with pain. Sometimes I feel that I am going out of my mind.

I opened my brother's letter from New Zealand. He wrote:

> I hope you are well. We are all well here. I hope you got the photos I sent you recently: Anne in bathing costume with myself and the kids on the beach. Colin is getting to be a great rugby player. I could send you some newspapers but I suppose you wouldn't like them. They are all full of rugby

and I don't think that would interest you. Still, if it would, say the word. The weather here is as good as usual. It's not very unlike the weather in the Old Country. Anne is always asking about you. Do you remember the time we went off fishing and left her and Mary together? Ever since then she asks for you a lot. I suppose you are still reading as much as ever. I don't find much time for reading myself. We are thinking of going to Australia for our holiday later on. Why don't you come out here yourself sometime? You'd be very welcome as you know and we could show you the sights. There's plenty of room in the house. But I suppose you won't come. The plane wouldn't take long to bring you out. The children would like to see their uncle of whom we talk so much. Flora is doing well at school, you would be proud of her. I think she might end up as a teacher some day. She gets good grades in her subjects and she's also good at sport. She was chosen for her hockey team and she had a part in the school play at the end of term. She reads a lot too, like you. You would like her. Well, if you do want the newspapers let me know. But as I say they're mostly about rugby. And if you want to come out you have only to say the word.

Hermit, where are you sleeping tonight. On your stone with your rope about your middle like an ancient monk lying down in the light of the moon?

And Janet, where are you sleeping? In your murderous innocence, also in the light of the moon, not the marble moon of the Greeks but the moon of romance, a moon that transforms you into a princess in a fairy story with a knife between your thighs. Or a poisonous rose.

While the whole village sleeps, the only sound the barking of a dog; the village with its ills and joys, with its closed rancours and its open happinesses, with its ancient sorrows and its lethal struggles, eels everywhere squirming and writhing in that sea of moonlight.

8

I determined to do it and I did it. At three in the morning I got up from my bed and set off to the hermit's hut. Of course I didn't want anyone to see me and that was why I waited till then. The village was not like the city, it would not have people walking about it at that time. People went to bed late – about midnight – but you wouldn't see them again till the late morning. I had never been about at night in the village before, or rather so early in the day. The place was so quiet sleeping under the moonlight. I went along the road: once a cat ran from one side to the other but I saw nothing else and all I heard was the sound of the stream which flowed quietly along to the sea. I didn't know what I was going to see; surely the hermit would be asleep. And in any case his door would be locked. I didn't know why I thought this but I did. I myself have never locked the door but for some reason I was sure that he would lock his. At the place where the huts were it was said that there once used to be a ghost. Once a young man from the village was coming home from the town and he said he saw it. It was walking towards him and its face was green. He arrived at his parents' house in a state of shock. He was home on leave at the time. Shortly afterwards he went away and his ship was blown up in the Pacific and he was drowned. But I wasn't afraid of ghosts and have in fact never believed in them. I didn't even believe in the young man's story.

It was strange to be up and about at that hour in the morning. It almost gave one a feeling of power as if one held the destiny of the village in one's hands, in one's mind. People are so helpless when they are asleep, so defenceless. I felt like a burglar creeping about the night. What treasure was I seeking, what golden hoard? I kept on the grass verge of the road as if it was necessary for me to make as little noise as possible. I wondered what I would say if I met anyone. Perhaps I might say that I couldn't sleep. And that was true. I didn't sleep well. After my wife died I didn't sleep for a month though I took sleeping pills every night. Still, it was unlikely that I would meet anyone.

The village itself looked strange in the moonlight as if it had been painted in yellow. I hated yellow. It reminded me of sickness and of old faces and of autumn and of the neon lights of the city. I felt as if I myself were coloured a sickly yellow, as if I were suffering from some sickness such as jaundice.

Eventually I reached the hut and slowly went up to it. As I have said I didn't know what I was doing. I peered through the window but there was complete darkness. I put my ear to the door as if I were a doctor sounding someone's chest, someone who was dying of an incurable disease. As I did so I saw in the light of the moon that there were names and drawings on the door. The drawings were of naked women and of Cupids and hearts with arrows stuck in them. I tried to imagine those airmen going up into the sky in their planes, all rushing out from the hut and setting off into the blue sky at the time of the Battle of Britain. Of course none of them had done that at all. I was only remembering old films. And on the door too someone had carved the name of Vera Lynn. It was strange to think of the hermit lying in such a hut, as if at any moment he might take wings and set off into the sky, masked and helmeted. Into that freedom, that false freedom. *Per ardua ad astra.* Beyond that hut I could see the Standing Stones shadowy in the moonlight, ancient and undecipherable. The tinny hut looked like an accordion, yellow and black. I wondered whether the hermit was lying there asleep in a bed or on the floor in a blanket. I nearly knocked on the door as if I wanted to ask him a question though I didn't know what I should ask him. Perhaps I should ask him, What is the meaning of the world?

Perhaps in fact he was one of those airmen returned again to the huts out of nostalgia. But I knew this wasn't true. I knew that he had nothing to do with planes or the war. His war was a different one. He had perhaps been wounded in some irretriev-able way and that was why he didn't speak. It would be so easy to take a plane up from that hut and set off into the illimitable blue, it would be too easy. All the time I stood there I didn't hear a sound. For all I knew there was no one there at all. For all I knew the hermit was sleeping outside and watching me at that very moment.

I turned away from the door and made my way home quickly as if someone was after me, as if I was being hunted. I actually began to run, looking behind me to see if anyone was following me, but I didn't see anyone. All there was was the moon high in the sky like a big stone and the shadows and yellowness. When I got to my room I was panting as if I had committed some terrible crime. I lay in my bed sleeplessly thinking of him lying in bed, not realising that a stranger had been looking at him through the window, listening at his door. I was ashamed of myself. I was frightened of something that was happening to me that I did not understand.

9

I don't think I have yet mentioned Kenneth John, though I did intend to, since he becomes important later. Kenneth John is older than me and has been married in the village for many years to a woman he met after he had given up sailing, late in life. He says himself that he has been everywhere, China, Australia, New Zealand, South America. 'In China,' he once told me, 'they leave food for the dead people. They think they will rise again and eat it.' And he looked at me with his small wrinkled face. 'That's right,' he would add, 'they do that. And they leave drink for them as well at the graves. Would you believe that?' And I would pretend that I hadn't heard any of this, since he clearly enjoyed telling an 'educated' man something new.

'Women,' he would say, 'they're no use on board ship. What use are they to any man? Wasn't it a woman who ate the apple? Doesn't it say that in the Bible? And it was because of them that sin came into the world.' At other times he would tell me that Edgar Wallace was the best writer in the world. According to him, he had read all his books.

'But there's nothing in the world like being on a ship on a fine day with the water stretching away from you on all sides, no land to be seen anywhere. In my youth I used to climb up into the sails. Up the masts. And I would look up and the sea was miles below. And sometimes you would see porpoises playing in the water.

'Have you noticed,' he would say earnestly, looking into my face, his thin red nose almost quivering and his teeth, discoloured by tobacco, clearly visible. 'Have you noticed,' he would say, 'that women never play? They're so serious all the time. That's the thing I have against them. Women,' and he would spit on the ground, 'what use are they to man or beast?

'When I came home first I wouldn't have anything to do with the land. I would go up to the town and I would watch the ships coming in and going away. I would stand there for hours and think of all the places the ships might be going to. And it took me all my time not to go on board one of them and sail away in it. But I was married then and I couldn't do that.'

He had pictures of sailing ships in his house and he and his wife would sit by the fire and he would tell me stories and his wife would say nothing much except that at intervals she might sigh heavily and murmur, 'He could have been a captain. He could have been a captain.' They said that she was very hard on him and made sure that he kept the house clean. One day I went in and found that all the pictures of sailing ships had been taken down and new wallpaper put up. I never saw them again. In the East, he would say, the women went about with veils on their faces and they would look down at the ground. They would never look up at you at all. They were very obedient in the East. 'But when I got married first I didn't want to stay in the house at all. I would walk about the village and sometimes I would go out fishing on a boat that I had. But it was like being on a pond and I gave it up. There was no excitement at all, no excitement.

'But I'll tell you about women. They have no humour in them. The things they worry about, like whether you are wearing a good suit or not, things like that, and whether the floor is clean. And one day I broke an ornament and she went on about it for months.

'And why do we settle down? Let me ask you that. You're an educated man. You tell me that.'

'I don't know,' I said.

'Well, I'll tell you,' he said, his little rusty moustache quivering. 'It's because we're frightened. That's the reason.

And don't let anyone tell you different. That's the reason and the only one. There was a boy once who went up to the top of the mast and he started screaming. He was frightened, you see, looking down into the water. That's the way we are. But I was never frightened up in the mast. Never.

'We're frightened, that's why we take up with women. I used to go into port and enjoy myself and get drunk. There was a lot of fighting and drinking in those days. But I would have ended up as a drunkard, you see. But in those days I didn't care. And so, I thought to myself, do I want my freedom so that I'll be a drunkard? And what do you think is the best thing?' he asked.

'To have your freedom and not be a drunkard,' I said.

'You can't have the two of them,' he said. 'Not at all. You can't have the two of them. Women. They've caused all the trouble in the world. We're frightened and we don't know what the world is about. That's the truth. No one knows what's right and what's wrong. You read books and you find that out. When I came home first I didn't want to have anything to do with the land. I was like a man in a cage. I used to go up and down the village as if I was on the deck of the ship. Why can't we have a house on water, on the sea? They have that in some countries. That's what I would like, a house on the sea. They have that in China and some places.' And he would spit in the fire. And then he would say, for his stories were always the same, 'Do you know the strangest thing that ever happened to me? One night I went into this bar in Australia. Myself and some of the boys from the ship. And do you know who I saw there sitting in the bar? It was Squinty. You remember Squinty, he had a squint eye. Well, he saw me and I was going over to speak to him but he turned away from me. He wouldn't even recognise me. He was playing dominoes with some people and he was wearing an old ragged coat. And he came from the same village as me. He didn't want the people at home to know what he had become. He had gone to the dogs, you see. To the dogs. He must have been drinking hard. A lot of these boys never write home, you know. No one hears of them, they go to the dogs and they drink. Well, he didn't speak to me and he had been brought up with me. And he was drinking wine. Imagine. He was like a Frenchman, drinking wine. And he just turned away from me. It was a queer thing.

'Well, that night, I went into the lavatory in that pub and I looked in the mirror that was there. I had been drinking, you see, and my face was red and my eyes were red. And I said to myself, "Where are you heading for, boy? Where are you sailing your ship?" That was what I said, "Where are you heading for, boy?" And that was why I got married. My wife is older than me and she had been looking after her parents, that was why she didn't marry before. She was very sweet to me at first, she wouldn't say anything about my suit then. Nothing but, "You do what you like, Kenneth John, you always do that anyway." That's what she used to say. But then she began to buy things for me, handkerchiefs and things like that. Then she would buy shirts and at last she bought me a suit. And ever since then I've been in a cage. Women. What can you say about them? They brought sin into the world. The Bible teaches you that. But you've never seen a woman on board ship, have you? They would be no good. They would be putting on their lipstick while water was coming in in a storm. You have to have some give and take on board a ship if you don't want a fight. That's what I say.'

And his wife would murmur, as she sat by the fire, 'He could have been a captain, you know. He could have been a captain.'

10

On a fine day our village looks very peaceful and lovely. The blue sea is in the distance, with perhaps a ship passing by, smoke coming out of its funnel, and behind us there is the moor which is wine-red with heather. In the early morning you can hear cockerels crowing from here and there, their red claws sunk in the earth, their coloured brassy heads extended. Sometimes too you hear a dog barking. The Clamhan, in front of the house, may be hammering a post into the ground or mending a net in front of his door. Or at this time of year you may see people going down to the corn which is yellow in the sunlight. As the sun comes up, small boys start running about. As the day

passes and it gets hotter, you may see them building tents. I
don't know why they do it, but on the very hottest days you will
find them sitting inside these tents and trying to make fires just
like Red Indians.

And beside me Murdo sits regarding his unfinished house.

Practically every morning I go over and talk to him after I
have got up and have had my breakfast (which usually consists
of a cup of tea and a slice of bread). I don't eat much for
breakfast. I offer as usual to help him but he says as usual that
he doesn't need any help. His two daughters who have now left
school are usually going about the outside of the house with
pails and pans. They are not pretty, are in fact spotty with very
thin legs.

Today he tells me about a big stone that he has taken home
on his barrow the day before.

'There were hundreds of worms below it,' he tells me.
'Hundreds of them. All so red. I could have killed them all but
I left them for the birds.'

I thought: the birds will make songs from them. There are in
fact few animals to be found around here. No foxes, rabbits,
weasels. Hardly any wild life at all. And no trees. I miss the
trees. That is why I often think of Edinburgh. For some reason
I specially associate trees with university days. But this is a bare
bleak island especially in winter when it's wet and misty.

'What are you doing today?' Murdo asks.

'Oh, I've got a few letters to answer,' I say. I have no croft and
this means that time passes very slowly for me. I am driven to
reading and writing, since I don't visit many houses in the
village apart from Dougie's. As I'm talking to Murdo the idea
comes to me that I could buy milk from Janet's parents. They
sell milk and are one of the few families in the village that have
a cow. It strikes me as a good idea. In the distance I see a cow
eating some clothes on a clothes line at the far end of the village:
that was what brought the idea into my mind. I can't make out
whether it is Stork's house or that of the two sisters Maclean,
one of whom has been lame all her life, practically, from polio.
Sometimes I find the mornings here exhilarating and most
beautiful; other times I find them boring. There is a rhythm

about the place, a slow deep sometimes exasperating rhythm. People talk slowly, chewing every word and releasing it as if it were a precious possession whose extinction in air is to be mourned. Language almost becomes like tobacco which is as much chewed as smoked.

'Ah, well,' says Murdo, 'it's going to be another fine day.' And I say that in my opinion it probably almost certainly will be. And I know that all we are doing is making sounds, that silence embarrasses us after a while, and we are not using language at all but making comforting motions. I look down at Murdo as he sits on his stone: there are red hairs in his nostrils. He looks like a large plump red animal. He is, as I have said before, like a man surrounded by tombstones. And I try to penetrate his mind but I often feel that he has no mind to penetrate. He has never thought about the world, about its meaning. He is, it seems to me, perfectly suited to his environment in a way that I shall never be. His environment makes on him the few demands that he can easily cope with. Day after day he rises from his bed and day after day he takes out his barrow and brings his stones home. It is almost as if he has forgotten what the stones are for, as if the house itself which is his ultimate aim has receded into the distance and it is only now and again that he recalls that the purpose of gathering the stones is for building the house. A slight breeze ruffles his canvas jersey which moves slightly about his big belly.

After a while he says, 'Isn't that Kirsty there setting off to the shop?' It is indeed. Then he says, 'I hear that her daughter is in London.' He looks at me slyly. 'I hear she's on the streets there. Someone from the village saw her.'

I was in London myself once. I remember it as a vast place glittering with cinemas and theatres and people with braziers selling nuts late at night on the streets. That was a long time ago when I was at a Conference.

A long time ago too Murdo was in the War, in the Fusiliers he says himself. He says that he didn't like the French, that they were tricky and lazy, not like the Germans. I can't imagine him ever having done anything that required rapid movement but I suppose that he must have been young once as we all were.

'Well,' he says at last, 'this won't do,' and he levers himself slowly to his feet and goes to his barrow. His hands must now be cracked and broken with the weight of the vast stones that he brings home.

'And I'd better be going too,' I say. At least he has something definite to do every day: I don't even have that. He spits on his hands and then takes the handles of the barrow and sets off to the moor again. I watch him as he plods steadily along. Then I turn back into the house.

After a while I take out my writing pad and my pen and write to my brother. The phrases flow easily. They are always the same phrases. My brother is a salesman in New Zealand and I really don't know him very well. Even when we were young I didn't know him: he was much more active than me and though younger he always beat me in fights. I was amazed at times by his aggressiveness and frightened by his mad possessiveness for property. We used to play sometimes in the attic of my parents' house and he would turn somersaults over the rafters which I couldn't do.

Now I have little to say to him but I feel a certain obligation to write. 'Everything here is as usual,' I write, feeling at the same time that the phrase is perhaps slightly too literary, too stilted. I have no gossip to give him. I merely tell him that all is well, that I hope his children and wife are well, that I am sure he is busy and so on. We don't communicate more than I communicate with Murdo and his work appears to me to be precisely as useful as Murdo's.

The only event that has happened is the arrival of the hermit but for some reason I don't tell him about it. I don't tell him how much I hate that mirror image of myself, which is yet stronger than me, at the end of the road. I don't tell him of my obsession with that being, because I have so little to do. I don't tell him that the reason I hate the hermit is because I am frightened I will become like him, for at the moment at least I still hold on to language, though it is possible that that too may go. I don't however want the New Zealand papers, I tell him. Rugby is the very least of my interests in life, it is certainly far on the periphery.

My brother was always far better at sport than me. I was never any good at any sport, neither football nor shinty, nor any other game that the boys used to play. I was never any good at rock climbing or jumping across streams. Perhaps that is why I became a schoolmaster in the end. I can't at any rate imagine myself as ever having been a salesman. That would be the final indignity of all.

I seal the letter slowly and after I have done that I turn to one of my paintings. The painting shows a thin Van Gogh-like figure sitting on a thin gaunt chair while above it as if about to jump on it a picture of a wild cat. On the wall which is red there is a framed picture of a violin.

II

I went to see Janet's parents to ask them about the milk. When I went in, the mother and father stood up from the table where they had been eating but Janet remained where she was. She continued eating, her head downcast, concentrated on her plate. O, my dear, chewing your bacon and eggs, so shy and sweet. Her father said, 'Come in, come in. What a stranger you are!' And he held out his hand. His wife, flurried and red-checked, was wiping her hands in her apron.

It wasn't often that they saw the ex-headmaster of the school in their house. I didn't know them very well – they lived at the far end of the village – all I knew was a story about her husband who used to go about selling fish that they found him one night drunk in a ditch, his horse and cart at the side of the road, the horse patiently cropping the grass. Now of course he had a van.

'Would you like something to eat?' he asked me.

'Yes, something to eat,' said the mother, as if she had just thought of it.

'No, thanks,' I said. 'As a matter of fact I came to ask a favour.'

All this time Janet was eating her bacon and eggs and drinking her tea. They had put a chair out for me and I sat down and they sat down but of course they wouldn't continue with their food. I shouldn't have come at that time, I thought, they took their meal later than me.

'And what favour is that?' said her father. 'I'm sure if we can help you we will.'

'Surely, surely,' said his wife, mumbling downwards at the table.

'Well,' I said, 'it occurred to me the other night that you sell milk. And I would like to buy some. I'm getting tired of the milk I have. I would like really fresh milk.'

They both smiled now that they knew that the favour didn't make a great demand on them. Janet looked up at me for the first time, her fork and knife still in her hand. I suppose I thought even Juliet had to eat sometimes, while the tragedy raged around her. There was a spot of yellow egg on her lip.

'Oh, I think that could be arranged,' said her father. 'I'm sure we could do that. Couldn't we do that?' he asked his wife.

'Oh, surely, surely,' she said. 'Surely,' she repeated. She was about the same size as her daughter but her jowls had begun to grow fat and gross and there were lines round her eyes.

'I was thinking,' I said, 'that Janet could leave the milk at the foot of the path when she was on her way to school.'

Janet gave me another piercing glance and then looked down at her plate again.

'I'm sure Janet would do that,' said her father. 'I don't see why she shouldn't do that. She's passing the house every day anyway. You'll do that, Janet, won't you?'

'Yes, that will be all right,' said Janet speaking for the first time.

'Well, that's fine then,' said her father. 'That's fine.'

'Well then . . . ' I prepared to get to my feet and leave.

'You can't go without a wee one, eh?' he said looking at his wife and then away from her. She pursed her lips but said nothing.

He poured me out a large dram and one for himself.

'Since you won't take anything to eat,' he explained. 'Your good health then. It's better than milk anyway.' His wife glanced at him for a moment and then glanced away again.

'Your health,' I said and drank.

Janet was still eating, her small composed head with the black hair bent over the plate.

Her father said laughingly, 'She'll bring the milk all right if she can stop thinking of Dolly.'

'Dolly?' I said.

'Oh, he works on the fishing boats,' said her father. 'They're thinking of getting married. He's a nice boy.'

'But the young ones nowadays,' said her mother in a sudden rush of nervous words, 'look for a house and washing machine and TV straight away.' It sounded as if she spoke that short speech often.

Dolly, dark and threatening, on the fishing boat.

'That's right enough,' said the father as if placating his wife for having taken the whisky. 'It's not like in our day. They want everything at once nowadays. And they marry so young. Still, maybe it keeps them out of mischief.'

'Oh, I'm sure she'll remember the milk all right,' I said. Janet looked at me again quickly and directly as if she had discovered some hidden meaning in my words.

'Yes,' said her mother, 'that's what they all do. They marry without thinking. And then they find themselves without a house or furniture. But Dolly is a nice enough boy.'

'I'm sure he is,' I said.

I put down the glass and got to my feet. 'Well,' I said, 'thank you for the dram. I didn't expect it and as you say it's better than the milk. Janet will bring the milk then?'

'Oh, you can be sure of that,' said her father. 'You can be sure of that.'

I went out of the house wishing in a way that I hadn't visited them. But as I had sat there in their kitchen while they ate their food a thought had hovered around the depths of my mind, a vague shape, a fish from the shadows, and it had something to do with Janet and her approaching marriage. But I couldn't think exactly what it was. It was a phantom thought without substance. But I felt that I knew Janet. I felt I knew her utterly and completely. And the thought had something to do with that feeling.

But I had been shaken by the news of her approaching marriage, if it were true, though after all it was natural enough that a girl like her in the ripeness of her youth, a fruit on the tree, would soon marry. And Dolly, this boy without a shape or a face, this enemy from the sea, would enjoy her. Well, youth must go its own way though it was bitter to think of it. How bitter it was to think of it.

And her parents looked so ordinary too, so ordinary and covetous. For even I could not miss the fact that they had jumped at the chance of selling the milk to me. And all her mother could think about was washing machines, houses and TV sets. Perhaps Janet was like that too. I was sure she was. In the mornings when she got up she probably switched on Radio Luxembourg, listening to the disc jockey with his false voice introducing songs about Love to people who lived in streets that he didn't know but pretended that he cared for. Ah, I thought, the whole world is a cemetery and among the gravestones there walk the young ones with their Japanese transistors, small as diamonds, while a voice which could be the voice of anyone tells them that love is a song, that it consists of flowers and furs, that disease and cancer are for the old, that the young lovers walk armoured in crystal and carrying boxes of chocolates to the world's end. And that always waiting for the young girls are boys like Dolly, ordinary and loveable and uncomplicated and faithful, thinking only about fish and TV sets, huge dark oceans and washing machines.

12

Shortly after this a strange thing happened. Kenneth John, whom I have already mentioned, left home. It was just before five o'clock in the evening, about the time that the bus passes through our part of the village on its way to town that I saw him walking down the path from his house, carrying what I was sure was a kitbag and wearing a dark well-pressed suit and a jaunty dark hat. He seemed for the moment much younger and spryer than I had ever seen him. As he walked down the path his wife shouted after him, 'Come back, Kenneth, come back.' It must have been her voice penetrating my room through the open window that brought me in turn to my own door to find other villagers at their own doors watching. It was an almost Victorian scene, for by this time there were two women against whom Kenneth's wife was leaning in a state of collapse while at the same time she was shouting and crying. I had never seen anything like it in the village in my whole life. But the crying and shouting seemed to have no effect upon Kenneth John who proceeded on his way with a youthful jauntiness, without looking back, presenting an adamantine back to those behind him involved in the Victorian scene.

For some reason that I didn't understand till afterwards I took it on myself to run down to the road to try and reason with him. Perhaps deep in the back of my mind was the envious thought that he should not be allowed to leave behind him all that made life precious and poisonous to him, especially at an age when all confidence in himself should have long ago been burned out in the ashes of defeat. So I half ran along beside him as he made his way to the bus-stop, trying to keep up with him as in the past I had tried to keep up with bigger boys when we were on our way to school. The large red sun was shining dead ahead of us as we walked along, Kenneth John silent, his hat tipped back slightly on his head as in the days of his youth when he had set off for Hong Kong, San Francisco and Valparaiso. He didn't speak to me at all. And behind me his wife was shouting and crying while the two women, one on each side of her, sustained her.

'Where are you going?' I asked him. 'What do you think you're doing?' But he didn't answer.

'Have you any idea where you're going?'

Still he didn't answer.

A white handkerchief flowered from the pocket of his jacket and he looked very spruce and composed as if he had come to a definite conclusion about his life.

'You can't leave your wife like this,' I insisted. 'She has always done her best, hasn't she? She has done what every wife in the village does. She has looked after you all these years.' My voice sounded hollow and false as if I were creating for the moment opportunist reasons for him to return to his world.

'You don't have anywhere to go,' I said. 'You'll regret it.' But he remained silent as if he knew he was listening to lies or as if he did not recognise my right to speak at all. In a short time the bus would be coming and it would be too late.

'You're too old,' I said, 'you can't go away now.' And all the time I was talking to him I was thinking perhaps of myself, that what he was doing was what I should have done, and I was afraid that he would succeed in doing what I myself had failed to do. We walked on steadily side by side till finally we reached the bus stop, where we halted. He turned away from me and looked back to see if the bus was coming.

'Think what will happen to your wife,' I continued unashamedly. 'Think what her life will be like without you. She has always done her best. You can't deny that. It's an illusion,' I said, 'you're not young any more. San Francisco and Hong Kong are in the past. You can't go back there. They won't take you.'

And as I spoke I heard the bus coming. His wife was now rushing towards us, large and fat. She was standing beside us, tears streaming down her fat decaying face, while she looked at him, spruce and jaunty, with longing and amazement. As the bus stopped and the driver leaned down, Kenneth John, still in silence, climbed the steps and walked to the back of the bus and sat down. The driver gazed from me to his wife and back again in astonishment and seemed to be about to say something but then he put his foot on the accelerator and drove off leaving the two of us standing in the middle of the road watching the bus, red and lumbering, make its way to town. Kenneth John didn't even look back to wave.

I helped his wife up the path to her house and left her there with the two women who had been helping her before. Then I returned to my own house as empty-hearted as if I had suffered a defeat. For a long time I seemed to hear Kenneth John's wife crying. She didn't really understand what had happened. I knew it was the hermit's fault. I knew that it was his apparently free life, brooded upon by Kenneth John, which had caused this dash for an illusory freedom. She didn't know this because she lived in the flesh but I who lived in the spirit knew what was happening. I knew what illusory flag he was following on his way to his youth and Hong Kong. I knew what danger the hermit represented to the village. That poor penniless man

would find himself haunting the shops and streets of the town
as well as the quays and the ships, and would discover to his
cost that he was now not a figure of the future but rather a
figure of comedy and pathos in a world which had left him
behind.

And the poor woman he had abandoned didn't even know
what had happened to her. She didn't know the true significance
of the event. Soon she would waken up and find herself alone by
the fireside and as if stunned would mope and moan, comforted
by women who were secretly laughing at her. In fact the whole
village would turn on her a face of apparently comprehending
sorrow while there would be another face beneath that one, of
revengeful laughter. A Janus Hallowe'en mask.

And yet I couldn't help admiring Kenneth John, if he was in his
right mind and not sleepwalking into the past. But perhaps he
hadn't been in his right mind. Perhaps his apparent composure,
his hat set at a cocky angle, his spotless suit, were all disguises for
a final desperation which was almost suicidal in its deeper
meaning. He had stepped out of the village into nothingness. He
was hanging over the water, high in the swaying mast.

13

After some time the Clamhan who stays opposite me came up
to the house. Most of the time he sits at the door wearing
spectacles and mending a green net so that he looks like a
spider intently weaving, his spectacles glittering.

'What did you think of that, eh? Eh?' he said.

'I don't know what to think of it,' I said.

'No,' he said, 'no.' And then, 'He was never interested in the
land, you know. Never. Or in the peats. He didn't care for
them. Imagine him going away like that though. He had some
spunk, eh? Some spunk.' As if pleased with the word, like a girl
with a new necklace, he repeated it. As if he had found a new
shining word. And this was not my imagination, for the
Clamhan was the local bard who composed songs about any
event, unusual or comic, that happened in the village. Such as,
for instance, his song about the cart that had fallen down,

loaded with peats, while the horse broke one of its legs. Perhaps he was thinking of composing a song now. Perhaps this was what he did, immersed in his green net all day.

His small eyes peered at me.

'Nothing's gone right since that hermit came,' he said. 'I wonder what he does with himself all day. Do you know anything about him?'

'No,' I said.

'I wonder what he eats. Do you think he's got the Pension? They say that he goes to the well for water since there is no water in the house. And there's Murdo. He'll never finish his house.' And he glanced over at the pile of chaotic stones. 'He was in the army with me, you know. Always idle. He never finished anything. And what do you think of Kenneth John, eh? Who would have believed it?' His little eyes darted about all the time, as if he were a bird perched on an invisible twig.

'What is happening to the village at all?' he said. No one was coming out of Kenneth John's house. Already it had taken on the appearance of a grave.

'I'll tell you something,' he said. 'She had him on a tether. Maybe I would have left her as well.' His own wife was large and heavy and submissive. 'Maybe,' he repeated, 'I would have left her years ago. But I don't know. I don't know if I would have the courage. The strength. I don't know.' And he gazed down at the ground and following his eyes I too gazed down at the ground to see his large shapeless boots with the dust of the road on them.

'He mentioned the hermit to me, you know,' he said. 'He mentioned him to me once. He said that he would like to stay in the house by himself just like that. He never settled down, you know. He always wanted to be sailing. He had no time for the land. I don't understand that. I don't understand that at all. Still,' he said, 'I was never away from the island like him. The ones who were away from the island never settled down. Think of Kirsty's daughter. She never settles down.' And he looked at me askance with his small glittering eyes.

And I was thinking, I never ran away. In spite of everything I never ran away: that must count for something surely. In our mortal accounts that must count for something. Perhaps what lay between us was love after all, in spite of the cancer, in spite of the pain.

'Did he say anything to you while you were talking to him?' he asked.

I looked up startled, as if I had forgotten that he was still there. 'No,' I said, 'he didn't say anything. Nothing at all.'

'That's funny,' he said, 'that he shouldn't have said anything. It's funny, that. You would think he would have said something.'

'What should he have said?' I asked.

'I don't know,' he repeated. 'You would think he would have said something.'

'Well,' I said decisively and almost angrily, 'you can take it from me that he didn't say anything.'

What are you angling for, I was thinking. Are you trying to get hold of some saying that you can use for your poem when you can get round to composing it? His small bald head glittered in the light, like a small round stone.

'I just thought,' he said, 'that he might have said something.' I was too tired to repeat what I had already said and anyway we both stopped talking as we saw Kenneth John's wife making her way to the peatstack. Her body was bent as if under a great weight. She stood for a moment at the peatstack as if wondering why she was there. Then she put out her hand slowly as if in a dream, and withdrew two peats. She stared down at them for a while and then still very slowly and with bent back she made her way back to the house. His gluttonous quick eyes followed her movements.

'Well,' he said, 'well . . .'

'I'm sorry,' I said, 'I have to leave you now. I have things to do.'

'Of course, of course,' he said. 'Of course.' I went into the house without looking at him and I poured out a very large whisky and drank it in one gulp. It was very bitter and raw. When I was finished I could have smashed the glass against the wall. For a long time I stood there thinking of many things. Then I went up to the room where the violin was and I got it down. I played a little, with joy and sorrow. I drew the bow rapidly across the strings and it was as if new confident feelings sprang up in me. I played as I watched the Clamhan make his way down to his house and his eternal green net. Then I laid the violin down on the table – heart-shaped, coffin-shaped violin – and I almost wept for us all, for our strange hectic appalling lives. For poor Kenneth John's wife who at that very moment was probably sitting next door staring into the fire which she had composed from her black peats.

14

The following morning as usual I went down to the foot of the path to collect the milk from Janet. She was as usual cool and lovely, wearing yellow, her black hair contrasting strongly with her dress. I held the bottle of milk in my hand as I said, 'Another fine morning.' She said it was.

I continued, 'I've been thinking about what your mother said when I was at your house.'

She looked at me without speaking.

'About marriage and so on,' I said. 'It's true that people need money before they marry nowadays.' I just wanted to talk to her and didn't really know what I was talking about. Cool mornings, how I love you before the sun rises demanding decisions. 'One needs a house,' I went on. 'It must be even worse now, more expensive. Furniture and so on. When are you thinking of getting married?'

'I don't know yet,' she said. 'We aren't even engaged.'

'Oh,' I said, 'I thought . . . But still, it won't be long, a girl like you.' I thought I could see the cool wheels of her mind turning in the still early morning. After what seemed a long while she suddenly said in a hard cold voice, 'There's a suite I saw in the town. It's a red suite. Two chairs and a sofa. I've never seen one like it anywhere. That's what I would like to get.'

'A suite,' I said.

'I saw it in the window of a shop in the town,' she said. Dead ahead of her the sun was red and strong in the sky. A suite of clouds overhead.

'How much does it cost?' I asked.

'Two hundred pounds,' she said. And then she added, 'I must

be going or I'll be late.' And she set off at her brisk pace, her lovely cool body moving so freely. In the early cool morning. Towards the red sun. A suite at two hundred pounds. Why had she mentioned that? I considered it and as I was considering it the hermit rode past on his bicycle on his way to the shop for his messages. At least that was what I assumed. It was the first time I had seen him close to. He rode past me, his eyes fixed straight ahead, looking neither to right nor to left. Janet had turned her head to look at him but he hadn't looked at her. He was sitting upright on his bicycle, the belt of rope around him. Coming out of the red sun he looked like Death in his dark dirty clothes. His face looked tanned and unlined. Was the brown complexion from the sun or was it that he was naturally dark-skinned? He was like a man I had once seen who cleaned chimneys and had a small black dog running after him as he rode along on his bicycle. And he looked so contented, so silent, so harmonious. As if he was happy enough to rest in his silence. His coat was very long, almost touching his shoes. 'How do you live?' I spoke to him in a whisper. He never bought whisky or beer, just bread and cheese and butter and so on. Maybe he was a monk or a holy man. He hadn't looked at Janet at all. He was much stronger than me.

I returned slowly to my house, the bottle of milk in my hand, thinking about the red suite which Janet had seen in the shop window and whose like was not to be found anywhere. Her voice had sounded hard and greedy as she spoke. Even in the dew of the early morning which hung on flowers with its silver bells wobbling there was greed and hardness.

The hermit passed out of my sight on his way to the shop with his piece of paper in his pocket.

15

On the Friday night I went to visit Dougie as I often did. Sometimes we played chess and sometimes we just sat and talked. I had forgotten that his brother and wife were home on their annual summer holiday from Edinburgh but when I did go in, there they both were.

'Come in, come in,' said Dougie. His house is the largest in the village and with its large windows gives a wide panoramic view of the sea. His brother Edward and his sister-in-law Lorna got to their feet from the sofa on which they had been sitting as I entered. Edward is a commander of some sort in the Navy and is a silent perceptive tall darkish man who bears about with him the easy manner that is common to successful people. His wife on the other hand looks a bit neurotic and stringy and restless. She drinks vodka. After the usual greetings, I was given a drink.

'And how are you enjoying your holiday?' I asked them.

'Oh, fine,' said Lorna. 'We were out fishing in a boat today.'

'We didn't catch anything,' said Edward.

'Like me,' I said. 'I fish in the loch but I never catch anything either.'

I like sitting in the evening with professional people, preferably ones who have come from outside the village and are there only for a short time. I should have preferred to talk about books, art, music and even philosophy but one can't have everything. Lorna pretends she's cultured but she isn't, though she goes to the theatre quite a bit as her husband is often away from home. She told me that Edinburgh is as beautiful as ever and just as cold.

Dougie said to her, 'Of course you know that Charles's wife came from Edinburgh, but she settled here quite happily.' I was surprised that his own wife wasn't in the room till I remembered that there was an evening service on in church. He looked flushed as if he had been drinking rather heavily before I had come in. We talked about Edinburgh for a while, Edward silent as usual.

'I go to quite a lot of things at the Festival,' said Lorna. 'But there's so much. It's impossible to see it all.'

I envied her for that. To be able to see all the drama that one wanted to watch, to hear all the music that one wished to hear, and to see films and read books, that would have been my ideal life. But of course it was impossible.

'It's quite often the case,' she said, 'that people who come from the city settle down happily in the country.' She was referring to my wife.

'Yes,' said Dougie, 'she settled down happily here. I don't know whether she missed Edinburgh at all.'

'A little,' I said. 'She missed it a little. Especially in the spring.'

'I should like to stay here all the time,' said Lorna sipping her vodka.

I discounted what she said. They all spoke like this when they came home for their annual holiday but they would have been driven out of their minds by boredom if they stayed for more than a month and especially if they remained during the winter.

So much of language is lying, polite lying but still lying. The difference between men and animals is that men lie, animals don't. This thought came to me quite clearly as I listened to her bubbling on.

There were so many definitions about the difference between men and animals but this one came to me quite effortlessly. Man is the animal who lies. I sipped my whisky meditatively till Dougie suddenly said, 'The hermit was in today. He was getting his provisions.'

'Hermit?' said Lorna looking up.

'Oh yes,' said Dougie, 'didn't I tell you we have a hermit? No one speaks of anything else here these days.'

He went over and refilled our glasses, all except Edward's, who said that he was quite happy. One could never tell what he was thinking. He let his wife do all the talking and sat quietly listening. One couldn't imagine him saying or doing anything rash. One could however quite easily imagine him in a coldly computerised ship absorbed in instruments.

'Isn't that interesting?' Lorna said to him. 'A hermit. Imagine that. And, tell me, does he stay entirely by himself?'

'He does,' said Dougie, 'in one of those huts the RAF used to have. And he doesn't speak to anyone. He had the same routine today,' he said, turning to me. 'He took a piece of paper out of his pocket with the messages written on it but he didn't speak. Funny thing, the people are turning against him. The children were shouting after him after he got on his bicycle.' As he was speaking Dougie's voice was becoming slurred and lazy.

'I can imagine it,' I said.

'And another odd thing. Stork's wife went in front of him in the queue, though she had no right to. But you know her. And he just accepted it. I wondered what he would do. He just smiled but didn't say anything.'

'Is he dumb or something that he doesn't speak?' Lorna asked.

'Not at all,' said Dougie. 'He's not at all dumb. He just doesn't want to speak at all.'

'That's really odd, isn't it, Edward,' said Lorna. One couldn't imagine her not speaking.

'It is,' said Edward.

'Still,' said Dougie, 'if he's got the money I'm not going to refuse him his provisions.'

'Well,' I said, 'I suppose you're right.'

'How do you mean?' said Dougie, as if he had detected some hint of argumentativeness in my voice.

'It's just,' I said, 'that he doesn't seem to care for the village. He belongs to it and he doesn't belong to it. He's a villager and he isn't.'

'Well,' Dougie answered, 'he's a man anyway. He's a human being.'

'I suppose,' I said, 'it depends on how you define a man.'

'I don't understand,' said Dougie again.

'Well,' I persisted, as if driven by an inner compulsion, 'a man is someone who lives in society. He can't be said to live in society.'

'That's true in a way,' said Lorna as if thinking deeply and trying to follow what we were saying. Her husband was taking it all in, his hand round his glass which had still quite a lot of whisky in it.

'Yes,' said Dougie, 'but you're not going to say that because he doesn't bother with the village I shouldn't sell him provisions.'

'And there's another thing,' I said. And I told them about Kenneth John and what the Clamhan had told me.

Lorna looked at me in astonishment or pretended astonishment. 'Well, there seems to be goings on without doubt. And where is he now?'

'I don't know,' I said and then speaking to Edward, 'He used to be in the Merchant Navy, you know, in his youth. He was all over the world. Hong Kong, Valparaiso, the lot. He's well over seventy now and he just went and left his wife like that. He took the bus and he wouldn't speak to anyone and he went off to town and no one's heard of him since.'

'Isn't that extraordinary?' said Lorna, finishing her vodka. 'Isn't that quite extraordinary?' Her husband agreed that it was.

'You say he was over seventy?' he said.

'Yes,' I said, 'and he left his wife. He had apparently been saying that he should be like the hermit, fancy free. Of course he never really settled down.'

'More of us should do that,' said Dougie jokingly as he refilled the glasses again, including mine. 'More of us should do that. Leave our wives, I mean. A lot of people want to do that.'

'Do you want to do that?' said Lorna to her husband.

'No, I'm quite happy. In any case, I'm in the Navy already.'

'I'll tell you something though,' said Dougie whose voice was becoming even more slurred and his face redder. 'It's a question of principle, isn't it? I mean if the hermit – whoever he is – wants provisions from me I'm bound to sell them to him. Else why was I fighting the Germans, tell me that.'

'That's a point,' said Lorna brightly, looking from me to him as if she were watching a tennis match.

Dougie repeated what he had said.

'After all, we're living in a democracy, aren't we? At least, that's what they call it.'

Democracy, I thought. Is cancer a democracy? Cancer is what destroys the unity of the cells, the Greek polis. Maybe the hermit was a cancer. Was that what he was?

'Still,' I said, 'if a lot of people start to leave their wives because of him that will be something else again. You won't find the women talking about democracy.'

Dougie was about to say something, I felt sure, about women not being democratic anyway but then looking at Lorna he stopped himself in time and merely remarked, 'Well, all I can say is what did I fight the Germans for? I'll tell you,' he went on forcefully, 'I fought the Germans so that hermits can buy their groceries at my shop even if they don't want to speak to me. That's why I fought the Germans.'

'And quite right too,' said Lorna as if to a child. 'Quite right too. Though on the other hand Charles has some right on his side as well. Still it was odd about that old man.'

'It was,' I agreed. 'It was very odd.'

I was looking out of the window at the moon which was rising bright and stunningly clear above the sea. Pure lovely moon, pure merciless moon. There was a long pause in the conversation which no one seemed to wish to break. I felt comfortable and yet at the same time I was restless. Soon I would have to leave. That is what is so odd about lonely people, they want to be alone and yet they do not want to be alone. There were times when I needed solitude like food and drink and other times when I couldn't bear it.

The fact was I didn't particularly care for Lorna or Edward. They seemed to me to be artificial superficial people who could not see and did not wish to see anything profound. They were made uncomfortable by deep discussion. I was much more interested in Dougie than I was in them, though he was being rather incoherent about the Germans.

Suddenly he said, looking at me in what he imagined must be an affectionate roguish manner, 'I hear that you're getting your milk every morning.'

'Oh,' I said, 'that's true. I thought I'd buy fresh milk every morning.'

'And very nice too,' said Dougie as if he were back in his wartime barracks again and using the sort of language he might have spoken then. 'I wouldn't mind getting her in the corn,' he said. 'Still, every man to his own taste.'

'And who is this?' said Lorna, looking at me almost roguishly. 'I detect something.'

'Oh, you can detect something all right,' said Dougie. 'She's a stunner. Mind you, she's pretty young.' And he laughed. I was angry but remained smooth on the surface.

'There is nothing in it,' I said, 'but a pure business transaction.'

'Ah, you old rogue,' said Dougie again. 'There's depths to Charles that you wouldn't believe,' he told the others, going over to pour himself another whisky. 'She's a stunner. A real hum-dinger.'

This went on for some time till finally around eleven o'clock I said I would have to go.

'You don't have to go yet,' said Dougie. 'The night's still young.' In the old days I would have left even earlier when my wife was alive and in fact there was really no reason why I should be leaving at eleven o'clock as I could stay in bed as long as I wished. Nevertheless I wanted to leave. The pressure of words without meaning was beginning to tire me. And also I was wondering if other people were saying or hinting what Dougie was saying and hinting. With him it was just words and not for a moment did he believe that there was any truth in what he was saying but other people in the village might be less charitable. The trouble was that though as far as I was concerned nothing had happened, the desire was there, and this was what prevented me from being angrier.

The moon above the sea which I could see so clearly through the large window reminded me of her, the circles of light on the water. Great white breast of the moon, lovely unattainable Diana, stunningly lovely.

I insisted on leaving. At the door Dougie said that I must not be offended by his chatter as it was all a joke. He seemed suddenly drunk and pathetic while behind him stood his brother so cool and remote and collected.

Perhaps, I thought, the village does this to us. It doesn't present us with enough challenges, it allows us to run to seed.

Astoundingly, Lorna put her face up to be kissed and as my eyes approached it, it looked grained and rutted like a close-up picture of the moon. There was a smell of stale perfume from her and altogether she reminded me of a string bag such as one might carry home from a shop. Edward's clasp was cool and faint. They were still standing at the door when I left. I wondered what they would say about me in my absence. Poor Charles, Dougie might say, he's getting old and narrow-minded. Imagine saying all that about the hermit! But I knew that Dougie was serious about democracy and the Germans, he was fair and straight and kind. Maybe, I thought vaguely, I shall come up against him. Perhaps he too is my enemy. Or rather perhaps I am his enemy. I waved and then they went into the house and the square of light closed.

And I began my walk home.

As I walked along I thought of myself as a tramp without destiny, without purpose. I had worn my best suit to visit Dougie as I always did on a Friday but nevertheless I thought of myself as a tramp. The fact was that since my wife died I had had trouble even with maintaining my clothes in a reasonable condition, quite apart from my trouble with cooking. I couldn't be bothered with darning my socks and often I just threw them away when they were holed and bought new ones. A lot of my jackets had buttons missing and I couldn't be bothered sewing new ones on. And this was really absurd since I had all the time in the world but at the same time I couldn't spare the time to sew buttons on jackets or darn my socks. I could hardly be bothered making food for myself.

As I walked along I could see the hermit's hut in the distance. Perhaps he was now sleeping quietly and peacefully while I was walking along the road to my lonely house, restless, yet not wishing to go back to it. The sky above was bright with moonlight. Even the Greeks, it occurred to me, must have had trouble with their cooking and their clothes. But of course nothing of that was mentioned in their philosophy. They seemed so wholly concerned with the merciless mind, like the moon that raced between the clouds, remote and hard, and so goldenly unlike the stones which Murdo took home for his house. Imagine what it must be like to compose a house of moons.

And as I walked along thinking of the hermit and his hut and the planes rising from it into the night sky on their unimaginable missions, black planes headed for their destiny of dumbness and silence, I heard above the noise of the running stream another sound. It was the sound of dancing. I halted and listened. Every Friday night the young people would dance to the music of the accordion at the end of the road. They had been doing this for generation after generation – at first it had been the melodeon – and they were doing it tonight. The wheel circled, night was an affair of whiteness and perfume, the ring of erotic flesh. And I myself in the past had sometimes joined in the dance. And many of the girls with whom I had danced had now become old and flabby and fat and had varicose veins. But now if I were to enter that circle they would all withdraw from me as if I were a ghost and the accordion player would stop playing and there would be a dead silence. But in the old days it hadn't been like that. In the light of the autumn moon the world appeared brave and brilliant, the future lay before us all, our feet derived strength from the earth as we danced and we were young. There was no disease in the world, no sorrow, nothing but certainty. The dance was the symbol of eternity which re-peated itself endlessly. Now it was merely a nostalgic charm. But perhaps that was the image I should have been seeking for, the image of the dance, not the image of silence and dumbness. If only one could live forever in the world of the dance, if only we had the luck. But, no, I didn't even dance very well and now I wouldn't be able to dance at all. Time had slowed me down, made my body stiff. I would find it undignified to dance. I would be too aware of those forces which were like a high wind trying to break up the dance. How could one be so innocent again? How could one have the fierce animal eye that gazed at the moon and tried to stare it down?

And as I walked along I thought that if I had a bomb I would destroy this village where my idealism had died. Here my heart which had burned with fervour had turned to ashes. It was all the fault of the village and its people. They too easily had lost their vision of the dance and because of that I had lost it too. The dance to them was frivolous, it was a stage in their lives which had to be transcended so that they could settle down and raise families and cultivate their land. But what, I thought, if the dance itself is the centre of the world? For in the dance we do not consider what other people may be thinking about us, we are not looking for hidden meanings in their conversations. In the dance we put out our hand and we grasp another hand and the two hands are mortal and warm. We are all together in the dance creating together whatever our souls and minds are like, an image of harmony. In the centre of the dance there is no fear, no horror. There are no skulls staring at us from the centre of the dance and no cries of pain are heard.

And these thoughts and wishes brought me to the house and to my own door. I have to say at this point, if I have not said it already, that when I go out I always leave the door unlocked: there is no history of stealing in the village. I switched on the light and there sitting in my chair was my wife. She had always sat there and for a moment in my slightly drunk state I didn't find it wholly odd that she should be there. She always used to sit by the fire knitting or sewing in that very chair with the blue cover on it.

Then the whole world turned over again and it wasn't my wife, it was Janet.

I looked at her in amazement, almost buckling at the knees. She had clearly been waiting there patiently for me in the chair by the unlit fire, her legs crossed perhaps as they were now.

'My parents think I'm at the dance,' she said.

I looked from her to the window and then I walked over and drew the curtains. What would happen to me if anyone saw her there. She was wearing a white dress and her long black hair flowed down behind her back.

'I haven't much time,' she said.

I went over to the cupboard and poured myself a whisky.

'Would you like one?' I asked.

'No thanks,' she said.

I now knew why she had come. With my whisky in my hand I walked over to the bureau in the corner of the room and took out my money. I didn't care how much I was giving her and I poured the notes in her lap. It was the two hundred pounds for the red suite, that was what she wanted. She counted the money carefully and put it in her handbag which lay on the floor beside the chair.

I drank the whisky quickly and she said: 'Where do we go?'

I put the glass down on the table, my lips dry. It was impossible that she should be there and yet she was there in her white dress with the pure glow of youth on her face.

I went into the bedroom and she followed me, shining palely in the darkness. I drew the curtains in this room too, shutting out the light of the moon, though I could still hear the dancing.

I undressed and climbed into bed. My legs seemed scrawnier than usual, my skin unhealthy looking. She stood over at the dressing table looking briefly in the mirror in front of which my wife had used to sit in the mornings and at night. This was the bed the two of us had shared for so many years.

She climbed into bed and her flesh felt cool and marbly. I put my arms around her in the darkness. The desert had blossomed with water.

'I haven't got much time,' she whispered again.

She had come out of the darkness for two hundred pounds for a red suite, for its cheap rays. I had plenty of money. I didn't grudge that. I grudged the torment of my soul that had led to this.

It took only fifteen minutes, that was all. When it was over she got up and dressed again in front of the mirror. There was a comb there which she used: in it were still a few grey hairs. I looked at her while she was dressing. She was like a fish, lively and cool. She seemed to have forgotten about me. After a while she was completely dressed again, this child, this cool child.

'Shall I close the door after me?' she asked as I lay there.

'Yes,' I said.

She pulled the door behind her and then I heard the main door close.

I felt corrupted and yet light as if some great weight had been lifted from me. Forgive us our sins . . . I imagined her making her way home like a thief through the night while the dance continued. I nearly got up to take some more whisky but after the door had closed I stayed where I was. I knew that would be the last time, the only time, that she would never come again, but my heart was humming with joy. After a while I fell asleep still hearing, before I dropped off, the music of the accordion and the sound of the dancers' feet.

16

The following evening Kenneth John came back to the village on the bus.

I didn't talk to him that night but the following day I was able to. He was sitting in front of his house on a chair which his wife had set out for him and he looked diminished and shorn as if some vital part had been removed from him. As I came over his wife looked at me and for the first time I realised that she didn't like me very much. There was a hard hostile gleam in her eye which however she masked immediately. She brought me out a chair as well and I sat beside Kenneth John: she had given him a pillow to lean against but hadn't brought one for me. After a long while he began to talk, at first almost to himself and then later to me.

'I tried to get a job on a ship but I couldn't get one. I went down to the quay and there were some men there but when I told them what I wanted they just laughed. I told them I had been to Hong Kong and Valparaiso and that I had been on the big sailing ships up in the rigging. They said that they didn't have sails on ships nowadays. They called me "old man" and told me that I should go home. And I'm sure none of them had ever been to Australia or New Zealand or any of those places. "You can't go to Valparaiso, old man," they said, "you're too old." They didn't realise,' he said, turning to me at last, 'the thirst I felt. The day we went to San Francisco, years ago, I saw the bridge shining in the sun and I couldn't believe that the world could be so beautiful. There was a slight haze too, a slight blue haze. But the bridge was shining. They didn't understand the thirst I had to see that place again. And every day I saw them and they said the same thing. They used to call me Valparaiso Jim. And I used to see them loading and unloading the ship and in the evening I would see it setting out. It was so big and white. But they just laughed at me.

'At first I walked about the town but I didn't see anybody I knew. Nobody at all. It was like being in a new country. People just going to the shops and walking along the pavements and their eyes looking into themselves and they were all so gloomy.

'And I stayed in this house run by a Mrs Malloy, a small greedy woman. She wouldn't even let me watch the TV. And the house inside was all dark and there was a smell of polish and cabbage. And there were pots with shiny plants in them and big leaves. I used to sit in my room every night and watch the walls, there was nothing else to do. And I'm sure she didn't clean the dishes properly. I'm sure the dishes were dirty. She wouldn't even wash my clothes unless I gave her extra money. I just had forty pounds altogether, I didn't have much money. It was funny, wasn't it, after leaving here, I ended up in a room watching the walls. On the wall there was a painting showing three deer on a mountain side and it looked like a painting I had seen on a train a long time ago. I think she must have stolen it from the train, that's what I thought. She was a small sour-looking woman and I didn't like her at all. The furniture was very dark and the house was dark. She didn't seem to draw the curtains aside and there was a smell of cooking. She wouldn't even darn my socks for me. I didn't like her at all. Not at all. And there was no one in the town I knew. I was used to a hot water bottle every night and she wouldn't even let me put the fire on. She said I could go to the lounge but there was no one in the lounge and it was full of old furniture.

'And, in the mornings, I would go down to the quay. The weather was so beautiful, there's never been a summer like it, and there were boats in the bay and I would ask these people if I could get a job. In the early morning I was full of hope. But they still laughed at me. And they told others about me and they laughed at me as well. Valparaiso Jim they called me. They had no pity for me at all. I said I didn't want any pay while I was on the ship. All I wanted was bed and board but they had no pity on me at all. I thought that everybody had been at San Francisco at some time or another. But no, they hadn't, not one of them had been, and it didn't worry them. They were happy where they were and all they thought about was making their money for the day and then going home at night. They said I should go home and put my feet up at the fire. You're too old, they said. You're too old for San Francisco. But one of them seemed to understand and he took me in for coffee one day and he said that he had a family and three children. You should go home, he told me. Look at me, he said, I've never been to San Francisco, not even once. And you're better off than me. You've been at least once. And that was true too. I hadn't thought of that before. What he said was right enough. But I still had this thirst. That's what they don't understand, the thirst. I didn't want to lie down and die and that's what they wanted me to do. But they didn't have any pity.

'And when I went back to the house at night there was no TV and there was no fire and this woman wouldn't even wash my clothes. And sometimes in the morning there would be a queue at the bathroom. And there was a man who never spoke to me, he read the paper all the time, even at his breakfast. And there was a smell from the house, a smell of polish and cabbages and some other smell that I have never smelt before. It was an old smell, it almost made me sick.

'And at night I used to look at the picture with the three deer on it. They were green deer and they were on this brown mountain and there was an old gold frame to the picture. And in the lounge there was an old piano and no one ever played it. You had to be at your breakfast at a certain time and if you weren't there you didn't get any. I didn't like the place at all and I didn't like the woman. She also asked me for my money in advance. I couldn't help thinking of the old days when you had somewhere to go. When you're young there's always somewhere to go. I didn't have anywhere to go there, I couldn't even walk the street because I didn't know anybody. I never met anybody all the time I was in town, nobody at all. They were all strangers and they were looking ahead of them and they looked so worried and so old. It wasn't like that in San Francisco.

'You know, I always thought that everybody had been in San Francisco at some time or another and there were these people and they hadn't been and they didn't want to go.

'So one morning I got up and I looked out the window at the bay where the ships were and I knew that I would never get to San Francisco again. I would never be on board a ship again. So I put all my clothes in my case and I told the woman I was leaving and I left the house and I went down to the bus. I didn't even go to the quay in case I changed my mind when I saw the ships.

'So I came back home and I knew all the time as I was sitting in the bus that I would never leave the village again. But I'll tell you something, I can get a hot water bottle now and I can watch the TV and I don't have to sit in a lounge. It's funny how those things mean so much to you. I knew that I was old and that all my youth had gone. Sometimes you don't realise that till it's very late in life. I've realised it now.'

He turned and looked me full in the face. 'I'm home now,' he said, 'for the last time.' A wisp of sand blew about us and I thought of the little girl who had come from school and said that she had gone to the window of the hermit's hut and she had heard him singing.

He was altering things because he was there, his existence was an affront.

'I'm sure you did the right thing,' I told Kenneth John. 'I'm sure you did the right thing.' But my heart felt empty as I said it. How could the knowledge of the right thing make one feel so shorn and diminished, so totally void?

17

When the minister, the Rev. Murdo Mackenzie, came to see me I thought at first that he was looking for money. I never of course go to church and haven't done so for many years now. The minister is a very thin man with a cadaverous face, one of those faces that Highland ministers have, grained and deeply trenched so that they look like portraits of Dante in his old age. When he came in I asked him to sit down but he gazed vacantly at the chair and didn't sit on it. He paced about the room nervously, sometimes passing his hand across his eyes as if he were dazzled by an enormous problem.

'I suppose you are wondering why I came to see you,' he said at last. For one frightening moment I thought it might have something to do with Janet and that he was going to warn me about the terrible moral consequences my sin might involve me in. But it wasn't about that at all. As a matter of fact I had nothing against this particular minister. He had never pestered me to come to church as some of them do and as far as I knew he was a very competent minister, visiting the sick regularly and making no distinction between the rich and the poor.

'As a matter of fact,' he said, 'I came to you simply because you do not attend church. I couldn't tell my congregation or my elders because they wouldn't understand.' He paused for a long moment staring into vacancy then sat down in a chair and almost immediately got up again.

'It's difficult to tell you this,' he said. 'Very difficult. I don't know where to begin. It's so strange. So strange. Nothing like it has ever happened to me before.'

I waited patiently. I knew now that whatever it was it had nothing to do with Janet or me. I wondered, if he had known about that, whether he would have come to consult me. Almost certainly not.

'Well,' he said at last, as if preparing to take the brunt of a large cold wave, 'I suppose I'd better tell you. You'll probably think I'm mad, utterly mad, and perhaps I am. You see, I always prepare my sermons in advance of the Sunday. I like writing them out, I get a great amount of pleasure out of my little efforts. I feel that I am creating something, you understand.' I nodded. I was sure he must feel like that about his trivial orations.

'I spend quite a lot of time preparing them,' he continued. 'I write them down in longhand and sometimes after that if I have time I type them. I don't just use headings for my sermons. No, I write the whole sermon out. The sermon I was preparing this week was on God and His gift of His son to us and how, sinful though we are, God has thought it expedient to save us out of His great mercy. There is nothing unusual about the sermon. In fact I have often used a similar kind of sermon before. O I believe in God and in Christ. When I was in the pulpit the words would pour out of me like a fountain. For what after all is a minister unless he has the gift of words? I don't mean the gift of language, for few have that, but the gift of eloquence, the gift of words. It would certainly be odd if you had a minister who couldn't speak, who couldn't use words. A minister needs words and he needs hope. What would his congregation think of him if he had no hope and he couldn't preach? He would be like a thorn without sap, he would be a useless plant in the desert. He would be nothing.' He looked at me keenly and I thought I knew what had happened. He had lost his faith. I had often wondered what would happen to a minister if he lost his faith. Most of us at some time or another lose our faith in what we do, we find our work absurd, we feel that our motions and operations in the world are meaningless and dispensable. But what if this happened to a minister whose business after all is faith, and who must rest in it or be without function?

'I know what you're thinking,' he said. 'You're thinking that I've lost my faith. It's not as simple as that. For, as I said, what is a minister without a voice, without words? If silence descended on a minister what would he be? Nothing. Nothing at all. Do you understand?'

'I'm not sure,' I said.

'Well, I'll tell you what happened,' he said. 'I wrote my sermon and then I tried to speak it. Aloud in my room, standing up, as if I were talking to the congregation. I was talking about God and Christ and the fact that the Son of Man was born in a stable. Well,' he said looking at me with horror, 'I tried to speak the words and no words would come out of my mouth. It was as if I had gone dumb. I thought at first that I was suffering from some sickness, some disease, but no, for I am speaking to you now, am I not? And I could speak to my wife and children. But whenever I tried to speak the words of that sermon it was as if I had gone dumb.'

'This sermon about God and Christ?' I said.

'Yes,' he said, 'about the blessings of God.'

'And did you mention in it,' I asked ironically, 'the blessing of pain which has been granted to us?'

'No,' he said, 'I didn't mention that.'

I was silent for a long time. The stable and the hut. The dumbness and the hermit.

The wings ascending to the sky.

The words written on paper.

Was I going out of my mind? The minister paced about my house like an animal in a cage. Understanding nothing.

First there was Kenneth John and now there was the minister.
It was like a plague, a language dying.

The big stones in the mouth.

'Well,' I said, 'you should tell the congregation that you've got a cold, that you're hoarse, and maybe the words will come back to you later.'

'But it might happen to me again,' he said.

'It won't,' I said. 'It won't. You just tell them that you're hoarse.'

The soul of the village dying. Not that I cared about the minister but it was as if I owed a debt to the village. Truth moving restlessly about my room, dumb.

The white Greek moon in the sky like a stone screaming. And its dumbness lying on the earth. The veins and tentacles dead and finished.

'Everything will be all right,' I said. 'It's just a momentary crisis. It happens to all of us at some time or another. Sometimes when I was teaching I felt the same, as if I didn't want to say anything, as if for that time I had nothing to say.'

His eyes pleaded with me.

'Is that true?' he asked.

'Of course it's true,' I said. 'It happens to all of us at some time or another. The dark night of the soul.'

'Well,' he said, 'I feel much better. I'm glad I came.'

'That's because you talked about it,' I said. From the closed grave the soul rose fluttering. When the stone moved.

After some time he left looking much happier. But he left me thinking hard.

The hermit would have to leave the village, that was certain. I would have to save the village. And no one else could save it except me. No one else knew the extent of the threat, the potential damage. It wasn't that I was concerned with the minister. Much of what he said seemed to me false and irrelevant. But what if this happened to others? If the silence of the dead descended on the village? If people grew too tired even to speak to each other, if language, that necessity of the human being, failed? No village, no society, could survive that. I didn't need the minister but others did. His words for them were significant and important. And what if they failed? It was as if the influence of the hermit extended outwards like a cold ray without his knowing it. Or perhaps he did know it.

Truth lay perhaps in silence but it was not a human truth. Human truth lay in lying speech. And who in the village knew this except me? Who would be able to deal with this but me? Only I saw what was happening because it was what I mistakenly wished to happen. Dougie didn't understand it with his talk about democracy. This had nothing to do with democracy, this was a fight to the death. The silence of death. Snow falling over the village dulling its traffic. The roads that joined us together slowly being throttled.

After the minister had gone I sat for a long time thinking. I couldn't think what to do but I knew that something must be done. And I would have to do it myself. Even if I passed the limits of morality, even if I struck deep at my own image. The monster of silence would have to be driven out of the village, even by corrupt means. Later perhaps someone might understand why it had been necessary but more probably no one would: there would be no biographer to tell of my achievement since the people for whom I was acting as benefactor didn't themselves understand the problem. This was a metaphysical question, and they lived in the physical world of stone and corn and hay and houses.

But no solution came to me. The hermit had apparently harmed no one. I couldn't hire the policeman to drive out a metaphysical criminal. I thought of that opening chapter in Frazer's book where one prince hunts another one in the dark wood, the new god taking over from the old, while the moon poured down its equal rays.

But I felt so tired. And there was no one I could talk to. Not to Murdo, not to Kenneth John, not to Dougie. Not even to Kirsty. Her narrow brutal mind would be of no use here. This needed much greater fineness, much deeper cunning.

And I thought too, Why shouldn't I leave him where he was? After all when he left what would I have to think of? That black silence of his, so attractive to me, would perish with his disappearance and I would be alone. The moon was now rising in the sky. O my Greek volumes, why don't you bring me an answer to this unanswerable question, with your brimming knowledge, your endless fertility? Why don't you bring me your manifold gifts? But this question went beyond those texts. There was a deep loch and there was a thought which needed to take the bait but the thought wasn't rising to the surface clear and strong. Still, it might come to the surface eventually.

It would have to. I stared directly into the face of the moon which was as pure and direct and strong as Janet's face and that was the last vision I had before I fell asleep, still searching for that thought, that solution which would permit me to rid the village of the hermit who was to a great extent myself, and yet more dangerous and much stronger than me.

18

And as I slept I dreamed of my childhood. It returned to me in all its clarity and fullness. I saw again my father and my mother, my father so silent and large and my mother so quick and busy and demanding. She seemed always to be running about the house with a duster, or washing, or drying dishes, or sweeping the floor. A vivid insect presence in her blue gown with the white flowers printed on it. And always saying to me, Keep at your books. You have to get on in the world. What is there here for you? Look at all those other boys. What are they doing but wasting their lives fishing and crofting? You keep at your books.

While my father, slow and silent, said nothing and did nothing to protect me from this quick demanding presence which wouldn't leave me alone, which would not let me ripen in my own darkness but was always shining its sharp little torch on me. Always without cease. And my father was so slow and heavy and perhaps lazy and silent. It seemed to be an effort for him to speak, as if he had allowed my mother to speak for both of them. It was she who was proud and small and quick, who was alert to insults, even imagined ones, from the villagers who didn't like her because of her ambition. He on the other hand seemed to have no sense of honour but he got on better with them than she did. In a way he was like Murdo Murray but deeper, more vulnerable. He wasn't at ease in his environment but perhaps more so than she was. She saw her environment as something hostile, she confronted it with her quick agile mind and her quick body: she was always improving it, cleaning it up, tidying it. And my father would sit by the fireside reading the paper and he didn't protect me at all. He would hardly touch me except that now and again he might lay his hand on my head absently in passing, but he would say nothing.

Eventually he withdrew to a shed where he kept his loom and there he would play his ancient dark music among a smell of oil, his feet on the treadles, his hands busy. He was like a big composer in the half darkness, a sort of Beethoven, heavy and silent and dull. I would go there and watch him and marvel at his quick skill as he made the cloth, but in the house he was so quiet.

And my mother would say, Keep at your books. And I wasn't allowed out at night hardly at all in those years. All the other boys of the village including my brother whom she had given up as far as education was concerned would play football and shinty and go bird nesting but I stayed in the house reading and writing. She didn't understand what I was studying but had a superstitious reverence for it all and made sure that I kept at it. And all the time my father would sit by the fireside sometimes sleeping, sometimes looking at a newspaper, or at other times he would be down at the shed or sometimes he would stand at the door gazing outwards perhaps at the sky, perhaps at some imagined land of his own. And this quick insect hummed about me and would not let me alone. It cleaned everything up and tidied my life and kept it on course. And I brought home all the prizes from school and she would place the cups on the sideboard and show them to visitors till I grew tired of her as they did too. They disliked her for her ambition, they much preferred my father, he was much more like themselves than she was. She was like a sliver of wood in a fingernail, never resting. And my father would play the music of his loom, dark and silent and dull, till one day he had a heart attack while he was in the shed. His body toppled off his seat and he lay under it, his eyes sightless and gazing upwards and it was I who found him. And I remember the humming of the large black flies about the shed on that summer day with the door open to the fragrance of flowers outside.

He was buried, and I was left to the mercies of my mother who became very religious. She would even look in the Bible for texts which would prove to me that study was important. It was as if my father had never been, as if that dark music was buried forever in the dark earth.

And the world passed me by with its perfume for others but for me nothing but books. My mother's small sharp beak was always probing at me. Till one day she also died. Before she died I used to sit at her bedside listening to the business of her breath which was like an accelerating train. She was very brave. Even then she told me to keep at my books lest, I suppose, she should feel betrayed in eternity. She told me that death dues were in a drawer in a dressing table and that there was money there for her coffin as well. She wasn't afraid to die, she thought that she had done her work in the world by bringing me up to study books which she did not understand, though her faith was great. 'I am going to that place where there is rest and calm,' she said.

And I thought that perhaps there too she would be going about dusting heavenly tables and making sure that the saints kept at their theology.

I was then twenty years old and in university. While home one Christmas I had taken a girl to the house but after she had left my mother said, 'She won't do for you. She smokes.' And after that I never brought anyone home. I cried when she died. I cried more than I had cried for my father. I hadn't really known my father, that dark musician of the flesh. My mother's quick agile spirit had however sustained me, she had taught me the way to go though at times I hated it. And after all but for her would I ever have read the Greek authors? Would I ever have listened to great music, would I ever have seen great works of art? And that, in spite of the pain, is something. And also in spite of the fact that she herself had never looked at a painting in her life nor ever listened to Mozart or any other composer. Her favourite magazine was the *People's Friend* where after a great struggle the nurse eventually married the surgeon who had never noticed her till finally she had helped him in that Great Operation. But her will was indomitable and her ambition without end.

So I wept for her more than my brother did, for he knew that she had found him wanting and therefore he resented her.

And my mother is always clearer in my mind than my father is, he who had never shielded me from her remorseless light, who sat in his dumbness and his hopelessness. At least she had been optimistic. She had looked into the future and made me a schoolmaster. But at least she had been conscious of a future. My father had only been conscious of a past.

Once in Edinburgh I went to the zoo and in it I saw in a corner of a cage a great hulking bear lying down in its dark stink. In another cage I saw a leopard or perhaps a panther pacing restlessly up and down. And I wished to say to the bear, Why don't you get up from there? Why do you accept the darkness and the stink and the servitude? And I far preferred the leopard with its restless proud pacing. And also I liked the birds with their quick movements and their colourful plumage and their beaks that seemed to question the world around them. All that perhaps was dreams. But I did not like the dark bear. I wished to be like the leopard, optimistic and angry and agile.

For the bear had never used its strength but the leopard used all its energy without surrender to the end.

When I woke up I knew perfectly well what I must do. The idea came to me in my sleep.

19

'I don't believe it,' said Dougie.

'You heard what she said, that she was . . . '

'Attacked. I heard her and I don't believe it. The man is, was, quite harmless.'

'We have to believe her,' I said, 'and anyway after that the villagers wouldn't have allowed him to stay.'

'I can see *that*,' said Dougie. His eyes were cold and hard and hostile. 'Did you see his eyes?'

'His eyes?'

'Yes. When he set off on that bicycle of his again. It was like watching a refugee that I'd once seen in Europe. The same expression on his face.'

I didn't tell Dougie, but I did remember his expression when he set off again, upright on his bicycle in his dark clothes with the belt of rope around his waist. And the villagers standing watching him, hostile and threatening. The hermit's eyes had turned for a moment to look at me as if by strange magic the hermit had recognised his true enemy. After all, really, he had done nothing to me. And that perhaps accounted for his expression.

'I must say again,' said Dougie, 'that I don't believe it, that she was attacked. That man would never attack anyone. He has no possessions at all, did you notice? That was the hellish thing. He had nothing. He set off again. With nothing. And where was he going? And if he goes somewhere else will the people there also put him out? And we never,' he said, 'found out anything about him. He spoke to no one and no one spoke to him. He could be a fool or a genius – he could be anybody.' And he looked at me with horror.

Well, I had used the corrupted to get rid of the corrupted, I thought. Sometimes such things are necessary, sometimes ethics themselves have to be poisoned in order to create health.

'There didn't seem to be anything wrong with Janet that I could see,' Dougie repeated. 'She seemed to me self-possessed enough.'

'Why should she say she had been attacked unless she had been?' I asked innocently.

'I don't know but I have an idea,' he said. And there was the glitter of hate in his eyes.

The village would now be silent. It would now return to its ancient ways, it would not be disturbed. The mirror image of myself would have left it, expelled forever.

'What the hell is he going to do?' said Dougie again. 'I can't stand thinking about it. Wandering about forever on that bicycle.' I thought for a moment that he would weep.

But what in fact he did was to turn away.

'I don't think it would be a good idea if you came to the house again,' he said.

I didn't say anything but watched him go. Now I myself was truly alone, but then loneliness was something to be suffered in the service of one's kind. I knew that Dougie would be relentless and that his sense of fairness might not let him rest. But Janet wasn't going to talk. After all she had plenty of money now.

I looked at Murdo's unfinished house, I heard the music of the sea. I turned back into the house, feeling as if I didn't wish to talk to anyone. I thought of my wife, then of Janet, sitting in the chair by the fire, as I poured myself a whisky. No one understood what had happened. Not even Dougie understood that. It was true that like him I saw the figure of the hermit setting off into nothingness on his old bicycle. But it was true that it was necessary to make a refugee. I had saved them from silence at the expense of my own silence. I laughed bitterly as I sat down by the fireside. Even Kirsty would congratulate me. Even the minister. And yet I had a frightening feeling of emptiness as if I were suffering from a strange disease. What else could I think about now, now that that hut had no inhabitant, now that questions of metaphysics had been removed from me?

As I sat there for what seemed to be hours the day became dusk and then slowly the moon rose in the sky. I looked at it. It was dazzlingly white and clear, a brilliant stone, it was the eye of a Greek god or goddess. It was the stunning beauty of the mind, it had no physical beauty. It no longer reminded me of Janet, it was pure intellect. For Janet had been only an evanescent being, a sparkle of moonlight on the water. It was the cold stony mind that illuminated its own dead world remorselessly, its own extinct craters. I imagined the hermit cycling along in its light forever.

The house was extraordinarily peaceful as if by an act of will I had banished all the fertile ghosts. It had an unearthly calm as if I were floating on a dumb sea of solitude. I found myself humming to myself as if I had come to the silence of myself. I went to the bookcase and took out a book and began to read. Strangely enough I didn't realise at first what book it was. Then I saw that it was the Bible. I turned to the New Testament and began to read,

'In the beginning was the Word . . . '

The Impulse

Yesterday morning a most odd thing happened to me. I was walking down one of the streets of our small town – which has a population of 7,000 or so – when just as I approached the paper shop . . . or rather as I was about to approach the paper shop which is quite near the police station but on the other side of it, I saw on the window of the police station a large notice which read, *Wanted for Murder*. Now this is the extraordinary thing. I stopped, and I was just about to walk into the police station to give myself up when I thought for some reason that as it was Sunday the police station would not be open, and therefore I did not go into it. (I was in fact on my way to get the Sunday papers.) But the strange thing is that at that moment when I saw the notice I thought it applied to me, and, as I said, I nearly went into the police station to give myself up as a murderer, though I didn't know what sort of murder it was or who had murdered whom.

And I have been thinking about this for a whole day and night while my wife has been doing what she always does on a Sunday, that is, cooking the dinner and resting and sometimes reading a paper or a book.

And my problem is: whom am I supposed to have murdered? Now I consider this not only an interesting question but more deeply an alarming question. For I have never murdered anyone, that is to say, I have not shot or strangled or poisoned or in any way physically attacked any human being in my life. And yet I nearly surrendered myself to the police as a murderer. How is this to be explained?

It was a fine warm spring day – one of the best spring days we have had yet this year – and I was in fact perfectly happy and I was whistling as I walked down the street, and then I came to the police station and what I said happened happened.

Now most people would, I think, describe me as an ordinary person and I would call myself so. For instance, I am not very intelligent: I find the simplest crosswords and puzzles in the Sunday papers difficult. I have an ordinary job, that is to say I own a small grocery shop, and my wife works there with me. We have run this shop for the past thirty-four years. Naturally we have felt threatened by the new supermarket in the town but we have survived by working very hard. I met my wife at a dance many years ago and shortly after this we were married. She was then nineteen years old and I was twenty-three but this was all right as I have always believed that the husband should be older than the wife and if possible wiser. I had never slept with anyone before I met her. I thought her beautiful and sensible and this she has turned out to be. She is a good cook, she is extremely practical, she has brought the children up to be well-mannered and quiet in the presence of strangers, she works hard in the shop though it is in fact I who do most of the paper-work. It is true that sometimes I have seen her standing behind a counter as if lost in a dream, such that I have had to wake her up with a brisk word. When she falls into these dreams she seems to look younger and she is invariably looking out of the window at the time. Our window looks out on to the bay. At nights too when she is in bed with me I have heard her murmur strange names which might be the names of people or of places. But when I mention them to her in the morning she does not appear to know what I am talking about. Naturally this does not take place every night. It is very often during the summer that this happens, when the nights are warm, and the moon is shining brightly and there are perfumes of flowers from the neighbouring park.

I would say, I think, that I have been a good father. My children are of course away from me now. One is an engineer and the other, less bright perhaps, is a salesman. We see very little of them now since they are both in England but when they were growing up I was kind though strict. For instance, if James (the engineer) misbehaved I would patiently explain to him why misbehaviour was wrong and what the consequences might be; for example, that if God exists, as He does, He might punish him either by day or by night or at any time when he least expected it. I would say the same to Colin though in fact he did not listen so patiently. In his case, I would sometimes be forced to use direct punishment such as sending him to bed in the dark for I have never believed in physical chastisement.

My wife and I therefore live together on our own for most of the time.

We still work hard, even though we are old, and are respected by the townspeople. Sometimes, indeed, we are invited to dinners, though we are not seated in the most prominent places. My wife, I think, does not like this, though she does not complain at great length as so many wives do. For instance, she might wear a new black velvet dress which she has just bought and find that very few people speak to her and that she is at the lowest end of the table. Nor can she talk, therefore, on subjects that interest her for she is in fact much more intelligent than me and the only reason why she doesn't do the paper-work is that it bores her. I, on the contrary, am not bored by paper-work and in fact I quite like doing it for I have, as I myself recognise, a plodding but steady mind.

Thus we are, on the whole, contented.

Naturally we do not speak to each other as much as we used to. When she talks to me I grunt a lot, especially if I am reading the paper. But I understand and I think she understands that we are no longer young and that therefore some magic which we once had will not return. After all we are mature people. It would not be natural for us to be hugging each other all day or murmuring endearments to each other. These things are for youth, not for old age. And quite apart from that I feel tired when I come home from the shop and nothing suits me better than putting my feet up and smoking my pipe.

It is true that my wife does not appear so beautiful to me as she once did. But then I myself am not very handsome and have never been so. I often wonder why she married me in the first place but when I ask her, all she will say is, 'You cannot explain these things.' And indeed one cannot. For I myself cannot explain why I married her except that it seemed inevitable at the time. And of course she was very pretty and others were after her. I consider myself lucky that she married me.

Our life has been a struggle but whose life has not been? There have been weeks and months when we had to work very hard and when we talked endlessly in bed about how we would survive at all. Sometimes she would tell me that I must buy more exotic delicacies for the shop such as cheeses and small tins of caviare and at times I have been persuaded to do so but in general I have relied on customers who do not have much money. There have been times when they have let me down and not paid me for months, sometimes even years: some of them have not paid me at all.

Also in the early years of our marriage, my wife would say to me, 'Why don't you advertise in a better way? Do something surprising to draw attention to the shop.' Or at other times she would say, 'Why don't we emigrate?' But the children were growing up and I could neither take risks nor emigrate and on summer nights the strange names of her dreams would become more and more numerous and mysterious and unintelligible. And on summer mornings I would catch her looking in the mirror as if she were watching her beauty passing.

Thus I would say that we have led an ordinary life, not very different from the lives of most other people, and perhaps more secure and more stable.

We are both now well over sixty and when I look at my wife I see little sign of what she once was and when she looks at me I am sure she sees little of what I once used to be. In a few years we shall both be dead, and no one will remember us for we cannot write poetry or music or make speeches. Then they will take us to the local cemetery and bury us beside each other for I have already bought the ground in which we will both lie.

It is also true that five years ago my wife began to sleepwalk for a number of nights but ceased to do so as abruptly as she had begun. It was a great joke between us, for one of the things she did was to take flowers from a vase which we have in the living-room and take them quite gravely to bed with her, while water dripped across the floor as she blindly carried them along. Neither she nor I understood why she did this but as I say she stopped doing it when she realised that because of my anxiety about her I was hardly getting any sleep.

Thus it is not clear to me why I should nearly have walked into the police station yesterday morning.

However, I shall not tell my wife about it for I feel that she is settling down quite happily now for our last few years together. She has become much quieter and to tell the truth I can read my books in peace. She no longer tells me stories of people she has met at whist drives, and their strange ways. Nor is she liable to flash out in sudden bursts of rage as she sometimes has done in the past after a particularly tiring day with some of our more harassing customers. She no longer wishes to go out much, nor is she in the habit of buying new dresses designed to impress other men's wives. I myself have never felt that I needed to impress anybody. I was brought up to be well-mannered and quiet and to know my station in life.

I shall simply have to forget that impulse which came over me yesterday on that fine spring morning when I was whistling as I walked down the street. I think it would never have occurred if it had been a wet dismal day or if it had been any other day except a Sunday. Nevertheless I do not understand it. It would certainly have been embarrassing if I had gone in and met Inspector Munro whom I know very well and whose wife is a regular customer. I don't know what I would have done but I would probably have invented a story to account for my presence. I suppose however he would have considered it odd just the same, as he must be a trained observer since after all he is a policeman.

The only thing I can think of is that it must have been a slight aberration such as old people are prone to. None of our family has ever been a murderer or a thief.

But I think that in future I must avoid the police station in case I succumb to that impulse which I nearly succumbed to yesterday. It might be better if I ceased to read the Sunday papers altogether and confined myself to the books that are already in the house, most of which I have read over and over already. In any case, my wife seems quite happy that I should be with her most of the time and I find her company more relaxing than I did when we were young and facing the storms of life.

Timoshenko

When I went into the thatched house as I always did at nine o'clock at night, he was lying on the floor stabbed with a bread knife, his usually brick-red face pale and his ginger moustache a dark wedge under his nose. His eyes were wide open like blue marbles. I wondered where she was. The radio was still on and I went over and switched it off. At the moment she came down from the other room and sat on the bench. There was no point in going for a doctor; he was obviously dead: even I could tell that. She sat like a child, her knees close together, her hands folded in her lap.

I had regarded the two of them as children. He had a very bad limp and sat day after day at the earthen wall which bordered the road, his glassy hands resting on his stick, talking to the passers-by. Sometimes he would blow on his fingers, his cheeks red and globular. She on the other hand sat in the house most of the time, perhaps cooking a meal or washing clothes. Of the two I considered her the simpler, though she had been away from the island a few times, in her youth, at the fishing, but had to be looked after by the other girls in case she did something silly.

'Did you do that?' I said, pointing to the body which seemed more eloquent than either of us. She nodded wordlessly. As a matter of fact I hadn't liked him very much. He was always asking me riddles to which I did not know the answer, and when I was bewildered he would nod his head and say, 'I don't understand what they are teaching at these schools nowadays.' He had an absolutely bald head which shone in the light and a sarcastic way of speaking. He would call his sister Timoshenko or Voroshilov, because the Russians at that time were driving the Germans out of their country and these generals were always in the news. 'Timoshenko will know about it,' he would say and she would stand there smiling, a teapot in her hands.

But of course I never thought what it was like for the two of them when I wasn't there. Perhaps he persecuted her. Perhaps his sarcasm was a perpetual wound. Perhaps, lame as he was, sitting at the wall all day, he was petrified by boredom and his tiny mind squirmed like the snail-like meat inside a whelk. He had never left the island in his whole life and I didn't know what had caused his limp which was so serious that he had to drag himself along by means of two sticks.

The blood had stopped flowing and the body lay on the floor like a log. The fire was out and the dishes on the dresser were clean and colourful rising in tier after tier. The floor which was made of clay seemed to undulate slightly. I felt unreal as if at any moment the body would rise from the floor like a question mark and ask me another riddle, the moustache twitching like an antenna. But this didn't happen. It stayed there solid and heavy, the knife sticking from its breast.

I knew that soon I would have to get someone, perhaps the policeman or a doctor or perhaps a neighbour. But I was so fascinated by the woman that I stayed, wondering why she had done it. Girlishly she sat on the bench, her hands in her lap, not even twisting them nervously.

Suddenly she said, 'I don't know why but I took the knife and I . . . I don't know why.'

She looked past me, then added, 'I can't remember why I did it. I don't understand.'

I waited for her to talk and after a while she went on.

'Many years ago,' she said, 'I was going to be married. He made fun of me when Norman came into the house. He said I couldn't cook and I couldn't wash, and that was wrong. That must have been twenty years ago. He was limping then too. He told Norman I was a bit daft. That was many years ago. But that wasn't it. Anyway, he told Norman I was silly. Norman had put on his best suit when he came to the house. He wasn't rich or anything like that. You don't know him. Anyway he's dead now. He died last week in the next village. He was on his own and they found him in the house dead. He had been dead for a week; of course he was quite old. He was older than me then. Anyway he came into the house and he was wearing his best suit and he had polished his shoes and I thought that he looked very handsome. Well, Donald said that I wasn't any good at cooking and that I was silly. He made fun of me and all the time he made fun of me Norman looked at me, as if he wanted me to say something. I remember he had a white handkerchief in his pocket and it looked very clean. Norman didn't have much to say for himself. In those days he worked a croft and he was building a house. I was thirty years old then and he was forty-two. I was wearing a long brown skirt which I had got at the fishing and I was sitting as I am sitting now with my hands in my lap as my mother taught me. Donald said that I smoked when I was away from home. That was wicked of him. Of course to him it was a joke but it wasn't true. I think Norman believed him and he didn't like women smoking. My brother, you see, would make jokes all the time, they were like knives in my body, and my mind wasn't quick enough to say something back to him. Norman maybe didn't love me but we would have been happy together. Donald believed that his jokes were very funny, that people looked up to him, and that he was a clever man. But of course he . . . Maybe if it hadn't been for his limp he might have carried on in school, so he said anyway. I left school at twelve. I had to look after him even when my parents were alive.

'It didn't matter what I did, it was wrong. The tea was too hot or too cold. The potatoes weren't cooked right or the herring wasn't salt enough. "Who would marry you?" he would say to me. But I think Norman would have married me. Norman was a big man but he was slow and honest. He wasn't sarcastic at all and he couldn't think like my brother. "She was in Yarmouth," Donald told him, "but they won't have her back, she's too stupid. Aren't you, Mary?" he asked me. That wasn't true. The reason I couldn't go to Yarmouth was because I had to stay at home and look after him. I was going to go but he made me stop. He got very ill the night before I was due to leave and I had to stay behind. Anyway Norman went away that night and he never came back. I can still see him going out the door in his new suit back to the new house he was building. I found out afterwards that my brother had seen him and told him that I used to have fits at the time of the new moon, and that wasn't true.

'So I never married, and Donald would say to me, if I did something that he didn't like, "That's why Norman never married you, you're too stupid. And you shouldn't be going about with your stockings hanging down to your ankles. It doesn't look ladylike." '

I remembered how I used to come and listen to the News in this very house and it would tell of the German armies being inexorably strangled by the Russians. I would have visions of myself like Timoshenko standing up in my tank with dark goggles over my eyes as the Germans cowered in the snow and the rope of cold was drawn tighter and tighter. And he would say to me, 'Now then, tell me how many mackerel there are in a barrel. Go on now, tell me that.' And he would put his bald head on one side and look at me, his ginger moustache bristling. Or he would say, 'Tell me, then, what is the Gaelic for a compass. Eh? The proper Gaelic, I mean. Timoshenko will tell you that. Won't you, Timoshenko? She was at the fishing, weren't you, Timoshenko?'

And he would shift his aching legs, sighing heavily, his face becoming redder and redder.

'He thought I knew nothing,' she said. 'Other times he would threaten to put me out of the house because it belongs to him, you see.' She looked down at the body as if he were still alive and he were liable to stand up and throw her out of the house, crowing like a cockerel, his red cheeks inflated, and his red wings beating.

'He would say, "I'll get a housekeeper in. There's plenty who would make a good housekeeper. You're so stupid you don't know anything. And you leave everthing so dirty. Look at this shirt you're supposed to have washed!" '

Was all this really true, I wondered. Had this woman lived in this village for so many years without anyone knowing anything about her suffering? It seemed so strange and unreal. All the time we had thought of the two as likeable comedians and one was cruel and vicious and the other was tormented and resentful. We had thought of them as nice, pleasant people, characters in the village. We didn't think of them as people at all, human beings who were locked in a death struggle. When people talked about her she became a sunny figure out of a comic, blundering about in a strange English world when she left the island, but happy all the same. We hadn't imagined that she was suffering like this in her dim world. And when we saw him sitting by the wall we thought of him as a fixture and we would shout greetings to him and he would shout back some quaint witticism. How odd it all was.

'But I knew what was going on all the time,' she continued. 'I could follow the news too. I knew what the Germans were doing, and the Russians. But he made me out to be a fool. And the thing was even after I heard of Norman's death I didn't say anything, though he said a few things himself. He told me one day, "You should have been his housekeeper and he wouldn't have been found dead like that on his own. But you weren't good enough for him. Poor man." And he would look at me with those small eyes of his. They had found Norman, you see, by the fire. He had fallen into it, he was ill and old. He hadn't been well for years. I often thought of taking him food but Donald wouldn't let me. After all we're all human and a little food wouldn't have been missed. I used to think of when we were young so many years ago. And when I was young I wasn't ugly. I wasn't beautiful but I wasn't ugly. I used to go to the dances when I was young, like the others. And of course I was at Yarmouth. He had never been out of the island though he was a man and I was only a woman and we used to bring presents home at the end of the season. I bought him a pipe once and another time I got him a melodeon but he wouldn't play it. So you see, there was that.'

There was another longish silence. Outside, it was pitch black and there was ice on the roads. In fact coming over from my own house I nearly slipped and fell but I had a torch so that was all right.

I wasn't at all afraid of her. I was in a strange way enjoying our conversation or rather her monologue. It was as if I was listening to an important story about life, a warning and a disaster. I remembered how as children we would be frightened by her brother waving his sticks from the wall where he was sitting. And we would run away full tilt as if we were running away from a monster. Our parents would say, 'It's only his joking,' and think how kind he was to go out of his way to entertain the children, but I wondered now whether in fact it might not be that he hated children and it wasn't acting at all, that cockerel clapping his sticks at us as we scattered across the moor.

Maybe too he had been more in pain than we had thought.

The trouble was that we didn't visit the two of them much at all. I did so, but only because I wished to listen to their radio to hear the news. Also, I was a quiet, reserved person who was happier in the company of people older than myself. But I hadn't actually looked at either of them with a clear hard look. To me she was a simple creature who smiled when her brother made some joke about Timoshenko, for his jokes tended to be remorselessly repetitive. It didn't occur to me that she was perhaps being pierced to the core by his primitive witticisms and it didn't occur to me either that they were meant to be cruel and were in fact outcrops from a perpetual war.

Suddenly she said to me, 'Would you like a cup of tea?' Without thinking I said 'Yes,' as if it was the most natural remark in the world while the body lay on the floor between us. I was amazed at how calmly I had accepted the presence of the body, though I had always thought of myself as sensitive and delicate. But on the other hand it was as if the body was not real, as if, as I have said, it would get to its feet, place its sticks under its arms, and walk towards me asking me riddles. Naturally however this didn't happen. And so we drank the tea out of neat cups with thin blue stripes at the rim.

'I had to give him all my saccharins,' she said, 'because he liked sweet things. It's a long time since I've had such a sweet cup of tea.' I noticed then that she had put saccharins in my tea and I realised that this was the first time that I had had tea in her house. She was in a strange way savouring her transient freedom.

'I remember now,' she said. 'It was the Germans and

Timoshenko. The Germans had been trying to destroy Russia. I knew that, I'm not daft. And now the Russians were killing them. I heard that on the six o'clock news. And Timoshenko, he was doing that, he was winning. It was then that I . . . ' She stopped then, the cup at her lips. 'I remember now. It was when it said about Timoshenko and he said the tea wasn't sweet enough. That was when I . . . I must have been cutting bread. I must . . . '

She looked at me in amazement as if it was just at that moment that she realised she had killed him. As she began to tremble I took the cup from her hands – it was spilling over – and put my arm around her and comforted her while she cried.

The Spy

She has just left me, she has taken her case and gone, and I am sitting here drinking whisky and thinking for the hundredth time that we are living in a spy story, all of us. I know I'm drunk but I see this quite clearly. When I look back on it all I see it with the clarity of the insane, though I'm certainly not that. As a psychiatrist I've seen something of the way the minds of the insane – and especially those of schizophrenics – work, and I know that sometimes they have visions. I have visions myself. Perhaps it is the whisky but I think not, perhaps it is what is about to happen, but no, I have thought of this for some time now. She turned at the door with her small case in her hand, for the last time. She was about to say something but decided against it after all. She is going to that large painter Rank, whom she met at a party some months ago. I wish I had never taken her there. He is so much larger than me, more flamboyant, more vibrant, so much a filler of space and he is so positive about his work. And I think it is probably very good. I think I know something about painting, though Vermeer is my favourite painter. I don't on the whole like modern stuff, my mind is too orderly for that. Anyway I suppose that, like her, he paints abstract paintings, colourful and fragmentary, and he has such belief in himself and such a loud voice that he makes me feel weak.

She is of course much younger than I am. I met her first when she was one of my patients for a while, though there was really nothing wrong with her. She was recovering from a love affair that had gone wrong and she said she wanted to be straightened out. These were her very words. At first I didn't think a great deal about her. She seemed smallish and dark and rather untidy and I should say clumsy. She looked a bit odd and was at the time working in one of those ridiculous Health Shops where they have copies of the works of Herman Hesse, and stuff in bins which looks like bran. She also for a while wore beads and a long brown coat which trailed the floor. She had run away from home some years before and had kept herself alive somehow or other in London: I gathered that she had found it difficult.

She was the sort of girl that grows on one. One day she didn't turn up at all and I felt a certain emptiness which I couldn't account for. I suppose really the reason why she has been attracted to Rank is that she has something of the same quality that he has, that is, the idea that the future will take care of itself, a spendthrift bravado. She had read in an undisciplined manner; and indeed I thought her mind was a mess, full of the most extraordinary mixture of Salvador Dali and silly Eastern philosophies. She herself of course painted. She talked incessantly and asked about the Vermeer reproductions I had on the wall. She said she had drunk a lot after her break with a student, who had been studying law and who had given her the push.

'I find your placc so restful,' she would say and lie down on the couch and close her eyes. Indeed once or twice she went to sleep and I would look down at her and feel a deep pathos as if she were a waif of the storm and needed protection. There was, as I have said, nothing obviously wrong with her. It was just the fact that she had been jilted that had caused her symptoms of sleeplessness, etc. 'He had these dull parents,' she said, 'and they wanted him to marry someone respectable. Deep down, that was what he wanted to do himself. I could see it happening but at the end I didn't care. You know.' As a matter of fact I didn't know. Not at all. But she thought I did, and that was flattering. At that time I had never felt mental anguish. I thought of myself as a god ministering to the incomprehensibly sick. I couldn't understand why a jilting should have done all that to her. 'I cried for two whole days,' she said once, 'and then I went out and got absolutely sloshed. I drank two bottles of gin. I nearly killed myself.' And I would look at her not knowing what she was talking about.

I am not very good at describing people so I can't give you

any good idea of what she looked like or the way she would bounce into a room in her slacks – she always wore slacks – and plump herself down on the sofa, her hands supporting her head, and look at me like a schoolgirl. She seemed absolutely open and helpless. Even her eyes were like that. They looked large and innocent and questioning and ready for experience.

'I don't know how you can do it,' she would say to me. 'I mean listen to all this and look so calm. Day after day. You must feel like a bin with people unloading stuff into you all the time.' What she didn't know was that the calm had become a kind of callousness. Nothing surprised me but nothing touched me. Once she brought me some of her paintings but I didn't think much of them, though I pretended I did and in actual fact bought one. She would follow me with her eyes as I sometimes walked up and down the room thinking. She was very untidy, as I have said. She wore slacks and jerseys which always looked soiled with paint. She didn't seem to care about her appearance and this was a great part of her attraction. She always seemed breathless as if she had been running somewhere. At the beginning she wore her Eastern gear but as she grew to know me better I noticed that she would come in the clothes in which she had been painting.

'Have you ever looked at a red bus on a spring day?' she would say as if she had made a great discovery. 'That great red cube moving along the street. I should like to paint a red bus or a pillar box. That's what it's all about.' And she would plump herself down and sometimes I would talk. I think at first she admired my mind though God knows it's a pretty dull one in comparison with hers. I would talk to her about ideas of various kinds and she would listen or pretend to listen. She never gave the impression of being bored though I think she must have been. I didn't know then her subconscious cruelty. On the surface she wasn't at all cruel; she seemed, in fact, totally unaware of what impression she was making and this was what attracted me. I had seen enough of sophisticated ladies all beautifully dressed. The world – my world – is full of them. They don't want to be cured of anything. My consulting-room is a place where they can pass the time and show off their knowledge of psychiatry.

I think the first day I realised I loved her was on a particularly wet day in November when London looked very dark indeed. She was standing by the window and she seemed to be shivering and I looked down at the rain falling so heavily and I said, 'I'll drive you wherever you want to go.' But as I was unlocking the door of the car I thought, 'No, I don't want to drive her to some godforsaken flat. I'll take her home.' I needed a drink after a heavy day and I suggested this to her. To my surprise she was delighted. She couldn't drive herself and she snuggled into her seat, her small white face looking like that of a Madonna. After I had switched on the electric fire, and we had warmed ourselves (I need a lot of warmth in winter) she wandered about my large house commenting on this and that. 'How on earth do you have time to read all these books?' she said when she saw my library. 'And where did you get these African masks? And these paintings – you must be filthy rich.' I am, as a matter of fact, pretty rich. I am a good psychiatrist and I inherited money. My father was a surgeon and a stern abstemious man. He left me this house in which I'm now drinking. I cooked her some food and we drank some wine but we didn't go to bed or anything like that. I remember that she curled up at my feet like a kitten and stared into the fire and said, 'What space you've got. How easy it must be to work in this large house. Why, if there was someone living with you you wouldn't need to see them at all. I suppose you have a housekeeper too?' I said there was a woman who came in every day and did for me and that the house didn't really need all that keeping up. I didn't mess it up. I felt like the good fairy in a story showing off all my riches and clearly this house and my way of life were strange to her.

The things she paid attention to were odd. For instance, there was a blue paperweight which attracted her: I gave her that. And there was a framed poem of Lorca's on the wall about a gipsy, which she would recite over and over. It had of course been translated. She had never heard of Lorca and had only the vaguest idea of the Spanish Civil War. I realised that I was much older than her but I wondered whether I was wiser. Normally I would have been working on my critique of Alder in the light of recent ideas but I decided that I wouldn't do any work that night. She left at ten o'clock and I drove her to her flat where she stayed with three other girls.

After that I took her out quite a lot, mostly to restaurants. Once or twice I took her to the theatre but she preferred the cinema and she would take me to the most terrifying films where violence was shown in close-up, and the blood seemed more than just technicolour. She was especially fond of Scandinavian films infested with sex and nudity but I'm afraid that I couldn't understand them. They always had an air of meaning more than they stated and of being more modern than they actually were. They all seemed to be about young people disporting themselves by lakes and stripping to the waist whenever the opportunity offered. I'm not sure whether she understood them either, but she liked them. In a strange way I thought of them as Rousseauistic back-to-nature tableaux which smelt strongly of corruption, not of innocence. I learned however that the theatre bored her and so did Shakespeare. She was totally truthful in her reactions to everything and I discovered that I myself was a bit of a hypocrite. Did I really like Shakespeare as much as I thought I did? Probably not. We also saw a memorable performance of *The Spy who came in from the Cold*. Saturdays we would drive out of the city and picnic.

We were married a year ago yesterday. Even now I can hardly understand how it happened. I think one of the reasons was that one night we were in a restaurant and she smiled at the younger waiter who was pouring the wine. He was a glamorous young fellow with very fair hair and startlingly blue eyes. I think he must have been Nordic. At the moment for the first time in my life I felt the most intense pure pain of jealousy. I had never felt jealousy in my whole life before. I had been out with women but I hadn't felt jealous of them; my feelings had not been committed. I hadn't realised what she had meant when she told me about her jilting. Now I knew. Some being up there was taking revenge on me. I didn't let her know what had happened but at that moment I asked her to marry me. I worked out that I would rather have her near me than have her wandering about without my knowing what was happening to her or whom she was with. Incredibly and almost casually she said she'd like that and continued to drink her wine.

'But I won't wear a ring,' she said. 'I have a thing against rings.' Again I was stabbed by jealousy but I said that that would be all right. It wouldn't be a church wedding anyway. Looking back now I can see that from that moment I was glancing round the restaurant wondering if anyone was spying on us, if anyone wanted to take her away from me. Human eyes became important to me. I had been walking before that moment casually through a wood, now I was aware of the other animals. Now there was something of mine that I wanted to keep. Before, I hadn't felt like that at all. My house was full of valuable things but it had never occurred to me that anyone would steal them. And not being alive they weren't unpredictable, they wouldn't walk away to another house. Now, however, I was afraid. I sensed the eyes all around me. I sensed that they were avaricious and watchful, searching for my weakness. The world, I thought, is full of spies. They want to drain us of our secrets and strengthen themselves at our expense. They want to enlarge their territories. But her eyes at any rate appeared innocent.

I didn't know what I expected when I got married, but certainly the word 'idyllic' could on the whole be applied to the first few months of it. I continued with my work during the day and my writing at night, and Brenda painted. It was almost as if she had been looking for space in which to paint. She would, as far as I understand it, paint all day without eating much at all. By this time I had got a permanent housekeeper in and I told her to make sure that Brenda ate something after she had spoken to me about her lack of interest in food. 'She gets into an old smock and paints all day, sir,' she said. But Brenda assured me that she never ate anything much and her health did not seem to suffer. I would look at her paintings and certainly they seemed to be gaining in some sort of power, though as I have told you they were mostly abstracts and I don't understand them much. This fever of painting went on for about six months and we were happy. We were sexually happy and we had much to tell each other. She would talk to me about her paintings and I would tell her about my patients, especially a potential psychopath called Wilson who I felt sure would have been quite happy if there was a war on but, as there wasn't, he was extremely miserable. However, he spent most of his weekends with a gun shooting rabbits and, for all I know, sheep. She seemed particularly interested in him and asked me questions about him and I told her about psychopaths, that they had no moral sense at all, that they had never developed a proper public persona, that they were like outsized children with a young child's intense egotism and capacity for hatred.

We didn't go out much in those days at all, we seemed to be sufficient for each other. I hadn't realised that this was possible but I found myself incredibly happy. The only way I can describe it is by saying that everything seemed to taste better, the food, the air, everything. It was as if whole areas of me had come alive. I would get up in the morning and actually sing in the bathroom and I had a new zest for my work. Everything that I did turned to gold. I was a sensuous Midas. Not that I was interested so much in money but it was as if Brenda had opened me out like a new country, with new trees growing there and birds singing on the branches. It was almost as if I had taken a strange new drug. Even the furniture seemed sparkling and new. And yet Brenda most of the time was untidy in her painter's smock, her hands stained with paint. She talked incessantly about what painting was, how it must be sensuous, how the mind was not important to it. Even my article on Adler began to take shape though at that time it was more of a critique than a rhapsody. I didn't at that time believe that people tried to gain power over each other, certainly it didn't seem to be so with us. In short, I was in love, and I would recommend the experience to anyone. For though as I said we didn't go out at all, we seemed to live in a world that we had made ourselves. We explored each other. She explored my abstract mind and I explored her personality, sensuous and rich. I think now that at that time she found something useful to her in the abstraction of my mind. Perhaps it gave her work a discipline, a backbone.

But of course such an existence couldn't last. It isn't in the nature of things to do so. Life overtakes us again when we are least ready for it. Now and again I could see signs of a waning. Once she said to me, 'I don't understand how you can be so interested in such boring authors.' And she would point at my row of books. I didn't at the time really understand that she in fact did find these people boring and I took the remark as a joke. But she had no intellectual curiosity at all, I mean she wasn't interested in ideas. She was interested in people such as Wilson and she was interested in flowers and plants – I had a rather neglected garden – and she was interested in strange odds and ends lying about the house, even pieces of wood which had been found on the seashore. But ideas immediately, as she said, turned her off. In fact sometimes I couldn't understand how she could be interested in me at all. She also would remark that I didn't know anything about painting, that if I thought Vermeer was good I had no taste. 'He's so cold,' she would say. But it was Vermeer's intellect and logical space that had drawn me to him in the first place. I realised that, but I didn't realise that this meant that the two of us were unalterably opposed.

After six months were over, I sensed that she was growing restless. She wasn't painting at all now but according to Mrs Gray prowled about the house picking things up and putting them down again, glancing at a book and laying it down, smoking and drinking. There was no sign of a child on the way and I had a feeling that perhaps there wouldn't be, not that I myself was particularly interested. I knew that we had entered a second phase, especially when she referred more and more often to Lorca's poem about the gipsy. We had our first serious quarrel after I had taken her to a party which a married couple whom I knew were giving. This was the first time we had visited anyone since our marriage. This may sound incredible but it's true. We simply didn't have time and we were so preoccupied with each other and with our work which seemed to flower so naturally.

It was the usual sort of cocktail party which is a high hum of noise where people hold drinks in their hands and look superior, imagining brilliant things they might say except that they can't think of them. I talked for some considerable time to Bell and his wife. Bell is said to be the most brilliant exponent of his own esoteric branch of logic in the Western world but he is also a very nice, quiet man who has a very nice, quiet wife. Strangely enough I had forgotten about Brenda as we discussed whether logic itself is emotionally based and whether even in logic we find the things we are looking for. Bell agreed with me, though I had the feeling, as always with him, that he was talking most of the time at a level which I couldn't follow. I enjoyed the discussion and it was only afterwards I realised that I had been starved of intellectual conversation. After a while he said to me, 'I think your wife is over there,' and his voice sounded very considerate as if he were talking to a sick man.

At that time I was so sure of Brenda that I ignored what he had just said and continued with my remarks. Still looking at me in that quiet, almost pitying way, he said, 'I was once shown an article by a friend of mine on logic and I couldn't find anything wrong with it. Yet I knew that it was wrong just the same. I just knew.'

'How can that be?' I said.

He shrugged his shoulders and didn't speak. And I knew that I had missed the point of what he had been telling me. I turned away, saying goodbye politely, and almost bumped into Professor Train who was bumbling along in his usual shambling manner. I didn't want to speak to him and made my way over to where Brenda was supposed to be. On the way I met my hosts again, James Drew and his wife. Drew is a surgeon who knew and admired my father, and his wife is also a doctor. He is a smallish, red-faced man and he said,

'Glad you could come. We haven't seen you for ages.'

'No, indeed,' said his wife. 'We are so glad to meet Brenda at last. Why, you've been hermits.'

I couldn't see Bell any longer. He would be listening patiently to the inane chatter of some woman with a long cigarette-holder in her hand. The funny thing was that I couldn't get out of my mind the idea that when he was talking about logic he really was talking about my wife. I had heard rumours over the years that he and his wife were on the point of separation but that this hadn't happened so far. I could see that he had been drinking heavily.

Drew was saying that we must come and see them soon and his wife was nodding agreement. At that moment I had a terrible feeling that Brenda had left me and had gone home. I felt utterly unnerved and lost as if I saw the party for the first time from her point of view. All these people were old, they did not belong to her generation. They were all intellectuals. What could she say to Professor Train if she came across him leaning towards her with his old-world courtesy and talking about the Byzantine Empire?

What could she say to Bell, reserved, taciturn and desperate? Or even to Drew and his wife who had set this jiggling affair going to mitigate their own boredom? She was like a child in the woods, with the Red Indian hairband that she insisted on wearing.

I felt oppressed as if I had made a major mistake. Spies everywhere. Bell and Drew spying on me, wondering what I was doing. Eyes following me. Looking at eyes. Eyes devouring eyes. The whole room was infested with eyes. I thought that perhaps a painting could be made in which there would be a forest of eyes, eyes ravenously searching for some miraculous advent. Eyes weary and red, eyes glittering and cold, eyes starved of experience.

And people who believed in nothing but were looking for belief. Even Bell believed in nothing. That logic itself was emotionally based, to believe such a thing ... And his wife hovering around him, not sure of what he was talking about. Having an IQ of that level. What torture it must be! Imagine being a professor of that most obscure branch of logic! Why? Why should a man confine himself to that? But at least I had Brenda. I needed her.

And finally I saw her. She was sitting on the floor at the feet of a big man with flaming red hair who was holding forth to a group around him. She looked rather drunk and there was a globular glass beside her on the floor.

The man was saying: 'The day of the narrative is over. What

we have now is not a logic of thought but a logic of images. You see it everywhere, in literature, in music, and in art. And in the cinema. Go out into the city and see that. I mean all the lights flickering on and off. They don't constitute a narrative as perhaps the village did in olden times. What we see are flashes. We connect them quickly. Even driving a car you can see the same sort of thing. You react to flashes of signals, from everywhere around you. You haven't got the time to connect them into a continuous narrative. In the old days perhaps you might have the time but not now. You had leisure and you could stroll down the street or wherever, but not in the city. In the city you realise your knowledge is partial, you only know fragments, you react to these. And that is what modern painting is about, it is about the city. It is about these signals that we live by . . . '

As if aware that I was there, Brenda looked round and then turned away again. I knew that she was angry but at the same time that she was interested. I didn't want to sit beside her on the floor so I stood where I was and listened to this red-haired man, this demon, who went on and on and on, exhausting everyone around him except apparently Brenda. He had the look of a man who believed in what he was saying and people reacted positively to this because they themselves believed in nothing. A primitive force emanated from him. I knew that he was a painter and I knew why Brenda was listening to him. He was putting into words for her what she had sensed herself, the fragmentary isolation of painting, the sense of travelling without destination.

As the night wore on and we all sat there and some eventually left, he still went on and on, forceful, brutal. By half past eleven he had got on to psychology and its relation to painting. He was saying:

'Freud of course tried to analyse painters.' (Was it my imagination that he was looking at me in a challenging manner?) 'He had the temerity to try his ideas out on Leonardo da Vinci. He worked out from one painting that da Vinci's allegiance was divided between two mothers and from his continual swirling drawings like women's hair that he was a homosexual. The point is however that he knew things about da Vinci before he started. But what if he had known nothing about da Vinci?' By this time people were beginning to leave. Eventually I was still waiting for Brenda and the painter who were both getting steadily drunker. Suddenly Brenda stood up and said,

'This is Trevor Rank, the painter. This is my husband. He's a psychiatrist.'

We looked at each other and disliked what we saw. I hadn't intervened in what he had been saying about psychology at all. I don't like speaking in public. I'm a private person. And I recognised that Rank was a totally irrational person who would not be interested in reasonable discussion but in brutal swiping at an opponent. I nodded curtly in acknowledgement, and so did he.

Brenda walked beside me in silence to the car and we both got in. As she settled down, I heard her say very loudly, 'Thank Christ that's over.'

I didn't say anything. We drove in silence through the streets of fragmentary lights. It was true enough what the man had said. Reds and yellows made patterns against the rain. The traffic lights flashed on and off. I felt we had come to some sort of crisis. We spent the rest of the journey in silence but I felt Brenda seething beside me. And I myself was angry as well. I should never have taken her there. These people were too old for her. And I wished to God that she hadn't met Rank. I felt there would be trouble from that direction. Her pose of the disciple sitting at his feet affected me strongly. I sensed that I had lost some control over her. Or rather I felt that our period of idyllic happiness was over. As I manoeuvred my way through the coloured streets which might very well turn into a painting I knew that the next few months or weeks would be decisive. She had stopped painting and her inspiration had run out, and she was looking for fresh inspiration. Rank had provided her with an ethic which might help her but she might need to see him again.

When we finally reached the living-room she poured out a whisky and drank it quickly. She had taken off her coat in a frozen silence.

'These people,' she said at last, 'are mummies.'

'I thought they were quite pleasant,' I said peaceably. 'They liked you.'

'Like me,' she said, 'like me? Who cares whether they like me or not? And you went off and discussed some abstruse point or other and left me to take care of myself.'

'I'm sorry,' I said. 'I shouldn't have done that. But you seem to have found someone interesting.'

'You're dead right,' she said, 'he's interesting. All your friends seem to be dead from the waist up. They wouldn't even speak to me. Just because I was wearing my hairband, I suppose. If I hadn't heard of some creep called Wittgenstein or somebody like that I wasn't quoted.'

'I'm sorry,' I said again, 'but you must admit that your friend Rank is a bit boring too. At least, I found him boring. He went on and on, didn't he?'

'But I noticed that you didn't interrupt him,' she said viciously. 'He was taking your psychology apart and you just stood there and took it. You didn't open your mouth.'

'I knew he would be irrational,' I said. 'I knew he wouldn't be interested in argument for argument's sake. He's only interested in winning, not discussing.'

'That's because he believes in what he's saying,' Brenda snapped. 'That's the difference between him and the rest of the creeps there. He is creative and he actually has ideas. These other people whisper all the time. They know so much they're dead. I felt I was in a mortuary.'

'Some of them,' I said, 'happen to be the best in the world in their own field.'

'What fucking field?' she said. And she laughed. I realised that she was a little drunk and tried to be reasonable but I too was tired and needled. After all I hadn't liked the adoring looks she had cast at Rank. And even now as she threw herself back in the chair, her usually pale face even paler, I knew that she was necessary to me. But I also knew that that would not be enough.

'I'm sorry,' I repeated, 'I should have looked after you.'

'I didn't need to be looked after,' she shouted. 'And don't keep saying you're sorry all the time. You sound Japanese. It's the smug class-consciousness of these people I can't stand. There they are, drinking and eating and whispering their stories and theories about some bloody philosopher or other and they don't know what's going on in the world. They haven't any guts.'

'You're a bit drunk,' I said. 'You'll see more in perspective in the morning. And perhaps you'll see my side of it. After all, they're my friends too. And you did stay with that fellow all the time, didn't you? It didn't look nice.'

'Nice?' she said scornfully. 'And that fellow, I may tell you, is one of the best painters in London. I don't understand what the hell he was doing there in the first place.'

'In a morgue,' I said sarcastically. 'Are you coming to bed?'

'You go,' she said.

'All right,' I said. And I did go. I waited for a long time but she didn't come. It must have been over an hour before she did come to bed and she turned her back on me and went to sleep immediately. I stayed awake most of the night thinking of Wilson, my psychopath, and his terrifying mind. If she had spoken to him as she had spoken to me she would have been dead by now. She was relying on my gentlemanliness, that was it. I was the Kennedy to her Krushchev. We were poles apart and did not recognise each other. Nevertheless I loved her. I could not bear the thought of Rank speaking to her. But what could I do? I would be working in my office and she would be free, without any painting to do at the moment. Things were going to be bleak, if not totally black. I'd better ask the housekeeper in future what she had been doing during the day. Spying. Spying on each other. That's what we all did. Rank's hot angry eyes drilled into me as I lay on my bed watching the darkness turn into dawn, lighting up the innocent, heavy furniture.

The quarrel couldn't have come at a worse time as I had to go to Paris the following week to take part in a conference. I had to read a paper on Adler whose ideas I was beginning to take more seriously. Sex and power, I hovered between the two. The morning I left for Paris she was all right. It was almost as if she thought that her three days without me would help to stabilise her. She was loving enough the night before. I had, I thought, got her back.

I phoned twice from Paris but she wasn't in either time.

I drove impatiently from the airport but she was at home when I arrived. She welcomed me lovingly enough, as if she were compensating for some guilt. I asked her what she had been doing but she was very vague. She hadn't painted anything, I knew that, for her fingers were perfectly clean. There was an air of purpose and freshness about her and I knew that it was nothing to do with me. She was looking out of fresh windows and her excess of purpose was what she donated to me. The house seemed strange and she too seemed to be strange. I had a feeling that she had been seeing Rank when I was away but she didn't mention his name. She didn't ask me anything about Paris or my conference and I knew that she felt no jealousy. I didn't like that for I felt jealous about her. After the people I had met at the conference she seemed young and alive and vibrant. She didn't seem at all restless but I felt she wasn't listening to me half the time. She went to bed early and after she had done so I went through her untidy handbag and found in her diary a phone number ringed in red. I rang the number and the voice at the other end was Rank's. I put down the phone without speaking.

As I went along to the bedroom I was shaking with jealousy. I think that if I had gone in then I would have strangled her, but luckily for me or her I didn't go in. I turned at the door and went back to the living-room and began to drink steadily. I can't describe the intensity of the jealousy I felt that night. It was as if my whole body were being pierced by knives, as if I were in a fair delirious with lights and some gipsy were throwing blades at me. I drank and drank for my whole body was one raw nerve. If in the past I had been an Olympian studying people as objects, I was paying for that now. I couldn't sit still. I walked up and down the room all night shaking and trembling. I thought I would put her out of the house and throw her suitcase after her, but I knew that I couldn't live without her. She had infected my blood. She was making me into a gipsy suffering torments of passion. I tried to control myself, be the rational person I thought I had always been, but it was no good. I didn't even put the fire on but drank and drank. I was punishing myself for some terrible sin. Behind me stood the figure of my father, righteous and unforgiving, an armour-plated ego. And beside him stood my mother who was to leave him one day. I felt as if I was on a treadmill which would repeat that experience over and over. That was why I hadn't married till late, but the repetition was beginning. She had come into my house to spy on me. God knows what she had been telling Rank about me. They had probably had many a good laugh at my expense. She was a spy in my house. I was the country whose secrets she was selling to someone else, another country. Rank and I were two countries like Russia and America, and between us went this spy, a gipsy carrying documents across shifting frontiers. I couldn't stand it. My torment was appalling. My hands shook as dawn approached and she was lying in her bed, probably sleeping like a child. I could have killed her but I waited. I waited and I bled to death.

I had thought that perhaps the two of us might reach some mode of compromise but I had been wrong. She had only married me for the experience and because she had been a bit depressed at that time, but now she was returning to her true self, the traveller and spy without allegiance to anyone. Even Rank she might later desert when she had exhausted his knowledge. I thought very deeply that night as if I were in a hallucination. I knew that I would have to make concessions. I had decided by the time the morning came, grey and sickly, that I would make these concessions. I was a territory weaker than hers. I had to make a treaty for the moment if that was achievable. Later we would see, for deep inside me was the unforgiving voice of my father, hollow and echoing. He hadn't taken to drink, he had simply worked harder. Perhaps the turning of the knife in his patients was his therapy. As I sat in the armchair I found her Red Indian hairband beside me and wept like a child.

We are sitting at the table in the morning and I am putting marmalade on toast. Sunlight is buttering the table and Brenda is saying:

'I can't stay here all the time. Artists need their freedom, they need to work. I need to wander about. And you don't need to set Mrs Gray to spy on me. I need to wander about the streets, to look at colours, to walk in supermarkets, to stand at piles of fruit. I need the freshness.'

'But you had his telephone number in your book,' I said.

'There you are, spying again,' she said. 'You still don't understand. He's my guru, I learn from him. It's not sexual, at least not yet,' she said frankly.

'How do you mean, not yet?' I asked, my knife in mid-air about to descend on the butter.

'What I said. You haven't bought me, you know. You must let me be myself. I let you be yourself. I let you do your work. I don't bother you. You must let me do the same. I know it sounds like a cliché but artists aren't like ordinary people. They need air, they don't want to be disciplined. You like things to be in their places. I like disorder, that's the difference between us. And, by the way, why didn't you come to bed?'

'I didn't feel like it,' I said. It was such a beautiful morning and yet there were knives in my chest. I was like a bone case full of needles.

'I thought you knew all I've been talking about without being told,' she said. 'I thought you knew about artists. You said you knew about paintings. I don't suppose you think they come out of the sky. That was why I was attracted to you. I thought you would have enough maturity to give me my freedom. You must know that artists are like gipsies. I haven't got proper work to do. Art isn't a trade. I need to be open to everything.'

I looked at her for a long time and much passed through my mind then. 'All right,' I said, 'have your freedom, provided that you don't betray me.' I felt that the word 'betray' sounded old fashioned but I didn't withdraw it. 'Go about the street and pick up your inspiration. No one is stopping you from doing that. But don't fall in love with Rank, that is all I ask.' I didn't know as I spoke whether I would have the strength to give her all the freedom she wanted.

'I didn't go to bed with Rank,' she said. 'All I did was talk to him. I felt low and he gave me some ideas and conversation.

Surely I can do that. Look at all the women you meet at your job, I don't feel jealous of them.'

I nearly said, 'But you can trust me,' but I didn't say so. I felt myself slipping into a marsh full of strange flowers and evil odours. The world was slipping away from me, the abstract world which has nothing to do with painting or sensuousness.

'Look at these rolls,' she said, 'how white they are, how beautiful. I could make a still life of this breakfast table.'

The thing was she looked as wild and attractive as ever and as unselfconscious. 'That colour,' she said. 'What colour would you say marmalade is? Have you ever thought about that? And its taste. It's like nothing else on earth. Nothing at all.'

She illuminated the world for me, she was a series of detonations, she was my fate and my doom. She was halfway between my child and my wife, it was as if I could be seeing her off to school.

'I tell you what,' she said. 'In return for the party you took me to, I'll take you to another one. What do you think of that?'

'Will Rank be there?' I asked.

'He might be,' she said. In spite of her protestations I thought she had been to bed with him. I didn't believe what she was saying to me now. His large presence dominated the house, it was as if he was a huge gigantic being shouldering his way through its order. When I thought of his body lying on top of hers, drilling into it, its power and its savagery, I was almost screaming with rage. I was a long silent scream. Her buttocks entranced me, her round firm breasts, to have allowed anyone else near them was like having a needle stuck in my loins. How far I had come from the cool world of Vermeer with its maidservants and milk jugs and its laughing soldiers. How far I was from the domestic Dutch world of his paintings.

'All right,' I said, 'I'll go,' thinking again of Wilson. I wondered where he had spent his weekend, what animals he had shot, in what woods and fastnesses he had stalked. What animals he had spied on till they had been delivered to his gun.

When I drove to the office I watched the policemen directing the traffic and thought that they were spies giving incomprehensible signals in code. Eyes and hands were agents of change and direction. Even my patients were spying on me. They were laughing at me secretly behind their hands, behind their bland, masked large faces. And no one more so than Wilson who seemed to be saying to me, 'I am the true real person. The rest of you are hypocrites. You falsely believe that you are keeping the world together but deep down you are starving to be like me. You are killers. One day I shall be a killer in reality; I shall drink blood. Now it's animals I kill, later it will be people. The rest of you are sick to death fighting your instincts. I am going to give way to them. Soon now. Soon. Now I shoot foxes and rabbits. Later I shall kill men.'

And I knew that in one way he spoke the truth. The previous night I might have killed her. We all have an adamantine selfishness at the core. Think of Keats watching sparrows and musing at their purpose. They were hunting for worms or building their nests; he was writing his poetry. On the ladder of creation how were they different? We are all out to save ourselves, to keep our comfort and our pride. We may talk about civilisation but that is because it happens to be convenient to us at the moment.

Wilson told me of a weasel he had seen. 'The weasel,' he said, 'is the fiercest killer of all. Did you know that he will attack a human being? He is like a flash of fire. Dynamite. I saw him spring on a rabbit and I waited till he had killed it. Then I shot him. A very fine shot if I say it myself. Then I squeezed his body with my bare hands. It's so thin and small and yet so vicious. A weasel will defy you. I squeezed it to death.'

The noise was shattering, my ear-drums seemed to be bursting. There was a strange sickly smell in the air, and I wondered if it was drugs. Instead of standing about as people had done at Drew's party they were sitting or lying on the floor and in corners under the red lights some couples were embracing and as far as I could see having sexual intercourse. The room seemed to be full of savages – buttocks, breasts, hairy pale faces everywhere. It was like a Cubist painting, like *Guernica*. No one paid me the slightest attention though they must have wondered what someone like me, dressed so decorously, was doing there. I looked at Brenda and she was gazing around her with parted lips. She had clearly come home. She threw her long coat into a corner of the room and sat like the others on the floor. I did the same though I felt uncomfortable. Lights were flashing all around me, the banging noise of the record player was tearing me apart. The tenement room itself was perched high up, in a poor area of the city, and we noticed that the walls as we came in had been chalked with gang slogans. Beside me a girl with incredibly blonde hair like corn and blank eyes like stones was squatting.

I didn't know what I was doing there and no one spoke to me though Brenda had left me and was talking to a tall fellow who was wearing a long brown ravaged fur coat. In the middle of the group was a small fat man who was staring straight ahead of him into space as if he were looking at a screen. On a table there were some drinks. We had brought some ourselves – apparently we had been expected to – and it had been placed with the rest. I felt completely out of it, and all I could think to do was crawl over and get myself a whisky while the tremendous music beat at me.

For a while there seemed to be talking and chatter. I could hardly make out the words though I gathered that many of the people there were students. Brenda was waving her hands animatedly as she talked to the fellow in the fur coat who looked distant and bored. But this didn't seem to worry her at all; in fact she looked perfectly happy. It was a long time since I had seen her face so purely radiant. She also was drinking what I took to be gin or vodka and I remembered what she had once told me about drinking two bottles of gin in one day. 'I was absolutely stoned out of my mind,' she had said. 'It was heaven. I couldn't paint, of course. I wonder what other painters do when they can't paint.'

Suddenly as if they were all responding to a signal all of the tribe – I could only think of them as that – got to their feet and began to sway and dance to the music, their faces pale and cool and dreamy. They were incredibly beautiful and mindless, like long stalks on which the faces were set like flowers, utterly abstracted, immune to the mind. They didn't exactly dance, they swayed and thrust to the sound of the music. It was pure experience I was seeing, it was beyond thought. And among them was Brenda. She too was swaying to the music and I could have sworn that she looked straight into my eyes without recognising me.

This swaying and thrusting went on for a long time and then suddenly it accelerated, with the movement of an orgasm. I looked at Brenda in horror. She was thrusting her pelvis forward as if she were engaged in sexual intercourse and all the time her face was a dreamy mask as if she were drugged. She was living totally in the body which she accepted not as mortal and subject to death and disease but as a precious and living possession which would allow her to enter her own heaven. There was something obscenely automatic about her movements as if she were copulating during sleep and it terrified me more than the horrors of my mind. She had gone away like the others to another world which my mind wouldn't allow me to enter or experience.

Even though I was drinking there was a part of my mind which was ticking away like a watch, cataloguing, remembering. I was looking at a painting composed of images which was alive like an organism. Everything was fragmentary and no longer narrative as the man had said. And then, just as I thought this, there was the man himself – having just come in – standing beside me on his way towards the dancing.

'Well, what do you think of it, then?'

He was staring at the dancers with an almost mad smile on the whitish face below the red hair. He towered over me, pure brutal energy equipped with a high-powered brain as well, and I knew that I couldn't compete.

'It's strange,' I said, and my words seemed to fall hollowly at my feet.

'You would say that,' he said mockingly. 'I could have sworn that you would use that word.' And then he was gone, shouldering his way into the group and standing in front of Brenda, the two of them then swaying towards each other, thrusting their bodies forward, twisting like snakes. If this is the Garden of Eden, I thought, then the snakes are the correct occupants and

I am the alien devil looking on. I drank more and more as the rhythm of the music deepened and quickened and became more and more loud. The room with its red light swayed about me, the sickly smell increased. I felt as if I was going to vomit. I was the only person not dancing except the fat man who was still staring into space, squatting on the floor like a Buddha.

I had the most curious sensation of staring at something that I could never hope to understand, something that I half envied and considered dangerous. I could hear myself discussing this later with someone: 'Of course this is where Hitlerism came from. D. H. Lawrence started it off. It's the end of our tradition, Homer and the rest. It's the Dionysiac frenzy, the Bacchanalian syndrome which destroyed Greece.' But I certainly didn't feel Apollonian. I felt as if I were in some underground cavern thousands of years ago when people with rigid brows populated the caves. I fixed my eyes on a girl's long green belt which swayed in front of me and then I got up and sought the lavatory. When I came back they were all sitting on the floor again and Rank was talking to Brenda. He had his right arm casually over her right shoulder.

There was a long silence which made my head ache even more than the noise. It was as if the savages had been transformed into monks, as if they were waiting now for some revelation. Brenda was looking across at me and smiling secretly. It was as if she were saying, 'Well, I went to your party and now you have to come to mine. What do you think of it? I left you on your own as you did to me. What do you think of that?' Suddenly I got up and stumbled out of the room, and down the stairs. I remember that they were unlit and I had to use my lighter a lot to light my way in flashes. The last glimpse I had of them, Rank was stroking her hair. I wasn't going to fight him. He would have won anyway. It would not have been rational.

I steered the car through the night blazing with its reds and yellows, like an emporium of the East. I half expected to see women in veils walking past and Arabs talking at street corners. The night was a desert, lit by inane contingent lights. I managed to reach home safely, put the car in the garage, went upstairs, and climbed into bed. I went out like a light.

When I woke up the same stabbing pain returned as I remembered what had happened. Brenda, incredibly enough, was sleeping beside me like a child. I had no recollection of her coming to bed or when she had returned or with whom. She was sleeping peacefully, an arm thrown across the yellow coverlet. I shook her awake and said, 'When did you come home?'

She woke blinking, and said, 'I was given a lift home. I came back at three.'

'Who gave you a lift?' I asked.

'I don't know his name,' she said. 'Anyway his girl friend was with him so it's all right.'

'It wasn't Rank?' I asked, shivering as if with fever.

'It wasn't Rank,' she said. 'You left early, didn't you?'

'There was no one to speak to,' I said.

'It was the same at your party,' she replied. 'It was incredible. I haven't enjoyed myself so much. We had such discussions.'

Discussions. I wondered what she meant by 'discussions'. I knew what I meant by the word. But I didn't think that was what she meant by it.

'I left you with Rank,' I said accusingly.

'I know,' she answered, 'but there were others there as well, you know.' Suddenly she kissed me and said, 'You mustn't be so jealous. Jealousy is no good. You must learn to trust me.'

But I couldn't trust her. She was a gipsy who moved across frontiers, restlessly. I had a feeling deep within me that she had been with Rank and the knowledge was driving me insane.

'What are we going to do?' I said.

'Going to do?' she said in a surprised voice. 'What do you mean, "going to do"?'

'Well,' I said, 'we can't carry on like this. Are you going to be attending parties like that regularly? I don't understand the people there. I have nothing in common with any of them.'

'You don't try to have anything in common with them,' she said. 'You should try. You've led too sheltered an existence, that's what's wrong with you. You think that because you talk to your patients you know everything, that you've seen everything. You don't understand what creative people are like.'

And truly I didn't. I didn't understand these people and I was sure that most of them weren't creative. They seemed to me like savages who had surrendered reason. They seemed to be down and outs, drop-outs from society. I looked on them as exotic phenomena, who were turning and savaging the tree of light which had illuminated the ages.

'Why did you marry me?' I asked her at last.

'It's an experience,' she said unhesitatingly. 'Everything is an experience. Why do you always want a reason for everything? Why don't you just live? You should learn to live from day to day. Christ Himself said that, didn't he?'

Perhaps Rank was her Christ and these hairy people with their sandals and long coats were his disciples.

She sat up in bed and said, 'That's what's wrong with you. You're always looking for reasons and purposes. Can't you see that that's ridiculous? Just live in the moment, that's what you need to do. Just enjoy.' There were dark shadows under her eyes and her pale face was almost luminous.

'I know,' I said, 'but human beings can't live like that. Animals live like that. But not human beings. In any case there are moments when one is bored. One must endure these times.'

'Why?' she said. 'Why can't one go out and get lost in something else? You could retire now if you wanted to. You've got plenty of money. Why don't you? Are you frightened or something?'

I was indeed frightened. I would miss those voyeuristic glimpses into the satanic depths and she knew it. She could probe more deeply in her apparently innocent, sleep-walking way, than anyone I knew.

'Everything could be all right if you let it,' she said. 'Why are you so angry just because I enjoyed myself? How can you love me and be so angry?'

I got up from the bed and pulled the curtains aside. It was autumn again. It wouldn't be long till our year would be past. I could feel the tang of autumn in the air, I could see the trees losing their crowns and the leaves turning brown. I could feel my crown leaving me.

'All right,' I said, but I couldn't tell her about the pain that was pricking me continually. I couldn't tell her how I felt about Rank, invader of my private realm, I couldn't tell her how I was being flayed alive.

'Where are you going today?' I said.

'Oh, I'll walk around,' she said carelessly. 'I have a few ideas.'

'I'm glad,' I said.

'Yes,' she said, 'I got some ideas last night. I didn't realise you had gone till much later.'

I didn't want to go to my work but I felt that I ought to. I didn't want to lie down in my bed and drop out like those others. That wasn't my nature. I hated staying late in bed. Perhaps, I thought, in the world that is to come and is almost upon us, the congenitally idle who are able to bear the ravages of time will be the masters and those who need routine will be the slaves.

I thought of an experiment which had been done with rats, how if you put three rats in a cage with a machine which will release food if a lever is pressed, one rat will do all the work while the other two will sit back and eat. And this has nothing to do with class structure or the worker rat being terrorised by the other two. It is just that this particular rat seems to need to work, it is the responsible one.

I felt old and lost as I put on my clothes. I was one of the workers, one of the slaves, one of the inferiors. She was the master or mistress. She could live in the world in a way that I couldn't. I was trying to master the world, she ignored it.

When I turned away to go down and make my breakfast she was already asleep.

And so time passed. Autumn was resplendent in its marvellous colours. The year was going out in a blaze of colour and again I had to go to Paris but this time I didn't tell her when I would be back. More and more I felt the world as a spying machine.

She had married me to spy on me. What was she saying about me to her friends? She was learning that my world was as frail as she had thought. Reason was disintegrating, was being eaten alive by jealousy. Ideas were becoming pale and tired. I was betraying that world to her. I was a traitor to my own kind. Why else had she married me? I had surrendered to her because she was careless and unpredictable and irrational, but she hadn't surrendered to me. She had no weakness that I could see. She would move on with the secrets stolen from my house, built so flimsily on reason and principle. I was the weak one, she was the strong one.

When I returned from Paris and that conference of old spectacled idealistic confused murderous colleagues, I drove up to the house which was in darkness. I switched on the lights and went systematically through the house but she wasn't there. Her clothes were still there, she hadn't flitted in the night, that at least was true. I picked up the phone and put it down again. Then I dialled Bell and asked him if he knew Rank's address. He told it to me. I felt that he knew exactly what was happening, that almost alcoholic logical genius, that ghostly passenger in a world which had almost gone. He was like an insect whose wings were fading away because there was no need for them any longer.

I drove to Rank's house in a fury of rage and possessiveness. I rang the bell and Rank came to the door gigantic and red-haired. I said, 'Is my wife here?'

He looked at me mockingly for a long time as if I had said something unutterably bourgeois. 'Yes,' he said. 'Brenda is here.'

I followed him into the room. She was sitting on the floor by the fire as she had so often sat with me. She looked up when I came in and then down at the floor again. Her face seemed paler than usual and there were black shadows below her eyes. There was about her an air of the corrupt schoolgirl.

'Would you like a drink?' said Rank.

'No,' I said. 'Are you coming home?' I said to Brenda.

For some time she said nothing and then she got up and made for the door.

'You're frightened again,' said Rank to her. 'You're frightened of being left alone.'

But she wasn't that at all. I knew her. She was stronger than Rank, than me.

I took her arm and I said to Rank, 'Would you kindly leave my wife alone?'

He looked at me mockingly. 'My wife,' he said, scornfully. 'My wife! The old possessive thing. Why don't *you* leave her alone? If you left her alone she might learn to grow. She might even learn to become a good painter.'

She stood watching the two of us as if waiting to see the issue of our battle. My mind felt clear as crystal.

'And what will you put in place of possessiveness?' I asked.

'In its place?' he said, seeming to look at me directly for the first time. 'I'll tell you. Freedom to live as we are. You aren't trying to build a prison, are you?'

'And you,' I said, 'do you never feel possessiveness, jealousy, envy? Or are you a god?'

'No,' he said, 'I don't feel jealousy, and I'm not a god.'

'Then,' I said, 'you aren't poor and human like the rest of us. And those who aren't human are gods or animals.'

'Good old Plato,' he said. 'The phantom saint of the West. The man who wanted artists out of his republic.'

'I give you that,' I said. 'Nevertheless, what do you want? A race of gipsies?'

'Shall I tell you what I think?' he said. 'Since you wish to know. I think we are about to enter an era of Darwinism. I think that in this era men will have to fight for their wives as they did many years ago. I think the light of reason is going out. I think that you will have to fight for her. Are you willing to do that? Otherwise marriage will not protect you.'

I thought he was quite evil, but I wouldn't fight him. It was too great a loss of dignity. I wasn't afraid of him but I didn't want to appear silly.

'Well,' I said to Brenda, 'what do you think of all that?'

She looked at me without speaking and then she laughed and I knew that her laughter was a comment on my world. I knew that I had sold my world out to her because of my weakness. Well, I thought, it may be that. I may side with your world in ways that you won't understand. She laughed a pure innocent evil laugh in that room with its paintings all round the walls. Her laughter was joyous and free, like the laugh of a gipsy. It knew nothing of the real complications of the world or the mind. I had betrayed my world to her and I was being punished for it.

I went out and later she came home. She stayed with me for that week. She said she would do that and then she would leave.

I am sitting here drunk. She has gone out the door. We are living in a spy story. And what is she? She is a double agent. She has left my country for that other country. I look at my watch: soon she will be at his house. I pick up the phone and dial Bell's house. He will be drunk as usual but he belongs to my world. Wilson with his gun is perched at the window of an empty house opposite Rank's. I think it will be a good idea to have her shot just as she is about to seek asylum at Rank's embassy. Wilson is happy to do it. I shall be talking to Bell when the shot is fired. In any case they will never have any reason to suspect Wilson. He will get away all right. I am dialling now. I hear Bell's phone ringing and ringing but there is no answer. Well, in that case I shall have to phone somewhere else. I think I shall phone the Professor and he will tell me about Byzantium. Ah, he is answering. As he answers and I put some inane questions, I can hear the shot ring out in my mind. She staggers just as she is about to enter the embassy. I keep him talking and steady my voice. No, I say, I don't know much about the Byzantine Empire. Wilson will have left by now, carrying his long narrow case. No, I say, I don't know about the Byzantine Empire, but I'm willing to learn.

The Brothers

First of all, I should like to say that I don't believe in ghosts, and yet some strange things have been happening to me recently. And you won't understand them unless I tell you something about myself. I am a writer, and I was born and brought up in the Highlands of Scotland where, I may tell you, you can hear plenty of ghost stories. For instance, there was the man who used to get up from the ceilidh in the middle of the night and who would come back much later, his shoes and trousers dripping: he had been carrying the coffin of someone who had not yet died and who perhaps was telling a story at that very ceilidh. Imagine what it must have been like to be such a man. Anyway, I myself don't believe in these stories, though I have heard them often. My father told me once that he nearly turned back one night when passing a cemetery after seeing a green light there, but he carried on, and found that it was the phosphorescence from fish lying in a cart which had been put in the ditch by the drunken driver. I believe that, but I don't believe in ghosts.

However, let me say that when I was old enough I left the Highlands and came to Edinburgh and began to write stories and novels in English. I left the Gaelic world wholly behind me, because I suppose I despised it. If you ask me why I despise it it is partly because of these silly ghost stories and partly because of the simple unsophisticated mode of life of those people whom I have little affection for. In fact when I was growing up they seemed to laugh at me. I have even written articles attacking that placid unchanging world which knows nothing of Kafka or Proust or the other great writers of the world. I would never go back there now, so I live in my untidy flat in Edinburgh seeing very few people and working at my books, some of which have been published. I have set none of them, I may say, in the Highlands. After all, what important insight could I get from there, from people and a culture which have not moved into the twentieth century?

All was going well until recently when one night, working on a book about Joseph and his brothers – after all, I don't see why Thomas Mann should be the only person who is allowed to write about the Bible – I came down to the living-room where I had left my typewriter. I remembered quite clearly at which point I had stopped writing. Joseph was standing in astonishment gazing at the pyramids and comparing them to the hills of home and, exiled in a strange land, feeling very small against that hewn stone. The moonlight was shining on my typewriter making it look like a yellow skeleton against the window. I switched on the light and picked up the pages which I had typed. I began to read them, remembering in my mind, insomniac and restless, the cadences which I had aimed for and which I thought I had achieved. However, with an astonishment as great as Joseph's when he was regarding the pyramids, I suddenly found that I was reading Gaelic.

Now there is absolutely no question but these pages had been written in English. I had spent too long over the words not to know that. However, as I read these Gaelic sentences, rougher and more passionate than my English ones, I had a strange feeling that I had read them before somewhere. I stood there astonished in the silence. There was no sound in any of the other flats or on the street outside. I looked carefully round my now brightly-lit room but it seemed exactly the same as when I had gone to bed. My Penguins were arranged carefully round the walls, and my typewriter was on the table. I stared at the pages knowing that I must be going out of my mind. But I was absolutely certain that though these pages were familiar I had not written them. They seemed to be saying in Gaelic that Joseph had abandoned his land for another land and that in doing so he had betrayed his own. Someone must have typed these pages but who could that someone have been?

No living human being could have entered the flat and certainly no one could have typed the pages without my hearing them. On the other hand, no one could have typed them and brought them into the flat as a practical joke. I am very fearful and I lock the windows, and the door is always locked. But not only that, my English pages had disappeared. Whoever had done this had not simply translated the original pages, but had rather substituted his Gaelic pages for my English ones. And yet since that person was not me it must have been some spiritual being; in other words a ghost. I felt for the first time a draught as of cold air all round me even in the bright electric light. I went to the door but it was still locked. I switched on all the lights in every room but they were undisturbed and the windows were all locked as I had left them.

I came back to the room and stood looking down at the Gaelic pages. They were even written on the same kind of quarto paper as I had used myself and the typing was not unlike mine. But it was slightly different, the touch was lighter and surer. There were fewer erasures. The cold wind did not go away. I felt threatened as if some being whose name and form I did not know understood all about me and was determined to destroy me.

I made coffee and stayed up all night, I was too frightened to go to bed. I went and got my red and green dressing gown and sat by the electric fire, though I could ill afford to waste all that electricity. But there was nothing else that I could do. I listened to the silence, terrified that that ghostly being would return and type while I sat there. What was I going to do? Carefully I put the case back on the typewriter and stared at it as if hypnotised. I was afraid that I would fall asleep and that the ghost would type more while I sat transfixed there like a mummy. But nothing happened and when morning dawned sickly and pale I looked again at the pages. They were still in Gaelic. My English ones had irretrievably disappeared.

The following day I summoned up enough courage to burn the Gaelic pages and start again on my English version. I re-typed as far as I could remember what I had already done and went on to describe the sophisticated world of Egypt. I knew little about the country but imagined the kind of civilisation that would have produced those vast inhuman monuments. I invented a slave market at which Joseph was sold, I wrote about himself and Potiphar's wife. I may say that I had difficulty here since my sexual experiences have been limited and I know whom to blame for that. At five o'clock, satisfied with my work, I made some coffee and at that moment I heard it.

The sound was coming from the next room where I keep my record player. It was the voice of a well-known Gaelic singer and she was singing a song about the murder of a younger brother by an older one. I rushed into the room, spilling my coffee as I went. There was the record player plugged in and there was the record which I'd never seen in my life spinning on its black circuit. I switched the machine off and removed the record. Though I had never seen it, I had of course understood the words. I passed my hand across my brow and put the record down on the floor. I closed the cover of the record player and sat there dismally in the dull afternoon whose light was already fading from the sky. I didn't know what to do. I could have gone out to see a film or a play but I didn't fancy coming back to my flat in the middle of the night. I switched on all the lights again. I heard no one moving about the room. My jazz and classical records were still in their places. I trembled with fear and anguish.

Suddenly I rushed back into the room where I had left my latest English pages. I picked them up. They were all in Gaelic and without erasure. I read them with horror. They said that Joseph had been condemned to death and was lying in prison waiting for the end. This too, of course, was in the story. After all, it is one of the great stories of the world. My mother had told it to me many years before in a voice of rigour and appalling judgment. But since then I had read Thomas Mann.

I saw him quite clearly sitting in prison, the light about him dim and grey and his face quite blank. It was as if he was a white page waiting to be written on. All around him was Egypt which he had learned to love and whose language he spoke. I saw the walls of the prison and written on them were graffiti in a language which might have been Egyptian since they did not appear to be composed of any language that I had ever seen. He was dressed in his coat of many colours.

I sat dully at the typewriter with these pages in my hand. They were strong, powerful pages, in fact better than mine, simpler and perhaps cruder. It's difficult to explain why they were so much better, but I think it must have been because their language was less abstract. They seemed to have caught the intonation of a language that Joseph might have used, perhaps Hebrew, perhaps Egyptian. They even incorporated the words of the song I had heard on the record player. If I had had somewhere to go I would have rushed out that moment on to the street. But I had no friends in Edinburgh. Its vast stony houses were anonymous enough for me to be able to write among them in privacy, but they were not places for friendship. I stared at the light draining out of the sky and I was more frightened than I had ever been in my whole life, or rather I was frightened in a different way from that in which I had been frightened before. I felt like a statue which was also trembling. I made more coffee and kept all the lights on but I was on edge, as if waiting for a fresh incursion into my life which I had thought orderly. I waited there helplessly, as a cow waits to be poleaxed. I remembered seeing that once back in the Highlands and I had hated it. Now I was the victim myself in all that bright light. I knew I would have to stay up again all night. I would be frightened to lie in my bed among the cold stiff blankets, waiting for the dawn to appear. And as I waited I knew that some spirit was moving about me, determined to destroy me. I put the last page of the Gaelic script in the typewriter as if I was propitiating an angry god. And I sat there like that for a long time, shivering though the fire was warm.

It must have been about seven o'clock at night that I suddenly felt a terrible anger with whatever malevolent being was about me. The curtains were drawn, the electric fire was on, there was lots of light. Suddenly I took the Gaelic pages out of the typewriter, screwed them up and threw them into the wastepaper basket. I knew exactly why I had done this. I knew that I must not surrender at this point or I would surrender forever. Why should I allow this being, whatever it was, to tell me what I ought to do, how I ought to write? I was only doing what I thought I ought to be doing. Did I not have free will?

What law stated that some ghost or other from another world should command my mind? The anger I felt was pure and ardent and innocent. If I wished to abandon my homeland, if that was what I was doing, why should I not do so? Indeed, in doing so was I not being an exception? Was I not in fact setting out to create a new being? That is, the exile who is able to speak from another land and in another language? I had been betrayed by my own land. What therefore did I owe it? I too had been mocked by my own brothers, if I could call them that. Well then, let me stay in my Egypt. Let me adopt it as my promised land. Let my ambitions be fructified there. After all, wasn't Egypt the pinnacle of achievement? And in Egypt could I not gather my corn together and feed my rustic brothers who came down there from my own lost land? What was wrong with that? Wasn't that what the Joseph story taught, that the murderous brothers were dependent after all on the dreamer who lived in another and more powerful country?

So, out of my pure anger, I tore the Gaelic pages out of the typewriter and threw them into the wastepaper basket. And I waited. That's precisely what I did. I waited. I knew that something would happen though I did not know what it would be. I was frightened, yes, but I was angry too and the clean wash of my anger anaesthetised for a while my fear, at least as long as I could hear people passing on the street in my adopted city. I listened to those feet passing and I felt in my own country. I even summoned up enough strength to start typing again in English. I wrote how Joseph left the prison because he was able to interpret the dreams of the baker and the butler. I thought of myself as Joseph, the dreamer who had such great powers.

And the night passed and became more silent. Once I had to leave the room where my typewriter was and go to the bathroom. For a second, as I opened the door, I thought I saw a figure in white flashing past me, but I decided that it probably was an illusion. It seemed to me that the figure was dressed in a white robe which had an oriental look about it. But, as I have said, I decided that it must have been an illusion. Not an illusion however was the intense cold I felt as I left the room and all the time I was in the bathroom. And worse was when leaving the bathroom I looked in the mirror and saw my own face there. It seemed demonic and lined and white. I could hardly recognise myself. It was as if I was waiting for something to happen, something devilish and horrifying. I went back to the room, trembling again, and when I did so I saw that the pages in the typewriter were written once more in Gaelic.

I withdrew my eyes from the pages as if afraid that they contained sentences which would destroy me. My English pages had again disappeared. I looked down at my hands, wondering perhaps if I myself was the author of what was happening to me. But I could learn nothing from them. They looked innocent and bland. I looked at the clock. It said eleven. The noises on the street seemed to have stopped and there was an oppressive air of waiting about the flat. I went right through it and checked that every light was switched on. I waited as if listening for songs but I heard nothing. I went back and sat down again in my chair which seemed to have turned into a gaunt throne. Was I indeed Joseph, sitting in that alien chair? The wood on which I sat seemed to be rotting as if small animals were eating into it. There were the marks of teeth. I saw in my hand cows eating each other, cornstacks devouring one another. I was afloat on the river of time. I can't tell the visions I saw that night. It was as if I was in the centre of Egypt and there were snakes and cats all round me. They opened their mouths, and their teeth and fangs snapped at me. The throne or chair tottered. The furniture swayed. The pages seemed to turn into tablets, solid and white.

Suddenly I thought, what if the story of Joseph could have a different ending? And I was terrified. After all, I hadn't believed in the Bible, or had thought of it only as fiction. Well, if it were fiction, then alternatives were possible. Who was this Joseph anyway but an arrogant fellow who thought that he was better than his brothers? Wasn't that the case? Weren't the brothers justified in getting rid of him? I hadn't thought of that before, and yet wasn't that what the Gaelic typed pages had been telling me? If that were so, then the Joseph story could be turned inside out. Joseph had deserved everything he had got. He had deserved his Egypt. I imagined outside my room the tall stone buildings as if they were pyramids. Inside them were all the buried kings, the tyrants and despots. He had joined them. He had taken his robe down to Egypt and seen it encrusted with gold before his eyes. He had entered that alien time and place.

I sat trembling. After a very long time I brought myself to look at the Gaelic pages. They said in prose stronger than my English:

> Joseph was a traitor. His journey was arrogant and aristo-cratic. We brothers believe that he betrayed us, that he hated our language and our way of life. We speak for the oppressed and inarticulate countrymen who live in the small places far from the city. We come to see him not because we wish to eat his corn but rather because we wish to destroy him utterly. He hated us, therefore we must hate him.

I listened and as I listened it was as if the whole flat came alive with sounds. These sounds it is difficult to describe. Partly they were of music that I thought I had forgotten, fragments of songs about sailing ships and men exiled from their own land. Partly they were the sounds of cows mooing on early, almost forgotten, moors. Partly they were the sounds of human voices at street corners. Partly they were voices telling stories. Partly they were my own voice heard so long ago. And the night darkened and lengthened. The curtains shivered in the draught. My mind was a mosaic of different sentences, some in English, some in Gaelic. My whole body was sweating as if with an incurable fever. I remember getting up and for no reason shifting the position of the green-faced clock on the mantelpiece. There was a dreadful coldness all around me, though the two bars of the electric fire were on. I looked at the telephone as if it were a snake about to strike. For some reason or other I thought of all the family photographs I had destroyed.

And I sat on my throne in the middle of the night. And as I sat there listening to the sound of feet on the road I clearly heard steps which seemed much more purposeful than the ones I had heard earlier on. I can't describe why I felt this. It was something to do with the fact that the sounds made by the feet seemed to reinforce each other as if three people were walking along together, and as if they were making for a predetermined rendezvous. But at the same time the sound seemed curiously alien and echoing. The footsteps were purposeful and foreign and hollow, and they were, I was sure, making for my door. In a sudden panic I arose from my chair and pulled the bolt across the outer door, which was already locked. I don't know why I did this since I knew that locks and bolts would not keep these beings, familiar and fatal, out. But I did it anyway and went back to my room and shut that door as well. I waited by the fire, shivering. I was alone and afraid. There was no question of that.

When I happened at that moment to glance at the page still in the typewriter, the machine began to move of its own accord. I may say at this point that I had been so terrified by all the things that had happened that I almost accepted this strange event. I had once seen a teleprinter almost supernaturally receiving messages from a different place, miles and miles away, and as I accepted that so I accepted this. The typewriter was writing in capital letters WE ARE COMING FOR YOU JOSEPH WE ARE COMING TO TAKE YOU HOME. I cannot describe the menace that these simple words seemed to contain. What did HOME mean? The grave? The words leapt out at me in their large threatening capitals. They seemed to emanate from a different world, one far from mine. And simultaneously I heard drunken voices coming from behind my door. The drunken discordant voices were singing a Gaelic song or what seemed to be one. I can't wholly describe that song. It was, I thought, Gaelic and yet there were cadences in it of another country, an oriental country. I could almost have thought that the cadences might have been Egyptian. They were aureate and intricate and yet below them I could hear quite clearly the words of the Gaelic song, just as I had heard them many years before in my own home. It was a Gaelic song and yet the words seemed to come not through mouths but rather through snouts. I imagined at the door, just outside, three snouts raised to the moon. At the same time I sensed a menace such as one might feel – not from an animal but from a being other than animal or man, a being from another world, a world that existed long ago with its irrational gods and stiff hieratic clothes.

I stared at the door which was painted a bright yellow. My room is painted in two colours: two walls are black, the other two are yellow. When I looked at the yellow door it was as if I was looking at a screen that divided me from another world. It was as if the door was not made of wood but of a fine delicate skin which blazed with the power of the sun. And it was a skin that I knew would not survive if those beings, alive and barbarous and drunken, were to decide to burst through it. Their song was a lament and a song of triumph. It was menacing and despairing and fruitful. Suddenly, as I looked, words began to appear on the door, some in Gaelic and some in English and some in a strange language that I did not know. It was like the writing on the wall that had appeared to Belshazzar.

Then there was silence for a while. The drunken voices ceased. I knew that they were giving me time, and I did not know what I was going to do with that time they had given me. They had come down from their hills and they were waiting for me to act. They were waiting for a gesture from me. What would that gesture be? For I knew that these were not my real brothers, not the brothers I had been brought up with, not the brothers whose toys I had shared or smashed, not the brothers with whom I had bedded in that cramped house so long ago. These were other brothers. And their song was a menacing song.

I looked down at my clothes and found, to my surprise, that I was wearing not my cloak of many colours but a coat of pure yellow, the colour of the door. If I wanted to save myself I knew what I must do. Did I want to save myself? And was it only an instinct for self-protection that drove me to my action? That in itself would not be enough. No, it wasn't wholly that, perhaps not that at all. It wasn't just that, for as I listened I heard the Gaelic tune again, and my blood seemed to move with it, warmly and purely. I walked slowly to the door but it was as if I were dancing. A strange perfume seemed to fill the entire room. It wasn't however the perfume of the east, it was more local perfume, such as I had smelt so long ago. It was the perfume perhaps of heatherbells, of brine. It was harsh and pure and severe and it suffused my whole body. It was a perfume that I seemed almost to remember.

As I moved towards the door the words on it changed their shape and became not fragmentary but wholly Gaelic. I knew that outside the door my brothers were waiting. I knew that I must welcome them not with hauteur but with deference. I must not be the successful Egyptian but the humbled Hebrew. I knew that it was I who was the sinner. My eyes pierced the door which was like skin and on the other side I saw my brothers broken by defeat and starvation but still human and rustic and brave. It was to them that I must offer myself, not to the alien kings and an alien land. It was to them that I must, if necessary, be the sacrifice. In the silence of the night which trembled with so many stars I walked towards the door and felt my body gain energy and power. It was as if I was a king, a real king, because I had ceased to think like one. I reached the door. It had ceased to be skin and was wood again. I opened it but there was no one there.

I looked around me. The typewriter sat on its own in the moonlight. I sat down at it in the peaceful night and began to type. The words were Gaelic and flowed easily and familiarly, as if I were speaking to my brothers who had sung drunken songs outside my door. I looked down at my clothes and found that they were all one colour. I dreamed as I wrote and my dream was reflected easily in my words. I seemed to see faces, worn and lined, and they were more beautiful than any other faces I had known. I seemed to hear their language and it was their language that I wrote. It was rough and yet it was my own. It was their voices speaking through me, maimed and triumphant and without sophistication. I seemed to see the moonlight shining on the corn, ripe and yellow, the colour of the door. To their starving faces I brought joy as I wrote. And inside me was their song. I sat in my yellow robe at my yellow typewriter in the yellow room. And I was happy. I overflowed with the most holy joy.

The Incident

Why do I remember the incident so clearly, even in my fiftieth year? I throb with rage and rancour when it wells up in my mind. No, not my mind, my soul rather. It took place between my brother and me, my brother who is now at the other end of the world, in Kenya to be precise, married with five children, photographs of whom he sends regularly. The cottage where we grew up seems almost like a fairy hut in a dream, struck sometimes by thunder and lightning and at other times ringed by daisies. It has a slightly slant look and in winter time I think of it mounted by waves of snow.

And yet I don't suppose it was like that at all. My brother was older than me and most of the time we got on well together. For instance I remember him bringing to me from the town a chocolate with twenty-four squares in it and we ate it together in the one bed, for there were only two beds in the house. Another time I remember him sitting side by side with a redhead in a house in the village, and thinking how slatternly and vulgar she looked. But of course he was much more responsible than me. I dreamed and read, and he acted. I mean he acted in the world. He was the one who scythed the corn, and gathered the peats. He was the one who took apart, the very first night, the gun he had been issued with in the Home Guard (or LDV) during the last war. Later he became an officer in the army.

My life is a string of these incidents which stick in my mind like a row of beads, lights across a bay which I have never really seen but which I continually imagine. For instance, did I imagine a Santa Claus in red hood and fur coat who visited our house? Did I imagine that I once dressed up at Hallowe'en as a beast with a green face? Probably I have imagined it all. Have I even imagined this incident? No, I don't think so. For surely it would not return to me so often if it was purely imaginary. Anyway, I must tell you that I was a great reader of books. How often have I looked out through the dripping window panes of our cottage across to the sea which was slate grey and menacing, thinking of some book or other which I was immersed in! He, I am sure, has completely forgotten the incident even if he ever remembered it. His gaze on the contrary is fixed on the future and the ladder by which he climbs ever upward. My gaze is fixed on the past. I search for a flash from a stone or a leaf and that scrutiny is my whole life. That is why I so often return to my origins and why he has never written to any of his cousins or friends. I don't suppose I really like him.

Sometimes I think of myself bringing two pails of water home, and I also apply this image to the artist, who brings home from wells, where the cows stare at their reflected horns, his stories and legends, making sure that not a drop spills. My brother was much more daring than me. One night we waited for him, my mother and I, as he made his way across the moor from a neighbouring village in a storm of quick bitter lightning. Yet it didn't seem to frighten him. I could never climb to the roof of the house but he could. Even in the army he did daring things, daring direct things, because he felt the responsibility for doing them. I have always avoided responsibility.

And as I say, if I were to remind him now of this incident he wouldn't even remember it, it is so utterly trivial. And yet isn't it these incidents, so trivial in themselves, that we remember, that perhaps shape our destiny? We go up a road that we hadn't intended taking and we catch a glimpse of a red dress, or a car disappearing into the distance. And these moments are defined forever, engraved indeed on our minds. I have seen that happen, often and often. For instance, not so long ago I saw a boy's anguished face as he was taken into an ambulance whose blue light was flashing. I remember that, but I can't remember what I read in newspapers or in journals.

As you can see, I'm trying to create a philosophy, to define the importance of the incident even though it is trivial. I have a feeling it has shaped my whole life since it always returns to me, and that puzzles me. Why should something so minute become such a perpetual nagging pain? Why should it, at moments when I am involved in thought or our ambiguous relations in the world, flash out to me so startlingly?

It was a summer morning, or at least I think it was a summer morning. I have an impression of light. On summer mornings I used to get up early and walk about the house, my feet cold on the linoleum. It was as if I was waiting for someone, some guest. Such joy, such inexpressible joy. Walking about my crooked cottage where sometimes a mouse squeaked among the barrels of meal. It is therefore a summer morning, and I am reading a book. No, it is not exactly a book, it is a magazine, it is one of those yellow magazines which have such a strange distinctive smell. To the cheap paper there clings a yellow smell, for each colour has its own smell. It is a Western. It tells the story of Wild Bill Hickok. My brother is beside me in bed and he is leaning on his elbow looking at my book. He is not reading it, he is just looking at it. And it is a summer morning full of light.

I have reached the point where Wild Bill Hickok is pursuing outlaws across a mountain range. I don't know and I can't remember what American state it was, it might have been Kansas or Montana. Perhaps it was Montana. Anyway the mountains are covered with sage perhaps and they are blue for it is evening. Sometimes from our own house I could see a blue mountain and in the evening the sun setting behind it. The mountain was blue changing to black and sometimes it was purple. And slowly the sun would set behind it.

Anyway my brother began to fight with me for no reason at all, simply because of an unpredictable energy which had something to do with the summer morning. I have often such strange impulses myself. For no reason. As for instance in childhood one would be walking along the road and suddenly one would break into a run, flashing one's bare feet along the grassy verge as if one were competing against someone. But who? So he began to fight with me, no, not fight, tussle rather. And that was all it was at first, a tussle. Then as the tussle continued it became more serious, it swelled into a struggle for supremacy. We rolled over and over, each trying to get the other underneath and pinion the other's arms so that he would lie crucified below one. And our teeth would grit themselves, and we would breathe heavily, and we would say, Do you surrender? And a lot of the time I did surrender. For I knew this was my vocation in life, to surrender. I didn't have as much pride as my brother. And on this particular morning he tore the magazine into little pieces. Otherwise I might have been able to put it together again. But he tore it into very small pieces which drifted across the floor like snow.

And suddenly I began to cry. I remember this quite clearly. I cried and cried. And even now I almost cry when I think of it. For I was crying because I would never know what had happened to Wild Bill Hickok. I can still see him climbing the mountain in pursuit of the outlaws, his gun drawn, tall against the skyline, but I can't see the end of the story.

Of course I know that he won, of course I know that he killed them all, but I can never be really sure since the ending of the story was torn. I can smell some plant, perhaps sage, I can see the cactus and the mountain blue in the evening, but where has Wild Bill Hickok gone? Well, he is still preparing to cross the mountain after the outlaws but he will never catch them. He is caught in mid-flight. And why should that torment me? And why in my fiftieth year should I remember the incident so vividly that it brings tears to my eyes? All I can say is that it happened. All I can say is that that yellow paper is still rank and strong in my nostrils at this very moment as across the years we can remember certain tunes which have the power to raise for us whole areas of our past in their pristine dew and agony or happiness. I write to my brother in Kenya and congratulate him on the birth of his children but, below all that, I remember this incident. And it was so trivial that it ought not to be memorable. Yet all I can say is that if even now I could get the ending of that story on the cheap yellow paper I would give a great part of my real life in exchange for it, even the photographs of his children playing cricket, even much that I myself have endured and enjoyed and gloried in.

Listen to the Voice

For the past year he has been writing a book and for the past year he has been dying. In fact the disease, cancer of course, seems to have blossomed in harmony with the progression of the book. He will not show it to me till it is finished. It is a book about existentialism: Sartre, Camus, and the rest. He has been reading them thoroughly for many years in his spare time as a French teacher in the school where I myself taught. I have retired, in the natural order of things, and he has retired because of his illness though he has been keeping up a gay battle to the end. I have not been surprised by this. He has always been a man of immense intelligence and courage, a rare combination. I have known for years that his marriage was not a happy one (his wife did not understand his passion for research). She is a very ordinary common woman from England and he should never have married her. They met, I think, when he was at Oxford in the first dew of his youth. (At that time I believe that he was a dedicated left winger, anti-Franco, and the rest of it. The transition from left wing politics towards absurdity must show something about his life.) He has had to put up with a lot from her, not simply indifference but active malevolence and petty spitefulness. I have seen him humiliated by her in company though he smiled all the time. The humiliations were constant and searching, and might take the form of suggesting that he had not done as well as he should have done financially, or even of questioning his intelligence (he was not very practical), or of perfectly placed stab wounds with regard to money. When I have visited him I have treated her strictly as an enemy in whose custody a prisoner happens to be. She hates me as much as she hates him and for the same reasons, that I am like her husband in that I genuinely do not care for material things, I cannot understand why people should need more than one simple meal at a time. In fact the two of us have been unpopular with the staff of the school because at a certain meeting called to discuss possible strike action we spoke up against the greed of the society in which we live. Naturally we failed to persuade our colleagues to adopt our principles (they genuinely seemed to think we were cranks since we talked of money as being a superficial gloss), but our stand didn't make us popular. Simmons in particular was our bitter foe. He is a devious though apparently bluff fellow who is not only his own worst enemy but everyone else's as well. I cannot tolerate his hyprocrisy, and he has the scorned woman's ability to strike neatly at the underbelly.

Anyway we were both interested in our hobbies, he in his Existentialism and I in my literature. I mean in the novel and in poetry. He has always respected my mind and I have respected his. I have never written anything creative of course. How could one have the temerity to add to what is already there, unless what one writes is necessary? And I have never felt the pressure of the necessary. I listen to a great deal of music. I hear the note of necessity even in the flawed opulence of Wagner and overwhelmingly in the apparent simplicity of Mozart. But never within myself. I even wonder why he has decided to write his book. It is in a way unlike him to commit his dreamed perfection to paper. I know that he has taken a certain pleasure in the composition of examination papers and the preparation of notes on French writers but I never thought that he would actually write a book. Certainly not on anything as complicated as Existentialism.

More recently he has been moved to hospital where he has been getting intensive radiation treatment. I hate hospitals but I have been going to see him every Sunday afternoon. His bed is at the far end of the hospital, in a very distant ward, and I pass old people staring into space with dull eyes. His table beside the bed has the usual assemblage of grapes and oranges: no one ever dreams of bringing him a book to read. But in spite of the heavy atmosphere, relieved only by the sparkling presence of the nurses who know he is doomed, he has managed to finish his own book. We talk about various things. Once we had a long discussion on Keats and wondered how far tuberculosis animates the creative soul. He seems to think it does, though I feel it almost blasphemous to think that without the presence of tuberculosis Keats would never have been a great poet. Still, he lies there in all that white. He knows he is going to die. I suppose being an existentialist – for he holds the beliefs that they hold – he will die in a different way from those who do not hold such beliefs. He sees neither priest nor minister. I sit in my rather shabby coat – for the ward is sometimes rather cold – beside his bed. I do not think about justice or mercy. What use would there be in that?

His long haggard face, like one of those windows that one sees in churches, is becoming more and more refined each time that I visit him. The book, it seems, will be his last justification. It may be that he thinks he will posthumously justify his life to his wife, if the book turns out to be a good one. I know that she couldn't care less, as far as the content goes, but in his strange way he loves her. What could she know of the literature of France? It is only people like himself who have shed the world who can know about literature. In fact he is beginning to look more and more like a saint as the weeks pass. The pure bone is appearing through the flesh. One day I almost said to him, 'What is it like to die?' but I caught myself in time. In any case the nurses are often hovering about. Some of them are pupils whom he has taught. He told me that one of them (one of the dimmer ones in fact) had gone to the trouble of speaking to him one day in halting French. He felt that this was a compassionate gesture and so indeed it was. His eyes filled with tears as he told me about it. 'And yet,' he said wonderingly, 'she couldn't do French at all.' I don't think he told his wife about the incident.

He was of course a perfectionist when he was teaching. 'No, no, no,' he would shout, 'that is not how you say it. Not at all.' I could hear him two rooms away. 'Listen again. Listen. You must always listen. Listen to the voice.' And he would say the word over and over. The inflexion must be exactly right, the idiom must be perfect. Perhaps it was that lust for perfection that brought on his cancer. His own daughter had been one who had not flourished under his teaching (she was intelligent but rebellious), and his wife had never forgiven him for that. 'But,' he would say to her, as he told me, 'she isn't as good as the others.' However it happened that one of the others had been the daughter of one of her bitterest enemies and how could one expect that she could reconcile herself to his honesty? 'Women,' he would say to me, 'can't be impersonal. You cannot ask that of them.' How much futile quarrelling was concealed under that statement. For his daughter was now working in a shop, Frenchless, resentful, single.

How and why had he taken up Existentialism? I don't know. Was it perhaps that he was driven towards it by the absurdity of his own life? How can one tell why some writers and systems of thought attract us and others don't? (The other night I had a visitor from the chess club and there were two tarts on a plate, one yellow and one pink. I asked him which one he wanted and he said the yellow one. I myself had preferred the pink one. How can one explain that?) He hadn't of course been in the war either. And neither had I. (Yet I suppose the system of Existentialism, if one can talk of it in terms of a system, emerged out of the last war.) We had that in common. But there are differences too. For instance he has a good head for figures. I remember the marking system he once worked out in order to be fairer to candidates. The head-master couldn't understand it and so it was left in oblivion. I couldn't understand it either.

And so he is dying in this ward with the walls whose paint is coming off in flakes. And quite a lot of his former pupils visit him. It is surprising how many of them have done well for themselves. I do not mean that they have done well materially (though many have done that as well). What I was thinking of more precisely was that they have kept their minds true to themselves. One of them is now a Logic Professor in America and a leader of thought in his own field. I can't say that all of them have done as well as that but at least they have kept their integrity. What is even more striking is that they bring their wives along with them, however briefly they may be in town. He lies there like a medieval effigy, hammered out of some eternal stuff, and he listens to them and they listen to him. He has a great flair for listening and they tell him a great deal. In his youth he used to take them on expeditions, sometimes to France, and he and his pupils would talk into the early hours of the morning under other skies. Naturally, I wonder whether he did this because he wished to get away from his wife. I think this is partly true though perhaps he did not realise it himself. He did far more of this extramural activity than I ever did. I have never liked people as much as he has done. I have never had any warmth of nature. It has always struck me as strange that such perfectionism could be combined with such a liking for people.

He hasn't really had much in his life, an embittered wife and daughter, and that is all, apart from his schoolwork. And his book. That is not really very much to bear with one into the darkness of the absurd. Yet what else could he have done? How could he have known in those early days that his wife would turn out as she did? How could he have done other than take the side of his inflexible perfectionism against his daughter? Some men are lucky and some are not. I think one may say that he was not. Though naturally he doesn't believe in luck. I remember one revealing incident. There was a boy who wasn't able to get into university because his French was weak. He spent all his spare hours with him after school for weeks and months and managed to get him a pass in the examination. A year afterwards, the boy was working in a bar, he had simply gone to pieces after he had reached university. He had done no work at all. That was bad luck. Or was it bad judgement?

He is lying there and his book is finished. He has spent all his time on that book since his enforced retirement. He spent many years on it before that. He will take it with him into the final darkness. It may perhaps be a present for his wife, his last cold laurel. He may hold it out to her with a final absurd gesture, his lips half twisted in a final smile. To leave such as her the last product of his mind, the one least capable of understanding it! That would certainly be irony. Even now she may be thinking that she can make a little money from it. How else could one think of a book, of anything, but in terms of money?

I have been reading it. In fact I have read it all.

Last night I did not sleep. I read and reread the book. I searched page after page for illumination, for a new insight. The electric light blazed into my tired eyes, the bulb was like one of his sleepless eyes. Was it like a conscience? I revolved everything so slowly. O so slowly. After all we are human beings, condemned to servitude and despair. We are rags of flesh and bone though now and again pierced by flashes of light. I looked round my own monkish room. After all what had I done with my life? I didn't even have a wife or daughter. I thought of the world around me and how people might condemn me if they knew. They would condemn me out of their own shallowness, precisely because they were committed to no ideal and walked swathed in the superficial flesh. In fact at one time during the night while I was studying a page for the third or fourth time I heard on the street below the music of a transistor, though I could not make out the words of the song that was being sung. I supposed it was something to do with love and had travelled here from Luxembourg.

But not merciless love. No, love with all the mercy in the world. Love that would forgive anything because there was in the end nothing to forgive. Love that had no knowledge of the knife. But only of the tears. The light blazed on page after naive page. He had been too long in teaching. His mind had adjusted itself to immature minds. It was as if the book had been written for a Lower Fifth Form. All had been explained but all had been explained away. Sartre and Camus had lost the spring of their minds, the tension, they had been laid out flat on the page as his own body had been laid on its white bed. All was white without shadow. There was no battle. The battle had been fought elsewhere. The battle had been fought against his wife and daughter in the real world of money and teaching and jobs. The energy had gone into that. I stared for a long time at the book. After all, were we not poor human beings? After all, what was our flesh against the absurdity of the skies?

I walked to the hospital carrying the book. It was a June day and the birds were singing and the air was warm. The windows of the hospital were all open and the air was rushing in, scented and heavy. The whole world was in blossom. On the lawn there were some old people in chairs being sunned and tanned before being replaced in their beds. The sky was a mercilessly clear blue without cloud. I walked along the whole length of the ward and he was waiting for me. He would want to know what I thought immediately.

I handed him the book. I said to him quite clearly, aware of everything, 'It's no good, James. It's just no good.' The book lay between us on the bed. 'It's too naive,' I said. 'There are no new insights. None at all.'

Without a word he held out his hand towards me. And then he said equally clearly, 'Thank you, Charles.' I felt as if we were two members of a comic team as I heard our names spoken, two comedians dancing on a marble floor somewhere far from there.

He didn't say anything else. We started talking about other things. Three days afterwards he was dead. When I heard this I stared for a long time out of the window of my flat as the tears slowly welled in my eyes. No one can ever know whether he has done right or wrong. I stared around me at the books and they stood there tall and cold in their bookcases. I went and picked up a Yeats but I could find nothing that I wanted and I replaced it among the other books.

At the funeral the wife ignored me. Perhaps he had told her not to publish the book and she had guessed what had happened. Simmons was with her and he also ignored me. Later I heard that he had been advising her to get it published. I thought that if James had been alive this would have served as a true example of the absurd, his wife and Simmons in such an alliance. The two of them stood gazing down into the grave at the precious despised body and mind disappearing from view, she rigid and black, Simmons large and stout. As I turned away my shoes made a dreadful rustling noise on the gravel.

The Exorcism

I have just finished wrestling with a saint and I am very tired. For it is clear to me that a saint may act as a devil in his human affairs and because he is a saint may easily lead people astray. For one may think that one is imitating the saint when one is in fact imitating the devil in the saint. But ... I think it is the tiredness that is making me go on like this and I had better begin at the beginning.

I am a Professor of Theology at a college in Edinburgh. I am a round, rather fat, good-natured and, I think, nice man. When I wake up in the morning I am nearly always happy, for I exist in a harmony which I believe is the harmony of God, His universal music. I have never doubted this. Not that I ever had any special dramatic experience which proved that this harmony existed, I have always known it. Perhaps my secure childhood had something to do with it, a large rambling house, a garden in which the birds seemed always to sing, a father who was ample and good-humoured, and a mother who, loving him, loved me as well. I suppose really there is something to be said for success in the world and my father, himself a Professor of Theology before me, was successful in that he was doing the work which like myself he was born to do. Happy this kind of succession, and lucky those who benefit from it. He was not a tortured man: on the contrary, like me he existed inside the divine music whose notes were composed of books, garden, a loved wife, sunny days, and nights without the necessity for remorse. Sounds emerge from childhood, of pots humming on cookers, of mowers whose sleepy hum enchanted the June days, of laughter, of a pervasive busy world in which I budded and blossomed. Sights I recall of trams rocking down their rails, of the castle ancient and magical and theatrical on its hill, of colours almost excessively clear in a northern light.

So I grew up admiring my father and followed him as naturally into his world as if I had been born to do so. My student days were happy, I loved books and I recall sitting in gardens in white flannels reading theological and Latin books while the bees hummed about my deckchair. I don't suppose all those days were like that but that is how I recall them. There were poignant thorny moments as when my father died, closely followed by my mother. I married a woman rather like my mother and settled into my college world, a perpetual student, loved, I think, and loving. I think I may say that I have exercised a beneficent influence and that through me others have been brought to hear the harmony which composes the world. I can think of few people who have been as lucky as me. I have never suffered from the obligatory fashionable angst so zealously pursued in literary reviews, and that is because I have never divided man into body and spirit: both seem to me to form an indissoluble whole. I have never wished to do any other work than I do, or to be other than I am. Why should I be other than happy?

In general my students have been normal like myself. They have studied here, and thereafter gone out into the world to transform it according to their lights, and to bear with them, into whatever gaunt or lovely corner, an echo of the music which they have heard while briefly, almost too briefly, we have been together. Many of them, whom I have been conscious of, have gone on to the sombre battlefields of the world and I have often received letters which revealed minds and souls at the edge of sanity, frenzied notes which spoke of the devil and his fierce diamond will opposing them in the night as well as the day. I have felt it my duty to answer all these letters and to restate from this calm place the beliefs which have sustained me and my father before me. At times I have felt that perhaps I also ought to be in those embattled places but my inner voice has told me that my best work is being done where I am. And so all was well till I encountered Norman MacEwan.

Now Norman MacEwan was from the islands, and I had

better make quite clear at the beginning what I thought of him, and what I knew of the environment that had created him. First of all, he was very pale and intense and neglectful of his appearance. There was a bony aspect to him and a disharmony of clothes. His collar was often soiled, his tie disarranged, his hair long and floppy. He was not at all clever: on the contrary he had to work very hard at his books to keep up, but that may be because he had the kind of mind that needs to fasten on words and ideas till he has finally torn the flesh from the bones. He had no distractions that I know of, at least in his first year; he had no interest in music or the theatre or the cinema, and he read no books except the ones that were recommended. Sometimes on Saturday afternoons he would go out preaching to local layabouts. I once saw him near Princes Street Gardens, his hair flopping in the breeze, his right hand jabbing downwards through the air, all intensity and vivacity, while past him there walked a trampish looking man in a long overcoat whose shoulders and head were crowned with pigeons.

Of course he had come from an environment different from mine. In the bleak islands God is a hard schoolmaster, with the cane always ready to lash at the poor hand. He is the thorn and the lightning, and not at all the civilised artist or composer. He forgives no one and certainly not the introverted divinity student such as Norman MacEwan, only son of a widowed mother whose husband had spent his days and nights in a haze of drink, disoriented and Celtic, though whether this was endemic or whether it was reaction to his wife's harsh religious beliefs, who will now know? All this I found out from a minister friend of mine who came from the islands. But at the time I saw in front of me a bony tense unhappy boy who certainly did not hear the harmony I heard and was, I thought, impatient with the civilised books I lent him, and which he chewed at into the early hours of the morning. He seemed to be searching for some other harmony, some bleaker blacker globe of a harsher drama than I could supply him with.

I took him to the house one evening but I am afraid that he said very little and was so nervous that he spilt his tea all over the carpet and finally rushed out, head down, as if he had committed some unforgivable sin.

It looked to me at this early stage as if he would quite simply exhaust himself. I had the impression that he neither ate nor drank, that he spent his days rushing along the street (coat flapping, for he wore a long unfashionable brown tweed coat), that he felt he had found himself in a city rather like Sodom, attractive and terrifying and seductive, and that there was no place for him in the college at all. No place in the world even. I must confess that I wondered at times whether in fact he would take to drink as his father had done, but I hadn't quite realised how deep his mother's prohibition had bitten. In fact she sometimes came down to see him and to make sure that he was keeping to the right path. I never met her myself but I heard that she appeared in a black coat, remorseless and rigid and unyielding, and had a number of things to say to the landlady about certain aspects of her boarding house.

I may say that I was rather worried about him. I felt that his spirit was beating steadily against his flesh, as his own island waves beat against the cliffs, and that this force would destroy him if it did not find its form. He sat sulkily on the bench along with other students but at no time did his face flower into visionary understanding, nor did his clumsy bony body relax. All the time he seemed to be searching for some gift that I could not give, and by his undeviating remorseless stance adding a contemptuous gloss to my lectures. I grew almost to dread him as if he were my conscience accompanying me continually in visible form. I had in fact nothing to offer him at all. For the first time in my life, I felt almost in despair. I avoided his eye, and my words gradually lost their resonance, confronted by that stony gaze. My own inner harmony was being steadily dislocated. Till one day the miracle happened.

At a certain stage in the course I felt it obligatory on me to tell my students something about Kierkegaard though he is not in fact a theologian (if he can even be called that) who appeals to me much. I feel that in a sense his biography intrudes too deeply and that there is a certain fake element in his nature which I cannot quite focus on. However, as I explained to my students that day some of Kierkegaard's ideas, as well as some of the biographical data which I thought necessary to inform them of, I saw for the first time that stony gaze become intent and almost glowing. I have never in my whole life seen such a total conversion proceeding so nakedly before my very eyes. I can even recall the smells of that day, the varnish from the desks, the freshness of the green leaves penetrating the open windows, the scent of blossom. Truly a harmony of the natural day and of ideas as well.

I told them of how Kierkegaard's father had cursed God on a hill in Jutland, of his success in business as a hosier, of the nickname Soren Sock which had been cast at the hunchback boy at school, of the brilliant dandy who had kept the salons laughing, of the affair of Regine, whom he had been engaged to, and finally of the ideas, the world of the aesthetic and the ethical giving way to that of the existential. I told of the early Socratic irony, followed by the crucified tormented exhortatory prose, of the pseudonyms which were sloughed as he progressed, of the consciousness of power and the exceptional, of the death bed scene where he had expressed his happiness. All this I told them, and as I spoke I felt I had done a terrible thing, that I had introduced this boy to a saint so flawed that he might destroy him. But may I say how much I envied Kierkegaard at that moment, that he could affect a human being so much, that out of the death of the spirit he could bring him alive again? I was fair to Kierkegaard though I myself feel that he demands too much of men, that he has in fact divided the harmony of the body and the spirit, and reintroduced a terrible medievalism into the world.

Still, how can I forget how the boy's face brightened as if at last and for the first time in his life he had entered on his kingdom and come home?

When the lecture was over he came up to me and asked me if I could lend him some of Kierkegaard's books. I gave him some and he thanked me and then rushed slantingly away with that walk of his as if he were breasting a high wind, bearing his treasures with him. I shivered slightly wondering how that strong salty food would affect him, and it was as if I was frightened, as if across the lecture room had fallen a dark chilly shade. If my memory is not deceiving me I think that even on that day he was wearing his long trailing brown tweed coat.

I may say that after I had loaned him the books I didn't see him again at my lectures for a week or two. I was rather worried about this but when I asked a fellow lodger of his – also a student – if there was anything wrong, for I still had the feeling that I had done something irretrievable, he assured me that there wasn't but that MacEwan was still reading the books. It was a beautiful summer and, uneasy as I had been made by MacEwan's presence in my class, I didn't set out to investigate further. As I lectured to my students that month of May while the world of nature blossomed around the walls of learning – so that the ivy itself seemed to be in bloom – I felt Kierkegaard's presence as an intrusion, as if the devil himself had entered the Garden of Eden.

In any event I didn't see MacEwan again till after the vacation. I didn't know what I had been expecting to see, for his gaunt thorny presence had been forgotten during the long hot summer when I had relaxed from the book on which I was working, a history of the college. I had perhaps thought that in the Jutland of the islands he had become more thistly and sullen than he had been before, that the narrow intensity of his nature had been made more extreme and perhaps sharpened into a bitterer stake. It has always surprised me on my visits to these islands that such a paradisal landscape can produce such unhappy unstable men.

However, I was quite amazed to find that when MacEwan joined my class I did not recognise him. His hair was still as long as ever but it looked combed. Instead of a tie he was wearing a silken floppy reddish scarf mottled with green. He was even clean-shaven and altogether in his brown sports jacket he looked summery and almost radiant. The sullenness had disappeared from his voice which now sounded mocking and alert. He gave me back my books and said how much he had enjoyed them. I asked him whether he wished to discuss anything in them but he said, almost with a patronising smile, that he didn't, as if he had decided to assign to me the part of the vacuous liberal churchman in Kierkegaard's demonology. I can't say that I liked him any more than I had done previously, but my dislike now was founded on different causes.

Nor did his transformation stop there. The essays he wrote for me became lighter and what I can only call flippant, and he developed a gift for the superficial epigram such as when in one of them he said that the church was no longer even the opium of the masses, it wasn't even their cup of tea. I was brought up short by this statement because its style didn't seem to be his at all. It was rather as if a dandyish imagination, brittle and heartless, was beginning to speak through him. Even his writing blossomed into flowery ornamentation, which had once been gaunt and rigid and vertical. He began to introduce quotations from poets and novelists and to my surprise I learned that he had been reading Dostoevsky and Nietzsche. But more surprising than that was that he suddenly began to take part in plays, favouring world-weary sophisticated parts. He would typically be standing in corners of the stage, letting fall witticisms as he languidly smoked a cigarette. He even joined the Debating Society and would deliver short startling brittle speeches which often contained attacks on the contemporary church. At one which I attended I heard him remark that if, as Eliot had written, the whole world was a hospital endowed by a ruined millionaire, inflation had certainly made things worse. It was this kind of remark both arresting and shallow that antagonised and puzzled me. I couldn't understand how one who had come from his environment could effect such a transformation in his personality. I gathered that he had ceased to write home and that he even spoke of the islanders in a mocking manner. His father too had, according to him, been an atheist. My impression had been that he was just a drunkard. In class however he remained silent when he condescended to come. A lot of the time he didn't appear to be listening at all, at other times he listened but smiled in a world-weary manner, as if he was contemptuous of the quality of my mind. I found this rather irritating since I knew that my own mind was much more powerful than his (though still mediocre) but as I have sometimes encountered students of this kind, that did not in itself worry me. What began to worry me was that he would talk of his acting – this information I got from his fellow lodger again – as if he were a second Olivier and of his debating as if he were a second Demosthenes. In fact, I must admit that I was rather confused.

However, for the second time, something happened which encouraged me. Apparently he had started going out with a girl. As a matter of fact, the girl was a student and I happened to know her because her father was a Councillor, a man affable enough but not, one would say, imaginative. She was what one would call a nice girl (she was in fact studying Arts with a view to becoming a teacher) when one means that she is quiet and undistinguished. Her talent wasn't really for scholarship but rather for domestic and more mundane affairs. As her mother was dead she looked after the house and sometimes had to arrange dinners for her father's guests. She was a dark-haired girl who nevertheless looked presentable enough but who was rather silent in company, and the social functions must have been agonising for her. She played the piano rather well but in a sentimental manner, and was very good at arranging flowers in vases. In another century she would have married young and made a good wife and mother, but in this one it was decreed that she should study Latin and History in order to teach children. She was, I think, fond of her father who was a rather pompous vacuous man with a loud booming voice but kind enough in his way, and fond of his daughter. They lived in a large house set in an extensive area of ground in an exclusive area of the town, that is to say, not far from where I live myself.

Naturally I don't know very much of what went on between her and Norman and much of what I shall say will be guesswork though part will be information which I gained one way or another. If one wonders first of all where he met her, then, as far as I could find out, it was at the dramatic society where she acted as a maid in one of the more sophisticated plays that was staged. If one wonders what she saw in him, then it must be that at this stage she may have been attracted by his dandyish negligent manner and by that slightly alien sensitivity which one often finds in islanders. If one wonders what he saw in her then it

must be that she was the type of girl who would listen
uncritically to him, admire him, and be easily deceived by the
plumage without seeing to the bone underneath. I cannot
imagine what they would talk about but I am sure that the talk
would have mostly come from him, for he had grown to like the
sound of his own voice. As I say, my knowledge of the girl was
not very deep. I had occasion to see her father because I am on
a committee which has been set up to preserve the area in which
I live from the erection of a particularly horrible office block. I
had talked to her a few times and then as the office block
became more threatening I had visited him oftener and seen her
more frequently. I must say that she blossomed as time passed,
there was more purpose about her motion, she talked to me
once about the future in a more involved way than usual and she
even asked me some questions about ministers' wives. (I assumed that this had something to do with Norman MacEwan.)
She had a very earnest nature and one felt that where she gave
her heart there would be no disloyalty and no shadow of
treachery. One day we talked briefly in the garden of her house;
her hands were folded in her lap while on a branch in front of us
a bird's breast vibrated with the intensity of its singing; and as
she talked and I looked at her, I felt less tranquillity than fear.
(By this time of course she knew that I was Norman's teacher
and whatever he had said to her about me, probably unfavour-
able, she knew that I was at least close to him.) I don't know why
I felt such fear. I knew that MacEwan wouldn't have visited the
house much if at all, and that he would not have impressed the
father, for I was sure that he would be rather gauche, rebellious
in a half-baked manner or superciliously showing off his learning. Still, MacEwan had looked much happier recently in class,
and more human. He had even spontaneously thanked me for
the loan of some books and the ironical note was no longer so
evident in his essays which seemed to have a more pervasive
warmth than in the past. Indeed they began to show signs that
he was thinking in terms of a possible future and of the real
world and his responsibilities in that world. He would discuss
more mundane matters such as one might imagine a minister
being involved with. Thus on the whole I was encouraged.

One day quite by accident I happened to meet the two of them in the College grounds. MacEwan had taken her along to show her over the college. He was I thought rather startled when he saw that I knew her, and he looked at me in a considering manner after he had found this out. I asked her what she thought of the college and I noticed her turning to him as if she expected him to tell her what to say. He mentioned something about Cambridge in a large manner and I said diplomatically that MacEwan was promising enough before he met her but that now I was sure his promise would be fulfilled. She smiled at me gratefully. I was rather worried at the way in which she responded so naively to his rather florid pronouncements (for he was acting the lord of the manor a bit) and wondered if it was perhaps the authoritarianism of the islands that she was responding to as indeed she responded to her overbearing father. I asked in an indirect way whether he had been at their house yet but apparently he had not. I thought he was going to say something contemptuous about councillors but wisely he didn't. On the whole I got the impression that he liked her and perhaps even loved her, that he liked showing off before her (he had a long monologue about his performance in a play by Wycherley), and that she looked on him with a certain reverence. That was the last time I saw them together. I remember I looked back as I was leaving and I saw him bending over her as she sat on a bench. It was almost as if he was whispering in her ear and I was disturbed by an image which sprang out startlingly in front of my eyes in that place of leaves and shadows. It occurred to me that I knew little about either of them but what little I knew did not dispose me to augur a confident future for either of them, or both of them together.

I didn't see her again till she came to see me on an autumn day. She seemed agitated and looked as if she had been crying. In her hand, screwed up, she was carrying a piece of paper which after she had given it to me I discovered was a letter from MacEwan. I don't know why she came to me, unless it was that perhaps I might know something more profound about the writer than others did. It was a very abrupt letter but the handwriting was rather shaky. When I say that it was abrupt I don't mean that it was short but the tone of it seemed abrupt. I noticed that the handwriting had changed again and was what I can only call a compromise between the tall stiff calligraphy he had affected at the beginning and the flowery ornamental script he had been using more recently.

It read as follows:

Dear Helen,

After much reflection and deep anguished thought I have come to the conclusion that our affair cannot prosper. I feel in myself that which is exceptional striving to break the bonds which limit it. More and more I wish to break off my dandiacal existence and enter the world of the spiritual which calls me with its continual note. I feel condemned to be like a single tree in whose branches no birds are fated to sing. When I started going out with you it was because I had succumbed to my feelings of loneliness. I was wrong to do that. I should never have allowed myself that weakness since I do not belong to myself. I belong to the world of the spirit and the spirit will not let me be. I cannot bring myself to use the word 'husband', it seems so alien to me. Nor can I use the word 'wife' which others can so glibly use. My lips can't form either of these words. I do not *want* to be an exception. I wish to marry like everyone else but I feel that I'm different. Why else can my lips not form those words? I feel it would be better if you were to find someone more ordinary than me, someone who would provide you with love and who would not be continually thinking of the world beyond this one. I think it would be better if we did not meet again, however anguished this must make me. Please do not think that I do not love you. That is not it at all. On the contrary, I love you very much as far as my nature is capable of love. But I feel that my road must be a lonelier one, a more difficult one. Perhaps some day we shall meet again. I shall always think of you.

With sincerest regards,

Norman MacEwan.

(The name was signed with a large flourish.)

At that moment I knew what I must do. I took the almost weeping girl out to my house in my car and left her with my wife. As we drove along I would look sideways at her and notice how now and again tears would brim her eyes and deep in my heart I cursed MacEwan. When I had left her in the house after explaining the situation to my wife in a few words, I got into my car and went in search of my student. I remember staring bleakly at the autumn trees that lined the side of the avenue and wondering whether I had the strength for the confrontation that was necessary. I had never before been called to such a task and perhaps my resources were not equal to it.

I found his flat in a crowded part of the city and rang the doorbell. A large woman with a Roman nose came to the door and when I asked her if MacEwan was at home admitted that he was. I asked her if I could see him. She said she would get him but added that he might be working as he had come in late the previous night. I waited stubbornly, feeling the tides of anger rising steadily in me, far away from my own quiet avenue in the centre of the turbulent city.

After an almost insulting interval, Norman appeared at the door. We stared at each other in a hostile manner but I was pleased to see that he looked haggard and unshaven.

'I should like to see you on a matter of some urgency,' I said and my voice sounded pompous even to myself. 'Not here,' I added. 'I should be glad if you would come for a drive in my car.'

'If you like,' he said quite casually, his ill face sullen and bristly.

In silence we got into the car. I said nothing at all and neither did he as we drove out from the centre of the city and headed towards a quiet area where there was a wood in which I often walked when I wished to think. He stared rigidly ahead of him and I with gritted teeth concentrated on my driving, trying to think how I might open our conversation later.

Finally we reached the wood and I got out and he followed me. The trees were in glorious golden foliage and now and again I could hear twitterings from the trees. Once I saw a grey squirrel scampering up a trunk half in shadow and half in sunshine.

I stopped and thrust the letter at him. He glanced at it knowing what it was, and handed it back without speaking.

'What does that letter mean?' I said to him, my anger rising again.

'It means what it says,' he said in a voice which was almost impertinent.

We came to a bench in the middle of the wood where there was a sunny clearing and I said to him, 'I would be grateful if you would sit there for a moment while I talk to you. I think better when I'm walking up and down.'

I paused for a moment to collect my thoughts and then I said to him, 'First of all, I should like you to tell me what you think of me.'

He looked startled for a moment and then said quite finally, 'I believe that you are interested in comfort. I believe that you have betrayed the church.'

'And what then do you believe the church should be doing?' I asked him.

'I believe,' he said in the same positive voice, 'that the church should be much more extreme than it is. I believe in sin, I believe in hell. I do not believe in fatness and port.'

'And now do you mind if I tell you what I think of you?' I told him, catching at that moment a glimpse of a pheasant of the most incredibly complicated stained glass colours walking through the wood.

He nodded bleakly, his stubbly face seeming more hollow-cheeked than usual in the varying sunlight and shadow.

'Well, then,' I said with the same conviction as he had shown, 'I think you have a mediocre mind.'

He made as if to say something but didn't, though a nerve in his jaw quivered.

'You asked for honesty and truth,' I said to him, 'and I am giving it to you. You have a mediocre mind in that there is not in it the slightest glimmering of originality. Oh, I know that you have your dramatic and debating successes and that now and again you bring to birth with premeditated labour a *bon mot* or two. I know all that but that is not originality. I am not original,' I said. 'I am mediocre. The difference between us is that I have recognised this but you haven't. Of course you're young and it is hard for you to accept what I'm saying but you will have to eventually. If not now, then later.'

He gazed at me with his stony gaze though now and then I saw the nerve twitching in his jaw. He was no Isaac to me and I no Abraham (as in the story by Kierkegaard) but I was determined on this murder, this necessary murder, just the same. I must not be moved by pity of his pallor, that was irrelevant.

'I said,' I continued, 'that you have a mediocre mind. If you accepted this you might do better. There are very few people with original minds. You are not one of them.' Suddenly I lashed out at him, 'You are no Kierkegaard.'

There was a silence in which I heard a cuckoo crying its double note, pure and excessively joyful.

'Let me refer you to your letter. Do you know that you have used in it a phrase by Kierkegaard, that phrase about the lonely tree? Kierkegaard's "solitary pine". That was the phrase he applied to himself after he had jilted Regine. Tell me something,' I said. 'Why did you turn to drama after you had been so strict and inward in your early days here?'

He did not reply but looked straight ahead, tense and pale.

'Shall I tell you all of it? Well then, you read that Kierkegaard in his youth was interested in the theatre, that he was something of a dandy given to *bons mots*. That was why you changed, wasn't it? You were imitating him, weren't you?'

He still said nothing.

'I believe that was quite deliberate and conscious on your part,' I said. 'But that part wasn't evil. That was harmless enough. I repeat, that part was harmless enough.' I waited for him to speak but he still said nothing. In that wood there was a dead colour about his skin, a ghostly almost fishlike hue.

'Shall I tell you what was truly evil?' I continued as if hammering nails. 'You discovered Helen. Where did you meet her?'

There was no answer. A greenness from the leaves mottled his white face.

'You set out to meet her. You set out to find a girl who would fulfil the correct qualifications of your story. She must be the daughter of a Councillor. Oh, I know that Regine's father was not a councillor in our sense of the word but perhaps you didn't know that. You waited till you found someone who would love you and who would be normal and unambitious and conventional. That I consider evil. For why did you set out to find her? You did so in order that you might jilt her so that you might fulfil the law of Kierkegaard for that was exactly what he did. He went further than you in that he engaged himself to Regine, and when broken-hearted she wrote to him he sent her a cold letter and went out of his way quite deliberately to show himself to her in a cold light.'

Suddenly he burst out, 'It was necessary, to continue the life of the spirit.'

'Nevertheless,' I said, 'I believe that Kierkegaard was grossly mistaken. I believe that he acted in a criminal manner.'

'Criminal?' He stood up at last facing me and vibrating like a gaunt bird. 'Criminal! How could the foremost genius of his age be a criminal? A saint?'

'I say criminal,' I repeated, 'because I mean criminal. Whenever did the life of the spirit demand that one destroy a human heart and its faith?'

'Christ Himself left his mother,' he said fiercely.

'Christ,' I said, 'was God. His mother was only the momentary flesh he inhabited. But in any case Christ did not elaborate a whole net of deceit.

'I repeat, Kierkegaard was a criminal. He imposed himself on this girl, so much younger than himself, and having done so, he withdrew from her. Spirituality does not excuse the criminal.'

He turned away from me as if implying that I did not understand what I was talking about.

I went on, 'And what will happen to you? I have already said that you are no Kierkegaard. What sort of life will you live? Alone? You don't even have the resource of literature to hide you from reality. You are not a genius. You are an ordinary person. You do not belong to the world of the exceptional. You haven't the strength to endure that world. You are not wounded enough. Listen,' I said, 'listen to the birds. Look at the loveliness of this wood. Why don't you enjoy the world?

Because one is committed to the church one doesn't need to be wretched all the time. You,' I said, 'are possessed by a flawed saint. Possession, that's what it is. As if one were possessed by a devil.'

He turned round and faced me full in the light. 'Possession?' he said. 'How can one be possessed by a saint?'

'You are possessed by that part of the saint which is the devil. Listen,' I said, 'have you read Kierkegaard? Have you read of his intolerable loneliness, of his penance? Have you read of the time when later he met Regine on the street? Have you read his words: "If I had had enough faith I would have married her."? Did you realise the terrible genius that could have made him endure all that? You haven't got that gift. And only that gift is enough. Without it you cannot take up the burden.'

He sat on the bench and put his head in his hands. I waited but did not touch him. I said, 'She loves you, you know. The two of you could be happy together. You could be married. People do that every day. It's not an intolerable burden. I myself have been married for many years. It is not the end of the world. And what will happen if you don't marry? Helen will be tormented.' Suddenly at that moment I was possessed by an almost medieval vision. I don't know what caused the power to rise in my breast. It may be that the leaves all about me and Norman in his pose of the brooding monk reminded me of a missal where such pictures are shown, but I shouted in a loud voice:

'Kierkegaard, come out of this man! Leave him to his own life. He is not like you, he doesn't have your terrible gifts. Leave him alone.'

There was a long silence in the woods through which after a while I again heard the throb of a bird's song and then I was aware that Norman was sobbing, that his body was being shaken and torn as if by a snake that writhed deep within him. I forced myself to watch him, calling on all the resources of harmony and happiness that I had, so that it was as if for a moment I saw my father's shade encouraging me with large benignity. The sobbing continued for a long time, then Norman raised his exhausted white face. He looked at me and there was no longer in his eyes that impudence and intolerance. They were in fact calm and tired.

I looked at him for a long time knowing that the agony was over. It was a victory but an empty victory. And even in the midst of the victory how could I be sure that this was not indeed a second Kierkegaard, how could I be sure that I had not destroyed a genius? How could I be sure that my own harmonious jealous biography had not been superimposed upon his life, as one writing upon another, in that wood where the birds sang with such sweetness defending their territory?

I looked down at him white and exhausted. The exorcism was over. He would now follow his unexceptional destiny.

Macbeth

I think it must be a detective I am talking to, or who is talking
to me. He belongs to what is laughingly called the real world.
He is a greyish man and this is a greyish room, not unlike a
dressing-room I was in once when I was starting on my career,
and he is on the whole quite kind. He speaks to me as if I were
a child, which is perhaps what I am. That may be why I thought
Greta was in love with me though she wasn't. I have often
thought that certain people were in love with me though they
never were. Perhaps that is one of the occupational hazards of
being an actor. And maybe it is because I am a child that I
thought Duncan, no, I mean Charles, was simply an old man
when in fact he was so much more. I thought that if I could kill
him on stage I ought to be able to kill him in reality. The
detective doesn't understand that, he lives in the real world,
and he almost certainly has a wife and children, both of which
I have lost because of Greta so that now I am a tramp in a grey
room. I got the play the wrong way round and even Butler
deceived me. The lust I suffered from, the lust . . .

Why is he asking me such banal questions? My name,
doesn't he know it? Does he never go to the theatre? Has he
never heard of Ralph Cameron? Has he never seen it in lights
in this merciless city which I have often walked through at
night, obsessed by lust and injustice? That that old man
should have Greta as well as everything else, his genius, his
fame! That that beautiful dark harmonious woman should
belong to him, as well as everything else! And his flattery of
me. What did it mean after all? Nothing. And night after
night I killed him on stage with his grey hair, his grey face.
And night after night I nearly killed him in reality to the
applause of my insatiable invisible audience. And night after

night she whispered in my ear, 'Kill him, kill him, and you will be king.' I left my wife and children because of her, I left my terraced house, the grapefruit in the morning, the suffocating doors and windows because of her. And she would say to me in that world beyond the stage, 'Later, later I will leave him.' And she would tell me he was impotent, though hardened in kingship for so long. I mounted her in hotel rooms when he was not supposed to know, though he did know, and I didn't know that he knew. And if he hadn't known Butler would have told him. Butler, my Banquo. I dug my spurs into her beautiful black body. And 'Later, later,' she would say, in that country of Macbeth, bare ruined foggy Scotland, from which I myself came those many years ago. We played each other's murderers and victims, she Lady Macbeth, I, Macbeth, and her old husband the old swaying Duncan.

He is of course – I mean Charles Lawson, her husband – our greatest actor. He is better than Gielgud, has more daring. His Duncan – what can one say about it except that it is perfect? When I stab him, just before I stab him, having entered the room from my mistress's, his wife's, room, he opens his eyes at me and smiles. He smiles into my face, he isn't asleep at all when I stab him, and at that moment it is as if he is surrendering to the new king. The smile is saying, 'Take the kingdom, take the throne, and much good may it do you.' The critics raved about that moment, that slow half mocking smile, and then I stabbed him as if his smile had to be eradicated from the face of the world, since one could not live if such a smile were possible. And then along that shadowy corridor I returned to his wife, my mistress, and we embraced on stage in a feverish passionate embrace as we had done in hotel rooms so often before. And now I am alone, I have nothing, I am being questioned in a place very like the first dressing-room I ever had. All sound and fury signifying nothing.

He was my master, he found me in Scotland, and he brought me to London, he taught me everything, he taught me how to speak, how to stand and do nothing, how to stand and do much. He didn't want to play Macbeth. 'I am too old for the part,' he said, and he smiled at me his fanged genius smile. But then he is a man possessed by perfection. Possessed. How clearly I now see that.

The grey man opposite me is saying,

'You played the part of Macbeth?'

'Yes.'

'And Charles Lawson played the part of Duncan?'

'Yes.'

'And Mrs Lawson played the part of Lady Macbeth?'

'Yes.'

'She is West Indian, is she not?'

'African.' (Sometimes I swear her body had a bluish tinge like a grape.)

'And she was your mistress?'

Why should I answer that? It seemed to be so. For her I left my wife and family, for her I sought the kingship of my native land. Wherever we went all turned and looked at her, that was one disadvantage. She was a queen, far more than I was a king. 'Genius,' she would say, 'is difficult to live with. He is obsessed. How can one live with an obsessed man?' How indeed? My wife gazed at me as if poleaxed across the breakfast table. And how I pitied her. Christ in heaven, how much I pitied her and how much I pitied myself! For my lust and my loss were so painful to me. 'A giant's robe upon a dwarfish king.'

'*Macbeth* is a play about sex,' Charles would say, for he directed as well as acted. 'Macbeth has to prove his manhood. That is what the play is about.' And I would look at her and smile. How often had I proved my manhood on her. I was dying of proving my manhood. She in her black skin, wearing her white panties. Panties for a queen. 'Sex,' he would repeat, almost panting, 'that is what the play is about. She offers him herself if he will kill Duncan.' And he would smile his aged crocodile smile, his dry face cracking like a desert. Thus that autumn passed. In the afternoons I would kill him in my dreams and in the evenings I would kill him on stage with my loving trusty dagger. Never again such happiness and such anguish. That she should love me, that she should show me she loved me. I learned about her in reality, I explored her body, and what I learned in reality I would put into practice on the stage. But I knew nevertheless that something was wrong and some nights I would walk the streets of London, those merciless lights, and know that I was lost. I would ache for the barrenness of Scotland. The autumn had bare boughs and no birds sang.

And once in a pub I confided in Butler, my Banquo, and he said: 'I'm terribly sorry, old boy, but everyone knows about it.'

'Does Charles?' I said.

'Shouldn't think so, old boy.' He's six feet four inches tall and later in the play I kill him, stabbing at his cool remote unhelmeted head. 'You can't help it, old boy,' he said, but he went and told Charles. I, on the other hand, believed in the truthfulness of art, I mean I believed in life as if it were art which of course it isn't, though this grey detective who is making notes doesn't know that. I believed that people, especially in the same profession, shouldn't go around telling tales on each other. I now know that art has its politics too, as autumn has its songs. And I returned to Scotland in spirit to get my theatrical queen, I who had left there poor and distressed so many years ago till Charles, I mean Duncan, rescued me. He had saved me and I had repaid him by sleeping with his wife. Still, what else could I do? The doom was on me. From the first day I went to his house and she served up drinks with some sort of tall collar round her neck. And he said, 'My wife,' and glanced at me. That old man and that young black woman. It was incredible, it was obscene.

'I'm so pleased to meet you,' she said. 'I've heard so much about you.' And she crossed her long beautiful black legs. Christ in his blue heavens. So it happened with her after the *Macbeth* run began and I was being hailed as the greatest, squat and poetic, a doomed Scot blundering among lights and shadows. The lights and shadows of London. And I swear that one night after coming out of a restaurant I saw the three witches standing at a corner and laughing at me. How could I imagine that I deserved her? My doom and my queen.

Question: 'And I believe that he had helped you in your career.'

'Yes.'

Question: 'Would you say that you were jealous of him?'

Jealous? I burned. I was on fire. I couldn't stand the two of them in bed together. 'No,' she said, 'he doesn't have the energy left over.' But how was I to know that she wasn't lying? I dozed in an inferno beside my pale wife, my children coughing in the next room. Where are they now? Maybe with Butler. He liked her, I don't know. I don't know any longer the difference between the real and the unreal. I know nothing. I waited for Macduff to behead me and I didn't care, at the head of my ruined army. And for her, her suicide was always unreal. How could she ever commit suicide even in a play?

And that night . . .

Question: 'You stab him usually in that scene, don't you?' 'Yes.'

And this time I really did. For I thought that the time had really come for us to be together. Especially as Charles was setting off for America taking her with him. He was going to do Iago and she would be Desdemona. Didn't I say that he was a genius? Perhaps he had married her so that some day she might be Desdemona and he might be Iago. He was entirely capable of it. A genius lives in a world of his own, he is already deep in the future anyway. And I was deep in the past. I looked at her. She was dressing. 'America,' I said.

'Yes,' she said. Perhaps she would be more at home there, I thought. After all she is African. I wept and I raged. 'Come with me,' I said. 'We will go anywhere you like. The country. We two alone will sing like birds in a cage.'

'I can't,' she said. 'After all, look what he has done for me. I have given so little in return.' And after she left I drank and drank and Duncan arose in front of me swaying like a snake. If only the dagger were a real dagger. If only . . . And again I saw Butler and he said, 'Of course, old boy, it was all set up.'

'Set up?' I said as he towered above me, all six feet four of him. How sure of oneself one must be when one is six feet four.

'Set up?' I said.

'Of course, old boy. Charles's interpretation of the play was that it was basically sexual. Right? Now he had to get a highly sexed performance from you two. So he let you make his wife your mistress and she played along. He knew all the time, of course. You gave the performance of your life. It almost made us uncomfortable, you know. You knew her so well, I mean in the biblical sense.'

The world opened beneath my simple Scottish mind. How could it be possible that a man could do this, a husband, with his own wife? I couldn't see beyond that border. To give his own wife for a performance, greater love hath no man than this. I think I must almost have spun on my stool.

'Are you all right, old man? No, of course an ordinary man wouldn't do it, but a genius might.'

I staggered into the lights of London. I walked through the desert for what seemed to be twenty years, that is, the period since I had met Charles first. And I knew that it was true. His head towered from posters. What would a woman, even a black beautiful woman, supply him with that could assuage that divine hunger? Night waxed and waned. I found myself, a jongleur, a jester, among dustbins on which the moon shone theatrically.

And it was then that I decided to kill him. But that morning I asked him about America and he said, 'I'm sorry, Ralph, but there's no part for you. I've got another fellow for Othello. I would say that fresh blood is needed, wouldn't you? I think your innocence would be out of place there.'

And that night, Inspector or whatever you are, I killed him. I didn't even ask how a black Desdemona would fit into his play: but that's genius for you. He didn't smile. No, that night he didn't smile. From Scotland I plunged my direct simple dagger into his heart.

Question: 'And you tried to kill her as well?'

'Yes.'

'But Butler saved her?'

'Yes.'

Of course they don't behead one now, I know that. They put you in prison.

Well, let America receive her. The sere and yellow leaf, Inspector, waves at my window.

Leaving the Cherries

All that morning she picked cherries from her cherry tree. She dropped them in a pail which she had hooked to a branch of the tree and when she had filled the pail she put the cherries in little green baskets ready to be given to her friends. She only took the really ripe cherries, leaving the unripe ones till later. She did this every year and she got plums in exchange or sometimes cakes and scones. She and her friends would phone each other quite often though they didn't visit. And she was even cutting down on the phoning since the telephone costs had gone up again recently. Quite a lot of her friends were widows like herself but some had their children living near them either in the city or on the outskirts. When she was standing on the ladder she looked over the wall of her garden at the road where the cars streamed ceaselessly past, going to America and coming from America; there seemed no end to their passionless purpose. Some had trailers behind them, some boats. They were nearly all big cars and some stopped at the garage opposite, near which men with red helmets were working on the road. She imagined Canada as a country inhabited as much by cars as by people. When her husband was alive the two of them used to go up-country quite a lot at weekends. They nearly bought a place out there on the way to the canyon but the lots were expensive and growing more so every day. She looked up into the sky and saw a red breasted and red winged plane looping the loop. It would turn over and over and just when it seemed as if it was out of control it would start climbing again. Its red was brighter than that of the cherries which were now turning a tan colour as they ripened. Below her she could see the lawn parched by the monotonous sunlight but she could not use her hose as the water was rationed. She did not like to see the ground as parched as that, it made her body ache. Below the tree where she was working there were cherries which the birds had dropped, some half eaten and some with only the kernel left.

When she had put the cherries in their small green baskets she took the car out and drove to Woodwards. She had some difficulty in parking but eventually found a place among the acres of other cars whose glass was sparkling in the sun. The roads were packed with cars, some honking at her as she drove along carefully and slowly. Once a merging truck came straight at her and she had to move quickly out of the way. She drove over the long flagged bridge from which according to the radio a man had thrown himself the previous night into the water below. They had found no identification on him. What a way to die, she thought, diving from a bridge. But people died in all sorts of ways. Think for instance of all those drug addicts who haunted the parks and gardens and sometimes came out at dusk and killed people.

When she got into Woodwards she walked around for a long time looking at hats, jewellery, dresses. She couldn't afford any of them but she liked looking. Soon she might have to sell her house and move into a flat as many of the other widows had done. She wouldn't like a flat on the ground floor; many of them were broken into. She would probably get quite a high price for her house if she sold it, for it had five rooms altogether as well as a bathroom and kitchen and she had looked after it carefully though she was on her own. Once she saw a woman in a large green hat who bought lots of hats and dresses and she wondered whether she was some sort of film star. But even film stars had their troubles, their marriages were always breaking up, and many of them became alcoholics. Thank God that had never happened to her. She never drank anything apart from Seven-up and coffee, not even if she was invited out. There was nothing really that she wanted to buy in Woodwards even if she could have afforded to. In the middle of the store she suddenly stopped, wondering when her friends would get the cherries, for they were at their very ripest. Not everybody could grow good cherries. Of course she didn't mind if they came and collected the cherries themselves. Some of them often did that. If she was away they would come with their pails and fill them and sometimes leave a note, sometimes not. And sometimes other people, who had no right to, came and collected cherries. They seemed to know when she was away from home. And recently she had an argument with the man next door about one of her trees.

For weeks now the weather had been very hot. Every morning it was misty - so that the cars had to use their headlights - and then the mist cleared away and the sun came out like a sword. Her son and daughter who had been visiting her for three weeks had gone back to Los Angeles where water was left at the doors in cartons just like milk, because it was so scarce. Her daughter had made a funny remark about the house and there was mention of a will but she had ignored that, not that it was emphasised in any way. Not at all. In fact it might have been her imagination. They seemed to plan years ahead, these young ones. The children had liked the cherry tree, sometimes it seemed to her that the tree represented the only reason for her existence, that that was all she was good at, providing cherries. If she didn't have cherries to give people in baskets, what would her life be like? People had told her that she should sell the cherries, put a sign up outside her house saying that there were cherries for sale, but she wouldn't dream of doing that though she had seen cherries being sold at the roadside and in the stores and they weren't so good as hers. No, not even if she got two dollars for them would she do that. It would be like picking money from the trees. Sometimes she would take a book out and sit in a chair in the shade of the cherry tree and read it, though not so often recently.

She looked up at the sign in the store which told her where everything was and went down to the next floor on the escalator though she didn't like escalators very much. There was that funny jump you had to take at the end after the smoothness of the descent. She thought of the other Woodwards the gunmen had robbed recently, stripping the cash from all eight tills and disappearing. Strange how they could get away with that. She wondered if she had left the money for the milk on the mantelpiece as usual but she definitely remembered locking all the doors including the door of the basement where she had left the cherries in their little green baskets. But she had left the ladder still standing against the tree. She went over to the counter and bought her purchase, then made her way to the rest-room. She felt sweaty. She wished she had taken a bath. Driving through the intense hot traffic took a lot out of her but then on the other hand if she didn't have a car what would happen to her? And she wasn't getting any younger.

When she got into the wash-room she was relieved there was no one else there. She felt quite cool. She went to the mirror and tidied her hair and washed her face. Then she opened the parcel, took out the shotgun, put it to her mouth and shot herself.

from
MURDO
and other stories

In the Castle

The road seemed to last for miles as it headed towards the castle with the green sweeping lawns around it on which there strutted peacocks with blazing colours and small crowned heads.

Trevor thought that Mary looked a bit better and calmer. He drew the car to a halt and they got out, she as usual clinging to her handbag in which as he knew there was a mess of disordered stuff. She looked pale and hunted, almost haunted, in her yellow dress which he noticed was creased at the back. In the old days she wouldn't have been so untidy.

'Tickets first,' he said in his artificially cheerful voice, and they queued in a room whose walls were covered with lances, swords and guns, arranged in orderly array.

Having got the tickets he led her into the first room, passing Americans in their white suits carrying cameras slung over their shoulders. He heard the continuous murmur of mixed languages, French, German, and, he thought, Swedish. A little Jap with a creased face stood by himself. Nowadays Mary didn't speak much: their frightening screaming quarrels had passed. She seemed to have retreated into a world of her own and this worried him just as much as the quarrels.

'Well then,' he said cheerfully, 'this is the first room.' She gazed up at the deers' skulls and antlers on the wall. They looked so frail that they might at any moment break into powder and fall on the floor.

He looked at the deers' skulls and then at Mary. When had the irretrievable damage happened? Was it some time in her lonely childhood – when she had been the old child of an ageing doctor and his younger wife? Or was it after she had married him? Certainly her childish rages were a continual accompaniment to their marriage. That he himself was severe and unforgiving and humourless he knew. That perhaps she thought she had come down in the world in marrying him he also thought he knew: after all, lecturers were not as rich as doctors. And then there had been the tradition of alcoholism in her family: her mother had been in hospital for it once or twice. The doctor, her father, sat in his chair and smiled constantly as if he accepted the incurable world as it was. And Mary had grown up in her secret world. He himself had three brothers and a sister, and so he considered that normality had been rubbed into him, as a pebble takes its shape from the onslaughts of the waves.

They were now standing in a room in which there were a lot of eighteenth-century paintings. At what seemed to be open-air picnics women sat in long green or red dresses, with a cloth spread before them on the ground. The trees around them had inherited the calm of that passionless age. The firescreens too showed eighteenth-century paintings in which similar women sat easily in their composed worlds. On the mantelpiece was a clock of black marble which to his amazement told the right time as if the servants in the castle wound it up every day.

'Isn't that beautiful?' he said, but she turned away. If only she would speak, make even the slightest comment. Her large famished eyes took everything in but at the same time put it into secret drawers of her own with special locks. He almost felt like hitting her. And yet he had loved her and he still loved her. It was true she came from a different world, not a world as palatial as this, but at least one higher than his own. But that was no excuse for her deep griefs. The historian in him was ticking off, date by date, the articles he saw, though not evaluating them. He had never been interested in money and neither had she. How appalling her silences were, her frowning wrinkled brow. He had a wild vision that she would burst into a rage where they were and shout and scream at the tourists who were so grave and correct and earnest, speaking their foreign languages.

My love, my love what has happened to you? Was it my fault? Have I left you too much alone?

Through a window he saw the proud peacocks staring, it

seemed, towards him with their fathomless stupid eyes. Just like the dull aristocrats who had run this castle.

They stood in a room full of snuffboxes and packs of eighteenth-century cards larger than those he was familiar with. She stared down at one of them as if it were infinitely precious. On the walls were portraits of young aristocratic girls, smiling arrogantly from within their gilt borders. What had they ever done but sew and play the harpsichord, rather badly. How wasted their lives had been. And then he noticed that she was staring with particular interest at one painting. It showed a typically red-faced aristocrat in a kilt handing a pheasant he had just killed to his little daughter, who was stretching her chubby hands towards it as if it were a new toy. Her mother smiled complacently from the far edge of the picture. At the other edge there was a stiff slightly bowing servant, perhaps a gillie. Stupid buggers, he thought, what vulgarity, what stony-headed power.

And he hated these aristocrats and their families. It might have been better if he and Mary had had children but they hadn't and that was it. He supposed that in a way it wasn't a bad thing, for it allowed him to concentrate on his researches. But imagine having a child like that with such greed on its face as it stretched its tiny hands towards the pheasant whose colours seemed to be fading in the duke's hand. Long thin laths of people, wooden-headed possessors of empire, with their horses and their dogs and their servants who ticked away like black clocks till the time came to strike.

As he looked at Mary he thought that her face glowed, as if the picture belonged to a world she loved, a world of the masculine and the cruel and the fixed. He drew in his breath sharply and apologised to an American who was trying to get past him.

He felt in need of a pee. He should have gone to the toilet (loo, as his wife said) before he started on the tour.

'Come on,' he said gently, and then as she made no move he repeated the words. It was only then that she stirred out of her dream, still staring at the picture as she left the room, to enter another one in which there was a bed with matching chairs covered by a wine-red material. At the head of the bed and also on the chairs there was stitched or carved a yellow coronet. It was as if for a moment he expected that someone would be lying on the bed, as if he had burst suddenly into a private room, and there, perfectly still, her golden hair strewn on the pillows, would be a duchess fast asleep. Who had lain on that bed before, he wondered. It represented the sweat of history though now it looked so calm and familiar. The bed of sweaty bodies, of irrational sex, the stews of the past. And that bitch Elizabeth flaunting her smallpoxed body to the ambassadors of so many nations. Sex used as politics and economy, in the service of diplomacy. He was shaken by rage and rancour. His sister stood mockingly in front of a mirror in their crowded house.

Doctors, doctors, he thought, why didn't you cure that too when you cured the plague?

The next room was full of books. He bent down and looked at them, as they lay against each other untouchably on their shelves. He studied the frail copy of the Solemn League and Covenant, trapped in its case, trying to distinguish the familiar words in the ancient fading script. A letter from Charles I to his friend Lord George Murray wished him to supply him with men for the defence of the kingdom. And there was a letter from Mary, Queen of Scots just before she had put her fair hair on the block with such unflinching nerve. She talked, of all things, about sewing. And the letter was in French. His wife was looking at it now, with her frowning wrinkled brow. Of course she knew French just as he did himself, but the writing was so crabbed, so small . . . How could one ever distinguish it? The headman stood behind her for a moment there with his axe and his black mask, and the black clock of history ticked on . . .

His wife's fair hair streamed over the ancient page, her pale narrow neck exposed, showing the blonde hairs at the back. We are perpetual students, he thought, listening to a Frenchman talking volubly to his son, explaining something to him. A costumed American woman leaned down with a pince-nez . . .

My love, my love, this is history and it has all to do with us. From this we have come, we were servants – or rather I was a servant – of these impermeably stupid people, dying and fighting in their mess of blood. I don't want that to happen to you. But secretively and profoundly we waited, we the servants, till the time came, and then we shoved them off their seats and thrones with one big heave. Even your class, he thought, even yours.

He heard her voice from the past screaming at him. What is this business of class that you're always on about. Can we not just be human beings?

And himself. It's easy to say but we served them for centuries and what did we get? Their absent stupid stares like those of peacocks or pheasants.

Now they were standing in front of a portrait of Lord George Murray, dead at Loos, having fought bravely to the end at the head of his small company, with his chestful of medals dangling. There he stood with his big moustache, his sword stiff at his side, while the new machine guns were ready to mow him down. But he had his horse, hadn't he? And he had his sword and his invincible belief in himself and in the lady who waited at home, sewing, sleeping beside her dressing table with the coroneted brushes. How the stupid unwinking eye of the moon stared down at her.

Oh they had courage, right enough. Certainly they had courage, the courage of the dinosaur. He glanced at the scorched bullet mark in a red uniform and admitted that at least about them. They had taken the salmon and the deer, they had stared through their servants as if they were panes of glass, but they had certainly fought. One must give them that. They had been stupid and fearless and masculine. They were big stones in the torrent of history. Even Claverhouse whose pitifully thin armour was on show had been that, daring, romantic, idiotic, irrational. Those petty quarrels, those shrieks and screams, those terrible bleedings, how they had faded into the past. They were in the end trivial.

'Mary,' he said, 'I have to go to the toilet. I'm bursting.' She looked at him with her swimming blue eyes, saying nothing. 'I won't be long,' he said. 'You'll be all right.' But on his way to the toilet he couldn't resist going into one or two other rooms, feeling free now that he wasn't with her. In one of the rooms he examined a beautiful self-sufficient pistol of an earlier age, its perfect lines exciting him, well-preserved and oiled as most of the things in the castle were. Why, they must still have an army of servants. He rushed into the next room and had a quick look round. Here there were fans with Chinese women bending towards each other in a sky of deep black, wide sleeves on their arms, their hair black, their necks willowy and white.

He ran to the toilet pushing his way past the tourists. And there he was standing in front of the mirror, his face gaunt and haunted. Beside him standing above the white tile was a large American whose camera banged against his side. They glanced at each other and then looked away. Trevor washed his hands carefully over and over and then dried them in the draught of warm air, waiting till all the drops had faded and his hands were clean and fresh. Then he walked back the way he had come. He found the room with the documents in the glass cases but she wasn't there, though there were many foreigners – descendants of the duke's enemies – leaning down to read the indecipherable script.

He turned back and went into all the other rooms between the one with the documents and the toilet, but she wasn't in any of them either. She must have gone back then to see something she hadn't had time to study properly. What could it be? Her image became confused in his mind with that of Mary, Queen of Scots, that of the strutting peacocks on the lawn. O my God he thought something must have happened to her. She may have fainted. Her voice echoed in his head, 'You're always going on about class. Nothing but class all the time. Can't we live in peace?' In peace, in peace. Images of royalty, of aristocracy were all about him. The stupid heads gazed from their frames. The willowy necks bent over streams. The salmon bodies wriggled in nets. Coronets everywhere, everywhere lances and swords and guns, evidence of death, of violence. If only she is safe, he thought, if only . . . Because I love her with my gaunt unforgiving face, and my sharp weasel mind. The scorched bullet hole leaped in front of his eyes. So the thin armour had not been enough to keep the enemy out. It had worked its way through the aristocratic trappings.

And then he entered the room where the bed and chairs were. He had to fight his way through a crowd of tourists, shouting and screaming inside his head, Get away, you bloody American, what are you doing here anyway? Get back to your own country, to your pseudo-democracy and take your filthy pictures with you or take the castle with you stone by stone in your temporary luggage which has crossed a million frontiers.

There seemed to be hundreds of people and they were all quiet. When he got to the front he saw her. She had crossed the rope and was lying on the bed, her head on the pillow, the coroneted headboard above her, and she was clutching in her hand – what? A letter. Had she broken the glass cases as well? But when he looked he thought he recognised his own handwriting. Probably one of his love letters to her from their courting days when each had written to the other, 'I'll never leave you,' a sort of promise. There she was lying staring up at the ceiling, perfectly at peace, the letter in her hand, as if she were an effigy in an untouchable armour, and the tourists stared at her in perfect silence as if she belonged to the bed, in her wrinkled stockings (for she had thrown her shoes off) an image almost of the Sleeping Beauty. My God, he thought. My God what shall I do now? And he stared helplessly with the others at her who was so beautiful and distant, almost as if she were a perfect stranger, a frozen historical woman. Only a pulse in her throat beat and her breast rose and fell quietly. That was all that told him she was alive and that she was his wife.

The Missionary

The missionary walks through Africa
  thinking of God above.
Everything here is black but God is white
The waterfalls have distant leonine faces
  but God is near and warm.
Sometimes he doesn't know why he is there –
  in Africa in Africa
  with every particular star
  shining on his head
But he has faith O he has faith enough
  that in that bush in that resplendent bush
  there is no snake with diamond head
  and quick unchristian fangs
And so the missionary walks through Africa
  and all around him grow the hectic leaves
  pulpits of violent green.
And all around him he is watched by eyes
  that never heard of Paradise
How cool and white his collar is
  that circle of white bone.
For the missionary lies at last
  in that huge untitled waste
As if he wasn't there
  the trees that haven't heard of God
  grow about his bony head
  and all his pale ideas die
    in Africa in Africa
  where every thought is green.

One day the Reverend Donald Black decided to leave the ministry and go as a missionary to Africa. When he was living in Scotland he was always writing letters to the newspapers asking why the Sabbath was not being kept, why planes flew about the sky on Sunday, and why the ferries were operating. He believed that Sunday was truly God's day, the day on which the Lord had rested, as if in a manse contemplating the elegance and beauty of His creation. As a matter of fact the manse he lived in was old and damp, and the ground around it, which could hardly be dignified with the name of garden, was choked with wildflowers. Here the unmarried minister would write his sermons, which usually dealt with obscure points of doctrine that his parishioners found great difficulty in following. In spite of that the minister read diligently in thick books, many of them ancient and discoloured, and written in double columns.

He was a small sturdy man with quick alert eyes. When he visited his parishioners in his old car he liked to argue with them, and then after he was finished put up a prayer for all the inhabitants of the house. His prayers were usually long and difficult to listen to, for he had the unfortunate habit of stopping in the middle of sentences, unable to think what the next words should be. In fact he had no eloquence at all, and sometimes felt that God was unfair to him, since after all he believed firmly in the Bible and contended that every word in it was true. Why then had God not endowed him with flowing speech? Even when he was preaching from the pulpit, tall and bare below the long transparent windows through which in summer a greenish light penetrated from the leaves outside, these halts and stoppings would embarrass him. It was probably because of his lack of eloquence that he decided to become a missionary. In moments of despair he would remember Moses who according to the Bible had been something of a stutterer, but who nevertheless had led his people out of the corrupt lands of Egypt.

In fact he thought of Britain and Scotland as corrupt. The pure milk of the Gospel had gone sour, the houses were dens of iniquity, the streets dark with sin and blood. He dreamed of a place where the children would be well-behaved, the people upright and innocent, the blandishments of civilisation absent, the soul without taint. He thought that God had abandoned his country, that there was disorder everywhere, and the law itself cracking under the strain.

Since he was unmarried, he would sacrifice himself to the uncorrupted natives of Africa who had been saved by distance from the Sodom and Gomorrah of the west. One dark dismal day he left Scotland behind him and on a fine hot day arrived at the village where he was to be a missionary. There he found waiting for him a small church and a small congregation. Noticing that the church was surrounded by foliage and vegetation, the first thing he did was to cut down as much of it as possible so that the church could be seen, white and bare, in its fated place.

He had learned the language of the tribe before he had left Scotland, for he considered that such knowledge was of the greatest importance. Hadn't Luther translated the Bible into German? Perhaps, he thought to himself, I shall learn eloquence in another simpler language which has the freshness of novelty and not the staleness of advertising.

The first night he slept in the church he felt a little home-sickness but this did not last long and after a few days Scotland was to him as distant and hazy as its bluish mountains seem on a misty day, insubstantial, vague, almost incoherent. But the heat of Africa beat on him like a hammer.

When he rose from his bed on the first day he went off to see the chief of the tribe, who was sitting outside his hut on a chair which had once been European. He wore on his head a sort of leafy crown, and carried in his hand a stick which the missionary assumed was meant to be a sceptre. He had calm, merry eyes which regarded the missionary as only one of many who had come to his tribe. If he thought Donald rather small in stature he didn't say so but was courteous and benign.

Toko – for that was the chief's name – greeted him in his own African dialect and Donald replied in the same language.

'How many Christians have we here,' he asked him.

Toko began to count serenely on the fingers of his hands and after a while said,

'Twenty.'

Donald was surprised at this small number for he thought that there would have been more.

'That is so,' said the chief gravely, 'and I myself am one of them. I know about Adam and Eve and about the snake and

also about John the Baptist whose head was cut off at a dance.'
He flashed his teeth in a wide white smile and laughed. 'I also
know about heaven and hell,' he added.

This won't do, thought Donald. They know all about the
violent parts of the Bible but they do not know the pure milk of
it. He looked inside the large hut and saw a number of women
sitting cross-legged there in an attitude of eternal patience.
They were naked to the waist and in the half-darkness he could
see their drooping breasts like pale fruits. They were however
wearing grass skirts.

How shameful, he thought. But though the heat was almost
unbearable he himself didn't remove his collar which he considered to be a symbol, and a defence against the laxity of the
people and the vegetation.

A few children were playing on the road but they unlike the
women were totally naked and completely brown.

'Isn't it time that these women wore clothes,' he asked the
chief. 'Especially as you yourself are a Christian.'

'That would be impossible,' said the chief serenely, 'because
it is very hot and also they have no clothes to wear.'

Donald didn't say any more about this, and left the topic
lying there ticking away like a watch that he must later adjust.

All around him there were other huts and sitting in front of
them men and women who regarded him with the same
profound eternal look, as if they had been there forever and
would be there after he had gone.

'I shall expect the Christians tomorrow in church,' he said
and turned away.

What am I going to do here, he asked himself, and he looked
at the trees which were heavy with their fruit. His collar was
biting into his neck which was wet with sweat as was his whole
body encased in its black clothes. Thinking that he was the only
person there who was really black, he walked among the
sheaves of shadows till he arrived at his church. Once he looked
back, only to see that Toko was still sitting in his European
chair clutching his sceptre which was only a curved stick. The
shepherd of his flock, thought Donald. But he could have
sworn that the chief was secretly laughing at him.

The following day, arrayed in his robes, Donald climbed into the pulpit and stood looking down at his black congregation, their faces calm and shining and impenetrable, their breasts naked.

'There are two things we must remember,' he said. 'One is the Law and the other is the Grace. Christ said that he came to fulfil the law which the Pharisees had made intolerable.' He stopped, for it occurred to him that they might not have heard of the Pharisees, and in the blatant unhypocritical light of this country they seemed very far away.

'At any rate,' he continued, 'there is only the one God. He exists in the heavens and also in our own souls.' They regarded him with kind uncomprehending eyes.

'God is like a judge. He commands us not to make graven images, not to steal and not to commit adultery. You know all these things already for my predecessor must have told you.'

Hearing shouting outside the church he asked them what it meant. A small sturdy man with sad eyes told him that some of the youth of the village came to the church regularly to mock the Christians and call them 'the white ones'. The missionary left the pulpit and strode out of the door into the unabated sunlight. He saw in front of him a group of tall gangling boys who had been throwing stones and pebbles at the door. 'Get out of here,' he shouted. 'Get out of here at once,' and his face was so red and his whole body so bristling and hostile – as if he were swelling like a cockerel that crows with inflated breast at dawn – that they ran away at great speed, not once looking back. Then he returned to the church.

When the service was over the small man who had told him about the boys stood up and said that the previous missionary had allowed them to ask questions after the sermon.

'Do you have any questions then,' asked Donald who loved argument of any kind.

'I have a question,' said the small man. 'My name is Banga. A man belonging to the tribe has taken my wife away from me. I would like to cut his throat but I wanted to ask you first since you are a Christian.'

'The Bible tells us that killing is forbidden,' said Donald, 'and that what we must do is turn the other cheek. Christ did not struggle when he was crucified, even though he wept a little in the Garden of Gethsemane. I am sure that God will punish that man in his own good time. Where is your wife now?'

'She is with him in his hut and she has put me to shame.'

'Well,' said Donald, 'I will speak to that man. What is his name?'

'Tobbuta.'

'She will return to your house, never fear,' Donald said with great resonance and conviction. 'For it is the law that whom God has joined together no man dare put asunder. It tells us that in the Bible, and it is the teachings of the Bible that I have come to instruct you in. If necessary I shall myself drag her home to you.'

'But,' said Banga in the same even sad voice as before, 'I should cut his throat anyway.'

'I will put the matter right,' said Donald firmly. 'You leave it with me. There will be no killing. Everything will be settled according to the law.'

When he had finished a girl with large eyes and shining youthful breasts, who was sitting in front of him, said:

'My father is very old. He is ninety-four years of age and he is blind, deaf and bad-tempered and he spends most of his time in bed. We don't have enough food for him and when we do give him food he complains and says that we are trying to poison him. We are very poor and don't have much food for ourselves and what he eats is taking away from the younger ones. What does your mastership say?'

'What is your name?' Donald asked, as he watched the sunlight throb in her black hair.

'Miraga.'

'Well, Miraga,' said the missionary turning his eyes away from her firm breasts, 'God, as I said, does not want us to kill anyone, least of all our father whom we are told to respect. Respect thy father and thy mother that thy days may be long on the earth, that is what God says. I hope I will never hear you saying anything like that again. Are you listening to me?'

'Yes,' said Miraga, 'but he is old and we have no food in the house. The children are hungry. I myself am hungry.'

'There are things in the world more important than the body,' said Donald. 'The body passes but the soul remains.' But when he looked around him he saw no white and fluttering soul, benign though faint, but only the shining black bodies and the green light on the windows. I am a bachelor, thought Donald despairingly, how much do I know about the world? Especially how much do I know about women? But then the thought, which did not seem blasphemous, occurred to him, that Christ was a bachelor also, though his father was a carpenter and not, like his own, a minister.

His father's ferocious beard seemed to glare down at the girl's naked breasts which seemed to tremble in front of his eyes. Miraga Miraga Miraga. The name brought to his mind water and daybreak and sun on tranquil rivers.

'Does anyone else have a question?' he asked.

'Yes,' said a big slow man who clutched the seat in front of him as he stood up. 'My name is Horruga. We hear in the Bible the story of how Peter cut off the ear of a soldier. What was the reason for that?'

'He had no right to do that,' said Donald briskly. 'Christ himself reminded him that he had sinned. Surely my predecessor told you that.' When he mentioned his predecessor they began to look at each other slyly as if they had an unfathomable secret which like children they were unwilling to divulge.

'You did listen to him, didn't you?' he asked.

'Oh yes oh yes,' they all replied like children chanting in a primary class. 'Oh yes.'

'Well then,' said Donald, 'I hope you learned from him.'

When he was about to leave the church at the end of the sermon he saw that left on top of one of the seats there was an image of Christ carved from wood and that the image represented a plump smiling man with a crown on his head and what appeared to be an animal like a deer in front of him. It looked suspiciously like the chief but he knew that it was meant to be Christ because of the yellow rays that shone from the crown. He threw it out into the strong barbarous sunlight which beat on the street with an even eternal heat.

Can I bear this heat? he asked himself. It is like hell itself. He

looked down at his hands which were already turning brown.
The collar was chafing his neck as usual.

He was about to eat one of the fruits from a neighbouring
tree when he heard someone shouting, 'They are poisonous.'
When he lowered his eyes from the tree and looked into the
darkness of the sun he saw after a while that it was the witch
doctor who had spoken and that down his face red and black
stripes poured. His face like that of the chief was laughing.

That night he found by chance a diary that his predecessor had
been keeping and after a short struggle with his conscience he
began to read it, justifying his action on the grounds that he
might find out more about the work ahead of him. He read by
the light of the lamp, lying in the bed which was in the church
itself. While he was doing so it occurred to him that he did not
know anything at all about his predecessor, his appearance, his
beliefs, his thoughts, and this troubled him a little, but he soon
forgot about it as the contents of the diary occupied his mind
more and more.

This is what he read:

17 March.   I have arrived at this place at long last. Though
Britain was dark and melancholy, this country is hot and
bright. I think I will like it.

18 March.   Today I spoke to the chief. He tells me that there
are only ten in the congregation. When I preached to them I
felt faint and helpless in this land where the sun is so torrid
and where there are few shadows.

20 March.   What can I do to help them? I am not a doctor, I
am not a builder, I am not even a cultivator of the land. Is
the gospel alone enough for them? These thoughts never
occurred to me when I was in Britain but I can see that this
tribe is poor and hungry and that I myself lack the skill to help
them in their daily routine. I feel lonely, wretched and
helpless. Who can feed the hungry on the gospel alone?

22 March.   I told them about Abraham and Isaac and they
understood the story perfectly. I feel there is no point in

teaching them divinity or theology. They need flesh on the bones of the Word and the soul here is ghostly and white as if it did not belong. Yesterday I saw the witch doctor in his array and I thought he was laughing at me. Nevertheless all the people I meet are kind, but it seems to me that they think of me as a child whose actions have no real relevance to their lives. They humour me. My books have lost their meaning as if the sun were too strong for them and yet that should not be since the Gospel originally came from the hot lands of the East. The fact is that I feel superfluous here.

23 *March.*   The chief and the doctor prayed for rain today. I reminded the chief that he was a Christian and he admitted that he was, but at the same time pointed out that the tribe could not exist without water. I myself in the secrecy of my heart put up a prayer for rain but no drop fell and the sky remained as blue and expressionless as ever. The loneliness grows worse. I am like a ghost moving about in the dark. This place frightens me though the people remain kind and thoughtful.

2 *April.*   There was a fight between two men here yesterday and I stopped it. When I woke up this morning I heard that one of the men had been found stabbed during the night. If I had not stopped the fight would this have happened? Would the man be still alive? My principles are unsuited to this country. And yet if I lose them what remains to me?

3 *April.*   I cannot conceal it any longer. The intense heat is arousing sinful passions in my heart and body and every day I see the women half naked and desirable. Would I be a better missionary if I succumbed to these lustful thoughts? If like a king from the Old Testament I got me a wife from among them? At night I lie awake listening to the cries of the beasts in the distance. They seem so natural to this land which is barbarous and wild. I feel that I am being burned by a fire that will eventually devour me. I read St Paul constantly.

22 *April.*   When Regina walks about the village she is shown a certain respect as well as causing secret tittering laughter. She herself makes demands on me. She wants jewellery,

bright ornaments and ribbons, the miscellaneous contents of our ruined western civilisation, in order to differentiate herself from the rest of the tribe. She cannot understand why I am so poor. Therefore I am placed in a dilemma. If I were to give her these things – which of course I don't have – I would be surrendering to the world, and yet if I don't she will leave me. Now she wants my collar because she finds its whiteness attractive. She exists in pride and desires riches: she is like a child lusting for toys. At the same time she is natural as water, the water that I used to see when I was in Britain, but of which there is a great scarcity here. Where has my soul gone? It seems to me that it is moving faintly among the green vegetation which repeats itself forever. Or it is like an eel shining in the drained river beds with a dead gleam. Her black face on the pillow beside me shows no shadow of thought, no cloud heavy with rain. I am like a shell empty and without the noise of the sea. What am I doing here? Why did I come in the first place? Was it to escape from Europe as if I were fleeing from Sodom and Gomorrah? And look what has happened to me now. They demand nothing of me – they are like children – but more and more I feel myself existing on their charity. Is there no precious gift that I can give them? My Bible perhaps. But what should they do with these white pages? Is God Himself black in this country?

13 April.   I know now what I am going to do. I am sure of it. It is not, I hope, blasphemous, though it might be construed as such. It came to me in a dream troubled by writhing limbs, clouds, lions and rocks. I think that the witch doctor knows of my purpose, the stripes on his face are glowing with pride and victory. There is no point in writing any more.

And the diary ended there.

Lying on his bed Donald wondered what the missionary's confident purpose had been. He felt the church as a shell floating on the darkness, thin and powerless. And about him he heard the howlings of animals. His body was pouring with sweat and he would have liked at that moment to be back in Europe, in that corrupt continent of ancient crowded streets, of ingenious crooked paths. How am I going to pass the time here, he wondered. I am like a superfluous lily growing in the darkness that I do not understand and that frightens me. He put the diary under his pillow and composed himself for sleep. It seemed as if there was a tall white waterfall humming in his mind and that when he looked into it he saw cunning kind faces coiled as if in a secret conspiracy.

The following morning he went in search of Banga's wife in order to bring her back to her husband. Tobbuta's hut was deep in the forest whose leaves cast a deep green shade, though now and again the sunlight made a wavering glimmer between the trees. Donald followed the faint continually renewed path which human feet had made among the vegetation, hearing now and again the whistling of unseen birds. O world which God has made, he said, how beautiful you are, how abundant with blessings. After a while he saw two or three huts in a glade in front of him and asked a small naked boy which one was Tobbuta's. The boy pointed and he walked towards it, sensing all the while that he was being watched by curious vague eyes.

Tobbuta was sitting in front of his hut carving a piece of wood with a knife.

'I have come to take Banga's wife back to him,' said Donald.

Tobbuta raised his head and looked at him. Then without speaking he indicated to him the inside of the hut where in half-darkness Donald could see a woman sitting with two little girls beside her.

'You will have to come back to your husband,' he told her. 'I have an order from the chief. I have come to fetch you.'

The woman screamed as if he had pierced her with a knife or as if she were a wild animal in the forest transfixed by a suddenly thrown spear. The two girls grasped her hands with a fierce frightened grip, staring at Donald as if he were an enemy who had come white and blatant out of the safe darkness and greenery outside.

'Come,' he said. 'Your husband is waiting for you.'

She rose slowly to her feet and went out and he could hear her talking to Tobbuta in a low dead voice. Tobbuta was still sharpening his piece of wood and the woman stood beside him, obedient and slightly bowed, like a cow that waits for the axe to fall. The two girls stood beside her, gazing up at her with an intent gaze.

The missionary thought that what was happening had happened before, that he was standing in the middle of eternity where events are motionless and without meaning, that Tobbuta had been carving his wood forever, and that the world was heavy and fixed without profundity or purpose. The bodies of Tobbuta and his wife were solid in the sunlight, time had ceased to flow, they were images present to him and yet distant at the same time.

When he left, the woman and her two children walked in front of him. Tobbuta raised his head momentarily and looked at him, the knife glittering in his hand. The woman took nothing with her, she walked into the forest bare and without possessions. In the heavy silence they walked through the trees, she ahead of him with her children, he behind. It was as if he was bringing some quarry home from hunting, a wounded deer for instance that had not yet died.

He saw her black legs, her black thighs, ahead of him and he thought, I do not know anything about her, her existence is dark to me, she is anonymous and black. But the Bible supports me with its white pages, it shines among the rank green secretive foliage. Her body was stately and proud, inviolate and self-contained. Is it love that I am destroying, he wondered, but no voice answered him and now and again the girls would look at him with frightened yet obedient eyes.

He made them stop in the middle of the forest and knelt and prayed among a tangle of dried roots, feeling a weight on his spirit as if a terrible catastrophe were preparing itself in the silent forest. He prayed for a long time, the other three waiting patiently, as if wondering what he was about, but the forest was impervious to his prayer and his eyes were continually drawn to a group of ants carrying huge burdens across the dry roots.

When he rose to his feet at last he offered the woman some water but she refused to take it, looking at him with an indifferent gaze. It occurred to him that the forest itself was like a church with its tall green columns, its damp aisles. He tried to talk to her as if he were trying to rid himself of an unintelligible guilt. 'I'm sorry,' he repeated over and over, 'but you have sinned. God has seen your sin and he has sent me, his servant, on this errand to you.' But her eyes were still indifferent and dead, as if she did not understand what he was talking about, as if his words were as random as the patches of light that the sun sometimes cast on the foliage around him. She accepted him as she would have accepted a thunderstorm or lightning from the sky or a flood from a river. He was like a natural hazard that she did not even try to fathom. He noticed that there were stripes on her back as if someone had at one time beaten her fiercely and he felt the whip so tightly in his hand that he clenched his teeth.

God help me, he prayed, but there was only the greenness around him and in places the blue of the sky above him.

Sometimes he thought that some terrible event was about to happen, he had a deep premonition in his bones. And now and again he would glance behind him as if he were expecting Tobbuta with raised knife to appear out of the forest. But he saw no movement at all among the becalmed leaves. Why then do I feel this ominous trembling in my stomach, he asked himself, unfastening his collar because of the windless heat.

At last they reached the hut where Banga was waiting. I have finished my work now, he thought. I have delivered my message. He left the woman, her head bent and obedient in front of Banga, and when he looked back once he thought that the four united people were like black images sunk in eternity and that he himself was a ghost wandering with messages about a world that he did not understand. When he reached the church he prayed again: O God I do not feel at ease in this land, I do not understand what is happening around me. I am feeling the pangs of the flesh. Even today when I was walking through Your forest I trembled when I saw her black thighs and her breasts. It is You who must help me in this mysterious country, in this darkness that continually enfolds me, though the sun is so strong.

When he had ended his prayer he began to wash his hands

over and over and then his face. He removed his collar which was chafing his neck. When he looked in the mirror he saw the mark that the collar had left and it reminded him of the scars on the woman's back where a whip had lashed her. Love, what is love? Tobbuta had not tried to keep her after all and it was probably he who had beaten her. The chief's order had frightened Tobbuta and that was why he had surrendered Banga's wife to him.

He began to read the Bible as if searching for a story that would duplicate the one in which he had just been involved, and was so immersed in it that he hardly noticed the descending darkness and it was only when he heard the distant melancholy roaring of the beasts that he put the book down. He had found no tale that spoke to him of similar circumstances: the Bible was like an inscrutable stone darkening in front of him.

On the following day the weather was as hot and calm as it had always been and when the missionary stood outside the church in the morning he felt like a chief surveying his own territory. But at that very moment of tranquillity and poise when at last he felt at home in the freshness and the growing light of the country to which he had come, he saw Banga coming towards him at a stumbling run, and suddenly the street was full of watching people. Banga was holding a knife in his hand and Donald saw with fear and horror and at the same time an inevitable knowledge that there was blood on it. This is a drama, he thought, as he saw the silent people, this isn't really happening, this has been staged for my benefit, and Banga is the chief actor. But the latter sank down on his knees in front of him, the knife still in his hand, and lifted a face which streamed with tears.

'I killed them,' he screamed, while his body shook as if with fever. 'I killed them all.' He offered the missionary the knife as if suggesting that he should kill him, but Donald backed away. What is this drama, he was thinking. Is he doing this because he feels he has betrayed Christianity or our teachings.

'She cried all the time,' Banga was saying, 'and the children cried as well. She wanted back to Tobbuta. And I raised the knife and killed her, and after that I killed the children because they wouldn't stop crying. The shame was choking me. The shame was in my throat.'

He bent his head and shook with sobs. The missionary backed further away and then slowly and heavily as if he were trudging through water or a dream made his way towards Banga's hut following the drops of blood. He stopped for a moment at the door in a dazzle of sunlight and after a while went in. He saw them all lying on the floor: their throats had been cut and their faces looked grey from the leakage of blood.

He began to tremble violently and then knelt as if to pray, but when he was trying to put words together his teeth chattered so much that he couldn't make a sound. The words as before were breaking apart and he could not put them together.

He rose and returned to where Banga was still on his knees in the dust of the road. He saw the chief coming towards him and with the coldness still in his body was able to ask him, 'What are you going to do?'

'He must be put to death,' said the chief calmly. 'Isn't that what Christianity teaches us?' The missionary looked at him with horror as if he thought that the chief was mocking him but the latter's expression was as tranquil and settled as the morning itself.

Donald began to pull his collar off with frantic hands and finally threw it on the road where it lay round and white like a ring that has been cast aside or lost. He didn't know what to do or where to go.

All the time he was staring at the chief with a wild mad gaze and trying to speak but not succeeding.

'My fault, my fault,' he shouted at last and at that very moment he saw Banga, who was still kneeling on the road, thrusting the knife deep into his chest and falling on the ground.

He began to scream, 'I should never have come here. Never. Never.' He ran away from the dying Banga and from the chief with no destination in mind, and at last found himself in the middle of the damp green forest where there was a deep silence .

and he could hear no bird singing. His body was shaking and he had no control over it. He looked dully at the uniform green around him and no thought dawned in his mind, which was as empty as the blue cloudless sky that he had left. He thought of the prayer that he had put up in that very forest when he was returning with Banga's wife and children and began to cry with sorrow and rage.

After a while he saw the chief coming towards him and stopping beside him and looking down at him where he was lying on the ground. He raised his head to him as Banga had raised his to him.

'What are you going to do?' said the chief. 'You can't stay here.'

Fat man with your throne and sceptre, the missionary thought, are you going to tell me what my destination and purpose should be now? The chief's question rose in front of him like that phantom waterfall of which he had dreamed, that had poured endlessly among the heat.

'You can come back with me,' said the chief quietly. 'If that is what you want. Banga's hut is now empty and you can stay there if you wish.'

How wise you are, how subtle, the missionary thought. Who else would have thought of that? You are more than the owner of a ruined European chair and a stick. Was that what he wanted, to stay in Banga's house. There was a sort of fatal appropriateness in what the chief had just said, that he should go and live among the blood and sin and guilt that he himself had created and which would never wash away.

He rose and stood upright in the middle of the forest.

'That is what I shall do,' he said firmly.

The two of them returned to the hut through the forest. While they were walking the missionary threw off his shoes, leaving them behind him on the path which had been worn by so many feet. He felt the soles of his feet warm on the clay and he was like a child again barefoot in a Scottish summer.

They stopped outside the hut. 'The bodies are no longer there,' said the chief. 'You can stay in it. The floor has been cleaned.'

He turned away and the missionary entered the hut. There were a few clay plates, and a bundle of twigs and branches for a bed. The bareness appealed to him, in a strange way healed his spirit. This is my study, my dining-room, my bedroom, he thought, as if he were repeating a litany. He lay down on the bed like a prisoner in a cell, ready to pay for his crimes. He lay down on what had once been a marriage bed. He fell asleep almost immediately and did not waken till the darkness had fallen. He could not see his watch, and feeling for it, loosed the strap and smashed the dial again and again against the clay floor of the hut. Then he fell asleep for the second time.

When he woke in the morning he didn't at first know where he was. The sun was shining beyond the open door but inside the hut it was dark. He rose from his bed and saw that beside it there was a pot full of water and a bunch of yellow fruits that weren't at all like the ones he had seen on the trees. He washed himself and ate one of the fruits that tasted like a coconut and had some substance like milk inside it. He did not wish to do anything and sat in front of the hut as he had seen the natives do, now and again looking at the church which appeared remote and superfluous, its bells dumb. He told himself that he might as well let his beard grow and he considered this an important decision.

He felt time lying on him like a cloak that rests heavily on the shoulders. He had no desire for anything, the future did not trouble him in any way. As he watched the street which was at first still and bare, he heard the sound of instruments being played, and then he saw people coming towards him dancing, dressed in colourful clothes and feathers. They were carrying something, and it took him some time to realise that it was the bodies of the dead, wherever they had lain during the night. The bodies were covered with flowers, and lying on trestles. The dancers were making a noise that was melancholy and gay at the same time, and he saw with a bitter pang of pain that among them were the Christians whom he had seen in the church. Without thinking he rose and followed them as they made their way into the forest, dancing all the time as if they were taking part in a festival.

They danced and sang for a long while till at last they reached a glade deep among the trees. When he looked up he saw that the branches of the trees were thick with bones, shining among the leaves, white still bones like musical instruments.

The crowd stopped and he saw the witch doctor emerging from it and making signs above the bodies, while at the same time the people kept up a low harmonious murmur like the twittering of birds.

With thick ropes made of the branches of trees they began to haul the bodies up into the sky till they were lying among the other bones, while still maintaining their singing and dancing, and now and then taking little steps as birds do, or spreading their arms as if they were wings.

The music and the blueness of the sky and the dancing seemed to make death itself joyful and it occurred to him that this tribe had, in their natural motions, been little affected by Christianity. They were presenting the bodies to the birds, transforming them to music in the middle of the forest. When the bodies were safely in the trees, they began to make obeisance to them, again spreading their arms as if they were wings.

He was so absorbed in the sight in front of him, which seemed so natural and cheerful, that he did not at first notice that the chief was standing beside him, till the latter spoke in a soft voice, saying,

'This will bring your home to your mind,' and he looked at the missionary with a wise ancient gaze.

'That is so,' said the missionary, thinking of the burials in Scotland on cold days with a sharp wind, and the men clad in their black stiff clothes.

'That is natural,' said the chief.

'Do you believe in the soul then?' asked Donald.

'The soul?' said the chief. 'The soul is like the music of birds.'

'I thought you were a Christian,' said Donald probingly.

The chief did not directly answer the question but said, indicating the crowd, 'They think that what Banga did was natural. It was natural for him to kill his wife and children, and natural for him to kill himself. They understand that.'

Natural, thought Donald to himself, looking up at the bodies which he could hardly see because of the thickness of the foliage.

'Why did Banga's wife leave him?' he asked.

'He was beating her,' said the chief and then, without irony, 'After he became a Christian his temper became worse. Did you not see the stripes on her back? He talked about the soul and became idle.'

And that was natural as well, thought Donald. Everything was natural, the forest, the music, the dancing and even the chief in his purple feathers.

All the time the chief was gazing at him with sharp searching eyes and all the time Donald was thinking, Is everything then natural? What then of the Law?

He saw Tobbuta coming towards him and the chief whispered to him, 'He will try and kill you. You have put off your collar and you are now like anybody else. You are a natural enemy.' And again there was no hint of irony in his voice.

Tobbuta's face was a black uncomplicated mask. The crowd looked at him carelessly as if his rage too was natural.

He is going to try and kill me, thought Donald, and I don't care.

Tobbuta stopped in front of him, taking out two knives one of which he handed to him. Donald gazed at the knife as if he did not know what it was. Then he threw the knife on the ground and stood where he was, without weapons, Tobbuta raised his knife which was a dazzle of light among the greenness, and at that moment the missionary felt something strange happening to him. He did not want to die.

After all that had happened he did not want to die. The urge for life poured through him like water, like joy, like music.

He seized Tobbuta's wrist and began to twist it, using every ounce of strength which he possessed, thinking of the days when he had been a hammer thrower at the university which was now so far away. Tobbuta twisted and twisted like a fish at the end of a rod and the missionary fought for his life. The veins stood out on his forehead, a great wrath was blinding his spirit.

I do not want to die, he said to himself, squeezing Tobbuta's wrist, and he thought it absurd that he should lose his life so far from his own home while at the same time the bodies covered with flowers were waiting for the birds to come. It would be a ridiculous finale.

At last he heard a crack as of bones breaking and he saw Tobbuta looking down at his wrist which hung helplessly at his side.

'Ah,' said the crowd, and their sigh was like a breeze moving gently about the forest.

Tobbuta turned away and tried to stab himself with the knife which he held in his uninjured hand, but the missionary took it from him and threw it deep among the leaves. Tobbuta turned his mad tormented face towards him and then ran away through the crowd without looking back.

'Everything is natural,' said the chief in the same low voice as he had used already.

As if nothing had happened, the crowd began to sing and dance as before, and the missionary went in search of Tobbuta.

He found him at last sitting by himself against the trunk of a tree and when the missionary approached him he tried to rise to his feet, staring at him with a defiant angry look.

He thinks I've come to finish him off, thought the missionary, and he's not frightened.

He stood in front of Tobbuta and asked, 'Did you love her?' Tobbuta nodded without speaking.

'Why then did you let me take her away?' Donald asked.

'We couldn't disobey the chief,' said Tobbuta. And he began to cry, the tears streaming down his face, his body shaking.

'I didn't know that,' said Donald. 'I didn't know it.'

The two of them sat beside each other for a long time, and when Donald left Tobbuta appeared calm and peaceful. As he walked back he thought he was being watched by secretive eyes but he saw no one. He returned to his house wondering what Tobbuta would do now. Would he kill himself as well?

When he reached the hut there was a girl standing in front of it and he recognised her as the one who had asked him the question about her old bad-tempered complaining father.

Her face shone in the sun, her breasts were bare, her legs looked strong and muscular, and she wore nothing but a belt of leaves about her waist.

He was filled with lust: she was like a black Venus rising from a green sea of leaves.

'The chief told me to come,' she said simply, staring at him with a direct challenging gaze.

He took her by the hand and together they entered the hut. They lay on the bed of twigs and branches and she was like a fish turning and twisting in foam, in a waterfall, in tormented glimpses of water and sun.

Miraga Miraga Miraga.

Everything is natural, the voice told him. The birds are singing, the bodies are rising from the dead, there is music in the forest. And the black fish is turning in the water. The world is black and natural and beautiful, it is mysterious and abundant, its shadows are cool in the sunlight.

He threw the water away from his shoulders as he turned in the river. His white soul put on flesh among the fruitful shadows.

When she rose from the bed she set out fruit for the two of them and he ate his ravenously. The juice flowed down his growing beard.

'Are we always going to eat fruit?' he asked her.

'You will have to get meat,' she told him contentedly as if she were already a housewife at ease in her own house and with her own lawful husband.

'Get meat?' he said.

'Yes.'

'Tell me about that burial,' he said.

'What about the burial?'

'Why do you put the bodies up in the trees?'

'It's a custom of the tribe. That kind of burial has always been our way.'

She said nothing more and he knew that her knowledge did not extend further than what she had told him.

'What are we going to do every day?' he asked, thinking about time which would grow around him continually.

'There is nothing to do, but to bring the water from the well and to get the meat.'

'What sort of meat is that?'

'The meat of the deer, of course.'

'Where is it?'

'In the Long Grass.'

'Tell me about your tribe.'

'About our tribe? We believe in the birds, in the deer. We believe that our dead speak to us in the songs of the birds. I don't know anything else. And our tribe has been there forever.'

'What happened to the missionary who was here before me?' he asked.

She looked at him with astonishment. 'He died,' she said. 'He went to live in the forest and he died.'

'Is that true?'

'Yes,' she said. 'And tomorrow you will go to the Long Grass. It is not far from here.'

The same even intense heat was beating down on the earth, merciless, dry.

'We didn't have much rain this year,' she said. 'Perhaps the grass will not be so long as it used to be.'

'Is that a bad thing?' he asked.

'Of course.'

'But what can I do,' he asked. 'I can't hunt. I've never hunted in my life.'

'You can pray,' she said innocently without malice. 'That is what you can do.'

I am a spear in their hands, he thought, a spear in the war that is always going on, the war against starvation and disease.

'Is that why you came?' he asked. 'To buy my help?'

'The chief sent me here,' she answered simply.

The chief. What sort of man was he really. Old and wise, strong and intelligent, keeping the tribe together day after day, he was alive in time, in darkness.

'Come,' she told him and he found himself swimming in the dark waterfall again, among the shadows, among the lightning that poured about him, an eternal spear piercing a cloud without end.

'I can't leave you now,' he said stroking her hair. She looked at him with calm fathomless eyes.

'In the tribe,' she said, 'it's a law that I must leave you if you cannot win meat for us both.'

'Leave me?' he echoed.

'That is the law,' she answered. 'It is natural.'

But what of love, he almost shouted, what of loyalty, pity, are they too dependent on the world of plenty and abundance, are they unnatural?

'That is why,' she said, 'Banga's wife left him. He wasn't winning meat for her. His wife and children were hungry. That is why he began to beat her: that is why he became a Christian. He thought that he might learn magic from the Christian church that would help him to kill deer.' Donald nearly laughed aloud. Banga had gone in search of the soul in order to provide for the flesh!

'He thought that there was big magic in the church,' she repeated. 'When the other missionary died we had a good wet season.'

She sat in front of him like an idol of ebony, cut out of time, heavy, strong, potentially fertile.

My shadow, my black flower, my darkness from which all that is abundant and powerful flows.

He felt himself like a white worm inside that darkness.

He knew that this wasn't love, this was lust alone, and behind her, behind time, he saw a white church rising with white slender turrets, a large church, a cathedral.

But how would he win meat for her?

He who had never used a spear in his whole life.

He put his arms around her and said, 'What would I do without you,' as he buried his face in her hair. 'I would be completely alone in this strange place.'

Your breasts, your legs, the perfume that pervades you.

Your flesh, your flesh.

The deer running about the glade like rays of sunlight, and he himself pursuing them with the spear of truth.

He sensed a shadow falling across the doorway and when he looked up there was the chief with a rifle in his hand. 'I brought you this gun,' he said. 'No one in the tribe can use it. It will help you in the Long Grass.' The missionary seized the gun joyfully. How kind the chief was, how thoughtful. But why were his eyes so mocking, so distant? What was he thinking about? And again he had the uneasy feeling that he was merely a white puppet in this man's hands, that he was being pushed out of the darkness into the sunlight. They looked at each other, each holding an end of the gun, and it seemed as if the chief were handing to the white man a treacherous secret weapon.

But at that very moment a ray of sunlight flashed across the old wood of the gun and everything was clear and simple again. When the chief left he himself kissed Miraga, and while he did so his hand rested on the gun that lay between them. Slowly her hand crept forward and also touched the gun as if by doing so she was showing the purest trust in his ability to provide for her. And he was filled with a sudden and almost holy joy.

Early in the morning they left the village, he and ten other tribesmen including the chief himself, they carrying spears, he his gun. They walked silently through the forest, the missionary following the others. There was dew still on the ground and now and again he would see a bird peering through the mist, grey and wet, a ghost of a bird sitting on a branch with folded dripping wings. The whole world was like the ghost of a world, like a misty thought, the leaves silent and motionless under the wet heavy grey mist. There was no sight or sound of any animal, only the intent tribesmen moving silently forward, now lost and now found by his eyes. Donald thought, This is the meaning and marrow of existence and not preaching a dry sermon from a pulpit: this is natural, that other is unnatural. Though man may not live on bread alone he needs bread as well. The soul grows from the body as a flower from the earth, as a bird sings out of the mist. The hunters ahead of him were half running half walking at a steady pace, bending forward into the whitish mist ahead of them. No one spoke.

We are tied by an invisible string, thought Donald looking at the slightly wet gun in his hand. Inside the gun death was waiting, quiet and ready and exact, almost dapper. In a short while it would give a bark, and a deer would fall. And it occurred to him that he had never killed any animal in his whole life. Apart from Banga and his family, that was, and his face twisted in a painful smile. But a gun was simpler than that, pitiless, without feeling. The gun had come from Europe, from that white world that moved so confidently into the future. It had come out of that light and not from the darkness of Africa, it did not have the dirt of roots about it, it was clean and calm and elegant and self-contained.

At that moment they came to the end of the forest and the tall grass was in front of them, a vast sea of green: and he knew that they would soon see the deer. Past him as a ship passes another in mid-ocean he saw a tranquil yellow body glide, eyes gold-coloured and sunny, and he knew that it was a lion. He almost raised his gun and fired at the royal mane, but the lion was lost in the grass as quickly as it had appeared out of it. He clutched his gun firmly, feeling, strangely enough, no fear at all. He thought the others had not seen the lion, for they continued on their way without deviation, bent to the earth, the grass climbing their bodies like a river or a green stair so that sometimes he could hardly make them out at all.

But he sensed that the grass was alive with animals, that it was shifting and seething like a green silken flag around them, for now and again he would catch glimpses of eyes, claws, heads, and he felt as he had felt when moving through a cornfield once in his distant youth. And yet at the same time he would ask himself, What am I doing here? But he knew what the answer was: he was there because Miraga wanted food, and her body, like his own, was dependent on it. They existed in a green waving seething chain.

They were almost swimming through the grass which rose above their shoulders and was wet with dew. He raised the gun above his head so that it would be clear of the wetness and he thought wryly that if anyone were watching he would only see a gun moving above the grass, tall and bare, with a purposeful motion of its own.

The chief was making signs to him and the missionary saw that they had almost come out of the grass and that in front of them was a long wide river which was green with the reflection of the grass. Without sound the river flowed, a wide snake on which the sunlight flashed. In the distance the missionary thought he could hear the persistent thunderous noise of a waterfall, but the river itself was placid and smooth.

They were now near its bank though still hidden in the long wet grass and when Donald looked he saw a sight that he had never seen in his whole life and that he would probably never see again. The bank was crowded with deer of all kinds, horned and unhorned; with small and large gold-coloured animals; with zebras whose beautiful mortal stripes leaped out of the light.

On all of them the sun flashed as they stood quietly drinking, a friendly congregation. The only noise in the whole universe was their drinking, their lapping of the water from the river.

How helpless, beautiful, strange, they looked in the rays of the sun in that far place, thought Donald: it was as if they had leaped at that very moment into history, as if they had not existed at all till he and the other tribesmen had arrived, as if they were in some way a startlingly abrupt answer to their desire for meat. Rich abundant flesh glittered and gleamed in front of them in the multitudinous light. Now and again Donald would see a deer lift its head from the water and then look dreamily ahead of it as if it were seeing a sight invisible to anyone but itself among the foliage that came down to the further bank of the green sluggish river. Then it would slowly and almost regretfully lower its head again.

Flesh, flesh, his body was crying and his soul was saying, How beautiful they are. He raised his gun and aimed it. At the far end of the gun he saw a back, flanks, a head. He saw a spear curve out of the grass, hang in the air for a moment, and then quiver into the body of a deer, and at that very moment he fired. When the noise fell out of the sky the deer began to scatter, wildly making a huge thunder about him, shaking the very ground on which he was standing. Spear after spear plunged out of the sky, hovering, needling the wax-coloured flesh, and the gun fired again and again. And the deer moved hither and thither as if dazzled and not knowing what to do. There was blood on the earth, and in the water into which some of the animals had fallen. His companions had now jumped out of the grass but the deer were running away at full speed as if at last they had identified their enemy. There was tumult and noise about him, heads rising out of the grass, tormented and frightened, and then suddenly disappearing. In a short while there was complete silence.

They all walked out of the long grass and looked down at the dead animals. Of these there were only five altogether. He himself stared down – the gun in his hand emptied of its cartridges as an animal of its litter, and it was as if he had forgotten it. He saw black breasts panting and sighing, swelling and fading, he saw faint distant eyes gazing at him as if out of eternity, he saw blossoms of blood opening on the flanks of the animals and he stood above them, compassionate and just. After all death was a part of life. And then he saw the ten tribesmen looking at him. And he knew that he should not have fired the gun so quickly, that all he had succeeded in doing was scatter the quarry, that they had expected far more meat than was now lying, some of it still alive, on the bank of the river.

For a long time they looked at him in silence and he knew that he had made a terrible mistake. Their gaze was directed at him like so many spears, though they did not speak. And then the thought came to him; I shall be shamed in front of the tribe. Perhaps I should kill all the witnesses now. But he knew that he could not do that and in any case his gun was empty. His throat was sick with humiliation and he could not meet their eyes. Can I never do anything right in this country? And then the question rose in front of him as tall as the grass itself. What if Miraga leaves me now that I haven't brought home the meat that she wanted? He looked around him continually as if searching for some salvation from the grass or from the river, but they remained as they always were, in their own silence. Heavily he bent down and hoisted a deer from the ground, one of his companions taking the other end, and together, though separate, they began to make their way back to the village.

He was standing in front of the hut, the chief beside him. 'I'm sorry,' he was saying over and over, 'I'm sorry sorry sorry.

What will I do now? Will Miraga leave me?' And he began to shake as if he were in high fever.

'I don't know,' said the chief gravely.

Donald knelt in front of him. 'I do not want to lose her. I'll do anything.'

'The people are angry,' said the chief. 'I shouldn't have given you the gun,' and it occurred to Donald: perhaps he gave me the gun for a deep reason of his own. He knew what was going to happen. But he said aloud, 'What can I do? I'll do anything.'

He was on his knees in a net of shadows while the chief looked down at him.

'We will have to go to war for our food then,' said the chief. 'We will have to fight another tribe and take the food from them.' He gazed blandly and innocently at Donald.

'War?' said Donald.

'Yes,' replied the chief. 'The deer won't return till next year, and we cannot do without meat.'

My soul that was once white is growing dark again, thought Donald. When will this confusion and trouble end?

'All right,' he said. 'I can use the gun in the war.'

'Good,' said the chief, 'good.' And he left. Donald went into the hut where Miraga was sitting. When he entered she didn't speak to him. He kissed her but her lips were cold. 'If you leave me I am lost,' he told her but still she didn't speak: she was a statue of black marble.

He went out again restlessly and sat in front of the hut as he had seen the natives do, but it wasn't long before he got up and went into the hut again.

'Tell me,' he said, 'what happened to the other missionary.'

'He died.'

'How did he die?'

'He killed himself.'

'That's not right,' said Donald fiercely. 'I'm sure that's not right. Tell me what happened.' And he was so angry that he was ready to kill her.

'Tell me the truth,' he shouted.

'When the rain didn't come,' she said, 'he offered his body as a sacrifice. He was crucified on a cross. In the forest. His bones are among the other bones. He said that he wasn't doing any good in this country and so he sacrificed himself. When he died the rains came and the grass was green and wet again.'

He threw her away from him and thought that what she had said must be true. That must have been what the missionary meant by the entry in his diary, by his confident unnamed resolution.

'And the rains came,' he said meditatively.

'Yes.'

'Why did the chief send you to me?' he asked.

'He commanded me. I don't know.'

He looked deep in her eyes.

'Do you love me?'

'Love?'

She didn't understand what the word meant. He had failed to provide her with meat and the meat was so closely connected with love that she found it difficult to focus on what he now was. Neither provider nor lover.

'It doesn't matter,' he said and he went out again to sit in the sun which poured from the sky with a ruthless barbarous light. He realised that both the chief and the witch doctor were his enemies and yet he knew that he could not leave Miraga.

He was entrapped by the flesh, and the soul like a lost bird was flying about the forest.

He went into the hut again. 'You won't leave me, will you?' he asked humbly. 'I will go and fight with the tribe. You will be loyal and stay here?'

'Everything is natural,' she answered and her mind and soul were closed against him.

In the Old Testament, he said to himself, it tells how the kings sacrificed to God before they went out into battle. Should I do that too?

'We put our father out of the house,' said Miraga quietly.

'What?' said Donald, filled with fear and horror.

'We put him out of the house. My sisters and I.'

'Where is he?' said Donald.

'In the forest. We put him out when we realised that there wouldn't be enough meat for all of us.'

My fault my fault again, thought Donald with anguish. She put her arms around him and began to kiss him. 'Wasn't that the right thing to do?'

He felt her breast on his own, her heart beating against his.

'No, it wasn't right,' he shouted. And all the time she was trying to pull him down on the bed.

'It wasn't right.'

And then he was again in the darkness which was full of blood and agony and happiness and the roaring of animals. He was turning in the river, throwing the water away from him.

'The witch doctor told us it was right,' she said, her lips nibbling his ear. He rose from the bed and washed his face in the bucket of water. In his mind's eye he saw the old man sitting like a bird in the middle of the forest. I should go and find him, save him, he thought, but he felt too tired to do so. A weight of sun and shadows was all about him.

It was as if his gun fired again and again and again and the old man with his closed senile beak fell from branch after branch on to the forest floor.

All the time the drums were beating and the witch doctor was dancing with antlers on his head. Drums, drums, dancers circling, now and again giving a high thin piercing cry as if they had been pierced by spears. They danced around the ring of fires, and then threaded them, in and out, with their sweating naked bodies. The missionary's feet were almost moving, on the point of dancing, and in that place he knew that he could have let all his repressed emotions dance themselves out to the four winds, give them their freedom. He saw one strong muscular man in particular lost in a fantasy of war of his own, his mouth open, his face a glazed mask, his right hand thrusting a spear again and again into the empty sky.

'That's Morga,' the chief whispered in his ear. 'He is the bravest of the tribe. Last time he killed ten men.' Donald gazed at the rapt sweating vacant face, the thrusting spear, the eyes which had lost their humanity and had gained in its place the lust of an animal or a demon.

He couldn't remember when he himself had danced last.

Was it at the corner of the road on an autumn night when the moon was full and red in the sky, like a hen brooding? Autumn; dancing, girls, the moon: and a bridge. He looked up into the sky and there was the moon, distant, white, calm, a white plate, sailing about the heavens. It seemed to remind him of his home, distant, cold and white. My own world, he thought, the world that I abandoned. I am a stranger in this land. He felt dizzy, and almost touched the chief for support lest he should fall down. The dance, the dance, and the witch doctor looking at him now and again, with his striped body, his long pointed antlers, while Morga danced in his secret fever of battle.

'They are praying to their god,' said the chief. 'They are praying that he send them a lot of birds, for the souls of their dead enemies go into the bodies of the birds.'

A departing shower of birds like leaves in autumn setting off to warm distant lands, leaving behind them the bare stubbly fields, the reaped corn. The moon in the sky and the dancers dancing, Donald's body began to shake to the sound of the drums which seemed to have penetrated his skin, which seethed inside him like milk inside a churn.

Shall I let myself dance, he thought, shall I descend into darkness with the enchanted Morga? And at that very moment a piercing thin cry poured between his lips, a howl of freedom. He was like a bird flying about, looking for light in the dark, seeking the sun. His feet were beating on the ground, all his anger, resentment, fear, hatred, was pouring out of his body as dirty water pours down a sewer pipe: all jealousy, malice, enmity pouring out of him, leaving his body empty and light like a shell that contains a new music. He was among the crowd in the darkness, he was with them, he was in communion with them, he would never be alone again, he was leaving behind him the solitude of Europe (the advertisements that blow about the streets in the wind), he was leaving that white naked desolation behind him. Once he had been a single spear in the world, pushing through time, the prow of a ship. But now he was part of the crowd, part of the blood, of the sound of the drums, of the sweaty entranced bodies. He saw his mind departing like a ray of moonlight, going into hiding among the deep dense dark leaves, and he himself was in the safe darkness. Why had he never sensed that safety before? Why had he been so long alone, fighting against time when this warm rich life was present in the world? But now time itself had left him (for time was a sickness, a plague) and he was at last in Africa. He was at last in the middle of the true music. He saw himself from afar, as if he were millions of miles away, and the witch doctor was laughing through the coloured bars of his face. He heard himself shrieking and crying as the others were doing, and the noise he made was like that which he had heard at night in the church from the wild animals that infested the woods. He was in a ring of joy, of freedom, and the moon was spinning and spinning faster through the dark clouds, entering them and emerging cleaner and whiter and wilder than before.

He had a spear in his hand and he was thrusting it into the sky. I am coming, I am the black hero, I will destroy whiteness. I am alive in darkness, I am in the undergrowth of the forest, my white roots are pushing through the blackness. The water of freedom was pouring through his body, he was like a waterfall which sings tall and eternal in the forest, the music was running out through his beak. He was so light that he could almost fly.

And at that moment the drums stopped, there was an enormous silence as the world steadied in its course, and the witch doctor was making a sign to the crowd. There he stood, powerful and triumphant, in his antlers, in the red and white stripes that poured down his face, and then he was pointing at Donald with a commanding finger. Words were coming from his mouth, surely he didn't . . .

'Pray,' said the witch doctor. 'Pray for us.'

'Pray,' he said, 'to your own God that our enterprise be successful and lucky.' And his face was a white blaze of triumph, of glory, of power, like a moon that shines with transcendent light.

Donald stood where he was in the middle of the forest, inside the rings of fire, in a silence that seemed to throb with the absent music.

Miraga, Miraga, Miraga, what will I not do for you?

For your body, for the freedom that you have given me, for your thighs, your breasts, your mouth, your lips.

'Pray,' said the witch doctor insistently, and Donald felt someone put an animal's mask over his face. It stank of an ancient rank violent smell.

Kneeling on the earth he began to pray. 'May God assist us in our expedition, may he give us victory over our enemies . . . ' The words came out of his mouth hesitantly as they had done before he had come to Africa, they were like stones in a black river.

But he prayed and when he rose to his feet he felt as naked as a bird in winter, its wings shivering. He felt as if there were red and white stripes pouring down his very soul.

The tribe followed a path through the forest that they had obviously followed often before, the chief leading, followed by Morga and then by Donald. They were all maintaining an easy half-run which did not seem to tire them at all.

Now and again a bird would rise screaming out of the trees and then angrily make its way to another branch on which it rested. Donald was trying not to think at all. Would he be able to kill anyone? And what of the children and the women? But it was his responsibility that there was a shortage of food and therefore there was no alternative but to do what he was doing.

Now and again the chief would glance behind him as if he wished to see whether Donald was still there and then, satisfied, turn his head to the front again.

Donald had no idea what sort of tribe they were going to fight, but it occurred to him that he could safely keep his distance, for he had a gun - he would never, he knew, have used a spear - and the thought comforted him, though its hypocrisy was evident. He gripped the gun more tightly as if it were in a strange way his saviour. He had to get food or Miraga would leave him: that was all he must consider.

The chief stopped and made a signal for silence to the rest of the tribe, for they had now come on to a bare open place in which there were rocks, hills, rivers, but no trees. The tribe became even quieter than it had been, if that were possible.

Donald heard the noise of a waterfall and felt that he was back in Scotland again, for the landscape looked Scottish, broken, rough, bare of animals.

He suspected that they were approaching their destination and felt a sharp sick pain in his stomach. And at that moment he saw the waterfall, the waterfall of his dream, tall and white and overwhelmingly powerful.

Something is going to happen to me here, he thought, in this very place. My soul is to be tested here.

The waterfall was so clear in front of his eyes that he began to tremble with fear. He looked around him but all he saw were black expressionless faces concentrated on the task ahead of them as if they were tranced masks. And it occurred to him that the whole mission was a dream, that he wasn't in Africa at all but in Scotland, that there was no chief of a tribe running so easily ahead of him, that the only reality was the pouring waterfall. And then there happened the moment of proof that his soul had foreseen.

Morga suddenly shouted and they all saw a small black boy running as it were out of the heart of the waterfall as if he had been disporting himself in it or perhaps drinking from its very centre. And they knew by his sudden flight that he had seen them. Both Morga and the chief turned to look at Donald and at the gun in his hand and he recognised as if it were a predestined fact that he was the only one who was able to prevent the boy from returning to warn his tribe.

As if in a dream he stared down at the gun. As if in a dream he raised it to his eye, steadying it as much as he could for the trembling of his hands. The boy was running and he himself could see the fugitive with absolute clarity. The boy became larger and larger, almost filling the sights. Now and again he would turn and look behind him and it seemed to Donald that he was gazing particularly at him. He had only to pull the trigger and the boy would fall to the ground. The waterfall poured in front of him, ghostly, tall and resonant, and the boy was ahead of him and Miraga's face winked momently out of the waterfall and then faded back into it. The whole tribe had come to a standstill and were looking at him, and he heard a cry like that of an animal leave his throat and hover above him in the air.

'I can't, I can't, I can't,' he was shouting over and over again. The chief glanced at him and then took the gun from his hand and fired. 'Go on boy, go on,' he heard himself shouting, and then the gun fired again. But the boy was still running, zigzagging from side to side as if he knew perfectly well what sort of death was being aimed at him. And in a strange way Donald felt that the boy who was running was himself. It was he himself who was fleeing at the far shelter of the waterfall, it was he himself who was trying to save his life, it was his own breath that was being inhaled and exhaled. And then the boy was safe, disappeared from view, and the missionary still in the dream saw Morga's spear hover over him. But the chief barked something, like the report from a gun, and with an angry expression Morga put his spear down again.

He turned away and then the chief turned away and as the latter did so it was almost with a pitying reluctance as if Donald were a loved apostate from his church or one whom he had failed to convert. The whole tribe turned away and Donald felt such pain as he had felt once when he had become converted and his friends had mockingly left him.

He found himself lying on the ground staring up at the sky. He was broken, empty. He put his hands to his cheeks to feel with amazement the thick growth of hair which had sprung there so quickly, like vegetation. He lifted the gun that the chief had thrown on the ground, and returned home, following his feet.

He knew that his failure was fatal, that he was without home, without country, almost without name, and that his body hardly cast a shadow on the earth. He walked slowly, commiserating with himself, having forgotten the battle towards which the tribe was heading. Without surprise he came to the glade in which he had seen the bodies being buried in the trees and saw in front of him a skeleton as diminutive as a child's. There was nothing left but the bones, for the beaks like sewing machines had stripped them clean and though it was only bones he knew it was the skeleton of Miraga's father. The arms – or the bones where the arms had been – were extended away from the central spine as if they had been in search of something, an impossible mirage of food, and he gazed down at the horizontal ladder which they made without thought or feeling. All this seemed natural. He looked at the bones for a little while and then he left the place.

He was going back to his own hut, to Banga's bequeathed home, the only one he now had and by his side he carried the gun, dumb, absurd, without meaning.

'Why have you come back?' Miraga asked him. 'What's wrong?'

He didn't answer her directly but said, 'If I leave this place will you come with me?'

'Leave this place?' and her voice was an incredulous echo of his own. It was clear that the idea had never occurred to her in her whole life, that the thought was inconceivable, beyond the limits of her imagination.

'Yes,' he said, 'leave this place.' And there was anger in his voice. Why couldn't everything be simpler than it was?

'I can't,' she repeated. 'Why are you back?'

'I came home alone.'

'Why?'

'Why, why why,' he shouted. 'Why are you always asking questions.' And there was an enormous barrier between them, they belonged to two worlds. She was going out of the door when he stopped her. 'Where are you going?'

'I'm leaving.'

'You won't leave here,' he shouted and threw her on the bed. He was screaming, his voice high and trembling like the voice of a boy. He would have liked to put his hands around her throat and throttle her. The only connection between her and him was violence. She lay on the bed like a stranded fish, her eyes wide with fear.

'What are you going to do?'

'Are you coming or aren't you?'

'No. I can't. No one has ever left the village. It has never happened.'

'You stupid bitch,' he shouted silently, his throat choked with fear and rage and shame. He was out of his mind with terror.

And all the time he was thinking how beautiful she looked, lying there on the bed, her breast rising and falling.

'What are you going to do?'

'I will find another man.'

He raised the gun to his eye and saw her clearly through the sights. He was trembling with anger and frustration. For a long time he looked at her and then threw the gun down on the floor and scrambled out of the hut.

He didn't know where he was going and he only looked back once to see if she was at the door but she wasn't. The place where she should have been was empty. He walked past the church and then, as if a memory had struck him, returned and stood gazing at it, white in the sunlight. He thought of the pulpit, the seats, the cross on the pulpit cloth, large and blue; it was not an oasis but a mirage in the desert of his mind. He noticed that the leaves were growing luxuriously round the windows, almost hiding them from view. Then he began to run into the forest where he felt cool and sheltered. There was no destination in his mind, he felt neither hunger nor thirst. He was a ghost drifting about the day. He ran and walked and finally found himself standing in front of the waterfall.

He stood and looked at it as if he were asking it a question in the hot dumb day. It was like an eel that twists and turns, a white fraying rope, foaming and torrential. He sat in front of it as if he were a pupil in front of a teacher waiting for the latter to tell him the meaning of the world. He thought of his youth, of his father with his flowing white beard. He thought of his home, of the journey on which he had come.

The waterfall was pouring and pouring and giving him no answer, a white snake in the day. Its senseless music was all around him. What have I done to my life, he thought, this unrepeatable life? But the waterfall continued its rotation. The soul, the soul, the white soul where has it gone? This land has destroyed me. It has maddened me. And the waterfall poured down and he looked deeply into it. He would have liked to have sat there forever, fallen asleep there. He thought of the chief and knew that he had been his enemy from the beginning, all he had wanted to do was keep his tribe together. He had played on the previous missionary's sense of uselessness, it was all so natural.

He heard a voice in his mind and it kept saying over and over, everything is natural. Rage, hatred, malice, death, they are all natural. Even love is natural, and a ray of pain stabbed him, as deep as a spear. Natural, natural, natural, the birds were twittering, the waterfall was saying. That waterfall had been there from the beginning of the world, it had been there before he had been born or had thought of coming to Africa. It had been there in his days of the natural man and then after his conversion. The waterfall had in a strange way been waiting for him, confronting him with its absurd question. All the time that he had been talking about the Sabbath – and where were the Sabbaths now? They were all intertwined into one long tedious day – the waterfall had been waiting and laughing. That senseless froth and foam had been rotating.

And all the time that he himself was sitting there, the battle was going on elsewhere: two tribes were fighting, one to retain its food, the other to capture it. The lion was killing the deer. And then at that very moment as if it had stepped out of his mind on dainty natural feet a white deer descended from a hill above, went into the waterfall and began to drink from it. Now and again it would raise its head meditatively and look at Donald. It didn't seem at all frightened. How beautiful you are, thought Donald, how beautiful and elegant and calm. Perhaps I shall sit here forever like a Saint Columba in Africa. Perhaps people will come to me and be blessed from my corruption that will never again be washed clean. Perhaps the deer will come and lick the hand that carried the gun. But the deer suddenly turned away and was no longer there.

Donald looked after it and then saw a figure coming towards him. His heart leaped with joy for he thought it was Miraga. He began to wave and shout, 'I'm here, I'm here.' And the echo shouted among the rocks above the noise of the waterfall, 'I am here.' The figure was steadily approaching and then he saw with a sinking of the heart that it was not Miraga. In a short while Tobbuta was standing beside him.

'I saw you,' he said.

Are we going to fight now, Donald asked himself, tiredly. Is this what we are going to do? Will this never end, this wheel of water?

But Tobbuta began to pour a torrent of words out of his lips. 'I can't sleep,' he was saying. 'I can't rest. I am going mad. I came to speak to you,' and he went on his knees in front of him. 'Ever since Banga killed my sweetheart I can't sleep.' Tears were pouring out of his eyes. 'I want your God to help me. I want to be a Christian. I tried to kill myself, but I couldn't. I tried to become a Christian before but my nature was too fierce.' He showed Donald a carving that he had made. And then Donald knew that this was the carving he had been working on when he met him first. 'She didn't want me to become a Christian because of what happened to Banga. But now I know that I have sinned. Your God is punishing me.'

Donald looked down at him, and heard behind him the music of the waterfall and he laughed. His laughter was a repeated echo among the rocks. His vast laughter resonated among the hollow rocks. He went down on his knees while still laughing. And in that strange moment when the whole world came to a stop and he could no longer hear the waterfall at all, he knew that it wasn't the chief who had won, that it wasn't he who had woven the rope around him. He knew that it was God who had done that. Murder and death had been a plague around him simply in order that Tobbuta would be saved.

'Who are you,' he asked, 'that deserved all this?' But the face in front of him was expressionless and black.

On his knees he began to pray. 'I am in Thy hands,' he said, 'in Thy hands. You are here even in Africa, even in the darkness. Your voice is deeper and more mysterious than that of the waters.' And the words came smoothly without hesitation from his mouth.

And the sound of the waterfall was becoming stronger and louder. He rose from his knees and felt on his back a heavy joyful burden. He put his hand out to Tobbuta. 'Come,' he said.

He turned and looked for a long time at the village from which he had come. 'Come,' he repeated. 'Everything is natural. Everything is forgiven.'

At the Fair

The day was very hot as had been most of the days of that torrid summer and when they arrived at the park where the fair was being held she found that there was no space for her car: so she had to cruise around the town till she found one, cursing and sweating. It was at times like these, when she felt hot and prickly and obscurely aggressive, that she wished Hugh could drive, but he had tried a few times to do so and he couldn't and that was that. It wasn't a big car, it was only a Mini, but even so there didn't seem to be any space for it anywhere, and policemen were everywhere waving drivers on and sometimes flagging them down to give them information. However after half an hour of circling and backtracking, she did manage to find a place, a good bit away from the fair, and after she had locked the doors the three of them set off towards it. In the early days, before she had got married, she hadn't bothered to lock the car at all. Even if a handle fell off a door, like the one for instance that wound down the window, she didn't bother having it repaired, and the back seat used to be full of old newspapers and magazines which she had bought but never read. Now, however, it was tidy, as Hugh (though, or because, he didn't drive) kept it so. He also polished it regularly every Sunday, since he didn't do any writing on Sundays, finding that three hours a day for five days in the week satisfied whatever demon possessed him. She herself worked full-time in an office while he stayed at home writing and making sure that their little daughter who was not yet of school age didn't burn herself or fall down the stairs or do anything that endangered her welfare.

It was a Saturday afternoon and it was excessively hot, but in spite of the heat Hugh was wearing a jacket and this irritated her. Why couldn't he be like other men and go about in his shirt sleeves; why must he always wear a jacket even when the sun was at its most glaring, and how could he in fact bear to do so? She herself was wearing a short yellow dress with short sleeves which showed her attractive round arms, and the little girl was wearing a white frilly dress with a locket bouncing at her breast. She looked down at her tanned arms and was surprised to see them so brown since she had been working all summer at her cards in the office catching up with work caused by Margaret's long absence. But of course at weekends she and her husband and the little girl went out quite a lot. They drove to their own secret glen and sometimes sat and picnicked listening to the noise of the river, which was a deep black, muttering unintelligibly among the stones. The blackness and the noise reminded her for some strange reason of a telephone conversation which had somehow gone wrong, spoiling instead of creating communication. Sometimes they might take a walk up the hill among the stones and the fallen gnarled branches and very rarely they might catch a glimpse at the very top, high above them, of a deer standing questioningly among trees. She loved deer, their elegance and their containment, but her husband didn't seem to bother much.

The little girl Sheila was taking large steps to keep up with the two of them, now and again taking her mother's hand and gazing gravely up into her face as if she were silently interrogating her, and then withdrawing her hand quickly and moving away. She talked hardly at all and was very serious and self-possessed. In fact it seemed to her mother that she was more like what she imagined a writer ought to be than Hugh was, for he didn't seem to notice anything but wandered about absent-mindedly, never listening to anything she was saying and never calling her attention to any interesting sight in the world around him. His silence was profound. She had never seen anyone who paid so little attention to the world: she sometimes thought that if a woman with green hair and a green face walked past him he wouldn't notice. That surely was not the way a writer ought to be.

Anyway he wasn't a very successful writer as far as sales went.

He had had two small books of poetry published by printing presses no one had ever heard of except himself, and had sold one short story to an equally unknown magazine. She had long ago given up trying to understand his poetry. He himself wavered between thinking that he was a good poet as yet unrecognised and a black despair which made her impatient and often angry with him. In any case the people they lived among didn't know about writing and certainly couldn't have cared less about poetry: if you didn't appear on TV you weren't quoted. They lived in a council house in a noisy neighbourhood which seemed to have more than the average share of large dogs and small grubby children who stared at you as you went by.

The fair was really immense and she looked down at her small daughter now and again to make sure that she hadn't got lost. She sometimes worried about her daughter's silences, thinking that perhaps they were a protection against the two of them.

Hugh said to her, 'We could spend a lot of money here, do you know that? There are so many things.'

She was suddenly impatient. 'Well, we only get out once in a while.' She knew that Hugh worried about money because he himself hardly earned anything, and also because his nature was fundamentally less generous than her own. He had given up working two years before, just to give himself a chance to see if he could succeed as a writer. Before that he had worked in a library, but he complained that working in a library was too much like writing, and in any case he was bored by it and the ignorant people he met. As far as she could see nothing had in fact happened since he gave up writing, for when he wasn't writing he was reading, and he hardly ever went out. He would sit at his typewriter in the morning but most of the time he didn't write anything or if he did he threw it in the bucket. When she came home at five she would find the bucket full of small balls of paper. She herself knew very little about literature and couldn't judge whether such work as he completed was of the slightest value. She sometimes wondered whether she was losing her respect for him: his writing she often thought was a device for avoiding the problems of the real world. On the other hand her own more passionate nature dominated his colder

one. Before she met him she had gone out with other men but
her resolute self-willed character had led to quarrels of such
intensity and fierceness that she knew they would eventually
sour any permanent relationship.

As they walked through the fair, pushing their way among
crowds of people, they arrived at a stall where one could throw
three darts at three different dartboards, and if one got a bull
each time would win a prize.

'Would you like to try this?' she asked him.

'Not me. You try it.'

'All right then,' she said. 'I'm going to try it.' She took the
three darts from the rather sour-looking unsmiling woman
who looked after the stall and stood steady in front of the
board. She was always a little dramatic, wanting to be the
centre of attention, though she didn't realise this herself. She
didn't know about darts, but she would try to get the bulls, for
she was very determined and she didn't see why she couldn't
throw the darts as well as anybody else.

'Ten pence,' said the woman handing her the darts with a
bored expression.

A number of other people were there, and she smiled at them
as if saying, 'Look at me. I don't know anything about darts but
I'm willing to try. Aren't I brave?' She threw the first dart and
missed the board altogether. She laughed, and threw the
second dart which this time hit the outer rim of the board. She
looked proudly round but her husband's face was turned away,
as if he was angry or ashamed of her. She drew back her round
pretty tanned arm and threw the dart and it landed quivering in
a place near the bull. She turned to him in triumph but he had
moved on, little Sheila clutching his hand. There was some
scattered ironic applause from the crowd and she bowed to
them with a flourish.

When she came up to him, he said, 'You didn't do so badly.
But these darts are rigged. Some of them don't stick in the
board. All the fairs are the same. They cheat you.'

'Oh cheer up,' she said, 'cheer up. We came here to enjoy
ourselves.'

Two youths carrying football scarves in their hands went

past and whistled, and Hugh's face darkened and became stormy and set. She smiled, aware of her slim body in the yellow dress. She hoped that he wouldn't settle into one of his gloomy childish moods and spoil the day. He looked quite funny really from the back, as he had had a haircut recently: most of the time he wore his hair long like an artist's or a poet's but today it was much shorter, showing more clearly the baldish patches at the back.

'All fairs cheat you,' he repeated as if he were worried about the amount of money they might spend, as if he were busy adding a sum in his mind. For a poet, she thought, he brooded rather much on money, and far more so than she did. Her philosophy was a simple one: if she had enough for the moment she was quite happy. But today she didn't care, she actually wanted to spend money, positively and extravagantly, as if by doing so she was making a gesture of hope and joy to the world. As they were passing a machine which emitted cartons of orangeade when money was inserted she bought three and they drank them as they walked along. She threw hers away carelessly on the road, but Hugh and Sheila waited till they came to a bin before depositing theirs.

The heat was really quite intense and she was annoyed that he showed no sign of removing his jacket.

What had she expected from marriage? Was this really what she had expected? Before her marriage she had been lively and alert and carefree but now she wasn't like that at all. She was always thinking before she made a remark in case she said something that would wound her husband, in case he found buried in it a sharp intended thorn which he would turn over masochistically in his tormented mind.

They came to a shooting stall and she said, 'Would you like to try this then?'

'Well . . . ' She put down the fifteen pence and he took the rifle in his hand, looking at it for a moment helplessly before breaking it in two. The woman gave him some pellets which he laid beside him, inserting one in the rifle after fumbling with it shortsightedly for some time. He snapped the broken rifle together and took aim: it seemed ages before he was ready to fire. She kept saying to herself, Why are you taking so long? Why don't you fire? Fire.

He sighted along the rifle and fired, and one fat duck in the moving procession fell down. Again he aimed steadily and carefully, at one point putting the rifle down in order to wipe the sweat from his eyes, but then raising it and firing. He looked extremely serious and concentrated as if there was nothing in the world he liked better than shooting down these fat slow ducks passing in procession in front of him. And again he knocked one down. So he had a talent after all – another talent, that is, apart from his poetry. He steadily aimed and again hit a duck.

'What do I get for that?' he asked the woman excitedly.

The woman pointed without speaking to a miscellany of what appeared to be undifferentiated rubbish but which on examination defined itself as clay dishes, cheap soiled brooches and a teddy bear.

'Take the teddy bear,' Ruth suggested and he took it, handing it over proudly. She in turn gave it to Sheila who gravely clutched it like a trophy.

'I didn't know you could shoot,' she said as they walked along together.

'I used to go to fairs when I was younger,' he replied, but didn't volunteer any more. She was proud that he had won a prize though it was a not very plush teddy bear and she put her arm momently in his. He seemed pleased, and relaxed a little, but she wished that he would remove his jacket.

'The prize wasn't worth the entry fee,' he commented as they walked along.

'That's true.'

'All these fairs are the same. They cheat you all the time.'

She knew that what he was saying was true but she thought that he shouldn't be repeating it so often: after all there were more things that they could talk about than the deceitfulness of fairs. When she had married him his conversation had been less monotonous and more enterprising than this, but she supposed that sitting in the house all day, every day, there wasn't much new experience flooding into his life.

A woman on toppling heels and wearing blue-rinsed hair walked past them.

'Did you see that woman?' she asked. 'Do you see her hair?'

'What woman? I didn't notice.'

'It doesn't matter,' she sighed.

Yet he had aimed carefully and with great concentration at the ducks as if more than anything else in the world he had wanted to shoot them down. He was pretty well as quiet as Sheila most of the time; she herself wasn't like that at all, she liked to talk to people, that was why she worked in an office. She liked the trivia of existence. She would take stories home to him at night but he hardly ever listened to her or suddenly in the middle of what she was saying he would talk about something else. He might for instance say, 'Do you think poetry is important?' And she would answer, 'I suppose so,' and immediately afterwards, 'Of course it is.' And she herself would have been thinking about her boss whose wife had visited him in the office that day and how he had shown her round as if she had been a complete stranger. Or about Marjorie who had told her how she had thrown a frying pan at her husband with the eggs still in it.

And he would say, 'It's just that sometimes I wonder. Sometimes I . . . ' They had come to the Hall of Mirrors and she said, 'What do you think? It costs fifteen pence.'

'I don't know. What do you think?'

Why was he always asking her what she thought? She wished he would accept some responsibility for at least part of the time. But, no, he would always ask, 'What do you think?' If only once he would say what he himself thought.

She didn't know what a Hall of Mirrors would be like but she said aloud, 'Why not?' It was she who always walked adventurously into the future, throwing herself on its mercy without much previous thought.

'Come on then,' she said. 'Let's go in.'

Hugh and Sheila followed her into the large tent.

It was hilarious. When they entered they saw two people whom they assumed to be husband and wife doubled over with laughter in front of a mirror, the wife pointing at her reflection and unable to utter a word. The husband glanced at the three of them and at her in particular, raising his hands to the roof as if saying, 'Look at her.' Hugh stared at his wife angrily and she thought, 'To hell with him. Can't I even look at another man?'

Then she turned and looked in the mirror. Her body had been broadened enormously, her legs were like tree trunks, and her large head rested like a big staring boulder on massive shoulders. It was like seeing an ogre in a fairy story, in a world of glass, a short wide ogre so close to the earth that he might have been planted in it. She began to laugh and she couldn't stop. Even Sheila was laughing and crying: 'Look at Mummy she's so fat.' She looked so rustic in the mirror as if she had lived all her life on a farm and had only gained from it a disease which gave her eyes a staring thyroid look, and her body the appearance of someone suffering from advanced dropsy. The man smiled at her again – as if caught up in her simple laughter – and Hugh glowered at the two of them.

Then he himself turned and looked in an adjacent mirror. This particular one elongated his body so that he seemed very tall and thin and his head with its frail brow was like a tall egg on top of his stalklike body. He smiled without thinking and she laughed from behind him and so did Sheila, clapping her hands, and shouting: 'Daddy's so thin. Look at Daddy.' She moved from mirror to mirror. In one she was squat and heavy and lumpish, in another her legs were as thin as the stalks of plants, climbing vertically to her incredibly shrunken waist. And all the time Sheila was running from one to the other excitedly. Hugh wasn't laughing as much as she was, he seemed rather to be studying the reflections as if they had philosophical or poetical implications.

Most of the people in the tent were laughing so loudly and with such abandon that they were like occupants of an asylum, rocking and roaring and leaning on each other, hardly able to breathe. But though she laughed she didn't abandon herself as helplessly as they did. And Hugh gazed at the reflections gravely as if they were pictures in an art gallery which he was trying to memorise.

She looked down at her slim body in the yellow dress as if to make sure that she wasn't after all the distorted woman in the mirror, the gross heavy-rooted peasant with the swollen arms and the swollen legs. And all around her was the perpetual storm of laughter and the rocking red-faced people. And suddenly she too abandoned herself, doubled over, banging her fist on her knee, shrieking hysterically at the squat figure, making faces at her. Tears came into her eyes, she wept with a laughter that was close to pain, and in the middle of it all she saw the reflection of her husband, tall and incredibly thin, with the immensely frail tall egg perched on his shoulders, gazing disapprovingly at her.

She couldn't stop laughing, it was as if a torrent had been released in her, as if she were a river in spate. And beside her the man and his wife were doubled over with laughter, their faces red and streaming, the man making faces in the mirror to make his reflection even more macabre.

Finally she stood up and made her way to the door, Hugh following her with Sheila. He was silent as if he felt that she had betrayed him in some way.

'Didn't you like that?' she asked him. 'It was really funny.' And she began to laugh again, this time more decorously, as if at the memory of what she had seen, rather than at its present existence. Why on earth did he never let himself go? Ever? She was angry with him and gritted her teeth. She supposed that even when he had been working in the library he had been like that, sad and serious, gravely spectacled, a source of tall disapproval when women borrowed their romances or thrillers. But how on earth had he learned to be so dull?

The two youths who were wearing striped green and white scarves came back up the road again, shouting. Hugh pulled Sheila aside out of their way, turning his eyes from them.

Damn you, damn you, she almost shouted, why didn't you go straight on? But she knew that he shouldn't have done so and that she was being unreasonable, for after all the creatures she had just seen were quarrelsome, irrational, and violent. But was that what writing did for you, sitting day after day in your room and then drawing aside from the rawness of reality when you emerged into it? Oh my God, she thought, what is it I want?

Joy, life . . . She listened to the steady beat of the music which animated the fair. In the old days she used to dance such a lot, now she didn't dance at all. She even knew some of the tunes they were playing, nostalgic reminders of her youth. Paper roses, paper roses, she hummed to herself, as she walked along. But why couldn't he take off his damned jacket? There were men passing all the time with bare torsos tanned to a deep brown and looking like gipsies, while by contrast Hugh seemed so pale even in this gorgeous summer because he never left his room. Damn, damn, damn. If only one was a gipsy, wandering about the world in a coloured caravan, without destination, without worry.

She wanted to dance, to sing, to shout out loud. But she didn't do any of these things and she merely walked on beside Sheila and Hugh looking as demure as any of the other women she met, a member of an apparently contented family, while all the time the beat of the music throbbed around her and inside her.

They came to a place where there were small cars for the children to drive and she asked Sheila if she would like to go on one of them. Sheila gravely nodded and then paid the man with the money her mother gave her, stepping with the same unhurried gravity into one of the cars which ran on tracks so that there was no danger. Ruth watched her daughter as the latter gazed around her with the same unsmiling serious self-possessed expression and when one of the other little girls began to cry Sheila gazed at her with a faint distaste. It worried Ruth that her daughter should be so unsmilingly serene and while she was thinking that thought Hugh said, 'She's cool, isn't she?'

'Isn't she?' Ruth hissed back and Hugh turned to her in surprise.

'I'm worried she's so cool,' Ruth continued in the same hissing tone. 'She never smiles. She's like a robot.'

'What's wrong with being cool?' Hugh asked her.

'I don't know. Maybe she's like you. Maybe she'll be a writer.'

'What do you mean by that?' said Hugh, his face pale.

'What I said. Maybe she should be a writer. Isn't that a good thing? Maybe a writer doesn't have to have emotions.'

'I don't understand what you're trying to say.'

'Oh skip it,' said Ruth impatiently and watched her daughter driving past with the same unearthly competence and composure as she had noticed before, self-reliant, never bumping into anyone, never making a mistake.

'Anyway,' she said aloud, 'what does your writing mean? This is the real world. What have you got to say about this? About the fair? You haven't said anything. I don't think you've noticed a thing.' She was hissing like a snake and all the time he was staring at her with his pale hurt face among all the tanned people. Perhaps he thought the fair vulgar, beneath him; perhaps he thought that the music which recalled her youth to her was indecorous, inelegant, raucous.

They watched Sheila driving round and round in her small yellow car.

'It's because I don't drive,' said Hugh.

'No,' she almost screamed. 'It's nothing to do with that. Nothing at all to do with that. It's your lack of feeling, your damned lack of feeling. She's getting like you. Look at her. She's like a robot, don't you see?'

'No I don't see. She's self-contained, that's all. But I don't think she's like a robot.'

'I don't care what you say, I know.'

'Do you want me to stop writing then?' he asked plaintively.

'You do what you want. Anyway I don't think writing is the most important thing in the world, as you seem to.'

And all the time there throbbed around her the beat of the music, heavy, sonorous, plangent. Her body moved to its rhythm. And her daughter revolved remorselessly in her small car.

'You're shouting,' said Hugh. 'People are hearing you.'

'I don't care. I don't care whether they hear me or not.'

The cars stopped and she leaned over and pulled Sheila towards her. She walked off ahead, Sheila beside her. It was as if she wanted to get into the very centre of the fair, its throbbing centre, in among the lights, the red savage lights, so that she could dance, so that she could feel alive, even in that place of cheating and deception, crooked sights, bad darts.

He was so dull, always asking her if poetry was important. And what should she tell him? Why was he doing it if he doubted its value so much? The fair was important: one could sense it: its brash reality had all the confidence in the world, its music was dominating and without inhibition. It was doing a service to people, even though the prizes were cheap and without substance. The joy of existence animated it, colour, music.

What's wrong with me? she asked herself. What the hell is wrong with me? She watched a girl and a boy walk past, arm in arm, and she felt intense anguish like the pain of childbirth.

She hated her husband at that moment, he looked so pale and anguished and out of place. If only he would hit her, say something spontaneous to her, but he looked so perpetually wounded as if he was always trudging home from a war he had lost. The only time she had seen a look of concentration on his face was when he had been firing at the ducks.

She saw a great wheel circling against the sky with people on it, some of them shrieking.

'I think I'd like some lemonade,' she said aloud, and they walked in silence to the lemonade tent.

While they were in the tent a drunk man pushed his way past them swaying on his feet and muttering some unintelligible words.

'Hey,' she shouted at him but he pretended not to hear.

'Did you see that?' she said to Hugh. 'He pushed past. He had no right to do that.' She was speaking in a very loud voice because she was so angry and Hugh looked at her in an embarrassed way. She wanted to stamp her heels into the man's ankles: but she knew that Hugh wasn't going to do anything about it and so she said, 'I don't think I want any lemonade at all.'

'That bugger,' she said, referring to the drunk man, hoping that he would hear her, but he seemed to be rocking happily in a muttering world of his own.

Before she knew where she was – she was walking so fast because of her rage – she found herself away from the fairground altogether and in an adjacent park where she sat on a

bench, seething furiously. When her husband finally caught up
with her and sat beside her she felt as if she could pick up a stone
and throw it at him, so great was her frustration and her
loathing. Sheila sat down on the grass, cradling the teddy bear
in her arms and saying into its ear, 'Go to sleep now. Go to
sleep.' Its unblinking eyes with their cheap glitter stared back at
her. She seemed to have forgotten about her parents altogether
and was in a country of her own where the teddy bear was as real
as or perhaps more real than her parents themselves.

'Why didn't you want lemonade?' said Hugh.

'If you must know,' she replied angrily, 'I didn't take it
because that man got ahead of us in the queue and you didn't
do anything about it.'

'What was I supposed to do about it? Start a fight?'

'I don't know what you could have done. You could at least
have said something instead of just standing there. You let
people walk all over you.'

'What people?'

'Everybody.'

'Perhaps,' he said, 'I should get a job then. It's quite clear to
me that you don't want me to be writing.'

'What on earth . . . ' She gazed at him in amazement. 'What
on earth has that to do with what I'm talking about? I don't care
whether you write or not. You can carry on writing as long as
you like. I don't care about that. It doesn't worry me.'

'You think I'm a failure. Is that it?' he asked.

'I don't know whether you're a failure or not. You're never
happy. You're always thinking about your writing. And yet you
never seem to see anything that goes on around you. I don't
understand you.'

'And what about you? Do you see everything?'

'I see more than you. You don't care about the real world.
You really don't. You didn't really want to come to the fair, did
you? You think it's beneath you.'

'No,' he said, 'it wasn't anything like that at all. It's just
that . . . Oh, never mind . . . '

Sheila was still talking to the staring teddy bear, quiet and
self-possessed as she sat on the grass in front of their bench.

In the old days the two of them had gone out together and they would lie down beside the river that flowed through the glen and she would think that Hugh's silence was very restful. But they would talk too.

What did they talk about in those early days that passed so quickly? Days passed like hours then, now hours seemed as long as days. She didn't even know what he did with himself when she was out working, and even when she came home at night with her fragments of news he didn't seem to be listening or, if he was, it was to some inner voice of his own, and not to her. She knew that she was jealous of that inner voice that tormented and obsessed him, that it was a part of him that she would never know, deep and dark and distant. What inner voice was there anyway beyond the fair, beyond the passing people and the music? She stared down at the grass which was green in places and parched in others. If Sheila hadn't been there she might have walked away but she was there and she couldn't leave her.

Sitting beside each other on the green bench they stared dully down at the ground. Eventually she got up. 'We might as well go back and see the rest of the fair,' she said. 'After all that's what we came for.' Hugh got to his feet resignedly and followed her as did Sheila, cradling the teddy bear in her arms.

When they returned to the fair, she asked Sheila if she would like to go on the swings. She paid for her and watched her settle herself on one of them, she herself standing on the ground and watching her from below, while Hugh was silent at her side. Sheila sat on the swing turning round and round with the same unnaturally quiet self-possessed air. Sheila terrified her. She wondered if, while she was away at work, Sheila was learning to be like her father, distant, without feeling. Maybe Hugh was taking her away into his own secret unhuman world. She wanted to rush up to the swing and stop it and take Sheila into her arms and say to her, 'This is the real world. This is all the world there is. Don't you smell it? Don't you hear the music? Enjoy it while you can. This is your childhood and it won't come again.'

She turned and glanced at Hugh, but he was staring ahead of him, hurt and wounded, as if into a private dream of his own.

God, she thought, what is happening to us? Maybe I should leave him. Maybe I should take Sheila with me and leave him. Maybe I should take her into the centre of the fair and teach her to dance.

The swing had come to a halt and gravely as ever Sheila stepped off and walked over to her parents still clutching her teddy bear. She stopped beside them, staring down at her brown shoes, shy and serious.

Ruth took her by the hand and in silence they moved forward.

'Would you like to go into the Haunted House?' she asked Hugh but he didn't answer. She didn't want to go by herself, as she was superstitious and believed firmly in ghosts.

What had that Hall of Mirrors meant? What had been the significance of it? She had looked so squat and earthbound there. Was that what she was really like who once had danced with such abandon and joy?

She thought, I'd like to go to a dance just once. Just once to a dance so that I would let myself go. But Hugh didn't like dancing. I should like to listen to music, she thought, the music of my early days when I had my freedom, before that silence descended. He has done more harm to me than I have done to him with his tall thin spiritual body and his brooding mind. If I had only known before my marriage . . . If only . . . But it was too late.

She was still alive but dying. The flesh – surely that was superior to the spirit, the soul.

There must be dancing in the world, joyousness and music.

But Hugh walking beside her was not speaking. She knew that he was hurt and angry, she could tell by the pallor of his face, by his compressed lips. What had he learned at the fair? Had he had any ideas for a poem? She didn't like his poems anyway, she didn't pretend to understand them, she was not a poseur as some people were. There were lots of people who would say that they liked a poem even if they didn't understand it, in order to be 'with it'. She, on the other hand, was the sort of person who would speak out, who had definite opinions.

She wasn't enjoying the day one little bit, she knew that:

everything was so hot and sticky. She wanted to be at the centre of things just once, she wanted to do something dramatic, something that she would remember in later years. She wanted to throw perfect darts, hit a perfect target . . . No, on second thoughts, she didn't even want to do that, she merely wished to laugh and enjoy herself and have a happy untidy day so that she could go home and plump herself on the sofa and say, 'Gosh, how tired I am.' But that wasn't likely to happen.

The three of them walked together but she seemed as far away from the other two as she could possibly be. And all the time Hugh remained wrapped in his silence as in a dark mysterious cloak.

They came to a tent outside which there was a notice saying SEE THE FATTEST WOMAN IN THE WORLD. She stopped and looked at the other two and said, 'I want to see this. Even if you don't,' she added under her breath. She paid forty-five pence for the three of them and they entered the tent. Sitting on a chair – she thought it must be made of iron to sustain the weight – there was the fattest grossest woman she had ever seen in her whole life.

The head was large and the cheeks were round and fat and there were big pouches under the treble chins. The breasts and the belly bulged out largely under a black shiny satiny dress. With her huge head resting on her vast shoulders the woman was like a mountain of flesh, and in close-up Ruth could see the beads of sweat on her moustached upper lip. The hands too were huge and red and fat and the fingers, with their cheap rings, as nakedly gross as sausages. Crowned with her grey hair and almost filling half the tent, the woman seemed to represent a challenge of flesh, almost as if one might wish to climb her. Ruth gazed at the immense tremendous freak with horror, as if she were seeing a magnification of some disease that was causing the flesh to run riot. Sunk deep in the head were small red-rimmed eyes, and in the vast lap rested the massive swollen hands. And yet out of this monstrous mountain, vulgar and sordid, there issued a tiny voice saying to Sheila:

'Do you want to talk to me, little girl?'

And Sheila looked up at her and burst out laughing.

'You're just like Mummy in the tent,' she shouted. And she ran over and clutched her mother's hand, laughing with a real childish laughter. Pale and tall, Hugh was watching the woman and Ruth thought of the vast body seated on a lavatory pan in some immense lavatory of a size greater than she had ever seen, and as she imagined her sitting there she also saw her spitting, belching, blowing her enormous nose. She was sickened by her, by her acres of flesh, by the smell that exuded from her.

She imagined the fat woman dying in a monstrous bed, people bending over her as she breathed stertorously, beads of sweat on her moustache.

And Sheila was still laughing and shouting, 'She's just like you, Mummy,' and tall, with egg-shaped head, Hugh gazed down at her, ultimate flesh seated on its throne.

Ruth felt as if she was going to be sick; the image in the mirror had come true in the stench of reality; the legs like tree trunks, the large red hands, the sausage-like fingers were there before her. She ran out of the tent, the bile in her mouth, and Hugh followed her with Sheila. In the clean air she turned to Sheila and said, 'There's the Big Wheel. Do you want to go on it? Your father can go with you if you like.'

'All right,' said Hugh, as if some instinct had told him that she wanted to be alone.

She watched them as they got into their seats, and then from her position on the ground below she saw them soaring up into the sky, descending and then soaring again. She waved to them as they turned on the large red wheel. And Hugh waved to her in return but Sheila was staring straight ahead of her, cool and self-possessed as ever. Up they went and down they came and something in the movement made her frightened. It was as if the motion of the wheel was significant amidst the loud beat of the music, the crooked guns and darts. As she saw the two outlined against the sun she knew that they belonged to her, they were her only connection with reality, with the music and the colour of the fair. If something were to happen to them now what would her own life be like? She almost ran screaming towards the wheel as if she were going to ask the operator to stop it lest an accident should happen and the two of them,

Hugh and Sheila, would plummet to the ground, broken and finished. But she waited and when they came down to earth again she clutched them both, one hand in one hand of theirs.

'That's enough,' she said, 'that's enough.'

The three of them walked to the car. She unlocked the door and got into the driver's seat, Hugh beside her wearing his safety belt, and Sheila in the back.

Sheila suddenly began to become talkative.

'Mummy,' she said, 'you were fat in the mirror. You were a fat lady. You had fat legs.'

Ruth looked at Hugh and he smiled without rancour. They were sitting happily in the car and she thought of them as a family.

'Did you think of anything to write about?' she asked.

'Yes,' he said but he didn't say what it was he had thought of till they had reached the council estate on which they lived.

He then asked her, 'Do you remember when we were at the shooting stall?'

'Yes,' she said eagerly.

'Did you notice that the woman who was giving out the tickets had a glass eye?'

'No, I didn't notice that.'

'I thought it was funny at the time,' Hugh said slowly. 'To put a woman in charge of the shooting stall who had a glass eye.'

He didn't say anything more. She knew however that he had been making a deliberate effort to tell her something, and she also realised that what he had seen was in some way of great importance to him.

What she herself remembered most powerfully was the gross woman who had filled the tent with her smell of sweat, and whose small eyes seemed cruel when she had gazed into them.

She also remembered the two boys with the green and white football scarves who had gone marching past, singing and shouting.

She clutched Hugh's hand suddenly, and held it. Then the two of them got out of the car and walked together to the council house, Sheila running along ahead of them.

The Listeners

He came back in the night when the castle was dark and he could not make out the blaze of rhododendrons, azaleas, roses, and the blue haze of bluebells. He knew the place of old: he knew where the lily pond was and the two green seats on which the visitors would sit. The general and his daughters would be in bed, for the rooms were unlighted. In the darkness his uniform was invisible and he felt as if it were flowing with blood. He had grown up not far from this castle; he had on one summer's day, rank and shadowy, played with the two girls when his gamekeeper father had taken him round the grounds. O salmon that I am not allowed to taste . . . But that had been a long time ago and his father was dead. 'They're no' bad,' he would say about the general and his daughters, 'But they dinna understand.' Didn't understand what? In those days he himself didn't understand what his father had meant but now he knew. In those early days the general would come out with his field-glasses and look around the land which he owned and controlled. He would stand there in front of the door under the stone towers, with his white moustache and bullet head glinting in the sun. The daughters were white and ghostly like figures from Greek legend.

He stood there in the darkness while the leaves of the trees moved and the stars made a little light in the spaces that the wind made. It was almost but not quite dark. He felt the scent of the flowers all round him but they did not calm his mind. Nothing calmed his mind now not even the quotations from his favourite Latin authors when as a second lieutenant he had suffered the infamy of the trenches. 'O Palinurus too easily trusting clear sky and calm sea you will lie on a foreign sand, mere jetsam, none to bury you . . . ' Even now in the darkness under the moving leaves a quotation came to him: 'Come praise Colonus' horses and come praise *the windy dark of the woods' intricacies* . . . ' He himself couldn't afford a horse: he had never been in the cavalry, only in the infantry. What had that fool general said: 'A cavalry charge will soon put a stop to their machine guns.' And the horses had gone flying into the mouths of the cannon, graceful, doomed, their heads raised in a classical perfection. O woods of Colonus . . .

He was a small boy again in those grounds, watching the general so superbly confident among his regimented flowing acres. And the girls who were like pictures of Greek heroines on those fabled vases. But the blood rose in his mouth again, his soul was a pheasant blundering about the woods. He could feel the blood flowing down his uniform, darkening his trousers, it was as if he had been shot on the wing. I am Palinurus, I trusted too much in that clear sky, that calm sea, that blaze of rhododendrons, azaleas, hyacinths. That garden which though I did not own it I left behind.

My rage is so great that my teeth are tightening on my tongue through which my blood is flowing.

I was never happy in the mess, I didn't have enough money. Their loud-mouthed bluster was too much for me, their red faces. I felt only hatred when I thought of those soldiers who were my friends pierced, beaten, lashed, starving, dying, thirsty. The general was only one among many with a stone head like a stone ball on a gatepost.

He stood at the big door, heavy, unyielding. Above him a tree creaked as if it were a soul in torment, as if it were trying to speak. Why had he come? Surely he didn't want to speak to them, especially when the castle was dark and they were all in their beds. Underfoot, the grass was thick and rich. O lord I could lie there, I am so tired, the blood has been flowing out of my body, my bones are insubstantial. My blood is flowing away like water, like the river in which I used to fish for salmon when I was a boy in spite of my father's gamekeeping. That too was a game, the hooked salmon, landing on the bank twisting and pale, the blood draining from it. The water flowed through him among the cool shadows under the trees. Of course they had shown him some respect for he had turned out to be a good classical student. His father had gazed at him in surprise and perplexity but they had tried to make up to him: not that they cared about the classics or about anything else, but they had thought that that was the thing to do. They had spread their net, they had laid down their snare. He knew that now though he didn't know it then. At the time he had been flattered by their interest: the girls too had been deferent. 'And this is Hugh, the great classical scholar.' Though he was only the son of a gamekeeper, old and bent, not understanding either his son or his masters and who now lay dead under his grey stone in the churchyard. 'O Palinurus too easily trusting clear sky and calm sea . . . ' It was his father whom his love focussed on, caught between himself and them, uncomprehending but knowing all there was to know about wind direction, shadow, leaf motion, prints of animals. Even now he could almost feel his presence in the wood guarding it for his masters from his own kind. Betrayer and guardian, hunter in Hades on behalf of his corrupted clients. There they were, upright, stony, eternal, shooting the pheasants on the wing . . . Father father you too were in your war and I thought of you often in the trenches, poor principled man who could get no other job than the one you had, guarding the acres that you yourself and your own kind ought to have had. But you never thought of that. All you would say was: 'They're no' too bad but they dinna understand.' You, like me, would walk about this place in the dark. The only difference is that my blood is flowing and yours is not.

He stood at the big wooden door and listened, and he could hear the whispering, the nervous mocking whispering. Who were they laughing at? At him or his father? Setting down their snares in the dark. As he stood at the door he could hear them whispering in what seemed to be a susurrant Latin, a deep dark language like black water in a river pool. What were they saying and whom were they speaking to in their black watery language? ' . . . the windy dark of the woods' intricacies . . . ' He listened. Was it Latin they were speaking? Surely not. And yet again they might be speaking Latin in order to mock him. Professor, they might be saying in Latin, how easily you were deceived, how easily you let us pull the wool over your eyes, bright though you thought you were. Of course they had done it for centuries and they would do it for centuries more. How did he think they had gathered their acres in? How did he think they defended themselves but by the deep cunning they had learned over the years, water spreading slowly, unnoticeably, leaving their pale salmon on the bank. Even his very Latin they would use against him, even the images of his mind. They sent their daughters out dressed in their classical white as if they were flowing down a vale where Pan played his seductive pipes among the leaves and the flowers and the carved fountains. They knew what they were doing all right. None could defeat them, they were water without shape, protean, adapting itself to the new ground. Didn't he understand that? Would he ever understand it?

No, it is not Latin they are speaking, he told himself, it is German. Inside their houses these are the secret spies. They didn't really want us to win, the stone-headed generals, they wanted the Germans to win, they wanted to echo their Prussian acres with their own. They have more in common with the Germans than they have with you, poor soldier. Both of them, the mirrored generals, belong to the deep Prussian darkness, with their thorny helmets, they are both aristocrats to the bone, on their large deep dark horses. And the whispers became louder and louder, more and more urgent. They were Germans whispering in a deep dark linguistic well, they were a writhing snake-pit of language. I can tell them by their square words, he thought, I can tell them by their secret mockery. And he was again the wraith from which the blood was steadily leaking.

He banged on the door angrily. 'Tell them I came,' he shouted. 'Tell them I came to bear witness to the dead. Tell them, all those aristocrats of Hades, that I have come from a still lower place. Tell them that one day they will wake and their castles will be on fire, their minds will be burning. They will rush out into the rhododendrons burning. Tell them that.'

But there was no sound, and the whispering had ceased. The general and his daughters were sleeping upstairs in their stony bedrooms and they had heard nothing. 'Tell them,' he shouted again. And the whispers had ceased as if the beings who had made them were huddled together in the hallway in active secret venomous consultation. 'Tell them that,' he shouted and then he turned away from the locked door into the wood. No lights had come on in the house. He went back into the darkness, almost floating as if his body had been drained by the shouting and the banging. Into the darkness he went, his uniform pouring with blood, his father behind him. Ah, I found you, you were poaching, were you not? No no no I was only telling them. You were poaching, said his father in his double voice. And then his father too was gone and there was only himself and his uniform peeling away like the bark of the tree and the last shine receiving him, like the ghostly pallor of a dying salmon, and there was a voice speaking gently and faintly from a distance, from a lectern of green. 'O Palinurus too easily trusting clear sky and calm sea you will lie on a foreign sand, mere jetsam, none to bury you . . . ' Aie Aie shouted the red-faced men raising their glasses of wine the colour of blood.

'You wait you wait,' he shouted. 'You wait.' And his soul for the moment hovered like an eagle's, its angry beak extended over the acres, dark and bloodstained, which might once have been his own but which now belonged to the secret-voiced Germans.

Mr Heine

It was ten o'clock at night and Mr Bingham was talking to the mirror. He said 'Ladies and gentlemen,' and then stopped, clearing his throat, before beginning again, 'Headmaster and colleagues, it is now forty years since I first entered the teaching profession. – Will that do as a start, dear?'

'It will do well as a start, dear,' said his wife Lorna.

'Do you think I should perhaps put in a few jokes,' said her husband anxiously. 'When Mr Currie retired, his speech was well received because he had a number of jokes in it. My speech will be delivered in one of the rooms of the Domestic Science Department where they will have tea and scones prepared. It will be after class hours.'

'A few jokes would be acceptable,' said his wife, 'but I think that the general tone should be serious.'

Mr Bingham squared his shoulders, preparing to address the mirror again, but at that moment the doorbell rang.

'Who can that be at this time of night?' he said irritably.

'I don't know, dear. Shall I answer it?'

'If you would, dear.'

His wife carefully laid down her knitting and went to the door. Mr Bingham heard a murmur of voices and after a while his wife came back into the living-room with a man of perhaps forty-five or so who had a pale rather haunted face, but who seemed eager and enthusiastic and slightly jaunty.

'You won't know me,' he said to Mr Bingham. 'My name is Heine. I am in advertising. I compose little jingles such as the following:

> When your dog is feeling depressed
> Give him Dalton's. It's the best.

I used to be in your class in 1944–5. I heard you were retiring so I came along to offer you my felicitations.'

'Oh?' said Mr Bingham turning away from the mirror regretfully.

'Isn't that nice of Mr Heine?' said his wife.

'Won't you sit down?' she said and Mr Heine sat down, carefully pulling up his trouser legs so that he wouldn't crease them.

'My landlady of course has seen you about the town,' he said to Mr Bingham. 'For a long time she thought you were a farmer. It shows one how frail fame is. I think it is because of your red healthy face. I told her you had been my English teacher for a year. Now I am in advertising. One of my best rhymes is:

> Dalton's Dogfood makes your collie
> Obedient and rather jolly.

You taught me Tennyson and Pope. I remember both rather well.'

'The fact,' said Mr Bingham, 'that I don't remember you says nothing against you personally. Thousands of pupils have passed through my hands. Some of them come to speak to me now and again. Isn't that right, dear?'

'Yes,' said Mrs Bingham, 'that happens quite regularly.'

'Perhaps you could make a cup of coffee, dear,' said Mr Bingham and when his wife rose and went into the kitchen, Mr Heine leaned forward eagerly.

'I remember that you had a son,' he said. 'Where is he now?'

'He is in educational administration,' said Mr Bingham proudly. 'He has done well.'

'When I was in your class,' said Mr Heine, 'I was eleven or twelve years old. There was a group of boys who used to make fun of me. I don't know whether I have told you but I am a Jew. One of the boys was called Colin. He was taller than me, and fair-haired.'

'You are not trying to insinuate that it was my son,' said Mr Bingham angrily. 'His name was Colin but he would never do such a thing. He would never use physical violence against anyone.'

'Well,' said Mr Heine affably. 'It was a long time ago, and in any case

> The past is past and for the present
> It may be equally unpleasant.

Colin was the ringleader, and he had blue eyes. In those days I had a lisp which sometimes returns in moments of nervousness. Ah, there is Mrs Bingham with the coffee. Thank you, madam.'

'Mr Heine says that when he was in school he used to be terrorised by a boy called Colin who was fair-haired,' said Mr Bingham to his wife.

'It is true,' said Mr Heine, 'but as I have said it was a long time ago and best forgotten about. I was small and defenceless and I wore glasses. I think, Mrs Bingham, that you yourself taught in the school in those days.'

'Sugar?' said Mrs Bingham. 'Yes. As it was during the war years and most of the men were away I taught Latin. My husband was deferred.'

'*Amo, amas, amat,*' said Mr Heine. 'I remember I was in your class as well.

'I was not a memorable child,' he added, stirring his coffee reflectively, 'so you probably won't remember me either. But I do remember the strong rhymes of Pope which have greatly influenced me. And so, Mr Bingham, when I heard you were retiring I came along as quickly as my legs would carry me, without tarrying. I am sure that you chose the right profession. I myself have chosen the right profession. You, sir, though you did not know it at the time placed me in that profession.'

Mr Bingham glanced proudly at his wife.

'I remember the particular incident very well,' said Mr Heine. 'You must remember that I was a lonely little boy and not good at games.

> Keeping wicket was not cricket.
> Bat and ball were not for me suitable at all.

And then again I was being set upon by older boys and given a drubbing every morning in the boiler room before classes commenced. The boiler room was very hot. I had a little talent in those days, not much certainly, but a small poetic talent. I wrote verses which in the general course of things I kept secret. Thus it happened one afternoon that I brought them along to show you, Mr Bingham. I don't know whether you will remember the little incident, sir.'

'No,' said Mr Bingham, 'I can't say that I do.'

'I admired you, sir, as a man who was very enthusiastic about poetry, especially Tennyson. That is why I showed you my poems. I remember that afternoon well. It was raining heavily and the room was indeed so gloomy that you asked one of the boys to switch on the lights. You said, "Let's have some light on the subject, Hughes." I can remember Hughes quite clearly, as indeed I can remember your quips and jokes. In any case Hughes switched on the lights and it was a grey day, not in May but in December, an ember of the done sun in the sky. You read one of my poems. As I say, I can't remember it now but it was not in rhyme. "Now I will show you the difference between good poetry and bad poetry," you said, comparing my little effort with Tennyson's work, which was mostly in rhyme. When I left the room I was surrounded by a pack of boys led by blue-eyed fair-haired Colin. The moral of this story is that I went into advertising and therefore into rhyme. It was a revelation to me.

> A revelation straight from God
> That I should rhyme as I was taught.

So you can see, sir, that you are responsible for the career in which I have flourished.'

'I don't believe it, sir,' said Mr Bingham furiously.

'Don't believe what, sir?'

'That that ever happened. I can't remember it.'

'It was Mrs Gross my landlady who saw the relevant passage about you in the paper. I must go immediately, I told her. You thought he was a farmer but I knew differently. That man does not know the influence he has had on his scholars. That is why I came,' he said simply.

'Tell me, sir,' he added, 'is your son married now?'

'Colin?'

'The same, sir.'

'Yes, he's married. Why do you wish to know?'

'For no reason, sir. Ah, I see a photograph on the mantelpiece. In colour. It is a photograph of the bridegroom and the bride.

> How should we not hail the blooming bride
> With her good husband at her side?

What is more calculated to stabilise a man than marriage? Alas I never married myself. I think I never had the confidence for such a beautiful institution. May I ask the name of the fortunate lady?'

'Her name is Norah,' said Mrs Bingham sharply. 'Norah Mason.'

'Well, well,' said Mr Heine enthusiastically. 'Norah, eh? We all remember Norah, don't we? She was a lady of free charm and great beauty. But I must not go on. All those unseemly pranks of childhood which we should consign to the dustbins of the past. Norah Mason, eh?' and he smiled brightly. 'I am so happy that your son has married Norah.'

'Look here,' said Mr Bingham, raising his voice.

'I hope that my felicitations, congratulations, will be in order for them too, I sincerely hope so, sir. Tell me, did your son Colin have a scar on his brow which he received as a result of having been hit on the head by a cricket ball.'

'And what if he had?' said Mr Bingham.

'Merely the sign of recognition, sir, as in the Greek tragedies. My breath in these days came in short pants, sir, and I was near-sighted. I deserved all that I got. And now sir, forgetful of all that, let me say that my real purpose in coming here was to give you a small monetary gift which would come particularly from myself and not from the generality. My salary is a very comfortable one. I thought of something in the region of . . . Oh look at the time. It is nearly half-past eleven at night.

> At eleven o'clock at night
> The shades come out and then they fight.

I was, as I say, thinking of something in the order of . . . '

'Get out, sir,' said Mr Bingham angrily. 'Get out, sir, with your insinuations. I do not wish to hear any more.'

'I beg your pardon,' said Mr Heine in a wounded voice.

'I said "Get out, sir." It is nearly midnight. Get out.'

Mr Heine rose to his feet. 'If that is the way you feel, sir. I only wished to bring my felicitations.'

'We do not want your felicitations,' said Mrs Bingham. 'We have enough of them from others.'

'Then I wish you both goodnight and you particularly, Mr Bingham as you leave the profession you have adorned for so long.'

'GET OUT, sir,' Mr Bingham shouted, the veins standing out on his forehead.

Mr Heine walked slowly to the door, seemed to wish to stop and say something else, but then changed his mind and the two left in the room heard the door being shut.

'I think we should both go to bed, dear,' said Mr Bingham, panting heavily.

'Of course, dear,' said his wife. She locked the door and said, 'Will you put the lights out or shall I?'

'You may put them out, dear,' said Mr Bingham. When the lights had been switched off they stood for a while in the darkness, listening to the little noises of the night from which Mr Heine had so abruptly and outrageously come.

'I can't remember him. I don't believe he was in the school at all,' said Mrs Bingham decisively.

'You are right, dear,' said Mr Bingham who could make out the outline of his wife in the half-darkness. 'You are quite right, dear.'

'I have a good memory and I should know,' said Mrs Bingham as they lay side by side in the bed. Mr Bingham heard the cry of the owl, throatily soft, and turned over and was soon fast asleep. His wife listened to his snoring, staring sightlessly at the objects and furniture of the bedroom which she had gathered with such persistence and passion over the years.

The Visit

When Helen and Tom had got into the car, Tom suddenly asked, 'Did we bring a bottle for them?'

'Yes,' said Helen proudly. 'I've got it in a bag on the back seat.'

'That's fine,' said Tom clicking the safety belt around him.

Helen never wore a safety belt for it never occurred to her that anything would happen to her in a car. Tom on the other hand took the long-headed business view, for after all he was a businessman. His imagination however was less powerful than hers and confined itself to premonitions of the collapse of his business, the hotel and the chalets. For this reason he worked very hard, and insured himself against all eventualities. Helen would have preferred to spend their money immediately but Tom took out more and more insurances. What do we want with money in our old age? Helen would ask him and he would answer, Well, we might fall ill and we would need the money. His bland face was adamant against her.

Ah well, said Helen, ah well. For she never quarrelled, never even wanted to start a quarrel. She loved her children and was content to be with them. In fact she didn't really like to leave the house much: she would have liked to spend Tom's money on a summerhouse where she could sit all day. Or perhaps even on a swimming pool where she could laze and drowse, face upward, on the hot days of July and August, staring up at the sun, golden and fierce in the sky, in the hard empty blue sky.

'Well thank God we brought the bottle,' said Tom. 'At least they can't say we were drinking all their drink.'

'No,' said Helen. Tom drove very competently, as he did practically everything except those things that depended on the imagination. For instance he couldn't tell the children bedtime stories, but she could and did. She had invented a country called Daffodil Land. In this country everything was yellow, the grass, the buses, the roads. Even the flag, the newspapers, the books, were all yellow. The children loved the story and its endless possibilities for disguise and mystery.

'Tell us another story about Daffodil Land,' they would shout at night while Tom would stand about foolishly. At moments like these she thought that he looked very vulnerable, not to say foolish, and sometimes she had great difficulty in keeping herself from laughing at him. But there was no question that he was a good provider. He drank sparingly and smoked not at all, though she did both. However he was always hinting that she should smoke less so that they could save more money for that phantom paradise of their old age when they would live on the fat of the land. She couldn't imagine herself as old, nor could she imagine Tom as old. Why was that, she wondered, as she watched the cars passing them, and to her right the cows grazing in a field, a calf nuzzling its mother furiously. Tom's gaze was directed straight ahead of him.

She wondered vaguely whether she loved him and could not understand what the word meant. Then she had her attention distracted by a black-faced lamb that seemed to be staring straight at her. How beautiful and innocent lambs were. Like children who didn't cry too much.

She didn't really want to visit Tom's brother but both of them felt it a duty especially when they were periodically invited as now. Tom slightly despised his brother who didn't make as much money as he himself made. If Helen had her way she wouldn't leave her house. After all what was there to attract one in the outside world? Tom's head, neat and polished, stared straight ahead. His cheeks were healthily red, his hair cut short.

'Was it whisky you got or vodka?' he asked suddenly.

'Whisky,' she said.

'That's all right then. Teddy's on the whisky. He was on the vodka for a while but he's on the whisky now.

'I saw Gibbon today,' he added. 'He bought quite a lot of sherry.'

'Oh,' she said, 'perhaps he's having a party.'

'He was looking a bit sloshed,' said Tom. He drove very carefully, keeping a steady forty and never going over it. 'Not like him to buy sherry.'

'True,' said Helen. Sherry, she thought. What can one possibly say about it.

'I can't understand it,' she said aloud.

'Neither can I,' said Tom. 'It's all very odd. If it had been anyone else but Gibbon. But he bought four bottles.'

'Four bottles,' Helen echoed.

There was a wasp buzzing about her ear and she wished to kill it, it was making so much noise.

'Would you mind if I opened the window and let this wasp out?' she said.

'Not at all,' said Tom, swerving to avoid a huge lorry that bore down on them.

'Bugger you,' she said to the wasp under her breath.

In spite of the open window the wasp didn't fly out. Stupid bloody thing, she said under her breath but not aloud.

If we don't speak too much, she often thought, we will be safe. They drove past the church with its towering becalmed weathercock and headed up the brae. On both sides of them were little neat houses very like each other, with little gardens, and prettily painted gates. She thought that she wouldn't like to live in any of these. To have to emerge from the door every morning and talk to the women on both sides of her, why that would be awful. It would be like living in one of those clocks with the small Dutch figures – such aproned housewives, such upright bearded men – which came out promptly and tidily when the clock struck.

Teddy's house was in front of them. It was a long wooden Swedish-type house which looked almost black, and in front of it there was unworked black soil which had not been turned into a garden. Teddy was not interested in gardening, he was more interested in talking. In fact he would have quite liked to live in a flat though his wife Ruth wouldn't have allowed him.

The car drew up and there, suddenly in front of them, were Teddy's two children running breathlessly. Oh my God, thought Helen, not again. But she bent down and kissed them just the same. William, small and sturdy like a midget bricklayer or boxer, stood gazing up at her almost hostilely, a red wooden train under his arm. Then he rushed away from her without speaking. Miriam smiled winningly and took her hand and making little premeditated steps guided her into the house. Behind her Tom carefully locked the car doors. She felt him behind her as a slow steady presence bearing the bottle wrapped in brown paper which she had forgotten about.

Teddy was waiting at the door, Ruth behind him. They all kissed each other and then Teddy said, 'Come away in.' They went into the large living-room with its red suite, the clock white and gilt on the mantelpiece, the children's stuff lying on the floor in front of the fire.

'How are you?' said Teddy as they sat down. 'You look well, Tom. Still gathering in the shekels, eh? Good old Tom.'

Tom smiled and crossed his legs, first pulling up his trousers carefully. Helen sat in the chair nearest the fireplace.

'Outside,' said Ruth to her daughter. 'Go out and play.' Without saying a word, though looking disappointed, Miriam left.

She has such control, said Helen to herself. They always do what she tells them to do . . . It's odd. There are people like that. And yet she never raises her voice.

'I see you've got your priorities right,' said Teddy accepting the bottle and removing the brown paper wrappings. 'How's business?'

'Fine,' said Tom.

'Good, good, that's good. And there's Helen looking as cool as ever. Well now, what will you have? Whiskies all round or would you like something different?'

'Vodka for me if you have it,' said Helen.

'And for me for a change,' said Ruth.

'Oh?' said Teddy inquiringly, adding, 'Whisky for Tom and for me a very large one. Do you know folks I have a terrible desire to get drunk. Mackinnon's been acting up again. This time he's wanting more interviews. And there's no one to interview. How would you like to be interviewed, Tom? Have you anything to tell the masses?'

Helen noticed that in a small cupboard beside her there was as usual a pile of *Time* magazines. It seemed to suggest that Teddy kept up with the latest sharp-eyed insightful journalism.

'Ah,' said Teddy, leaning back in his chair. 'Now we're all settled.'

He doesn't really think about us at all, Helen thought. He is interviewing us. His attitude is that of a reporter to his newsfind.

'I think,' said Teddy, 'that we should go to a party later. What are your reactions to that? I know of a place we can go to. Do you want to go?'

'Not us,' said Tom. 'We have to get back in one piece.'

'Oh don't worry about that. Wait till you've drunk enough and you'll want to go. Won't they, Ruth?' Ruth smiled her usual impassive smile and said nothing.

'As I was saying then, Mackinnon's latest gimmick is to interview people. He called me into his office on Monday. "Maxwell," he said, from the quarterdeck, "we need more interviews. The biographical angle. That's what we really need." And the fact is that there's no one I can interview. Who are these imaginary people, I ask myself. Give me one name. Can you give me one name, Helen?'

'Stewart,' said Helen. 'Why not Stewart?'

'Stewart, that pompous jumped-up ass. His photograph's in the paper every week anyway. You must be joking. What about you, Tom?'

'I can't think of anyone at the moment,' said Tom, sipping his whisky. Teddy had already finished his.

'Come on, guests,' he said, 'hurry up. Ruth's got a cold buffet for us later, haven't you, darling?'

'Yes, darling.'

It seemed to Helen for a moment that a spark flared between the two of them and then vanished into the air.

'Come on then, I'll refill your glasses. The fact is I feel as if I want to get drunk. Come on, Tom, Helen. No, you'll just have to take it. In these days of inflation grab what you can. Uncle Teddy's feeling in a generous mood.'

He poured more drink into their glasses and continued:

'I mean, what can you say about Mackinnon. If he didn't exist someone would have to invent him. He'll be wearing a green eye-shade next, if it wasn't that he is Protestant. He actually thinks that journalism consists of "quipped Harold", and "expectorated Ted".'

'He keeps saying that he'll leave but he never does,' said Ruth as if she were talking to Helen alone.

'If I was making as much money as Tom here I'd leave,' said her husband. 'No question of that. Come on, Tom, tell us. Do you make eight thousand a year?'

'Eight thousand. You must be joking,' said Tom, speaking out for the first time. 'Eight thousand?'

'Well, you've got these chalets. You must be making a packet. Have you noticed, Helen, that nobody talks about anything but money nowadays. It's like a disease. And quite right too. Except Tom, of course. He never talks about money. That's because he has it. Do you know that in the old days, when the plague was on, people who were infected used to try and give it to those who weren't. I wish they would do that with money. Anyway, I . . . ' And he stopped.

'Oh, but you must be making a reasonable salary,' said Helen quietly.

'Reasonable salary? But how do I make it? There's Tom and he doesn't have a master. He can wander round his estate, and I have Mackinnon breathing all over my shoulder day and night, asking for things to be changed, checking the phone bills, sniffing around the toilet paper. My God, to think that I have sold my soul for this. A mess of pottage right enough, whatever the hell that was. A mess, anyway.' He leaned back in his chair triumphant after his speech.

'Don't believe him. He really likes his job,' Ruth repeated, thin-lipped.

'Like my job? How could I like my job? True, I'm out in the real world, I know what's going on in the district, I get a gobbet of news now and then, but, my God, like it? How could I like it? As long as you have a master you can't like your job. There's Tom now. He can stop work any time he likes. Tell me, Tom, what is the difference between us, is it brain power, or a different kind of brain, or low cunning on your side? The fact is,' he said, turning to the others, 'I was the clever one at school. I always got the prizes. I was the one they expected a lot from. And this bugger here didn't do a stroke, never got a pass in a composition, and look at him now. I don't understand it. I just DO NOT UNDERSTAND IT. Come on, folks, some more drink. Refills coming up. Helen, are you all right? Of course, you're all right. But I mean it, I really mean it, how did my brother do so well. There he is with a hotel and chalets and there I am with a rotten bugger for a boss. There is no justice in the world.'

He slumped back into his chair and then jumped up again. 'And there's another thing. Any money I get the income tax take off me. And Tom here's got an accountant, haven't you, Tom? I bet you claim for the phone bills, the fire, everything. You hardly pay any tax, isn't that right? How do you do it?'

'Well,' said Tom, 'I'll tell you something, if we had a Tory Government we'd be better off.'

'Tory Government be buggered if the ladies will excuse me. If we had a Tory Government people like me would be down the drain, and that's a fact. Did you think of that? No, of course you didn't.'

'Well,' said Tom, smiling expansively, 'we'd have some law and order. Look at all the delinquents you get nowadays going about.'

'Delinquents, my arse. They aren't the delinquents, Tom. They're just small fry. The real delinquents are in the Tory Party. The delinquents are people like you evading your tax. That's who the delinquents are.'

'Yes,' said Helen, 'you're right. I'm not for the Tory Party.' Her head felt tight and hot. She had heard all this talk hundreds of times before, all this artificial drama, this storm in a teacup. It was how people lived.

'Didn't you know,' she said to Teddy, 'that we're all saving up for our old age. That's Tom's theory anyway.'

Ruth looked at her as if she was surprised by her statement. Ruth of course never spoke, never gave any hostages to fortune. When she came to think of it she didn't really know anything about Ruth. She seemed to have no weaknesses precisely because she never spoke.

'For your old age?' said Teddy incredulously. 'My God, I can't even save up for now. And there's the two of you gathering your money in. How lucky can you get? I should have . . . '

I should have married someone like Helen, Helen thought. That's what he was about to say. Just because my family had some money. In those days Tom had a motor bike and looked young and adventurous but he had turned out to be like everybody else, like her father, like her mother, concerned about money. How sickening it all was. If it weren't for the children I couldn't stand living. If it weren't for their unpredictability.

'Well,' said Tom, 'it's true about law and order. The crime figures have gone up since they abolished hanging. What would you do about it, then?'

Ignoring all the previous conversation Tom had steadily held to his own obsession with the same kind of resolution and tenacity as he brought to the making of money.

'Tom, I don't care about that,' said Teddy. 'They can hang as many of them as you like. All I'm saying is that for poor people like me the Labour Government is the best we have. They've handled the unions, haven't they? They've kept them in line. And I'll tell you something, that's one thing the Tory Government can't do. Mackinnon's a Tory and, my God, look at him. He's a bloated capitalist, if ever there was one. No one more bloated than him. He thinks the world belongs to him, that he can walk on the water with his shooting stick. He thinks of me as a black, I can tell you that.'

'You're quite right,' said Helen, 'keep at him.'

'To think,' Teddy mused sadly, 'that my little brother would turn out to be a Tory. Why I can remember the days when we couldn't rub two pennies together. Oh come on Tom, you can't really believe what you're saying.'

'Oh, but he does,' said Helen. 'Of course he does. He's saving up for his, our, old age.' Her voice slightly trembled. She felt she had been drinking too much.

And here was Teddy again with the bottle.

'Oh come on Helen, your capitalist friend here can drive you home and see what happens when the police stop him under a Labour Government. He'll get his law and order then all right.'

'Don't you worry about that,' said Tom. 'I'll sort them out. Don't you worry about that.'

'With bribes, eh?'

'I don't know about that but I'll sort them out.'

'You know, Helen,' said Teddy, 'there were days when Tom and I used to go fishing because we didn't have enough food in the house. And we had this old rod and bent hooks. And we'd sit there by the river and fish. It's like that bit from Burns, what was it again?

> We twa hae paiddlt in the burn
> frae early sun till dine
> and seas atween us braid hae roared
> sin' auld lang syne.

Or words to that effect. And see him there now in his classy suit. Just look at him.'

'Oh shut up Teddy,' said his wife. 'Why don't you just shut up? You're always taking the mickey.'

'Not at all. I'm just reminiscing. Seas atween us twa hae roared sin' auld lang syne. Old Burns had the words for it right enough. Even journalists are allowed to reminisce, you know. You should hear old Mackinnon at it. Public school, rugby, bean feasts, the lot. But it's true. All the talk now is about money. In the past people used to talk about religion. Now they talk about money.'

There was a silence and then Ruth said to Helen,

'And how are the children?'

'Fine. And yours.'

'Fine. And how are you keeping yourself?'

'I'm fine too.'

Teddy looked at his wife quickly as if he thought that she had been tactless and then turned again to Tom.

'What's your latest idea, Tom? After the chalets, I mean.'

'Are you speaking as a reporter or as a brother?'

'Oh, as your brother of course.'

'Well, then I can tell you that I have no ideas,' and Tom giggled slightly as if for the first time he had said something witty.

'I'll believe that when I see the removal men taking your stuff away.'

Removal men? What was that about removal men? Helen thought about men in black coats and black gloves taking everything away and then there would be nothing left for their old age. My God, I'm going to be sick, she thought in a panic. But she stayed where she was and smiled. Tom wouldn't want her to make a fool of herself. Not in his brother's house anyway. It would be so much better to be back with the children. My head, my head so tight, I need air.

'As a matter of fact,' said Teddy, 'as I told you earlier on we're thinking of going on to a party. Later, of course, after the buffet. Have you got the food then, Ruth. The loaves and the fishes?'

'Of course. Do you want it now?'

'Naturally we want it now.'

And he gave her a quick secret husband's smile, like a Belisha beacon flashing on and off for a moment.

'She likes doing this, you know,' he told the other two largely. 'Don't think you're putting her out in any way. She likes nothing better than making and arranging food. Other people arrange flowers, Ruth arranges lettuce and beetroot. What about you, Helen?'

'No, I don't like making food particularly,' said Helen smiling through her almost cracking mask. 'Tom can tell you that if you ask him. There's a lot that Tom can tell you.'

Teddy gazed at her in surprise and then his face moved away from her into the distance, returning slowly so that she almost asked, 'Have you come back from the party already?'

'I don't believe it,' he said laughingly. 'But it must be the quality of the brain. I mean there's Tom and he left school with O levels and I had four Highers. And look at him now. What do you think, Helen. Is it a special sort of brain?'

'Probably.'

'Well, now, that's interesting. A special kind of brain eh? I think what it is is this: you think of money all the time and then it comes to you. Your brain is a magnet for the money. Most people don't think of money all the time, but Tom does and therefore money obeys him. It gravitates towards him as to its natural master. Ah, well, here's Ruth with the nosh.'

He busied himself with plates and cups and saucers till they had all been served with coffee or tea and food.

'That,' he said, 'is egg sandwich. That is cheese sandwich and that, I think, is paté. Eat up and drink up for tomorrow we die and we all go to meet Mackinnon, the old bastard.'

He doesn't mean anything by it, thought Helen, as she helped herself to an egg sandwich. It's all talk. Mackinnon could be anybody, anything, he is only a symbol for the frustration that is bothering him. It could be thistles, spikes, needles, sharp points of ordinary existence. People talk about substitutes for their real worries. We live in metaphors and that is all Mackinnon is, a metaphor – an inflamed monster who gathers about him like seaweed the destitutions and rancours and envies that we secretly bear with us all the time. We live in metaphors, as in the old days before I met Tom and I used to read poetry by myself in the attic. Before all this useless and aimless heat.

'I think,' said Teddy, 'that I haven't been ruthless enough. That's what it is. I am too much a liberal at heart, I see too many sides to too many questions. And I talk too much. Have you noticed that Tom doesn't talk much? He sits there and listens. He's wondering what he can do with us. Isn't that right, Tom? He studies and he considers. That's why he's rich and I'm poor. That's all there is to it. The liberal brain is rotten to the core. Still, I've got to go on,' putting his hands out towards Ruth and almost falling on to the sofa.

'You watch it, Teddy, or I'll belt you one,' said his wife. 'Poor brain or not.'

'OK OK, you're stronger than me. I'm weak. Everybody's strong but me. How's about me interviewing you, Tom? Like for instance, question one, where did you make your money?

Second question . . . Oh, sorry, old pal, I think I'm just drunk.
It's just this money question. One can't think about anything
else nowadays. It's like a cancer in your head. Watching every
penny. Was it always like this? Shoes, toys, shirts, did one have
to think about them all the time and how much they cost? I
suppose one must have done – except in the Golden Sixties. Ah,
the Golden Sixties when even *Time* magazine was interesting
and you had great reporters. The Golden Sixties. Why, I used
to leave the electric light on all the time and run hot water all
day. We used to spend like drunkards, we were millionaires.'
His face became clear and tranquil as if he were looking back to
that time and that place where all had been simple and no one
worried about a tomorrow.

'Are you all right?' Helen asked suddenly.

'Yes, I think so. I think I'm all right.'

Tom looked at his wife but he didn't say anything. His face
was redder than usual and he seemed embarrassed by his
brother's outburst. She knew that the revelation of emotion
upset him. I wish I was home, she thought, I didn't really want
to come. Ruth is watching me all the time and so too is Teddy
with his unsleeping journalist's eye, though he is very drunk.
We're all drunk, we had better not say too much, we must hide,
hide. And at the moment Tom said,

'It's all a question of how you sell yourself, Teddy.'

'What do you mean, how I sell myself?'

'What I said. If you put a high value on yourself then other
people will put a high value on you as well. You would get on
better with Mackinnon if you thought more of yourself.'

'More of myself,' said Teddy. 'What do you think I am, a
diamond? A car? By God, I muck about the garbage and I can't
find any gold dust, that's for sure. You go on as if people were
objects.'

'He always talks like that,' said Helen in a conciliatory voice
though her head was tight and hot.

'Well, aren't they?' Tom asked drunkenly. 'Aren't they? Isn't
that what they are? They sell their labour on the market. Some
sell themselves better than others, that's all I say. You've got to
face up to reality, Teddy. If someone comes to inquire about

my chalets I don't take the first person I get. I look at their shoes, their clothes, I listen to them. I watch how they sell themselves, how confident they are. Some are more successful than others at selling themselves, that's what I think.' His smile succeeded in being pleasant and embarrassed at the same time.

Ruth also smiled, looking from Tom to Helen and then back again. She's studying us, thought Helen, she's wondering what our marriage is like. And she never opens her mouth. How can she keep it shut for so long? Has she nothing to say, or is it something else? I hate people like that, they are like stones with no mouths. And yet her children obey her without question. How odd. Or perhaps how right. I think I am feeling sick, she thought, I think I am going to be sick.

'Like Watergate,' she heard Teddy say. Talk talk talk. Nothing but open mouths and people talking. They spoke because they had to speak, because they were there. I talk because I am here. She wanted desperately to put her insight into words but could find no break in the conversation.

Did Teddy fantasise that he might have dug the Watergate story out of the secret recesses of Washington?

There he sat so sleek and careful though he was pretending to be revealing his innermost thoughts all the time. Yes, we are like objects, we manipulate each other all the time.

'I . . . ' she got up.

'What is it?' said Ruth.

'The bathroom. I'm just going to the bathroom.' Teddy and Tom mistily swathed in the Watergate story didn't seem to notice that she was leaving the room.

'I don't see what was wrong with it,' Tom was saying. 'They made a mountain out of a molehill.'

'A mountain out of a molehill?' she heard Teddy saying and then was out of the room with such a feeling of relief, as if she were leaving a ship that was going on the rocks. But she didn't go to the bathroom. She went out by the back door and there she saw a field of daffodils spring out at her in yellow. The children were playing with a red ball and they came running over.

'The daffodils,' she told them, 'let's hide in the daffodils.'

'Let's, let's,' shouted Miriam, but William stood staring at her, foursquare like a workman.

'So that they won't see us,' said Helen. 'They won't see us if we really lie down and hide.' She lay down and pressed her face against the tall daffodils. From the midst of all that scent and colour the house looked dark, almost black.

Somewhere they are walking, free and tall, the queens without worries about money. No one can see them among the daffodils with their yellow flags. She crouched down and felt moisture on her face.

In our old age we are safe, in the cage of our old age no one will get at us.

She felt as if she were diminishing and withering, into the safe country of the daffodils. Down down with the children among the yellow flowers, safe in her shrunken old age.

She saw the adults coming and she hid more and more deeply. They were coming from Washington, from Watergate, from the city of cherry trees and corruption, they were walking across the lawn, weighing the problems of the world. There was Teddy with his journalist's eyes gazing down at her, wicked and sharp. There was Ruth, her face flat and expressionless as a stone. And there was Tom, red-faced and impatient. He can drive home, she giggled, he can drive home. I am staying here.

Boo, she shouted at them, boo, boo boo. And the daffodils pale and tall were about her. She was the queen and they were the black square people coming from their eternal conferences trying to keep the world going till she was old enough to be rich and without care.

from

MR TRILL IN HADES

What to do about Ralph?

'What on earth has happened to you?' said his mother. 'These marks are getting worse and worse. I thought with your father teaching you English you might have done better.'

'He is not my father,' Ralph shouted, 'he is not my father.'

'Of course, having you in class is rather awkward but you should be more helpful than you are. After all, you are seventeen. I shall have to speak to him about these marks.'

'It won't do any good.'

How sullen and stormy he always was these days, she thought, it's such a constant strain. Maybe if he went away to university there might be some peace.

'He has been good to you, you know; he has tried,' she continued. But Ralph wasn't giving an inch. 'He bought you all that football stuff and the hi-fi and the portable TV.'

'So I could keep out of his road, that's why.'

'You know perfectly well that's not true.'

'It is true. And anyway, I didn't want him here. We could have been all right on our own.'

How could she tell him that to be on your own was not easy? She had jumped at the chance of getting out of teaching and, in any case, they were cutting down on Latin teachers nowadays. Furthermore, the pupils, even the academic ones, were becoming more difficult. She had been very lucky to have had the chance of marrying again, after the hard years with Tommy. But you couldn't tell Ralph the truth about Tommy, he wouldn't listen. Most people, including Ralph, had seen Tommy as cheerful, humorous, generous, only she knew what he had been really like. Only she knew, as well, the incredible jealousy that had existed between Jim and Tommy from their youth. Almost pathological, especially on Tommy's side. It was as if they had never had any love from their professor father who had been cold and remote, hating the noise of children in the house. They had competed for what few scraps of love he had been able to throw to them now and again.

She couldn't very well tell Ralph that the night his father had crashed his car he had been coming from another woman, on Christmas Eve. She had been told that in the wrecked car the radio was playing "Silent Night".

Of course, in his own field Tommy had been quite good, at least at the beginning. He had been given a fair number of parts in the theatre and later some minor ones on TV. But then he had started drinking as the depression gripped and the parts became smaller and less frequent. His downfall had been his golden days at school when he had been editor of the magazine, captain of the rugby team, actor. What a hero he had been in those days, how invisible Jim had been. And even now invisible in Ralph's eyes. And he had been invisible to her as well, though she often recalled the night when Tommy had gate crashed Jim's birthday party and had got drunk and shouted that he would stab him. But he had been very drunk that night. 'I'll kill you,' he had shouted. Why had he hated Jim so much even though on the surface he himself had been the more successful of the two? At least at the beginning?

She should have married Jim in the first place; she could see that he was much kinder than Tommy, less glamorous, less loved by his father, insofar as there had been much of that. But she had been blinded by Tommy's apparent brilliance and humour, and, to tell the truth, by his more blatant sexiness.

Of course he had never had any deep talent, his handsomeness had been a sort of compensatory glow, but when that faded everything else faded too. She herself had been too complaisant, declining to take the hard decision of leaving him, still teaching in those days, and tired always.

To Ralph, however, his father had appeared different. He had been the one who carried him about on his shoulders, taught him how to ride a motor bike, how to play snooker (had even bought a snooker table for him), taken him to the theatre to see him perform. Even now his photograph was prominent in his son's room. She had been foolish to hide from him the true facts about his father's death, his drunken crash when returning home from one of his one-night stands. She should have told him the truth, but she hadn't. She had always taken the easy way out, though in fact it wasn't in the end the easy way at all.

And then Jim had started to visit her, he now a promoted teacher, although in the days when Tommy had been alive not often seen except casually at teachers' conferences, but very correct, stiffly lonely, and certainly not trying to come between her and his brother, though she knew that he had always liked her. She had learned in the interval that kindness was more important than glamour, for glamour meant that others demanded some of your light, that you belonged as much to the public as to your wife. Or so Tommy had used to say.

She remembered with distaste the night of the school play when she had played the virginal Ophelia to his dominating Hamlet, off-hand, negligent, hurtful, almost as if he really believed what he was saying to her. But the dazzled audience had clapped and clapped, and even the professor father had turned up to see the theatrical life and death of his son.

But how to tell Ralph all this?

That night she said to Jim in bed,

'What are we going to do about Ralph?'

'What now?'

'You've seen his report card? He used to be a bright boy. I'm not just saying that. His marks are quite ridiculous. Can't you give him some help in the evenings? English used to be his best subject. In primary school he was always top.'

'I can help him if he'll take it. But he won't take it. His English is ludicrous.'

'Ludicrous? What do you mean?'

'What I said. Ludicrous.' And then, of course, she had defended Ralph. No one was going to say to her that her son's intellect was ludicrous which she knew it wasn't. And so it all began again, the argument that never ended, that wasn't the fault of anyone in particular, but only of the situation that seemed to be insoluble, for Ralph was the thorn at their side, sullen, implacable, unreachable.

'I'm afraid he hates me and that's it,' said Jim. 'To tell you the truth, I think he has been very ungrateful.'

She could see that herself, but at the same time she could see Ralph's side of it too.

'Ungrateful?' she said.

'Yes. Ungrateful. You remember the time I got so angry that I told him I had after all brought him a television set and he shouted, "You're a bloody fool then."'

'You have to try and understand him,' she said.

'It's always the same. He won't make the effort to understand. His father's the demi-god, the hero. If he only knew what a bastard he really was.' Always making fun of him with his quick tongue, always taking girls away from him, always lying to his distant father about him, always making him appear the slow resentful one.

That night she slept fitfully. She had the feeling that something terrible was happening, that something even more terrible was about to happen. And always Ralph sat in his room playing his barbarous music very loudly. His stepfather would mark his eternal essays in his meticulous red writing, she would sew, and together they sat in the living-room hearing the music till eventually he would tell her to go and ask Ralph to turn it down. She it was who was always the messenger between them, the ambassador trying hopelessly to reconcile but never succeeding. For Ralph resented her now as much as he resented Jim.

She couldn't believe that this could go on.

Ralph sat at the back of his stepfather's class, contemptuous, remote, miserable. Quite apart from the fact that he thought him boring, he was always being teased by the other pupils about him. His nickname was Sniffy, for he had a curious habit of sniffing now and again as if there was a bad smell in the room. But, to be fair to him, he was a good, conscientious teacher: he set homework and marked it and it really seemed as if he wanted them all to pass. But there was a curious remoteness to him, as if he loved his subject more than he loved them. Nevertheless, he was diligent and he loved literature.

'This, of course, was the worst of crimes,' he was saying,

sitting at his desk in his chalky gown. 'We have to remember that this was a brother who killed another one, like Cain killing Abel. Then again there is the murder in the Garden, as if it were the garden of Eden. There is so much religion in the play. Hamlet himself was religious; that, after all, was the reason he didn't commit suicide. Now, there is a very curious question posed by the play, and it is this' (he sniffed again),

'What was going on between Gertrude and Claudius even while the latter's brother Hamlet was alive? This king about whom we know so little. Here's the relevant speech:

> 'Aye that incestuous, that adulterate beast,
> with witchcraft of his wit, with traitorous gifts,
> won to his shameful lust
> the will of a most seeming virtuous queen . . . '

The point was, had any of this happened in Hamlet's lifetime? He meant, of course, King Hamlet's. Had there been a liaison between Gertrude and Claudius even then? One got the impression of Claudius being a ladies' man, while Hamlet perhaps was the soldier who blossomed in action, and who was not much concerned with the boudoir. After all, he was a public figure, he perhaps took Gertrude for granted. On their answer to that question would depend their attitude to Gertrude.

The voice droned on, but it was as if a small red window had opened in Ralph's mind. He had never thought before that his mother had known his stepfather before the marriage which had taken place so suddenly. What if in fact there had been something going on between them while his father was still alive? He shivered as if he had been infected by a fever. He couldn't bring himself to think of his mother and stepfather in bed together, which was why he had asked for his own bedroom to be changed, so that he would be as far away from them as possible.

But suppose there had been a liaison between them. After all, they had both been teachers and they must have met. True, they had been at different schools but it was inconceivable that they hadn't met.

O God, how dull his stepfather was, in his cloud of chalk.

How different from his father who inhabited the large air of the theatre. What a poor ghostly fellow he was in his white dust.

But the idea that his mother had known his stepfather would not leave his mind. How had he never thought of it before?

That night, his stepfather being at a meeting at the school, he said to his mother,

'Did you know ... your husband ... before you married him?'

'I wish you could call him your stepfather, or even refer to him by his first name. Of course I knew him. I knew the family.'

'But you married my father?'

'Yes. And listen, Ralph, I have never said this to you before. I made a great mistake in marrying your father.'

He was about to rise and leave the room when she said vehemently, 'No, it's time you listened. You sit down there and listen for a change. Did you know that your father was a drunk? Do you know that he twice gave me a black eye? The time I told everybody I had cut myself on the edge of the wardrobe during the power cut, and the time I said I had fallen on the ice? Did you know where he was coming from when his car crashed?'

'I don't want to hear any more,' Ralph shouted. 'If you say any more I'll kill you. It's not true. You're lying.'

For a moment there he might have attacked her, he looked so white and vicious. It was the first time he had thought of hitting her; he came very close.

Her face was as pale as his and she was almost swaying on her feet but she was shouting at him,

'He was coming from one of his innumerable lady friends. I didn't tell you that, did I? I got a message from the police and I went along there. He had told me he was going to be working late at the theatre but he was coming from the opposite direction. He was a stupid man. At least Jim is not stupid.'

He raised his fist as if to hit her, but she didn't shrink away.

'Go on, hit me,' she shouted. 'Hit me because you can't stand the truth any more than your father could. He was vulgar, not worth your stepfather's little finger.'

He turned and ran out of the house.

Of course it wasn't true. That story was not the one his mother had told him before. And for all he knew the two of them might have killed his father, they might have tampered with the brakes or the engine. After all, a car crash was always suspicious, and his father had been a good if fast driver. His stepfather couldn't even drive.

He went to the Nightspot where some boys from the school were playing snooker, and older ones drinking at the bar. He stood for a while watching Harry and Jimmy playing. Harry had been to college but had given it up and was now on the dole. Jimmy had never left town at all. He watched as Harry hit the assembled balls and sent them flying across the table. After a while he went and sat down by himself. He felt as if he had run away from home, as if he wanted to kill himself. He was tired of always being in the same room by himself playing records. And yet he couldn't bring himself to talk to his stepfather. The two of them were together, had shut him out, he was like a refugee in the house. He hated to watch his stepfather eating, and above all he hated to see him kissing his mother before he set off for school with his briefcase under his arm. But then if he himself left home where could he go? He had no money. He loathed being dependent on them for pocket money, which he used buying records.

He hated his mother as much as he hated his stepfather. At other times he thought that they might have been able to live together, just the two of them, if his stepfather had not appeared. Why, he had loved her in the past and she had loved him, but now she had shut him out because she thought he was being unfair to her husband. He was such a drip: he couldn't play snooker, and all he did was mark essays every night. The house felt cold now, he was rejected, the other two were drawing closer and closer together.

'How's old Sniffy,' said Terry as he sat down at the same table, Frank beside him. They, of course, were unemployed and Terry had been inside for nicking stuff and also for nearly killing a fellow at a dance.

Then they began to talk about school and he had to sit and listen. Terry had once punched Caney and had been dragged away by the police. No one could control him at all. Frank was just as dangerous, but brighter, more cunning.

'Have a whisky,' said Terry. 'Go on. I bet you've never had a whisky before. I'll buy it for you.'

The snooker table with the green baize brought unbearable memories back to him, and he said,

'Right. Right then.'

'I'll tell you another thing,' said Terry. 'Old Sniffy's a poof. I always thought he was a poof. What age was the bugger when he got married? Where was he getting it before that?'

Frank didn't say anything at all, but watched Ralph. He had never liked him. He had belonged to the academic stream while he himself was always in one of the bottom classes, though he was much brighter.

'A poof,' Terry repeated. 'But he's having it off now, eh, Frank?' And winked at Frank. Ralph drank the whisky in one gulp, and tears burned his eyes.

'Old bastard,' said Terry. 'He belted me a few times and I wasn't even in his class.'

The two of them took Ralph back to his house. Then they stood around it for a while shouting at the lighted window, 'Sniffy the Poof, Sniffy the Poof.' And then ran away into the darkness. Ralph staggered to his room.

'What was that? Who was shouting there?' said his mother. 'Some of your friends. You're drunk. You're disgustingly drunk.'

But he pushed her away and went to his bed while the walls and ceiling spun about him and the bed moved up and down like a boat beneath him.

He heard his mother shouting at his stepfather, 'What are you going to do about it then? You can't sit here and do nothing. He's drunk, I'm telling you. Will you give up those exercise books and do something?'

Later he heard his mother slamming the door and heard the car engine start, then he fell into a deep sleep.

At breakfast no one spoke. It was like a funeral. He himself had a terrible headache, like a drill behind his right eye, and he felt awful. His mother stared down at the table. His stepfather didn't kiss her when he left for school: he seemed preoccupied and pale. It was as if the house had come to a complete stop, as if it had crashed.

'You have to remember,' said his stepfather when talking about *Hamlet* that morning, 'you have to remember that this was a drunken court. Hamlet comments on the general drunkenness. Even at the end it is drink that kills Hamlet and Claudius and Gertrude. Hamlet is at the centre of this corruption and is infected by it.'

His voice seemed quieter, more reflective, as if he was thinking of something else. Once he glanced across to Ralph but said nothing. 'I'm sorry,' he said at the end of the period, 'I meant to return your essays but I didn't finish correcting them.' A vein in his forehead throbbed. Ralph knew that he was remembering the voices that had shouted from the depths of the night, and he was wondering why they had been so unfair.

'Something's wrong with old Sniffy,' said Pongo at the interval. Ralph couldn't stand the amused contempt the pupils had for his stepfather and the way in which he had to suffer it. After all, he had not chosen him. His stepfather never organised games, there was nothing memorable about him.

When he went home after four, the door was unlocked but he couldn't find his mother. She was neither in the living-room nor in the kitchen, which was odd since she usually had their meal ready for them when they returned from the school.

He shouted to her but there was no answer. After a while he knocked on her bedroom door and when there was no response he went in. She was lying flat out on the bed, face down, and was quite still. For a moment his heart leapt with the fear that she might be dead and he turned her over quickly. She was breathing but there was a smell of drink from her. She had never drunk much in her life as far as he knew. There was a bottle of sherry, with a little drink at the bottom of it, beside her on the floor. He slapped her face but she only grunted and didn't waken.

He didn't know what to do. He ran to the bathroom and filled a glass with water and threw it in her face. She shook and coughed while water streamed down her face, then opened her eyes. When she saw him she shut them again.

'Go way,' she said in a slurred voice. 'Go way.'

He stood for a while at the door looking at her. It seemed to him that this was the very end. It had happened because of the events of the previous night. Maybe he should kill himself. Maybe he should hang or drown himself. Or take pills. And then he thought that his mother might have done that. He ran to her bedroom and checked the bottle with the sleeping tablets, but it seemed quite full. He noticed for the first time his own picture on the sideboard opposite the bed where his mother was still sleeping. He picked it up and looked at it: there was no picture of his father there at all.

In the picture he was laughing and his mother was standing just behind him, her right hand resting on his right shoulder. He must have been five or six when the photograph was taken. It astonished him that the photograph should be there at all for he had thought she had forgotten all about him. There was not even a photograph of his stepfather in the room.

And then he heard again the voices coming out of the dark and it was as if he was his stepfather. 'Sniffy the Poof, Sniffy the Poof.' It was as if he was in that room listening to them. You couldn't be called anything worse than a poof. He heard again his mother telling him about his father. A recollection came back to him of a struggle one night between his mother and father. She had pulled herself away and shouted, 'I'm going to take the car and I'm going to kill myself. I know the place where I can do it.' And he himself had said to his father, 'Did you hear that?' But his father had simply smiled and said, 'Your mother's very theatrical.' For some reason this had amused him.

She was now sleeping fairly peacefully, sometimes snorting, her hands spread out across the bed.

And his stepfather hadn't come home. Where was he? Had something happened to him? At that moment he felt terror greater than he had ever known, as if he was about to fall down, as if he was spinning in space. What if his mother died, if both of them died, and he was left alone?

He ran to the school as fast as he could. The janitor, who was standing outside his little office with a bunch of keys in his hand, watched him as he crossed the hall, but said nothing.

His stepfather was sitting at his desk on his tall gaunt chair staring across towards the seats. He was still wearing his gown and looked like a ghost inside its holed chalky armour. Even though he must have heard Ralph coming in he didn't turn his head. Ralph had never seen him like this before, so stunned, so helpless. Always, before, his stepfather appeared to have been in control of things. Now he didn't seem to know anything or to be able to do anything. He had wound down.

Ralph stood and looked at him from the doorway. If it weren't for his mother he wouldn't be there.

'Should you not be coming home?' he asked. His stepfather didn't answer. It was as if he was asking a profound question of the desks, as if they had betrayed him. Ralph again felt the floor spinning beneath him. Perhaps it was all too late. Perhaps it was all over. It might be that his stepfather would never come home again, had given everything up. His gaze interrogated the room.

Ralph advanced a little more.

'Should you not be coming home?' he asked again. But still his stepfather retained his pose, a white chalky statue. It was his turn now to be on his own listening to his own questions. Ralph had never thought of him like that before. Always he had been with his mother, always it was he himself who had been the forsaken one. On the blackboard were written the words, 'A tragedy gives us a feeling of waste.' Ralph stayed where he was for a long time. He didn't know what to do, how to get through to this man whom he had never understood. The empty desks frightened him. The room was like an empty theatre. Once his father had taken him to one in the afternoon. 'You wait there,' he said, 'I have to see someone.' And then he had seen his father talking to a girl who was standing face to face with him, wearing a belted raincoat. They had talked earnestly to each other, his father laughing, the girl looking at him adoringly.

No, it could not be true. His father hadn't been at all like that, his father had been the one who adored him, his son. What was this ghost like when compared to his father?

He couldn't bring himself to move, it was as if he was fixed to the floor. There was no word he could think of that would break this silence, this deathly enchantment.

He felt curiously awkward as if his body was something he carried about with him but which was distinct from his mind. It was as if in its heaviness and oddness it belonged to someone else. He thought of his mother outstretched on the bed, her hair floating down her face, stirring in the weak movement of her breath. Something must be done, he couldn't leave this man here and his mother there.

Slowly his stepfather got down from his desk, then placed the jotters which were stacked beside him in a cupboard. Then he locked the cupboard. He had finished marking them after all and would be able to return them. Then he began to walk past Ralph as if he wasn't there, his gaze fixed straight ahead of him. He was walking almost like a mechanical toy, clumsily, his gown fixed about him but becalmed.

Now he was near the door and soon he would be out in the hall. In those seconds, which seemed eternal, Ralph knew that he was facing the disintegration of his whole life. He knew that it was right there, in front of him, if he couldn't think of the magic word. He knew what tragedy was, knew it to its bitter bones, that it was the time that life continued, having gone beyond communication. He knew that tragedy was the thing you couldn't do anything about, that at that point all things are transformed, they enter another dimension, that it is not acting but the very centre of despair itself. He knew it was pitiful, yet the turning point of a life. And in its light, its languageless light, his father's negligent cheerful face burned, the moustache was like straw on fire. He was moving away from him, winking, perhaps deceitful. He saw the burden on this man's shoulders, he saw the desperate loneliness, so like his own. He felt akin to this being who was moving towards the door. And at that moment he found the word and it was as if it had been torn bleeding from his mouth.

'Come on home,' he said. 'Jim.'

Nothing seemed to be happening. Then suddenly the figure came to a halt and stood there at the door as if thinking. It thought like this for a long time. Then it turned to face him. And something in its face seemed to crack as if chalk were cracking and a human face were showing through. Without a word being said the ghost removed its gown and laid it on a desk, then the two of them were walking across the now empty hall towards the main door.

Such a frail beginning, and yet a beginning. Such a small hope, and yet a hope. Almost but not quite side by side, they crossed the playground together and it echoed with their footsteps, shining, too, with a blatant blankness after the rain.

The Ring

In my secondary school in those years long ago, when I wore shorts and could feel the wind on my knees, the main romance was that between Mr MacColl (whom we called Frothy) and Miss Simpson. Mr MacColl taught mathematics and the reason we called him Frothy was that when he got into a rage, which he often used to do because for instance we couldn't understand the (to him) pristine obviousness of Pythagoras' Theorem, he foamed at the mouth so that if you were sitting in the front seat spittle beaded and bubbled on the desk. His face would become a bright red, like a cockerel's, and then after a while white as chalk. Strangely enough, for all his angry outbursts, we rather liked him, for we knew that his rage was not directed at us personally but rather at the abstract beings who had failed to learn that which was so evident to him; but who could however still be saved. And indeed on good days, he would be quite cheerful and even joking, and we would feel protected and secure in his world of triangles and circles and parallelograms. At the same time we thought of him as a comic figure whose trousers were always above his ankles; and sometimes he would say ludicrous things like,

'Watch this blackboard while I go through it again,' and we would smile and giggle behind our hands; and I could swear now, looking back, that these clumsinesses were intended, or if not intended, that he himself saw them as being as funny as we did. All in all, we liked him as much as we liked any teacher in the school, though he belted us quite often, for we knew that in his own way he loved us. Yes, I think I could put it as high as that.

Miss Simpson on the other hand I was never taught by, for I didn't take science, but I remember her as being short, rather squat, and yellow-faced. I have a vague memory that she was also splay-footed.

The romance between the two of them, for they must have been well over forty when I first knew them, had been a source of gossip and merriment in the school for many years, and indeed I had heard even my older brother talking about it. Sometimes a boy or girl would come into Frothy's room with a note: Frothy would study it for a while and then write an answer making sure that it was well sealed. We could tell from his later behaviour whether the note had contained good news or bad. The messenger would smile significantly at us while Frothy was reading the note, and then we knew it had come from Miss Simpson.

I don't know where Frothy stayed (some teachers stayed in the Hostel, but I don't think he was one of them). I think he would have lodged with a landlady in the town: he certainly didn't own a car, or a bicycle, and I think he walked home from school to where his home was.

I myself had a great love for geometry in those days. I adored the inflexible order of the proofs, the fact that parallel lines never met, that triangles were always composed of 180 degrees. One knew where one was with geometry, it was a world of security and happiness, which sprang no surprises, and I always associated it with summer and the warm sun shining on the desk. That such a settled world should exist beyond the tangle and whirl of adolescence was an unexpected gift. It was as if when one had finished a geometry problem one was locking a safe, hearing a satisfactory click.

For this reason I got on well with Frothy, and I liked him though in common with the other boys I considered him eccentric and comic: one could however never admit that one had any feelings at all for a teacher. So there I would sit at my desk in my shorts and Frothy would glance at the proof I had so elegantly created, and find it good. In fact I think I must have entered that world of geometry as a shelter against the difficulties which I had at home at the time, though these are irrelevant to my story. At any rate what I remember best is the safety of those days: Frothy pacing about in his torn gown, the windows bright with light. In a strange way I felt that such days would never come again, and that I owed Frothy their harmony and richness.

There is one thing I forgot to say and that is that during his paroxysms Frothy would cough a lot, his face reddening, and then after the bout of coughing was over, he would pop a pill into his mouth, though none of us knew what this pill was for.

However, one afternoon, he told me to come with him outside the room, and there with great secrecy asked me if I would go on a message for him to the chemist's and get him some Beecham's Powders. It seemed to me odd that a teacher should ask a pupil to do this, it was a confession of bodily weakness that came queerly from a teacher who by definition was a being without illness or frailty. After all, teachers were invincible beings who appeared at the beginning of a period and left at the end of it: in a sense their gowns suggested that they were not human beings at all, like the rest of us. Nor did they ever ask if there was anything wrong with us. The flesh had nothing to do with teaching, one never saw a teacher who was really ill.

However I did go for the powders to the chemist's and all the time I was walking along the street, now and again giving a sudden little skip, I giggled to myself. What a story I would have to tell the others. Frothy sending me for Beecham's Powders. What an extraordinary thing, how essentially funny it was. Nor did it occur to me to wonder why Frothy had sent me rather than anybody else. Had he perhaps thought that I would be different from the other boys and keep my story to myself? If he had thought that he was very much mistaken. And also I took my time on the errand, for I believed like all the other boys that one should never do anything for a teacher with any enthusiasm. I therefore walked slowly down the street, passing the shop where I used to buy *Titbits* and *Answers*. I waited outside the chemist's for a while watching a yacht in the harbour riding up and down on the waves, tethered to its anchor.

When I had got the Beecham's Powders, I put them in my pocket along with the change that I had received from the chemist, who wore a white gown and had an abstracted air like a busy doctor. I didn't have a watch in those days and I kept looking at the clock which was fixed on top of the Town Hall. I wanted to make sure that the period was up before I got back, not because I didn't like geometry, but rather because it was what the boys would have expected of me.

When I got back to the school, the period was over, as I had calculated, and Frothy had left the room. I walked along to the staff-room to find out where he was. All along the corridor the windows were open and the fresh breeze was blowing in. And then I suddenly noticed that at the far end of the corridor, and just outside the staff-room, Frothy and Miss Simpson were standing. I stopped and waited, for I didn't want to intrude on them. As a matter of fact, Frothy's back was turned to me and I could hear him talking in a low passionate voice to Miss Simpson. They were so engaged in their conversation that they didn't notice me. Miss Simpson, like Frothy, was wearing a gown which was white with chalk: she looked like an old splay-footed bat. Frothy's quick speech continued, but Miss Simpson didn't appear to be listening. I couldn't move and pretended to be looking out of one of the windows while at the same time I was thinking that I could gain some information which I would tell the other boys from my class. Their voices were now raised and finally Miss Simpson strode away in the other direction, her gown flying about her. Before she did so she flung something on the stone floor of the corridor, and it rolled along till it came to rest against the wall. I looked down. It was a ring, and it had a red stone in it. It was not unlike those rings that I used to see in Woolworth's when I visited it at the lunch break in order to see if there were any good books I could buy. The sun flashed from the gold of the ring, from its circle.

I went up to Frothy who still had his back to me and said, 'Please, sir.'

He turned on me a face bereft of all expression, a totally empty face, and one which was deathly pale.

It was as if he didn't recognise me.

'Please, sir,' I said again.

Then it was as if his face assumed expression, became firm and set, knowledge returned to the eyes, and he said,

'Oh, it's you, Turner.'

'Yes, sir, please, sir.' And I handed him the Beecham's Powders and he took them and waved away the change which I offered from my sweaty hand. It seemed to me at that moment that he was not like a teacher at all, and that his lips were trembling.

I nearly said to him that the ring was lying on the floor and that if he wanted me to I would retrieve it for him but I didn't say anything. I moved away from him, as from something irretrievably stricken, and ran with the light steps of youth to my next class. I suppose he must have bent down to get the ring, for no one found it later, but I didn't see him doing it.

I was trembling with excitement all through the next class which was Latin, and where I wrote down a long list of irregular verbs. After the period was over I told the others my story. They would hardly believe me, and my news ran through the whole school: the engagement had been broken off. That, I was told, was the significance of the thrown ring. In any case pupils later noticed the abstraction and bad temper of the two protagonists. What a story – a broken romance, a romance that was finally over. And so it proved. They were never seen together again. And never again did Frothy send anyone for Beecham's Powders, as far as I know.

Some hope that he had nourished finally died that day and he became fiercer and fiercer. No, he did not love us any longer, he hated us, he was determined that we would learn about algebra and geometry, not for our own sakes but for his own. The number of passes increased and, as they did so, so we grew to hate him more and more. Then as I climbed the school, shedding my shorts and wearing trousers, I forgot about him, for we now had a different teacher.

Today I opened the paper and read that Frothy had died in an old people's home in the town where he had taught. I had heard vague stories about him, that he had become odder and odder, his rages more and more incoherent, the pupils uncontrollable and hostile. No one however dared to be unruly in Miss Simpson's class. I thought of him sitting in a chill breeze outside the old people's home, shadows shaped like parallelograms at his feet while his hands trembled under a red blanket. I often wondered what the quarrel had been about but I never found out. I despised myself for the horrid little squirt that I had been and decided to go to his funeral.

It was a fine summer's day again, and there were only a very few people there, not even Miss Simpson, whom I would certainly have recognised even after all those years. I had hoped that there might have been a representation from the school but there wasn't. The only person I met there whom I knew was Soupy who had been in the same class and was now a reporter on the local paper. As the coffin was being lowered into the ground I said to him,

'Tragic, isn't it?'

'Yes,' he said. Then he glanced at me in a peculiar way and said, 'It was you who found the ring on the floor, wasn't it?'

'Yes,' I said.

'That was the day they broke off the engagement. I heard you handed it to him and he burst out crying. He had sent you for a tonic or something, isn't that right?'

'That's not true,' I said. 'He didn't burst out crying.' And I was suddenly angry with Soupy for getting all the facts wrong.

'It doesn't matter,' he said catching up with me. 'Do you know that he had a stroke the year before he was due to retire. Miss Simpson never went to see him. She's still quite fit, I saw her the other day. She was striding along the front looking like a boxer. She wore tweeds and had a dog with her. Are you coming for a drink?'

'Sorry,' I said, 'I haven't got time.' And I left him.

The chemist's I had bought the Beecham's Powders from was no longer there. In its place was a grocer's shop.

It seemed to me that the best thing about geometry was it never lied to you, which is why I myself am a mathematics teacher as well. It has nothing to do with pain or loss. Its refuge is always secure and without mythology.

Greater Love

He wore a ghostly white moustache and looked like a major in the First World War which is exactly what he had been. On our way to school – he being close to retiring age – he would tell me stories about the First World War and the Second World War, for he had been in both. As we were passing the chemist's shop he would be describing Passchendaele, walking along, stiff and erect, his eyes glittering behind his glasses.

'And there I was crouched in this trench, with my water bottle empty. I had somehow or another survived. All my good boys were dead, some of them up to their chests in mud. The Jerries had got hold of our plans of attack, you see. What was I to do? I had to wait till night, that was clear. When the sun was just going down I crawled along the trench and then across No Man's Land. I met a Jerry and the struggle was fast and furious. I am afraid I had to use the bayonet. But the worst was not over yet, for one of my sentries fired on me. But I eventually managed to give him the password. After that I was all right.'

He would pause and then as we passed the ironmonger's he would start on another story. He taught chemistry in the school and instead of telling his pupils about solutions or whatever they do in chemistry, he would spend his time talking about the Marne or the Somme. He spoke more about the First World War than about the Second.

Once at a school party there was a quarrel between him and the Head of the English Department, who also had been in the First World War and believed that he had won it. He questioned a statement which Morrison had made. It was, I think, a question of a date, and they grew more and more angry, and wouldn't speak to each other after that for a year or more. As I quite liked both of them, it was difficult to know whose side to take.

The headmaster didn't know what to do with him, for parents came to the school continually to complain about his lessons, which as I have said consisted mostly of accounts of his adventures in France and Flanders. The extraordinary thing was that he never repeated a story: all his tales were realistic and detailed and one could almost believe that they had happened. Either these things had been experienced by him or they formed part of a huge mythology of legends which he had memorised, but that had happened to others. I was then Deputy Head of the school and it was my duty to see the parents and listen to their complaints.

'He will soon be retiring,' I would tell them soothingly, 'and he has been a good teacher in his time.' And they would answer, 'That's all very well but our children's education is being ruined. When are you going to speak to him?' I did in fact try to speak to him a few times but before I could start he was telling me another of his stories and I found, somehow or another, that there was no way in which I could introduce my complaint to him.

'There was an angel, you know, at Mons and I saw it. It was early morning and we were going over the top and we saw this figure with white wings bending over us from the sky. I thought it must have been an effect of the sun but it wasn't that. It was as if it was blessing us. We had our bayonets out and the light was flashing from them. I was in charge of a company at the time, the colonel – Colonel Wilson – having been killed.'

This time I was so interested that I said to him, 'Are you quite sure that it was an angel? After all the rays of the sun streaming down, and you I presume being in an excited frame of mind . . . ?'

'No,' he said, 'it wasn't that. It was definitely an angel. I am quite sure of that. I could actually see its eyes.' And he turned to me. 'They were so compassionate, you have no idea what they looked like. You could never forget them.'

In those days we had lines and the pupils would assemble in the quadrangle in front of the main door, and Morrison loved the little military drill so much that we gave him the duty most of the time. He would make them dress, keeping two paces between the files, and they would march into the school in an orderly manner.

A young bearded teacher called Cummings, who was always bringing educational books into the staff-room, didn't like this militarism at all. One day he said to me, 'He's teaching them to be soldiers. He should be stopped.'

'How old are you?' I asked him.

'Twenty-two. What's that to do with it?'

'Twenty-two,' I said. 'Run along and teach your pupils French.'

He didn't like it but I didn't want to explain to him why his age was so important. Still, I couldn't find a way of speaking to Morrison without offending him.

'You'll just have to come straight out with it,' my wife said.

'No,' I said.

'What else can you do?'

'I don't know,' I said.

I was very conscious of the fact that I was fifteen years younger than Morrison.

One day I said to him, 'How do you see your pupils?'

'What do you mean?' he asked.

'How do you see them?' I repeated.

'See them?' he said. And then, 'They are too young to fight, yet, but I see them as ready for it. Soon they will be taken.'

'Taken?'

'Yes,' he said. 'Just as we were taken.'

After a silence he said, 'One or two of them would make good officers. It's the gas that's the worst.'

'Have you told them about the gas?' I said, seizing on a tenuous connection between the First World War and chemistry.

'No,' he said, 'it was horrifying.'

'Well,' I said, 'explain to them about the gas. Why don't you do that?'

'We never used it,' he said. 'The Jerries tried to use it but the wind was against them.' However he promised that he would explain about the gas. I was happy that I had found a method of getting him to teach something of his subject and tried to think of other connections. But I couldn't think of any more.

One day he came to see me and said, 'A parent called on me today.'

'Called on you?' I said angrily. 'He should have come through me.'

'I know,' he said. 'He came directly to me. He complained that I was an inefficient teacher. Do you think I'm an inefficient teacher?'

'No,' I said.

'I have to warn them, you see,' he said earnestly. 'But I suppose I had better teach them chemistry after all.'

From that time onwards, he became more and more melancholy and lost-looking. He drifted through the corridors with his white ghostly moustache, as if he was looking for a battle to take part in. Then he stopped coming to the staff-room and stayed in his classroom all the time. There were another three months to go to his retirement and if he carried on this way I knew that he would fade away and die. Parents ceased to come and see me about him, but I was worried.

One day I called the best chemistry student in the school – Harrison – to my room and I said,

'How is Mr Morrison these days?'

Harrison paused a moment,

'He's very absent minded, sir,' he said at last. We looked at each other meaningfully, he tall and handsome in his blue uniform with the gold braid at the cuffs of his jacket. I fancied for a terrible moment that I saw a ghostly white moustache flowering at his lips.

'I see,' I said, fiddling with a pen which was lying on top of the red blotting paper which in turn was stained with drops of ink, like flak.

'How are you managing, the members of the class, I mean?' I said.

'We'll be all right, sir,' said Harrison. Though nothing had been said between us he knew what I was talking about.

'I'll leave you to deal with it, then,' I said.

The following day Morrison came gleefully to see me.

'An extraordinary thing happened to me,' he said. 'Do you know that boy Harrison? He is very brilliant of course and will certainly go to university. He asked me about the First World War. He was very interested. I think he will make a good officer.'

'Oh,' I said.

'He has a very fine mind. His questions were very searching.'

'I see,' I said, doodling furiously.

'I cannot disguise the fact that I was unhappy there for a while. I was thinking, "Here they are and I am not able to warn them of what is going to happen to them." You see, no one told us then there would be two World Wars. I was in Sixth year when the First World War broke out and I was studying chemistry just like Harrison. They told us that we would be home for Christmas. Then after I came back from the war I did chemistry in university. I forgot about the war, and then the Second one came along. By that time I was teaching here, as you know.'

'Yes,' I said.

'In the First World War everyone was so young. We were so ignorant. No one told us anything. We were very enthusiastic, you see. You recollect of course that there hadn't been a really big war since the Napoleonic War. Of course there had been the Boer War and the Crimean War but these were side issues.'

'Of course,' I said.

'You were in the Second World War yourself,' he said, 'so you will know.'

But as I had been in the Air Force that didn't in his opinion count. And yet I too had seen scarves of flame like those of students streaming from 'planes as they exploded in the sky. I felt the responsibility of my job intensely. Though I was so much younger I felt as if I was the older of the two. I felt protective towards him as if it was I who was the officer and he the young starry-eyed recruit.

After Harrison had asked him his questions Morrison was quite happy again and could return to the First World War with a clear conscience. Then one day a parent came to see me. It was in fact Major Beith, a red-faced man with a fierce moustache who had been an officer in the Second World War.

'What the bloody hell is going on?' he asked me. 'My son isn't learning any chemistry. Have you seen his report card? It's bloody awful.'

'He doesn't work,' I said firmly.

'I'm not saying that he's the best worker in the world. The

bugger watches TV all the time but that's not the whole explanation. He's not being taught. He got fifteen per cent for his chemistry.'

I was silent for a while and then I said,

'Education is a very strange thing.'

'What?' And he glared at me from below his bushy eyebrows.

I leaned towards him and said, 'What do you think education consists of?'

'Consists of? I send my son to this school to be taught. That's what education consists of. But the little bugger tells me that all he learns about is the Battle of the Marne.'

'Yes,' I said, 'I appreciate that. But on the other hand I sometimes think that ... ' I paused. 'He sees them, I don't know how he sees them. He sees them as the Flowers of Flanders. Can you believe that?'

His bulbous eyes raked me as if with machine-gun fire.

'I don't know what you're talking about.'

I sighed. 'Perhaps not. He sees them as potential officers and NCOs and privates. He is trying to warn them. He is trying to tell them what it was like. He loves them, you see.'

'Loves them?'

'That's right. He is their commanding officer. He is preparing them.' And then I said, daringly, 'What's chemistry in comparison with that.'

He looked at me in amazement. 'Do you know,' he said, 'that I am on the education committee?'

'Yes,' I said, staring him full in the eye.

'And you're supposed to be in charge of discipline here.'

'I am,' I said. 'I have to think of everything. Teachers have rights too.'

'What do you mean teachers have rights?'

'Exactly what I said. If pupils have rights so have teachers. And one cannot legislate for love. He loves them more than you or I are capable of loving. He sees the horror awaiting them. To him chemistry is irrelevant.'

For the first time I saw a gleam of understanding passing across the cloudless sky of his eyes. About to get up, he sat down again, smoothing his kilt.

'It's an unusual situation,' I said. 'And by the nature of things it will not last long. The fact is that we don't know the horrors in that man's mind. Every day he is in there he sees his class being charged with bayonets. He sees Germans in grey helmets. He smells the gas seeping into the room. He is protecting them. All he has is his stories to save them.'

'You think?' he said looking at me shrewdly.

'I do,' I said.

'I see,' he said, in his crisp military manner.

'He is not like us,' I said. 'He is being destroyed by his imagination.' As a matter of fact I knew that his son was lazy and difficult and that part of the reason for that was the affair the major was carrying on with a married woman from the same village.

He thought for a while and then he said, 'He has only two or three months to go, I suppose. We can last it out.'

'I knew you would understand,' I said.

He shook his head in a puzzled manner and then left the room.

The day before he was due to retire Morrison came to see me.

'They are as prepared as I can make them,' he said. 'There is nothing more I can do for them.'

'You've done very well,' I said.

'I have tried my best,' he said.

'Question and answer,' he said. 'I should have done it in that way, but they didn't know enough. One should start from the known and work out towards the unknown. But they didn't know enough so I had to start with the unknown.'

'There was no other way,' I said.

'Thank you,' he said courteously. And he leaned across the desk and shook me by the hand.

I said that I hoped he would enjoy his retirement but he didn't answer.

'Goodbye for the present,' I said. 'I'm afraid I shall have to be away tomorrow. A meeting, you understand.'

His eyes clouded over for a moment and then he said,

'Well, goodbye then.'

'Goodbye,' I said. I thought for one terrible moment that he would salute but he didn't.

As a matter of fact I didn't see him often after his retirement. It was time that chemistry was taught properly. Later however I heard that he had lost his memory and couldn't tell his stories of the World War any more.

I felt this as an icy bouquet on my tongue. But the slate had to be cleaned, education had to begin again.

The Snowballs

'The minister, the Reverend Murdo Mackenzie, and his son, Kenneth, will be visiting the school tomorrow,' Mr Macrae told the boys of Standard Seven. 'I want you to be on your best behaviour.' They sat two to a seat in a room which was white with the light of the snow.

'That is all I have to say about it,' he said. He unfurled a map which he stretched across the blackboard. 'And now,' he said, 'we will do some geography.'

The following day was again a dazzle of white. Mr Macrae took a watch from his breast pocket and said, 'They will be here at eleven o'clock. It is now five to eleven and time for your interval.' They rushed out into the playground and immediately began to throw snowballs at each other. They would perhaps have a longer interval today and then Mr Macrae would blow his whistle and they would form lines and march into the room.

Torquil shook his head as he received a snowball in the face and then ran after Daial, whom he hit with a beauty. The sky was clear and blue, and the snow crisp and fresh and white.

At eleven o'clock they saw a stout sombre man clad in black climb the icy steps to the playground, a small pale boy beside him. They stopped throwing snowballs for they knew this was the minister. He halted solidly in the middle of the playground and said,

'This is my son Kenneth. I shall leave him with you for a while. I am going to see Mr Macrae.' He had a big red face and a white collar which cut into his thick red neck. Mr Macrae was waiting for him at the door and they saw him bend forward a little as he welcomed the minister into the school.

'Come on,' said Torquil to the small pale Kenneth. 'You can

join in if you want.' Kenneth seemed at first not to know what to do, and he stood uncertainly in the middle of the playground, while all around him the boys whirled and shouted and threw snowballs. Then he too began to throw snowballs and after a while he was enjoying himself hugely, and his pale face glowed with colour. He got a snowball in the back of the neck but he gave another one back, though he slipped once or twice being not at all sure on his feet. He ran almost like a girl with his hands in front of him. The interval passed quickly and then just at the moment that Kenneth had received another snowball, this time on the cheek, Mr Macrae and the minister appeared at the door.

They saw the minister stride wrathfully forward after saying something to Mr Macrae and still with the same uninterrupted stride descend the icy steps, his hand in his son's hand, and disappear from view. Mr Macrae blew his whistle and they all lined up, still red and panting from their exertions. As they stood in line they saw that Mr Macrae was trembling with rage and his face was white.

His moustache bristled as he shouted,

'So you threw snowballs at the minister's son, eh? Eh? I will teach you.' While they still waited in line he went furiously back into the school-room and emerged with a belt. 'So that you will know what you are being belted for,' he said, 'you are getting it for throwing snowballs at the minister's son. You have made me a laughing stock. The minister's son is at a private school and is not used to such behaviour. You have shown yourselves to be hooligans, that's what you have done.'

'Hold out your hand,' he said to Daial, who was at the head of the line. They heard the belt whistle through the air six times. 'Now your other hand,' said Mr Macrae. Torquil waited. He was sixth in line. He knew that the belt would be very sore on such a cold winter's day. He spat on his two hands in preparation. Swish went the belt and the more he belted the more fierce became Mr Macrae's rage.

While he was waiting to be belted Torquil said to himself, 'Kenneth was enjoying the snowballing. Why are we being belted?' But he knew that the belting didn't have anything to do with Kenneth, it had to do with the minister, and perhaps not even with the minister but with Mr Macrae. Deep within himself he felt the unfairness of it: twelve of the belt for throwing snowballs, that was not right. Ahead of him he heard the Mouse whimpering quietly and saw him bending down, wringing his hands as if he were in unbearable pain. Mr Macrae now reached him and said, 'Hold out your hand, boy,' not 'Torquil' but 'boy.' He did so and the first stroke had a sting that made him wince. The second one was worse and by the time that the sixth one came he felt that his hand had been cut. He gritted his teeth as tightly as he could. 'The other hand,' said Mr Macrae, his small pale moustached face fierce and determined. The belt rose and fell, rose and fell. For one crazy moment Torquil thought of withdrawing his hand and then decided against it, even though he was as tall as Mr Macrae if it came to a struggle. Then it was all over and they were back in the classroom again.

They sat down in their seats and for a while Mr Macrae turned his back on the class, breathing heavily as if still not satiated.

Many of the boys were wringing their hands under the desks and the Mouse was still whimpering quietly.

'That's enough,' said Mr Macrae and the Mouse stopped whimpering.

The boys opened their poetry books and they read round the class.

> 'A wet sheet and a flowing sea
>   a wind that follows fast
> and fills the white and rustling sail
>   and bends the gallant mast
> and bends the gallant mast, my boys,
>   while like the eagle free
> away the good ship flies and leaves
>   old England on the lee.'

Mr Macrae beat with his ruler on the desk as if it was a metronome.

'There's témpest in yon hórned móon,
    and líghtning in yon clóud
But hárk the músic máriners
    the wínd is píping lóud.'

Suddenly he seemed to have become jolly again and to have forgotten the belting and the snowballing.

'The wind is píping lóud, my bóys,
    the lightning fláshes frée,
while the hóllow óak our pálace ís,
    our héritage the séa,

Torquil put his hand up.
'What is it, Campbell?'
'Please, sir, I want to go to the toilet.'

'All right then, all right then,' said Mr Macrae in the same jolly voice. Torquil left the room and went outside into the whiteness. It was snowing gently and the flakes broke like stars on his jacket and his white trousers. The toilet at the back of the school was cold and draughty, and there was no lock on the door. The water poured down the walls. He stood there for a while contemplatively peeing, his hands so raw and red that he had difficulty in unfastening and then fastening his fly.

After a while he left the toilet and went into the school again. As he was coming in the door he saw Mr Macrae standing there, while from the classroom whose door was shut he could hear the boys chanting in unison,

'O for a sóft and géntle bréeze
    I héard the fáir one cry
but gíve to me the snóring bréeze
    and white waves héaving hígh.'

'And white waves heaving high,' said Mr Macrae jocularly. 'So you will throw snowballs at the minister's son.' And he made to hit Torquil on the bottom with the belt, but Torquil slid away and was hit on the head instead. For a moment a phantom fighter turned on Mr Macrae and then he was back in the classroom again, sitting in his seat. Mr Macrae was now in a good mood and shouting,

'And bends the gallant mast, my boys. Can't you see it, boys, the ship with all sails set crowding across the ocean? The storm can do nothing to her for as we are told in the poem the good ship was tight and free. What is the hollow oak, Torquil?' Torquil looked up at him out of the gathering swaying darkness into which he abruptly fell, the ocean closing over him.

'Torquil,' shouted the headmaster and then there was complete darkness. Later he felt himself being set on his feet. Cold water was streaming down his face. Mr Macrae was speaking to him nervously.

'Are you all right, Torquil?'

'Yes, sir.'

'Good, good. You can go home then. Did you hear me? You may go home. Tell your father I shall be along later.' Torquil stood on the floor, no longer swaying.

'Fine, fine,' said Mr Macrae, 'it was an accident, you understand.'

Torquil left the classroom and walked across the playground and down the steps and then turned left to go home. The snow was still falling, very lightly, on his jacket. Soon it would be Christmas, he thought.

When he went in the door his mother looked up. Her hands were white with flour.

'I'm not going back,' said Torquil.

'What did you say?'

'I'm not going back. Ever,' said Torquil.

'I am going for your father,' said his mother, and she went into the byre where her husband was busy with harness.

'Torquil has come home,' she said, 'and says he's not going back to school again.'

Her husband raised his grave pale bearded face and said,

'I will see him. Tell him to come in here.'

She went back into the house and told Torquil,

'Your father wants to see you in the byre.'

Torquil went into the byre where his father was waiting. The smell of leather calmed him: he would like to learn how to plough. Next spring he would ask his father to let him.

'What is all this?' said his father. 'Sit on that chest.' Torquil sat down.

'Well, then,' said his father.

Torquil told him his story. He tried to tell his father that the worst part of it was not the belting but the difference between him and the minister's son, but he couldn't put into words what he felt. He put his raw hands under his bottom as he sat on the chest. His father didn't say anything for a long while and then he said,

'Mr Macrae is a good man. He is a good teacher.'

'Yes, father,' said Torquil.

'The one before him was too slack.' Then he stopped. 'I will think about it.' Then, 'Mr Macrae is a good navigation teacher,' he added as if this was as important. 'Go inside now.'

At half past four Torquil saw Mr Macrae heading for the house on his bicycle, a small figure on which the snow was falling. Through the window, itself almost covered with snow, he saw him approaching and then his father going to meet him. He couldn't hear what Mr Macrae was saying but saw that he was gesticulating. His father stared at the ground and then shook his head. He seemed to be much calmer than Mr Macrae who was like a wasp humming about a bull. Then after Mr Macrae had talked a great deal, Torquil saw him get on his bike and ride away. After he had gone his father sent for him.

'You are not going back to school,' he said. 'You will work with me on the croft. We will say no more about it.'

Torquil saw that his mother was about to say something but his father looked at her and she bent her head to the plate again.

That spring Torquil was allowed to help his father with the ploughing which was harder than he had thought. The plough refused to go in a straight line, the patient horse tugged and tugged. Seagulls flew about the sparse ground, and a fresh wind was in his nostrils. Sometimes as he walked along he could hear a voice in his head saying

> And bends the gallant mast, my boys,
>   while like the eagle free

> away the good ship flies and leaves
> old England on the lee.

The black earth turned and the blades were hit by stones. He felt as if he was captain of a ship, his jersey billowing in the breeze.

'You'll come on fine,' said his father and then to his mother that night. 'He's coming along fine.'

When he was eighteen years old, because there was no employment, he decided to emigrate to Canada. He stood on the pier, his father and mother beside him. The ship's sails swelled in the breeze.

'You will be all right,' said his father. 'You have a good grounding in navigation. Mr Macrae saw to that.'

'Yes,' Torquil agreed.

He went on board the ship after kissing his mother and shaking his father by the hand. As the ship sailed away from the pier he saw them standing there with a lot of other people who were seeing relatives off. The sails swelled and soon they were far from shore and the island was a long line of green with lights twinkling here and there. Then it could not be seen at all.

He had a hard time of it in Canada for it was during the thirties that he emigrated. Sometimes he slept in doss-houses, sometimes he worked on the railway tracks. At nights he and the other boys from Scotland kept themselves warm by dancing the Highland Fling. His underclothes were in rags and one morning in spring after washing them in a stream he threw them away. Eventually he reached Vancouver and there got a job as a Fire Officer. He trained hoses on charred bodies in burnt rooms.

One night at a ceilidh in another islander's house he had an argument with him about the Garden of Eden.

'It wasn't an apple that was mentioned,' he said. 'It was just any fruit. I'll show you.' And, after asking him to get his Bible, they both studied it. It didn't mention an apple at all. It simply said the Tree of Good and Evil.

'You know your Bible sure enough,' said the islander whose name was Smith, and who was lame because of an accident on the grain elevators.

Torquil didn't say anything.

'The funny thing is that I never see you in church,' said Smith.

'You will never see me in church,' said Torquil.

But he didn't say why not. It seemed to him strange that he felt no anger towards Macrae whom he still regarded as having been a good teacher, especially of navigation. Sometimes when it was snowing gently he would see the belt descending, he could hear the words of that poem which he had never forgotten and he could see the thick neck and face of the minister.

'No,' he repeated, 'You'll never see me there.'

The Play

When he started teaching first Mark Mason was very enthusiastic, thinking that he could bring to the pupils gifts of the
poetry of Wordsworth, Shakespeare and Keats. But it wasn't
going to be like that, at least not with Class 3G. 3G was a class of
girls who, before the raising of the school-leaving age, were to
leave at the end of their fifteenth year. Mark brought them
'relevant' poems and novels including *Timothy Winters* and
Jane Eyre but quickly discovered that they had a fixed antipathy
to the written word. It was not that they were undisciplined –
that is to say they were not actively mischievous – but they were
thrawn: he felt that there was a solid wall between himself and
them and that no matter how hard he sold them *Jane Eyre*, by
reading chapters of it aloud, and comparing for instance the
food in the school refectory that Jane Eyre had to eat with that
which they themselves got in their school canteen, they were
not interested. Indeed one day when he was walking down one
of the aisles between two rows of desks he asked one of the
girls, whose name was Lorna and who was pasty-faced and
blond, what was the last book she had read, and she replied,
  'Please, sir, I never read any books.'
  This answer amazed him for he could not conceive of a world
where one never read any books and he was the more determined
to introduce them to the activity which had given himself so
much pleasure. But the more enthusiastic he became, the more
eloquent his words, the more they withdrew into themselves till
finally he had to admit that he was completely failing with the
class. As he was very conscientious this troubled him, and not
even his success with the academic classes compensated for his
obvious lack of success with this particular class. He believed in
any event that failure with the non-academic classes constituted

failure as a teacher. He tried to do creative writing with them first by bringing in reproductions of paintings by Magritte which were intended to awaken in their minds a glimmer of the unexpectedness and strangeness of ordinary things, but they would simply look at them and point out to him their lack of resemblance to reality. He was in despair. His failure began to obsess him so much that he discussed the problem with the Head of Department who happened to be teaching *Rasselas* to the Sixth Form at the time with what success Mark could not gauge.

'I suggest you make them do the work,' said his Head of Department. 'There comes a point where if you do not impose your personality they will take advantage of you.'

But somehow or another Mark could not impose his personality on them: they had a habit for instance of forcing him to deviate from the text he was studying with them by mentioning something that had appeared in the newspaper.

'Sir,' they would say, 'did you see in the papers that there were two babies born from two wombs in the one woman.' Mark would flush angrily and say, 'I don't see what this has to do with our work,' but before he knew where he was he was in the middle of an animated discussion which was proceeding all around him about the anatomical significance of this piece of news. The fact was that he did not know how to deal with them: if they had been boys he might have threatened them with the last sanction of the belt, or at least frightened them in some way. But girls were different, one couldn't belt girls, and certainly he couldn't frighten this particular lot. They all wanted to be hairdressers: and one wanted to be an engineer having read in a paper that this was now a possible job for girls. He couldn't find it in his heart to tell her that it was highly unlikely that she could do this without Highers. They fantasised a great deal about jobs and chose ones which were well beyond their scope. It seemed to him that his years in Training College hadn't prepared him for this varied apathy and animated gossip. Sometimes one or two of them were absent and when he asked where they were was told that they were baby sitting. He dreaded the periods he had to try and teach them in, for as the year passed and autumn darkened into winter he knew that he had not taught them anything and he could not bear it.

He talked to other teachers about them, and the history man shrugged his shoulders and said that he gave them pictures to look at, for instance one showing women at the munitions during the First World War. It became clear to him that their other teachers had written them off since they would be leaving at the end of the session, anyway, and as long as they were quiet they were allowed to talk and now and again glance at the books with which they had been provided.

But Mark, whose first year this was, felt weighed down by his failure and would not admit to it. There must be something he could do with them, the failure was his fault and not theirs. Like a missionary he had come to them bearing gifts, but they refused them, turning away from them with total lack of interest. Keats, Shakespeare, even the ballads, shrivelled in front of his eyes. It was, curiously enough, Mr Morrison who gave him his most helpful advice. Mr Morrison spent most of his time making sure that his register was immaculate, first writing in the Os in pencil and then rubbing them out and re-writing them in ink. Mark had been told that during the Second World War while Hitler was advancing into France, Africa and Russia he had been insisting that his register was faultlessly kept and the names written in carefully. Morrison understood the importance of this though no one else did.

'What you have to do with them,' said Morrison, looking at Mark through his round glasses which were like the twin barrels of a gun, 'is to find out what they want to do.'

'But,' said Mark in astonishment, 'that would be abdicating responsibility.'

'That's right,' said Morrison equably.

'If that were carried to its conclusion,' said Mark, but before he could finish the sentence Morrison said,

'In teaching nothing ought to be carried to its logical conclusion.'

'I see,' said Mark, who didn't. But at least Morrison had introduced a new idea into his mind which was at the time entirely empty.

'I see,' he said again. But he was not yet ready to go as far as Morrison had implied that he should. The following day however he asked the class for the words of 'Paper Roses', one of the few pop songs that he had ever heard of. For the first time he saw a glimmer of interest in their eyes, for the first time they were actually using pens. In a short while they had given him the words from memory. Then he took out a book of Burns' poems and copied on to the board the verses of 'My Love is Like a Red Red Rose'. He asked them to compare the two poems but found that the wall of apathy had descended again and that it was as impenetrable as before. Not completely daunted, he asked them if they would bring in a record of 'Paper Roses', and himself found one of 'My Love is Like a Red Red Rose', with Kenneth Mackellar singing it. He played both songs, one after the other, on his own record player. They were happy listening to 'Paper Roses' but showed no interest in the other song. The discussion he had planned petered out, except that the following day a small girl with black hair and a pale face brought in a huge pile of records which she requested that he play and which he adamantly refused to do. It occurred to him that the girls simply did not have the ability to handle discussion, that in all cases where discussion was initiated it degenerated rapidly into gossip or vituperation or argument, that the concept of reason was alien to them, that in fact the long line of philosophers beginning with Plato was irrelevant to them. For a long time they brought in records now that they knew he had a record player but he refused to play any of them. Hadn't he gone far enough by playing 'Paper Roses'? No, he was damned if he would go the whole hog and surrender completely. And yet, he sensed that somewhere in this area of their interest was what he wanted, that from here he might find the lever which would move their world.

He noticed that their leader was a girl called Tracy, a fairly tall pleasant-looking girl to whom they all seemed to turn for response or rejection. Nor was this girl stupid: nor were any of them stupid. He knew that he must hang on to that, he must not believe that they were stupid. When they did come into the room it was as if they were searching for substance, a food which he could not provide. He began to study Tracy more and more as if she might perhaps give him the solution to his problem, but she did not appear interested enough to do so. Now and again she would hum the words of a song while engaged in combing another girl's hair, an activity which would satisfy them for hours, and indeed some of the girls had said to him, 'Tracy has a good voice, sir. She can sing any pop song you like.' And Tracy had regarded him with the sublime self-confidence of one who indeed could do this. But what use would that be to him? More and more he felt himself, as it were, sliding into their world when what he had wanted was to drag them out of the darkness into his world. That was how he himself had been taught and that was how it should be. And the weeks passed and he had taught them nothing. Their jotters were blank apart from the words of pop songs and certain secret drawings of their own. Yet they were human beings, they were not stupid. That there was no such thing as stupidity was the faith by which he lived. In many ways they were quicker than he was, they found out more swiftly than he did the dates of examinations and holidays. They were quite reconciled to the fact that they would not be able to pass any examinations. They would say,

'We're the stupid ones, sir.' And yet he would not allow them that easy option, the fault was not with them, it was with him. He had seen some of them serving in shops, in restaurants, and they were neatly dressed, good with money and polite. Indeed they seemed to like him, and that made matters worse for he felt that he did not deserve their liking. They are not fed, he quoted to himself from *Lycidas*, as he watched them at the checkout desks of supermarkets flashing a smile at him, placing the messages in bags much more expertly than he would have done. And indeed he felt that a question was being asked of him but not at all pressingly. At night he would read Shakespeare and think, There are some people to whom all this is closed. There are some who will never shiver as they read the lines

> Absent thee from felicity awhile
> and in this harsh world draw thy breath in pain
> to tell my story.

If he had read those lines to them they would have thought that it was Hamlet saying farewell to a girl called Felicity, he thought wryly. He smiled for the first time in weeks. Am I taking this too seriously, he asked himself. They are not taking it seriously. Shakespeare is not necessary for hairdressing. As they endlessly combed each other's hair he thought of the ballad of Sir Patrick Spens and the line

> wi gowd kaims in their hair.

These girls were entirely sensuous, words were closed to them. They would look after babies with tenderness but they were not interested in the alien world of language.

Or was he being a male chauvinist pig? No, he had tried everything he could think of and he had still failed. The fact was that language, the written word, was their enemy, McLuhan was right after all. The day of the record player and television had transformed the secure academic world in which he had been brought up. And yet he did not wish to surrender, to get on with correction while they sat talking quietly to each other, and dreamed of the jobs which were in fact shut against them. School was simply irrelevant to them, they did not even protest, they withdrew from it gently and without fuss. They had looked at education and turned away from it. It was their indifferent gentleness that bothered him more than anything. But they also had the maturity to distinguish between himself and education, which was a large thing to do. They recognised that he had a job to do, that he wasn't at all unlikeable and was in fact a prisoner like themselves. But they were already perming some woman's hair in a luxurious shop.

The more he pondered, the more he realised that they were the key to his failure or success in education. If he failed with them then he had failed totally, a permanent mark would be left on his psyche. In some way it was necessary for him to change, but the point was, could he change to the extent that was demanded of him, and in what direction and with what purpose should he change? School for himself had been a discipline and an order but to them this discipline and order had become meaningless.

The words on the blackboard were ghostly and distant as if they belonged to another age, another universe. He recalled what Morrison had said, 'You must find out what they want to do', but they themselves did not know what they wanted to do, it was for him to tell them that, and till he told them that they would remain indifferent and apathetic. Sometimes he sensed that they themselves were growing tired of their lives, that they wished to prove themselves but didn't know how to set about it. They were like lost children, irrelevantly stored in desks, and they only lighted up like street lamps in the evening or when they were working in the shops. He felt that they were the living dead, and he would have given anything to see their eyes become illuminated, become interested, for if he could find the magic formula he knew that they would become enthusiastic, they were *not* stupid. But how to find the magic key which would release the sleeping beauties from their sleep? He had no idea what it was and felt that in the end if he ever discovered it he would stumble over it and not be led to it by reflection or logic. And that was exactly what happened.

One morning he happened to be late coming into the room and there was Tracy swanning about in front of the class, as if she were wearing a gown, and saying some words to them he guessed in imitation of himself, while at the same time uncannily reproducing his mannerisms, leaning for instance despairingly across his desk, his chin on his hand while at the same time glaring helplessly at the class. It was like seeing himself slightly distorted in water, slightly comic, frustrated and yet angrily determined. When he opened the door there was a quick scurry and the class had arranged themselves, presenting blank dull faces as before. He pretended he had seen nothing, but knew now what he had to do. The solution had come to him as a gift from heaven, from the gods themselves, and the class sensed a new confidence and purposefulness in his voice.

'Tracy,' he said, 'and Lorna.' He paused. 'And Helen. I want you to come out here.'

They came out to the floor looking at him uneasily. O my wooden O, he said to himself, my draughty echo help me now.

'Listen,' he said, 'I've been thinking. It's quite clear to me that you don't want to do any writing, so we won't do any writing. But I'll tell you what we're going to do instead. We're going to act.'

A ripple of noise ran through the class, like the wind on an autumn day, and he saw their faces brightening. The shades of Shakespeare and Sophocles forgive me for what I am to do, he prayed.

'We are going,' he said, 'to do a serial and it's going to be called "The Rise of a Pop Star".' It was as if animation had returned to their blank dull faces, he could see life sparkling in their eyes, he could see interest in the way they turned to look at each other, he could hear it in the stir of movement that enlivened the room.

'Tracy,' he said, 'you will be the pop star. You are coming home from school to your parents' house. I'm afraid,' he added, 'that as in the reverse of the days of Shakespeare the men's parts will have be to be acted by the girls. Tracy, you have decided to leave home. Your parents of course disapprove. But you want to be a pop star, you have always wanted to be one. They think that that is a ridiculous idea. Lorna, you will be the mother, and Helen, you will be the father.'

He was astonished by the manner in which Tracy took over, by the ingenuity with which she and the other two created the first scene in front of his eyes. The scene grew and became meaningful, all their frustrated enthusiasm was poured into it.

First of all without any prompting Tracy got her school bag and rushed into the house while Lorna, the mother, pretended to be ironing on a desk that was quickly dragged out into the middle of the floor, and Helen the father read the paper, which was his own *Manchester Guardian* snatched from the top of his desk.

'Well, that's it over,' said Tracy, the future pop star.

'And what are you thinking of doing with yourself now?' said the mother, pausing from her ironing.

'I'm going to be a pop star,' said Tracy.

'What's that you said?' – her father, laying down the paper.

'That's what I want to do,' said Tracy, 'other people have done it.'

'What nonsense,' said the father. 'I thought you were going in for hairdressing.'

'I've changed my mind,' said Tracy.

'You won't stay in this house if you're going to be a pop star,' said the father. 'I'll tell you that for free.'

'I don't care whether I do or not,' said Tracy.

'And how are you going to be a pop star?' said her mother.

'I'll go to London,' said Tracy.

'London. And where are you going to get your fare from?' said the father, mockingly, picking up the paper again.

Mark could see that Tracy was thinking this over: it was a real objection. Where was her fare going to come from? She paused, her mind grappling with the problem.

'I'll sell my records,' she said at last.

Her father burst out laughing. 'You're the first one who starts out as a pop star by selling all your records.' And then in a sudden rage in which Mark could hear echoes of reality he shouted,

'All right then. Bloody well go then.'

Helen glanced at Mark, but his expression remained benevolent and unchanged.

Tracy, turning at the door, said, 'Well then, I'm going. And I'm taking the records with me.' She suddenly seemed very thin and pale and scrawny.

'Go on then,' said her father.

'That's what I'm doing. I'm going.' Her mother glanced from daughter to father and then back again but said nothing.

'I'm going then,' said Tracy, pretending to go to another room and then taking the phantom records in her arms. The father's face was fixed and determined and then Tracy looked at the two of them for the last time and left the room. The father and mother were left alone.

'She'll come back soon enough,' said the father but the mother still remained silent. Now and again the father would look at a phantom clock on a phantom mantelpiece but still Tracy did not return. The father pretended to go and lock a door and then said to his wife,

'I think we'd better go to bed.'

And then Lorna and Helen went back to their seats while Mark thought, this was exactly how dramas began in their bareness and naivety, through which at the same time an innocent genuine feeling coursed or peered as between ragged curtains.

When the bell rang after the first scene was over he found himself thinking about Tracy wandering the streets of London, as if she were a real waif sheltering in transient doss-houses or under bridges dripping with rain. The girls became real to him in their rôles whereas they had not been real before, nor even individualistic behind their wall of apathy. That day in the staff-room he heard about Tracy's saga and was proud and non-committal.

The next day the story continued. Tracy paced up and down the bare boards of the classroom, now and again stopping to look at ghostly billboards, advertisements. The girls had clearly been considering the next development during the interval they had been away from him, and had decided on the direction of the plot. The next scene was in fact an Attempted Seduction Scene.

Tracy was sitting disconsolately at a desk which he presumed was a table in what he presumed was a café.

'Hello, Mark,' she said to the man who came over to sit beside her. At this point Tracy glanced wickedly at the real Mark. The Mark in the play was the dark-haired girl who had asked for the records and whose name was Annie.

'Hello,' said Annie. And then, 'I could get you a spot, you know.'

'What do you mean?'

'There's a night club where they have a singer and she's sick. I could get you to take her place.' He put his hands on hers and she quickly withdrew her own.

'I mean it,' he said. 'If you come to my place I can introduce you to the man who owns the night club.'

Tracy searched his face with forlorn longing.

Was this another lie like the many she had experienced before? Should she, shouldn't she? She looked tired, her shoulders were slumped.

Finally she rose from the table and said, 'All right then.'

Together they walked about the room in search of his luxurious flat.

They found it. Willing hands dragged another desk out and set the two desks at a slight distance from each other.

The Mark of the play went over to the window-sill on which there was a large bottle which had once contained ink but was now empty. He poured wine into two phantom glasses and brought them over.

'Where is this man then?' said Tracy.

'He won't be long,' said Mark.

Tracy accepted the drink and Annie drank as well.

After a while Annie tried to put her hand around Tracy's waist. Mark the teacher glanced at the class: he thought that at this turn of events they would be convulsed with raucous laughter. But in fact they were staring enraptured at the two, enthralled by their performance. It occurred to him that he would never be as unselfconscious as Annie and Tracy in a million years. Such a shorn abject thing, such dialogue borrowed from television, and yet it was early drama that what he was seeing reminded him of. He had a quick vision of a flag gracing the roof of the 'theatre', as if the school now belonged to the early age of Elizabethanism. His poor wooden O was in fact echoing with real emotions and real situations, borrowed from the pages of subterraneous pop magazines.

Tracy stood up. 'I am not that kind of girl,' she said.

'What kind of girl?'

'That kind of girl.'

But Annie was insistent. 'You'll not get anything if you don't play along with me,' she said, and Mark could have sworn that there was an American tone to her voice.

'Well, I'm not playing along with you,' said Tracy. She swayed a little on her feet, almost falling against the blackboard. 'I'm bloody well not playing along with you,' she said. 'And that's final.' With a shock of recognition Mark heard her father's voice behind her own as one might see behind a similar painting the first original strokes.

And then she collapsed on the floor and Annie was bending over her.

'I didn't mean it,' she was saying. 'I really didn't mean it. I'm sorry.'

But Tracy lay there motionless and pale. She was like the Lady of Shalott in her boat. The girls in the class were staring at her. Look what they have done to me, Tracy was implying. Will they not be sorry now? There was a profound silence in the room and Mark was aware of the power of drama, even here in this bare classroom with the green peeling walls, the window-pole in the corner like a disused spear. There was nothing here but the hopeless emotion of the young.

Annie raised Tracy to her feet and sat her down in a chair.

'It's true,' he said, 'it's true that I know this man.' He went over to the wall and pretended to dial on a phantom phone. And at that moment Tracy turned to the class and winked at them. It was a bold outrageous thing to do, thought Mark, it was as if she was saying, That faint was of course a trick, a feint, that is the sort of thing people like us have to do in order to survive: he thought he was tricking me but all the time I was tricking him. I am alive, fighting, I know exactly what I am doing. All of us are in conspiracy against this Mark. So much, thought Mark, was conveyed by that wink, so much that was essentially dramatic. It was pure instinct of genius.

The stage Mark turned away from the phone and said, 'He says he wants to see you. He'll give you an audition. His usual girl's sick. She's got . . . ' Annie paused and tried to say 'laryngitis', but it came out as not quite right, and it was as if the word poked through the drama like a real error, and Mark thought of the Miracle plays in which ordinary people played Christ and Noah and Abraham with such unconscious style, as if there was no oddity in Abraham being a joiner or a miller.

'Look, I'll call you,' said the stage Mark and the bell rang and the finale was postponed. In the noise and chatter in which desks and chairs were replaced Mark was again aware of the movement of life, and he was happy. Absurdly he began to see them as if for the first time, their faces real and interested, and recognised the paradox that only in the drama had he begun to know them, as if only behind such a protection, a screen, were they willing to reveal themselves. And he began to wonder whether he himself had broken through the persona of the teacher and begun to 'act' in the real world. Their faces were more individual, sad or happy, private, extrovert, determined, yet vulnerable. It seemed to him that he had failed to see what Shakespeare was really about, he had taken the wrong road to find him.

'A babble of green fields,' he thought with a smile. So that was what it meant, that Wooden O, that resonator of the transient, of the real, beyond all the marble of their books, the white In Memoriams which they could not read.

How extraordinarily curious it all was.

The final part of the play was to take place on the following day.

'Please sir,' said Lorna to him, as he was about to leave.

'What is it?'

But she couldn't put into words what she wanted to say. And it took him a long time to decipher from her broken language what it was she wanted. She and the other actresses wanted an audience. Of course, why had he not thought of that before? How could he not have realised that an audience was essential? And he promised her that he would find one.

By the next day he had found an audience which was composed of a 3A class which Miss Stewart next door was taking. She grumbled a little about the Interpretation they were missing but eventually agreed. Additional seats were taken into Mark's room from her room and Miss Stewart sat at the back, her spectacles glittering.

Tracy pretended to knock on a door which was in fact the blackboard and then a voice invited her in. The manager of the night club pointed to a chair which stood on the 'stage'.

'What do you want?'

'I want to sing, sir.'

'I see. Many girls want to sing. I get girls in here every day. They all want to sing.'

Mark heard titters of laughter from some of the boys in 3A and fixed a ferocious glare on them. They settled down again.

'But I know I can sing, sir,' said Tracy. 'I know I can.'

'They all say that too.' His voice suddenly rose, 'They all bloody well say that.'

Mark saw Miss Stewart sitting straight up in her seat and then glancing at him disapprovingly. Shades of Pygmalion, he thought to himself, smiling. You would expect it from Shaw, inside inverted commas.

'Give it to them, sock it to them,' he pleaded silently. The virginal Miss Stewart looked sternly on.

'Only five minutes then,' said the night club manager, glancing at his watch. Actually there was no watch on his hand at all. 'What song do you want to sing?'

Mark saw Lorna pushing a desk out to the floor and sitting in it. This was to be the piano, then. The absence of props bothered him and he wondered whether imagination had first begun among the poor, since they had such few material possessions. Lorna waited, her hands poised above the desk. He heard more sniggerings from the boys and this time he looked so angry that he saw one of them turning a dirty white.

The hands hovered above the desk. Then Tracy began to sing. She chose the song 'Heartache'.

> My heart, dear, is aching;
> I'm feeling so blue.
> Don't give me more heartaches,
> I'm pleading with you.

It seemed to him that at that moment, as she stood there pale and thin, she was putting all her experience and desires into her song. It was a moment he thought such as it is given to few to experience. She was in fact auditioning before a phantom audience, she and the heroine of the play were the same, she was searching for recognition on the streets of London, in a school. She stood up in her vulnerability, in her purity, on a bare stage where there was no furniture of any value, of any price: on just such a stage had actors and actresses acted many years before, before the full flood of Shakespearean drama. Behind her on the blackboard were written notes about the Tragic Hero, a concept which he had been discussing with the Sixth Year.

'The hero has a weakness and the plot of the play attacks this specific weakness.'

'We feel a sense of waste.'

'And yet triumph.'

Tracy's voice, youthful and yearning and vulnerable, soared to the cracked ceiling. It was as if her frustrations were released in the song.

> Don't give me more heartaches,
> I'm pleading with you.

The voice soared on and then after a long silence the bell rang.

The boys from 3A began to chatter and he thought, 'You don't even try. You wouldn't have the nerve to sing like that, to be so naked.' But another voice said to him, 'You're wrong. They're the same. It is we who have made them different.' But were they in fact the same, those who had been reduced to the nakedness, and those others who were the protected ones. He stood there trembling as if visited by a revelation which was only broken when Miss Stewart said,

'Not quite Old Vic standard.' And then she was gone with her own superior brood. You stupid bitch, he muttered under his breath, you Observer-Magazine-reading bitch who never liked anything in your life till some critic made it respectable, who wouldn't recognise a good line of poetry or prose till sanctified by the voice of London, who would never have arrived at Shakespeare on your own till you were given the crutches.

And he knew as he watched her walking, so seemingly self-sufficient, in her black gown across the hall that she was as he had been and would be no longer. He had taken a journey with his class, a pilgrimage across the wooden boards, the poor abject furnitureless room which was like their vision of life, and from that journey he and they had learned in spite of everything. In spite of everything, he shouted in his mind, we have put a flag out there and it is there even during the plague, even if Miss Stewart visits it. It is there in spite of Miss Stewart, in spite of her shelter and her glasses, in spite of her very vulnerable armour, in spite of her, in spite of everything.

In the School

They came in to the school through a window, Terry handing the can of petrol to the other two who were waiting on the floor of the boiler-room down below. It was the evening of a fine summer's day, and the school was empty, for it was the holidays.

Terry, the mad one, walked along the corridor first, the other two behind him as they always did, and always had done. Usually Terry was shouting and playing about but tonight he was quiet, at least at first. It had been his plan, for he hated the school, he hated it with a bitter hatred and he wanted to destroy it. He hated the teachers, he hated his parents, he hated the whole world. He was a burning simmering fire of hatred, always on the edge of explosion, and it seemed to him that fire was the only answer to the fire inside him. Time and time again he had been belted, for he was either fighting other boys in the school – when the force inside him demanded violence, as if it were a demon from hell – or he was demanding money with menaces, for he was poor, or he was creating some novel or ancient kind of trouble in the classroom. The very last day of term he had fought a boy in the cloakroom and had broken his nose. The boy had looked at him that second too long, but it was enough. Terry hated anyone staring at him, as if he were a freak or something. He had been given six of the belt and that had been his farewell to the school, the headmaster standing at the door shaking his dim wormy head, the belt in his hand.

Terry hated the school because he didn't want to be there in the first place, especially after getting up in the morning to the interminable quarrels between his father and mother ('Get off my back,' his mother would shout. 'Why don't you shove off?'), the crowded house where the other three children would fight each other as well. He never had any money or if he had it was money he had screwed out of pupils, usually first year ones, who did not dare to report him to their parents, and usually said that they had lost it. He had a job in Woolworth's for three weeks before he was found carrying a hundred cigarettes home, concealed beneath his jersey. Sometimes he would go into insane rages and beat his fists against a stone wall till the blood came.

He walked on, swinging his can, and suddenly out of the quietness began to shout obscenities, completely forgetting where he was or what the dangers might be: or maybe it was, thought Roddy, that he didn't care, that he wanted teachers to appear so that he could fight them.

The other two, Roddy and Frankie, followed him as they had always done, Frankie indeed imitating Terry's walk. Frankie was like a small cinder, ginger-haired and pale, without Terry's flamboyant madness but with hard deep cold eyes. The two of them admired Terry because he didn't care for anyone, and if he was belted he never cried, he held his hand out disdainfully as if belting were an awful bore which he despised. Nothing mattered to Terry, he was a spark of hatred, he was the king. Time and time again they had seen him do things that they themselves would never have dared to do. They had seen him square up to Baney, the Chemistry teacher, and Baney had backed down, only saying weakly that he would send Terry to the headmaster, but he never did. They had seen him break calmly in half the ruler the Mathematics teacher had given him and sit back in his seat arms folded. They had seen him setting fire to a girl's hair at the back of the Assembly when the headmaster had been going on about Jesus and the disciples who had been ordinary men. They knew very well what the headmaster had been really saying, they were the ordinary fishermen and the headmaster was one of the top ones like Jesus. They weren't stupid, they knew what was going on all right, they could read between the lines though they couldn't read the lines themselves very well. And that guff at the prize-giving by that fat git that there were some people who didn't win prizes but that didn't make them any worse than the ones who did: they knew just the same what would happen if their mothers or fathers tried to get on to the platform where the women with the flowered hats sat, and the men with the bald heads and blue suits.

They walked along the corridor as far as the Maths room into which they looked at the crummy equations which were still on the blackboard. The Maths room was not their target but nevertheless Terry urinated all over the boxes full of exercise books in the corner. He did this patiently and steadily, playing arcs of water up as high as the desk and then onwards as far as the door.

'Hey,' he shouted to Frankie, 'you get along to the Art room and get paper. We need paper for the fire. Piles of the stuff.'

Frankie turned and went, for he was used to acting as Terry's message boy, he was like a legate sent to the provinces by his commander. The last they saw of him was when he swaggered through the door of the Maths room on his way upstairs.

After he had urinated Terry got a piece of chalk and first rubbing the equations off the board began to draw what purported to be the teacher's sexual organs in considerable detail. He spent the whole fifteen minutes on this, his tongue stuck out, absolutely concentrated on his task, as if he were an artist who had forgotten where he was. At times not happy with what he had done, he rubbed it all out, and began again. After a while he drew back from his masterpiece, studying it with an appraising scrutiny as if he were in an art gallery and said, 'Hey, that's great, Rod, ain't it? Ain't that great?' Roddy nodded for unlike Terry he believed that too much talking was sissy and he modelled himself on Clint Eastwood. 'Ain't that great,' Terry said again and began to dance up and down among the boxes of books like a Zulu. Sometimes Roddy thought Terry was crazy, like the time he had jumped off the bus which was going at thirty miles an hour so that he wouldn't have to pay his fare, and he had rolled over and over on the street like a cat. In his phantom Mexican hat and lethal black uniform, Roddy wondered whether Terry would have done the same thing if a car had been coming, and concluded that he probably would have.

They left the Maths room, Terry giving a final look at his masterpiece as if reluctant to leave it, since no one would see it till the school started again after the holidays. The school was ominously quiet and it bothered Roddy though it didn't seem to bother Terry at all. Like Terry, Roddy was used to noise and movement, either the movement of the world outside – traffic, shouting, fighting – or the noise of the family in the crowded tenement where he lived. He hated total silence about him though he himself never talked much. He hated those periods of silent reading when that bag Simmons made them read *Kidnapped* or *Treasure Island* and you felt as if you could scream, the room was so quiet. The tension built up inside you so that you had to clench your teeth to prevent yourself from howling like a wolf. He wanted to stand up and throw a brick at Simmons, to kick her in, to flatten her long quivering nose. Sometimes she would look up from her own reading – for she read with them, 'to set a good example' – and a stare of naked hatred – the more bitter for being unseen by anyone except themselves – would pass between them across the room. Oh, he knew she hated him all right and she knew that he hated her. She didn't want people like him, she wanted people who were interested in books, who did what they were told, who sucked up to her in their new uniforms. Who cared about books anyway, the letters of the words were so hard to focus on. It was like trying to see the number of a bus on a wet day when the streets were glistening and your shoes and socks were soaking. The letters danced about in front of his eyes, like that red cloak he had seen them passing in front of the bulls on the telly, he would like to batter them stupid so that they would stay still. He identified himself with the bull, not the toreador, he would have liked to sink his horns into that dancing poof.

They stopped, this time outside the gym, and as they did so Terry suddenly said, 'Frankie's taking a long time. What the hell's happened to him?' And Roddy felt again that strange ominous silence of the school He suddenly had the weird thought, Why don't they protect it, defend it? It must be because of something that he didn't know about. The entry had been too easy, the silence too prolonged. The school looked so defenceless, there had been no obvious attempt to keep people like him and Terry out. It was odd. They listened but they could hear nothing, not Frankie, not anybody. The stillness was appalling and the school was so clean, the floors were newly washed and there was a smell of disinfectant everywhere. The two of them stood there in the middle of the silence.

Suddenly Terry followed by Roddy turned into the gym and that too was silent. From the stage end they looked down the length of the polished floor, at the tiers of slats which climbed the wall like a weir, at the ropes which were tied together, at the horse and the buck, at the box with the yellow footballs, at the roof with its acreage of glass.

Terry put down the can of petrol and said, 'Let's have a game. One against one.' And with his usual vividness and mad spontaneity he stripped off his jacket and shirt to make two goalposts at one end of the gym while Roddy had to do the same. Then they got a yellow ball out of the box and they began to play in the vast gym all by themselves on that summer evening. Terry did things like that – he sometimes forgot what he had come to do – but you couldn't cross him, he might turn on you and beat you up, out of the blue, or even knife you. You didn't know what he might do next, he was like a spark carried on a strange wind of his own.

Terry played like a madman with ferocious energy. He believed that he was a great footballer, though he wasn't, for he was too unco-ordinated. He believed that he was playing in the World Cup and that thousands of voices, like one, were applauding in an untranslatable language of their own. He pushed Roddy away with all his strength, committing every foul that was possible, at one time tripping him up as he was about to score.

'That was a penalty,' said Roddy.

'Penalty my arse,' said Terry, 'you don't have penalties in a one to one, you stupid bugger.' And the two of them stared into each other's eyes, but it was Roddy's eyes that fell first, confronted by the savage undeviating glare that shone out of Terry's gaze. At moments like these Terry seemed to forget who you were, that you were his mate, and he would be ready to do you. His whole body and his whole mind were concentrated on winning. He hacked at Roddy's feet when he had the ball, he elbowed him fiercely, at one stage he nearly bit him, and all the time he would be weaving up and down as he had seen players do in the World Cup.

Then after he was winning two-one he flopped down on the floor of the gym, and said, 'That's enough. I'm shagged out.' And he stayed there for a while, staring up at the glass roof where there was a small bird flying about, after coming in through a broken pane. It beat at the glass but it couldn't get out.

'Stupid bastard,' said Terry, looking up at it. Roddy lay down beside him and thought that once he had lain like that in the past when his family had gone for a day to Loch Lomondside: and he had a memory of water flowing, and a few white clouds floating about like ice-cream. Suddenly as they lay on the wooden floor Terry began to punch him and then the two of them were rolling over and over, kicking and gouging, till finally Terry was on top, his mad eyes glaring into Roddy's and it seemed for a moment as if he would choke him to death. Then the craziness drained out of his eyes and he got to his feet, put on his shirt and jacket and prepared to leave the room.

Roddy did the same. On their way out Terry retrieved the petrol can.

And then Roddy said, 'Where's Frankie got to? Where the hell . . . ' The silence enfolded them again, the eerie silence.

'Maybe the wee bugger's gone home,' said Terry. 'Maybe he didn't have the guts for it.'

But Roddy wasn't sure about that. For a strange moment he thought he saw out of the corner of his eye a flash of black like a bird's wing passing, but that was impossible. That must surely be impossible.

'You go and have a dekko,' said Terry. 'You go. See if Frankie's there.' No no no something deep in Roddy said. No no no and it was like the voice of a bird, a big black bird.

'Come on, Terry,' he said, 'let's get it finished with. Get the petrol on and let's get out of here. Frankie's gone home, that's what it is.'

But Terry was adamant. 'No, you go and have a dekko.' And

he stood there solidly, the can still in his hand. 'I'll be in Grotty's room. That's where we start it. Bring the paper. Bring Frankie and the paper. I'll be there. Right?' He was like a commander giving orders to his staff or to the troops. 'You get along there.'

And all the time the voice was telling Roddy not to go. The place was too quiet. There was something funny about it. There was no noise anywhere, not even a tiny creak. Even the slats in the gym, climbing up to the roof, had looked oddly still, and the ropes hanging down like snakes. And the buck standing in the centre on its own. Everything looked unprotected and waiting. There had been no real smell there as there used to be from the boys as they waited to start their exercises. There had been no human stink of dirty socks. There was only the neutral smell of disinfectant everywhere.

He stood at one end of the corridor glancing back at Terry and at that moment Terry looked like an ape swinging the can of petrol in his hand. Christ, what were they doing there, as if they had all the time in the world, as if they were on a visit or a tour of the place? Why hadn't they just put it on fire as they had meant to do? But this place was like a church, as silent as a church, but instead of incense there was only the smell of polish and disinfectant.

He was frightened. He should just turn and run but he couldn't because Terry was there and Terry would get him later, there was no escape from him. You couldn't get away from Terry. You hated and admired him at the same time. He himself hated Terry but in a different way from that in which the teachers hated him. He hated him because he had never beaten him. Even in the gym Terry had cheated and he had to take it because there was nothing else he could do. Terry made his own rules: for instance he had decided to stop playing when he was leading two-one.

Oh, bugger it, he must go and get the paper and if Frankie had been playing about, then he would do him. If he couldn't do Terry then he would do Frankie. He turned abruptly away. Terry was laughing like a maniac at the far end of the corridor with the can in his hand.

Terry watched Roddy go. He would wait there till the two of them came back, he couldn't do anything without the paper. He stood against the wall and laid the petrol can down in front of him. He stared along the corridor and could see nothing, just the wall painted a bilious green. It was like the wall of a prison he had once seen in a film, blotched and patchy. He waited. He wished he had a watch but he didn't have one – he'd lost the one he had nicked from the jeweller's – other people had watches but he had none. Other people had football strips but he had none. Other people had hi-fis but he had none. He waited. And up above there was silence. He fancied for a moment that there were guards up there as there were in prisons on the films. No Frankie, no Roddy. For a second he thought he saw something flicker but no that couldn't be right. He waited and they didn't come. He knew that they could have gone along the top and down another stair and out of the school that way: perhaps the two of them had got the shakes and run home.

The buggers. Everyone left you in the end, even your mother and father. Everyone looked out for himself. If it hadn't been for his fire of hatred and strength he would have been ground down to the earth long ago. If it hadn't been for the rage that smouldered inside him and never went out, ready at any moment to burst into flame, he would have been finished.

You had to fight for yourself or people would get you. Or if they didn't get you they would betray you. You couldn't trust anyone. You had to fight for everything, for every scrap of property. Like that headmaster: he thought he was up there with Jesus and you were down here with the fishermen. They all thought you were stupid but it didn't seem to occur to them that you thought they were stupid. He himself wasn't stupid, he knew he wasn't stupid, not deep down inside himself. It was the stuff you had to do that didn't make sense. It made you scream with rage keeping you here doing things like maths and English which didn't have anything to do with anything. He'd never heard anyone speak like they spoke in the books. His father and mother never spoke like that. And what were these triangles in aid of. He'd never seen one outside school in his whole life. Anyway he could sort his father out now. One night he had held a knife at his throat when he was lying in bed. He had asked him for money and his father had whispered, 'You'll find it in my jacket.' He wouldn't have been able to do that if his father didn't have a bad back.

He passed his hands over his eyes. He couldn't allow himself to do that when the other two were there. They would think you were weak if you told them you got headaches now and then. You always had to show that you weren't weak, you had to keep it up all the time. Bugger them. They must have gone home. He'd just have to go to Grotty's room himself and hope that there was paper there. Because they had betrayed him he felt bitter: he felt as if he wanted to burn them down as well as the school. He wanted to see them running like rats among the flames like in that warehouse they had broken into one Sunday and set on fire. There was nothing like a fire, it was so really powerful, nothing could stand against it, it was great when you made it yourself and you saw it coming into action like a servant, especially in those old buildings when the rats ran about in the flame and the smoke, and the little buggers didn't know where they were going.

He walked along the corridor carrying the can in his hand and arrived at the Latin room. He never took Latin, they said he was too stupid, but one day when he was making a noise in the room next to it, jumping up and down on one of the desks, the Latin teacher, Grotty, had come in and taken him out and given him six. He hadn't forgotten that, especially as the Latin teacher didn't have people like him in his class, and he only took the best, though he had belted him just the same after he had made sarcastic remarks about him first in front of the class, using long words that he didn't understand. Barbaric it was, he wouldn't forget that.

He arrived at Grotty's room and looked round it. The desks here were clean with no names carved on them, there were pictures of temples and people with skirts on the walls, and on the board were words which he didn't understand. He went up and looked at them.

INSULA he spelt out aloud and then he spat at the word.

What the hell sort of word was that? Who wanted to know about these bloody words, the other ones were bad enough. He spat again and again and then finding a black gown hanging on a nail pussy-footed about in it for a while like a poof or a ballet dancer, before finally tearing it into ribbons, sometimes using his teeth. He found a piece of chalk and scrawled stuff all over the desks and sometimes there were not only single words but sentences, almost the beginning of a story, his story. The only Roman he had ever heard of was Julius Caesar and he wrote on one desk JULIUS CAESAR WAS A POOF and burst out laughing crazily. It never occurred to him that no one would see what he had written.

Then in a frenzy of activity he began to gather desks together. He pulled at the handle of the weakest-looking cupboard till he opened it and a pile of old dusty papers – examination papers – came pouring out. He picked them from the floor and then put them inside the desks and prepared to pour petrol over them, but then a thought struck him and he got the wastepaper basket which was made of wicker, and put that in the desk as well, among the papers, standing out of them.

As he was doing this he thought he saw a black flicker again but paid no attention as he was too busy with what he was doing. The familiar lust was growing in him like sex. Sometimes the fire as it swirled and grew and changed shape was like a bint's body moving and curvaceous. It was like one of those bints you saw on the TV sometimes, advertising chocolate or a drink. He bent over the desk as if over an experiment and his mind was totally focussed on what he was doing. He was like a Frankenstein, he suddenly thought, and he flashed two of his teeth like fangs at the desk piled with papers. For the moment he had forgotten about Roddy and Frankie, he would sort them out later anyway. He would put the boot in. He was like a mad scientist bowed over the desk. He raised the can. And at that moment a movement flickered at the corner of his eye and he looked up. He turned and stared at the door and he saw him standing at the door in his black gown.

The man in the black gown was looking at him and the man

in the black gown had no face, and the gown was dusty and had holes in it. Terry screamed and threw the petrol can straight at him as he ran for the door. He went through the dusty gown, right through it, and the can rolled along the corridor spilling the petrol as it went. It rolled along the polished floor. Terry ran along the corridor at full speed as if he were making for an invisible tape, his tongue hanging out, his eyes rolling in his head. Then at the end of the corridor he saw another man and he had no face either. Terry turned back and the other man, the one from the Latin room, was walking towards him. Terry stood in the middle of the corridor not knowing where to go. Then he saw more and more of them. They were coming out of the classrooms, out of the walls, like huge black insects. All of them were in dusty black gowns and they had no faces or if they had they were the colour of chalk. Terry stood there and watched them, his breath going in and out. Steadily and unhurriedly at a grave pace they came towards him. He cowered down on his knees in the corridor. They made a ring round him and they looked down at him. He stared at his own hands which were beating like a fish against the floor. They stared down at him and they had no faces. He looked up and he screamed and he screamed and he screamed.

And his hands beat against the floor with all the life that was in them.

His hands beat on the floor in the silence.

Mr Trill in Hades

One afternoon Mr Trill, dead classics master of Eastborough Grammar School, found himself in Hades.

The journey across the river had been a pleasant one, for the boatman had been fairly communicative though he had a small stubby black pipe in his mouth from which he exhaled meditative smoke rings across the water.

Mr Trill was quite happy to sit in the stern and now and again like a boy dip his hand in the quiet waves. Nevertheless he was quite excited and asked the boatman a few questions.

'Did you have many going over this morning?'

'No, not many to speak of,' said the boatman.

Mr Trill was silent for a while wondering what sort of life this was, ferrying people from one side of a river to another, and perhaps not even having a holiday in one's whole life.

As if the boatman had understood what he was thinking he said helpfully.

'It's in the family, you see.'

In the family? Did that mean that the job passed down from father to son, or did it mean that the whole family took alternate turns at the job? He imagined a great number of ferrymen, each wearing a cap like this and each smoking a black pipe, unless of course there were women who could also, he assumed, be able to carry out the task of being a ferryman.

'The class of passenger has gone down,' said the ferryman. 'You don't get the same type now.'

'I can believe that,' said Mr Trill and in fact he did believe it.

Even in his own school since comprehensive education the quality had deteriorated, and he hadn't been very fond of the last headmaster who was a large bearish barbaric man, a comedian among the dignified photographs of his renowned predecessors.

'I can tell the intelligent ones from the unintelligent ones,' said the boatman pulling steadily at the oars. 'You're one of the intelligent ones. You turned the board over so that I could see the white side, according to instructions. Some of the other ones wait there all day not knowing what to do. How am I supposed to know that they are there if they don't turn the board over? That is what I would like to know.'

'That's very true,' said Mr Trill. 'That's very true,' he muttered again.

'One of them,' said the boatman, 'stayed there all day and he hadn't the gumption to turn the board over though our instructions were staring him in the face. When I crossed over – because my son who has sharper eyes than I have saw him – do you know what he said?'

'No,' said Mr Trill, 'what did he say?'

'He said it was my job to make sure that he was there. You should be reported, he said to me. But I knew he didn't have any class. His suitcase had an old belt round it.'

He was silent for a while and then added, 'He was going to report me. You're all the same, he said, you ferrymen, lazy good for nothings. All you want is your obols and you don't care about the passengers. I suppose you'll be putting in for a rise next. I nearly told him to go to hell . . . but it didn't matter as he was going there anyway.'

'I can see that,' said Mr Trill who hadn't laughed, since he didn't have much sense of humour. When he was teaching he would stride into the classroom, the Vergil open in front of him, and without raising his eye from the book ask someone to read. Sometimes there might be a long silence and only then would Mr Trill know that the person whom he had asked to read was absent. He had a long Roman nose and a shock of gingery hair and the energy of a dynamo. His landlady thought he was crazy and he himself didn't like women or bingo. He had never married. His father had also been a classics master who had married a girl employed in the school canteen. She had taught him about carpets, curtains, furniture and paint.

'Well, here we are,' said the boatman, 'and there's your case.'

Trill felt in his pocket but found he had no money for the trip.

'That's all right,' said the boatman. 'We're all on fixed rates now. Cheers.'

He turned back to the opposite bank and Mr Trill stood on the one where he had landed and looked about him.

There was a lot of mist and he couldn't see clearly where he was but the air was mild and gentle.

He didn't feel at all hungry after his trip and it occurred to him that he wouldn't feel any hunger as long as he . . . as long as he was in the place where he was.

'Well, well,' he said to himself, 'this is very nice. Very nice indeed and I don't feel at all afraid as I did when I left for the first time to go to university.' He walked forward and saw beneath him a valley in which he thought he could make out dim shapes here and there lolling about, some of them gazing into space.

He descended into it and found himself beside a number of people who were sitting talking to each other but who immediately stopped when they saw him.

One man with a red nose who seemed to be their leader asked.

'You new?'

'Yes,' said Mr Trill, thinking of the boarding school of many years before, the dormitory, the cricket matches, the basins with cold water.

'Thought I hadn't seen you before. My name is Aphareus. Served in the Trojan War . . . And my comrades here. The same.'

'Course,' he added, 'we're on our own here. The officers don't mix with the privates . . . '

'What do you do with yourselves then?' said Trill.

'Do with ourselves? There's no need to do anything with ourselves. We're quite happy here aren't we, old pals?'

Seated on the grass the others looked at him calmly.

Mr Trill inhaled deeply and said, 'You were in the Trojan War?'

'We were that, weren't we, old pals. We always stick together. Lived and died together. From Greece we all are.'

Naturally.

Achilles, Agamemnon, Hector, Ajax, those marvellous heroes, they had seen them all.

'Course we saw them. Served under Agamemnon. Didn't know his arse from his elbow. And we got news what happened to him. Took ten years to get into that bloody town. Course we died before that, most of us.'

What had it been like?

'To tell you the truth, they used to come out and we used to get out and fight them. There were as many gods there as soldiers, some taking one side, some the other. Most of the time we were pretty bored. Fighting, lying in bed, watching that wall for years, knew every stone of it. Course we had our own wall, too, all round the ships. All we wanted was to go home. But that was not to be. They had to make a wooden horse to get in there. I call that cheating but that was Ulysses for you. All he was interested in was himself. Bright as a needle, mind you, stocky little man. And there was old Agamemnon fighting with Achilles all the time, and bringing his own daughter out for sacrifice so that the ships could move. I'd have told the gods to stuff themselves 'fore I would do that.'

'But . . . ' said Mr Trill.

'Look around you, friend, whoever you are. Do you see that hill up there? That's where the officers are. They never mix with us, never talk to us. Have you had your entry noted yet?'

'No.'

'They'll do that right enough. They know all about us. Amazing how they didn't put the tags on you. We think it's something to do with that castle but no one's ever been in it, no one we know anyway. Do you see it over there?'

When Mr Trill looked in the direction the man was pointing he saw a big shape swirling indecisively in the mist.

'There's a river there,' said Aphareus. 'People have tried to cross it. But they never make it. No one knows what's in there. They say they have hounds patrolling all the time. Anyway, who cares? We're quite happy here. But to get back to that lot, they were pretty punk, acting like women all the time. Like little girls. Imagine taking all that time to a siege. And all done by a trick in the end, not good honest fighting, spear against spear, but a trick. It makes me puke to think of it. No strategy, just stand there and slog it out all the time, or retreat to the ships, our side, or to the town, their side. Agamemnon didn't know how to handle Achilles, that was the trouble. If it had been me I would have sent him home with his tail between his legs, like a dog. Year after year we sat staring at that wall and year after year our children grew up and we never saw them. And the officers divided the women among themselves whenever they got any. And when did we privates get women or wine, I ask you. I remember when I got killed I didn't mind it, the time had felt so long. I didn't care when I saw the spear coming at me, it went right through my shield, of course I didn't have a shield with ten layers as Ajax had. And the Big Boss himself had ten strips of enamel on his with a snake on it. Isn't that right, fellows, I didn't care?'

They all nodded their heads as if they had heard the story over and over again and would never grow tired of it.

'I'll tell you something, we could have finished the war for them ourselves but who listens to the likes of us? Tell you about Agamemnon. He used to come round and speak to us now and again. You could tell he didn't have a clue, a big red-faced fellow, very hearty but false. Ulysses and Nestor, they were the ones who were really running the show. But Agamemnon, he was always smiling and waving from his chariot but he didn't have a clue. 'You'll be home for the festivities,' he'd say, 'you trust me, lads.' And we didn't trust him at all. And who stood there year after year though it had nothing to do with them? Us. What did it have to do with us, tell me that. A whore and a man who couldn't keep his wife. Paris, you know, was always firing arrows, you hardly ever saw him with a sword in his hand. I'm telling you I would have knocked Agamemnon off and gone home, only I didn't think of it at the time. But then Menelaus was his brother, it was all in the family, not that Agamemnon ever thought much of Menelaus, about as much as Hector thought of Paris. They told us it was a patriotic war, patriotic my arse, and then they told us that it would make us all richer with all the plunder we would get. But who got all the plunder? I'll tell you, it was the officers, and who got a spear in his guts if he fell asleep on watch? I'll tell you, we did. But how could it make us richer, I ask you? I had a little piece of ground and a wife and children. What did I want with Troy? Nothing. And when I saw that man with the spear I was so bored . . . I didn't mind. I wasn't at all frightened. And yet to die like that so far from home, with all these dogs feeding off you . . . But the thing is that I didn't have any respect for Agamemnon. There he is up on that hill and Achilles sits on another hill. They hold court there and they never speak to each other except on a Friday. Hector and Achilles will speak to each other, funnily enough, but not the other two. And as for his daughter she's never approached him since he came here, though he was looking out for that. She's never forgiven him, he believed too much in the gods, you see. Rest of us didn't give a bugger. We're quite happy here, though, we don't mind. You tell him your story, Patroclus.'

'Not the . . . ?'

'No, no, this is a different Patroclus.' And they all laughed as if they had made a good joke.

'It was like this,' said Patroclus, a tall young fellow with glimmering fair hair. 'One day I seen her standing at a little window which was in the wall. I don't know what I was doing there on my own.'

'Picking daisies more than likely,' said one of his friends and there was more laughter.

'Anyway I seen her and I knew her. I don't know how I knew but I did. She wasn't what I would call beautiful. She had a sort of thin face with high cheekbones and a cropped head. Not much flesh to her. But they say that she must have had it somewhere else, if you understand me . . . Anyway she had Paris in a net. So I spoke to her. It was evening, late like. I just saw her there and everything was peaceful like, I went up to her same as I would go up to you and I said to her, Why don't you go back to Greece, just like that, I said to her. Why don't you go back to Greece? And all she said was, I wouldn't go back for all the world. And you could see she was enjoying herself. I wouldn't go back for all the world, that was what she said. Didn't I tell you that when I came back, lads?'

They all nodded their heads again, having heard the same story with avid hunger for century after century.

'I saw her plain as plain can be and she was standing looking out that little window and there was no blood in her cheeks at all, dead white she was, and I, thinking of all the lads here, said, Why don't you go back to Greece? And all she said was, I wouldn't go back for the whole world. And she was smiling all the time and she spoke in that upper class accent. And then, do you know it came to me, I was telling the lads about it, I knew then that they was all enjoying the war, all these officers and captains, they was enjoying the war, the war was passing the time for them, and they was making names for themselves . . . It was a short time after that that I was killed.'

Amazed by what he had heard, Trill rose to his feet and left the soldiers. Was that then what the Trojan War had been like? Had Agamemnon known nothing of strategy? Had he just been a big red-faced fellow who was telling the soldiers that they would be home in time for the festivities? Surely not. Surely that was not what Trill had read in the big Latin and Greek translations when he was still young and his parents were as usual quarrelling.

'What is that boy doing sitting there day after day?' his mother would say. 'And why is he letting all the other boys walk all over him?' Her beak snapped at him all the time while his father crept into his study for peace but even then she would put her snout round the corner and peck at him.

'And you too sitting in there reading and marking when there's painting to be done. When are you going to do something about the lawn and the garage?' And so he and his father would try to hide together in the study while the merciless fusillade stormed on. Carpets, curtains, ornaments, that was all his mother was interested in.

'All that rubbish that happened long ago, what is that to you? You don't go out and meet people, that's what's wrong with you. You're living in the past.'

And then she had started going to Bingo and he and his father had been left in peace, till she came home at night and then she would start again. 'I met the headmaster's wife and she wouldn't speak to me. Who does she think she is? Just because I used to work in the school canteen she thinks she won't speak to me. I can tell her that I did a good day's work with the best of them instead of sitting on my bum as she does, drinking coffee all day. I had to work for my living and I'll have you know that. I didn't sit in my room all day reading about the past. Tell me, what are you going to do about the car? Are you going to trade it in or not? That's what I want to know and that's what you've got to tell me.'

And her voice droned on and on and his father would look at Trill as if he was begging forgiveness for bringing his mother into the house in the first place. And Mr Trill would sit with his father as if he was his companion for he preferred to be with him than to be out playing with the rough boys who were always going on about sex and how long their things were.

That was at the beginning before he was sent to boarding school, but even then Mr Trill liked to haul out his big books from his father's shelves and try to read them.

'Why don't you get a proper big house?' his mother would say to his father. 'You've been in this house for years. I thought when we got married we would have a bigger house but no, not you. You just want to stay in this old house till they put you in a box and I'm ashamed in front of all the other teachers' wives. Why have they all got bigger houses than you? And why don't you put in for the headmaster's job? You've as much right to it as anyone else, isn't that true? You've worked hard enough. You slave there every night and no one can speak to you.'

And the voice would continue, the beak would clack and the two, father and son, would huddle together in the study. And sometimes his father would tell him stories such as the one about Orpheus and Eurydice, and Mr Trill would listen with bated breath. What a tragic beautiful story, that lady moving about Hades in white while Orpheus played his lyre to the cruel god.

And there he was . . . For Mr Trill had wandered till he came to a sunny glade in which there were flowers growing and trees like the rowans that he had seen in the country when he and his father had gone for runs in the car. The berries were blood-red too and the tree leaned over Orpheus with all its pliant branches, and he was idly strumming his lyre.

No longer could Mr Trill see the soldiers, talking to each other, it was as if they had receded into the mist and left him alone in the sunlight with the singer. His heart nearly burst with joy as he thought of his father telling him that famous story when he was a child, allowing him to enter that golden kingdom for a while, evading his mother's sharp beak.

And here he was beside the singer in Hades, on a sunny hill with a river flowing past, black and complex as if it were a telephone talking endlessly to itself.

Orpheus, the sad singer, who had been so badly treated by Pluto, here he was in the . . . no, in the spirit, and Mr Trill could ask him questions, and talk to him. How astonishing that was, when he remembered the cutting voice of his mother who thought that history was finished with, and whose whole concern was whether a certain painting matched the paper on the wall, and who didn't believe in the existence of heroes like Orpheus. No, on the contrary, she thought that all history was a dream, that everybody had his weakness which she would find out in order to bring him down to the level of everybody else, including her own. She would pick holes in him, who did he think he was anyway? She wouldn't like to see anyone putting on airs and graces in her presence. For she was as good as Trill's father any day, and don't let either of them forget that fact or think they were any different just because she had worked in a canteen. She knew the world just the same and knew what people were like and she was more practical than his father in spite of all his degrees. Let them both put that in their pipes and smoke it . . . And Mr Trill stood and watched Orpheus who was idly strumming on his lyre till the latter turned towards him a head which streamed with golden hair. How girlish the face looked, how white the skin. Mr Trill felt uncomfortable in the presence of the singer.

'I suppose you're another newcomer and you want to hear the story as well,' said Orpheus petulantly. 'Everyone wants to hear my story. It's part of the tour. Well, I suppose we might as well get it over with . . . What do you know of it already? Some of them know a little and some a lot. And then there are all those old fat sweaty woman who go on and on saying, "Poor boy, poor boy." If only they knew how ugly I thought they were . . . '

Over his naked legs lay his lyre which he was strumming and Mr Trill said, 'I know that your lyre was so entrancing that the stones and the beasts followed you. Isn't that right?'

'Yes, that's perfectly right,' said Orpheus tossing his hair carelessly. 'They did that. In those days I was certainly a good singer . . . And then I married Eurydice.'

'What do you mean?' said Mr Trill who was horrified to feel some doubt in his mind that this was really Orpheus for he didn't look at all like the singer as he had imagined him.

'Oh, it was nothing wrong with Eurydice,' said Orpheus. 'No man could have had a better wife. She was compassionate, kind, a good listener, a companion, and I loved her to excess.' He paused and Trill said,

'Why then do you blame her? You seem to me to blame her.'

'Blame her? No I don't blame her. There is nothing I can blame her for. If my friends visited me she was hospitable to them, and some of them were not all that reputable. Her love was flawless, perfect, there was no other woman like her. She was faithful, adoring, practical. If I wished to compose she would leave me alone, if I didn't she would talk to me. I never ever saw her angry. Would you believe that was possible; and yet I can tell you it was true. And at times I thought if she died that I would be helpless, without anchor, without rudder. If I came in drunk in the early hours of the morning she was always there waiting for me, but she never harangued me . . . And then she was bitten by the snake and she died.'

'And so,' said Mr Trill, 'you went to Hades to save her and bring her back to the world again.'

'That is what I intended to do,' said Orpheus. 'I played to Pluto in that land of minerals, I charmed even Cerberus himself. I crossed with Charon in his boat and brought my lyre to the country of the dead. And Pluto said to me, 'Now you can take her with you provided you do not look back.' Such perfection she had had, such restfulness, such repose. And she looked at me with such trust and complete love. How can I describe it to you or to anyone else? She stretched out her arms towards me with such longing. At that moment even the darkness seemed clear and piercing.'

'Well,' said Mr Trill, 'what happened? You were told not to look back and yet you did. Isn't that right?'

Orpheus seemed not to hear him but to be as it were listening to a voice deep within himself. 'So much I thought of in that moment. Never before had I played so harmoniously, so finely, as when I was going in search of Eurydice, when I didn't have Eurydice at all. Do you understand that? It was as if my whole soul had become part Hades, part Elysium, it was as if I needed Hades. And for the first time ever I thought about my singing and my poetry, for never before had I thought of it. It had been as natural to me as the wind in the trees. I had not suffered any sorrow. It was as if at that moment I suffered an agony greater than any I had ever suffered, as if I had to cross over into the shadows, and become self-conscious. And that self-consciousness was necessary to me. Everything seemed to happen in that moment.'

'What? What seemed to happen?' said Mr Trill. 'I don't understand.'

'I knew I didn't want Eurydice back.'

'What?'

'That's true. I didn't wish her back. If you can understand this, her perfection was too great for me, it damaged my poetry. Do you know what I did then? I placed my art, the development of my art, before my love for Eurydice. I needed to suffer, it was in my nature to suffer. If I had brought Eurydice back, I myself would have died, I myself would have gone to Hades.'

Mr Trill gazed at him uncomprehendingly.

'It was strange to see them with their bony hands pleading with me to save Eurydice: but what did they know of art?'

Orpheus crossed his naked legs disturbingly, and continued, 'I had to suffer all that there was to suffer, know all there was to know. That was my destiny. And my destiny was unavoidable. From the very first moment that I had sung and played, I knew that my fate was to continue with my chosen art. And in Hades I felt that my power was greater than it had ever been, and that I needed a perpetual Hades. I needed an unending search for Eurydice. And all that happened in a single moment, as we stared at each other across the space of Hades, in that dimness of iron and ghosts. How can one ever describe that gaze? And let me tell you something else, the most bitter part of all, Eurydice knew what was happening, what had happened, and she agreed with me. She loved me so much that she agreed with me. She did not complain nor make any other sign of entreaty. Does that not in itself tell of her perfection? How could I ever have deserved her?'

And Mr Trill recognised that unalterable selfishness of the artist, that shield and armour which not even human feeling can pierce and he mourned Eurydice, and her implacable generosity. And he heard Orpheus' voice as if in a dream.

'And so I emerged into the upper world, and the stones were whiter than they had ever been and the trees were greener. And I wandered among the dead of this world, the perverted, the fallen. There is no den or hovel that I have not visited, there is no practice that I have not attempted. And all my songs have been elegies for Eurydice for she is the perfection that I have not attained. She had to die before I could possess her, and every song is a fresh attempt on her virginity, an interrogation of her love. Her love,' he added hopelessly as if he did not know what the word meant.

'And I was determined that I wouldn't remarry. And so, well, I turned to others for my satisfaction, not women, if you get me. But they had their revenge on me in the end.'

'What others?' Mr Trill was about to say when he saw Orpheus's melting eyes resting on him and it was for a moment as if he was lost in a mist of desire, languid and faint. Those white legs, those girlish hands and neck . . .

'I . . . ' said Trill, 'I . . . ' It was as if he had entered a world which was dazzling yet corrupt, attractive yet unnatural, a total Hades of the spirit, in which Eurydice flowered poignantly among metals of a fierce flawed lustre. So this had been the reality of the story, this selfish passionate substance. For art to flourish, the human being must die, must stretch out its hands unavailingly, must accept death that another life be created, another music be made. Was there truth nowhere? Was every narrative ambiguous? Had the classic world been a deception?

'I . . . ' said Trill again and got to his feet and ran away as fast as possible on his short stumpy legs, away from Orpheus who, as if he had already forgotten him, went back to his strumming again.

What a narrow escape, thought Trill, there had never been anything like that in Eastborough Grammar, though in the boarding school it had been different. But what was happening to his knowledge of the classics? It was as if everyone was determined to tell him the opposite of what he wished to hear and know about.

At that very moment Trill heard a voice saying, 'Hullo, old chap,' and he looked and there, standing in front of him, was Harris. Here among the shades, Harris whom he had hated so much.

'Well, well, well, so this is Rosy,' said Harris, his flushed moustached face gazing down at him. 'I often wondered what had happened to you. Little Rosy whose head I used to plunge in the basin.'

'I'm going to run away,' thought Trill feeling a trembling in his legs. I'm going to disgrace myself and run away. But he didn't. He stayed where he was, in the swirling mist.

'It's all right,' said Harris. 'I'm not going to touch you. As a matter of fact I'd be glad of someone to talk to. It gets boring down here and I never seem to meet anyone I know.'

But Trill was seeing in front of him the faces of boys distorted with cruelty: he heard their laughter and felt again the cold harsh water on his face.

'Ah, those were good days,' said Harris amiably. 'Do you remember old Horace with his Latin and Greek? Silly old duffer. Never did me any good, that's for sure.'

'What did you do then?' said Trill tremblingly.

'Oh, I went into business. No need for Latin or Greek there, I can tell you. Did quite well.'

And his face faded and solidified, grew and withered.

'I don't believe you,' said Trill in a high squeaking voice. 'I don't believe you. You were always cruel and a liar. I don't

believe that you did well at all. I believe that you were a –
commercial traveller. That was all you were fit for. I hated you.'

'Yes, I suppose you did. I suppose you did but we're both
grown men now. We don't need to keep up that feud.'

'We do, we do,' shrilled Trill daringly. 'Of course we do. Do
you know that I had nightmares about you? Why did you
torture me so much? I didn't do anything to you.'

'Well, old boy, you looked so helpless, that was all, and it
passed the time. God, those essays we did, and those rules.
Lights out at ten. It was just that you were one of nature's
losers, old boy, that's all. All you were interested in was
handing in your comps all present and correct.'

'But I didn't do anything to you and you used to put my head
in the basin and tie up my bedclothes. Why did you do that?'

'I just told you. And anyway it's a long time ago. Why should
you keep those grudges going? I bet you ended up as a teacher
yourself. I can imagine you in the staff-room with your pipe in
your mouth marking your exercise books and having a quiet
look in class up the girls' legs. You were a bit of a sissy really.
No offence. We always thought that.'

'Who did? Who always thought that?' said Mr Trill, his
voice rising to a scream. 'Tell me that.'

'Oh, if you want to know there was Ormond and Pacey and
Mason, they all thought that. As a matter of fact, I saw Mason
not so long ago. He's a brigadier now. But I haven't seen any of
the others. I must say it's very lonely.'

'Mason always said you were an old liar,' shouted Trill, the
blood mounting to his face. 'He caught you out time and time
again. He said that you would become a commercial traveller. You
mark my words, he used to say, that stinker Harris will end up as a
commercial traveller. And that was when Mason was in the
Cadets. You were always trying to get out of them, weren't you?'

'They were so boring, old chap, so boring, all that dreary
marching. So Mason said that, did he? What else did he say?'

'He said he thought your parents lived in the slums. He often
told us that because he said why otherwise did your parents
never visit the school?'

'Did he now?'

'Yes, and there were other things too. We once saw your underpants and they were full of holes. Did you know that we called you Holy Harris? We never told you that 'cos you were a bully.'

'Well, well,' said Harris his face fading and solidifying. 'Isn't that interesting? You certainly find out things in Hades that you didn't know before. It's worth the visit. But surely after all those years you'll have forgotten about all that. I'll tell you what I'll do. I'll introduce you to some of the bigwigs. I've got a ticket here which allows you to see them. I can give it to you if you like. Would you like that?'

'No I wouldn't,' screamed Trill. 'I wouldn't. I don't want your ticket. You can keep your rotten ticket. You're a great big bully and you won't change and that's a fact.' And as he looked Harris's face changed and wavered and the tears started to pour out of his eyes and his hands began to tremble and his whole body which had looked so imposing became small and withered, and even the striped tie which he still wore began to disappear.

'Please, please,' said Harris holding his hands out in entreaty.

'No,' said the implacable Trill, 'no, no, no. I don't want to have anything to do with you. You're a bully and a cheat and a liar. And I can see your pants. Holy Harris, Holy Harris,' he chanted, and the bony knees of Harris disappeared and there was no one left in the wavering mist but Mr Trill himself who groped about as if looking for his own body while the fog swirled around him and in the distance he could vaguely make out the lowering castle with its towers and battlements.

He looked down at his body to see if his own knees were still there or if he was still wearing his navy blue uniform with the badge of the red lion at the breast and the word sequamur written on it, but no, he was wearing his adult clothes – his suit greyed a little by the ashes of his pipe – and he was himself again, just as if he were the old Mr Trill sitting in a chair in the staff-room filling in the Ximenes crossword or interlacing essays with red marks as if they were bars of blood across the page.

At that moment he saw a tall figure looming towards him out of the mist, and he started.

'Who are you?' he shouted. 'Do I know you?' But the figure passed on with a silent dignified walk. Mr Trill ran after it. 'Who are you?' he shouted again and though he didn't realise it he looked silly running about with his case as if he were a business man whose train had left without his knowing it and who was scurrying about in search of the stationmaster.

The figure stopped and looked at him. It was tall and imposing and as its lineaments solidified Mr Trill saw that it was a woman, majestic, implacable. He went down slowly on his knees and heard himself asking, 'Are you a goddess then? You are not Athene, are you? Or even Juno?'

'No, I am none of these,' said the figure. 'My name is Dido, and who are you?'

'My name is Mr Trill and I used to be a classics master at Eastborough Grammar, Dido,' and he was almost over-whelmed that he had spoken her name but he began to speak again quickly and nervously. 'I used to read poetry about you. "And I shall know it even from among the shades." You said that didn't you?'

'I can't remember. I suppose I might have done. I said many things.' And the lips twitched with a brief pain.

'But your story,' said Mr Trill, 'can I not hear your story? Look, we are alone. We will not be interrupted. I've been told so much that I feel is wrong, and perhaps you could tell me the truth about yourself and Aeneas. Is it true that he left you and sailed to Italy? Is it true about the cave where you met?'

'Yes, it is true, it is all true. But what use is it to talk of it now? In his own mind he had his duty to do, he had to sail away and found Rome. That, he said, was his destiny. Who can resist the will of the gods? I thought we might,' and her voice faded away. 'It was possible that my love might, but it didn't. He sailed away secretly in his boats. Perhaps that was the worst of all. He should have told me.'

'Perhaps,' said Mr Trill daringly, 'he could not bring himself to meet you again in case he could not continue with his destiny.'

'Perhaps. What does it matter now? He has sought me here, I have seen him hesitantly lingering as if he wished to speak to me, but I, what should I have to say to him?'

'But the founding of a new city, of a civilisation,' said Mr Trill, 'is that not more important than a private love? Rome became a great empire: it spread its power all over the world.'

'Is that true?' said Dido in an uninterested voice. 'Perhaps that is important.'

'And then,' said Mr Trill, 'it produced a great poet who wrote about you. I think his sympathies were with you.'

'With me? A Roman?'

'Yes.'

As if talking to herself Dido said, 'He charmed me with his stories. All the time that he was telling me of the fall of Troy, Carthage was being built. There was the sound of hammers everywhere. It was like a new beginning. I thought it would be a new beginning for us. But even while he was talking to me, even in the deepest moments of our love I knew that he was thinking of Rome.'

'The poet says,' Mr Trill persisted, 'that it was with a heavy heart Aeneas left Phoenicia, though he was filled with love and longing.'

'And I,' said Dido, 'was on fire when I saw his sails fading into the distance. It was as if I was burning. As a queen what should I do but kill myself? I had my own dignity too. Everyone has his dignity.'

'Yes,' said Mr Trill. And he was filled with hatred for that obstinate, god-obeying man who had set off in search of his own fame, leaving behind him a pyre that blazed on an abandoned headland. Was the creation of a new land, the pursuit of fame, narrow obedience to the gods, indeed greater than the love such a woman as this could give?

'There were some other words that the poet wrote,' said Mr Trill, quoting from memory. 'He wrote that you said,

' "If that wicked being must surely sail to land and come to harbour because such is the fixed and destined ending required by Jupiter's own ordinances, yet let him afterwards suffer affliction in war through the arms of a daring foe, let him be banished from his own territory and torn from the embraces of Iulus, imploring aid as he sees his innocent friends die and then after surrendering to a humiliating peace may he not live to enjoy his kingdom in happiness: and may he lie fallen before his time, unburied on a lonely strand." '

'I said that?' said Dido laughing. 'When did I say that? How could I speak like that? No, that was not how I felt. How should love speak like that? How should I wish such things for him? I thought you said that that poet spoke well of me? What I felt was not that. When I saw those ships sailing away and I heard around me the sounds of the hammers as Carthage was being built, it was not vengeance I felt, rather it was hopelessness, as if my world was coming to an end. Have you not loved? Do you not know what love is?'

'Yes,' said Mr Trill, 'I have loved.'

'If that is so then you must know that it is not anger one feels at such a moment.' She paused and then began again as if she were back in Carthage, 'It was a clear day and his men were pulling at the oars. Men were working around me excavating a harbour and others raising a temple and a theatre. The sea was so calm: it was the calmness of the sea that tormented me. He was sailing into the future and I was remaining there. Yet it was not anger I felt, it was the indifference of the day that tormented me. The sea was so calm, the day was so clear and pure and the ship was sailing away from me forever. Forever. And then I turned to the pyre and stabbed myself with my dagger.'

Men and women, thought Mr Trill, the ambition of men, their daily task, and the love of women. The one who hunts and the one who remains behind. It has always been like that. There has been the searcher for new horizons and the one who keeps the horizons stable. Dido's foreign black face blazed out of the dimness and he was struck for the first time by the knowledge that this was a clash between civilisations. How had he never thought of it before? The fixed seeker after knowledge, the sensuous one who in spite of protestations did not care for destiny, for the unsleeping arrow of fame.

'Was I not married to him,' said Dido, 'if not in name then in love?'

So many shades flickered around them, hungry, unappeased, and Mr Trill could imagine Aeneas hesitating, trying to summon up courage to speak to her, ready to explain with quick words. But deeper than any words was this woman's knowledge: she knew that when the choice came he had chosen the abstract not the concrete, and nothing he could say would make her believe otherwise.

This queen, this marvellous queen, who blazed out of this dimness!

'I will tell you really what I felt,' said Dido at last. 'When I struck myself with that dagger I felt, Even if he should come back now, I would be dead and he would perhaps be sorry. I killed myself like any ordinary girl whose lover has left her: and I had thought I was a queen.'

And she interrogated Trill with her marvellous eyes which shone like torches. 'Imagine it, I had thought a queen would die differently from the rest of the women of the world. But no, it was just the same. His kingdom was to me a trivial thing, and his gods unimportant. When I thought, Perhaps he will see my pyre and know it for what it is, it was then my heart broke. Do you understand that?'

'I think I do,' said Mr Trill.

'And do you understand, too, that that is why I do not speak to him. Words to him were everything. It seemed to me that I had listened forever to his words, and then it seemed to me that I had burned forever in that silence into which he sailed. I have thought much of that, that silence. It is now my weapon, as once it was his, on that day.'

There was a calmness and Mr Trill gazed into the heart of it and it was as if in the very heart of it he saw a wound opening wide, and enlarging itself slowly and inexorably. Yes, he thought, it must have been like that, that is exactly how it must have been. On the fine clear warm morning, apparently full of hope, that is how it must have been. Her loved one left her, and she was alone, while all around her the city was being steadily built by workmen who whistled and sang as they worked. In the city that was being built Dido killed herself. And Mr Trill was filled with hatred for Aeneas, as if he were his own most bitter enemy, so that he could almost have shouted out to the departing ships, Don't you know what you are doing? Can't you see the heartache you are causing? What are you trying to do to this woman? Is Rome a sufficient prize for a broken heart?

But even as he looked Dido had faded away and in her place was . . . Grace.

For ten years they had been going together, ten years during which he had taken her now to a classical concert, now to a theatre.

'Is it your night for going out then?' his landlady would say, her avid eyes fixed on him.

'Yes, Mrs Begg,' he would answer.

And so he would put on his coat, take his umbrella and set off down the stairs past the window which showed the tiny green on which washing was drying in the evening light.

And Grace would be waiting for him outside the door of the theatre or the concert hall, for she always arrived first. She was not at all pretty, he didn't expect that good fortune – nor indeed did he desire it – but she was pleasant, even-tempered, and always neatly but not showily dressed.

He would always buy her a box of chocolates though he himself wouldn't eat any, and after the play or concert was over they would go to a restaurant for their coffee and discuss the entertainment they had just seen.

'I didn't like his interpretation of Prospero,' or 'I felt that Miranda was just right,' Grace would say, for she taught English. And Mr Trill, whose knowledge of English literature was not great, would listen to her, puffing at his pipe and feeling amiable and contented.

He was not allowed to go to Grace's home, for her mother, who was still alive though old, had, according to her daughter, a nasty habit of insulting any men she brought to the house, especially one in the far past who had ridden a motor bike and worn a helmet which he laid down negligently on the sofa when he entered the room. Though a clerk he had a careless taste for adventure.

Mr Trill never kissed Grace, for he regarded his friendship with her as belonging to an equable maturity without emotional storms or tantrums. He was glad in a way that her mother existed for she would save him from having to confront the problem of marriage to her daughter. Now and again Grace would refer to a house as if it were quite settled in her mind that the two of them would one day live together, but Mr Trill would pretend not to hear such remarks. Their friendship, he believed, belonged to the world of the mind, and he was happy that it should remain there, and that her mother should like Cerberus guard her house so that he would be unable to enter it.

Thus, as they strolled along in the gentle evening light after the play or concert was over, Mr Trill existed in a mild radiance of the mind and spirit, feeling himself superior to all those men who for some reason which he could never understand were involved in passionate quarrels with their sweethearts or wives. Sometimes he would read in a newspaper that a girl had stabbed her lover in a jealous rage and he couldn't understand how this should be. Why did secretaries sob all day in offices when their boy friends had spoken a casual cruel word to them? Why did some of them kill themselves, or send vicious rancorous letters which dripped with poison and anger? Mr Trill himself didn't live in that world nor did, he was sure, Grace.

And so all was tranquil and peaceful and Grace was always equable and mild till her mother died suddenly of a heart attack. At first Grace had been prostrated and Mr Trill had sent some flowers. He had asked if there was anything he could do but she had told him that there wasn't, that it was really the sort of situation that he wasn't equipped to deal with: and he had blessed her perspicacity and thoughtfulness. Thus he did not learn anything about the mechanics of dying: he remained ignorant of the irrational guilt which Grace felt at actions done and left undone, he did not see her wandering about the house picking up a handkerchief of her mother's and then dropping it as if it were electrified. He did not see her sitting in church weeping while the coffin was being borne on the shoulders of four men to the waiting hearse. All these things had passed without his knowing them, nor did he see her on the sofa at night, her jotters abandoned at her side, while she shook with sobs or stared dully into space, knowing that there are things in this world which cannot be corrected.

The weeks passed and then they went out for the first time after her mother's death, to a concert given by members of the Cairo Conservatoire. As they sat in the second row watching the Egyptian conductor enter, and with a stern military gaze around the orchestra, invite them to a typically stormy Beethoven piece, Mr Trill knew that matters would never be the same again. He sensed that Grace's easy-going amiable nature had vanished and that contained within her was a storm of her own. Thus as the violinists rested their bows, though the trumpets sounded, he felt a chill in his bones as one sometimes does at the beginning of autumn: for Grace was silent and had refused the chocolates he had offered her. After the concert she invited him to her house but he refused to go as he said it was rather late and he still had some translations of Ovid to mark.

'So,' she said pulling on her gloves, as they stared at the empty cups in the restaurant, 'what are we going to do?'

'To do?' Mr Trill echoed, though he knew perfectly well what she meant. For a moment he was reminded of the story of Echo and Narcissus, how Echo had fallen in love with Narcissus but he had scorned her and she had faded away bodilessly into the depths of the wood while Narcissus sickened and died for love of his own ailing reflection.

'So are we getting married or not?'

'Getting married?' Mr Trill repeated.

'Yes, getting married. Are we or are we not getting married?' Her voice which had once been mild and amiable had suddenly grown harsh like the voice of a seagull that screams along the shore.

'I . . . ' began Mr Trill.

And then she had begun. It had not occurred to Mr Trill that this woman who had been in the past so tranquil should so suddenly become violent and stormy, bitter poisonous words pouring out of her mouth.

'Well, are we or aren't we? I have been going out with you now for ten years and you have never mentioned marriage once. It is true that you couldn't very well do so while my mother lived but now that she is dead I don't see why we shouldn't discuss it.'

Mr Trill thought it was rather indelicate of her to speak of her recently dead mother at such a moment and especially in a public restaurant but all he did was take his pipe out of his mouth, empty its grey ash into the ashtray and put the pipe back again into his pocket.

'Naturally,' she was saying, 'I believed that after ten years we could get married. Why else would I have gone out with you for such a long time? There were others I could have gone with but I chose to stay with you because I understood or thought I understood that marriage was in your mind, though we didn't discuss it. But now I want to know one way or the other especially as I deliberately protected you from the ugliness of death because I knew that you are not interested in such matters.' Her eyes which had been so mild were blazing with temper and it was almost as if he were seeing a woman transformed into a demon in front of his eyes. Such must once Medea have been like when tormented by her love for Jason, and a pleasurable feeling trembled within him.

'I . . . ' he began but before he could say any more she had risen to her feet and said, 'I know you now. You are afraid of marriage, of the world. All you want to do is sit in your corner with your books. As long as you have your stinking pipe and can discuss a concert or a play with me that is all you want. Naturally. I'm thirty-five years old and now I find,' and here she burst into tears though the restaurant was full of people 'now I find that you don't care.' Mr Trill looked around him with trepidation. Why, she was just like his mother, making a scene in public. She had the same unreasonableness. Could she not have waited till they had left the restaurant at least? But she didn't wait and she continued through her tears,

'All that time I was deceiving myself. I thought that when my mother died . . . But no. Not you. Not once have you made any single gesture or shown any tenderness. Anyone else would have demanded that he help with the funeral arrangements. But not you. You simply agreed with what I told you. Go back to your landlady then if you like her so much.'

This last statement astonished Mr Trill who had never thought of his landlady as other than his landlady, and who ate so little that he was hardly in the dining-room for more than ten minutes at a time gulping his food while his landlady who, he thought, knew nothing about his personal life brooded darkly about him and hoarded up the crumbs of information that he ignorantly gave her. What was Grace implying and why had she changed so much? It was as if he were listening to his mother again as she shouted at his helpless father who was trying to hide in his study.

'Please, Grace,' he said, 'can we not . . . ?'

'No, we can not. And don't "please" me. I have asked you a question and you have given me your answer and that's it.' All the time she was saying these words her pleading eyes were gazing at him as if belying the sentences that she was uttering and he saw her as she would be, a woman whom marriage had forever passed by. Nevertheless though he recognised this with his mind he didn't feel anything, nor had he any desire to touch her or comfort her. It was as if there was a cold glacial being at his heart like a tiny snowman who was gazing at this woman, and seeing her as having no connection at all with himself. And it occurred to him how extraordinary it was that one should have feelings, that one should laugh and cry, that one should be shaken by rage or jealousy. He felt fumblingly for his pipe but then left it where it was.

Then she left the restaurant, her white shawl round her shoulders, and he remained sitting where he was. At that moment he felt desolate as if something valuable were leaving him forever but at the same time he still made no effort to pursue her. After a very long time he got up and walked slowly home. The streets were yellow with light, the scholarly lamp-posts with their bent backs leaned over the pavement as if studying it, and Mr Trill trudged to his lodgings. He was tormented by an absence, for never again, he felt, would he be able to discuss concerts and plays with anyone in an atmosphere of peace and tranquillity. Never again would he have his evenings to look forward to. His landlady would ask him if he was going out and he would have to answer that he wasn't, and then her little eyes would glitter and she would begin to dig down into his life with her little wicked spade to find out why he no longer left the house on a Friday night as he had used to do. He would be naked to the world, without armour. But he gritted his teeth and walked on not even pausing to consider whether he should phone Grace in order to find out if she had arrived safely. He vaguely thought that she might kill herself but dismissed the thought immediately. That would not at all be like Grace. That night he lay in his bed sleepless and it was as if the room began to close round him, as if some grief, hitherto invisible, was drawing closer to him, ensconcing itself among his Greek and Latin books and casting a sad light over his jotters.

Grace never married, and continued with her teaching, her temper becoming more bitter and enraged. She still lived alone, as far as Mr Trill knew, in the house from which her mother had departed and among those yellow lights that seethed about the streets.

For a long time Mr Trill wandered about, after his meeting with Dido, confused in his thoughts and wondering if all his work on earth had been wasted, for he remembered with pleasure not unmixed with pain – especially in his latter years – the time he had spent in teaching. Some pupils he recalled with affection, some with dislike, but in general he was highly pleased – or had been until now – with his sojourn on earth, and with the work he had done there. And it was while thinking these thoughts that he came through the mist on a rugged hill and saw a man rolling a huge stone up it, his cheeks bloated, his teeth gritted. Whenever the man pushed the stone up the slope with great effort it rolled down again to the bottom, as if it were an animated being with a will of its own.

Why does he not stop, why does he keep on doing it? thought Mr Trill, as he watched in silence the man who hadn't noticed him. And of course he knew perfectly well who it was, it was Sisyphus.

And he knew also why he was doing it, it was because he had been condemned by the gods to do it. Why else would a man spend all his days and nights pushing a big boulder up a hill when it always rolled back relentlessly again? The gods, thought Mr Trill, the gods are our destiny. It is they who decide what we must do, and who keep us at it.

And yet he didn't wish to accept this reasoning. Was it the gods who had decided what he must do with his own life, what in fact he had done with it? Was it the gods who had decided what his father and mother must be like? Was it the gods who had decided that he must be born of such a mother and such a father, and that because of them he must do what he had done? Was the whole world, then, a huge machine, a huge boulder, dumb and bare, to which no one could appeal?

And, after all, had that not been the case with Achilles? Had he not been told that after killing Hector he was doomed, and had he not done it in spite of that?

And was it the gods who had decided that on a certain day he should arrive at Mrs Begg's house, lay his case down on the mat, press the bell, and that he would, after her acceptance, stay in her house for thirty years? Had all that been decided by the gods? Ah, Mrs Begg, were you too an instrument of the gods, with your pride in your house, your incessant scourings and washings, your ear for scandal, your meanness with fire in winter, and even with sugar during all seasons? Was there some god that decided that you and I should meet and perhaps made you think after my break with Grace that I should perhaps get married to you even if you had a moustache? Was it a god that guided me to Eastborough Grammar School on that day when my heart beat so strongly and I entered those alien gates and I laid my briefcase down for the first time in the staff-room and I hung up my coat for the first time on its predestined nail and I read the notices on the notice-board.

Is that so, thought Mr Trill as he watched Sisyphus make another effort with the stone. The mist gathered around him and there was Sisyphus in the midst of it pushing and moaning and grunting and then just when it appeared that the stone had reached the top it fell down again: and Sisyphus would stare at it for a long time and instead of giving up would summon all his energy and push and heave and grunt again while the muscles of his jaws stood out and his arms strained and his back bent into an arc and the brute stone without consciousness would almost grinningly confront him. How sick surely he must grow of that stone, without perfume, without grace, how he must hate and curse it. But, no, Mr Trill did not hear a word of anger, it was as if anger had been drained away over the centuries, as if long ago Sisyphus had forgotten the reason for anger, knowing that the stone would not hear him, nor the gods forgive him. How strange, thought Mr Trill, as he sat and watched him, how futile and odd. And as he watched he thought of the vanity of his own life. First of all there had been the quarrels with his parents – perhaps fated to meet each other – then there had been his sufferings in boarding school, then there had been his years of teaching, and in the middle of these his break with Grace.

Had it all been like the stone and Sisyphus then? Certainly, perhaps, the last years had been, though not the middle ones. In the last years it seemed that he had lost his love for his work, it seemed that the teachings of the classics had fallen heavy from his lips. But before that it had been different.

The horror of it all, this Sisyphus and the stone! And then Mr Trill did a strange thing. He leapt down from where he was and began to help Sisyphus to push the boulder. Side by side they pushed, side by side they puffed and panted, and almost they had reached the top. Next time, thought Mr Trill, surely next time will do it. Nor was he afraid that he would be attacked for what he was doing. All he thought of was that he could not bear to see this useless toil. We will do it next time, we really will, he told the silent Sisyphus: and then you can stop your work and you will be happy.

This time a really big push will do it.

Damn you, he shouted at the stone, while Sisyphus grunted and puffed, a gigantic yet curiously insubstantial figure in the mist. Damn you, damn you, we'll get you this time, bald senseless thing. Push push push till the veins stand up on your forehead. Work work work till all the examinations appear easy. *Amo amas amat . . . mensa mensam mensae mensae mensa . . .* O table, O chair, O stone . . . let life enter you, let you wing your way about Hades, fly about squeaking like a bat. Run about in the park, sing, dance . . . And he pushed as hard as he could and he shouted as he pushed and then, glory of glories, the two of them were up on the sunshine of the hill with the stone and it was lying there on the summit as if it was where it had always wanted to be. They stood there amazed, Sisyphus still in silence, his arms hanging at his side, the veins on them swollen and blue. Ah, ha, we got you at last, said Mr Trill, giving the stone a kick and only succeeding in hurting himself. You big, stupid, senseless dolt, you ignorant, inanimate lump. As Mr Trill triumphed over the stone and made as if to shake hands with the weary shade the latter looked at him with infinite sadness and then very slowly and carefully pushed the stone downhill again and Mr Trill heard it thundering and banging till at last it came to rest though echoing still with a loud thunderous sound. Then still without a word, Sisyphus descended the hill and prepared to begin his endless task again, while above him Mr Trill sat and thought.

On his green bench Mr Trill sat and thought. At first when he had retired from school he used to sit in his room reading but then as time passed he realised that Mrs Begg was growing more and more irritable when she saw him there (and sometimes he would have to leave it so that she would be able to bring her hoover and clean the floor).

It was strange how Mrs Begg's attitude to him had changed. In the beginning she perhaps thought that there was a possibility of marriage, and for this reason she would tell him fragments of the story of her life. (Her marriage to a train-driver who had died of a heart attack: she, still, according to herself, could get free railway passes to any part of the country that she wished to go to. However she never went anywhere, not even to her nieces and nephews in Surrey.) Mr Trill hardly ever listened to any of her stories or if he did it was only with half an ear and even now after thirty years with Mrs Begg he didn't know the names of any of her relations, or what they did, though he had been given the information often enough in the moments between soup and mince or while he was drinking his tea. Nor did he really know much about Mrs Begg herself. She existed for him in a vague world as a being which as far as he was concerned had no emotions of its own, no ambitions or destinations, merely a servant who was there to give him, in return for money, the little food that he required.

He never for a moment realised that even in Mrs Begg's heart there beat storms of rancour as when for instance he ate absentmindedly without comment or even left half finished on his plate a particularly fine pie that she had specially made for him: nor did he notice that some days she had tidied the room particularly well, or even left a vase of flowers in it. On the contrary she was like a slave belonging to Greece, a manual worker who allowed him, the lord, to conduct his silent speculations.

Thus it was when he left the school he found for the time a cold wind blowing around him as if Mrs Begg had decided that he would never leave and therefore she could treat him as she liked. She sometimes grunted when he spoke to her and made references to the sunniness of the weather, and would howl about his legs with her hoover when he was deep in Homer. Therefore Mr Trill took it into his head to leave the house in the mornings and only come back at dinner time: and as he was a creature of habit he always departed at half past nine.

The park was a large one with plots of flowers scattered here and there. In the middle of it there was a fountain in which a Cupid composed of white alabaster hovered, bow and arrow in hand, while waters poured endlessly out of its mouth. Here Mr Trill would sit on a green bench and watch the world go by. Sometimes an old man would come and sit beside him and the two of them would discuss questions of the day or rather the other man would talk and Mr Trill would half listen for he had no interest in politics and rarely read a newspaper.

'The country is going to the dogs,' successive old men would tell him. 'Even the young people aren't frightened of the police nowadays. They throw stones at you and shout names and what does anybody do about it? Nothing. It wasn't like that in the old days.'

And so he would listen to the same story, repeated over and over in various guises and various accents, of a world that was always peaceful with calm blue skies and perfect behaviour.

And he would grow tired of it all but he didn't want to cause a disturbance, so he would agree wordlessly, now and then nodding his head, but in truth weary of it all.

'I am becoming an old man,' he would think. 'And is this what I wanted from my life? Is this where I wanted to be?' And sometimes he wished that he had married Grace and at other times he was glad that he hadn't done so. But most of the time he simply felt lonely.

Once he had gone up to the school, and swore that he would never do so again. It wasn't that anybody had been unkind to him – on the contrary everybody had been very gentle and considerate – but it was as if they were talking to an invalid, as if their voices echoed around him with hollow solicitude. While they were talking to him, he sensed that they thought of him as an intruder, a sort of ghost who was no longer involved in the heat and the smoke. And even while they were speaking he felt them, as it were, glancing at their watches as if they were thinking how much they had to do, and that this old buffer was preventing them from getting on with it. The staffroom was no longer his staffroom, he himself had been replaced by a new younger man with fresh ideas, and he felt that he was a posthumous being moving about the circumference of the field on which the war was being waged. Even his old room had changed, it was less tidy than it used to be, there were pictures on the walls, and the desks were carved with new names.

So he decided that he would stay in the park and watch the flowers and if necessary endure the stories of the old men who were so implacable, stubbly and envious.

One day a little girl came over to talk to him. She had been playing with a paper boat in a pond but after she had finished she stood in front of him gazing at him with wonder in her eyes as if waiting for him to speak to her. But he found that he couldn't think of anything to say. If she had been older he might have offered to help her with her Latin – for that was all he could do – but as she was only four or five years old such an offer was out of the question.

Eventually she sat beside him on the bench swinging her legs and offering him her boat which he had looked at with surprise, unable to think of anything to say about it except that it was pretty.

'What is your name?' she asked him directly.

'Mr Trill,' he answered.

'My name is Margaret and my mummy is coming to get me. She is at the shops.' There was a long companionable silence while Mr Trill searched for some words to say to her but there was nothing at all that he could think of: not a single idea came into his head. In front of him the flowers blossomed and the gardener gazed at them, rake in hand, while the white Cupid with bow and arrow leaned gracefully into the blue day.

The little girl swung her legs which were clad in white socks. And Mr Trill gave her some sweets.

The following day she came back and the following day again and Mr Trill finding nothing to say gave her more sweets and she seemed quite happy to sit there beside him. Sometimes she brought a doll and sometimes a teddy bear and there the two of them would sit, Mr Trill now old and greying, looking out at the park, and the little girl clutching her doll with the red dress and the startingly blue eyes which stared unblinkingly out of the polished glaze of the face. And all the time Mr Trill was silent. The world of children was forever closed to him for he hadn't really understood them though he had taught them. To him they were beings who must be instructed in Latin, they didn't have minds or will or souls of their own. Nevertheless for some unfathomable reason the little girl came and sat beside him in perfect peace though now and again she would abruptly leave him in order to float her boat on the pond and talk to the gardener who seemed to have more to say to her than Mr Trill had. Sometimes she would take him into her confidence and tell him little snatches of her worldly affairs, though they were so difficult to understand that Mr Trill would let his attention wander, and indeed once she had stood in front of him stamping her feet and saying how stupid he was. Mr Trill had accepted this verdict quite calmly and without rancour as if it had a perfect justice of its own.

Once he had made a great effort – as if speaking were like the lifting of a great stone – and asked her where she stayed but he couldn't make out the answer and had left the question dangling where it was in the bright light.

She had even asked him whether he had a mummy or daddy but Mr Trill had pretended not to hear: it would have been too difficult for him to explain to her that they were both dead.

One morning when as usual he had sat down on the bench which happened to be rather damp as it had been raining the night before, a big man with an angry red face strode towards him. Mr Trill knew at once that he didn't belong to the middle classes, but rather to the ranks of the labourers. For all he could tell he might have been a miner or a bus driver or a dustman but he certainly didn't belong among those who work with paper and pen and ink.

'You the fellow who's always giving my daughter sweets,' said this craggy-faced apparition standing threateningly in front of Mr Trill and clenching and unclenching his fists as if he was prepared to hit Mr Trill on the nose there and then.

'I . . .' began Mr Trill. But before he could say any more the man – whatever his occupation was – had said,

'Well, I want it stopped. Right? Stopped. You understand.' And his stony head came quite close to Mr Trill's. 'Stopped you understand. Right. Kaput.' And Mr Trill had nodded his head violently whereupon the man had also nodded two or three times saying,

'I know your sort, mate,' and then had marched away leaving Mr Trill in a stunned silence. From that day on the little girl came no longer to the park and Mr Trill had to listen to more nostalgic commentaries on the age from old men – and sometimes old women with shopping baskets – and felt more and more lost and weary. It occurred to him that perhaps he ought to have been more combative when faced by the stony-headed man, perhaps he should have said that he wasn't going to be pushed around by the likes of him, but Mr Trill knew that he wasn't the sort who would ever say any such words and so he declined into melancholy and despair. He had never fought back when he was in school and he would never do so in his old age. But what terrified him most of all and prevented him for a while from returning to the park was that the stony-faced man had simply seen him as a dirty old fellow who was quite prepared to make a sexual assault on his daughter, even though he was wearing a good suit and perfectly good shoes and was a scholar who knew about Homer and Vergil.

The unfairness and injustice of life! Could the man not have seen that he wasn't like that at all but was on the contrary a person of refined tastes who knew Latin and Greek and would never have lifted a finger to touch his child? Was that not entirely visible to him as Mr Trill sat there on the bench. But evidently it hadn't been, evidently he had been assigned to a room in the man's mind in which old men, whoever they were and no matter what their occupation or past history, behaved like sexual maniacs whenever they saw a little girl.

How unfair, how unjust.

I am growing old, thought Mr Trill, I am growing old and tired. Autumn with its chill airs is gathering round me and its breezes are about to waft me to the place to which all men and women go in the end.

And so Mr Trill ceased to visit the park and was never quite the same again. When he went out it was to sit in the library among the other old men and stare with blank wonder at the busts of the big-nosed Romans that were perched on top of the shelves, while a newspaper lay neglected in front of him on the sloping table. And finally he never left the house at all.

As Mr Trill walked along it seemed to him that he did not feel at all tired. The air was mild, though not invigorating, and he felt as if he was strolling in the twilight through a fair, though here there were no bright lights. What had happened to that other girl whose name he could not now remember, whom he had once walked with in just such a balmy twilight when he was in university so long ago? Where had he met her? It must have been at one of the Greek or Latin classes. She was the first girl he had ever taken out. Or had he simply met her at the fair? She had, he thought he remembered, blond hair, and she had turned out to be a good shot with the crooked rifles that they supplied there. What had she won again? A plate was it, or a little doll? Something cheap anyway. They had gone on to the big wheel, he, Mr Trill, erect and dignified, turning over and over, spinning like a top, his heart in his mouth, while she had looked at him with a joyful triumphant smile. How difficult it was to grasp the past, and remember oneself as one had been. Continually one lifted photographs from dusty tables and the faces were like ghosts, inquiring, young, hopeful, belonging to an irretrievable world that one would never see again.

No, he could not remember her name, but she had been a student, that much was clear to him. He remembered her eye squinting along the rifle, the ducks marching placidly in line, and she picking them off one by one till they had dropped and fallen away. And all the time there had been that tremendous vulgar music, the rotation of clusters of coloured bulbs, the stands decorated with classical motifs, faces of wolves like those which had been involved in the foundation of Rome. The wheels turned dizzily in the twilight and the girls and boys passed by with vaguely white flowery faces, as if they were blossoms set on invisible stems. Had he been happy that night? Was that why he remembered it? He had rolled pennies across boards but they had never come to rest on the proper numbers: he had tried the darts but they had missed their targets. And all the time she had been at his side, laughing and happy. How long ago it all was. Had he ever really been at the fair or was it all part of his imagination? As the days darkened so the lights brightened, so the sharp-eyed women behind the stalls came into clearer focus as they handed out their fixed and corrupt guns. And even when she had won her prize how cheap it was. Yet the crooked rifles were raised to eternally hopeful eyes, the big wheel rose brilliantly over the horizon, the coins spun across the slanted board. The fattest woman in the world, the haunted house, the train-ride through the tunnel. How carelessly people spent their money as if it would last forever while the voices shrieked with happy laughter. In spite of the fact that one knew at every moment that one was being cheated, that the odds were stacked against one, that every gun was crooked, every dart was the wrong weight, that it was only by a colossal fluke that one won even the tawdry presents that stared so cheaply out at one – nevertheless one spent money like water, like a king, for a sordid little cardboard plate, or a picture of an unreal spring.

And then the slow walk home through the twilight as if one were swimming. He remembered standing with her – whoever she had been and whatever her name – under a blue light which illuminated the porch of her house. Her face turned blue in the light and beyond the porch was the garden with its flowers wet with dew. The big house towered above him, it was late, and there were no lights in the windows. It couldn't have been lodgings, it must have been her own house. Was his own face as blue as hers? In the distance he could hear the noise of a bus fading. Otherwise there was complete silence.

What had they spoken about?

'Thank you for a lovely evening.'

'Thank you for coming.'

Had they gazed into each other's eyes with the infinite longing of the young? How blue her face was, with its alien blotches of light. That sight he could remember clearly. The wheel had stopped turning and now they were standing on foreign earth again and facing each other in the silence where his heart beat. Had she put her face forward to be kissed? Had either he or she prolonged the conversation trying to think of something new to say while the magical silence lasted, the silence which was teeming with possibilities as a quiet loch with fish.

Where did you learn to shoot?

But all the time he was thinking something else. Should I dare or not? Should I kiss her? Have I the courage? Who are you, dear youth, whom I can hardly recall? Where have you gone? You are so clumsy, so hesitant, so pale. In your eyes there is an unfathomable hope, an innocence that will not return again. And you are standing there in the middle of the resonant silence. And if you kiss her perhaps that will change everything.

And he hadn't. He remembered that he had turned away, his feet making a rustling noise on the gravel just as, much later, they had done in the cemetery when his father had been buried and he with the others turned away. The sound of the gravel was life beginning again.

So he had left her without turning back, without waving, and he had heard a door closing gently behind him. And so he had walked home to his lodgings, to that house in which the old man – the landlady's father – still waited, with his sharp inquisitive ratlike face, and his little hostile grunt, as if he were a small Cerberus, waiting though not barking, just grunting feebly among the shadows.

And he had climbed the stairs and watched the moon through the windows of his attic room among the furniture which the spoilt cat sometimes scratched. He had lain on his back watching the moon with its terrifying scrutinising eye moving stormily in and out of the clouds, creating coppery shapes, figures with ruffs hammered out of cloudy copper, faces, monstrous bodies, wings. Beautiful moon, how long you have existed, moon of lovers, staring paralysing moon whose relentless eye seems to see into the heart of men, moon which Perseus swings on his arm as if it were a stone on the end of a sling.

The bathroom chain was pulled and then there was silence. The old man had finally gone to bed and the house was at peace. The blue face hovered in front of his eyes, distinct, untouchable, and he turned over, his head on the cold white pillow, a nocturnal monk. But in the morning he had forgotten all about it, and had gone to classes as usual as if nothing had happened, and he had turned to his books again, even to Catullus, as if the fair had never existed, as if the haunted house, the tunnel of lovers, no long existed. As if the blue face did not exist.

But it had existed. It had been another decisive moment in his life, a vision of reality which had faded as the blue light and the moon had faded. For he had not made any move, he had remained where he was, in the midst of his own existence.

He sensed a crowd of shades around him, and it seemed that they all had a definite destination in mind.

'Where . . . ' he began but nobody listened to him, as they pushed past him while he stood there hesitantly with his case in his hand.

Eventually he was able to ask a small wrinkled man what was happening.

'It's Agamemnon and Achilles,' he said. 'Every Friday they have a slanging match. Each one stands on his own hill and then they shout across at each other.'

'Every Friday,' said Trill in amazement.

'That's right,' said the small man. 'That's what they do. It's what you might call a tradition.'

Mr Trill followed him. Soon he found that a space of grass had been left vacant but that all round this area people were sitting or standing expectantly.

'Excuse me,' he said continually, as he tried to force himself towards the front. But there was no need for him to be so anxious for on both sides of the space there were two gradually sloping hills, and as he watched he noticed that first from one side there came a warrior dressed in armour of complete black followed by his minions. Could this then be the great Achilles? He was tall and towering and his presence felt like death itself, huge and invincible. It was as if there poured from him deep dark rays of menace and power which drained the life from the spectators. He was still wearing his helmet, also black, and carrying at his side a huge spear.

From the other side there appeared another tall man but less tall than Achilles. His armour was bluish and his shield flashed and glittered in the dim light. His face also appeared commanding but not with the inner authority that blazed contemptuously from the eyes of Achilles, rather with a power that had been bestowed on him by others.

They came to a halt each on his own hill.

'Ha ha,' said Achilles, 'so she killed you when you didn't expect it.'

And he laughed hugely while his minions echoed his laughter, some of them doubled over and slapping their knees.

'It's none of your business,' said Agamemnon but looking embarrassed as if he had been caught in a shameful act.

'Well, you deserved it,' said Achilles. 'You were pretty useless as a commander anyway.'

'I had to keep the army together and you were too temperamental to be of much help. You only helped when we were already winning.'

'That's a lie,' shouted Achilles angrily, 'and you know it. But then you were always a liar. You were being beaten back to the ships when I came to your assistance. And did you not send a messenger to me pleading with me to come back?'

'I only did that because the army asked me to do so.'

'Your army asked you! *Your* army!' said Achilles mockingly. 'And if it hadn't been for your pettiness in taking my concubine away from me I would have fought from the very beginning. The trouble about you is that you can't handle men.'

'And the trouble about you is that all you care about is your own vanity,' shouted Agamemnon. 'You only think about yourself. You the great "star" who must be humoured like a child.'

'Yes, and you spoke to me as if I was a child.'

'So you were, a child.'

'I wasn't a child. I was the one who killed Hector if you remember. I cut his head off and threw a dozen Trojans on the pyre to keep Patroclus company.'

'That may be but you sulked like a girl for years while we bore the brunt of the fight. Wasn't it Ajax who was the great warrior in those days?'

'Ajax! You were glad enough to send me presents and my concubine back when you needed me and when Hector was causing havoc at the ships. You were frightened that you would lose the war and go back home with your tail between your legs. You the great commander! But it was I who saved you and don't you forget it.'

'The fact is,' said Agamemnon, 'if Patroclus hadn't been killed you wouldn't have come out of your tent. He was your real concubine.'

Achilles's terrible eyes seemed to dilate and his whole body in his black armour swelled with rage as he shouted.

'Why, you pathetic little man, if it wasn't for me you would have lost the war and you know it. The whole army knows it. What did you or your famous brother Menelaus do when Helen was stolen from him? No, it was left to me to save your reputation. You may look terrifying to others but not to me.'

'My brother Menelaus fought as well as any man and later he enjoyed Helen when he took her back to Greece.'

'And what about your own wife? Did you enjoy her? What about her lover who held a dagger behind his back for you as they unrolled the red carpet? Why, you are nothing but a fool.'

And again the minions of Achilles laughed out loud clapping each other on the back and slapping their knees while the noise of their mockery was like that of a big stone rolling downhill.

'You may laugh,' said Agamemnon, 'but even you yourself had your weakness. You were not immortal as you thought you were. And after all what was your bravery but that which the goddess gave you?'

This thrust went down well with Agamemnon's followers who like those of the other side began to laugh immoderately. When Trill looked around him into the dimness he saw the spectators laughing too, some taking Agamemnon's side, some Achilles'. Their starved bored faces were twisted with hate and rancour.

'You were being cuckolded while you were away in the army wearing your campaign ribbons,' shouted Achilles. 'Your wife's lover served your wife as if she was a cow.'

'It's hotting up now,' said the small man with the bitter sharp eyes. 'Now they'll go at each other.'

'And what will happen then?' said Mr Trill.

'Nothing. They will just go back with their followers to where they were before. That's all.'

'You mean that they don't fight,' said Mr Trill.

'No. Not at all. Sh,' said the small man impatiently.

'You compare me to a girl in a tent,' said Achilles. 'It's you who were the girl fighting for ten years for a woman's tits. A whore like all the others.'

'And why then were you so fond of your own whore that you wouldn't fight because I took her away from you.'

'*You* took her away from me! Why you streak of dog's spit I could have killed you if I'd wanted to. In the end it was only by a trick that you won the war.'

'You were too stupid to think of a trick.'

'I wasn't as stupid as you. Walking around the camp with your staff and your papers. You were always jealous of me. You didn't want another soldier in the army as great as yourself unless it was Ajax who was as stupid as you. And at the end you got what you deserved, you self-important staff officer. You and your brother were both tricked by women. Ha ha ha.' And his laughter rolled like big stones among the phantom crowd.

'You are a laughing stock,' he shouted. 'Anyone who wears beautiful armour like you must be a laughing stock.'

'And you didn't want to serve under anyone else, isn't that right?' said Agamemnon. 'You didn't want to take the responsibility. You are nothing but a blockhead descended from a goddess as you say you are. Isn't that right?'

'No, it's not.'

'Yes, it is.'

'No, it's not.'

'Yes, it is.'

'No.'

'Yes.'

'No.'

'Yes.'

'Will they go on like this for a long time?' asked Mr Trill who was reminded of himself picking the petals of a flower in his youth and repeating the same monosyllables as these two great antique captains.

'Yes, they will go on like this till one of them gives up.'

'And which one gives up?'

'I never wait to see.'

'Do the others wait?'

'Some do, some don't.'

'I see.'

And Mr Trill got to his feet and wandered away till he could no longer hear the voices of the two soldiers. So this was what Achilles and Agamemnon had been like, shouting at each other like two bad-tempered boys.

What an extraordinary thing. Fighting each other over trivialities while the war raged around them. And yet perhaps that was how all wars were, life itself, even. He sat and thought about it for a long time. Was that really the substance of honour, fighting for the slightest thing, for a feather, for a rag of insult?

And all the time he had been thinking of them as two great invincible heroes who had fought for their country with complete dedication.

'No.'

'Yes.'

'No.'

'Yes.'

The words echoed back from his own childhood, from his schooldays, conkers on an autumn day.

He sighed heavily. What word, what picture, was now sacred, when all ideals were tumbling about him like a pack of cards.

He could hear the voice of his mother. 'What are you doing reading those books all the time? Why can't you look around you? There's a garden to be done and the shed to be painted. But no, you spend all your time reading. Idleness, if you ask me.'

And Mr Trill sat by himself in the dim shade, almost weeping, for it seemed to him that he had misspent his whole life, which had been a phantom one, far from the immediacies of the day. If only, he thought, if only I had enjoyed myself instead of locking myself away with my books. If only I had fought for my rights in the glare and heat of a life that after all only came once. His mother went out helmeted towards the street, to fight her little daily war against the headmaster's wife, who wouldn't speak to her. Her bony face thrust itself forward into the sunlight, and her knuckles whitened with rage, for the honour of the woman who had served in the canteen, with the scarf wound round her head like a flag among the dishes and the tables wet with tea and soup.

'O my God,' thought Mr Trill putting his head in his hands.

'I think,' said Mr Watt the new headmaster, the man whom Mr Trill called the Bingo Caesar, 'that it would be a good idea if that boy Anderson were not to be given seven periods of your time for Greek this year. What do you say?'

He's only been here for six months, said Mr Trill to himself. I don't like him, and I think he's an inadequate fraud, not in any way to be compared with the great Roman headmasters we had before him, but nevertheless I must try to make things easier for him. After all he must feel this himself, that in scholarship, gentlemanliness, elegance of thought, he is inferior, and so I must help him.

'What do you suggest then, headmaster?' he asked him. What a comedian this man was, how could he ever have believed that he would fill the shoes of those who had gone before him and who had emerged from the Graeco-Roman world as civilised and liberal beings. Why, this man had emerged from the world of – chemistry. He was large and bear-like, blunt and tactless, scholarship had not mellowed him nor made him humble. Perhaps his wife had pushed him to where he was now. Perhaps the undeviating road of ambition had showed him at last this post which was clearly too big for him.

'I suggest,' said Watt, 'that you take him along with your other class – the third year – and find room for him in that way.'

But then Anderson was a real find. He had a feeling for poetry and, for his age, an unsurpassed knowledge of the classical world. He was a quiet well-behaved boy who absorbed with a relentless omnivorousness everything that Mr Trill could say to him. It was he for instance who in mathematics had learned about algebraic symbolism on his own and was reading Bertrand Russell at the age of fifteen.

Could he, Mr Trill, teach him while in his room there were thirty other pupils who had no feeling for Latin at all?

I must not let my dislike for the headmaster influence me in any way thought Mr Trill. His own ambition had never been excessive. In fact it was others who had made him apply for the post of Principal Teacher.

One day he had arrived in a room where there were about ten people, some men, some women, who glanced down at papers as he entered dressed in his best brown suit and brown tie. One woman had looked up at last and said,

'Do you think an unmarried man can have any knowledge of children?'

Mr Trill stared at her and then spoke the immortal words which had been part of his legend ever since.

'Madam, Vergil never married as far as we know, and he wrote the greatest poetry in the Latin language.'

He heard someone – a man – snigger, and from that point there was no doubt that he would get the post.

'I'll take him with the third year,' he said.

'Thank you very much, Mr Trill,' said the headmaster and walked away whistling.

Later, in the staff-room, the young English master who made his pupils write poems about gangsters and cowboys remarked,

'I hear that our friend the headmaster is thinking of introducing our children to the industrial world. Princes of finance and bureaucrats from the town will talk to them once a week.'

By this time Mr Trill was taking Anderson for Greek during the lunch periods in a little room up a poky little stair.

At the beginning of the following session, when he examined the brochure that the school published every year he noticed that Greek was no longer available.

'Why,' he asked the headmaster, 'is there no Greek this year?'

'It's quite simple, Mr Trill, there was only one pupil last year and I feel that it is not right to spend so much time on one pupil. Do you not agree with that yourself? Would it not be better for you to spend your undoubted talent on the less classical elements of the school? I have decided that the junior classes will be given classical studies instead. I suggest you introduce them to Rome and Greece, perhaps tell them something about the kinds of clothes they wore, cookery for the girls and sports for the boys. And so on.'

He waved a vague hand and at that moment the telephone rang and Mr Watt, leaning back in his chair, spoke into it with great confidence while Mr Trill looked on.

Well, wasn't that right, thought Mr Trill to himself. Wasn't it right that as many as possible should be told something about the Roman and Greek world? It would mean however that he wouldn't be able to teach the poetry that he loved. Still, wasn't he being elitist and selfish in demanding that his own desires should be satisfied? On the other hand he couldn't understand what these lessons would be like. Was it simply a matter of filling in blank periods for those who did not wish to have anything to do with the classics in the first place?

Should he not really make a stand? But on the other hand how undignified that would be. After all he despised Mr Watt and the latter knew that. The question of the superiority of the classics was not in doubt. And what were his arguments anyway? Was he not simply admitting that he did not want the 'masses' to be educated in them. Mr Trill looked into Watt's small eyes and at the centre of them he detected a little gleam of hatred. Why was Mr Watt trying to destroy him? Was that what lay behind his manoeuvrings? Why should Mr Watt hate him? He had done nothing to him, in fact he had been very accommodating. Did the headmaster despise his subject then? Did he think that in the present day the classics were of no value? The words flowed into the telephone. How smooth this Watt appeared. Perhaps he, Mr Trill, should not have shown him any sympathy at the beginning when he came to school first. The walls were breaking, the barbarian was in charge.

'I . . . ' he began, but Watt was waving him away, his hand over the mouthpiece of the telephone, as if all had been settled. Had it been settled then? Should he not return and debate every inch of lost ground? From now on there would be no Greek in the school and this meant that if any bright boy wished to study Greek he would only be able to do it if Mr Trill tutored him in his own time. Well, he could do that. Matters hadn't reached such a pitch of greed and laziness that he couldn't do that. He wasn't so interested in money that he would refuse a plea for help. Mr Trill stood on the landing indecisively. Had he lost another battle? Of course he had and he knew it. But on the other hand those battles in the ditches were so undignified, so impure. He didn't want to be another rat in the wainscoting.

Still . . . and he almost turned back, but he didn't.

How had Mr Watt become what he had now become, a virtual dictator? And all the time, at least at the beginning, Mr Trill had felt sorry for him, thinking that surely he must feel his own inadequacy. But in fact he had been wrong. Mr Watt hadn't felt any inadequacy at all. He hadn't, in comparing himself with his predecessors, felt in any way inferior. How could that be, Mr Trill asked himself? It was so obvious that he was inferior, and yet he hadn't felt it. Was that because he was thick-skinned or because he actually was superior in some way?

I don't understand what is happening, thought Mr Trill. The liberal classical world is collapsing around us, and *nobody notices*. What an extraordinary situation.

He stared at the wall on which someone had written GOEBBELS EATS HAGGIS. The light poured through the glass roof on to him. Where am I, he thought, what is this place supposed to be?

And yet . . . and yet . . . perhaps it is right that I should try and teach the 'masses'. And if I don't what can I say? Others, he knew, would be cunning enough to find a purely objective way of defending personal territory, but he wasn't clever enough to do that. His honesty was his weakness. He knew nothing about people. It was quite clear that he hadn't understood Mr Watt at any rate. It was obvious that the two of them belonged to two very different worlds. The small cunning eyes bored into his again.

I should really be defending my own territory, thought Mr Trill, and yet there is a certain amount of truth in what he is saying. It is perhaps wrong to give Anderson seven periods of Greek a week.

That had a truth in it but on the other hand was that the real reason why Mr Watt had stopped Greek? Mr Trill took another step down the stair and stopped again. Perhaps he should still go back. But what was he to say? No, it was no longer important that one should love one's subject, that was romantic idealism. What was important was to fight for everything you could get, find a quarrel in a straw. He took another step downstairs.

'You have been very accommodating,' said Mr Watt later, 'in fact I would say that you have been the most accommodating and most civilised of all the teachers that I have dealt with. So therefore it is with a certain amount of trepidation that' – he rested for a moment on the Latin word – 'I approach you again.' Was it Mr Trill's imagination or did Mr Watt use longer words usually derived from the Latin than he had done in the past? Why, once or twice recently, he had come to his room to ask him about the derivation of a word like 'curriculum' and Mr Trill had been glad to expatiate, despising himself at the same time for basking in the warm glow of power.

'Well then,' said Mr Watt, 'you will have heard of my plans for talks to be given by professional local people on selected topics, for example the law, medicine and so on. The question arises about a room for them.' And he glanced round Mr Trill's large and airy room and at his small class.

'I was wondering whether you would be willing that they use this room during these periods. This would only occur once or twice a week. And you could have Mr Blake's room at that time. Mr Blake is free. He has a small chemistry room as you will know.'

I know what he is doing, thought Mr Trill. Eventually he will get this room entirely for Mr Blake, or entirely for these industrial and professional conferences and I will be teaching in Mr Blake's poky room till the end of my days. I know that this is exactly what he is doing. But what shall I say? Shall I say that he can find another room for his conferences, in which case he will tell me that there is no other room more suitable. Or shall I say that I am against these conferences in the first place? But how can you be? he will say. After all, these poor children cannot go out into the world blind and deaf.

And in any case, thought Mr Trill, does it matter where I teach Latin? Do I need a sunny room such as this one is and which I have inhabited for twenty years and which I love? Is this not selfishness on my part? Why, is my comfort to be more important than the future lives of the children as they set out on their journey through life?

'I don't mind,' he said. And again the small sharp eyes glittered with their lights of sharp hate, if that was what it was.

Who are you, thought Mr Trill, who are you really? My scholarship after all is no use to me in this world. All this time you weren't weak at all, all this time when I felt pity for you you knew exactly what you were doing. All this time when I wept for you because you were such a pigmy you thought of yourself as a giant. And perhaps you have gone home and discussed me with your wife and she has helped you to find my weakest spot, just like Achilles. How can I stand out against you, against these ratlike movements, with my shaken armour?

And so without argument Mr Trill surrendered more and more, till finally he had hardly anything at all left. Dressed in his dignity he found that dignity didn't count at all. The past was forever gone and only the present remained and the present was fashioned by these devious manoeuvrings.

Perhaps then he should have fought from the very beginning for every piece of chalk in his room, for every jotter, every desk. Perhaps that was what fighting and honour really meant.

And his father, by retreating into his study, had been wrong, and his mother by intuition had been right all along.

Hail to the Bingo Caesar, he shouted among the shades. And he raised an imaginary glass.

From a deep shade behind him he thought he heard the sound of weeping and there under a tree he saw a woman who was dressed in black. Above her flowed the dark distraught leaves.

'Who are you?' he asked.

'Andromache,' she replied.

'The wife of Hector?' he asked.

'The same,' she said.

'Why then are you weeping?'

'It is because of my fear,' she said.

'Fear of what?' asked Mr Trill.

'Not fear of death,' she replied. 'Not fear of death but another fear. A greater fear than that.'

'What fear is that?'

'Fear of loss,' said the woman as she shivered uncontrollably under the shadow of the leaves.

'Everyone knows,' she began, 'what happened to my husband Hector. Everyone knows that he had to go out to fight Achilles. I remember it very well. I helped him put on his armour on that never-to-be-forgotten day. He was trembling with fear but when I asked him whether he should still go out, he said, "I must, I must," over and over. I asked him why he should go out when he was frightened but he kept saying, "I must, I must," like a little child. That day was a day of sorrows. It was a beautiful calm blue day and the soldiers were gathered together to watch the fight for they themselves wouldn't have to take part. And my husband Hector put on his armour on that calm blue day with the mist in the air and I said to him, "Why do you have to go out and fight?" and he kept saying, "I must, I must." His mother Hecuba was there and his father Priam and to them he returned the same answer.

'And you know what happened to him. In spite of the fact that he ran round the walls of Troy to escape the terrible Achilles and finally had to turn and fight he was still carried about the dust of the plain tied to the victor's chariot wheels.' And she began to weep uncontrollably. 'And you know how Priam had to beg for my husband's body in order that it might be buried. And Achilles threw the bodies of many Trojans on to the same pyre as that of Patroclus. But that was not it. That was not what I was talking about. For there was much else that no one knows about.'

There was a long silence and it seemed to Mr Trill that she would not speak again but at last she said very slowly and quietly.

'Men do not know what women suffer. None of them knows that. For if they must go out and fight we must stay where we are. We must look after the children and we must knit and tidy and clean. The house or the castle must be kept, whether we know or not that the war will soon be lost and we ourselves will be taken prisoner or raped. Thus it was that while Hector fought I must keep the house together, and Priam and Hecuba were old.

'But it was not even that. It was worse than that, much worse. All day Helen went about the castle, young and beautiful, gazing into her mirror as if she were a girl. She was the centre of the world's attention, men fought over her. How could she not be happy? How could she not look on herself as valuable and important? Every day she would wake up in the morning and how could she not say to herself, "I am the centre of the whole world. Great armies are dying and fighting all the time because of me." On the other hand, I worried about my husband continually while I must give orders to the servants to keep the affairs of the palace running smoothly. And who was to say to me that the two great armies were fighting over me? No one was to say that, no one. Every woman must be encouraged and told that she is beautiful. But how could Hector do that when he was out fighting every day? When he was taking the responsibility for a whole kingdom? And all the time Helen was singing and dancing and happy in the house, for she knew that if the Trojans lost Menelaus would take her back again. All she had to do was keep herself beautiful for any eventuality, while I on the other hand lost my beauty every day because of the responsibility I was enduring. No one can know the anger and the rancour that I felt. Because of her my husband was going out to die, because of her my father and mother were trembling with fear, because of her Trojans were dying every day, and all she could do was sing and keep herself beautiful.

'One day I lost control of myself and I told her all this. And who took her side? I will tell you. It was Hector. One day I said to her, "Why don't you go and give yourself to Menelaus, and the Greeks can go home?" But she only looked up from her mirror and smiled for though she was beautiful she was stupid. I could have torn her eyes out. I could have scratched her face to make her less lovely than she was. But who was it who stopped me? It was Hector, my own husband. It was the same Hector who must go and die for her, for a girl – I cannot even call her a woman – who didn't care. What was it to her that I would be without a husband? She had seen many husbands die and one more wouldn't make any difference. And as she was the most beautiful girl in the world so Hector was the greatest soldier. And he loved her. O I know that he loved her. He told me that he didn't, he insisted that he didn't, but I knew that he did. A woman cannot be deceived. He saw me as old and wrinkled, and he saw her in the dew and blossom of her youth. How could he not love her? I have no proof that he slept with her, that I do not know. But I do know that he loved her. When he didn't think that I was looking at him, his eyes would follow her about the palace and she would walk with her swaying woman's walk. I knew what she was doing but Hector did not know. One night I accused him of being in love with her. I said that if he wished to leave me he could do so. If he thought me old he should find someone younger. "I am not keeping you back," I told him. For I was insane with jealousy. And why should I not be? I knew that he loved her though he refused to admit this to himself, and yet he was going out to die for her, leaving me alone to take all the responsibility. Who would blame me for my jealousy?

'I remember the morning he left and went out of the gate of the palace for the last time. Though he was trembling he looked heroic. The palace and the people depended on him. He knew that and everyone knew it. Only Priam and Hecuba and I were sure that he would not live, for who could survive an encounter with Achilles? His armour suited him, he looked handsome and radiant. Only I was aware of the fact that he had been trembling, for of course being his wife I knew everything. And then as he was leaving he kissed us all. He kissed me first and then Hecuba and Helen. Lightly, as it seemed to me, on the lip as if she were his sister. But that was only what he wished us all to think. I on the other hand knew that the kiss was a more meaningful one than that. I knew that she was the only one among us whom he would have wished to kiss with passion though he restrained himself. I knew that it was she alone whom he loved. And she too realised it and turned to me with her blazing triumphant eyes and at that moment I could have killed her. But being who I was I had to remain silent. I had to preserve my dignity to the end as Hector had to preserve his courage, the image of the great soldier and hero, even though he was going to his death and knew it. Never have I suffered so much in my life before or since, seeing my husband setting out to fight a great soldier and a god, for a woman younger and more beautiful than me, and knowing that he was setting out with a lie in his heart. How beautiful that day was, how blue, how calm, and how terrible was the beating of my heart. It was Helen who waved gaily to him as he turned for the last time with his puzzled face and his brow which I knew would be wrinkling under his helmet.

'My love my love I cried to him. And then I heard the scream, like the scream of an animal in agony, and when I turned and looked it was as if Helen was trembling with ecstasy as she might have done in the marriage bed. Her eyes were large and very clear and yet at the same time turned inwards on themselves and her lips were large and full and soft and her whole body was trembling as if at the height of love. I cannot tell you what I felt at that moment for I knew that she was an animal in heat and that she wished to go out and give herself to the victor Achilles in the prime of his courage and his triumph.

'I could have slapped her face, I could have bitten her ear off, but in spite of all my rage, I had to maintain my dignity, for there was much to be done, Priam and Hecuba to be looked after, and my child to be pacified. I could have turned into a stone that morning but I didn't.

'I could have dropped down dead where I was, but I could not afford even that, there was too much to do.

'And that is what broke my heart, that Hector loved Helen and he had gone out from me with a lie in his heart. Perhaps he had never slept with her but nevertheless the lie was in his mind. His love had passed from me to her, from age to youth.'

She became silent under the shadow of the leaves and Mr Trill felt a desolation in his heart as if it had been pierced. He wanted to say something but there was nothing that he could say. All he could do was bow his head in front of that suffering, while the woman's silence swelled and swelled as if it would overwhelm him totally. And there together they sat in the dark shade of the trees, each thinking his thoughts till finally with a deep sigh the woman rose and left him.

At the age of thirty-four Mr Trill had fallen in love with one of his pupils, a girl called Thelma who had long blond hair worn in a pigtail. At first Mr Trill did not know that he was in love for he had never been in love before. It was only when he realised that he was extremely sad when Thelma was absent from his class that he finally knew that he was in love. The only problem was that Thelma was at the most seventeen. Mr Trill began to re-read Catullus in his room at night but could find in that famous Latin poet only salacity and not the pure true language that he craved. For his love was agonisingly sweet and weighted with youth and mortality. It was as if Thelma's youth, its imagined pains and terrors and exquisite joys, was a sign of eternity that concerned itself only with the soul.

As he bent over her jotter to see how she had translated a passage from Livy that he had set, it seemed to him that a faint perfume wafted from her that did not belong to her as such but to a kingdom of which she was simply an emanation. And this was especially so on summer mornings when the mist had not yet been dispersed, and he saw her enter the room in her blue blazer and skirt as if she were not a woman at all, but the spirit of eternal youth, a youth that had forever passed from Mr Trill and which he could hardly remember.

In all the time however that Mr Trill was in love with Thelma he in no way made any advances to her since to him youth was sacred, and especially so as he was a teacher. Thus he sighed in secret and his heart bled in private. At night when he lay in bed he thought of Thelma as of some unattainable star which shone straight into his bedroom from unimaginable distances, a kind of Diana, a huntress connected with spring woods and delicate waters.

How happy Mr Trill was in those days and how well, in his opinion, he taught. It was as if he was inspired and his happiness in the presence of Thelma reflected on to her fortunate class. She was the daughter of a man who worked in the local agricultural office, though Mr Trill of course could not believe this. She was no more his daughter than she was Persephone. She was flesh and blood but she was more than that. Her perfume was that of the Muses as they disported themselves around Helicon.

He found ways of lending her books which in fact she did not read – books with titles like *The Greek Mind* or *The Thought of Greece* – but she was not interested in the classics, and her brightness was not in any case exceptional. Nevertheless Mr Trill saw signs in her exercises of a budding brilliance. In her presence words like 'mensa' and 'insula' had a music of their own, and, once gaunt and antique, became vernal and tender. Sometimes he would sit on his tall barren chair wondering how he could get through the day without seeing her again.

At times he would dream that he might some day marry her, but these times occurred only rarely for to him she was not a being of flesh and blood such that he could imagine her as a wife, whatever that might be like, but as an inspiration and guide through the banality of the days, a sort of Beatrice. If only she would remain as she always was, in that breathless moment when beauty is poised at its height before it begins to tremble and waver and finally fall like a dewdrop from a branch in the early morning when the gossamer webs are drifting in the breeze.

Not a sign however did Thelma give that she loved him in return or was at all occupied with these omens and portents of eternity. Not a sign did she give that his scholarship was devoted to her, that all he was and all he possessed he was willing to lay in a moment at her feet. If Mr Trill had been in the habit of going to school dances he would have attended them for her sake alone but he could not bring himself to do that, for his mirror, as he thought, taught him his unworthiness. Why, he had seen too much of the world for her to love him. He was soiled with knowledge and irony and rancour. And he was too old for her.

He existed in what only could be called a mist of love since his love had no reality in the world around him, was not anchored in it, and could not issue in any fruition. If she was spring he was autumn, and if she had suddenly said to him at some moment charged with significance that she was his forever he would probably have run away, his gown floating behind him. For he craved the pure and impossible which he saw only in her.

Not that some of the other pupils were not sharp-eyed and malicious enough to see what was happening. They all said that old Trill was in love with Thelma and teased her with their knowledge. And Thelma was in one way proud and in another embarrassed. For it could not be said that Mr Trill was handsome nor that his teaching though enthusiastic was interesting. Her own interests were in romantic books and horoscopes. Mr Trill, whose knowledge of classics was devoted and pure, would have been horrified if he had known the quality of the magazines that she devoured every weekend and how firmly she believed that the stars controlled her every action. If in fact she had been in love with Mr Trill she would have searched her horoscopes for signs and omens, she would have asked her aunt to read her tea leaves for her, she would have seen the whole world as an open book trembling with apparitions. The slightest action such as breaking a cup would have been prodigal of supernatural signals and her diary would have been as important to her as Vergil was to him. But Mr Trill remained in ignorance of that world of possible commotions and storms, pullings of hair and jealousies, for to Mr Trill the universe was an ordered place which now and again throbbed with lines from the great poets who had never felt in their whole lives despairs and terrors but had been inspired to their highest flights by the gods themselves.

Was it perhaps that Mr Trill, sensing that his youth was leaving him, committed all his feelings to that one girl representative to him of all youth, or was it that he was truly in love? Who can tell? It is certain that if she had been ill he would have been able – if he had been asked – to wait patiently at her bedside for hours and days on end. But as for her days of health what could he do during them? She was certainly pretty with her fair pigtail, her pale face with very blue eyes, her long slender neck, her blue blazer and her blue skirt. She was like a ship that is ready to leave harbour and enter the mist that shrouds all youth when it sets off on its journey. How he would have protected her in his imagination from that hollow journey from which he could see great suffering and difficulties springing, similar in fact to the ones that he had endured himself.

If he had only known her as she really was, her hurried glances at unfinished homework, her concern with hockey, her wish that one day she would have a pretty house, nice clothes and crystal vases, and her total attention to the banalities emitted by disc jockeys in the early hours of the morning before she went to school. If he had only seen her mind that was totally ordinary, and realised that never once did she think of Vergil after she had finished her set work for the day and that she panicked totally when she was faced by a difficult problem in mathematics. If he had seen her when she was dressing for a school dance pirouetting in front of the long mirror in the corridor. If he had seen her when she was quarrelling with her younger brother at breakfast every morning while she grabbed at the last minute the thin slice of toast that was her only sustenance at that time of day since she was looking after her figure. If he had seen her mind which was a storehouse of miscellaneous information and feelings, like an antique shop which is cluttered with all sorts of goods leaning crazily against each other, mirrors, mattresses, wardrobes, pillows and hundreds of other articles which have settled there as naturally as snow.

But he did not see this, he only saw her in his classroom when the sun shone through the window on to her hair, making it radiant and pure, flawless and perfect. If he had seen the treachery of which she was capable, the tantrums, the jealousies, but, no, he saw none of these.

Sometimes he tried to catch her eye, but she always looked away. Was it perhaps that she had not seen him? Was it that she was dreaming some impossible dream of youth? Was it, dreadful thought, that she did not really like him? But at least he could test that by marking her jotter, by being close to her, by, most daring action of all, sitting beside her at the same desk.

And soon she would be leaving the school altogether, soon she would be setting out on her temporal voyage after her eternity of dreaming, and he would never see her again. The days were passing and the end of the session was approaching. How his heart beat as if it wished to squeeze a value out of every passing moment. Soon the last bell would toll and she would walk out of the gates with her school bag over her shoulder, over her arm, among all the other ex-prefects and ordinary scholars. Soon she would enter the summer after her spring. And for these months, these weeks, these days, the desks glittered as if with a supernatural radiance, and Mr Trill spent himself on poetry and rhetoric. The days passed, the bells rang, the hours were devoured. Soon the school would be a dark place again without illumination. My youth, my youth, is going, thought Mr Trill.

And then one fatal day he passed by design the room which the senior girls were allowed to use during their free time. Perhaps he thought that he would catch a glimpse of her whom he loved through the half-open door. In front of him he could see the cracked mirror in which the girls studied their own reflections, and there standing in front of it was another girl, not Thelma, but someone else. Who? What was her name? Muriel? And Muriel, with coat flying about her as if it were a gown was parading in front of the mirror and saying,

'And now Thelma my dearest love, *carus cara carum*, will you please tell me what Vergil meant by these famous words which he once spoke when having a solitary pee in Italy. Will you please tell me that, my dearest Thelma?'

He couldn't see her face in the mirror because the glass was cracked and she for the same reason could not see him. Her capped head flashed and flickered, and her gown swung and floated. And from behind her, though he could see no one, he heard the happy clear laughter of Thelma, as if she were delighted with the performance which spotty-faced Muriel was giving. He stood transfixed. He . . . He could not go in, he would not give them that pleasure, he was too proud, too dignified for that. But if ever a heart . . . if ever a heart was broken it was his. Dazed he stood, the pain piercing his soul, and listened to the happy laughter as if it were coming to him from the depths of hell itself, from that inferno in which Vergil and Dante had travelled. His legs shook, his face was on fire. What a fool he had been, what an old fool. To think that he had ever credited that girl with any delicacy of feeling, to think that he had thought she would walk with him through these shining pages, so resonant with power and pathos. No, it was impossible. Never again, never, never again. Never again would he give his heart to anyone in order to endure such mockery. Muriel disported herself in front of the cracked mirror of that poky room and there just outside it, a frail eavesdropper, Mr Trill died.

And thus it was that when the pupils came to say goodbye to him he wasn't available: he had as he had written on the board been asked to take part in an urgent meeting. In fact he was

standing alone in the library watching them leave the school
for the last time, now and again turning back to look, and
waving their scarves in the air, as they entered the street on
which people talked and walked, and passed the shops in which
the transactions of the world were carried out. Mr Trill
hardened his heart forever and put on his Roman shield, while
at the same time he read that poem of Catullus in which he says
goodbye to his brother and which ends,

Et in perpetuum, frater, ave atque vale.

In his wanderings, still carrying his case as if he were a clerk in
a dimly lit office, Mr Trill had come to the banks of the river
again but at a different point from that at which he had landed.
It flowed sluggishly along through the pervading mist and
beyond it Mr Trill could see the vague mass of the castle about
which he had previously been told. It seemed to him that he
could hear from the thin mist the baying of hounds.

'Strange,' said a voice from behind him and when Mr Trill
turned round in a startled manner he saw a little man with a
wrinkled puzzled brow who was gazing at him with dull eyes.

'No one knows what goes on in there,' said the man. 'I've
often stood here and wondered. Some people go into that
castle and they never come out again. I've seen it happening.'
And he nodded his head wisely two or three times.

'That's odd,' said Mr Trill.

'It is indeed,' said the little man speaking rapidly like one
who wishes to convince his audience of an important idea.

'I have a natural turn of curiosity myself, my wife often used
to speak to me about it, and I have often stood here wondering
what is going on over there. I have seen people being ferried
across to the castle and for a moment when they land the
hounds seem to stop barking and there is silence but the people
never come back. Not once have I seen any of them returning.'

Mr Trill found it hard to place the man's accent; it was as if he
was pretending to be more educated than he really was. His
mind, attracted by puzzles – every morning in the staff-room he
had been in the habit of filling in a newspaper crossword –
brooded vaguely on the castle. Was there some secret connected

with it? Did some terrible fate belong to it, some obscene tortures? Was there even in Hades a group of people who managed the shadowy territory as if it were a real empire.

And if so who were these people and why were they never seen?

'Some people say,' said the little man as if he had understood Mr Trill's thought, 'that men's brains are taken out of their heads and stored in the cellars there.'

'Oh,' said Mr Trill shivering.

'But most of us just want to stay here,' said the little man sadly. 'We suffered enough while we were on earth.'

'That's true,' said Mr Trill. 'I can understand that and one could be happy enough in this place – even in this place.'

'Yes, indeed,' said the little man. 'However, perhaps you are different. Perhaps you are an adventurer and wish to see what is going on on the other side.'

'Not me,' said Mr Trill. 'I have suffered enough too and in any case there is more than enough here to puzzle me without looking for more.'

'Every man to his nature,' said the little man. 'For myself I have always been of an inquisitive nature and I spend a lot of my time here on the bank of the river thinking and wondering what is happening in the castle. But that is the way I am,' he said proudly. 'Not everyone is like that.'

He brooded for a moment and continued, 'Anyway, I'm not important. I was never important. There were millions like me when I was alive. But I always had this curiosity. When my fellow workmen were content to accept orders I would wonder if they were the right orders, do you understand me, and why they were being given. And many times I thought I could have done a better job myself.'

'I can appreciate that,' said Mr Trill absently.

'You are saying that but you are not listening to me much,' said the little man in a resigned voice. 'I understand that and I'm used to it. No one ever listened to me. I used to sit and people would talk around me and it was as if I wasn't there. This place now is full of gods and goddesses. But have you ever thought how hard it is for people like me to get up in the morning?' And he fixed Mr Trill with his dull eyes. 'There is nothing ahead of them, no glory, nothing like that. All they have is their work. Famous people have great events to look forward to. They have parties, and they get invited to dinners, but nothing like that ever happened to me. Our wives despise us because nothing important happens to them through us. And women like to be noticed, they like to dress up, to speak to important people.'

As he spoke the man seemed to become smaller and smaller, almost diminishing to the size of a dwarf, and Mr Trill thought that even his colour was changing as if from white to brown or even black. His brow too was wreathed with wrinkles which looked like tiny snakes.

'I can tell that you once were a man of importance,' said the little man. 'It's in the way you walk, the way you speak. But I never had any power. Sometimes when the day was stormy I didn't want to get up from my bed. I had to force myself to put my feet on the floor. My sons and daughters despised me, for I wasn't famous in any way. No one saluted me when I passed them on the street. In shops I was served last because even the shop assistants knew that I wasn't important. And if I tried to kick up a row they wouldn't listen to me, they ignored me as if I wasn't there. And sometimes I could hardly hear my own voice. Policemen pushed me aside and charged me with offences because I had no one to protect me. They would rough me up and then let me free and not even apologise. That happened to me once, it was a case of mistaken identity but the cops just said, "Don't you show your face here again, you little bastard." "And what about my scars," I said, "what about my black eye." "Your black arse more like. Clear off or we'll mark you for life." But of course they don't do that, they use rubber truncheons so they don't mark you. Why, even my wife didn't meet me off the ferry because she was ashamed of me. No one loved me all the days of my life. Can you understand what I'm telling you?' said the little man, who had almost become a hunchback in the dim light. 'All I saw of the world was my bench and my tools. And if I had an idea someone else would take the credit for it. Oh, they spoke nice to you but they took the credit just the same. If I told a joke

I always got the story wrong because of nervousness and no one could get the point of it. I was always flustered and I spoke too fast and so no one bothered with me. Even you aren't listening to me properly. You are saying to yourself, Why doesn't this fellow stop speaking? What is he on about? But I have thoughts of my own too and I'm not stupid. I was a good carpenter in my day, I have my certificate. There are a lot of the young ones now who don't have a certificate and couldn't care less, but I cared. I liked to make a piece of good furniture. Understand me? Are you listening? I took pride in my work but the others don't do that. Why I've seen them putting nails, would you believe it, in mahogany instead of joints. And have you seen their tables and their chairs? A dog wouldn't sit on them. And they talk and people listen to them, that's what I can't understand. They don't care about anything but they are listened to just the same. Even my wife didn't listen to me. Perhaps you've never had that experience. Perhaps you were never married. You don't look as if you were married. Oh, I notice things and I said to myself, as soon as I saw you, I don't think this fellow is married.

'Even my children laughed at me and because I was so small they would beat me up to get money for the gambling machines. When they grew up and were earning a wage they never gave me any of it; they would say, "We didn't ask to be born." They expected their food and lodging as if they had a right to it. And what about me I used to say to them, "Do you think I wasn't born?" They blamed me for their lives, for bringing them into the world. I was tortured by them, they made fun of me, they imitated me.

'My children and my wife despised me. What was there for me? Many a time I thought of killing myself but the good God has told us not to do that. And anyway I never had the courage. Do you know what the difference between the rich and the poor is? I've thought about it a lot and even more since I came here. The rich have a future, do you understand me, and the poor don't have a future. There was a star I used to watch in the sky in the morning before I went to work. It might have been Venus, I don't know. It was as sharp as a thorn. I used to hate that star and yet I looked for it every morning when I got out of my bed.

'Even when I died my family scrambled for the few things that I had. Do you know that they broke the joint of my finger to get my ring. See, I can show it to you.'

And he showed Mr Trill his broken finger as if it were a trophy. 'And they bought the cheapest coffin they could find. I knew about good wood and I knew it was cheap. But they didn't care. And how many were at my funeral? I can tell you. Six. My wife didn't come. She pretended she was too sick. Imagine that.

'Every day that passed was like every other day, except that some days if I had nerve enough I got drunk. But then my wife would shout and scream at me and say to me, "How do you expect me to pay for the hairdresser if you're going to be as drunk as a pig?" You tell me that. She was like a knife in my side. She didn't just want food and shelter. She wanted honour, she wanted people to look up to her. Why did I live at all, that is what I wish to ask?'

And the small man gazed up at Mr Trill with the large liquid eyes of a dog and Mr Trill could find no answer to his question.

'I thought so,' said the little man, 'I thought so. I don't blame you. I don't blame you at all. I don't blame anyone at all. This is how it is.'

And before Mr Trill could speak he had faded into the mist so that after a moment it was as if he had never been there at all, as if he were only an emanation of the mist, while behind him the castle glowered in the dimness, the castle whose purpose was obscure, and from whose environs hounds howled now and again, as if they themselves were questioning, with their wet snouts, the mist around them.

There was a blind blundering about him and Mr Trill recoiled as a gigantic figure loomed out of the mist, like a wrecked yet moving ship.

'Aargh,' said the mouth of the figure, and its words were strangled in its throat.

'I,' said Mr Trill about to run still clutching his case. 'I . . . '

'Aargh,' said the figure searching for him and laying a hand on his arm. The massive head leaned down towards him, in the middle of it a scorched single dead eye, piteously dead.

It was like the huge idiot that Mr Trill had often seen, in the town where he taught, in his vast flapping coat standing in the middle of the road and directing the traffic while sometimes the policemen looked on benevolently and sometimes drew him kindly away on to the safe pavement.

'You?' said the figure, lightly touching his arm.

'Mr Trill,' said Mr Trill in an agitated voice.

'Trill,' echoed the huge mouth. 'Trill.'

The word was like a big stone in its jaw.

'Noman?' said the figure, 'No man?'

'No,' said Mr Trill, 'not no man.' Surely this giant was not still searching for the nimble Ulysses even in the depths of Hades. 'Not Noman,' said Mr Trill thinking of the painting by Turner where Ulysses stood high on his ship, his arms spread triumphantly in victory while he waved his flag and around the ship sailors like dead souls milled, and on the left there was the darkness which the raw sun had not yet illuminated.

'Noman,' said the figure with a sigh. 'Alone was. Noman came, killed my sheep, killed my good sheep, ate them. Lucky I caught. Ate them.'

'What?' said Mr Trill. 'Did Noman eat your sheep? Was that why you . . . ?'

'Alone was, shepherd, harming noman. My lovely sheep. Ate them.'

'But,' said Mr Trill, 'that is not . . . '

'Got them . . . Ate.' The giant licked his lips as if he felt blood on them.

'Cheated me. Said name Noman.' His dead eye turned towards Trill, a waste circle.

And Mr Trill had a vision. Inside the cave the quick intelligence of Ulysses searched lithely, seized on the stick, grew an eye, liquid, smart, Mediterranean, put out the other savage eye, and blazed afresh as with the sharp vision of a fierce dedication to survival.

It was the new blue eye of the Mediterranean, European, scientific, piercing, single, egotistical.

'My sheep, lovely sheep,' said the pastoral giant. 'Killed them. Noman spoke. Lonely. His voice echoed.'

The massive hands had left Mr Trill's arm and they flapped about in the mist like grey claws, extinct, searching.

'Felt for them. Threw stones. Heard them falling in the water. Laughed at me.' He stopped as if he were listening to the laughter coming out of the darkness, echoing from all directions. 'Noman, noman, noman,' said the laughter. And that was what it was, thought Mr Trill, it was the laughter of Noman, the new Noman, the interchangeable Noman, the schemer who would survive, the nameless one, eternal salesman of the new moving world. Where Noman went no flowers grew but around the ancient giant there was a solid shadow, a place of ancient songs and foliage.

'Noman,' said the mouth. 'Talker. Little man. Mouth always going. Speaking. Took sheep away.'

The long sharp stick hissed through his eye and he was blundering about on the headland where the wind howled, the wind of his own land, dear to him, now blind, unseen. The sound of the wind was like the music of strings, singing about the lonely land, while Ulysses headed for the cities, devious, a blue eel.

'Noman,' sighed the giant. 'Cheated me. Caught him eating sheep. Ate the little men. Eye put out. Alone. Shouted Noman. Noman came. Noman didn't come.' He floundered about in the dead branches of language, puzzled, blundering, 'Noman didn't come, went on in ship. Noman came, of own people. Laughed. All laughed. Noman laughed. Every man laughed. Own people laughed. Brothers, sisters laughed. Noman laughed, laughter everywhere.'

And Mr Trill heard the laughter coming from all directions, thousands and thousands of little distinct laughters blending into one huge laughter as if like the sun on the Mediterranean the world was a bowl of sunny laughter. And through it moved Ulysses, a thin whip of survival, heading for his island, his mind ticking ceaselessly like a bomb, an infection returning home.

Laughter everywhere, the ironic laughter of the whole world, echoing Noman, the sea and the rocks laughing, as little Noman flourished his flag and the sails filled, and the sea waited, laughing ceaselessly. In the centre of the laughter was little vain Noman on whom the joke was as much as on the stranded giant, lost among his vast woolly sheep.

'Alone was,' said the giant with the words like pebbles in his throat. 'Night and day the same. Eye bandaged, people about me. "Who?" they said. "Noman," I said. And they laughed. Eye throbbed. Pain everywhere. In plain, on hills. Nothing seen.'

Tenderly Mr Trill touched the giant's arm. The monster sighed as if pleased. His vast blind head nodded in the air above, searching.

Mr Trill saw them all in their tribes, in the caves, huddled together, their sheep about them. The sun rose, the sun set, day after day: darkness came down, darkness dispersed. The fields were white, then black. Still they huddled together, rose in the morning, then tended their sheep.

Then Noman came. The island was seen by a new eye, a quick moving eye that investigated advantages, positions, vegetation, food. It moved about the island seeking to use it, falling now here, now there, like a torch, powerful and shining. It did not hear the music of the island, the antique tune that the wind made, had made for century after century. It was a famished restless eye that would not cease moving till death came. It did not see the antique heavy settled figures.

Noman was a stranger on the island, but it was as if it belonged to him, as if its politics were his, as if its future belonged to him. The sharp unjaded salesman seized on all things on the island as a woman picks up and adores her own dear ornaments, which are hers alone, which tell who she is. It is her house, every corner, every cranny, every little china figure. So the island was to Noman, for Noman was no man. He was the little figure lost in eternity but determined that eternity should echo with his mind.

'Noman,' came the voice out of the mist. And the huge stones fell into the water and beside the boat there was the thick darkness that not even Noman could illuminate. Though the rigging might hum, the darkness would always follow the ship like a stain, and no sunlight would ever darken it.

'Sorry,' said Mr Trill over and over.

'Name Sorry?' said the giant.

'No, name Trill, but sorry sorry.'

The giant gazed blankly down, among the thickets of language, a lost head. It sighed as if the words were painful to it, like the stick that it remembered, the sharp burning stick that hissed about its once serene ring.

'Sorry, sorry,' said Mr Trill, 'most sorry.'

The craggy head lowered and sighed among the mist.

'It is Noman that caused it,' thought Mr Trill. And it seemed to him that he had been given a tremendous revelation, so huge that he could hardly grasp it, as he could not grasp the grey giant who was so helpless beside him. The physical was manoeuvred by the mental, the body was guided by the mind. The headlands, ancient with music, surrendered to the intelligence. Ulysses was the blue sharp quick Mediterranean eel.

'Alone,' said the giant. And its voice echoed in the greyness. 'Alone.'

It bent its head down over Mr Trill as if seeking, and then with the same sigh, as if it had smelt from him, as well, the betrayals of civilisation, turned away, and blundered off like a big sad dog into the mist.

Mr Trill stood behind the lectern and made his last speech.

'There have been many changes since I came to this school. I would like to think that in the early days the influence of the Roman and Greek traditions was very strong but now all that has gone. In the old days we wore gowns but now hardly anyone wears a gown. I remember Mr Mason who taught history. He used to mark three hundred exercises a week. He was a man devoted to his studies, a true Roman. Sometimes I think that it wasn't Octavius who won at all but Mark Antony and that he brought Cleopatra to Rome: but I have only thought this in more recent times.

'I have been very happy here on the whole. My greatest delight was when some pupil or other came to me and asked me the meaning of the words in a poem, but that, I regret to say, was in my early career. However all is not yet lost and we pass the torch on to the young who will, we hope, keep it alight. As I stand here behind this lectern I feel I am only saying *au revoir*, not goodbye. The dead are always with us though we may sometimes forget that. A school is not a building, it is a communion of the living and the dead. Have we not added our tiny stone to the cairn that is perpetually being built? My father was a classics master as I am and he passed down his tradition to me. My mother . . . ' And here Mr Trill paused but didn't finish the sentence.

'I know that on days like these it is traditionally the case that we tell jokes. But I feel in too sombre a mood to tell jokes. For I see every day the barbarians approaching more and more closely to the walls.' And here he looked directly into the eyes of the headmaster. 'I see our traditions dying, discipline being eroded day after day. Is it our fault? Is it the fault of society? Who knows? Is it the treason of the clerks? I remember when I came here first the headmaster told me, "You must never sit down when you are teaching. How can a man teach well when he is sitting down?" I have never forgotten his words and I have always obeyed them. For when you sit down you begin to grow lazy, and laziness is our enemy. Laziness and despair. I have never despaired. In spite of everything I have always kept in front of me the example of the Romans, people like Brutus and Cato. For how can we live unless we have great exemplars to sustain us?

'I remember many years ago there was a boy in this school and he couldn't pass his Latin which he needed for getting into university. I spent my intervals and free periods teaching him. And he managed to pass after all, he managed to get into university. But what did he do when he got there? He started to drink and go out at nights instead of attending to his studies and the next I heard of him he was working as a conductor on the buses. At times like these one feels that there is no point in going on. But there *is* a point in going on. It is a struggle which must be renewed every day, and we must not fail the generations, though it is true it seems to me that the earlier generations were the most mature and the most hardworking. There is a responsibility on us all, that is why we become teachers in the first place. I could never imagine myself as other than a teacher.'

At the back of the room he could see the table laden with

cakes and tea and it reminded him that his mother had once served in a school canteen before she had married his father. Again he was about to say something about her but refrained.

'I often used to think about those teachers who left the school. What happened to them? They went out into the great wide world but what happened to them after that? Did they disappear from human view? No, they did not. Their work lies here and also in the hands of those who work and teach and turn lathes in the furthest corners of the earth. Perhaps even there our work is remembered, over the whole world. In some steaming jungle, on some ship or other, in an office, in the furthest east, perhaps our words and our instructions are still remembered. That is what I think, and that is my faith.

'But do not forget that civilisation is thin and fragile, that the barbarians are always beating at the gates, and we must be the guardians and the watchers, sentries at our posts as even Socrates was. As long as we exist perhaps night won't fall.

'When I came here first the pupils wore school uniform. Now they don't. These little things are significant, though some may not think so. When you think about it every little thing is significant. It is the addition of the little things that make up the quality of a civilisation, and a school too is part of civilisation, and is a leader and keeper of that civilisation.

'My name is Trill, as you know, and on the whole I am an insignificant man. But I am the guardian of the works of men more significant than me. I am the casket for their works and their teachings and so I become significant. And the same is true of all of us. When I come into the room I am not just Mr Trill, I am Vergil and Homer as well. This, when you think of it, is a great honour. Of course in the tenor of my life I have done some petty things, perhaps to some of you. I may even have argued about the peg on which my coat was hung, but nevertheless beyond and behind all this I am the guardian of the best minds of the ages. Isn't that a frightening responsibility? Sometimes, as you know, children will almost break our hearts because they do not seem to be listening to what we have to say to them. But in the end we shall prevail because that is what we must do, there is no alternative. There were times when I didn't feel like coming to school in the mornings and some of you may have felt the same yourselves. But I came just the same because every minute counts.

'I had this sense of urgency as if it had been left to me to save the souls of our younger generation. Was that, do you think, egotism or pride? Perhaps it was. So, before I leave, I wish to say to you that we must have this urgency. I know that many pupils used to laugh at me and say, "There is Mr Trill again, rushing along the corridor with his book open in front of him." But why did I do that? It was because I did not wish to waste a minute, for the battle is continually around us. Sometimes its sound is muted by the concerns of the day, but don't believe that it isn't there and that many people don't live and die in that battle. It too has its victims and its victors. It too has its flags and its cohorts and its generals. I was never one of the generals, I would have described myself as a corporal or even a standard bearer. But that didn't bother me. The only thing that bothered me was, Will I be found at my post? Will I be a watchman?

'And that is the final message that I would like to leave with you. We must do what we can the best we can. Nobody can ask any more from us.'

The speech ended to prolonged applause. However, though Mr Trill didn't hear them, there were criticisms. Morgan the Geography teacher for instance said,

'One would think he was Julius Caesar or Hannibal the way he talked. Everyone knows that he had no time for the dimwits, and these are the real test after all. He was lucky to have had the best of it. Coffee, Miss Scott?' He shook his hair back boyishly as he always did and Miss Scott said, 'Tea for me, Mr Morgan. I thought you knew that.'

During the brief meal the teachers talked about inflation, pay, bad pupils, shortage of accommodation, marks. Finally Mr Trill was left alone. When most of the teachers had left after saying goodbye to him, he himself slipped out. He walked along the empty corridors which the cleaners had already washed. His feet echoed with a hollow sound and it seemed to him that he was young again in that place which he had for so long inhabited. Voices returned to him from the dead, gowns rustled, the walls were clean and new again. He stood at the main door, pausing a moment before shutting it. Then he pulled the great ring of the handle behind him. As he walked across the playground it was as if he was dizzily coming into the world again, about to scream like a child which has just been born. He descended the steps and waited for the cars to pass. Then he crossed the road and went home to his lodgings.

'Who are you?' said Mr Trill as the figure emerged from the mist about him. But it did not answer, as it shyly gazed across the dark water.

Mr Trill felt a strange awe and ardour as if he were in the presence of a famous, almost divine man such as he had never seen in his life before. Head bowed, as if it were a monk, the figure studied the river with its fathomless modest eyes.

'I think,' said Mr Trill, 'I think you are Vergil himself.' And he went down on his knees as if to a god. The dark water, the swirling mist, were about the two of them as they met in the faded light.

'I think,' said Mr Trill, 'by your silence and your modesty that you are Vergil himself. I wish to tell you, I wish to tell you,' he stammered, 'that I think you are the greatest of all poets.'

'*Sunt lacrimae rerum mentem mortalia tangunt*,' he said, 'I think that is the greatest line of poetry that was ever written.

'The tears of things,' said Mr Trill as he gazed at the figure with love and respect.

'That is all past,' said Vergil. 'That is all over now. My work was inadequate. In comparison with divine Homer my work was nothing.'

'But the pity,' said Mr Trill, 'the pity, the divine pity.'

'That too is over,' said Vergil. 'My trouble was that I could never write narrative. I should never have written of Rome. I was never a public poet. Better for me to have written of my farm. I should never have written of great events. What were politics to me?'

Gazing sadly across the waters he said, 'I should have destroyed all my verse. It was not good enough. I did not have the divine sunniness of Homer and his good temper. The

best I could do were set pieces. I substituted style for content.
I was a decadent. All I wished was to be a private person.'

'Did you not then get pleasure from writing?' said Mr Trill.

'Pleasure? It was the greatest labour that one can conceive of.
Words slipped away from me. I could not keep them together.
I was alone, polishing and polishing, refining and refining.
How tired I was of Aeneas. Was he perhaps myself? If he
wasn't myself who else could he be? Religious, correct, boring,
what did I have to do with him? As one of your own poets has
written, the task made a stone of my heart, I was tired of him.
How is the founding of a country worth a lost love? How? I
betrayed myself. Is Rome worth one broken heart? Tell me
that. That is the question that has tormented me. Is the great
task, the great hero, worth the lives of the innumerable dead?'

'I do not know,' said Mr Trill.

'But is it? Think of it. Aeneas has to found Rome and what
was Rome? Think of what it became, the games at which
human beings were thrown to the lions while the emperors and
the mob cheered in their bronze and their rags. Was that worth
the death of one woman, one soul? How could I have written
the words, "But meanwhile Aeneas the True longed to allay
her grief and dispel her sufferings with kind words"?

'I tell you, I grew tired of him. He should have forgotten
about Rome. What was his duty but a terrible blindness? What
are all our duties in the end but that? I betrayed myself as a
poet. What were these boring battles to me when I wished to
write about the human heart? What is history but the deaths
that we need not share? That is why I wished the *Aeneid* to be
burned because in it I had been false to myself. Do you
understand? It wasn't the labour that I regretted nor was it the
technical revision that I needed another three years for. Not at
all. It was the central question that perplexed me and that I
couldn't solve. On the one hand there is the founding of a great
nation, which I believe in, yes, to a certain extent I believed in
it, for after all what else was there to believe in? But I was
seduced by the human and I understood that a great nation is
built over the bones of men and women. Night after night I
heard their cries as if they were trying to get in. My heart

trembled and shook with their cries and their pain and their tumult. How could I write poems, how could I? How could I fashion lines in the midst of all that pain? Tell me that, whoever you are. Here at least however I have some peace. I do not wish to speak of my poems again, they shriek at me with their bleeding roots.'

'No,' said Mr Trill, 'that isn't all there is, surely. Discontent everywhere. Discontent and smallness where one had thought was greatness.'

'I should not have stayed so long in my study,' said Vergil. 'I should have gone out into the world that Homer knew. I should have lived off the justice of the moment. Do you understand?'

He was silent at the water, and then turned to Mr Trill.

'It is not that I wish to be impolite. How could I wish that? You too have had your life. Perhaps you have lived off the justice of the moment more than me though perhaps you aren't a poet. So few of us have the nerve and the power to do what I have just said we should do. A line a day, that is all I wrote, perfecting, perfecting. And all the time I had a vision that I should follow the curve of the human heart. All my work was but a feeble approximation to my ideal. As we stand here, by this dark water, what are empire and bronze to me? I have thought about this for a long time while I have been here. Up above, the empire no longer exists and when it did exist it was only a shade. My greatest terror is that I shall meet Dido. What should I say to her? Tell me, whose side was I on? I betrayed myself because I made a case for Aeneas when there was no case for him at all. None. What has the king to do with the poet, what has the empire to do with him? Nothing. What has power to do with him? I tell you I should have burned that book with my own hands.'

As Mr Trill sat side by side with Vergil and gazed into the dark water it was as if he saw that all effort is vain, that all endeavour is without sense, that beyond statues and paintings and books there is the shadow of the dark stream which reflects nothing, thinks nothing and only is it itself.

'No,' he shouted, 'it is not true. Not true.' And his eyes

flashed as they had once used to do when he had entered the classroom with a copy of the *Aeneid* open in his hand while outside the window the traffic roared by. 'No,' he shouted, 'there is something left. Something remains.'

'What is it that remains?' said Vergil turning towards him his pale tormented face. 'All that can remain is the human heart and how have we treated it? How have we written of it? We set up systems and so we avoid writing of it. We do not attend to the trembling, the fear, the music of the human heart. I was seduced by armour and war because I myself was unwarlike, and I did not see the trap into which I had been led. I forgot about the terrors of the living. Rome was a curtain that hid the truth I should have seen. The human soul, that is what is important, the infinite tenderness.'

'And that you had,' said Mr Trill. 'Of all the poets that is what you had. The tears of things.'

And he thought that in one way he at least was like Vergil, he had never married, he had suffered the silence and the dispossession, like a tree that stands by itself without leaves, bare to the wind.

'No,' he shouted, 'you have not failed. How could you have failed when so many centuries later I still read your works?'

But the figure, fatigued and insubstantial, had faded away into the mist and Mr Trill could no longer see it. 'Dear God,' he said, 'what now is there left to me when even the author whom I loved best thinks that he has failed, when the heroes of my childhood turn out to be simple and egotistical men, when the monsters abuse the heroes for being hateful and aggressive. What is there left for me to do or say?'

And he sat with his case beside him on the bank of the river gazing deep into the dark water where no reflections were visible. Is the dark water the end of everything, he asked himself. Is that really true? The dark water where no fish lives, where no wave moves, where there is only motionlessness without end.

He gazed deep into the dark water and it changed as he looked, and he was lying in his bed again.

Mr Trill lay in his bed in the hospital staring at nothing. An old woman with a hoover was humming like a hornet round the ward. After a while Mr Trill began to study her. She had a scarf wrapped round her head and she wore a blue uniform and her nose was narrow and long. Where have you come from, thought Mr Trill, do you have children? When did you begin to work here? For some strange reason she reminded him of his mother, busy, distant, forever creating noise among the silence. Across the floor lay bands of sunlight, which streamed in through the window and among them the dust sparkled and moved as if it were alive. Through the windows he could see trees with golden leaves, and in the distance a moor which was turning brown. He lay in his bed knowing that he was going to die.

It all happened very suddenly. One moment he was reading in his room, the next his chest was a battlefield of pain which threatened to kill him. He had enough energy to knock on the wall before he fell. The next thing he knew he was in an ambulance and the next thing after that he was being operated on. A doctor was bending over him while he gazed upward at the ceiling. In a short while he was asleep.

The woman had now passed his bed and was hoovering the space in front of the next one. Mr Trill stared at the red blanket, at the man with the gaunt face who was lying under it, at the black grapes which lay beside him on the table. The man got visitors regularly, and Mr Trill got none except that his landlady came now and again. He would have liked visitors, even some of the pupils he had taught, even some of the teachers who had once been his colleagues, but no one came. It was as if he had already dropped into a big hole from which he could see no one, through which light would never again escape as the ring of gravity tightened.

So this is what death will be like, thought Mr Trill, and he was not frightened, only tired as if all the work he had done during his life had at last caught up with him. In fact sometimes he felt peaceful and content as if what was happening was happening to someone else, and not to him at all. Sometimes it was as if he was gazing down at himself from a position above the bed, and wondering what he was doing there. At night he could hear coughing, and nurses moved quietly through the dim light. Sometimes he would hear a man talking in his sleep, as if arguing with his wife or his employer.

There were bowls of flowers everywhere, not brought by visitors but donated by gardeners. There they stood brilliantly blossoming from the sparkling crystal, among the reds and white of the blankets and sheets. Now and again a nurse would pass with a trolley, and he would see her as a saviour among all the spit, blood, urine. At nights the nurses would laugh and shout as they entered a taxi on their way to a dance. Well, why shouldn't they enjoy themselves, how else could they remain sane, in a world of death and dying.

But now at this particular moment on this serene morning Mr Trill didn't feel at all frightened. It was as if like the season itself he was poised between growth and decline, blossoming and withering, as if his mind and soul were in balance, calmly accepting the justice that was about to come. I am about to die, he thought to himself, and this woman with the hoover will live, not forever, but perhaps for a long time yet. Perhaps her whole life has been spent like this, cleaning and hoovering. She has never aspired to anything else. I on the other hand wanted more, I aspired to train minds in the great poetry of the ages. And what use was it after all? Now I am alone and no one comes to see me. Of all those thousands I have trained no one comes to visit me. Well, let it be, let it be. The sunlight is indifferent to us all. We are who we are and that is all that can be said about us. He watched an old man, slightly healthier than himself, being helped by two nurses out of his bed to sit in the lounge and watch the colour television. He would sit there all morning, sometimes dozing off, sometimes staring ahead of him.

The old man tried to push the nurses away from him as if he thought that he could manage quite well on his own. His face was stern and bitter, as if he had not accepted what had happened to him, even though he was old. Shall I be a coward, thought Mr Trill, when I am about to die? Shall I thresh about on the bed? He had never seen anyone die, not even his father or his mother, and he didn't know what to expect. He wanted to die quietly and tranquilly, like a Greek or Roman hero who dispensed with life as if with a sword for which he no longer had any use.

Steadily the hoover hummed and brightly the sun shone on the floor. I never had time to notice this before, thought Mr Trill. How did I not notice how the dust moves like insects, how even the clearest sun contains a proliferation of dark grains? Perhaps this very day will be my last, this serene autumn day whose calmness is like that of great art, when all passion falls away and only the essential fullness of things is left behind. On this morning there was no 'tears of things', no '*lacrimae rerum*', there was only an almost holy calm.

I have never made a will, he thought. What will happen to my money? I have no one to leave it to. But he didn't care, the survival of his money after him didn't seem to matter. And he had saved a lot of money for he hardly ever spent any. There it lay, symbols and signs in his bankbook, and he didn't care. It was almost a joke, to leave all that complication behind. He felt like an exile who was looking back at the world as at a strange distant shore. The woman was now at the far end of the ward, the flex of the hoover trailing behind her like a black snake.

Mr Trill looked at the bed opposite. Above and behind it on the wall there was a brass plate which said that the bed had been donated by William Mason. Who now remembered him, whoever he had been? Perhaps he had once been a rich man, enthusiastic, competitive, red-faced, but now all that was left of him was the name, read by an ignorant man. Our ignorance is total, thought Mr Trill, our achievements minimal. We move about the world as if we were important, we fight and squabble over trivial things, we feel slighted when we are seated at the wrong table, and yet in the end all these things are unimportant. The universe is a huge, unimaginably huge, organism, in which we are as important as the dust in the sunbeam, flickering slightly and then fading from sight.

The hoovering had ceased and the ward was silent. I am lying here like an effigy, thought Mr Trill. Should I try to get up or not? But he did not wish to get up. He wished to lie where he was, resting, happy. The boy with the hole in his heart lay sleeping peacefully opposite him, his fair hair strewn over the pillows. It seemed unjust that he should suffer when he was so young.

Mr Trill looked out of the window which was open. He saw two boys throwing stones up into a tree so that the chestnuts would fall down. When they did so they put them in a bag which they were carrying. A minister with long hurrying strides passed the window. The sky was perfectly blue without a cloud in it. Early November was exact and accurate and clear. I am dying, he thought, and I have never loved anyone and there is no one who will grieve for me. My funeral will be bare and diminished.

Yet I am not frightened. Isn't that odd? It is as if all the time I was thinking not about myself but about someone else. He felt his heart pattering, and listened to it as to an old friend who was finally letting him down. Patter patter, hammer hammer, beat beat. They say that the heart is the centre of love, but I have never felt that. I never used to notice it much, it was there when I needed it. Now when it is failing me I notice it. How much we take for granted in this world, that we shall live forever, that our bodies will remain our indefatigable servants. He remembered the oxygen tent, the hard serious breathing, but again it was as if he was thinking of someone else, as sometimes one may look at an early photograph of oneself standing on a sideboard and one may not for a moment recognise it. He felt his face which was stubbly and unshaven, like a field of autumn corn. He wondered what he looked like. His pyjamas felt larger than they had previously done, so presumably he had lost weight. The watch had disappeared from his hand. None of his clothes were to be seen anywhere. It was as if he had arrived in the final place where all must be confiscated, where the only values are physical, how much of flesh and bone and blood can still survive.

The ward was beginning to waken up. Now he could see a nurse examining a thermometer, thin and silver in the sunlight. Very faintly he could hear laughter from the lounge where the colour television was. Soon perhaps they would get him out of bed and he would sit with the others staring at that oddly distant screen. The nurses would smile and laugh and joke, they would walk about with such great energy and speed, as if they did not wish their patients to have any time to think.

The world would assume the noise and din of normality. Nevertheless his heart was beginning to hammer again, as if a blacksmith were forging some new iron thing on an anvil of deep black, as if a train were accelerating steadily on an autumn day when the flowers are tall and red and wasteful beside the rusty rails. It was as if he was rocking from side to side down a forgotten siding. I am feeling dizzy, he thought, something is happening to me. Is this it then? Is that unimaginable pain going to pierce me again?

He waved frantically as no words would come out. The nurse continued to regard the thermometer as if it were a tiny silver fish she had caught and which she was studying for size. The rackety old train was bouncing up and down. Somewhere down there was a black tunnel which, when he entered it, would make the carriage dense and thick and dark so that he could no longer see the pictures on the wall, the blossoming flowers in their sparkling vases.

He waved again and someone came. Then they were all about him. A face was bending over him, fresh and young and inquiring. His face and that other face were very close, close enough almost to kiss. A hand was clutching at his own: he hung on as if he were clinging to the side of a raft. How marvellous, he thought, that we should help each other, that in spite of hatred and insult and anger there are those who rush to one's side when it is necessary. How marvellous that they are not simply professional people but that they expend their own precious store of love and pity on perfect strangers. How truly amazing the world is, how bad and how good, and how, in spite of all, more good than bad. It was now as if he was seeing flashes as from a tall lighthouse searching a dark sea. Steadily they came, then faster and faster.

At that moment it was as if he were a well full of water, of love, as if a full tide were rising inside him. I love you all, all you fallen ones, all you autumn ones. We are all in the same boat, but the lighthouse is sending out its flashes, mortal meagre hands are blessing me, hands which have curved round the handle of a hoover, examined a thermometer, emptied bed pans. We do not deserve such care, such love. In spite of their petty quarrels, their envies, the unambitious ones help one at the end. He felt tears slowly trickling down his face, and in front of him the young stunned inquiring face was also wet with tears. He wanted to say, It's not as bad as that. Though I'm dying I feel quite happy. Don't worry. The eyes were so dear and so fresh and so filled with light. They should not be seeing this, he thought. Then they were no longer there. There was nothing at all. And Mr Trill passed over into Hades.

Mr Trill was aware that the baying of the dogs across the other side of the water had ceased, and that a small boat was being rowed towards him across the water. When the boat had reached his bank, a figure signed to him to enter it. Mr Trill looked around him to see if the invitation was to someone else, out the figure, still without speaking, signalled to him more impatiently and, with his case in his hand, Mr Trill stepped into the boat. It did not take long to cross to the other side, and when they arrived the figure, unspeaking as before, led the way to the large building that Mr Trill could see crouched in the vague prevailing mist. They passed a quadrangle and entered the building by a large creaking door. As Mr Trill stood in the hall where the notice-boards were covered with notices, the figure silently slipped away.

As if knowing where he was, Mr Trill climbed the stair to the door of an office on which he knocked, hearing from an adjacent room the sound of typewriters. After a long pause a voice asked him to come in, and when he did so he saw that seated behind a desk there was a small harried man in a black coat.

'Ah, Mr Trill,' said this man, 'my name is Dubbins. I'm very glad to see you.'

Mr Dubbins rose from his seat and strode forward, putting out his hand. Mr Trill laid his case down and shook the hand extended to him.

'You may go along to the staff-room in a minute,' said Dubbins. 'We are happy to have you. Very happy.'

I have been here before, thought Mr Trill, or if I haven't it is very like a place which I have visited.

'You are surprised,' said Dubbins, 'but you need not be. We have various alternatives to offer you.'

'Alternatives?'

'Naturally. You may stay with us which is one alternative.'

'And the others?'

'Another is to go back to your earlier life and continue your work there.'

'And?'

'The other is to go back where you came from.'

'I see.'

'There seems to have been a flaw in our organisation. We should have picked you up earlier. Still, that can't be helped.'

'What did the others do?'

'Most chose to stay.'

'And what is done here?'

'Done? My dear fellow, nothing much is *done*. We read and discuss.'

'I see.'

'I think the best thing would be if I took you along. Do you not think so?'

'I don't mind.'

The headmaster looked round the office as if to make sure that he had forgotten nothing, and then the two of them walked along a corridor till they came to another door on which the headmaster knocked. When they entered, the occupants of the room stood up as if they were flustered by the unexpected honour of the headmaster's visit.

'This is Simmons,' said Dubbins, 'and this Morrison, this is Andrews and this Burbridge.' The names followed each other like a roll call, and finally Mr Trill ceased to listen. All of them had been reading books when he entered and he noticed that all the books were classics such as *The Iliad* or Catullus' poems.

Suddenly a small bald man began to speak. 'Headmaster, I don't think this is right. The place is becoming overcrowded already. Why are we bringing in another candidate? Soon we shall not have enough room for ourselves and our books.'

'This is Carter,' said the headmaster, 'and he is always complaining.'

In a corner by himself there sat another man whose face twitched continually.

'That's Harris,' said Dubbins, 'his nerves are bad.'

'Now,' he said, 'if you wish to stay with the rest you can do so. All you require is a seat. You will be able to get any books you like from the library, and read them and comment on them. Little discussions are held regularly. What's that? Ah, another of our storms.'

Mr Trill could hear what seemed like hail beating against the window, and beyond it the howling of the dogs. Beyond both of these there was the weird distorted cry of many voices.

'What is that noise?' he asked.

'It is the hail,' said Dubbins.

'And beyond that?'

'That will be the cry of the dogs.'

'And beyond that again?'

'I do not hear anything.'

Dubbins's bland composed face, turned towards him, seemed closed and distant.

'Am I to leave you here then?' he asked. 'We feel that we should all be together and that we should look after our own kind.'

Mr Trill looked down at the classics which were lying on the table and they seemed to him to be surrounded by storm and wind, shaking in the hail which beat on them. Otherwise there was silence in the room and all the other occupants, retired into the world of their books, appeared to have already forgotten about him.

'What did you say my choices were?' he asked.

'To stay here or go back to your life and teach there or go out into the place from which you came.'

'Are there no other choices?'

'There is one other, but no one has taken it so far.'

'And what is that?'

'To go back to life but not as a teacher. We allow this, but it is not a choice that we like anyone to take. That is why I did not mention it.'

'Why don't you like it to be taken?'

'We think of it as an admission of failure.'

'Failure?'

'We feel that it is an admission that what we are doing is not considered important.'

'I see.'

The man in the corner twitched uncontrollably.

Mr Trill looked down at a copy of Homer, then turned the pages idly. In the margin of the book there were pencilled comments. One said, 'Ironical?' Another said, 'An example of synecdoche?' A third one said, 'The hexameter as narrative technique.'

Suddenly as he was speaking an excited voice shouted, 'I have found it. I have correctly dated the *Georgics*.'

Heads turned towards the speaker simultaneously. One man said, 'The fool. Who does he think he is? That has already been done by Malonivitz.' Another said, 'I shall have to rebut whatever he says.'

The headmaster gazed smilingly at Mr Trill and said, 'See? Nothing but excitement.'

Mr Trill felt as if he was going to be sick. Even though the headmaster heard nothing he himself was hearing beyond the hail and the baying of the dogs the voices of many men shrieking in pain, cursing, tormented.

His mother stood at the door.

'Put that woman out at once,' shrieked Carter. 'She has no right to be here.'

But his mother stood stolidly there.

'This is outrageous,' shouted Carter. 'What is this place coming to? Nothing but deterioration day after day. Standards failing, texts inadequate, and now we have women. I shall, I shall . . . ' But foaming at the mouth he subsided for he could not finish the sentence.

Mr Trill thought of an army of synecdoches meeting an army of metonymies on a battlefield where vivid green and blue scarves waved. Ah, the billowing bronze of my unlived life! The wind that drives the similes before it.

But his mother had gone. She had lived among the little piercing needles of the day, stung, stinging.

'I shall go back,' he heard himself saying.

'To Hades?' said Dubbins.

'No, to the world in which I once lived. I shall return as something else.' There was a universal sigh of horror all over the room.

'As something else?' they sighed.

'Yes,' said Mr Trill.

'Are you sure?' said Dubbins.

'Quite sure,' said Mr Trill, 'if it is possible, that is.'

'But no one before has asked that he go back as someone else.'

'In that case I shall be unique,' said Mr Trill and he felt an odd pleasure.

'I shall go back without shield.'

'Without shield?' They all gazed at each other as if he had said something incomprehensible.

'That is so,' said Mr Trill. 'Naked and without shield. I shall watch the wheelbarrows.'

'What is he talking about?' they asked.

'The wheelbarrow and the stone,' said Mr Trill. 'With rain on it, perhaps sunshine. The train that travels through the day. The man who collects the tickets in his dirty blue jacket. The drunk in the restaurant. The Chinaman who dreams of Hong Kong. The lorry driver, the builder, the carpenter with the ruler in his breast pocket. The docker who heaves the cargo to the quay. The cloud that has lost its way, and to which the child points. The bin man who lifts the grooved ash can on to his shoulders. The lady standing at the corner with the neon light on her handbag. To all these things I pray, to the rain that falls, the sun that shines. To the temporary I give my allegiance.'

Suddenly there was no room there at all and Mr Trill found himself standing at a windy corner in a vast city selling newspapers.

'*Evening News*,' he was shouting. '*Evening News*.' A man with a rolled umbrella took a paper, threw money on the ledge and then slanted quickly away into the lights of the city.

'*Evening News*,' Mr Trill shouted. 'Terrible murder, terrible rape. Read about it in the *Evening News*.'

Men and women passed through the yellow lights. Mr Trill clapped his hands together in the cold. In the distance the high windows burned like stars and it seemed that they were all on fire, twinkling and guttering.

'*Evening News*,' shouted Mr Trill in a sudden access of joy, ready to dance up and down on the pavement. 'Read about the murder, the rape, the embezzling, the incest. Read about the rescue, the gift, the offer. *Evening News*, read all about it.'

Around him the lights winked and shivered. His boots were yellow in the light, he crowed like a cock, his bronze claws sunk in the pavement.

from
SELECTED STORIES

By their Fruits

My Canadian uncle told me, 'Today we are going to see John Smith. I'll tell you a story about him. When he was nineteen years old, and coming to Canada, the minister met him and he said to him (you see, John had been working at the Glasgow shipyards before that) the minister said to him, "And I hear you've been working on a Sunday," and John said to him, "I hear you work on a Sunday yourself." So when John was leaving to come to Canada the minister wouldn't speak to him. Imagine that. He was nineteen years old, the minister didn't know whether he would ever see him again. Now the fact is that John has never been to church since he came to Canada.'

My uncle was eighty-six years old. He had been allowed to drive, I think, during the duration of our holiday with him, and he took full advantage of the concession.

'They said to me,' he told us, 'you keep out of Vancouver, you can drive around your home area, old timer. Drive around White Rock.'

Every morning he took the white Plymouth from the garage, put on his glasses carefully and set off with us for a drive of hundreds of miles, perhaps to Hell's Gate or Fraser River. His wife was dead: in the garden he had planted a velvety red rose in remembrance of her, and he watered it devoutly every day.

Once in Vancouver we came to a red light which we drove through, while a woman who was permitted to cross in her car stared at him, her mouth opening and shutting like that of a fish.

'These women drivers,' he said contemptuously, as he drove negligently onwards.

Every summer he took the plane home to Lewis. 'What I do,' he said, 'I leave this lamp on so that people think I am

here.' One summer Donalda and I searched Loch Lomondside for the house in which his wife had been born but we
couldn't find it.

'She was an orphan, you know, and the way we met was like
this. She went to London on service and decided she would
emigrate to Australia, but then changed her mind when she
saw an advertisement showing British Columbia and its fruit. I
was going to Australia myself with another fellow, but he
dropped out so I emigrated to Canada instead. One night at a
Scottish Evening in Vancouver I saw her coming in the door
wearing a yellow dress. I knew at that moment that that was
the girl for me, so I asked her for a dance, and that was how it
happened.'

He fixed his eye on the road. 'Listen,' he said, 'you can drive
a few miles over the limit. You're allowed to do that.' His big
craggy face was tanned like a Red Indian's. It was like an image
you would see on a totem pole.

John Smith lived in a house which was not as luxurious as my
uncle's. He had a limp, and immediately my uncle came in he
began to banter with him.

'Here he is,' he said to his wife, 'the Widows' Delight.' My
uncle smiled.

'Listen,' he said to me, after he had introduced me. 'This
fellow believes that we come from monkeys,' and he smiled
again largely and slightly contemptuously.

'That's true enough,' said Smith, stretching his leg out on
the sofa where he was sitting. His wife said nothing but
watched the two of them. She was a large woman with a flat
white face.

'It may be true of you,' said my uncle, 'but it's not true of me.
I'm not descended from a monkey, that's for sure. No, sir.
You'll be saying next that we have tails.'

'That's right,' said Smith, 'if you read the books you'll see
that we have the remains of tails. And I'll tell you something
else, what use is your appendix to you, tell me that.'

'My appendix,' said my uncle, 'what are you talking about?
What's my appendix got to do with it?' And he winked at me in
a conspiratorial manner as if to say, Listen to that hogwash.

'It's like this,' said Smith, who was a small intense man. 'Your appendix is no use to you. It's part of what you were as an ape. That's what the books tell you. You could lose your appendix and nothing would happen to you. You don't need it. That's been proved.' His wife smiled at Donalda and at me as if to say, They go on like this all the time but below it all they like each other.

'A lot of baloney,' said my uncle, 'that's what it is, a lot of baloney. When did you ever see a man turning into a monkey?'

'It's the other way round,' said Smith tolerantly. 'Anyway the time involved is too great. Millions of years, millions and millions of years.'

'Baloney,' said my uncle again. 'You read too many books, that's what's wrong with you. You'd be better looking after your garden. His garden is a mess,' he said, turning to me. 'Never seen anything like it. All he does is read and read.'

'And all you do is grow cherries and give them to widows,' said Smith chortling. 'Did you know that,' he said to me, 'he's surrounded by widows. They come from everywhere: they're like the bees. And he grows cherries and gives them baskets of them. Did you see the contraption he's got to keep the crows away from the cherry trees?' And he laughed.

Donalda and I looked at each other. My uncle had a wire which he strung out through the window of the kitchen and on it hung a lot of cans and a big hat and when he saw any crows approaching he pulled at the wire and the cans set up a jangling noise.

'They're like the Free Church ministers, them crows,' said Smith, 'you can't keep them away from the cherries.'

My uncle once told us a story. 'When I came here first I used to drive a cab and I used to take a lot of them ministers around to conferences. And, do you know, they never invited me into any of their houses once? They would leave me sitting in the cab to freeze. That's right enough.'

'All that baloney about monkeys,' said my uncle again. 'That's because he's got hair on his chest. Mind you, he does look a bit like a monkey,' he said to me judiciously.

Smith got angry. 'You're an ignorant man,' he said. 'Just

because you were on the Fire Brigade you think you know everything. Do you know what he reads?' he said to me. 'He reads the *Fishing News* and the *Scottish Magazine*. He never read a book in his life. You wouldn't understand Darwin,' he said to my uncle, 'not in a million years.'

'And who's Darwin when he's at home?' said my uncle.

'Darwin?' Smith spluttered. 'Darwin is the man who wrote *The Origin of Species*. You're really ignorant. If you kept away from the widows you would know these things.'

'Do you think the widows are descended from the apes?' said my uncle innocently.

'Of course they are, and so are you.' Smith was dancing up and down with rage in spite of his limp.

'I never heard such hogwash,' said my uncle. 'Tell me something then. Do you swing from the trees in your garden instead of digging?' And he went off into a roar of laughter.

'Oh, what's the use of talking to you,' said Smith, 'no use at all. You're ignorant.'

And so the debate went on, though deep down we could see there was a real affection between the two men. When we were going home in the car my uncle would suddenly burst into a roar of laughter and say, 'Descended from the apes. Do you think Smith looks like an ape? Eh?' And he would laugh again. 'Mind you, where he comes from on the island they could be apes. Sure.' And he laughed delightedly again.

He was really rather boyish. He was always saying 'By golly', in a tone of wonder.

'Did you know,' he told us once, 'there's a woman here who comes from the island and her son-in-law is an ambassador. If you go to their house you'll find that the children have a room of their own with a billiard table and a television and everything else. And she sits there and makes scones as we used to do in the old days. You'd think she was back in Lewis. And when the kids come in, she says, "How much money did you spend today? Did you buy Seven Up?" And if they spent more than they should have, she gives them hell. And I once saw a millionaire in her house. Sure. He was walking along the corridor with a towel round him, he had been for a bathe, and that was all he was wearing. "That's a millionaire," she said to me. "That fellow?" I said. "Yes, that's right," she said. And he looked just like you or me. He said "Hi" to me as he passed. And there was water dripping all over the floor and all he was wearing was a towel.'

He had bought himself a cine camera and the last time he had been home to the islands he had taken some photographs. He showed us them one night and we saw figures of old women in black, churches, rocks, peat cutters, all flashing past at what seemed a hundred miles an hour. 'There's something dang wrong with that camera,' he muttered. Donalda and I could hardly keep from laughing.

All the time we stayed with him - which was three weeks - he wouldn't let us pay for anything. 'I won't be long for this world,' he would say, 'so I might as well spend my money.' And we fed on salmon and cherries and the best of steaks. And sometimes we would sit out in the garden wearing green peaked caps and watching the crows as they hovered around the cherry trees.

'When my wife was taken to hospital,' he said, 'I went to the doctor and I said to him, "No drugs. No drugs," I said to him. We never had a quarrel in our lives, do you know that? She was a great gardener. When we went out fishing on Sunday she would say, "Stop the car," and I would stop, though I drove very fast in them days, and it was a little flower she had seen at the side of the road.' He smiled nostalgically.

'This is my country now, you understand. I go back to the old country, but it's not the same. I've been to see the people who grew up with me, but they're all in the cemeteries. Sure. There was a schoolmaster we had and he used to go into a rage and whip us on the bare legs with a belt. Girls and boys, it was the same to him. But there's no one left now. Canada is my country now.' And he would look out the window at the men in red helmets who were repairing the road in front of his house.

The days were monotonously sunny. There was no sign of rain or storm. It was like being in the Garden of Eden, guiltless and without questions.

The night before we left many of the widows visited him, as did Smith and his wife. The widows brought scones, cakes, and buns, and made the coffee while he sat in the middle of the living-room like a king on a throne.

One widow said, 'You know what Torquil here said to my husband when he was building our house. He said to him, "I used to go duck shooting here when I came here first. It was a swamp." '

'And so it was,' said Torquil, laughing.

'He used to tell us, "The men here die young. The women live for ever. What they do is sell their houses and then they buy apartments in Vancouver." '

Another of the widows said to me, 'I saw one of your Highland singers on the TV. He had lovely knees.' All the other widows laughed. 'Lovely knees,' she repeated. And then she asked me if I knew the words of 'Loch Lomond'.

'Iain doesn't like that song,' said my uncle, largely. 'The fact is he despises them songs.' They gazed at me in wonderment. 'Iain doesn't like Burns either. But I'll tell you something about Burns. They say he had a lot of illegitimate children, but that was a lie put out by the Catholics.' He spoke with amazing confidence, and I saw Smith looking at him.

'I went home to Lewis,' said one of the women. 'The shop girls were very rude. I couldn't believe it.'

'Is that right?' said my uncle.

'As true as I'm sitting here,' said the woman.

Another one said, 'You've got lovely cherries this year.'

'Sure,' said my uncle, 'they're like the apples in the Garden of Eden.'

Smith suddenly pounced. He had been sitting on the edge of the company, brooding for a long time.

'It doesn't say that in the Bible at all.'

'What?' said my uncle. 'Of course it says that.'

'Not at all,' said Smith, 'not at all. It doesn't mention the fruit at all.'

'I beg your pardon,' said my uncle, 'it says about apples as clear as anything. Do you know,' he said, turning to the widows, 'I read the Bible every year from end to end. I know the names of all the tribes of Israel. The gipsies, you know, were one of the tribes of Israel.'

'It doesn't say that at all,' said Smith, 'not at all. You read your Bible and it doesn't say it was an apple. It doesn't name the fruit at all.'

'What does it matter?' said one of the widows.

'We all know it was a woman who ate the fruit,' said my uncle magisterially.

'It might even have been a widow,' said one of the women. And the others laughed, but Smith didn't laugh. He was muttering to himself, 'It doesn't mention the fruit at all.'

'Next thing you'll be saying it was a pair of monkeys in the Garden of Eden,' said my uncle. 'You'll be saying it was the apes who ate the apple.' And he laughed so hard that I thought he was going to have apoplexy.

'Do you have a Bible here?' said Smith apologetically.

'I can't find it just now,' said my uncle.

I myself couldn't remember what it said in Genesis. My uncle started on a story about how once he had seen a black bear and it was eating berries in Alaska. 'They're very fast, you know,' he said. 'You'd think they would be slow but by golly they're not. By golly they're not.'

Some of the widows asked us if we were enjoying our holiday and we said, 'Yes, very much.'

'That's because Torquil is driving them about,' said one of the widows. 'He's a demon driver, did you know that? His wife used to shout at him and she was the only person he would ever slow down for.'

What did I think of Canada, I asked myself. There were no noises there, no creakings as from an old house. The indifferent level light fell on it. It was like the Garden of Eden uninfected by history. It was without evil. Smith was still muttering to himself. His wife was smiling.

'My friend here,' said my uncle largely, 'believes in the apes, you know. He thinks that we're all apes, every one of us.'

The women in their fine dresses and ornaments all laughed. Who could be further from apes than they were?

'Apes don't make as good scones as this,' said my uncle. 'Do you think apes make scones?' he asked Smith.

Smith scowled at him. He was looking around the room as if searching for a Bible.

'But there's one thing about John here,' said my uncle, 'by golly he's got principles. Yes by golly, he has.'

As the evening progressed we did sing 'Loch Lomond',

' . . . where me and my true love will never meet again on the bonny banks of Loch Lomond.'

I saw tears in my uncle's eyes.

'Mary was from Loch Lomondside,' said my uncle, 'but I couldn't find the house she was brought up in. She was an orphan, you know. Iain and I went there in the car but we couldn't find the house.' There was a silence.

'The only person he would ever obey was Mary,' said one of the widows.

'Gosh, that's right,' said my uncle. And then, it seemed quite irrelevantly, 'When I came here first we used to teach Gaelic to the Red Indians. Out of the Bible. And they taught us some Indian, but I've forgotten the words now. They spoke Gaelic as you would find it in the Old Testament. Of course some men used to marry squaws and take them home to Lewis. They would smoke pipes, you know.'

Smith was still staring at him resentfully.

At about one in the morning they all left. The night was mild and the women seemed to float about the garden in their dresses. My uncle filled baskets of cherries for them in the bright moonlight.

'That's the same moon as shines over Lewis,' he said. 'The moon of the ripening of the barley.'

They were like ghosts in the yellow light, the golden light. I thought of early prospectors prospecting for gold in the Yukon.

'You mark my words, you're wrong about that,' said my uncle to Smith as he pressed a basket of cherries on him. They all drove off to a chorus of farewells from myself and Donalda.

After they had gone, I looked up Genesis. Smith was right enough. It doesn't mention the particular fruit.

At the airport my uncle shook us by the hand briefly and turned away and drove off. I knew why he had done that. I imagined him driving to an empty house. Actually I never saw him again. He died the following year from an embolism. He dropped dead quickly in one of the bathrooms of a big hospital in Vancouver. He firmly believed that he would meet Mary again when he died.

The plane rose into the sky. Shadows were lying like sheaves of black corn on the Canadian earth which was not ours. It was still the same mild changeless weather. I hoped he wouldn't look up the Bible when he arrived home for he prided himself on his knowledge of it, and it was true that he read it from end to end in the course of a year. Even the tribes he memorised. And in the fly leaf of the big Bible were the names of his family and ancestors, all those who had passed it on to him.

I recalled the men in red helmets working in front of the house. He would drive in carefully. Then he would back into the garage and take off his glasses and walk into the house. Sometimes one could see grass snakes at the door sleeping in the sun, and Donalda had been quite frightened of them. One day my uncle had hung one of them round his neck like a necklace. 'You see,' he said, 'it's quite harmless. Sure. Nothing to fear from them at all.' At that moment the camera in my mind stopped with that image. The snake was round his throat like a green necklace, a green innocent Canadian ornament.

Mac an t-Sronaich

The student saw Mac an t-Sronaich crouched by the fire at the far end of the cave.

'Of course,' said Mac an t-Sronaich, 'I am going to kill you.'

The student, who studied divinity and who had been on his way across the moor after a long journey, was frightened. Mac an t-Sronaich was wild-looking, had matted hair and a long nose. There had been stories of the murders he had committed and so far he had not been caught. He moved from cave to cave on the desolate moor and lived, it was said, partly on human and partly on animal flesh. After being sentenced for a crime on the mainland he had escaped and had sworn eternal enmity against society. The student trembled. He was tall and strong but looked pale.

'I am going to kill you,' said Mac an t-Sronaich, 'because there is nothing else for it. You've seen my cave. You will tell others.'

His red gibbering face glared from the smoke. He piled wood on the fire. He looked like a devil which had once haunted the student's dreams. God knew how he existed.

'Also I could do with some of your clothes. My own are in rags.' And he studied the student carefully.

'I can't believe it,' thought the student, 'I can't. I have travelled from Edinburgh, from the divinity college there, and here I am on this moor in the grip of a madman.'

He knew that Mac an t-Sronaich was a madman, though he talked rationally enough. How could one live like this and not be a madman? He knew that if he tried to run Mac an t-Sronaich would outrun him, at least the way he felt at the moment. And in any case it had been late evening when he had crossed the landscape of rocks and grass. Mac an t-Sronaich's eyes would be keener than his: they would find him in the dark.

Mac an t-Sronaich came and sat beside him, his big hooked nose prominent in his red face. The student recoiled from the smell which had something of fish in it, something of sweat, and something else unnameable. He looked strong as a bull, his flesh peering from among his rags like a moon through clouds. He wished to talk before he killed him. But then lonely men did wish to talk. The murderer was starved of conversation as he was often of food.

'Why should I not kill you?' said Mac an t-Sronaich. 'Tell me that.'

The student was paralysed with fear. He couldn't speak. It was like seeing a cat coming home triumphantly with a mouse between its teeth. Mice lived in such a world and so did cats. When they were eating they always looked around them in case they too were being stalked. The student had never imagined a world like this. To be killed like a mouse. To face that natural brutality.

'I see you are well-dressed,' said Mac an t-Sronaich, as if he were taking part in an ordinary conversation. 'No one has accused you of a crime and condemned you. Do you know what it is like to live here? The snow, the rain. The search for food. The traps. I have even eaten wild cat. Did you know that? Have you ever seen a wild cat? It's a terrible animal.'

The student couldn't think of a reason why Mac an t-Sron-aich couldn't kill him if he wanted. Mac an t-Sronaich was studying his flesh as if tasting its sweetness in advance. He had heard of cases where human bodies were hung up like the carcasses of pigs.

'The Bible,' he muttered, trembling.

'The Bible,' said Mac an t-Sronaich, snorting contemptuously. And he made a sudden grab for the student's bag. He removed the sandwiches of bread and cheese and began to wolf them ravenously. He lived on the edge of the world. Sometimes he might approach a village at night and kill a hen or a cockerel. Once he had even managed to drag a dead sheep away into the darkness. He was the murderer who lived on the circumference of lights and warmth.

The student could actually foresee Mac an t-Sronaich leaping at him. He could feel his hands on his throat, he could smell his stink. His own body flowed like water. He wished more than anything to be back in the warm room in the college listening to a lecture. The world of glosses, analysis, seemed far away. His books stood up in front of him. The voice of the lecturer droned like a bee.

Should he get down on his knees to pray for mercy? Should he plead for his life like a slave? And yet some pride made him not do it. What was the origin of that pride? And what was the origin of the idea that God had betrayed him? He had followed in His footsteps and now here he was in a smoke-filled cave like hell on the edge of a moor. It was crazy. It was beyond reality, logic. And then on the other hand he had nothing to bribe Mac an t-Sronaich with, no money. He had spent his last money on his journey home. Even now his parents would be waiting for him - his father was also a minister - in the halo of the lamp. And here he was in this cave face to face with a madman. The light of the fire made disturbing enigmatic patterns on the walls of the cave. An insane gibberish. And yet Mac an t-Sronaich sounded so reasonable.

'Don't think you can run away,' said Mac an t-Sronaich. 'I can run very fast. I've had to. You are my prey,' he said. And when he heard the word "prey" the student again had a clear image of a cat and a mouse. He felt his whole body naked and vulnerable as if his clothes had been peeled from his skin. For this, he thought, I have followed the teaching of the Lord, for this I have been peaceable, tried to be without sin, though that is not possible, formed myself in His pattern. I have never drunk alcohol, never smoked. I have remained a virgin till the time for marriage comes. He saw his father's head bent over the big Bible inscribed with the names of his own father and mother. He himself sat upright in his pew gazing up at his father every Sunday. The face was bell-cheeked, red, healthy.

'I see you're a student,' said Mac an t-Sronaich at last. 'You have books in your bag.'

'Yes, I am,' said the student, trying to keep his voice under control. He felt that his teeth were chattering in his head. He was aware of his bones, of his flesh, of the blood pouring through his body. Indeed the place looked like the product of a man's fever, monstrous, dreamlike. He pinched himself in the stomach to find if it was a dream or reality. It was more like a dream that he had once had, a dream of a place from which he could not escape, with a white figure confronting him, smiling. And behind the white figure was his bearded father. For some reason he was dressed in a butcher's smock.

Let me die, he thought, let my heart give way. I can feel it beating heavily. But I don't wish to be killed in the smoke and the dark.

'I've thought about things a lot,' said Mac an t-Sronaich. Incredibly, he was now smoking a pipe. 'To kill or be killed, that is the rule of the universe. You can see it everywhere. Sometimes we kill by the mind, sometimes by the body.' He puffed out chains of smoke which were lost in the half darkness. 'You live off me with your nice clothes. At one time I never thought I would kill anyone. The idea would have been abhorrent to me. But I did. For money and food. On this very moor. It didn't bother me as much as I had expected. Not at all. After all, what use was the man to the world: there are so many people alive. What use are you? Does it matter whether you live or die? The victory goes to the strong. That's what your Christ didn't understand. He poisoned the world, made us all into pale-faced women.' And he spat on to the floor. 'But I am not a woman. I see the deer in the summer-time fighting each other, locking antlers, and they die like that, locked together. Men attack each other too. I know you are frightened but you needn't be. It won't last long, I promise you. And you have knowledge, you see, you have knowledge of my cave. I can't let you go away with that. When I killed that first man he evacuated everything in his body. What a stink! But then when you look at a dead body it is like a log. It has no light in it. You see I'm on the edge of things here. But I hear things. Sometimes at night I listen at windows to the quarrels between husband and wife, quarrels to the death. I have seen children who are eaten up with desire of possessions. I have heard businessmen (you find businessmen too in villages) making false deals in the darkness. I have listened outside these cages.

It is as if they are inhabited by animals. That's where I get my entertainment from. I've eaten food in their kitchens while they are in their beds. I've crept in and out of their houses. And I have thought to myself, at least I am more honest than they. Do you understand?'

The student didn't answer. The murderer puffed at his pipe. It was like being at a ceilidh in a village, two men talking together contentedly. Why, the murderer might suddenly burst into song.

'And then again,' the murderer continued, 'people marry and when they do so they are no longer what they were. They are frightened. They sit by the fire and wonder what will happen to them when their partner dies. But I have outfaced a wild cat. Have you seen a wild cat?' The words poured from him in a torrent: his red cheeks glowed in the twilight. 'A cornered wild cat. And all I had was my bare hands.' He pointed at scars on the right one. 'I killed it as it was standing on end and its teeth were bared. That was an adventure. When people marry they no longer have adventures. There are the children at first and they have to be protected, and when the children leave there is the fear of loneliness. Have you ever thought that all we do is based on fear? I fear no one. Not even death itself. I've often been close to death here with fever and cold. I've seen a rabbit in the mouth of a weasel, which is thin as a string. I'm not afraid of death. Don't you be afraid of death either,' he said, almost gently.

His voice seemed to lull the student. And he thought, Why should I die? This is injustice. I didn't harm this man. Never. And he felt again the unfairness of the universe. And perhaps it was then that he forsook his God. In that smoke-filled cave his eyes were stung.

But the implacable Mac an t-Sronaich talked on. It was as if he hadn't seen a human being for twenty years. He was like Robinson Crusoe who has found a ship with a sailor on it.

'And the mornings,' he was saying, 'you cannot imagine what they are like. The sun, the dews, the flowers. The sweetness. Why, there have been times when I rolled in the dew like a hare. I have been so filled with joy. Have you ever felt such joy?' Only in the Lord, thought the student, only in His worn body yellow as parchment. Only in the psalms, in the holiness of a church, its peace and stillness. Only then. That was joy.

Mac an t-Sronaich tapped his pipe casually. 'I don't suppose you have any tobacco,' he asked.

'No,' said the student, 'I'm sorry, I don't smoke.'

'It doesn't matter. I can always steal some. People here often leave their doors open. It's amazing. They don't wish to admit that I can destroy their way of life. They want to hang on to it. They don't like to admit that I am different from them, that I can live without them.'

Suddenly the student was filled with anger. Why should this man kill me, he thought. I have never thought about it all till tonight.

Well, yes, I did hear of him. My mother especially warned me about him. She would say, Take your milk and go to sleep or Mac an t-Sronaich will get you. So Mac an t-Sronaich must really be quite old. The anger poured through the student's body like wine. Who does this murderer think he is? That he can rampage about this moor and kill anyone he likes. He looked around the twilit cave for a log but could see nothing he could use as a weapon. He felt his muscles tense. After all, he was not weak. He had thrown the javelin at the sports. He was in good shape, he had never drunk or smoked. Now he would have to fight for his life.

Better now while this holy anger possessed him before it drained away. Later, his body might be like water again.

He stood up.

'Where are you going?' said Mac an t-Sronaich.

'I am going away,' said the student.

'So that is what you are at?' Mac an t-Sronaich carefully tamped the fire in his pipe and advanced. It looked as if he had been doing this for years, advancing through the smoke with his red cheeks glowing.

'I cannot let you go,' he said to the student. 'You know that.' His beard was long and tangled, the muscles on his arms were huge. He put out his arms slowly. His eyes were on fire in the dark. The student stepped back. And then they were grappling with each other in the smoke that tingled and sparked.

It was the first time that the student had ever struggled with anyone. The arms of the monstrous murderer were about him, squeezing him, he was losing his breath. And then the most amazing thought came to him. Why, this is like love. This struggle is like love. Murder itself is like love. It is as if the cat is in love with the mouse as it flings the body up in the air, as it devours it, leaving violet-coloured intestines. He struck the arms away from him, and seized Mac an t-Sronaich by the throat with the frenzy of self-preservation. In order to save himself he had to be like Mac an t-Sronaich. He must empty his mind of books, ideas, become naked and pure.

'I shall not be killed,' he shouted aloud, 'I shall not be killed. I refuse to be killed.' And his voice echoed back to him.

And this extraordinary love that was involved in death almost overwhelmed him. Their legs were locked together but he would not let Mac an t-Sronaich's throat go. No, that was what he must cling to, the throat of this man who was not so young after all as he had been. Why, he must have been on the edge of that moor for years listening, mocking. He squeezed and squeezed. Mac an t-Sronaich managed to unlock his hands from his throat. He retched for a while and before he could recover himself the student was on him like a wild cat. He kicked him with his heavy boot right in the stomach. Then he jumped on top of him and held him by the throat again.

'I will kill you,' he shouted, 'I will kill you.' Never, never, had he thought he would be like this. Energies of the most astonishing kind flowed through him. Whose were these bell-shaped cheeks glaring up at him? His body was behaving with a logic of its own. Let him stop thinking, leave it all to his body, that was the secret. The long tangled beard thrust at him. He pushed the mouth slowly away from him with his hand.

This was the devil he had always wanted to kill, the devil that had tormented him, in the summer nights. Here he was in front of him, not abstract but concrete. He kicked again with his boot. Then he ran away into the darkness outside. He trembled in the silence watching the mouth of the cave. But no one came out. Instead he heard an insane laugh, and then a voice.

'Good for you, my friend.' The voice seemed to echo and

echo. Yes, he thought, I will sit and watch the cave mouth till I see a shadow across it. He fumbled around him in the dark and found a big stone. He heard the secret mutterings of the night. I must not fall asleep, he thought, I must not fall asleep. And so he watched the flickering mouth of the cave. But no one came out. Instead he heard snoring as if Mac an t-Sronaich had fallen asleep or perhaps he was just pretending.

If only I had a wall that I could keep between him and me, he thought, feeling at his torn clothes. He held his breath till eventually the dawn came up red and angry. All night he had stayed awake. Then when the light bloomed he ran as fast as he could across the moor. He knew after a while that Mac an t-Sronaich would never catch him. And yet he kept seeing him, following him at a distance, sometimes on his left, sometimes on his right, sometimes even ahead of him. The mouth was full of broken teeth, he cast a salty smell on the air, there were coils of worms about his body. The fire shone like the fires of hell. Sometimes the moor itself seemed to disappear and he was back in his room at the college or he was at home and his father's head was bent over the table, bearded and still as if carved from stone. And the voice of Mac an t-Sronaich screamed at him as he ran and ran. And his body was infected with rage and shame. Bestially the dawn glared around him. There were clouds like red hot cinders in the sky. The dew arose around him smokily. There were red flowers like wounds growing from between the stones.

Oh God, he thought, this world will never be the same again. I shall never return to my college now that I have, like the mouse against the cat, fought in my grey nakedness. He was like a white vulnerable root, which had finally been tugged out of the earth.

'My God,' he shouted from the bare moor, but no answer came from the sky. His voice hammered against it with a metallic sound. And then in the distance like an echo he seemed to hear the voice of Mac an t-Sronaich. And he saw again the enigmatic whirlings of the smoke in the cave. He knew that Mac an t-Sronaich was not dead and would never die. Even among the fog and lights of gas-lit Glasgow he might meet him. Even in his own house. Even in his own mirror.

I do not Wish to Leave

In the thatched house the fire was in the middle of the floor and they sat on benches around it in the smoke. There were six people altogether. This was the ceilidh house in the village, the one where on certain nights there was a gathering to tell stories, sing songs, sometimes play music. This was a tradition in the Highlands in the old days.

The host was called Squashy. At one time he used to be a shoemaker: now he was retired. He would sit by the wall watching the world go past, for his legs were very bad with arthritis, and he could walk only with the help of two sticks. He had never left the island in his life but he read a fair amount and thought that he knew more than he did. His favourite reading was about Egypt and the pyramids, the burials of the Pharaohs in big tombs which had been prepared by slaves, the murders of servants, the voyage of the king-god across the sky.

He was not married and lived with his sister. She had been at one time a servant on the mainland in a hotel but she was also rather simple-minded and wore stockings which accordioned down to her ankles. She deferred to her brother even though he had seen less of the world than she had. He treated her with contempt.

He was in fact speaking at that moment, saying ' . . . and do you know that they had mummies in those days. My sister here Mary doesn't know what a mummy is but the rest of us do, don't we? They used to take the bodies and make them into mummies, that's what they did in those days.'

'What did they treat them with, eh?' asked Cum, who was a big fat man wearing a fisherman's jersey. He was engaged in building his own house and had been so for years. He had a thin daughter with very thin legs who would meet the boys on Sunday among the corn.

'I don't know what they treated them with, I wasn't there, was I?' said Squashy shortly. 'But it was something mysterious, you can depend on that.' He shifted his bottom on the hard wooden seat. 'They were very clever people and what they put in their heads they put in their feet.' And he looked significantly at Cum with his small, angry red eyes as if implying, They would have finished your house years ago.

'That's true, it would have been something mysterious,' said Shonachan. Shonachan was perhaps forty years old. He came from an odd family who hardly ever left the house. There were seven of them altogether and he was the only gregarious one. The others would sit at windows gazing out on to the road: one in particular was shouted at and laughed at by the local children and he would shake his fist at them from behind the curtains. One sat in a corner of the house endlessly repairing fishing nets as if he were a spider. Shonachan found relief in his visits to the ceilidh house.

'And another thing,' said Squashy, leaning back against the whitewashed wall, 'another thing. They buried them deep in tombs so that no one would ever find them. And people tried to rob the tombs but they got lost among the passages and they were never found again.'

The others thought of this among the swirling smoke of the fire, their faces shining, for all of them believed in ghosts and mysterious events: why, there was supposed to be a ghost at the corner of the road. And also Alastair Macleod had seen a ghost the last time he was home from his work on the mainland and shortly afterwards he had died. Ghosts were not to be taken lightly. The fire shone on their faces and they imagined the false passages and the robbers lost among them.

'That may be true,' said John Smith consideringly. Curiously enough he had never been given a nickname by the villagers. He was the scribe who used to write their letters for them if they were at all official, and he would show them the letters, and they would all think what a clever man he was. 'Dear Sirs,' he would write, 'thank you for yours of the 21st inst.' Imagine that, the 21st inst. He had also been to America and he had many stories and had at times picked Squashy up on a number of points. But Squashy was like an eel in a river, difficult to catch.

'That may be true,' said John Smith. He looked around him with a judicial air. 'That may be true,' he repeated. Only he gave the impression that he didn't believe it.

'Of course it's true,' said Squashy, 'it's all in the books.' His books coloured the air around him with a foreign radiance and John Smith stared at him as if saying, 'Well, for the moment I will let you away with this. Many things happen in this world and I have seen them myself, having been to America, while you haven't been out of the island.'

Squashy continued, 'And another thing. The cat was their god and that's another thing that you find out. They wouldn't allow anyone to do anything to a cat.'

The sixth person, who was called Pat and who was also the local postman, listened carefully. Cats, eh, what was this about cats? Dogs perhaps, but not cats. Nothing had happened so far this night and he was comfortable, almost sleepy. But nevertheless the others were wary of him because of his reputation. Sometimes he thought that they would prefer if he didn't attend their ceilidhs. But being alone in the house he sometimes felt the need of company and he couldn't prevent himself from coming. It wasn't his fault that he was as he was. It was inheritance, it had been in his people. It was a sorrow and a triumph, that's what it was.

The cat glared at him from his seat beside the fire.

Oh, God, let me have peace, he thought, let it not happen tonight.

'The cat,' said Squashy, 'that was what they worshipped.'

'Imagine that, the cat,' said his sister.

Cum thought, One of these days I'll finish my house. My wife wants it finished. And yet the other day when I was shifting that big stone I felt a twinge. It's still there.

Pat listened. He enjoyed being in this social ring, damned though he was. He loved the glitter of the fire, the voices, the stories. Why, one day he would like to visit those pyramids in the desert.

'There's a lot we don't know about right enough,' said

Shonachan. He dreaded going back to the house where the hearth was often cold. He wished they had a housekeeper. And he was smoking far too many cigarettes. One of these days he would have to give them up or they would kill him. Full strength Capstans. In the mornings he coughed and coughed and spat and spat and he fought for breath and his chest ached. But what could he do?

With regard to yours, thought John Smith, with regard to yours, I have to tell you . . .

They don't know, thought Squashy, what my life is like sitting by the wall in the heat or the cold, my hands turning red round the sticks, thinking, thinking . . . Why did this have to happen to me? And this stupid sister of mine as well. That is another cross I have to bear. They don't know the length of my days and without Egypt where would I be? His little moustache quivered with self-pity.

And then it happened to Pat, they could all see it happening. He stood up and as if in a dream walked to the door through the smoke which loomed and drifted around him. Just like that it happened. Again. And he was frightened. Oh, he was frightened, but he was also compelled. From that warm circle, that ring of smoke and fire, he went out into the frosty night, for it was freezing heavily and the stars were clearly visible in the sky, twinkling and sparkling.

And they watched him with fear but they did not try to stop him. It was almost as if his eyes were closed. Then the door shut behind him and they were left alone.

There was a silence and no one looked at his neighbour. It was as if a dreadful death had fallen over the ceilidh house and they were all suspended in their individuality, like statues of Pharaoh.

Finally Shonachan spoke, 'Who is it this time?' he said. No one answered. All they knew was that it was one of them. And for a moment they felt mortal and cold in front of the fire as if death were at their breasts. Like stony effigies they sat there.

Pat went out into the night. The stars were twinkling and the ground was hard. He walked as if in a trance. There was no sound to be heard and the earth like an enchanted stone rang under his feet. How brilliant the sky was, so many stars like a huge city, each one answering the other in a brave bright language.

And then he saw them. They were coming from his left, the men in hard hats walking slowly. And they were carrying a coffin. He waited for them to come. The coffin was open and he could see the face. The funeral party walked slowly: it did not even stop at the stream. The stream was crossed, with the coffin. Pat's trousers were wet: he could feel the water making them heavy. They made their way towards the cemetery, taking short cuts, and all the time he could see the face in the coffin.

They laid the coffin down. There was a prayer, and after a while he turned back, walking again through the stream, opened the door of the ceilidh house, and entered. This was his sorrow and his triumph. They were all silent looking at him. They noticed the wet trousers and knew that it happened again. His eyes travelled over them like a light as if he were saying, I know you, I have power over you. But he did not speak and they did not ask any questions. They were vexed in their mortal individualism around the sociable fire. Death had come into the room. Each looked at Pat and thought, Is it me, is it me? But Pat gave no sign. He never did. He never passed his final judgment.

And the ceilidh broke up and they all went home.

Pat loved being a postman. He loved bringing letters to people who hadn't heard from their sons or daughters for years before. What a surprise, what a joy! He would never like to live anywhere else than where he lived. Why, when he was on his rounds, the birds would be singing in the sky, the stones glittered, the sun shone, red and brilliant. No one saw the world as he did carrying his bag around the village. The dew glittered, the trees bore their blossoms, and in the bag were the signs of hope, communications from the whole wide world. And now and again he would stop at a house and have a cup of tea and narrate the gossip that he had picked up. No, he could not live anywhere else. He had been to other villages but this was his favourite. He had never married, so attractive was his work and his life. Apart of course from that other shadow.

And if he were to marry would he gaze down one morning at the pillow beside his own and see death imprinted on the face of his wife? And perhaps one day he would even see his own face in the coffin. How could one know?

He walked on. A bare tree was reflected in the loch. In the summer its berries were like open wounds. Oh, how beautiful the day was, even though he carried his mysterious knowledge around with him. And that too was power, was it not? Of a sort. He knew, he knew . . .

John Smith took the letter from him and thought, I wonder if it's me. He studied Pat's face, but it was open and cheerful as usual. It can't be me then, thought John Smith. Otherwise how could he be so cheerful. Maybe I should propitiate him, ask him in for a cup of tea. On the other hand, he suddenly hated him. Why should he have been given that power? It was wrong, it was unhealthy, and it wasn't as if he was intelligent. And he glanced at his letter. It was about the croft, he could tell that right away.

Cum watched him from the roof of the incomplete house where he perched like a cockerel. Maybe I'll never finish it. That stone is in my breast. I may have injured myself. I may be dying at this very moment. Who knows? But I do know that the others look down on me, I know that. But if I don't finish this house what will my wife say? He hammered, and made no sign that he had seen Pat. He completely ignored him. He wouldn't speak to him. You are not going to tell me when I'm going to die, my friend. I have my rights too.

Shonachan didn't see him, for he was working away from the village, but Squashy watched him from the wall where he sat like an owl thinking about Egypt. His hands were red and glassy in the cold. Pat waved to him but he made no acknowledgement. You bugger, he thought, you're like a vulture, you perch on the bones of men. Was it his own bell-like moustached face that Pat had seen in the coffin? Should he shout to Pat and ask him? But he didn't, he had too much pride. After all, what was Pat but an incomer from another village, and there were stories . . . In fact he had been in many villages, that was a fact. He rested on his sticks like a wounded proud Pharaoh.

It might be me, thought his sister. And to tell the truth she didn't care. No one knew what it was like living with her brother with his mocking ways. It seemed to the outside world as if he coped well with his ailment but she knew he didn't. He was always complaining about little things. There wasn't enough salt in his porridge, not enough sugar in his tea. She wouldn't be unhappy if suddenly . . .

And Pat passed on less cheerfully. Something glacial, something frosty, had entered the air. Was it going to happen again as it had happened before? Some cold air was blowing towards him.

He humped his bag over his shoulder. What a glorious quiet frosty morning, so clear, so calm. Such a holy day. But he knew that face in the coffin and the knowledge was his grief and his pride. Some tried to bribe him, others not. Some had bribed him to tell, if they thought they would inherit money.

'Please tell me, Pat, is it Jim? The old monster. He's so mean.' And Pat would remain tight-lipped except that twice, twice only, he had released himself from his burden and the man had died. But was it destiny that had killed him or the revelation? Who could tell? And so Pat was like a crow traversing the countryside.

No, they will not drive me out, not again. One fine morning, as fine as any he had known, they were waiting for him. Cum, Shonachan, John Smith. The three of them.

They were standing in front of a gate through which he must pass on his round. They were frowning and hostile.

He tried to pass but they stood in his way.

Cum spoke first. 'Who is it?' he said.

Pat said, 'I can't tell. I am not supposed to tell. You know that.'

'You had better tell,' said Shonachan. For a man usually so calm he was aggressive. He wasn't smoking as many cigarettes as he had done.

'You'd better tell,' said John Smith.

But, no, he would not tell. He had made this mistake before and he would not do it again. No, he would not do it again. It was his secret. And the very telling might be the death blow.

'If you don't tell,' said Shonachan, 'you will have to leave and that's the end of it. We will not have you in the village.' The phantom taste of cigarettes bothered him.

So this was it happening again. It always happened. Always. And up to now he had never learnt. No one wanted a death-dealer in their village.

He stared at Cum, the bag over his shoulder. His red face shone in the day from the effort of carrying his letters and parcels.

Now he must make a new effort. He did not wish to leave. Not again. It was too late. He was getting old and he wanted to stay where he was. But to give birth to the monster, that was bad, for he knew that it might be the monster that killed.

The three of them stood in front of him: Shonachan with his slightly greying hair, John Smith like a civil servant, with his clever eyes, Cum, huge as the side of a house in his fisherman's jersey. It was a moment of tremendous silence.

He laid his bag down gently on the ground. If he told, what would happen? Would they attack him, would they drive him out just the same into the other villages. But he did not wish to go. All that was over for him. He would face them out this time, it was his own life that he was saving.

He thought for a long time and then he pointed at Cum, and he saw Cum's face disintegrating in front of him. 'You forced me to tell,' he shouted. Cum seemed to fall apart like the house he had never completed. His face quivered like a child's.

And then amazingly he saw the other two withdrawing from Cum, as if in horror, and turning ever so slightly towards himself.

The moment passed, he was safe.

The hostility had left the faces of Shonachan and John Smith. Indeed it was as if the three of them, these two and Pat himself, formed a new ring.

And they watched as Cum stumbled away from them like a wounded sheep.

'It's terrible,' said Shonachan, searching for his cigarettes.

'Awful,' said John Smith. And then to Pat, 'You saw him?'

'Yes,' said Pat, 'as clearly as I see you.' Much more clearly than anyone had seen the Pharaoh's mummy.

And yet and yet . . . In the service of death itself what could one do? To defend oneself? Knowing all of them . . .

'Yes,' he said, 'I saw him as clearly as I see you.'

The land around them became fresh and beautiful again. Shonachan saw it through the smoke of his cigarette. For Pat it was his joy and his triumph resurrected. No one would ever again drive him from it. He had done with his exile.

And in front of him as it were he saw Cum like the Pharaoh travelling through the sky like a god, huge and eternal, while John Smith was writing. Thank you for yours of the 14th inst. I have to tell you that after due consideration and much thought I have come to the conclusion that . . . The pen hung over the page. His clever eyes would never tire. But above him travelled the heavy, wounded, puzzled Pharaoh, his unfinished pyramid below him in the desert.

The Ghost

I

It was a bleak windy evening when they arrived at the hotel, situated by itself at the roadside with the bare moor behind and around it, he the artist and she the wife. At first they weren't sure whether the hotel was open, since it was still cold January, but in fact it was, and when through driving rain they ran to the door and pressed the bell a tall youngish man in tweeds appeared and told them that they could have bed and breakfast. They took the cases in from the car in silence and signed the register while the tweeded man who they thought was the owner agreed that the weather was grim, and, yes, he could provide them with a drink and, yes, they could have dinner.

They went into the lounge where there was a paraffin heater, black leather seats, and on the walls a number of landscapes which the artist glanced at with some contempt, for he himself painted in the modern style, that is to say, abstractly. They sat in silence staring at the heater: there was no one but themselves in the lounge.

Sheila the wife didn't speak: she knew that the holiday had been a disaster but she was unwilling to take the blame. Her husband looked at her now and again as if about to say something and then changed his mind. Even after the stormy crossing on the boat her blonde hair was carefully combed, her suit impeccable. He looked out of the window at the sea which was still tempestuous and restless, white waves foaming round the rocks.

They sipped their whiskies and sat in silence. Who would have thought that she would have turned out to be so religious and intolerant and dark? It was a part of her nature that hadn't shown clearly in Edinburgh. And as for himself, he hadn't realised that such places existed, such intolerant boring dull places where time oozed like treacle, where people would sit for hours staring into the fire, where the fear of death was everywhere, where life had been pared to the minimum, where his red velvet jacket blazed out of the grey monochrome like a scarlet sin. His head still felt as if it had been flayed.

'It was a bit of a disaster,' he said frankly, turning towards her.

'I thought you would say that,' she answered, and turned away again.

To tell the truth she had been frightened by the sight of her own true nature, concealed for so long in Edinburgh. And yet it was her nature and it had to be reckoned with.

'All those elders and ministers,' he said, 'those endless graces. I couldn't even show them my paintings. Imagine that. They thought they were idols and the work of the devil, they really thought that.' He truly didn't understand them, not at all. His own upbringing - free and sophisticated - hadn't prepared him for that darkness, that constriction.

'I felt,' he said, 'as if someone was squeezing me slowly to death.'

'I was brought up there,' she said, sipping her whisky very carefully as if she were already thinking of giving it up, and all this after a fortnight.

'I know,' he said. 'I hadn't realised . . . ' And then he stopped.

'Hadn't realised what?'

'How much of you belongs to that island. How you accepted it all, how clearly you are one of them.'

'I hadn't realised it myself,' she said. Of course they had only been married six months but even so, not to have known . . .

'But do you not see,' she insisted, 'that in a way they are right?'

'Right!'

'Their lives are ordered,' she said. 'They have order.'

So that was what she was looking for. Order. Certainly he couldn't give her that, not that sort of order. That sort of death.

'I felt so secure,' she said. 'All the time I felt so secure.'

After your chaotic life, she meant. After your terrifying disorder.

'They know where they are going,' she said. 'Where we are all going.'

Her blonde composed head turned towards him passionately. 'Don't you see? They are preparing. They are readying themselves.'

'For death,' he answered, seeing so clearly the black shawls around the breasts like black shields, the wind stropping the bare windy moor.

'The lack of colour,' he mused. 'That was the worst of all. Nothing but black and white. Nothing but sorrow and sighing. Nothing but fear. They are frightened to live.'

She was about to reply when the tweedy man came back in and said that they could have their food now. They followed him into the large deserted dining-room.

'Would you like some wine?' he asked her.

'No, thanks.'

'Well, I'll take some,' and he ordered a German wine that he had never heard of before.

They sat facing each other alone in the dining-room which had more landscapes on the walls. The island had almost killed him, it was only now that he was beginning to waken up. He wanted a theatre of the body, music, joy, colour. But she didn't want any of these things. It was as if she had returned to an aboriginal guilt on which she was feeding in silence as a trembling shorn Eve suddenly feels frightened of the apple in her hand, bitten and in such a short moment discoloured. He had a picture in his mind of the scoured streets of the island town, of the men and women in black, of the salt piercing wind, of the churches and cemeteries, of the barrenness and the blackness, of the psalms rising and falling like the sound of the sea.

Of her father saying grace, of the truisms endlessly delivered as if they were revelations from God. 'We are so hard-hearted,' he would say, 'there is no good in us.' He had felt as if he must free Sheila from a demonic world. But she had lowered her head like a cow about to be axed, and surrendered herself to that world as if returning to her helpless childhood again.

'Will steak do?' said the tweedy man. Steak would do. They ate in silence.

The two worlds – that bare one and the world of the artist – hung around them like contrary paintings. He felt as if he might never paint again. An old woman struggling against that eternal wind of death in her black clothes, that was what he might paint, nothing joyful. He felt tired to the bones and she was staring down at her plate. It was almost as if she expected him to say grace. The vanity. She had even stopped using perfume.

'I'm not saying anything against your people,' he said.

She looked up questioningly.

'But,' he said, 'God did not mean us to be like that. Surely he didn't.'

'How do you mean?' she asked, her eyes very blue and cold and distant.

'I felt as if I was being squeezed to death. It is not right to feel like that.'

'Aren't we all being squeezed to death?' she said. And yet in earlier days she had been so gay and happy. Perhaps too much so, he thought now, perhaps with too much desperation.

On their holiday they had met an alcoholic who lived alone and whose room was filled with empty bottles. But no one asked him why he had become an alcoholic. Everyone avoided him, they made no allowances for the temptations and the terrors. No one questioned himself, no one asked, 'Am I my brother's keeper?' He shuddered. And even now as he looked out of the window he could see the bareness and the storm and the rain lashing the ground, with its grey whips. Inside the house there was the wine on the table. He drank some more while she looked at him disapprovingly, though she said nothing.

He felt his hands clench as if around a paint-brush that could no longer paint pictures.

He felt as if he were fighting against some form of possession, possession by God. So many days they had sat by the fire, gazing into it as if into a mirror which showed scenes from the past, the dog asleep on the floor and now and again twitching in its sleep, the clock ticking, time devouring them. Ships on the stormy seas, bringing letters from America, from Australia, from the exiles.

He was suffering from culture shock. He remembered his own upbringing, the playing of the piano in the large sunny drawing-room, the reading of novels, the endless simple unprincipled traffic of the world. The art galleries. On the island he was the stranger, the enemy. No one would look at his pictures.

So much of what we do is vain, she said. And she was so beautiful, that was what was so heartbreaking. But the island would destroy her beauty, it would eat her alive, it would put shapeless clothes round her infernal breast. He drank some more wine. He wanted to get drunk, to forget about the cemeteries, the cold hard wind.

They had some trifle after the steak and he drank some more wine.

'This is quite an old hotel,' she said, 'really. They've modernised it. That's all.'

'Yes, perhaps you're right. And we're the only guests here.'

If only she would dance as she had used to do. But now he could see that her former frenzy had been an escape from herself, from the darkness. From that incessant flaying wind, from that devilish music.

'Don't you see?' she said eagerly. 'They have adapted. They have adapted to the bareness. There's no protection. Not even in art. Nothing protects us from mortality.'

'And all your – their – lives,' he said, 'they are preparing for death.'

'Yes,' she replied. 'It is another way of seeing the world. Perhaps it is the true way, without deception.'

'No,' he said, flushed with the wine. 'I won't allow it to be. It can't be. I want the vanity, the unpredictability, the perfumes, the mirrors.'

She flinched as if he had struck her. He drank some more wine. The tweedy man came in and asked if they would have tea or coffee. They would have coffee. He paused for a moment and told them that it was worthwhile keeping the hotel open in the winter because of the bar trade, that life here was very different from life in the south, that he hadn't begun to live till he came here. He shot and fished and boated. The artist fancied that he looked now and again at Sheila who, however, stared straight ahead of her. Her faithfulness mirrored his own. For a moment he thought that religion would make her even more loyal, more predictable and he felt contentment but not joy. A large dog came into the room and gazed at them with large tranquil eyes. Fidelity. Peace.

When they had had their coffee they sat a little longer and then Sheila said that she wished to go to bed, though it was still quite early. They climbed the stairs together and he fitted the key in the lock of the door. As he went in he had an impression of glass, another door perhaps at the end of the corridor. In the room itself there were twin beds, an oldish dressing table with a large spotty mirror, a wardrobe, and an electric fire which looked broken. He tried to fit some coins into the slot but failed. They undressed in silence, took their chill night-clothes from their cases and went to bed. He noticed that she was wearing a long chaste nightgown which he couldn't remember having seen before: perhaps it was an heirloom which had been given her when she was home. He stayed awake for some time staring up at the ceiling and then, feeling quite tired, fell asleep.

2

He woke up in the middle of the night and groped for the light to see what time it was. It was three o'clock.

'What are you doing?' said Sheila.

'I'm sorry,' he said, 'I didn't realise you were awake. It's three o'clock. Didn't you sleep?'

'Yes, I slept,' she said irritably. For some reason he had an impulse to be teasing and provocative and he said, 'Imagine. Suppose there's a ghost in the hotel.'

'What?'

'A ghost.' And then more daringly. 'Suppose we two are ghosts. Suppose the real you has gone out while I was sleeping and you are a ghost.'

'What nonsense.'

'But think of it,' he said. 'How do I know that you're not a ghost? How do you know that I'm not a ghost? How do you know that the real me hasn't gone out and that only my spirit is here?'

But he wasn't able to frighten her though he was almost frightening himself. All round the hotel on that desolate moor there might be ghosts shimmering in their long white chaste nightgowns. For a moment he really thought that perhaps she was a ghost as he listened to her breathing, a bed away in the darkness. If the two of them were ghosts, if time had changed during their sleep, in this room so old and dim with the ancient furniture!

What women had sat at that mirror who were now in all corners of the world or dead? What women or men had slept in these very beds and had wakened perhaps at three in the morning and had spoken to each other as they were speaking now? He felt himself sweating and wanted to put the light on again. Perhaps if he did so he would only see a skull lying on the bed next to him. But he was too frightened to switch it on and lay awake staring at the ceiling which he couldn't see. Hotels, how strange they were. Transients of all kinds passed through them, the old and the young, the sane and the insane, the crippled and the healthy. They all lay down in those beds and slept in them. They woke in the early hours of the morning and lit cigarettes and thought about their lives, wasted or fruitful.

'It's true,' he said in a whisper across the dark space, 'we could be spirits.'

'Oh shut up,' she said. And then she got up and switched the light on. 'I have to go to the bathroom.'

'All right,' he said, grateful for the light.

He watched her as she walked across the floor to the door. She was really very beautiful with her blonde hair streaming down her back. One would never have suspected that she had succumbed to the powers of darkness – or the powers of light. She pulled the door behind her and he was left alone again. All round him was absolute silence, the silence, he thought fearfully, of the grave itself. What if she never came back? What if she disappeared forever? What evidence would there be that she had ever been with him, if the tweedy fellow was involved in some ghostly complicated plot.

But she did come back, shutting the door behind her and saying excitedly: 'What an extraordinary thing.'

'What's so extraordinary?' he said.

'You know that glass door down at the end of the corridor,' she said, 'well, there was a woman standing behind it. She wore a black shawl and she looked quite old. Must be the owner's mother.'

'Funny,' he said.

'Yes,' she said, 'perhaps she can't sleep. She didn't look spooky or anything. I only had a glimpse of her. Maybe there's another bathroom over there, the family quarters perhaps, and she was going to or coming back from the bathroom.'

'I suppose so,' he said.

'I'm sure she can't sleep,' said Sheila. 'That's what it is. She was looking at me and then I had an impression of her turning away.'

'Perhaps you'd better lock the door anyway,' he said.

'All right,' she said, 'is that better?'

'Fine.'

'Well in that case,' said Sheila, 'I'd better get to sleep and so had you. You've a lot of driving to do tomorrow morning.'

'Okay,' he said. 'What did she look like?'

'Oh, just an old woman with a black shawl. She looked a bit hunchbacked. That was all. I don't know what you're going on about her for. The curious thing was that she looked vaguely familiar. Maybe I caught a glimpse of her in the hotel tonight without realising that I'd seen her.'

'It's possible,' he said.

Now that the door was locked he felt quite secure. He turned over on his side and almost immediately fell asleep.

He was awakened by the sunlight falling across the bed and into his eyes. Sheila was already up and sitting in front of the mirror tidying herself. He himself felt joyful and light hearted as he often did on a sunny morning, aware of a new unused world opening before him, alive with hope and cheerfulness.

When he got up he went behind her and put his arms around her. She shrank away from him, not much, but enough for him to notice.

'Don't be a clown,' she said, 'put on your clothes. You'll be cold.'

He did his Groucho Marx walk across the room as he had often done on the island while walking along the street, wondering if anyone would notice. But in fact no one had looked at him: perhaps they really thought he was a cripple.

'Oh, oh, oh,' he sighed heavily, imitating her father and glancing at her mischievously. But she didn't react in any way and only looked into the mirror searching for signs of approaching age. That, he thought, was good: at least she hadn't forgotten she was a woman. He padded round her, the sex fiend of the Highlands. 'An inconspicuous elderly man with a wooden leg and a mask has been taken into custody,' he intoned, 'for the murder of an old woman who had inflicted psalms on him for fifty years. Pleading justification the man said that she had a rotten voice anyway.' She didn't smile at first but then gradually did. He was happy again.

'I think,' he said in his normal voice, 'that we should take our cases down with us. Save us coming back to the room again after breakfast.'

'All right,' she said.

So they packed their night-clothes in their cases and walked along the corridor, he behind her.

He didn't know what made him turn as he was leaving the door of the bedroom behind him but in any event he did turn.

He stared directly towards the glass door at the end of the corridor and saw with horror, quite clearly, himself and his case, and she slightly ahead of him with her own case also reflected in it. As he moved and looked backwards the image moved with him.

With horror such as he had never known he realised that what he was looking at was not a glass door at all but a mirror.

His head spun but he had enough presence of mind to nudge her forward as she was about to turn and look at him. In that case (his spinning brain was telling him) what she had seen was not an old woman in black at the far end of a glass door but herself walking towards the mirror. And the vague sense she had of the woman turning away was herself turning in at the bedroom door.

She went into the bathroom on her way downstairs and he waited outside it, ready to prevent her for any reason from walking back along that corridor towards what she had thought was a glass door but what was in actual fact a mirror.

And as he sat there on a chair conveniently provided outside the bathroom the world turned round and round and finally came to a stop and he saw her as she would be in the future, old and clad in black exactly like that woman whom he had thought of painting as she breasted the sharp island wind. He stared straight ahead of him at a painting on the wall which showed a hill and a loch and a boat and its amateurishness seemed to gather about it like a black shadow descending from the badly drawn sky.

When she came out of the bathroom he picked up the case and walked down the stairs, she ahead of him. When the tweedy man asked them if they had slept well he said that they had. He wished to be away as soon as possible, ate little, and when his wife was about to ask about an old woman who might or might not live in the hotel he quickly sent the man off to make out the account for bed and breakfast.

Behind the wheel of the car, later, he drove at seventy miles an hour for mile on mile. Disapprovingly she sat beside him but said nothing. For a good part of the way he found himself looking in the mirror to see if there was anything following them but all he could see was a small yellow car with a small man in glasses at the wheel who was staring ahead of him unsmilingly. Beside him was his taller wife and behind both of them there sat upright a tall black dog which gazed ahead of it with an air of tranquil ownership.

The True Story of Sir Hector Macdonald

He became Major General Hector Macdonald, he who had been brought up in the Black Isle in the Highlands of Scotland. Apprenticed at an early age to a shopkeeper in Inverness he ran away to join the army in Aberdeen. Sent to Afghanistan he was promoted rapidly, reaching the rank of Colour Sergeant: and after two episodes where he showed conspicuous bravery he was sent for by General Roberts who gave him the choice of a VC or a commission in the Gordon Highlanders.

'Better a commission in the Gordon Highlanders than to be a Member of Parliament,' said the impeccable soldier. Nor perhaps did he realise then that to hold a commission in peacetime in the army of that day was to expose himself to expense that only a private income could cope with. And that to rise from the ranks to a commission was further to expose himself to humiliation and jealousy and envy.

And loneliness. Above all loneliness.

After the mountains of Afghanistan, after the bodies of the rebels had twisted slowly in the wind, he was ordered to South Africa to take part in the Boer War, a very different kind of war where the enemy were like ghosts, sharpshooters, brilliant amateurs.

At Majuba Rock he among others climbed at night to ensconce themselves above the Boer camp. Sliding about the rocks in hobnailed boots they entrenched themselves, digging wells for water. In the early morning one of the soldiers shouted to the sleeping Boers to come up and fight like men. There was a scrambling of Boers from their camp which became like a live anthill and then the rock became an inferno of heat and fire. As the British soldiers were picked off by the Boer sharpshooters the rock became a cauldron flowing with blood. Hector fought with his bare fists but was eventually overpowered, made prisoner, and had his sword taken from him. Later he was released and as a gesture of respect had his sword returned to him: the Boers recognised a brave enemy.

The First Boer War had however been a disaster.

Hector went to the Sudan to train native soldiers to fight the Dervishes. The Sirdar, called Kitchener, a hater of women, built a road along the Nile along which he sent his armour to avenge Khartoum. The desert was infested with flies but most beautiful at night with its millions of stars. From water-holes dead camels stared back at one. Kitchener's iron road drove undeviatingly for Omdurman, as he made his bullish rush at the enemy. The Mahmud was dragged behind a horse to pay for Gordon's death. Kitchener's army marched relentlessly forward supported by ships and big artillery. At night one could see the searchlights from the ships dividing the sky into sections. One could also hear the sleepless drums of the enemy. Maxims cut the Dervishes down and they lay like black sheaves while Kitchener made for Omdurman, not realising that many more of the enemy were hidden behind sand dunes. Hector or Fighting Mac as he was called was surrounded by them. Cool as an icicle he told his men with the harsh fury of the ex-sergeant that they must wait till the enemy were close before they fired, and his trained Sudanese obeyed him. His army was outnumbered by ten to one and caught between two forces. At that moment he invented a spontaneous dance of march and countermarch, retreat, advance, retreat, advance, while sabres cut and drums beat till they heard the pipes of the Cameronians, and the Dervishes – thirty thousand of them at the beginning – began to break. Later it was said that it was Hector who by his coolness had given Kitchener his victory.

Promoted to Brigadier General he was made Commander of the Bath and an ADC to the Queen, while Kitchener was voted thirty thousand pounds by Parliament. Hector who needed the money was instead given ceremonial swords, banquets, freedom of cities. Highland societies acclaimed him – 'Pray silence for Colonel Macdonald.' The Earl of Kincardine, the Duke of Atholl, were among the guests at these dinners. He had been promoted dizzily from private to the rank of a high officer but he was still lonely, perhaps more so now that envy became acute. After all had he not been just a leader of black troops? And was it not his training as a sergeant that had drilled his force sufficiently to save the hour at Omdurman?

He begins to write to a young boy whom he had met in Aberdeen. Again he is sent to fight the Boers in charge of the Highland Brigade who were in disgrace because they had run away at Magersfontein after they had been propelled in darkness to make a frontal charge on entrenched Boers who picked them off like ducks. Six hundred men had been killed in a few minutes. Lord Methuen stood on a platform and told them, 'Your primary duty is to the Queen, then to your country, lastly to yourselves.'

Hector himself drills his troops in sections like a sergeant but is wounded in the foot at Modder River while his unprotected men advance, again under the overall charge of the unimaginative and bullish Kitchener. The war was a stinking abattoir, the enemy was a taunting lightning on the hills.

Hector is given the charge of some gentlemen Volunteers and rages at them in pain and frustration: why can't these Boers stand and fight like honest men? Kitchener invents his concentration camps and in spite of comparative failure caused by his wound and accumulated fatigue. Hector is knighted and sent to Australia, and New Zealand, and finally to Ceylon, a post suitable to tired old superannuated army horses. From the latter place he was ordered home after rumours of homosexual adventures, the sin of David and Jonathan.

Roberts, himself happily married, didn't understand the loneliness which led to the offence if offence it was. King Edward, bulbous-eyed womaniser, understood even less. Hector was ordered back to Ceylon to face a jury of his peers. On his way there he stopped off at Paris where he took lodgings. One morning he went to buy a morning paper and there in the New York Herald found that the story about him had broken. He walked back to his lodgings and shot himself. His body was rushed hugger mugger to London in a plain coffin and from King's Cross was taken by train to Deans Graveyard where he was buried in a rainy grey dawn with only a few mourners present.

These then are the facts about this famous soldier, of whom it was said by grieving admirers that he was not dead, his coffin had been filled with stones, and that he was the Mackensen who fought in the German army in the First World War.

In such speculation I am not interested. I have a speculation of my own. It is Paris, city of culture, of books and poems and opera, in the early morning, and Hector Macdonald is walking along one of its streets in search of a newspaper. He is the simple flower of the British Empire, he has fought for it till he has grown weary, he has been a good linguist, but not a cultured man in the Parisian manner. He has committed the sin of Sodom and Gomorrah and his home village is biblical and puritanical.

No, I am not concerned with any of that. On the contrary I am concerned to follow this man down the Parisian street in the early morning. I imagine it as early morning, pearly grey. There he walks, stiff-necked, ramrod-backed, this Highlander who has become a world figure: and I imagine, for one can imagine such things, passing him on the other side of the street a young painter called Picasso perhaps with a brush in his hand. And Hector does not notice him, and Picasso does not notice him either. And Picasso may be thinking of a collage of bits of newspaper stuck on a painting, and it may be that he will use the same newspaper which has just told of Hector's disgrace. At any rate they pass each other on this pearly morning, the old soldier who has fought for the Empire, the flawed lonely man who has climbed into the sky only to be brought down like a pheasant by jealous guns: and the painter with the eyes as piercing as twin gun barrels.

Two worlds let us imagine, one dying, one about to be born.

And then as if the image has been frozen it begins to move again, and there is the crack of a gun in the very heart of the Empire, creating eddies of disturbance, spreading outwards. The coffin is hurried north in a weeping dawn – the initials HAM written on it – and Picasso returns to his studio. It is a day in March at the beginning of the twentieth century.

Chagall's Return

When I came home the cat was smiling and the walls of the house were shaking. The door opened and there was my mother in front of me.

'Who are you, my child?' she asked, and her eyes were unfocused and mad. There were other old women in black with her and they nodded to me over and over. I went to see a neighbour who was ploughing, and afterwards I took buckets to the well and brought in water. But my mother was still gazing at me with unfocused eyes and she asked me again and again who I was. I told her about the skyscrapers and the man with the violin, but she could understand nothing.

She kept saying, 'In the old days there were cows, and we were children. We would take them to the grass and there they would make milk.'

'I have brought you money,' I said. 'See, it is all green paper.'

But she looked at the paper unseeingly. I didn't like the look in her eyes. In the afternoon I took a walk round the graveyard near the house, and the tombstones were pink and engraved with names like conversation sweets.

There is nothing in the world worse than madness. All other diseases are trivial compared to it, for the light of reason is what illuminates the world. All that day I shouted to her, 'Come back to me', but she wouldn't. She wanted to stay in her cave of silence.

In this place I walk like a giant. My legs straddle the wardrobe, and the midgets around me speak with little mouths. My hands are too big for the table and my back for the chairs. I look into the water which I brought home from the well and it is still and motionless. But my mother's eyes are slant and the old women whisper to her. I nearly chase them out of the house but my mother needs them, I think, for they tell old stories to each other. I think they are talking about the days when things were better than they are now.

The cat's mouth is wide open and he smiles all the time as if his mouth were fixed like that.

'Who are you?' says my mother, over and over. She doesn't remember the day she stood at the door watching me leave, a bag over my shoulder, her eyes shining with tears. I used to see her in the walls of skyscrapers, a transparency on stone. My young days were happy, I think, before she went crazy. Now and again she says things that I don't understand. She speaks the words, 'Who is the man with the black wings?' over and over. But when I ask her what she means she refuses to answer me.

Night falls, and there is a star like a silver coin in the sky. I hear the music of violins, and the black women have left. But my mother's eyes remain distant and hard, and she stares at me as if I were a stone. A dog with a plasticine body is barking from somewhere and in an attic a man is washing himself with soap over and over.

One day in New York I saw that the sun had a pair of moustaches like a soldier home from the wars, and he began to tell me a story.

'I went to the war,' he said, 'and I was eighteen years old. For no reason that I could think of, people began to fire at me trying to kill me. I stood by a tree that had red berries and prayed. I stayed there for a long time till the sun had gone down, counting the berries. After that I went home and I was hidden by my sister behind a large canvas for the rest of the war. When the war was over there were no trees to be seen.'

Still my mother stares at me with her unfocused eyes. I see the whites of them like the white of an egg. She has terrible dreams. In her dreams she is being chased by a vampire, and just at the moment when he is about to clutch her she wakens up.

'Where are you, my son?' she cries. I rush in, but she doesn't recognise me. The greatest gift in my life would be if she recognised me, if the light of reason would come back to her eyes.

I wonder now if it will ever happen.

'I shall put tap-water in the house for you,' I say to her. But she doesn't answer. She only picks at her embroidery.

'And heating,' I say. 'And an electric samovar.'

'My father,' she says, 'was a kind man who had a beard. He was often drunk but he would give you his last penny.'

I remember him. He wasn't kind at all. He was drunk and violent, and he had red eyes, and he played the violin all night. Sometimes I see him flying through the sky and his beard is a white cloud streaming behind him. But he was violent, gigantic and unpredictable.

Where the sky is greenest I can see him. I go to the cemetery with the pink tombstones, and his name isn't on any of them.

What am I to do with my mother, for she shouts at the policemen in the streets? 'Get out of here,' she screams at them; 'this was a road for cows in the old days.' The policemen smile and nod, and their tolerance is immense for she cannot harm them.

The bitterest tears I shed was when she told them that when her son came home he would show them that she wasn't to be treated like a tramp. The old, black women come back and are always whispering stories about her, but if I go near them they stop talking.

'Is your seed not growing yet?' I ask my next-door neighbour.

'No,' he says, 'it is going to be a hard year. How is your mother?'

'Not well,' I say, 'she lives in a world of her own.'

He smiles, but says nothing. He was ten years old when I left this place with my bag on my shoulder. That day the birds were singing from the hedges and they each had one green eye and one blue.

I begin to draw my mother to see if her reason will come back to her. I see her as a path that has been overgrown with weeds. Her apron is a red phantom which one can hardly see and the chickens to which she threw meal have big ferocious beaks. Nevertheless, she does take an interest in what I am doing, though she cannot stay still, and her eyes are beginning to focus.

One day – the happiest of my life – she speaks to me again

and recognises me. 'You are my son,' she says, 'and you left me. Why did you leave me?' I try to tell her, but I cannot. The necessity for it is beyond her understanding, and this is the worst of all to bear.

That night before she goes to bed she says, 'Good night, my son,' and in the middle of the night she tucks the blanket about me to keep me warm. I feel that she is watching over me and I sleep better than I have done for many years. In the morning I am happy and wake up as the light pours through the windows. She is sitting by my bed with a shawl wrapped round her.

'Mother,' I cry, 'I am here. I have come back.' The windows change their shape as I say it. But she doesn't answer me. She is dead. She is a statue. She is solid and changeless. All that day I kneel in front of her, staring into her unchanging face.

In the evening one of her eyes becomes green and the other blue. I take my bag in my hand and leave the house. The birds are singing in the hedges and a man is walking through a ploughed field. I do not turn back and wave. The houses are turning into cardboard and the violins are stuck to their walls. I feel sticky stuff on my clothes, my hands and my face. I carry the village with me, stamped all over my body, and take it with me, roof, door, bird, branch, pails of water. I cross the Atlantic with it.

'Welcome,' they say, 'but what have you got there?'

'It is a nest,' I say, 'and a coffin.'

'Or, to put it another way, a coffin and a nest.'

Napoleon and I

I tell you what it is. I sit here night after night and he sits there night after night. In that chair opposite me. The two of us. I'm eighty years old and he's eighty-four. And that's what we do, we sit and think. I'll tell you what I sit and think about. I sit and think, I wish I had married someone else, that is what I think about.

And he thinks the same. I know he does. Though he doesn't say anything or at least much. Though I don't say much either. We have nothing to say: we have run out of conversation. That's what we've done. I look at his mouth and it's moving. But most of the time he's not speaking. I don't love him. I don't know what love is. I thought once I knew what love was. I thought it was something to do with being together for ever. I really thought that. Now I know that it's not that. At least it's not that, whatever else it is. *We do not speak to each other.*

He smokes a pipe sometimes and his mouth moves. He is like a cartoon. I used to read the papers and I used to see cartoons in them but now I don't read the papers at all. I don't read anything. Nor does he. Not even the sports pages though he once told me, no, more than once, he told me that he used to be a great footballer, 'When I used to go down the wing,' he would say. 'What wing?' I would say, and he would smile gently as if I were an idiot. 'When I used to go down the wing,' he would say. But now he doesn't go down any wing. He's even given up the tomato plants. And he imagines he's Napoleon. It's because of that film he says. There were red squares of soldiers in it. He sits in his chair as if he's Napoleon, and he says things to me in French though I don't know French and he doesn't know French. He prefers Napoleon to his tomato plants. He sits in his chair, his legs spread apart, and he thinks about winning

Waterloo. I think he's mad. He must be, mustn't he? Sometimes he will look up and say 'Josephine', the one word 'Josephine', and the only work he ever did was in a distillery. Napoleon never worked in a distillery. I am sure that never happened. He's a comedian really. He sits there dreaming about Napoleon and sometimes he goes out and examines the ground to see if it's wet, if his cavalry will be all right. He kneels down and studies the ground and then he sits and puffs at his pipe and he goes and takes a pair of binoculars and he studies the landscape. I never thought he was Napoleon when I married him. I just said *I do*. Nor did he. I used to give him his sandwiches in a box when he went to work and he just took them in those days. I don't think he ever asked for wine. Now he thinks the world has mistreated him, and he wants an empire. Still they do say they need something when they retire. The only thing is, he's been retired for twenty years or maybe fifteen. He came home one day and he put his sandwich box on the table and he said, 'I'm retired' (that was in the days when we spoke to each other) and I said, 'I know that.' And he went and looked after his tomato plants. In those days he also loved the cat and was tender to his tomato plants. Now we no longer have a cat. We don't even have a tortoise. One day, the day he stopped speaking to me, he said, 'I've been hard done by. Life has done badly by me.' And he didn't say anything else. I think it was five o'clock on our clock that day, the 25th of March it would have been, or maybe the 26th.

Actually he looks stupid in that hat and that coat. Anyone would in the twentieth century.

I on the other hand spend most of my time making pictures with shells. I make a picture of a woman who has wings and who flies about in the sky and below her there is a man who looks like a prince and he is riding through a forest. The winged woman also has a cooker. I find it odd that she should have a cooker but there it is, why shouldn't she have a cooker if she wants to, I always say. On the TV everyone says, 'I always say', and then they have a cup of tea. At the most dramatic moments. And then I see him sitting opposite me in his Napoleon's coat and I think we are on TV. Sometimes I almost say that. But then I realise that we aren't speaking since we have nothing to speak about and I don't say anything. I don't even wash his coat for him.

In any case, how has he been hard done by? He married me, didn't he? I have given him the best years of my life. I have washed, scrubbed, cooked, slaved for him, and I have made sandwiches for him to put in his tin box every day. The same box.

And our children have gone away and they never came back. He used to say it was because of me, I say it's because of him. Who would want Napoleon for a father and anyway Napoleon didn't spend his time looking after tomato plants, though he doesn't do that now. He writes despatches which he gives to the milkman. He writes things like 'Tell Soult he must bring up another five divisions. Touty sweet.' And the milkman looks at the despatches and then he looks at me and then I give him the money for the week's milk. He is actually a very understanding milkman.

The fact that he wears a white coat is neither here nor there. Nothing is either here or there.

And sometimes he will have forgotten that the day before he asked for five divisions, and he broods, and he writes 'Please change the whole educational system of France. It is not just. And please get me a new sandwich box.'

He is really an unusual man. And I loved him once. I loved him when he was an ordinary man and when he would keep up an ordinary conversation when he would tell me what had happened at the distillery that day, though nothing much ever happened. Nothing serious. Nothing funny either. It was a very quiet distillery, and the whisky was made without trouble. Maybe it's because he left the distillery that he feels like Napoleon. And he changed the chair too. He wanted a bigger chair so that he could watch the army manoeuvres in the living-room and yet have enough room for the TV-set and the fridge. It's very hard living with a man who believes that there is an army next to the fridge. But I think that's because he imagines Napoleon in Russia, that's why he wants something cold. And on days when Napoleon is in Russia he puts on extra clothes and he wants plenty of meat in the fridge. The reason for that I think is that the meat is supposed to be dead French soldiers.

He is not mad really. He's just living in a dream. Maybe he could have been Napoleon if he hadn't been born at 26 Sheffield Terrace. It's not easy being Napoleon if you're born in a council house. The funny thing is that he never notices the aerial. How could there be an aerial or even a TV-set in Napoleon's time, but he doesn't notice that. Little things like that escape him, though in other ways he's very shrewd. In small ways. Like for instance he will remember and he'll say to the milkman, 'You didn't bring me these five divisions yesterday. Where the hell did you get to? Spain will kill me.' And there will be a clank of bottles and the milkman will walk away. That makes him really angry. Negligence of any kind. Inefficiency. He'll get up and shout after him, 'How the hell am I going to keep an empire together with idiots like you about? Eh? Tell me that, my fine friend.' Mr Merriman thinks he is Joan of Arc. That causes a lot of difficulty with dresses though not as much as you would imagine since she wore men's armour anyway. I dread the day Wellington will move in. I fear for my china.

Anyway that's why we don't speak. Sometimes he doesn't even recognise me and he calls me Antoinette and he throws things at me. I don't know what to do, really I don't. I'm at my wits' end. It would be cruel to send for a doctor. I don't hate him that much. I think maybe I should tell him I'm leaving but where can you go when you're eighty years old, though he is four years younger than me; I would have to get a home help: he doesn't think of things like that. One day he said to me, 'I don't need you. I don't need anyone. My star is here.' And he pointed at his old woollen jacket which had a large hole in it. Sometimes I can hardly keep myself from laughing when I'm doing my shells. Who could? Unless one was an angel?

And then sometimes I think, Maybe he's trying it on. And I watch out to see if I can trap him in anything, but I haven't yet. His despatches are very orderly. He sends me orders like, 'I want the steak underdone today. And the wine at a moderate temperature.' And I make the beefburgers and coffee as usual.

Yesterday he suddenly said, 'I remember you. I used to know you, when we were young. There were woods. I associate you with woods. With autumn woods.' And then his face became slightly blue. I thought he was going to fall, coming out of his dream. But no. He said, 'It was outside Paris and I met you in a room with mirrors. I loved you once before my destiny became my sorrow.' These were exactly his words, I think. He never used to talk like that. He would mostly grunt and say, 'What happened to the salt?' But now he doesn't say anything as simple as that. No indeed. Not at all.

Sometimes he draws up a chair and dictates notes to me. He says things like, 'We attack the distillery at dawn. Junot will create a diversion on the left and then Soult will strike at the right while I punch through the centre.'

He was never in a war in his life. He was kept out because of his asthma and his ulcer. And he never had a horse in his life. All he had was his sandwich box. And now he wants a coronet on it. Imagine, a coronet on a sandwich box. Will this never end? Ever? Will it? I suffer. It is I who put up with this for he never leaves the house, he is too busy organising the French educational service and the Church. 'We will have pink robes for the nuns,' he says. 'That will teach them the power of the flesh which they *abominate*,' and he shouts across the fence at Joan of Arc and says, 'You're an impostor, sir. Joan of Arc didn't have a moustache.' I don't know what I shall do. He is sitting there so calm now, so calm with his stick in his hand like a sceptre. I think he has fallen asleep. Let me put your crown right, child. It's fallen all to one side. I could never stand untidiness. Let me pick up your stick, its fallen from your hand. We are doomed to be together. We are doomed to say to the milkman, 'Bring up your five divisions', for morning after morning. We are doomed to comment on Joan of Arc's moustache. We are together for ever. Poor Napoleon. Poor lover of mine met long ago in the autumn woods before they became your empire. Poor dreamer.

And yet ... what a game ... maybe I should try on your crown just for one moment, just for a short moment. And take your stick just for a moment, just for a short short moment.

Before you wake up. And maybe I'll tell the milkman, We want ten divisions today. Ten not five. Maybe that would be the best idea, to get it finished with, once and for all. Ten instead of five.

And don't forget the cannon.

Christmas Day

On that Christmas Day she was the only customer in the hotel for lunch. 'I shall take the turkey soup,' she said. The dining-room was very large and she sat at her table as if she was on a desert island. Above her head were green streamers and green hats and in the middle of the dining-room there was a green tree.

Somewhere in Asia the peasants were digging.

The fact is, she thought, I'll never see him again. He is irretrievably dead. The pain was inside her like a jagged star.

There was this particular peasant with a bald head and when he was finished digging he went home to his family and played the guitar. It might have been China or Korea but when his mouth moved she didn't understand what he was saying. To think, she mused, that there were all these peasants in the world, and all these languages.

She drank her turkey soup and watched the two waitresses talking, their arms folded.

She had watched him die for three weeks. His pain was intolerable. After that there were the papers to be checked. One day she had left the house with a case and gone to the hotel in which she now was.

There were millions of peasants in the world and millions of paddy fields, and they all sang strange unintelligible songs. Some of them rode on bicycles through Hong Kong.

'I love you,' he had said at the end. Their hands had tightened on eternity. When she withdrew her hand the pulse was beating but his had stopped.

She wished to change her chair so that she could not see the waitresses, but she was naked and throbbing to their gaze.

When she had entered her room in the hotel for the first time she had switched on the television set. It showed peasants working in the fields in the East. She had picked up the phone and wondered whom she could talk to. Perhaps to one of the peasants in their wide-brimmed hats. She had put the phone down.

There were twenty of them in the one house, children, parents, grandparents, aunts and uncles and they were all smiling as if their paddy fields generated light.

'I am thin as a pencil,' she thought. 'Why did I wear this grey costume and this necklace?'

She finished the turkey soup. Then she tried to eat the turkey. For me it was killed, with its red comb, its splendid feathers, its small unperplexed head on the long and reptilian neck. Nevertheless I must eat.

Wherever Tom had gone, he had gone. 'Put me in a glass box,' he used to say. 'I want people to make sure that I am dead.' But in fact he had been cremated. She heard that the coffins swelled out with the heat, but he had laughed when she had told him. 'Put me in an ashtray in the living-room.'

The smoke rose above the paddy fields and the peasants were crouched around it.

She left much of the turkey and then took ice-cream which was cold in her mouth. She was alone in the vast dining-room.

Christmas was the loneliest time of all. No one who had not experienced it could believe how lonely Christmas could be, how conspicuous the unaccompanied were.

From the paddy field the peasant raised his face smiling and it was Tom's face.

'Hi,' he said in a fluting Korean voice.

The green paper hats above her swayed slightly in the draught which rippled the carpet below. It seemed quite natural that he should be sitting in front of her in his wide-brimmed hat.

'The heat wasn't at all unbearable,' he said.

He took out a cracker and pulled it. He read out what was written on the little piece of paper. It said, 'Destiny waits for us like a bus.' Or a rickshaw.

The world was big and it pulsed with life. Dinosaurs walked

about like green ladders and bowed gently to the ants who were carrying their burdens. The peasant sat in a ditch and played his guitar and winked at her.

'I remember,' said Tom scratching his neck, 'someone once saying that the world appears yellow to a canary. Even sorrow, even grief.'

And red to a turkey.

She got up and went to her room walking very straight and stiff so that the waitresses' glances would bounce off her back. Who wanted pity when death was so common?

She sat on her bed and picked up the phone.

She dialled her own number and heard the phone ringing in an empty house.

'If only he would answer it,' she said. 'If only he would answer it.'

Then she heard the voice. It said, 'Who is that speaking, please?'

She knew it was Tom and that he was wearing a wide-brimmed hat.

'I shall be home soon,' she said.

She took off her clothes and went to bed. When she woke up she felt absolutely refreshed and her head was perfectly clear.

She packed up her case, paid her bill at the desk and went home.

When she went in she heard the guitar being played upstairs. She knew that they would all be there, all the happy peasants, and sitting among them, quite at home, Tom in his green paper hat with the wine bottle in his hand.

The Arena

It was at Pula that she had the vision that she would never forget. She had taken Paul there on the bus and he was rather tired as usual. Ever since his big operation he had been tired and at the end of their holiday he was going back to another operation. According to himself his boss had been rather kind and had said, picking up the phone that lay in front of him on the desk, 'Paul has been with us for thirty years. There is no question of this half-pay nonsense.' Paul worked as a clerk in the Civil Service and had never missed a day till his operation. He had been in severe pain for a while and no one knew what was wrong with him till the specialist had finally diagnosed it as an aortic aneurism. He had lost a lot of weight and looked thin and drawn.

When she looked back over the years she realised that their life together had been on the whole a peaceful one. But she wondered if in fact the disease had come because Paul was tired of his work though he used to tell her, 'When I first started I was happy. I can't tell you how happy I was. And then it all changed. We used to have a joke together in those days but now it's all different.'

He had many little anecdotes to tell her, such as the one about the day when quite young he had been doing an imitation of the manager, an imaginary pipe stuck in his mouth when the latter had put his head round the door and caught him. 'He was a man entirely without humour,' he said. 'And after that I beat him at billiards.'

But of course that had been a different manager from the one they now had. 'Another time,' he said, 'he made an awful speech on the retiral of a lady member of staff and I was the only one who clapped. He stared at me, I remember, as if he couldn't make up his mind whether I was laughing at him or not. His speeches were terrible.'

According to himself he had been a ball of fire in those days, fiery with wit and inventiveness. And he had told her the same stories over and over so much that she sometimes wondered whether her boredom was becoming unbearable. Still he had taken his illness with admirable stoicism, not complaining much, accepting his destiny with dignity.

But in a country like this one saw only the healthy ones, especially in summer and they all looked so beautiful and tanned beside Paul.

They bloomed with luminous health, they seemed to have the sheen of animals: while all the time the sun was a fierce bristly animal in a sky of unchanging blue.

As well as being a civil servant, Paul also umpired cricket matches on Sundays and she knew that he missed the cool green misty afternoons when in his white surgical coat he would stand there making decisions. He himself believed that umpiring was his real vocation: it certainly gave him more scope for decision-making than the Civil Service did.

A youth walked along in front of her. He looked dark and Italian and had the most beautiful arrogant buttocks. How self-confident he was, how extraordinarily alive and lovely. At that very moment she would have gone with him to a dance, a gipsy dance, to drink wine, to make love. She couldn't imagine him in the Civil Service sitting down at a desk day after day, picking up a phone and saying to a caller who perhaps had an upper-class accent:

'I'm sorry, sir, but we don't keep a record of that,' and the man with the upper-class accent saying contemptuously:

'But aren't you a clerk or something? Shouldn't you know that sort of thing?'

No, that youth would never be servile or slavish, he would never reach that stage in his life when he would become so depressingly proud and say, 'And Spence took up the phone and said, "No damn nonsense about half-pay. Mason's been with us for thirty years." '

She could imagine Paul leaning forward obediently, subserviently, the manager swivelling arrogantly in his chair in a careless arc as if he were on a machine at a fairground.

So many of these youths, so beautiful, so young, and herself growing old, and into her menopause. She dragged Paul along like a chain behind her: he clanked in the hot day of her mind.

Conscience-stricken that she had almost thought of him like a slave she pointed out a wallet to him in a window that they were passing and asked him if he wanted it but he didn't, he considered it too cheap and tawdry. He seemed to evaluate it with agonising slowness as if deciding whether it was like a cricketer who should be given out.

Finally, he said, 'It's not worth the money.' He was very good at converting lire and dinars into English money, far quicker than she was. But these days there was a faraway look in his eyes as if he was staring at the green ring of a damp cricket field.

No, he had never been a flashing batsman or a demon bowler, only a very calm considering umpire, one who was weighty and careful in his decisions: and perhaps he would never be an umpire again. Perhaps he would never stand in his white coat under an amateur sky.

Her body boiled with the heat and, she was ashamed to admit, desire. The two of them hadn't had sex for the last three months. Funny expression that, 'had sex' or 'made love' when what she really meant was what she imagined these foreigners as doing, devouring each other's bodies in the sun. Images of bodies clawed and mated and fought in her mind. They leaped ravenously out of dark secret corners into the arena of her sunlight. They were strong and powerful and had nothing at all to do with the calm fields over which her husband had presided in the intervals of his dedicated work for the Civil Service.

'Are you all right?' said Paul curiously. 'You seem to be sweating a lot.'

'It's very hot,' she said.

Her body seethed with the heat, she almost fainted with the savagery of the images that leaped about in her mind, no, not in her mind, in the secret caverns and hollows of her body. And she was ashamed of them as Paul slowly paced beside her.

No, she must confront the question: what would she do if Paul died? Would she marry again? Could she bear to be alone? She had never been alone in her life, she had come from a large noisy family, animated with anecdote and discussion, and she didn't really know what solitude was. Also, she had never been a reader, she had always been happier with physical things, the confused chatter of kids in the school canteen where she served. But the question nevertheless had to be faced. When they returned to England and he had his operation he might die and what would she do then? Could she stay alone in the house after the day's work was over, could she watch television endlessly? Not that she had anyone in mind to replace Paul, nor had she ever been intimate with anyone but him. She smiled to herself at the archaic oddity of the expression.

Could she perhaps fling up her job and do what she had always wanted to do, that is wander about like a gipsy? But that would be impossible, an idle dream. Even gipsies didn't live on air, they too needed food, drink, a bed. No she couldn't leave the little terraced house bought with Paul's blood and the garden which he kept so tidy. Nor could she abandon her job. Paul wouldn't have much money to leave, though he had now stopped drinking and smoking.

Did she love him? Did she truly love him? The question struck at her like a blow from the sun. She thought she loved him and was sure that he loved her. But what was real love like? Had she ever truly experienced it? Was love involved with sex? Could she love someone without having sex with them?

It was odd how grey his hair was becoming, she hadn't noticed the greyness so clearly before. And how dependent he was growing on her, he who had always planned the details of their holidays so meticulously, taking a pride in doing so. She did not like his new passiveness: it was significant and ominous. In the past he used to love working out itineraries, even keeping a diary. And now he had given all that up. It was as if he was sensing an eternity which had no need of notes.

And another thing, he never told her what happened in the office. In the old days he used to bring home a hoard of stories like the one for instance about the tramp who used to come to the office to collect his social security and say, 'You think I'm going to die and save you money but I'm not.' And he would glare fiercely around him, unshaven, gaunt, indomitable. She could imagine him, obstinate in his determination to stay alive.

Or he might tell her about Miss Collins and Mr White who hadn't spoken to each other for years because Miss Collins had arranged the chairs for a meeting without telling him about it beforehand.

Oh God, this tremendous heat, this desire, this unfocused lust. Did others suffer from this? Did others appear to walk calmly along while raging inwardly like beasts within their pale pelts? And why was she feeling that desire now, was it the heat that was causing it, or the threat of death, or was it that she was simply ageing?

'Are you feeling all right?' she asked. She was always asking the same question as if out of a sense of profound guilt that followed both of them like shadows. Paul was sweating, not her brimming natural sweat but a grey chilly sweat. Her sweat on the other hand was the bloom on the fruit about to burst, before it hangs and shrivels like a rag on a tree.

When Paul wore his umpire's coat he looked like a doctor or a waiter. Not that she had seen him umpiring for many years. He stood there in the green light and a man would be out - his wickets sent flying - or a catch would be granted. As an umpire, Paul had a certain power. But she didn't like cricket, it was very slow, it was so slow that it felt like an eternity happening in front of her eyes. All you could hear was sporadic clapping as if from a grave and then silence.

But that didn't disguise the question she had to face. Did she love Paul? And the most tremendous question of all was, would she be glad when he died? Would she be glad when she heard no more about the Civil Service or cricket? Would she be glad when she was no longer in the presence of his greyness?

'There it is,' said Paul suddenly.

'What?' she asked as if emerging from a dream.

'The amphitheatre,' he said.

And she saw it then, a big circular stone building with rows of arches and window spaces.

'Do you want to go in?' he asked.

Seeing that he was tired she was not sure what she should say, but he added, 'I think we should see it. It's the only worthwhile thing in Pula.'

Of course he would have read about it, of course he would know its history. If he had nothing else he had information.

As they paid and entered, the heat was appalling.

'Do you know the story about it?' Paul asked. 'Why it doesn't have a roof?'

'No,' she said.

His gaunt face softened. 'It's a charming story. It is said that fairies built the amphitheatre with big stones they carted from all over Istria. They began building it at night. However at cockcrow the fairies ran away and left the building without a roof on it.'

'How beautiful,' she said. In her mind's eye she saw bronze cocks crowing, pulsing throats outstretched, wings clapping. Paul had become animated for a moment: he was like a pupil showing off to a teacher. The cocks crew and the fairies flew away and there was no roof on the amphitheatre. The fairies like gipsies departed in the night, in their irresponsible glamour. If it had been Paul he would definitely have completed the roof, for he always finished what he began.

The stone around her was intensely hot. In front of her she saw the young men and women from all over Asia and Europe with their vibrant fragrant impudent bodies. The throbbing heat pulsed from the stone, from her body.

'Listen,' said Paul, 'to the right and left there were areas where wild animals were kept. They were released into the arena.'

'Did they fight each other?'

'They fought with the gladiators and the slaves. The front seats in the gallery were reserved for the important people, the patricians. There used to be a lot of women spectators. Some of them were the worst.'

'The worst?' she said.

'The most cruel.'

And the Civil Servants, she thought, where were they? And the cool umpires? She had a dim memory that there used to be someone important who raised or lowered his thumb, as the gladiator turned and looked up into the blinding sunlight, foreshortened, waiting for his doom to be signalled, his fortune to be told.

And at that moment she felt a storm of sound around her. The arena was a writhing medley of legs, arms, torsos, swords: the lithe lions eeled forward like cats stalking birds. Then they leaped in an arc of claws and teeth. She saw a gladiator on the ground and another one standing above him, his legs spread wide in an arrogant posture.

The one on the ground was Paul and his face was throbbing in the sun, especially a big blue vein in his forehead, and there were rays of blood across his cheek. The other one – but who was the other one? She couldn't see his face but his private parts were massive, his penis throbbed like a hammer between the two big bells, the colour of flesh. Far away was the green field and the cloudy sky. There was a man in a white uniform in the middle of the arena turning his thumb down over Paul. There was a chaos of gnawing beasts, jaws, teeth, and in the centre of it all a cockerel crowing. Her whole body throbbed with fire: she was a womb that burned and flamed. Her eyes were blind and hollow and made of stone, as she turned them on Paul. She was an empress, a sleek lioness. Somewhere in a stony room underground a man was scribbling furiously with a stony pen forever and forever, his brow wrinkled as if with puzzlement. He was bent over, keeping records of all the animals, he was making sure that the timetable of furious deaths was adhered to. Then she saw him rising slowly and ascending into the arena. A lioness, tawny and almost loving, was waiting for him. She sniffed and her eyes were golden and lazy and calm. Her mane was like a circlet of fire around her. She trotted towards him easily and he waited there quite tranquilly, his hands loose at his sides. He was scrutinising the lioness silently as if asking her a question.

Do you want me? Do you love me?

And the lioness trotted towards him. The empress was standing up. In a short while she would turn her thumb down or up. The crowd was roaring, itself like a wild beast, and the sun was a torrent of fire.

The man was looking into the eyes of the lioness. He was wearing a white coat, he was standing in the middle of the stone field.

Her loins shuddered and dampened.

Paul was leaning out of the sun and was saying to her, 'Are you all right? Are you frightened or something?'

She felt the tears streaming down her face.

'What's the matter?' he was saying over and over in a concerned voice. The lioness had shrunk back to its den. The fairies had flown away. The cockerel had started flapping its wings.

'Come on,' she said, 'let's go.'

It was too late. It was not a question of loving or being loved. The last blood had been and gone. This had been a country of the sun, merciless and hot, and she had missed it. In this country one didn't ask about love, one either loved or one didn't. The ring of stone which encircled her wasn't hers.

If you had been umpire here, she nearly said to him, if you had been umpire here what would you have done? This was no amateurish play on a Sunday, this had been an affair of life and death, of real claws, real teeth.

She looked down at her damp green dress, and nearly wept with the pity of it. She would stay with him till morning, till the roof of stone went on. She would not leave at cockcrow or in the middle of the night. She would not fly away on negligent wings.

The apples that moved ahead of her, these round buttocks were distant and belonged to another country. She dare not touch them, not in this ring of stone, in this arena from which the blood had departed.

The Tour

Daphne hadn't thought that she would enjoy herself so much, though at first she had been rather stiff and formal, finding it difficult to break the shell of her English private school upbringing, which had been followed by her marriage to Geoffrey, a captain in the British army who was now in Australia, posted there for a year. But as the bus tour progressed she found that it was impossible to keep herself apart from the rest of the passengers, however she might try to do so. And it really wasn't arrogance that was the armour that stood between her and the others, not at all, it was, she knew, her accent that separated them and made them suspicious of her. Her martial stiffness was odd and imperial and very British and they resented it in their inner being.

Yet it was odd how, unlike Geoffrey, she had liked Australia from the beginning, though it was in its dusty acreages so different from the green fields of England. She belonged, she thought, with a wry smile, to the world of that school in the film *Picnic at Hanging Rock* with its iron grey mistresses.

Geoffrey didn't like Australia, he thought of it as a country of beer-swilling yobs, of undisciplined soldiers. He had once related to her a story of what had happened during the war to an officer much older than himself, who had told him of it.

'He was standing at this railway station,' he said, 'waiting for a train, and he saw this mob of Australian soldiers walking up and down. None of them saluted him. So he gave them a bollocking. And do you know what they did? They marched up and down for the rest of the time, very stiff and proper, saluting him every time they passed him.'

She had tried not to laugh but she couldn't help it.

'What the hell are you laughing at?' Geoffrey had said in his stiff upright manner.

'Nothing, nothing,' she had replied between giggles. 'Nothing at all.' And Geoffrey had fumed at her, angry as if she were a green silly schoolgirl.

But she loved Australia. She loved its mystery, she imagined it as a childish book illustrated with pictures of dingoes, kookaburras, emus. The centre of it was an echo that wished to become a voice, that wished to say, 'I am me.' It had no ranks, no orders, it was an efflorescence of wild spiky flowers, and lonely marvellous deserts.

It was the retired schoolmistress whom she liked best of all. Whenever the bus stopped at a hotel she was the first to rush to the gambling machines – the one-armed bandits – that were to be found everywhere: and with the curious careless innocence of a seventy-year-old who no longer cared for convention, she would plunge her hand in among a cascade of coins. Her name was Casey and she belonged originally to Sydney where she had taught for forty years.

'Didn't you know that we Australians are a nation of gamblers?' she said to Daphne. 'Everywhere you go there are these machines.' Her hair was cropped and grey and she moved with great rapidity and animation like a little very positive animal.

'No, I didn't know,' said Daphne. Neither she nor Geoffrey had gambled in their lives. She knew that in any battle, if there was a battle, he would prepare for every contingency, he wouldn't make a move without checking and cross checking; she thought of him as a machine in a tight uniform, like one of those early redcoats.

And so she watched Miss Casey, who had never married, plunging her hands among the coins as if she were a virgin immersing herself in a waterfall in a land that was brilliant with sunshine.

'Luck is everything,' said Miss Casey, 'I have been lucky all my life. I loved my children,' as she called her pupils, 'and now I am enjoying myself. What is the point of not?' And she gazed at Daphne with a bland guileless eye, the eye of one who has transcended it with inward bubbling joy. She was the first to get up in the morning and was to be found exploring among the woods and the dew.

At first the hare-lipped Miss Cowan didn't speak to them at all. She sat by herself in the bus, staring out of the window, clutching her handbag. When she did at last speak it was on their tour of the wineries when they were all tasting different wines.

'You could spend all your days doing this,' said Miss Casey delightedly. 'I'm sure there must be some people who do it.' She sipped appreciatively. 'What do you think of this one?' she asked Miss Cowan, and Miss Cowan in words that one could hardly understand because of her harelip, answered, 'It's sweet.'

As a matter of fact Daphne disliked deformity of any kind; but that had been a hilarious day, seven wineries in one day, and the driver had smiled when they had asked him, 'Are you sure you can drive after all this?' Imagine it though, seven wineries in one day, it wasn't the sort of thing that Geoffrey would have approved of. Bad organisation he would have said, surely they could have organised the trip better than that! A whole day wasted at wineries! But even Miss Cowan blossomed and was in fact slightly tipsy on that blue marvellous day, and Miss Casey had been very animated.

Daphne enjoyed herself immensely though she was sorry for Miss Cowan. To think that she could hardly be understood by anyone! No wonder she kept silent, no wonder she withdrew from them all. It must be awful to try and speak and come out with these awful strangulated sounds.

Eventually there were five of them that went about together, herself, Miss Casey, Miss Cowan, and that ex-policeman from Glasgow, Mr Wilson, and his wife. He was a squat energetic interesting man who had served so he had said in Borneo before coming to Australia; his wife was quiet, slim, fair-haired. He was determined to enjoy his trip.

And so they sailed on the Murray River, and had a look in the museum at Echuca where Prince Philip in upright glassy splendour was to be seen among more macabre exhibits. Echuca was slummier than she had expected, the rag-end of a once prosperous town, though the paddle steamers were quaint and romantic and ponderous.

'Did you hear this one?' said Mr Wilson. 'There were these two Glasgow football supporters and they went to Italy and they went into a pub and one of them said,

' "What do you sell here?"

'And the barman said, "Chianti."

' "Whit's that?" said one of them. "We'll take a pint."

' And they took a pint each and they got very drunk and as they were staggering along one of them said to the other,

' "No wonder they carry the Pope about in a chair." '

They had all laughed, Miss Casey in short concentrated bursts like machine-gun fire, Daphne more decorously. Then she felt constrained to tell some of her own stories, for she felt that the Wilsons weren't sure of her, thought of her as a Southern English type.

She felt awkward beginning her story. 'It was one day,' she said, and then casually, 'My husband Geoff is an officer. And this general's wife came to visit us. This was in Australia. I had tried to talk to her, usual stuff I thought you should talk about to generals' wives, and she sat there, a big woman, and then after a while she got up and said,

' "See you later."

' And I thought,' she began to laugh, 'and I thought she was going to come back that same day. And when Geoff came home I was in a panic. I told him that I had gone out to buy a new dress because I didn't want the general's wife to see me in the same dress twice in the one day. And Geoff said,

' "Don't you know that saying, 'See you later' is like saying 'Cheerio'."

'But I had actually gone out to buy a new dress. Actually.'

And Miss Casey laughed and said, 'Of course you were not expected to know that.' She herself went on to cap the story with another one.

'There was this friend of mine who was staying in London. And she caught a cold and stayed in bed. A friend of hers, English, phoned her up and asked her to come and visit her. "No," she said, "I can't, I'm in bed with a wog." You see "wog" in Australia means a "germ".'

They had all dissolved in hysterical laughter though it

seemed to Daphne that some of the others had heard the story before. Miss Cowan making odd guttural noises, her moustache trembling at her lip.

'What she must have thought,' said Daphne, 'what she must have thought.' And she saw this proper woman in bed in a London hotel with a wog stretched at her side. 'Wog' was the very word that Geoffrey might have used about the Australians.

The bus crossed the border into Victoria which was much greener than the area from which they had come. It looked exactly like England, with its green fertile land; she could imagine a private school set here among the fruit trees.

And then there was the day they stopped at the Chinese cemetery. There was Chinese writing on the tombstones, indecipherable among the wild grass.

Miss Casey gazed at the cemetery in amazement. 'It's like seeing restaurants,' she said. 'Restaurants of dead people.' And Tom Wilson shouted, 'Made in Hong Kong,' while his wife looked on disapprovingly. Daphne thought Mrs Wilson didn't like her, fearing that Tom might get off with her, for she was young and girlish and upper class. Daphne didn't think that the Wilsons were well off though Tom was incredibly generous, insisting on paying for the drinks whenever they stopped at a hotel.

They wandered through the graveyard, Daphne saying to Miss Cowan, 'They don't look after their graveyards very well here, do they?' (thinking of the ranked stone doors of English graveyards), and Miss Cowan made her usual strangulated noises, like a radio not quite tuned to a station, and Daphne thought she heard her say that Australians moved on a great deal, wouldn't stay long in one place.

'I will tell you what happened here,' said Miss Casey, as if she were teaching the class from the centre of the overgrown graveyard. 'There was a lot of Chinese labour here at one time, and it was treated abominably. That is why this graveyard is so large. Look,' she said, 'this is where they made their offerings to the dead.' Miss Cowan in her dumb way bent down to interrogate the indecipherable language on the stones. Daphne briefly remembered her walk through the Chinese quarter of Vancouver and the Chinese signs on the telephone kiosks.

They stood silently in the graveyard among the wild overgrown grass, the sun hot on their heads like a burning helmet in the sky. We are all gathered here, thought Daphne, me from my leafy school, the Wilsons from Glasgow, Miss Casey the schoolmistress from Sydney, and Miss Cowan from I don't know where. All I know about her is that she has an invalid sister and that she goes on a bus trip once a year, with her harelip and her moustache.

And the sky was blue above them, and there were some brightly coloured birds flying from branch to branch, and the signs on the stones were inscrutably Chinese. The poor labouring foreigners came to this land, toiled and died, and were buried in a country which did not know enough to interpret their epitaphs. The Chinese had died indecipherably among the stones.

It was in silence that they went back to the bus but the silence didn't last long for Tom Wilson began to imitate their driver who also acted as their guide.

'And there straight ahead of us is Bare Hill,' he said. 'It is called Bare Hill because there is nothing on top of it. Once there was a winery but it fell into disuse over the years. On your left you can see Goat Hill because it was once inhabited by goats. You will notice that it has the shape of a big cheese.' And they all thought the commentary hysterically funny, Tom imitated the driver so well, he was so jolly, he drew new ideas and sights out of the air around him, out of this Australia which she was beginning to love so much. And already she had forgotten about the Chinese labourers and the cemetery. O how young she felt, how happy, how glad she had come: she felt so diaphanous and clean and leafy. And she could have waved a hand to make Miss Cowan speak. But Miss Cowan couldn't speak properly, you had to listen very patiently to her to understand her, it was as if she was trying continually to move a step up the evolutionary scale, like those animals and birds halted in their upward drive, these freaks, these speechless beings.

And on a night with a hard metallic moon in the sky like a yellow medal they played one-up with coins in a Club after the Anzac Day military parade. And Miss Casey played the gambling machines and won. So that back in the hotel that night, after they had seen the aged veterans marching, they had not wanted to go to bed. And miracle of miracles they had found a piano in the big hotel dining-room and Tom had bought them schooners of beer, and Miss Cowan had played for them. Such talent too! Who could have foreseen that Miss Cowan would be such a pianist. But she had been, and she had known all the songs, and Tom had sung 'Loch Lomond', while pretending he was wearing a kilt and in that Australian world with its images of Gallipoli they had listened to him singing of his country with sweetness and power. Then Daphne had been asked to sing and she couldn't bring herself to do so, with all her English reticence, that final barrier which she hadn't broken. Even Mrs Wilson, though reluctantly, had sung, though she herself hadn't dared to. Once she thought of singing 'Greensleeves' but considered it somehow unsuitable. She regretted that very much. But Miss Casey had flung her skirt about and had sung 'Waltzing Matilda' and finally they had a huge concert going in that big bare dining-room whose seats had been cleared to the sides, with Anzac veterans there, and Miss Cowan had tirelessly played the piano, and had been kissed by a large Australian with a fat belly and a lot of medals on his chest. Miss Cowan was really glowing, not having to speak at all, the centre of attention, a queen whose harelip had been forgotten. It was like a fairy story.

And so they had gone to bed very late and she had been restless and had stood at the window and seen through it a moon like a shrunken aboriginal bone, shining in the sky. And she had undressed and stood there white and pearly, thinking of green England, with Geoffrey standing at attention on a green field and herself about to play hockey, watched by a schoolmistress with short grey hair who was blowing a whistle for the game to begin. O Lord how beautiful this is, she thought, these lovely Scottish songs, these high roads and low roads, these ghostly soldiers, as Tom had explained them. And she was angry with herself because she hadn't sung

'Greensleeves' as she had intended to, for after all it was a beautiful song too. Her not singing it had been a betrayal!

And the moon hung there like a curved bone, ancient, aboriginal, the bone from which the world had been made, as if it were a continual interrogation, but really speechless and blank, the shape of Miss Cowan's mouth, but with no harelip on it. Miss Cowan who had played the piano so well; Daphne could play the piano too, and had been taught to do so, though she had left Miss Cowan to her triumph that night in her speechless glow. And somewhere not far away the Wilsons were sleeping and Geoffrey too was sleeping in his cold military bed and Miss Casey was dreaming of her pupils.

In the morning she was up bright and early and waiting for the bus. She felt a constraint in the atmosphere as if the Wilsons had been quarrelling during the night, as if Mrs Wilson had been saying to Tom, 'I don't like the way you talk so much to the snooty Daphne. Don't you realise that you are making a fool of yourself? She doesn't belong to our class. She is only amusing herself. And she wouldn't even sing, pretending that she didn't know the words.'

And in this atmosphere of constraint the bus made its way towards Beechworth, Ned Kelly country. From the bag in which she kept the koala bear she had bought for Shirley, her little daughter, she took the reproductions by Nolan and studied them while Mrs Wilson stared out of the window and Tom was unusually silent, a bearlike hulk which had been stood in a corner. How funny these paintings were, Ned Kelly with his box-like mask peering from between slim green tree trunks. And the funniest of all was the policeman, head down in a hole, only his legs, straight and blue, to be seen, while a quizzical bird perched on a precarious branch looking at him. The box-like mask was like a television-set. The butt of a rifle stuck in the ground had fingers at the end of it. Funny old surrealistic paintings. And Ned Kelly, the bandit, the anarchic chaotic Irishman, the one whom Geoffrey would have hunted down remorselessly, if he had been living at the time, Geoffrey like that policeman upside down in the hole, still so correct in his blue uniform. And perhaps Miss Casey herself had Irish ancestry with her love of gambling, her uncaring innocence, Miss Casey who had loved her pupils all her childlike life.

And Beechworth when they arrived at it was like an Old Wild West frontier town. And they saw the Rock Cavern with its glittering gems and minerals, a fairyland of colour. And the gold vault where the dummy with white shirt and black waist-coat weighed gold on a scales while behind him there was a green safe. Oh, it was really like another world, a world now of order which had once been anarchic. Why had it all disap-peared? Why had the men in tight blue cloth destroyed the green anarchic Irishry?

And they had wandered through the museum looking at the Ned Kelly stuff, the frail looking armour and guns. Why had she thought the armour would be more solid than it was? But imagine a man thinking of that, wearing armour. It took Irish imagination to think of that. It was so medieval and romantic among these spiky flowers so far from Westminster Abbey, and for that matter from Buckingham Palace in which bright aluminium-coloured armour still concealed Her Majesty's soldiers. But the frail armour of Ned Kelly was like a holed leaf with the rot of autumn in it. That frail armour, those horses, in the middle of Australia so long ago. So that she had stood beside Miss Cowan who was looking at the armour, the mask, with a strange longing, and suddenly quite out of the blue she had been startled by the thought,

That is what she wants, that armour. She has taught no pupils as Miss Casey has done, she has never married like Mrs Wilson and me, she doesn't have the armour to protect and conceal herself from the world. She wants to be secretive and hidden like myself long ago in those leafy woods round my private school, in my green leafy uniform and speaking my Latin; like Tom Wilson behind the sweetness of 'Loch Lomond'. Perhaps Tom doesn't like being in Australia, she thought, perhaps he really wants to go home, perhaps he will have to stay here forever, perhaps too his wife hates being here, for she often talks about her mother on some council estate in Glasgow, dying there, not to be seen again, among these stones with the indecipherable writing on them; perhaps she wants to be home with her, before she is laid to rest in that stony windy jungle. We are all exiles, frightened of the world. But she wasn't frightened of the world, she loved Australia, she loved its wildness, its strangeness, its unranked foliage. And she loved Geoffrey too though sometimes she couldn't stand his correctness and stiffness, she thought him comic in his uprightness, in his meticulousness, she saw him upside down in the hole, in his tight uniform while the mocking TV box stared at him from behind a tall green tree trunk, and the military abrasive kookaburra glared at him like the general's wife. And she thought of the emu she had seen in the zoo to which the driver had taken them and which was an albino and had to be kept apart from the other emus for they would have killed it because of its strangeness, like Miss Cowan, the separate one, the one who did not belong. And at that moment she touched Miss Cowan lightly as the latter stared at the mask and it was as if something in her own breast, her womb, overflowed, as if it were water, tears.

And they walked back in silence to the bus through the calm serene air of Beechworth, the Wilsons still not speaking to each other, Miss Casey lost in a dream of her own.

Oh, except that she did buy a towel for Miss Cowan on which were written the words of 'Amazing Grace' and Miss Cowan's gratitude was so excessive that she felt ashamed. To be going on bus trips year after year in order to rest for a while from the demands made on her by her invalid sister, but at least taking back with her this time memories of her hours at the piano, of Tom Wilson's horseplay, of the funny commentary, of the wineries, of the sail on Murray River, of the towel with its religious words, a gift freely given. The possible grace of speech that Miss Cowan took away from her enchanted stare at the mask set in the middle of the tamed town!

And that was the high part of the tour, that visit to the once wild land where Ned Kelly and his Irishry had taken on the establishment. The road unspooled through the evening: it was as if they all really wanted to go home now, exchanging addresses at the back of the bus. 'You must visit us,' said Daphne to her four friends, though she wasn't sure whether they would or not, whether they thought she really meant the invitation seriously. Rank was closing in on them like the evening. Imagine if Miss Cowan visited them and Geoffrey said,

'Why did you bring that woman here? Where on earth did you find her?'

And she would try to explain to him how longingly Miss Cowan had gazed at the armour. But of course he wouldn't be able to understand, ever. How could he be what he was, and also understand?

And Miss Casey who was now exhausted slept and the Wilsons were not speaking to each other and she expected that Geoffrey would say,

'Well, where did you go? Where did you sleep? Whom did you meet? Don't tell me that you didn't meet anyone. It was a stupid idea to go on that bus tour anyway. No one else but you would have done it. Could you not have waited till I got some leave?' No, the thought of the generals and the generals' wives stifled her, with their military kookaburra faces. She wanted to be a kangaroo, to take huge unexpected leaps into the blue. And Miss Casey slept and looked quite old in the dim light of the bus. And Mrs Wilson, she knew, was hostile to her, her secret though smiling enemy. She was keeping Tom from the real joy of his nature. The bars and gratings were everywhere.

The bus travelled on through the evening. The milestones were like little tombstones. Oh how she loved Australia with its mysterious femininity, not at all masculine as she had feared, as she had been led to expect. No, not at all, rather yearning to be itself, as Miss Cowan yearned for articulate speech, as Tom Wilson, large and bearish and funny, yearned to be the person that he really was.

She felt cool and fulfilled as if now she could sing 'Greensleeves': but the moment had passed. She should have sung it when she had the chance. And that young unmarried spectacled girl who worked in the Civil Service was sleeping in the seat directly in front of her. Oh the aboriginal brilliance of this land, its shining bone-like moon, the bone of our common existence, the boomerang moon curved like a horn.

And they all dozed and the bus was silent. Soon they would

be back in Canberra and Geoffrey would be waiting for her with the car, and the others would take buses or taxis. And Geoffrey would say

'Everything all right?' And she would be able to say to him that everything was all right except that . . .

Suddenly she said out of the silence to the four, 'You must really come and visit. I mean it. We must make a date.' But they didn't believe her. So she must make them believe her, she must set a specific date. And into the world of the generals' wives she must bring the harelipped Miss Cowan, the Wilsons from Glasgow, Miss Casey who had once taught pupils in Sydney, and also played the gambling machines. She must bring the wildness into the tame, the lame towards the healthy. She must not let Geoffrey overwhelm her. Nor the generals' wives. She must not be stifled.

'Let's make it June the 5th,' she said consulting her diary, in the dimness, by the light of that unutterably strange moon. 'You must come then.'

And they didn't believe her. And they didn't answer.

'June the 5th then,' she said as she took her case from the rack. And the others were still in the bus gathering their possessions together as she ran out to meet Geoffrey who was waiting for her, stiff and military and young, holding Shirley by the hand.

'How are you, old girl?' he said. But she watched for a while till the other four got out and joined the queue for the taxis, and she waved to them and they waved back. And then she was in the car and still waving.

'Your friends?' said Geoffrey sarcastically as he steered the car away from the bus station. And she said in a very distinct voice,

'Yes. They're coming to see me on June the 5th. I hope you have nothing fixed that evening.' Clutching her koala bear Shirley looked from her mother to her father.

'I must be military too,' thought Daphne. 'I must fight with stiffness in order to allow the flowing to enter.'

And later that night as she lay gazing up into the imperialistic face of her husband she thought, 'June the 5th it must be, will be.' And it seemed to her that she must be like a Ned Kelly and fight it out and this time win, peering out from behind the green slim tree trunks. And on that day perhaps Miss Cowan would learn to speak.

The Travelling Poet

One autumn day he stopped at my door. He said he was on a sponsored walk to raise money for a boy who needed medical treatment in America. He was also a poet and as he travelled, he read his poems in pubs, halls. He sold copies of them to pay for his lodgings.

He sat in the living-room and took out a bag with some of the booklets that he had published at his own expense. There were also letters from prominent people: 'Lord X thanks you for letting him see the enclosed but is sorry that he is not able to contribute to your appeal.' 'As you will understand Lady X has many demands on her resources and is sorry that she can only send two pounds at this time.'

His poems were bad. There was also a children's story about a fox which was not much better. He found out that I was a poet and asked for my opinion. I was hypocritical as usual.

It turned out that he had been in prison and that was where he had begun to write. His father had been a crane driver; his mother had been an alcoholic. He himself had been a heavy drinker but had according to himself stopped.

'When I was young,' he said, 'we were very poor. We used to beg for clothes. I have seen myself wearing girls' clothes.'

Imagine that, I thought, girls' clothes.

His wife had left him and gone to America.

'I used to be quite violent when I was young but not any more. I was in prison a few times.' This long journey to raise funds for the boy was in a way a rehabilitation for him.

He had cuttings and photographs from various local papers, with headlines such as the following: 'Ex-Convict Raises Money for Charity Mission'. And so on. He was very proud of these cuttings, and of his letters on headed notepaper, from the aristocracy, from Members of Parliament. He had even sent a copy of his booklet to Ronald Reagan, to Mrs Thatcher. I thought he had an adamant vanity.

He left me a story about the fox to read at my leisure so that I could give him an opinion on it when he returned.

As he travelled northwards he phoned me every night.

'I feel,' he said, 'as if you are interested, as if I'm in touch with home.' He discovered the luminousness of landscapes (he himself had been brought up in the city). One night he slept in a barn and when he had asked for a clock to get him up in the morning the farmer had told him, 'You have a clock. You wait.' The clock turned out to be a cockerel. 'Imagine that,' he said. He was happy as a sandboy. Another time he saw a fawn crossing the road.

'Tonight,' he phoned, 'I'm booked into the Caledonian Hotel. I shall pay for my room with some booklets of my poems.' He had already raised the almost unbelievable sum of £2,000. 'I ask for cheques so that I won't be tempted to drink the money.'

He also said to me, 'I mentioned your name to the landlady but she had never heard of you.'

Actually it bothered me a little that she had never heard of me. It also seemed to me that my visitor had become more dismissive of me, more sure of himself. After all he was not a very good poet, indeed not a poet at all.

Let me also say that I wished he had not come to the door. I had my own routine. I started writing at nine in the morning and finished at four. He had interrupted my routine and also put me in the position of being hypocritical about his poems. I had met people like him before. For instance, here is a story.

Another poet of approximately the same calibre as my visitor had accosted me once in Glasgow. He was unemployed, his wife had left him, he had smashed his car, his father was dying of a stroke, and his mother of cancer; he had been cut by a razor when he was a bouncer in a night club; he had been charged with sexual assault; he had fallen out of the window of a second storey flat after taking drugs. Now it might be considered that such a person might turn out to be a good poet but in fact his poems were very sentimental and didn't reflect his life at all. Such is the unfairness of literature. What can you do for such people who have experienced the intransigence and randomness of the world and cannot make use of it?

My visitor disturbed me. I imagined him as I have said learning the luminousness of the world, coming across pheasants, foxes, deer; rising on frosty mornings among farm steadings; setting out in the dews of autumn; writing his poems ('I have no difficulty at all: I can write four poems a day easy'); meeting people.

One night he phoned me and said that he was going to have an interview with the Duke of – . The local paper had asked to take a photograph of the two of them together.

Alcoholism is a terrible thing. I know a talented man who is in the entertainment world and who often does not turn up at concerts etc. because he has been inveigled into taking a drink. It was really quite noble that this 'poet' was taking his money in cheques so that he would not be tempted into using it to buy drink. Drily he toiled on, changing his poems and booklets into cheques, having as far as I could see nothing much of his own at all.

I can't write. Isn't that odd? Most days when I sit down at my desk I have no difficulty at all in writing something. But from the time that this poet called on me, I have written nothing, I have dried up. I think of him plodding along a dusty road, stopping at a hotel or a boarding house, negotiating with the sharp-eyed owner, paying for his keep with pamphlets, poems. What a quite extraordinary thing. Nevertheless I should have had nothing to do with him. And I am paying for it now. This is the first time I've ever had writer's block. What does it mean?

Maybe he won't come back. He hasn't phoned so often recently and when he does he sounds more independent, as if the two of us were equals.

Last night he phoned. He had run into another writer in a pub. This writer decorated the wall of his room with rejection slips. He didn't think he was getting fair treatment because he was a Socialist. He dressed in a Wild West outfit. He was 'quite a character'. 'Listen,' I nearly said to my visitor, 'don't be deceived by him. He is a bad writer. I can smell his amateurism a mile away. People like that always dress in an outré manner, they always say that they are not understood. Avoid him. Listen to me instead.'

I started writing when I was about eleven. I believe that routine, hard work is the most important thing in any art. I sit down at my desk every morning at nine. Without a routine all writers and artists are doomed. I have never been an alcoholic. Writing is my life: that must be the case with all artists.

I should have asked him how he had got involved in his walk to raise money for a boy who is dying and is to be sent to America where the 'poet's' wife is. Maybe she left him because he didn't make any money, because he insisted on taking part in such outlandish projects. On the other hand she might have left him when he was in prison. 'They were very good to me in prison. It was there I met the man who illustrated my booklet. I had five hundred printed. Who is your publisher? Do you think you could interest him in my poems, my story about the fox?'

A startling statement he had made was, 'This is all that I have left, my writing.'

When I was younger I actually used to taste the excitement of art. I remember days when myself and my current girlfriend would travel on a green tram in Aberdeen. Mornings were glorious. I used to shout out lines from Shakespearean plays in cemeteries, among the granite. 'The great poet,' I used to say, 'is always on the frontier.'

Later I went back to Aberdeen and had the following fantasy. My earlier self met me on the street wearing a student's cloak. He was with a group of his friends. They passed me in the hard yellow light laughing, and probably never even noticed me. Perhaps they thought of me as a prosperous fat bourgeois. My earlier self didn't recognise me but I knew him. He was as cutting and supercilious as ever.

I don't think my visitor will visit me on his way south. He hasn't phoned for a week now. He is probably lost in admiration for his genuine artistic friend who is so daring. I feel sorry for him. Really he's so innocent with all his talk of cockerels, barns, deer. I am sure he will have another copy of the story of the fox and not ask me for my opinion. Perhaps his companion has heard of me, dismisses me.

Once before my wife left me I saw a small knot of weasels, a mother weasel with her tiny family, crossing the road. They looked like notes in music.

Another thing I have discovered about myself, I hate the cold. And the rain.

Autumn is passing and he hasn't come. I have heard nothing more of him. Perhaps he did after all use some of his money for drinking. Perhaps he has returned to prison. Perhaps he went berserk one night, was arrested. It is not easy to travel alone, and one's wife to be in America. There is no such thing as goodness: aggression must out. The greater the creativity the greater the aggression if thwarted.

It is winter. There is snow on the ground, he certainly won't come now. And I have not written anything for two months. I begin to write and I fail to continue. The reason my wife left me was that she said I didn't speak enough to her, about ordinary things. As a matter of fact I found that I couldn't speak about ordinary things: I would try to think of something to say but couldn't.

Listen, let me tell you a story which I read in some book or other. There was a mathematician in Cambridge who knew that being over forty he could no longer do original work in his field. So he spent his time making up cricket teams to play against each other. One cricket team would have names beginning with B such as Beethoven, Brahms, Balzac. Another one would have names beginning with A such as Joan of Arc, Aristotle, Archimedes. One day he received a letter from India which contained a number of incomprehensible equations, and he threw the letter into the wastepaper basket. However in the afternoon he usually went for a walk with a friend of his (also a mathematician) and he told him about the letter and the equations. The result was that they retrieved them from the wastepaper basket. It turned out that they had been created by a young Indian genius who had never been taught orthodox mathematics. He was taken over to Cambridge and died young. It is said that his last words were, Did you notice that the number plate on the ambulance was a perfect cube?

Now I'm sure that man had no small talk.

Who in fact is the boy and what disease is he dying of? Maybe my visitor faked the whole business in order to make money. But no, I don't think so: the story is true. He showed me a newspaper cutting which described the boy but I didn't read it very carefully. I have difficulty with detail and especially with people's names.

He must by now have collected £3,000 with his bad poetry. What an extraordinary thing.

Actually up until the very last moment I didn't believe that my wife would leave me. I used to say to her, 'You won't find anyone else as interesting as me.' She picked up her case and took a bus. And never said another word to me. I waited and waited but she never phoned. I tried to trace her but was unsuccessful. She was quite beautiful: she will find someone.

Actually she used to weep over stories on the TV. She would dab at her eyes or run to the bathroom. At first I didn't realise what was happening.

Every night I gaze up the road before I lock the door. I am waiting for my poet but he never comes. He has become a mythological figure in my mind like the Wandering Jew. His bag is full of undrinkable cheques. His mouth is dry. He cannot afford the money for the phone. All the money that he collects he puts in his bag which swells out like a balloon. Maybe that's it, he can't afford to phone.

> Or he has gone home.
>> Or his wife has come back to him.
>>> Or he has shacked up with his Wild West friend.
>>> Or he has become so stunned by the beauty of
>>> the Highlands that he will never leave them
>>> again.

And here I am making money out of his wanderings. By means of this story. Whereas he . . .

I imagine the boy in a hospital in America. He is being

watched over by doctors, surgeons. They are all looking at a clock. 'Soon he will come with the money,' they are saying to the boy. 'You must trust him. Till then we can't treat you.' And he swims across the Atlantic with his bag of cheques. He fights waves, he pacifies the ocean with his bad poems. Out of the green water he coins green dollars. And the boy's breathing becomes worse and worse and the doctor says, 'He won't be long now.'

It has begun to snow. He is perhaps out in the snow in the Highlands, perhaps at John O'Groats with his bag. The snow is a white prison round him: he can't even take a nip of whisky. I feel sorry for him. He should come in out of the cold, he has done enough. He has had more courage than me. With his bad poems he has done more than I have with my good ones. I can see that. And he was just as poor as me.

My writer's block has persisted. I think I am finished as a writer.

The snow is falling very gently. A ghost tree clasps the real tree like a bridegroom with a bride. They have had the worst winter in Florida in living memory.

What a sky of stars. And yet I see them as if I was a spectator. I'd better shut the door, he'll never come, my muse in her girl's dress will never come again. I shall have to take account of that.

I heard a story today about a villager. He has run away with a woman much younger than himself and left his wife. It is said that he was the last person anyone would have expected to have done anything like that. What does he hope to gain?

What energy, what a strange leap. Will there not come a time when he will make a third spring and then a fourth one? As if Romeo and Juliet were still alive . . .

Last night I thought I saw him emerging out of the snow with his bag. When I went to the cat's dish there was a snail eating the food. Unless I take my bag on my shoulders I shall never write again. Unless I am willing to accept the risk of bad poems.

The phone rang but it was a wrong number.

Imagine first of all surviving in girl's clothes and then in bad poems.

I am sure that when the spring comes he will be happier. I can almost hear the ice breaking, the sound of running waters, the cry of the cockerel. The fox shakes itself out of its prison of snow. Meagre and thin. It laps at the fresh water. All around it is the snow with its white undamaged pages.

The Scream

The play lasted about an hour and took place in a small theatre off the High St in Edinburgh. The story of the play was not complicated. A prison had been burnt down in the night and there was an enquiry as to who had done it. The cast was as follows:

> The Governor – an idealist who hated brutality.
> The Governor's wife – who supported her husband as an honourable man but was also sex-starved.
> Two brutal guards – one tall and one small. They had ill-treated the prisoners, made them bend down and eat their own excrement. In the presence of the Governor, however, they always appeared reasonable and respectful, having only the welfare of the prisoners at heart!
> There was a cleaner who appeared at times dim-witted but at other times could discuss Marx: a homosexual prisoner who was beaten up by the guards in a scene of great cruelty: the man who headed the enquiry who was an ex-communist, drank a great deal and was in love with his secretary, a not particularly good-looking girl of great idealism: and finally a boy who had left Cambridge and who found himself plunged into 'real life'.

The audience liked the play. It started slowly and then built up to a claustrophobic denouement. But the enquiry didn't discover who had burnt the prison down. The part of the homosexual was acted by Jeff Coates, a young actor from Cambridge. In the pivotal scene he was fitted up with electrodes while the two guards tortured him.

One of their lines was 'the poof of the pudding is in the eating'. For the two guards were intellectuals too, clever, cunning, able to switch from viciousness to calm collected discussion especially when the Governor appeared, the Governor, tortured by moral doubts, whom they despised. After all what was a prison for but to convert criminals to goodness by torture?

Jeff Coates was changed by the play. At first he had not liked it very much. He thought the dialogue at times brittle, its poeticisms brilliant but perhaps esoteric. But gradually it took a grip of him, he felt himself inside a world of almost total evil. At coffee breaks he would speak only to the Governor and never to the guards. In the crucial scene he screamed a high piercing scream though of course it was only a pretence of torture he was suffering. At times however he felt he was being really tortured.

The trouble was that he was really a homosexual and that made it worse – or did it? He couldn't make up his mind. Was it indeed worse to be a real homosexual in that scene? (Also in the play he was attacked by prisoners.) He sometimes felt that the two guards really hated him, for neither was a homosexual. They made comments about his walk and these comments he accepted as belonging to the play. The women in the cast befriended him more than the men did, though of course he was not interested in them sexually. In the scene where he was being tortured he felt real hatred emanating from the two guards as if they were his most bitter enemies. Of course he had experience of being beaten up in real life, particularly in a public convenience in London, about two years before.

His scream was real, he thought, because it came from the centre of his being. And yet it was happening in a play. These men didn't really hate him, he told himself, they were merely acting, they obviously had to act as if they hated him. The Governor too in real life was stingy, sarcastic, embittered, not at all attractive. The two guards in real life were not at all intellectual: in fact he despised them. For he himself had read Artaud on the Theatre of Cruelty. The stage became very small each night. It shrank. Every night he waited to be tortured. It was almost as if that was the reason for his existence.

As time passed he became more and more solitary, arriving late, leaving early. He didn't want to see these contemptuous eyes nor did he wish to listen to the banal conversation of the guards. The scream was taking a lot out of him, he had to prepare himself for it, it shattered his whole being so that if there had been glass near him it would have cracked. He didn't wish to discuss the play with the others since in his opinion they didn't really know what it was about, they did not know what suffering was. Of course none of them had ever suffered except in fantasy. That at any rate was what he thought. He himself had suffered, especially on the day that his mother had discovered him in bed with a male friend of his. That was the worst. Her whole face had disintegrated: he would always remember that moment.

O none of them had really suffered. He himself had suffered, however. He was the one who was in the prison. The suffering was disguised by talk about morality, about Marx, but nothing could disguise the torture. And his scream, was it real or not? For after all he wasn't really being tortured. In fact the two guards used to make a point of asking him over to take coffee with them He was probably making a mistake in thinking that they hated him.

And he loved acting. He had acted many other parts as well as the part he was acting in this play. That was the awful and marvellous thing about actors, that they took on themselves the pains and sufferings of others. They brought to audiences the calmness of art at the expense of their own tortured spirits. He had acted kings, drunks, and most especially the dark blind figure in *The Room*, by Pinter. And in all these instances he had sought determinedly for the meaning of the text. When he was acting the part of Creon, he had thought, This city of Edinburgh is Thebes, we shall show it its plague, though there was in fact no appearance of plague in Edinburgh's theatrical façade, with its green light shining about the castle at night

To be an actor was to be a healer, a doctor. And the scream waited for him every night. In fact he had become obsessed by it.

He stayed in lodgings on his own. Every night he left the theatre and walked to them through the throbbing festival city, through the slums of the High St. After the scream he strolled through the streets, emptied of emotion, solitary. And he thought, the guards are at least uncomplicated. They are brutal, they have assessed the world as it really is. They had no imagination, they could not put themselves in the position of the weak, nor did they want to. He found himself hating them in return. Why had they taken these parts unless they were in a deep way suited to them? And this in spite of the fact that such an idea was stupid.

And as for the Governor, he despised him. The Governor had never protected him. There he was tortured every day while the Governor stood around like a moral priggish Brutus and the guards like Mark Antonies ran rings round him. They would spring to attention while prisoners bled in the cells. O how they laughed at that poor tortured libertarian in the burnt prison under the open sky! Who had burnt the prison? Was it perhaps the Governor himself? Or his wife? Or the cleaner who could discuss Marx.

And every night his own high scream was the peak point of the play. It rose to a crescendo, then died away to a whisper, to exhaustion. And the audience winced (or perhaps they loved it. Who could tell?) But none of them was unaffected. He saw to that. And when the play was over and the audience had left, he and the other actors would have their coffee and discuss the effectiveness of the night's work. And it became more and more demanding to create the scream. It wasn't easy to scream like that every night.

One night he waited behind till the others had gone. Then he went out into the street. It was a Saturday night and the air was mild. All round him he sensed the delirium of the Festival. There were lovers strolling hand in hand, there were men in strange colourful costumes, the world itself was a theatre. It was Romeo and Juliet he saw sitting on a bench, it was the old woman from *Crime and Punishment* who staggered drunkenly down the street. The city was a theatre at which the plague had not struck.

He walked with his usual mincing walk. He had never been conscious of it himself but he had been told of it. Actually he was still wearing his prison clothes for he hadn't bothered changing. Well, why shouldn't he? One night he had seen a tall man in a black gown walking towards him on stilts, with a skull instead of a face.

He now entered a street which was quite dark. The council was dimming its lamps in certain areas even during the Festival.

And then they were there. There must have been about six of them. They were wearing green scarves and they were shouting. They owned the street. They were like members of a crowd in one of Shakespeare's plays, perhaps *Julius Caesar:* but they were really vicious. It might be that their team had lost. Who knew? He and they were in the dim street together and they were marching towards him. Perhaps he should run? He thought about it but he didn't run. They were chanting. Their heads were shaved.

Poof, they shouted, poof they shouted again. They danced around him. Poof in his theatrical clothes. And they with their shaved heads on which Union Jacks had been painted. (One light in the alley like a spot light showed this to him.)

It had happened before. It would happen again. Those without imagination were upon him. The animals with their teeth.

Poof, they shouted, bloody poof. And then they were on him and beat him to the ground and trampled on him. And his glasses fell off and cracked, he could feel that. He looked upwards but he could hardly see them. All he could see was a kaleidoscope of colour. And he could smell the smell of alcohol. And then he screamed. And as he screamed the high piercing scream they ran away and left him in a quick scurry.

And he lay there on the street alone, listening to the noise they made as they left, and he thought, That scream, was it different? Was it different from the one in the play? Which was the real scream and which was the unreal one? The prepared or the unprepared? The, as it were, artistic one or the real one? And he thought, the artistic one was the real one. This was only an accidental one. This was not the scream of art, this was the one he had attracted by walking like a poof and taking that lane which he should not have taken and continuing to walk towards them as perhaps he should not have done. Had he been trying to learn more about the artistic scream by this one? He felt naked in the dim street without his glasses.

He would have to make his way back to his real landlady. And with his real face. And put ointment on his real bruises.

He staggered a little as he stood up, coming out of the scream. Everything was silent around him. No one had heard him. There had been no audience. How therefore could his scream have been more real than the theatrical one?

How?

The Old Woman, the Baby and Terry

The fact was that the old woman wanted to live. All her faculties, her energies, were shrunken down to that desire. She drew everything into herself so that she could live, survive. It was obscene, it was a naked obscenity.

'Do you know what she's doing now?' said Harry to his wife Eileen. 'She keeps every cent. She hoards her pension, she's taken to hiding her money in the pillow slips, under blankets. She reminds me of someone, I can't think who.'

'But what can we do?' said Eileen, who was expecting a baby.

Harry worked with a Youth Organisation. He earned £7,000 a year. There was one member of the organisation called Terry MacCallum who, he thought, was insane. Terry had tried to rape one of the girls on the snooker table one night. He was a psychopath. Yet Harry wanted to save him. He hated it when he felt that a case was hopeless.

'She won't even pay for a newspaper,' said Harry.

'I know,' said Eileen. 'This morning I found her taking the cigarette stubs from the bucket.'

The child jumped in her womb. She loved Harry more than ever: he was patient and kind. But he grew paler every day: his work was so demanding and Terry MacCallum was so mad and selfish.

'I've never met anyone like him,' said Harry. 'His selfishness is a talent, a genius. It's diamond hard, it shines. I should get rid of him, I know that. Also he's drunk a lot of the time. He said to me yesterday, "I don't care for anyone. I'm a bastard you know that. I'm a scrounger, I hate everyone." '

Harry couldn't understand Terry. Everything that was done for him he accepted and then kicked you in the teeth. He was a monster. He haunted his dreams.

The child kicked in Eileen's womb. She wanted it badly. She had a hunger for it. She wanted it to suck her breasts, she wanted it to crawl about the room, she wanted it to make her alive again.

And all the time the old lady hoarded her banknotes. One day Eileen mentioned to her that they needed bread but she ignored hints of any kind. She even hoarded the bread down the sides of her chair. She tried to borrow money from Eileen. She sang to herself. She gathered her arms around herself, she was like a plant that wouldn't die. Eileen shuddered when she looked at her. She thought that she was sucking her life from her but not like the baby. The baby throve, it milked her, it grew and grew. She was like a balloon, she thrust herself forward like a ship. Her body was like a ship's prow.

'I tried talking to him,' said Harry. 'I can't talk to him at all. He doesn't understand. I can't communicate. He admits everything, he thinks that the world should look after him. He wants everything, he has never grown up. I have never in my life met such selfishness. If he feels sexy he thinks that a woman should put out for him immediately. If he feels hungry he thinks that other people should feed him. I am kind to him but he hates me. What can you do with those who don't see? Is there a penance for people like that? What do you do with those who can't understand?'

The baby moved blindly in her womb, instinctively, strategically. She said to Harry, 'I'm frightened. Today I thought that the ferns were gathering round the house, that they wanted to eat me. I think we should cut the ferns down.'

'Not in your condition,' said Harry. He looked thin, besieged.

The old lady said, 'I don't know why you married him. He doesn't make much money, does he? Why doesn't he move to the city? He could make more money there.' She hid a tea bag in her purse. And a biscuit.

The child moved in the womb. It was a single mouth that sucked. Blood, milk, it sucked. It grew to be like its mother. It sang a song of pure selfishness. It had stalks like fern. The stars at night sucked dew from the earth. The sun dried the soil. Harry had the beak of a seagull.

'Last night he wouldn't get off the snooker table,' said Harry. 'There are others who want to play, I said to him. This is my snooker table, he said. It isn't, I said. It is, he said. You try and take it off me. And then he said, Lend me five pounds. No, I said. Why, he said. Because you're selfish, I said. I'm not, he said. I'm a nice fellow, everyone says so. I've got a great sense of humour. What do you do with someone like that? I can't get through to him at all. And yet I must.'

'What for?' said Eileen.

'I just have to.'

'You never will,' said Eileen.

'Why not?'

'Just because. Nature is like that. I don't want the child.'

'What?'

'I know what I mean. Nature is like that. I don't want the child.'

Harry had nightmares. He was on an operating table. A doctor was introducing leeches into his veins. The operating table was actually for playing snooker on. It had a green velvet surface. He played with a baby's small head for a ball.

The ferns closed in. In the ferns she might find pound notes. She began to eat bits of coal, stones, crusts. She gnawed at them hungrily. The old lady wouldn't sleep at night. She took to locking her door. What if something happened? They would have to break the door down.

The baby sucked and sucked. Its strategies were imperative. It was like a bee sucking at a flower with frantic hairy legs, its head buried in the blossom, its legs working.

Terry stole some money after the disco. He insisted it was his.

'You lied to me,' said Harry.

'I didn't lie.'

'You said you were at home. I phoned your parents. They said you were out. You lied to me.'

'I didn't lie.'

'But can't you see you said one thing and it wasn't the truth. Can you not see that you lied?'

'I didn't lie.'

'For Christ's sake are you mad. You did lie. What do you think a lie is? Can't you see it?'

'I didn't lie.'

'You'll have to go.'

The old lady had a pile of teabags, quarter pounds of butter, cheese, in a bag under the bed.

'You owe me,' she said to Eileen. 'For all those years you owe me. I saw in the paper today that it takes ten thousand pounds to rear a child. You owe me ten thousand pounds. It said that in the paper.'

'You haven't paid for that paper,' said Eileen. 'I've tried my best, don't you understand? How can you be so thick?'

'You owe me ten thousand pounds,' said the old lady in the same monotonous grudging voice. 'It said in the paper. I read it.'

'You are taking my beauty away from me,' said Eileen to the baby. 'You are sucking me dry. You are a leech. You are Dracula. You have blood on your lips. And you don't care.'

She carried the globe in front of her. It had teeth painted all over it.

Harry became thinner and thinner. I must make Terry understand, he kept saying. He must be made to understand, he has never in his whole life given anything to anyone. I won't let him go till I have made him understand. It would be too easy to get rid of him.

'Put him out,' said Eileen, 'abort him.'

'What did you say?'

'Abort him.'

'You said abort. I'm frightened.'

'Can't you see,' said Eileen. 'That's what it is. People feed and feed. Cows feed on grass, grass feeds on bones, bones feed on other bones. It's a system. The whole world is like a mouth.

Blake was wrong. It's not a green and pleasant land at all. The rivers are mouths. The sun is the biggest mouth of all.'

'Are you all right, Eileen? Oh hold me,' said Harry.

And they clung together in the night. But Eileen said, 'Look at the ceiling. Do you see it? It's a spider.' It hung like a black pendant. A moth swam towards the light from the darkness outside. The spider was a patient engineer. Suddenly Eileen stood on top of the bed and ripped the web apart. 'Bastard,' she said. 'Go and find something else to do.' The spider had chubby fists. It was a motheaten pendant.

Terry the psychopath smiled and smiled. He bubbled with laughter .

'Give me,' he said to his mother, 'ten pounds of my birthday money in advance.'

'No.'

'Why not? You were going to give it to me anyway.'

'And what are you going to give me for my birthday?'

'I'll think of something.'

'You won't give me anything, will you? Not a thing will you give me!'

The old woman stole sausages from the fridge, matches from the cupboard. She borrowed cigarettes from Eileen. The latter gazed at her in wonderment, testing how far she would go. The old woman began to wear three coats all at the one time. She tried to go to the bathroom as little as possible: she was hoarding her pee.

'The old woman will live forever,' Eileen screamed. 'She will never die. She will take me with her to the grave. She will hoard me. She will tie string round me, and take me with her to the grave. And the innocent selfish ferns will spring from me. And the baby will feed head down in it, its legs working.'

'No,' she said to Harry, 'I don't want to.'

'Why not? What's wrong with you?'

'I don't want to. It's like the bee.'

'What bee?'

'The bee, I tell you.'

'For Christ's sake,' he said. The bee sucked at her body. It sucked her breasts in a huge wandering fragrance.

'I don't know you,' said her mother. 'Who are you? Are you the insurance lady? I'm not giving you any more money. You're after all my money. Are you the coalman? Eileen should pay for that. She owes me ten thousand pounds. I saw that in the paper.'

'It will cost ten thousand pounds,' Eileen said to Harry.

'What will?'

'The baby. To bring it up. It was in the paper. I don't want to have it. It will want its own snooker table. It will smile and smile and be a villain.'

'You will have to go,' Harry told Terry.

'What for?'

'Because I can't do anything with you.'

'What do you mean? You'll be sorry.'

'Are you threatening me?'

'No, I'm not threatening you. But you'll be sorry. You'll wake up one day and say to yourself: Did I destroy that boy?' And Terry began to cry.

'You won't get anything out of me that way,' said Harry. 'I can see through your tricks. You will have to go.'

'All right. But you'll be sorry. You'll hate yourself.'

'I failed but he went,' said Harry to Eileen. 'And he started to cry before he went. Oh he's so cunning. But there comes a time.'

'A time?'

'Yes, a time to save oneself. It's a duty. I see that now. She will have to go.'

'She?'

'Yes. She'll have to go. There comes a time. I made a mistake. I shall have to act.'

'Act?'

'That's it. Act. She will simply have to go. We can't afford her.'

'What do you mean?'

'What I say. You've done enough. This is not asked of us. I can see that now. Tell her she will have to go.'

'You tell her.'

'Right. I'll tell her.'

The two of them were alone. The house seemed to close in on them.

'What's that?' she said.

'What?'

'The phone,' she said.

'It isn't the phone. You're imagining things. The phone isn't ringing.'

'Yes it is.'

'No, it isn't.'

The ferns shut off the light. The floor was a huge beach of sand. She saw the child crossing it towards her. It smiled.

'I love you,' she said.

'I love you,' she repeated.

'The Club is quieter now,' he said. 'Ever since he left. We know where we are. I'm putting on weight.'

'Yes, I see that.'

'It's much quieter. He kept us on our toes. Everyone is obedient.'

'Yes.'

The child cried.

'I love you,' she said. The circle closed again. The baby smiled and smiled and laughed and laughed. It wobbled on unsteady legs among the ferns.

'I'm wounded,' she said, 'between the legs. Between the legs.' And its hairy head blossomed there. 'Between the legs. I'm wounded,' she said.

In the operating theatre on the snooker table its wild cry came towards her. She cradled the globe of its wet head, which had streamed out of the earth. Her hands closed, opened.

'I love you,' she said. 'There's nothing else for it.'

The phone rang. There was heavy breathing. 'You'll be sorry,' said a voice.

'He never gives up,' said Harry. 'But I don't care.'

He has become remorseless, she thought. We have been infected. And she clutched the baby's head to her breast. We inherit the disease, she thought. The baby warbled in its own kingdom. 'Isn't he beautiful?' she said.

'Yes.'

And the baby burbled like an unintelligible phone.

On the Train

It was late at night when the train stopped at the platform and he boarded it. It seemed to be crowded with people of different races and colours, but there wasn't much noise or din. On the wall of his carriage was a painting by Constable, and on the other was a flyblown mirror. It was as if he had been waiting for this train for most of his life, though its destination was unknown.

As time passed, the light brightened the countryside through which the train was passing. Cows could be seen chewing grass in the fields, smoke rose from the houses straight into the sky. The train stopped at a station called Descartes, at one called Hume, and at another called Locke. Sometimes the stations appeared bright and colourful with little gardens, and on the platforms stood small pompous stationmasters with brightly polished buttons, and large watches in the fobs of their jackets. At other times the stations were striped with shade and light.

Now and again he would stroll down the corridor and look in through the doors of carriages. He would see men and women locked in each other's arms, or a man seated silently by his wife, staring ahead of him, or another reading a book quietly as if there were no one in the whole world but himself. Sometimes there was music on the train, sometimes not. Rabbis, ministers, gurus, many of them with beards, inhabited some of the carriages. He clutched his ticket as the train raced on through the bright sunlight.

For most of the journey the land looked clean and tidy, divided up into small farms and crofts. A reasonable sun shone on it. People sometimes waved at them from the fields, women with kerchiefs, many of them red or green, the men wearing caps. Once he thought he saw a man and woman in a glade and he could have sworn they were naked. At another time he saw a man wearing only a pair of bright yellow wellingtons fishing in a stream.

He thought of Death as a man with a scythe strolling among the land, perfectly natural, perfectly happy and contented. He would knock on a door and be welcomed like a long-lost exile. He would sit down at a table and be offered food. But later he became dim and smoky and his face could not be distinguished. And people would not let him into the house at all, as if he were a being from another planet, a hated stranger.

More stations passed, one called Leibnitz, then two called Kafka and Kierkegaard respectively. On the tops of hills he could see castles with parks winding around them; mornings sang and sparkled and so did afternoons. Children played and at other times carried huge books about with them like gravestones. They gazed at the smoke which was like transient breath.

He was aware of a man who was joking in a loud voice to his friends in the adjacent carriage. He seemed to have an immense fund of stories. 'When I was in the army,' he said, 'we were prevented from going to church on a Sunday by this corporal. So I hit him. I pushed his head into a barrel of water, and they sent me to Colchester. There I had to run everywhere between two policemen. I thought the most Christian thing was to hit him so that he would let us go to church,' and he laughed. 'I never liked authority much, but I'll tell you that corporal was sent to Easter Island after that. They got rid of him.'

He had many other stories, some of which involved playing practical jokes on a strict aunt of his.

And the train raced on. Sometimes there would be white men standing on the platforms, sometimes a Negro reading *The Times*, or an Indian reading a book. In another carriage he heard two philosophers arguing, one maintaining that children's programmes were the best on television. 'I never miss any of them,' he said. ' "Jackanory" is my favourite one.' His fellow philosopher gazed at him in horror. A tall man with a very narrow head talked about structuralism. Someone else compared *Treasure Island* with Marx's *Das Kapital*. He used the word 'precisely' a lot. He would say, 'It is precisely Squire Trelawney who is the most important person in the book.'

An African who spoke with an Oxford accent complained about his son. 'I told him if he didn't like the food he could leave the house.'

Time passed and he clutched his ticket more tightly. Some of the stations showed clocks which had stopped. Their faces blank and empty. There was a smell of mortality on the train. The evening was falling and he felt that his destination was approaching. He took his case down from the rack, excited by the thought. It was about another hour, however, before the train came to a gliding stop. On the platform were a number of soldiers wearing helmets which looked grey in the fading light.

'Come,' they said. 'Follow us.'

He grew more and more excited. At least something was happening. A gun was put in his hand and he found himself firing it indiscriminately into the crowds which were pouring from the train. People fell onto the platform, writhing with pain. He wanted to feel the pain. It seemed to him that he had read about people like himself who were perfectly happy doing what he was doing. Bang, bang went the gun and more and more people fell down. It was all very banal; there seemed no connection between his gun and their act of falling down. The world didn't change much, that was the extraordinary thing. Pop, pop went the gun and there was this contingent but not necessary flowering of blood. It was all quite ordinary. Even death was a cheat and didn't seem tragic or interesting at all. He opened his mouth and began to howl like a wolf. He jabbed sharp pins into his eyes till blood spurted down his beard. He jabbed and jabbed at his eyes while the train hissed behind him and he was enveloped in a cloud of sighing steam.

The Survivor

The survivor stood among the debris. There passed by him a ragged line of refugees with their possessions in carts. They stared straight ahead of them. Houses were burning, ash was being blown by a small dry wind.

The survivor stood perfectly still. He passed his hand across his body to test if he was really there. Yes, he was intact, and there was no blood on him. A jet screeched across the sky leaving a thin line behind it. He touched the back of his neck where the hat had left a hot sweaty mark. It seemed to him that the trail left by the jet and the mark on the back of his neck were related in some way.

As he watched the refugees he wondered why he was still alive. Their carts had red wheels: they were carrying their bloodied household gods with them. Why were they going from one place to another? It would be the same everywhere, wouldn't it? The whole world would surely vibrate with din, with pain.

He stared down at the headless body of a child. It seemed as obvious and as unusual as a stone. The ruin seemed normal, he could hardly remember when it had been otherwise. There had been soldiers racing about in trucks in their olive-green uniforms. They had taken out guns and shot people and then they had raced away again. They barked orders as if they knew exactly what they were doing, what they wanted. In situations like this it was perhaps best if one knew what one was doing.

Why me, he asked the sky above him. Why was I selected? And the question was unanswerable. There were millions and millions of people in the world and he had survived. He rubbed his face. It was still there. The headless body of the child didn't trouble him now as it did before. At least you are dead, he thought, you will have no further decisions to make – if you ever made any. He himself found it hard to make decisions. Why should he head north rather than south, west rather than east?

But in fact he found that he was heading west, away from the sun. For no reason that he could think of. He came across a tank lying on its side amongst a bank of flowers. It seemed as if the flowers were growing out of the tank. He stared at it for a long time, considering. Some lines came into his head:

The green tank grew among flowers while the sun shone blindly. But he didn't pursue the poem.

In the distance he could hear the sound of guns, thump after thump. Subconsciously he had walked away from them and that was why he was heading west.

I am a survivor, he thought, there must be a reason for that. Look at all the people who have been shot, bludgeoned to death, hacked, bombed . . . and here am I, alive.

He had taken off his hat and thrown it in a ditch. He was not recognisable as belonging to any side, any party. Blandly the sun shone blue above him. It was exactly the same as on the morning before all the attacks began.

He proceeded on his way, since there was nothing else to do. A big fat man with documents in his hand was running about shouting. 'Look,' he said, 'this is my visa. Everything is in order.' He stared into the survivor's eyes as if pleading with him. 'Tell me that I have done the right thing.' The survivor turned away. The fat man was weeping, turning out his pockets, offering him money. He thinks I am in charge, thought the survivor.

A week ago he had been sitting in a class in the open being lectured to by soldiers in olive-green uniforms. They had told him and others that they must learn to change their attitudes, support the regime. There were a lot of flags.

And then this class had been attacked out of the sky, and there was no one to tell him what he should do or what regime he should belong to. All around him now was a silence which palpitated with fear and hatred.

He stared into the mouth of an open cannon. He went up to

it and examined it. Its mouth was big, as if it would swallow him. Its body was shiny. He stroked it absently. He noticed that it was now cold. Its blunt solidity gave it a better right to be there than he had. It was fixed and unwavering in its place.

He saw white flowers in the hedges. They also were more authoritative than he was in his white shirt. They frothed and foamed with the life that was in them. They too extended their empire.

Below him on the ground he saw a snail with its aerials extended. He banged his foot on the ground in front of it and it came to a halt. Poor snail, he thought. You hear something but you don't know what it is. I shouldn't really be banging the ground like this, frightening you. The snail was velvety black. Its aerials were its only defences.

He walked on, leaving the snail behind him. In the distance he could see flames rising and falling, but there was no noise coming from them. People were burning among these flames, jumping out of windows perhaps, but there was only the silence. And he touched himself again: yes, I am here. My stomach has not been gutted, I have not been beheaded, though I have seen many beheaded with great curved swords. Who are these people who behead others? What kind of people are they? Maybe they don't realise what they are doing. Maybe they don't think as I do. Maybe they can't imagine what it's like to be beheaded, to suffer pain. Maybe they are burning with faith. I, on the contrary, have no faith at all. Maybe it is better to have faith and behead people than to have no faith at all. It is hard for me to feel the reality of things. Maybe the stones will shift and move eventually like clouds.

He remembered in the class a little man who had stared at him vindictively as if he hated him. What have I done to that man? he asked himself. The man had hit him across the face and prodded him with a bayonet. The bruise was still on his cheek. Why had the small busy man done that? He couldn't understand it. And yet the hatred had been as palpable as stench. Maybe he himself had a smell to which the soldier had responded with enmity. A smell of nothingness, of unreality.

He came to a fragment of wall. Set in the wall there was a

face, a Roman face, arrogant and haughty. The face stared out at him with dazzling cruelty as if he weren't there. The eyes were cold, empty. The head was proud, indifferent. It was like the face of an emperor. He touched the eyes gently, but not before he had seen some small busy animal running out of the wall and across what appeared to be an empty courtyard.

He came to a grassy verge along which he walked. He stopped when he saw a small blue flower there. He touched it gently as he had touched the sculptured face. It was tiny, beautiful, hermit-like. It was saying: I wish to be alone, quiet, studious. Its petals were indescribably soft. That was how I used to be, thought the survivor. I had my books, my teaching, my poetry. That was exactly how I was. He smiled at the small blue flower; for the moment, this was the reality. Its coolness comforted him. It was as if he had returned to a world before warfare, before secrecy. What a tiny flower which had somehow survived, like himself. It was like a mirror of himself. Beauty is secrecy, he thought – yet I wonder. It is too late for the blue flower. The blue flower is a lie.

And he was about to tear it out of the ground. He stretched his hand forward and touched it. It could not be allowed to live in such an illusion. He knelt before it in a predatory manner. At that precise moment there was an explosion – a big red flower blazing above him, about him. The mine must have been there all the time without his noticing it, mocking him. The world exploded in rays like one of the wheels of the carts carrying the old useless gods.

The Dead Man and the Children

The child gazed at me from the doorway, his eyes innocent as the sky. His head was alive with curls: he looked like a cherub in a picture by an Italian painter. Beside him was a little girl who suddenly stood up, climbed on the piano stool, and began to bang the keys. She looked as demented as a real pianist.

'We'll have to be going to the funeral,' said my wife. I agreed. The child's father, who was our son, put on his black tie while the child stared at him with the same innocent round eyes. His father lifted his son on to his shoulders: the child screamed with delight, pulling at his father's tie.

We drove to the church. The coffin lay at the front. The minister, who was a young man with a beard, said, 'There is no death: I am the Way, the Truth, and the Life. In my father's house are many mansions and if it were not so I would have told you.'

The man in the coffin was a relative of ours. In his life he had been generous and courageous: he had died in hospital from cancer bravely borne. Now he was at peace.

The child stood in the sunlight which flickered around him. He touched the little girl wonderingly and then moved away from her, staring at us, his thumb in his mouth. She found a can in a box and began to bang it on the floor. Neither of them could talk much.

The minister intoned words from the Bible. The dead man's wife came in and sat in the front flanked by her daughter and son-in-law who both looked serious. Her relatives were big men from the island, strong, and robust. They sat in a row behind her. 'How handsome they are,' my wife whispered. Big men, solid and strong: they came from the island and ate good food and worked hard and were not sensitive. It seemed to me that they looked like big stones which had stood on a moor since the beginning of time.

The minister was actually quite a small man but extraordinarily intense. He seemed really to believe that there was no death, that death is an alteration and not an end, that we go through a sunny doorway into another more perfect world.

The child and the little girl played with each other in the sunlight. Then they chased a rainbow-coloured ball behind a sofa, their heads close together. The girl was much more active than the boy, more, even, aggressive. The boy sometimes stared in wonderment at the world: how could there be guilt in such a world?

When we came out of the church (my wife, myself and our son) the space in front of and beside the building was congested. It took us a long time to manoeuvre our way out and reach the cemetery even though there was a policeman directing the traffic. We parked the car and walked between the tall steel gates. The streets of the graveyard were straight and clean: in the distance we could see the sea, which glittered and over which a wandering cold breeze moved hesitantly. In front of us were the strong men from the island, stolid and robust, wearing only jackets in spite of the bitter wind. Their faces were as craggy as rocks. Some of the women cried humbly into handkerchiefs. The men got into position around the coffin, each clutching a cord. The dead man's widow couldn't bear coming to the graveside – 'I have done my duty,' she said, 'I cannot bear it.' We shivered in the wind.

My son said, in the hearing of the big men, 'They are supposed to be handsome, these old men. Mother's glasses need examining.' They smiled affectionately like rocks cracking. The minister wasn't wearing a coat either: young and intense he spoke out of the cold wind. 'There is no death, I am the Way and the Truth, I am the gateway to eternal life.'

The two children were sitting beside each other examining a teddy bear, and poking at its shiny button-like eyes. They looked serious and intent in the sunshine of the kitchen. The man in the coffin had been young once too, he too had stared blue-eyed at the world. He had never expected that he would die in a strange hospital in the terrible city: he had wanted home but it was too late. All his life and even during his cancer he had been courageous: perhaps he had been acting a part, but his courage had nevertheless been real. 'I don't worry,' he would say, 'what's the point of worrying. If you worry you die and if you don't worry you die, so what's the point?' He used to sing songs in an affected voice, especially Irish songs and sometimes Italian ones.

The cords lowered the coffin slowly into the hole in the ground. I heard the thud as they were let drop on the wood; it seemed a very final sound. Am I doing this right, the people who were holding the cords would be thinking, I don't want to make a mistake, for the people round the graveside will be watching every move. Then the purple cloth was dropped on top of the coffin and then the wreaths. I could no longer see the coffin at all.

The broad men in front of us turned round and began to talk to us. They were going back to the island the following day: there was the land to be tended to and the cattle, now that spring was approaching. The boat trip would take five hours or so. They didn't seem at all cold in the strong bitter wind which blew in from the blue wrinkled sea.

The eyes of the child were intensely blue. They were like a serene guiltless sky. For ages he would stare at us unwinkingly as if judging us, as if saying, I dare you to stare back at me so unblinkingly. His hands tugged at his father's black tie. Then he stood in the sunlight and seemed eternal.

We walked away from the graveside talking. There was one woman in particular who couldn't remember the names of her relatives. 'Is that Donald or is it James?' she would say. 'I'm so stupid.' A man told of snow in the town from which he had come. 'Six inches,' he said. 'Here it is so mild.' 'How tall you have grown,' said one furred lady to our son. The big men were like moving stones. It didn't look as if any of them would ever die. There was so much to be done on the croft: a new tractor had just been bought and one of the sons used it a lot, playing a radio from it which could be heard all over the village.

The two children touched each other. 'Up,' said the little

girl, and my wife lifted her on to the piano stool where she began to bang the keys again while the other child clapped his hands, delighting in the din.

The man had been left in his coffin, which looked like a cradle. Perhaps he had stepped out of it and was elsewhere. Perhaps his soul, white as a gull, had flown into the sun.

The child sat in his high chair banging with his spoon. The little girl gazed at him: he banged and banged as if he were playing a tune. His father raised him up to the ceiling and he shrieked with laughter and excitement. The sun shone on the living-room lighting up the music set, the fireplace, the yellow brassy bin, the statuette of the Virgin, tall and white, with the child in her arms. She was holding Him out to the world: and yet He was the world.

The minister intoned, 'Nothing shall separate us from the love of God.'

We sang, 'The Lord's my Shepherd': it was not in the hymn book under the number the minister had said, but we all knew the words. They came back to us from our childhood, exact and true and poignant. Wasn't it strange that we knew them, though we didn't know that we did. My table Thou hast furnished in presence of my foes . . . The child made a paste of its food seriously and obsessively and then chucked some of it on the floor.

Our feet crackled on pebbles as we left the grave: nothing could be seen but the flowers. We asked each other about cars, distances. Some were going to the hotel for a meal, some were not. The men from the islands were going to the hotel. They spoke to us secretively in Gaelic: it was like belonging to a separate mysterious world. I couldn't help remembering the poem, The eternal sound of the sea, listen to the eternal sound of the sea. The dead man was sleeping by the sound of the sea. It was better for him to be here than in Glasgow in a stiff shroud, a stranger in a strange city.

The child banged his spoon against the plate. The little girl clapped her hands. They belonged to another world, or did they? They were secretive strangers. On the other hand they were like us and would become like us, but at the moment they looked beautiful and immortal with their cherubic curls. The cradle shone and glittered like a coffin. The child had a pair of yellow shoes, his first ones. Everything was honey coloured, even the sunlight that lay in bars across the floor.

The big tall men sat down at the table and ate heartily. Tomorrow they would return to their island. They laughed and told jokes from their childhood. The dead man seemed like a pretext for a feast, for laughter, for joy. How odd that death should bring us all together like this.

Bang, bang, went the spoon. The little girl clapped her hands. Maybe in the coffin the dead man clapped his hands too. Maybe he was like a tiny baby in his cradle, blue eyes reflecting the blue sky above him.

A Night with Kant

Each evening Kant went for a walk. And as he walked he brooded about the Categorical Imperative. It seemed to him that the Categorical Imperative was as fixed as the sun.

One night he saw a beggar beating up his woman, hitting her across the face over and over again. The beggar wore a long coat and his face was unshaven.

'Shall I tell him about the Categorical Imperative?' he asked himself, but decided against it, though the woman was screaming with a loud piercing voice.

'You old fart, I'll kill you,' the beggar shouted. One eye shone madly in his head.

Kant walked on in his neat suit. A watch ticked in his breast pocket. It seemed to him as he looked at the stars that the beggar and the woman were both necessary parts of the universe, as a mainspring was part of a watch.

Another time he saw a thief stealing along with a bagful of stuff he had taken from a shop in which a window was starred and broken.

'No, I'll not tell on him,' he thought. 'I will let him go on his way. Why should I interfere? I am not God.' The thief glared at him with piercing eyes as if saying, 'If you tell anyone what I have done I will kill you.'

Kant wondered what the mind of the thief was like, why he had stolen. He was troubled by the quick bright eyes, the eyes of a man who knew he was doing wrong and enjoying the sensation of it.

How beautiful the stars were, that glittering city which seemed like a remote reflection of a real city. He imagined the stars as the souls of the dead, glittering. How really happy he was to be doing what he was doing. There was no one happier;

he needed no other human being, he needed only his mind, the universe, that was all.

Yet sometimes he was disturbed by strange thoughts. What if the world that he was seeing was an unreal spectral world? What if there was nothing out there that he could trust? What if there had been no thief at all, no beggar, no screaming woman? But he put these thoughts away from him as quickly as they had come. Why should he need a witness? Why couldn't he depend only on himself?

Another night a policeman stopped him and said, 'Who are you? Why are you walking about the streets every night?'

'I am a philosopher,' said Kant. 'I am thinking.'

The policeman looked at him suspiciously.

'I thought, sir,' he said, 'that you were following that young girl.'

'What young girl?' said Kant.

'Never mind,' said the policeman.

Such a self-contained little man this was, such a funny precise man. Perhaps indeed he had been following that girl. You could never tell with these oldish people.

Kant wondered whether he should mention the Categorical Imperative to the policeman. He couldn't understand how the latter's mind worked. In fact it seemed to him that he didn't understand how anyone's mind worked, except perhaps his own. The policeman too he considered had a secret violent eye. He was beginning to wonder whether the world was more treacherous, phantasmal, than he had originally considered it to be.

Once he heard two women talking. One was saying to the other, gesturing furiously, 'One should stand up for what one believes in. Speak straight out, that is what I think.' Later he heard the same woman saying, 'It doesn't help to be blunt nowadays. It's better to kowtow and take your hat off to your superiors.'

Kant couldn't understand how people could be so irrational, so contradictory. He wondered if perhaps the world was divided into two groups, the philosophers and the others. Nor could he understand how people were so noticing of the world around them, more noticing than he was.

For instance he heard some men talking about a factory which had just been built. He had passed it every night and yet he hadn't even seen it. Yet these men had studied it in minute detail.

'They shouldn't have a building like that one there,' one man was saying. 'It's ugly, that's what it is. It doesn't fit in.'

And the other man who was bald and fat, said, 'They shouldn't have hired a local firm. Do you know that they take much longer to finish the work? They take advantage, that's what they do.'

Kant gazed vaguely at the factory with its many windows. How had he not noticed it before? And yet factories were useful, they produced commodities. It occurred to him that he knew nothing about the workings of bakeries, butchers' shops, nor did he know what butchers or bakers thought of, or how they conducted their lives. Yet he knew about the Categorical Imperative which they knew nothing of, and conducted their lives in ignorance of it.

What is wrong with me, he asked himself, how do I not have eyes like other people?

And it troubled him that he was so stupid as not to have noticed a factory like that rising from a site where before there had only been emptiness. Again he was stirred by vague guilty feelings. Could it be that these people knew more about the world than he did? Could it be that mice, dogs, cats and rats were more knowledgeable than he was? Could it be that people were secretly laughing at him because he appeared such a fool with his head in the clouds? Or perhaps at the same time as they thought this they also thought that he was a clever man, cleverer than they were themselves. And yet he didn't feel himself to be clever at all. On the contrary he felt himself to be stupid, stupider than the men and women who noticed factories, and were aware of the inner workings of machines.

Once he talked to a man whose job was building houses. 'You put the foundations in first,' the man said to him. 'But sometimes you get a fellow coming from headquarters and he will tell you that the foundations aren't deep enough, so you have to dig deeper. Dampness is one of the things you have to watch for when you are building a house. Condensation you have to look out for on windows. And you should make sure that the house blends in with its surroundings. All these things you have to remember. What do you do yourself?'

'Nothing,' said Kant, 'I am retired. ' He was ashamed to tell the man that he was a philosopher, that he sat in a study with books and pen and paper, and that he spent most of his time thinking.

'I hope to be retired myself some day,' said the man, 'but at the moment I can't afford to do that.'

'Why not?' said Kant.

'Well, it's like this,' said the man. 'It's to do with my wife. She says I would be in her way in the house. Women are funny, you understand.'

'Yes,' said Kant.

'You see,' the man continued comfortably, 'you have to treat them carefully, as if you were walking on marshy ground. One minute my wife is saying to me, "You're never at home to help about the house, you never put in shelves, you're too tired", and the next moment she's saying, "I don't want you to retire, you'd be in my way. Under my feet." And that's the fashion of it,' said the man philosophically.

'Take this place we're sitting in,' said the man. 'Now you watch that girl there, the one in the yellow apron. Her name is Gretchen and I know for a fact she comes from a poor family. And yet she will turn up her nose if you don't buy more than one cake. You have to watch the lie of the land, same as when you're building a house. Now yourself now you'll have experience of these things, I don't need to be telling you them. I would say now you had been a schoolmaster.'

'No,' said Kant. 'I don't think of myself as a schoolmaster.'

'Never mind,' said the man confidently. 'I can tell you were a scholar. I was never a scholar. All I ever read were instruction books.'

'Are they difficult to understand?' said Kant curiously.

'Not if you keep your wits about you,' said the man, who in actual fact wore glasses and in his stooping fashion himself looked like a scholar, and not a builder at all. 'I've seen instructions written in languages that I don't know but that doesn't bother me. I have a picture in my head of what the thing is to be like. Instinctive, you understand. Sometimes I don't need an instruction book at all. I'll tell you something,' he continued expansively. 'Once I was putting in plumbing and this contraption came along and I'd never seen one like it before. But I installed it just the same.'

'Is that right?' said Kant.

'Yes, it's right enough. I have this instinct, you understand. Ever since I was a child. Some people don't have it but I do. Now you take that factory out there. I wouldn't have built it like that, and I would have finished it quicker. I wouldn't have put in so many windows but you can't tell these people anything.'

After the man had left, Kant sat looking around him. Sitting in the café were two young people, the girl gazing into the boy's eyes adoringly. She clasped his hands in hers and began to talk animatedly about some party which they had attended the previous night.

'I saw her wearing the same dress before,' the girl was saying, while at the same time she stroked the boy's hands gently. 'The pink one.'

'Is that right?' said the boy, gazing abstractedly into the girl's eyes.

'Of course, silly,' said the girl. 'Didn't you notice? And another thing, she doesn't have to tell me that she's related to the Schumanns. I know for a fact she isn't.'

Kant stood up and went outside. He looked upward. The stars were numerous like seeds, and remote and beautiful and sparkling. Space and time. They were the conditions of man's existence.

He glanced at his watch. It was seven o'clock at night.

As he was walking along he was stopped by a young woman in a short skirt who said to him, 'I can show you a good time.' Her cheeks were artificially red and her legs were muscular and strong.

'The time is seven o'clock,' said Kant mildly. 'It is neither better nor worse.' The young woman looked at him in amazement and then tottered away arrogantly on her high heels. Kant was stirred by a regretful desire, so vague it was no more than a wandering breeze. And at that moment the Categorical Imperative was very distant indeed.

It was like a ghostly axle in the sky.

Around him were feverish images of colour which seemed to speak of freedom. And he felt very peculiar.

'What am I doing in this place?' he asked himself. 'How did I arrive in this street which I walk so punctually every night? I can't understand it.' And it seemed to him that he could have done something different, been something very different. But the shell that he had constructed round himself protected him, and only late at night did he hear howls as if from the centre of space itself.

Purity, purity, he said to himself. Purity is what I need. Simplicity. But how can one be a saint and live in the world? And he clutched firmly at his watch, that round golden globe on which he depended, in its exactitude. Always ticking like his heart. Except that unlike his heart it was renewable.

Another night he saw a woman walking along the street alone, and her nose was as long as that of a witch such as he had once seen in a storybook when he was a child. Yet what a fool he was. Of course there were no witches, and of course that specific woman was not a witch. On the other hand, as he passed her he felt that at any moment she would burst out cackling and shout disgraceful things after him. Of course she couldn't put a spell on him. Naturally not. Yet he saw her in space dancing with an imaginary illuminated broom which was like the Categorical Imperative.

There is something else, he thought, there is. Behind the stars there is something else, behind the houses there is something else. Deep in the earth, in the remote depths of the universe, there is something else. And it is laughing at me. It is mocking me. It is saying, Who do you think you are? It is saying, Look at that silly man with his watch, he thinks he understands it all. But I know, I know, the thing was saying, I know differently. Deep in the roots and in space itself I AM.

And Kant saw a green snake undulating in the sky, a phantasmal shimmering snake.

And he was suddenly shaken with fear. When he held his hand out one of his fingers was trembling. He gazed at it for a long time but it didn't stop shaking. It was like a magnetic needle that had gone crazy.

Once he saw two small children running away after snatching a handbag from an old woman. They disappeared into the darkness as if into a den. The old woman began to weep, and Kant went up to her, put his hand gently on her arm and said, 'Here's some money.'

But the old woman replied, 'No, indeed, I'll not take it. I have never owed anyone anything in my whole life.'

'What, who?' Kant muttered. 'I don't understand.'

'I've never owed a penny,' said the old woman sniffling yet indomitable. 'I saw them. They were two girls.'

'A girl and a boy,' said Kant.

'No, they were two girls,' said the old woman resolutely. 'They were about sixteen years old.'

'Not more than eleven,' said Kant. 'I'm sure they were not more than eleven.'

'Not at all, sixteen they were,' said the old woman definitely.

Suddenly Kant lost his temper and shouted, 'They were not more than eleven years old and they were both wearing red jackets.'

'Green,' said the old woman. 'As sure as I'm standing here it was green they were wearing. I still have my faculties, you know.' And she glared furiously at Kant.

'Green,' she said, 'and you must come and tell the police that.'

'No,' said Kant, 'I can't do that.'

What a fool the woman was. Of course the children had been wearing red, even allowing for the darkness. They had certainly not been wearing green. On the other hand she was one of the ones he had heard discussing the factory. In fact, she was the woman whom he remembered as saying that such a stink should not be allowed. He turned away from her in case she would force him to go with her to the police station; he had enough to do with his time. It seemed to him that the ground was trembling under his feet, that the universe was quivering like a morass, that perhaps it didn't exist at all. Why, that old woman might say that it was he who had stolen her money. He looked down at his suit, which was yellow in the light of the lamps. He seemed like a jester, a clown. He took out his watch and consulted it: it gazed back at him, reassuringly golden and round. A tranquil moon.

'A good time,' he heard the voice saying seductively. And the words, 'A good time', echoed in his head. And at that moment he saw her again. It seemed as if she was always there. She was smiling at him, hitching her skirt to show her thighs.

He walked towards her through the harlequin chequered night. 'Categorical Imperative,' said Kant restlessly in his sleep.

What is he talking about? said the young woman to herself as she examined his jacket. A poor Categorical Imperative he had been indeed. Why, he had fallen asleep like a child in her perfumed room. She stretched herself luxuriously, feeling energy like a strong red pulse in her body. She felt complete inside her envelope of flesh; she was very conscious of her own languorous motions. At that moment she wasn't aware of age or of time. With money, what could one not do? One didn't need to bother thinking about a future: the future would take care of itself. As she watched the sleeping philosopher it angered her that he should have money and she none. Or at least he had more than she had. She had such a beautiful body, such taut pointed breasts, and his body was not powerful or muscular at all. Ahead of her through the window she saw a single star winking in the sky. That might be Venus: she wasn't sure. Her mother had once told her, but she couldn't remember things like that. She took the golden watch from his pocket. She could sell it and this poor idiot would never notice its loss, or if he did he would not complain. She knew his kind, a respectable bourgeois to the very core.

The Maze

It was early morning when he entered the maze and there were still tiny globes of dew on the grass across which he walked, leaving ghostly footprints. The old man at the gate, who was reading a newspaper, briefly raised his head and then gave him his ticket. He was quite easy and confident when he entered: the white handkerchief at his breast flickered like a miniature flag. It was going to be an adventure, fresh and uncomplicated really. Though he had heard from somewhere that the maze was a difficult one he hadn't really believed it: it might be hard for others but not for him. After all wasn't he quite good at puzzles? It would be like any puzzle, soluble, open to the logical mind.

The maze was in a big green park in which there was also a café, which hadn't as yet opened, and on the edge of it there was a cemetery with big steel gates, and beyond the cemetery a river in which he had seen a man in black waterproofs fishing. The river was as yet grey with only a little sparkle of sun here and there.

At first as he walked along the path he was relaxed and, as it were, lounging: he hadn't brought the power of his mind to bear on the maze. He was quite happy and confident too of the outcome. But soon he saw, below him on the stone, evidence of former passage, for there were empty cigarette packets, spent matches, empty cartons of orangeade, bits of paper. It almost irritated him to see them there as if he wished the maze to be clean and pure like a mathematical problem. It was a cool fresh morning and his shirt shone below his jacket, white and sparkling. He felt nice and new as if he had just been unpacked from a box.

When he arrived at the first dead-end he wasn't at all

perturbed. There was plenty of time, he had the whole morning in front of him. So it was with an easy mind that he made his way back to try another path. This was only a temporary setback to be dismissed from his thoughts. Obviously those who had designed the maze wouldn't make it too easy, if it had been a group of people. Of course it might only have been one person. He let his mind play idly round the origin of the maze: it was more likely to have been designed by one person, someone who in the evening of his days had toyed idly with a puzzle of this nature: an engineer perhaps or a setter of crosswords. Nothing about the designer could be deduced from the maze: it was a purely objective puzzle without pathos.

The second path too was a dead-end. And this time he became slightly irritated for from somewhere in the maze he heard laughter. When had the people who were laughing come in? He hadn't noticed them. And then again their laughter was a sign of confidence. One wouldn't laugh if one were unable to solve the puzzle. The clear happy laughter belonged surely to the solvers. For some reason he didn't like them; he imagined them as haughty and imperious, negligent, graceful people who had the secret of the maze imprinted on their brains.

He walked on. As he did so he met two of the inhabitants of the maze for the first time. It was a father and son, at least he assumed that was what they were. They looked weary, and the son was walking a little apart from the father as if he was angry. Before he actually caught sight of them he thought he heard the son say, 'But you said it wouldn't take long.' The father looked guilty and hangdog as if he had failed his son in some way. He winked at the father and son as he passed them as if implying, 'We are all involved in the same puzzle.' But at the same time he didn't feel as if he belonged to the same world as they did. For one thing he was unmarried. For another the father looked unpleasantly flustered and the son discontented. Inside the atmosphere of his own coolness he felt superior to them. There was something inescapably dingy about them, especially about the father. On the other hand they would probably not meet again and he might as well salute them as if they were 'ships of the night'. It seemed to him that the father was grey and tired, like a little weary mouse redolent of failure.

He continued on his way. This too was a dead-end. There was nothing to do but retrace his steps. He took his handkerchief out of his pocket, for he was beginning to sweat. He hadn't noticed that the sun was so high in the sky, that he had taken so long already. He wiped his face and put his handkerchief back in his pocket. There was more litter here, a fragment of a doll, a torn pair of stockings. What went on in this maze? Did people use it for sexual performance? The idea disgusted him and yet at the same time it argued a casual mastery which bothered him. That people should come into a maze of all places and carry out their practices there! How obscene, how vile, how disrespectful of the mind that had created it! For the first time he began to feel really irritated with the maze as if it had a life of its own, as if it would allow sordid things to happen. Calm down, he told himself, this is ridiculous, it is not worth this harassment.

He found himself standing at the edge of the maze, and over the hedge he could see the cemetery which bordered the park. The sun was flashing from its stones and in places he could see bibles of open marble. In others the tombstones were old and covered with lichen. Beyond the cemetery he could see the fisherman still angling in his black shiny waterproofs. The rod flashed back from his shoulder like a snake, but the cord itself was subsumed in bright sunlight.

And then to his chagrin he saw that there was a group of young people outside the maze and quite near him. It was they who had been the source of the laughter. One of them was saying that he had done the maze five times, and that it was a piece of cake, nothing to it. The others agreed with him. They looked very ordinary young people, not even students, just boys from the town, perhaps six or seven years younger than himself. He couldn't understand how they had found the maze easy when he himself didn't and yet he had a better mind, he was sure of that. He felt not exactly envy of them in their assured freedom but rather anger with himself for being so unaccountably stupid. It sounded to him as if they could enter and leave the maze without even thinking about it. They were eating chips from brown paper, and he saw that the café had opened.

But the café didn't usually open till twelve o'clock, and he had entered the maze at half past nine. He glanced at his watch and saw that it was quarter past twelve. And then he noticed something else, that the veins on his wrists seemed to stand out more, seemed to glare more, than he had remembered them doing. He studied both wrists carefully. No, no question about it, his eyes had not deceived him. So, in fact, the maze was getting at him. He was more worried than he had thought.

He turned back down the path. This time something new had happened. He was beginning to feel the pressure of the maze, that was the only way that he could describe it. It was almost as if the maze were exerting a force over him. He stopped again and considered. In the beginning, when he had entered the maze in his white shirt, which now for some reason looked soiled, he had felt both in control of himself and the maze. It would be he who would decide what direction he would take, it would be he who would remain detached from the maze, much as one would remain detached from a cross-word puzzle while solving it in front of the fire in the evening. But there had been a profound change which he only now recognised. The maze was in fact compelling him to choose, pushing him, making demands on him. It wasn't simply an arrangement of paths and hedges. It was as if the maze had a will of its own.

Now he began to walk more quickly as if feeling that he didn't have much time left. In fact he had an appointment with Diana at three o'clock and he mustn't break it. It would be ridiculous if he arrived late and said, 'I couldn't come because I was powerless to do so. I was a prisoner.' She was sure to think such an explanation odd, not to say astonishing. And in any case if he arrived late she wouldn't be there. Not that deep down he was all that worried, except that his nonappearance would be bad manners. If he was going to give her a pretext for leaving him, then it must be a more considered pretext than that.

He noticed now that his legs were becoming tired and heavy.

He supposed that this was quite logical, as the stone would be absorbing some of the energy that he was losing. But what bothered him more than anything was the feeling that it would be a long time before he would get out of the maze, that he was going round in circles. Indeed he recognised some of the empty cigarette packets that he was passing. They were mostly Players and he was sure that he had seen them before. In fact he bent down and marked some of them with a pen to make sure of later identification. This was the sort of thing that he had read of in books, people going round and round deserts in circles. And yet he thought that he was taking a different path each time. He wiped his face again and felt that he was losing control of himself. He must be if he was going round and round in helpless circles all the time. Maybe if he had a thread or something like that he would be able to strike out on fresh paths. But he didn't have a thread and some remnant of pride determined that he would not use it, rather like his resolve not to use a dictionary except as a last resort when he was doing a crossword puzzle. He must keep calm. After all, the café and the cemetery were quite visible. It wasn't as if he was in a prison and couldn't shout for help if the worst came to the worst. It wasn't as if he was stranded on a desert island. And yet he knew that he wouldn't shout for help: he would rather die.

He didn't see the father and son again but he saw other people. Once he passed a big heavy man with large black-rimmed spectacles who had a briefcase in his hand, which he thought rather odd. The man, who seemed to be in a hurry, seemed to know exactly where he was going. When they passed each other the man didn't even glance at him, and didn't smile. Perhaps he looked contemptible to him. It was exactly as if the man was going to his office and the path of the maze was an ordinary high road.

Then again he saw a tall ghostly-looking man passing, and he turned and stared after him. The man was quite tall, not at all squat like the previous one. He looked scholarly, abstracted and grave. He seemed to drift along, inside an atmosphere of his own, and he himself knew as if by instinct that the first man would have no difficulty in solving the riddle of the maze but that the second would. He didn't know how he knew this, but he was convinced just the same. The maze he now realised was infested with people, men, women and children, young people, old people, middle-aged people. Confident people and ghostly people. It was like a warren and he felt his bones shiver as the thought came to him. How easy it had been to think at the beginning that there was only himself: and now there were so many other people. People who looked straight ahead of them and others who looked down at the ground.

One in particular, with the same brisk air as the black-spectacled man, he had an irresistible desire to follow. The man was grey-haired and soldierly. He, like the first one, didn't look at him or even nod to him as he passed, and he knew that this was another one who would succeed and that he should follow him. But at the same time it came to him that this would be a failure of pride in himself, that he didn't want to be like a dog following its master as if he were on a string. The analogy disgusted him. He must not lose control of his will, he must not surrender it to someone else. That would be nauseating and revolting.

He noticed that he was no longer sweating and this bothered him too. He should be sweating, he should be more frightened. Then to his amazement he saw that the sun had sunk quite far in the direction of the west. He came to a dead halt almost in shock. Why was time passing so rapidly? It must be four o'clock at least and when he glanced at his watch he saw that it was actually half past four. And therefore he had missed Diana. What a ludicrous thing. This maze, inert and yet malevolent, was preventing him from doing what he ought to have done and forcing him to do other things instead. Probably he would never see Diana again. And then the thought came to him, threatening in its bareness, what if he had chosen to walk into this maze in order to avoid her? No, that was idiotic. Such an idea had never come into his head. Not for one moment.

He looked down at his shoes and saw that they were white with dust. His trousers were stained. He felt smelly and dirty. And what was even more odd when he happened to see the backs of his hands he noticed that the hair on them was grey.

That surely couldn't be. But it was true, the backs of his hands had grey hair on them. Again he stood stock-still trying to take account of what had happened. But then he found that he couldn't even stand still. It was as if the maze had accelerated. It was as if it could no longer permit him to think objectively and apart from himself. Whenever a thought came into his head it was immediately followed by another thought which devoured it. He had the most extraordinary vision which hit him with stunning force. It was as if the pathways in his brain duplicated the pathways of the maze. It was as if he was walking through his own brain. He couldn't get out of the maze any more than he could get out of his own head. He couldn't quite focus on what he sensed, but he knew that what he sensed or thought was the truth. Even as he looked he could see young people outside the café. They seemed amazingly young, much younger than he had expected. They were not the same ones as the early laughers, they were different altogether, they were young children. Even their clothes were different. Some of them were sitting eating ice-cream at a table which stood outside the café and had an awning over it. He couldn't remember that awning at all. Nor even the table. The fisherman had disappeared from the stream. The cemetery seemed to have spawned more tombstones.

His mind felt slow and dull and he didn't know where to go next. It came to him that he should sit down where he was and make no more effort. It was ludicrous that he should be so stupid as not to get out of the maze which others had negotiated so easily. So he couldn't be as intelligent as he thought he was. But it was surely the maze that was to blame, not himself. It quite simply set unfair problems, and those who had solved them had done so by instinct like animals. He remembered someone who had been cool and young and audacious and who had had a white handkerchief in his pocket like a flag. But the memory was vaguer than he had expected, and when he found the handkerchief it was only a small crumpled ball which was now in his trouser pocket. He turned and looked at the flag which marked the centre of the maze. It seemed that he would never reach it.

He felt so sorry for himself that he began to cry a little and he couldn't stop. Water drooled from his eyes, and he wiped it away with his dirty handkerchief. There didn't seem to be so many people in the maze now. It was a stony wilderness. If there was one he could recognise as successful he would follow him like a dog. He would have no arrogance now. His brow puckered. There was someone he remembered as existing outside the maze, someone important, someone gracious, elegant, a magnet which he had somehow lost. She was . . . but he couldn't remember who she was. And in any case had she been outside the maze? Had she not always been inside it, perhaps as lost as he was himself?

Slowly and stubbornly he plodded on, no longer imagining that he would leave the maze, walking for the sake of walking. The twilight was now falling, and the café was shut. He could hear no sounds around him, no infestation of the maze, and yet strangely enough he sensed that there were beings there. If he could no longer escape from the maze then he might at least reach the centre and see what was there. Perhaps some compensating emblem, some sign, some pointer to the enigma. Perhaps even the designer of the maze sitting there in a stony chair. He set his teeth, he must not give in. He must not allow the thought to control him that he had no power over the maze, that in fact the power was all the other way. That would be the worst of all, not only for him but for everybody else.

And then quite ironically, as if the seeing of it depended on his thought, there was the centre, barer than he had expected, no emblem, no sign, no designer.

All that was there was a space, and a clock and a flag. The clock pointed to eleven. The sun was setting, red and near in the sky. It was a big ball that he might even clutch. The twilight was deepening. For a moment there, it was as if in the centre of the maze he had seen a tomb, but that couldn't be true. That must have come from his brooding on the cemetery. On the other hand it might be a cradle. And yet it wasn't that either. There was nothing there at all, nothing but the space on which the paths converged.

He looked at the space for a long time, as if willing something to fill it. And then very slowly from the three other paths he saw three men coming. They seemed superficially to be different, but he knew that they were all the same. That is to say, there hovered about the faces of each of them a common idea, a common resemblance, though one was dressed in a grey suit, one in a gown, and one in jacket and flannels. They all stood there quite passively and waited for him to join them. They were all old. One of them to his astonishment held a child by the hand. He stood there with them. Slowly the sun disappeared over the horizon and darkness fell and he felt the pressure of the maze relaxing, as if in a dream of happiness he understood that the roads were infinite, always fresh, always new, and that the ones who stood beside him were deeper than friends, they were bone of his bone, they were flesh of his disappearing flesh.

Uncollected Stories

On the Island

He's on the island. Jim Merrick, whom I hated, hate. I saw his head like a cannon ball emerging now and again from the froth of the waves, as he struggled towards the shore, after the ship had been smashed on the rocks. I saw no other. Even now he must be on some other part of the island: tomorrow I shall explore it when the night has passed and there is clear daylight.

Yes, I have seen his footprints in the sand. This morning I swam out to the wreck of the ship which is being tilted and smashed steadily against the rocks: luckily for me that I am a powerful swimmer. I carried a knife between my teeth in case I met him scavenging among the broken wood.

I scrambled over the ship, my heart beating and managed to get a hammer and nails as well as some biscuits and salted meat. I don't know how he missed the hammer for he was there before me, since I found scrawled on a miraculously whole mirror the words, 'I shall kill you Cruso.' He had spelt my name wrong for he is practically illiterate. Jim Merrick, whom I hated because he made my life a misery. Uneducated animal – like Jim Merrick whose life is in his head. I swam out through a mass of bodies rising and falling in the water: a bitter harvest.

He must be building his hut somewhere on the island as well, for there must have been more than one hammer: he wouldn't have gone back without one. It seems a large island with green hills and valleys and, I think, plenty of water. Perhaps it is because of the largeness of the island that I haven't as yet seen him after two days. Luckily I slept in the trees the last nights or he might have found me and killed me. All this day I shall spend working on my hut and he will, I suppose, be doing the same.

I hope he hadn't got a musket for if he has he is bound to kill me. I must make sure That I don't leave any traces when I climb the tree. I haven't seen any wild animals: he is probably the wildest animal on the island.

This morning I found written in the sand the words: 'It won't be long now.' His writing is clumsy and unformed even in sand.

I wish I had a razor so that I could shave. I have managed to kill a goat: he's probably done the same, since his instinct for blood is greater than mine. I saw some wild pig as well and coloured birds in the trees. The sky has been clear and blue and there has been no rain. I am chary of the herbs for they might be poisonous.

The problem is, how can I feel secure in my hut when I have built it, especially at night. It looks as if I shall have to go after him in order to gain peace; one of us may have to die. I hope it will be him, naturally, I read my Bible a lot.

I have seen him. Exploring the island, I saw him building a hut behind a clump of trees (perhaps he is frightened of me too, though I never thought of that before). He was naked to the waist, very brown, and he looked like a wild animal with his club head and his long quivering snout. I stood behind him for a long time though I didn't throw my knife which I could very well have done. But something, I don't know what it was, prevented me from doing so.

He was hammering nails in wood and whistling to himself, and his face, like mine, was unshaven. Why, I thought to myself, he looks even like me. We are both turning brown in this perpetual sun. I nearly went and spoke to him, my bitterest enemy, for I felt so lonely: I wished to hear the speech of men, for even he is a man. He looked so innocent and harmless, working at his hut, as if he were an animal building its lair.

No ship will come for a long time if ever. I know that. Already our own ship has sunk in the waves and the decks on which we once walked are covered with brine: the mirrors lie among the fishes. I don't know whether he managed to get hold of one but I couldn't find any except ones which were too big to be lifted. How shall I ever know that I exist? However, I shall know he exists. I fixed a wooden bolt on the door of my hut. But this morning when I woke up and went outside, I found carved on the wood the words, 'You can't hide from me Cruso.' He persisted in misspelling my name: I don't know why that should bother me but it does. I wonder why he didn't wait for me till I came out, and then attack me. But no, I saw no sight and heard no sound of him. His treatment of the cabin boys was scandalously cruel: that was why I had quarrelled with him for I can't stand injustice.

Also he is a brute. He eats like a brute, slurping his food, and he talks like a brute and he walks like a brute. He has the physique of a brute and I am ashamed to belong to the same race as he does. It is amazing to me that he can write at all.

Now that I know where he is I crawled towards his hut but he wasn't there. I left a stone with a note tied round it: he can't expect to have it all his own way. I didn't wait to see him read it. When I got back to my own hut he had removed the bolt from the door and he had urinated against the walls.

I have a vision of Jim Merrick in a large cage and I am feeding him till a ship comes. I see him pecking at his food with his large beak and I watch myself dressing him in coloured clothes. I am teaching him how to spell my name correctly: when he succeeds in doing so, I give him some more seed. What an extraordinary vision: I must be going out of my mind.

I caught a fish today. At night I left my hut and watched him under the large yellow moon but he did not appear.

He is sitting outside his hut on a large boulder carving some wooden object. I think it is a model of a ship that he is making, a ship with wooden sails. Perhaps in his dim way he liked that ship, perhaps he misses his authority over the crew. His head is bent over his model and he is muttering to himself: I have a feeling that he knows I am near. Suddenly he turns round and looks directly at the place where I am standing hidden by the foliage. And then he laughs, a dry delighted laugh.

Last night I slept in the trees again in case he came to the hut. He did come to the hut though I didn't see him and carved on the door, 'Not now. Sumtime.' I know what is happening: he too in his dim way has worked it out. He's playing a cat-and-mouse game in order to pass the time: at least it gives us something to do for if we didn't have that we wouldn't have anything. But he had deteriorated. I think. His face is hairy, he walks in a stooping manner like an ape, or like a scholar. Ha, ha. He always, like me, carries a knife.

On board the ship he always sang for he was happy to be a master of a kind: here he never sings, and neither do I. My lips are becoming stiff, and my mouth is closing like the grave.

Yesterday we pursued the same animal. We tugged at the flesh, one from each side, each with his knife. But we did not attack each other: we agreed wordlessly to divide the flesh in two parts. His face has become like that of a beast: I wonder if mine is the same. We dragged the half-carcases back to our huts. I think he sometimes sleeps in a tree too lest he should be caught off guard.

I have worked out that it is Christmas Day but it is not cold and snowy and icy as it used to be in that home that I once knew. Perhaps we should have a truce for we are both growing tired. But I'm sure he doesn't know that it is Christmas, so there would be no point.

He is building a boat. If he succeeds in that he will kill me. Last night I went and smashed it. I don't know what he will feel like when he sees the results of my handiwork. Maybe he will try to build one somewhere else, hidden among the foliage. But I must say that I haven't felt such joy for a long time as I did when I smashed that boat: my hammer flew about the wood with joy and exhilaration.

I started to build a boat myself but the same thing happened to mine: he smashed it.

So we are back to where we were before. The weather holds well, unchanging, blue. There have been no storms. I am sustained by the Bible which I think is on my side.

I have begun to talk to myself. Once I heard myself addressing myself as Merrick. That's very odd and I can't understand it. I wonder if he is doing the same, that is addressing himself as Robinson Crusoe.

Perhaps Merrick doesn't exist. Perhaps he was never on the

island at all and I scrawled these messages myself, though they appear to be from him. But surely that's not possible. Would I misspell my own name? Could Jim Merrick write at all? But he must have been able to, otherwise how could he have scrawled on the ship's mirror?

His name was certainly Merrick. I must write it on the flyleaf of the Bible so that I will remember it. JIM MERRICK. It sounds right enough, it sounds as if he existed. I am frightened. I have thought, what would happen if I went blind on a desert island. I have succeeded in making a bow and arrow, but so has he: I heard an arrow whistling past me today while I was gutting fish. But he must have intended to miss me. Tonight I shall fire one through his window, not to kill, as a warning merely.

I have a parrot in a cage. I speak to it and it answers. I say, 'Kill Merrick, kill Merrick,' and it imitates me in a rasping almost incomprehensible voice.

Yesterday when I came back to the hut the parrot had been killed. I know that he won't kill me. It isn't time yet. The parrot had been strangled and all the colour had drained out of the body. I wasn't at all angry, and that frightened me.

I waited till he had left his hut, and then I got hold of the carving of the ship with its wooden sails and masts and I threw it into the sea. I watched it float away so bravely, so almost freely. I also smashed a mirror I found in his hut: perhaps he is superstitious and my action will shake him. I wish his face had been inside it.

Yesterday we sat fishing about three hundred yards from each other. We did not speak. Murder on a desert island, that would be odd, I wonder if he would bury me, I wouldn't bury him. The thing is that he would be on his own if he killed me, and I would be on my own if I killed him. That is why we are playing with each other: but which is the cat and which is the mouse? I like nothing better now than banging the heads of fish against stones when I catch them, and yet I didn't used to be a cruel man. Am I turning into a Merrick?

He is a beast. He ought to be killed. He is an unjust brute and I am the Hand of God. I have seen his death written in letters of flame.

A Voice is telling me that I must kill him, he is polluting the earth. This place would be pure and innocent without him. I shall fly over him on wings of flame, on coloured wings. I cannot be harmed but he is the devil. He looks like the devil shambling along with his head bent, reading the ground, the signs of the day. Without him I would be able to sleep, the sky would be bluer, the day more secure. And yet . . .

Hear ye, hear ye. The prophet goes out armed. He speaks to the people, he brings the word of God. The unclean and the sinful and the brutish must be killed and sacrificed. The wrath of God shall be upon them. The heathen must be extirpated from the earth.

He is growing old. I can see that now and my triumph is complete. His hair is growing grey. He stoops as he walks along, like a philosopher, an ape, and a philosopher. It is an effort for him to work. He can no longer run after the animals, he moves at a stately almost rotund pace, like a large grey egg. I move slowly after him, and sometimes he moves slowly after me.

He is an old man. Who would have believed that Merrick would have become so old, who once shouted from the deck at the seamen in the rigging? He no longer attempts to build a boat, he has surrendered to reality and the place where he is will be his final place. Sometimes he sits on a rock staring into space. We stare at each other, we are old men, but it will be worse for him, for he has no inner life, he is simply a sick animal. His shadow follows me, his lips move soundlessly for he has nothing to say. Soon we shall die for no ship will ever come.

All day yesterday we sat and stared at each other, our knives in our hands. I think I fell asleep. I know he did. His beard reaches to his feet and so does mine. We are drawing closer to death. Who will die first and who will bury whom?

Night is falling. It must be thirty years now since we landed on this island resentful and burning with hate, but at least we were young. Now we are shadows of the evening. Soon we shan't be able to catch anything, not animals, not fish. Soon we shall just sit and die.

Today I found him unconscious by the water . He had been trying to drag a plank ashore and it floated in the salty brine in front of him, dancing. I looked down at him. There was no ship on the horizon. I could have killed him then. He was meat, just grizzly meat, tough and wrinkled, uneatable. His closed eyes and his pale flashes of flesh among the stubble and old rags made him look defenceless.

After a while he opened his eyes and looked up. I helped him to his feet and threw both knives into the sea where they sparkled briefly in the rays of the sun. We turned away from the water, crooked bent old men together. There was no help for it. We started to hack aimlessly and weakly at the wood to make a boat. We shall cook the food in turns.

The Button

One day the old man and the old woman stopped talking to each other. They sat for a lot of the time in the same room but they didn't speak. She would make the breakfast and the dinner and the tea and lay them at regular times on the table and they would both sit and eat but they remained silent. Neither would pass anything to the other, but each would stretch across to get the salt or the pepper or whatever was required. At night they would go to bed and turn their backs on each other and go to sleep.

And yet in their early days they had been lovers. They had married young and gone through life together as other couples had done. They had a house of their own and in those days they would discuss what furniture they should buy for it. They would go out and visit and talk to other people. They had a garden where flowers grew every summer and withered every autumn. They were the same age, grew up together and no one was surprised when they married, as they seemed destined for each other. They had children and he worked at his work and came home every night. They sometimes joked and sometimes quarrelled and sometimes they took life very seriously.

Then one day in their old age ceased to speak to each other. It was as if they had no longer anything to say to each other, as if they had run out of thoughts, and so their minds became secretive and inward. They each had dreams of what they might have done differently but they concealed these dreams from each other. He would sometimes read the newspaper and she would sew and they wouldn't speak. And in a strange way they felt comfortable with each other, their silence was not bristling and hostile, it was a silence of emptiness. It was as if they were waiting for the grave into which they would be lowered. Nothing particular had happened to cause this, they hadn't had a major quarrel. They were like clocks which had run down.

When someone came to visit them, which was rare, they spoke to the visitor but wouldn't speak directly to each other. The visitors noticed this and stayed away in order not to embarrass them. They didn't know what to make of it all since they themselves couldn't imagine a world without speech. Who could imagine it?

It was a most peculiar situation and yet after a while it became natural to the two of them. They would brush past each other on their way to a room and ignore each other as if each were a wardrobe or a chair or a table. They had in fact become like pieces of walking breathing furniture. And they did not feel this as an emptiness or a tragedy. The world had long become opaque to them. It had gone past the stage of significance or even of being a game. It simply was and they simply were. Perhaps after all they were closer to being plants. They almost ceased being aware of each other. And in a sense they gained a kind of freedom from this silence, though it was not a fruitful or creative silence. It was a silence of surrender. Speech had made them tired and they simply ceased being tired. This silence would have gone on for a long time except for a strange trivial accident, if accident it was. The old man always wore a jacket with three buttons on it. It was a grey jacket and he had worn it for thirty years. It was frayed in places and it had been repaired here and there. One day the old woman noticed that one of the buttons was hanging by a thread. For some reason this disturbed her and she wished to sew the button on again. The trouble was however that her husband wore the woollen jacket to bed as it was winter time and he never took it off. He even left his shirt on and sometimes his tie. Every day and every night she would see this button which was a black one hanging by the single thread and it became an obsession with her. She was afraid that the button would fall off and she would never be able to find it again. She would follow him about looking down at the floor or at the ground to make sure that it hadn't fallen. She almost spoke to him in order to point out the danger to the button. But in fact he seemed completely unconscious that the button was about to fall off. He had always been like that, not caring what condition his clothes were in. Often in the past she had to tell him to wear a fresh suit when he went out visiting. For he really genuinely didn't care how he was dressed. The button, black and round, became an obsession. She could see it in her dreams. It expanded and filled her consciousness. And sublimely ignorant of her thoughts he went about, not caring what happened to the button. She grew angry and simmered quietly. Why on earth couldn't he pay attention to important things like that? If he had only two buttons instead of three he would look untidy and people would think that she wasn't looking after him. But even that was not what bothered her. What really bothered her like a toothache was the lack of symmetry. It was the lowest of the three buttons and he would look silly walking about with the lower part of his jacket spread wide. The black button became as large as a globe. It became a whole earth, round and fatal and trivial. It hung from a single thread and at any moment the thread might snap. The button would fall to the ground and she would never see it again. There would never again be found a button exactly like that one. Also, her sight wasn't very good and if the button fell she would probably never find it again. Sometimes she had the greatest difficulty in not stretching forward and seizing hold of the button and tearing it off so that she could keep it and sew it on later in the summer months when he might shed the jacket. In the morning she would look for the button in case it had fallen off in the bed at night. And sublimely indifferent to what was happening to him, her husband would continue in his sloppiness, making the silence untidy and incomplete. What could one say about him except that he was insensitive, that he did not understand her feelings, that no matter how hard she looked at the button he didn't seem to notice, that he didn't appreciate the importance of the button in the universe but carried on reading his newspaper? Of what importance was the newspaper in comparison with the button? It was like an aching tooth whose pain could not be relieved. The world went by as an accident without speech but the button belonged to the past, it had a position in space, it demanded this position in space, it agonised and throbbed in this position. It was more important to her than anything in the whole world. She watched it as she might watch a sick child, she thought about it sleeplessly all night as her husband slept, or turned so extravagantly and thoughtlessly in his bed. She hung on the button as on the speech of a lover. No, it was no good, it would drive her mad.

One morning when she saw that the thread was about to snap she said to him, breaking the silence, 'I think that button needs to be sewn again or you'll lose it.'

He looked at her in surprise and then, like her, returned from the world of silence with regret and sorrow as if he had come home from a holiday in the unknown. After that they talked to each other as before. The button was sewn close to his woollen jacket. She no longer even noticed it, it had become part of the world of things. But they never again went back to their world of silence. They had come home again.

A September Day

It was a day in autumn when I came home from school in Stornoway, a town which was seven miles from the village. The sky was a perfect blue, and the corn was yellow and as yet uncut. I left the bus at the bottom of the road and walked the rest of the way home. I was eleven years old, and I wore short trousers and a woollen jersey both of which my mother had made for me. Even as I write, the movement of the fresh air on my legs returns to me, and the red radiance of the heather all about me. Every day I went to Stornoway on the bus and every day I came back. I began to think of myself as more sophisticated than the villagers. Didn't I know all about Pythagoras's Theorem and was I not immersed in the history of other nations as well as my own?

As I walked along the road I looked down at the thatched house where old Meg stayed. Sometimes one would see her coming from the shop with her red bloomers down about her big red fat legs. She went home to a house full of cats, hungry, ragged, vicious. Today there was no smoke from her chimney: perhaps she was lying in her bed. Her breath was much shorter than it used to be.

Outside his house old Malcolm was sharpening his scythe. I shouted, 'Hullo' to him and the scythe momentarily glittered in the sun as he turned towards me. His wife like a small figure on a Dutch clock came out and threw a basinful of water on the grass. 'Hullo,' I shouted as I felt myself coming home. Old Malcolm shouted in Gaelic that it was a fine day, and then spat on his hands.

The village returned to me again, every house, every wall, every ditch. It was so very different from Stornoway whose houses were crowded together, whose sea was thickly populated with fishing boats. I knew practically every stone in the village. At the same time I knew so much that didn't belong to the village at all.

Head bent over his scythe, Malcolm sharpened the blade, and I made my way home to the little house in which we lived. Very distantly I heard a cock crow in the middle of the afternoon, a traditional sign of bad luck. After it had crowed a dog barked and then another dog and then another one. Ahead of me stretched the sea, a big blue plate that swelled to the horizon on which a lone ship was moving.

'Huh, so you're home,' said my mother, 'you took your time.'

As my mother hardly ever went to town I came home to her as if from another land. She made me work at my books but the work I was doing was beyond her. Nevertheless she knew with a deep instinctive knowledge that learning was the road to the sort of reasonable life that she had never had.

'You're just in time to go out to the shop for me,' she said. 'You can have your tea when you come back. Get me some sugar and tea.'

I put my bag down on the oil-skinned table and took the money she gave me. I didn't particularly like to go to the shop, but at the same time I didn't strenuously object. As I was walking along the road I met Daial who had come home from the village school. Now that I had gone to the town school I was warier with him than I had been in the past. He asked me if I wanted a game of football and I said that I had to go on a message for my mother. He snorted and went back into his house.

When I had passed him, I met old deaf Mrs Macleod. She shouted at me as if against a gale, in Gaelic, 'And how is Iain today? You're the clever one, aren't you? Ask your mother if she wants to buy any milk. Anything going on in the town?'

I said I didn't know of anything. She came up and said, 'Your mother made that jersey, didn't she? I wonder what kind of wool it is. Your mother is a very good knitter.'

I squirmed under her hands. 'I'll have to get the pattern from her sometime,' she shouted into my ear. I almost felt my knees reddening with embarrassment.

When I left her I ran and ran, as if I wished to escape somewhere. Why were people always poking and probing? And yet I had been flattered when she said that I was the clever one.

I arrived at the shop and waited my turn. The shop sold everything from sugar to paraffin to methylated spirits for our Tilleys. Seonaid was talking to the woman who owned the shop and saying, 'Did you hear if war is declared yet? I'll take two loaves.'

'No,' said the other one.

I was gazing at the conversation sweets in the jars, and wished that I had money to buy some, but we were too poor.

'Nugget, did you say?' said the woman who owned the shop.

'Black,' said Seonaid. 'They won't wear brown shoes. Everything black or navy blue.'

'That's right,' said the shop owner. 'No, I never heard anything about the war.'

'That man Chamberlain always carries an umbrella,' said Seonaid. 'You'd think it was raining all the time.'

She turned to me and said, 'And how is Iain today? You're getting taller every time I see you. And are you doing well at the school?'

I murmured something under my breath but she soon forgot about me. I went to the door of the shop and I saw Peggy, a girl of my own age who was wearing a yellow dress. She also went to the village school.

'Hullo,' I said to her

'Hullo,' she said, looking at me with a slant laughing eye.

She was wearing sandals and her legs were brown. It was a long time since I had seen her and now I couldn't think of anything to say to her. She had used to sit beside me in Miss Taylor's class. She was the prettiest girl in the school. Once I had even written notes to her which Miss Taylor had never seen.

'Did you hear if war is declared?' I asked her, trying to look very wise.

'No,' she said, staring at me as if I were mad. Then she began to rub one sandal against the other.

'Are you liking the town school?' she asked, looking at me aslant and half giggling.

'It's all right,' I said. And then again. 'It's OK. We gamble with pennies,' I added. 'The school is ten times as big as the village school.'

Her eyes rounded with astonishment, but then she said, 'I bet I wouldn't like it.'

At that moment I looked up into the sky and saw a plane passing.

'That's an aeroplane,' I said

'I bet you don't know what kind it is,' said Peggy.

I was angry that I didn't know.

Suddenly Peggy dashed away at full speed shouting at the top of her voice, 'Townie, townie, townie.'

I went back into the shop lest anyone should see me. I was mad and ashamed, especially as I had loved Peggy so much in the past.

When I got home my mother said that I had taken my time, hadn't I? She began to talk about her brother who had been in a war in Egypt. 'He was a sergeant,' she said. 'But this time,' she continued, 'all the young ones will be in the war.'

I thought of myself as a pilot swooping from the sky on a German plane, my machine gun stuttering. I was the leader of a squadron of aeroplanes, and after I had shot the enemy pilot down I waggled the wings of my plane in final salute. He and I were chivalrous foes, though we would never recognise each other of because of the goggles.

'There's Tormod who'll have to go and Murchadh and Iain Beag.' She reeled off a list of names. 'There won't be anyone left in the village except old men and old women. I was in the First World War myself, at the munitions. Peggy was with me, and one time she pulled the communication cord of the train,' and she began to laugh, remembering it all, so that she suddenly looked very young and girlish instead of stern and unsmiling.

'The ones here will all go to the navy,' she said.

I hoped that the war wouldn't stop before I was old enough to join the RAF, or perhaps the army.

When I had finished my tea I went out. Daial was waiting and we went and played a game of football. Daial was winning and I said that one of the goals he claimed he had scored shouldn't be counted because the ball wasn't over the line. We glared at each other and were about to fight when he said he wouldn't count it after all. After we had stopped playing we began to wrestle and he had me pinned to the ground shouting, 'Surrender.' But I managed to roll away and then I had his arms locked and I was staring into his face while my legs rested on his stomach. Our two faces glared at each other, very close, so that I could see his reddening, and I could hear his breathing, Eventually I let him up and we ran a race, which he won.

I felt restless as if something was about to happen. It was as if the whole village was waiting for some frightening news. Now and again I would see two women talking earnestly together, their mouths going click, click, click.

I tried to do some homework but ships and planes came between me and my geometry. I was standing on the deck of a ship which was slowly capsising, looking at the boats which were pulling away. Not far from me there was a German U-boat. I remained on the deck for I knew that a captain always went down with his ship. The U-boat commander saluted me and I saluted him back. The water began to climb over my sandals, and my teeth chattered with the cold. I knew that the rest of the British Navy would avenge my death and that my heroic resistance would appear in the story books.

I looked up and my mother was standing looking at me with an odd expression on her face. However, all she said was, 'Get on with your lessons.'

'You wait,' I thought, 'you will read about me someday. Your sergeant brother won't be in it.'

I went out to the door, and saw Tinkan hammering a post into the ground. The hammer rose and fell and it looked as if he had been hammering for ever, his head bald as a stone bent down so that he didn't see me. In the distance I heard someone whistling. Why had Peggy called me a townie: there was no reason for that. But I would show her. Some day she would hear that I had died bravely winning the Victoria Cross or perhaps the Distinguished Conduct Medal. She would regret calling me a townie and in fact she might even show some of our notes to the man who came to write about me. Displacing the adverts on the front page of the local paper would be massive headlines: 'Local Hero Goes Down Fighting.'

I went over to the house next door and talked to Big Donald who as usual was wearing a blue jersey. He told me, 'There's no doubt of it. There will be a war in a day or two. No doubt of it,' he said, spitting into the fire. The globs of tobacco spit sizzled for a moment and then died. 'No doubt of it,' he said. 'And you'll see this village bare.'

'Thank God I don't have to go,' he said. 'But if I had been younger . . . ' and he made a sign as if he were cutting someone's throat with a knife. 'The Boche,' he said, 'were all right. But I didn't like the Frenchies. You couldn't trust a Frenchie. The Boche were good soldiers.' And he sighed heavily. 'Sometimes,' he added, 'we called him Fritz. But there's no doubt. We'll be at war in two or three days.'

I left him and stood at the door of our house before going in. I felt that something strange was about to happen, as if some disturbance was about to take place. Another plane crossed the sky and I stared up at it. It looked free and glittering in the sky, a quaint insect that buzzed up there by itself.

'Why aren't you coming in?' said my mother.

'I'm coming,' I shouted back, and as I shouted a dog barked.

I felt obscurely that the village would never be the same again, and it seemed to me that the standing stones which stood out in silhouette against the sky a mile behind our house had moved in the gathering twilight, with a stony purposeful motion.

'I'm coming,' I shouted again.

I went in and my mother arose from the table at which she had been sitting. She suddenly looked helpless and old and I thought she had been crying. 'Bloody Germans,' I thought viciously.

Suddenly my mother clutched me desperately in her arms and said, 'You'll have to carry on with your studying just the same.'

'Yes,' I said.

I trembled in her arms like the needle on a gauge. I was

rocking in her arms like a ship in the waves. Ahead of me through the window I could see the red sun setting like a cannon ball.

The Snow

On the first day that snow fell Lorna ran in and told her mother, who was washing clothes in the sink of the tenement kitchen.

'Come and see, mother,' she said in her flat Rhodesian voice.

'I haven't the time just now,' said her mother, who thought, So this is what we've come back down to, after that other dream. I can't even afford a washing machine.

'But, mother, I've never seen it before.'

'You go and look at it then.'

Lorna ran out and left her, and her mother was left alone, squeezing water out of the socks. John would be selling insurance at that very moment, lucky to have got a job at all. To start again wasn't easy, on a thousand pounds, all they could take out. Her heart was almost breaking, and if it was not for John and Lorna she would not have been able to go on. For it was from a tenement that she had started, and to a tenement she had now returned.

Those who had determined to stay would be still living in their big houses, or strolling under the jacaranda trees, singing their new Rhodesian songs which blossomed more strongly as the fighting came closer.

We shouldn't have come home, she thought, we should have stayed in the dream till the end. What is life after all but taking risks, and is it enough to have life if it is to be life in a tenement?

Though in fact the people in the tenement, Mrs Smith, Mrs Bruce, Mrs Scott, all believed in the rightness of her cause. 'The British people are behind you,' they told her while studying her bare rooms with satisfaction. 'These blacks are getting too big for their boots.' It was funny how it was the poor who supported them: they themselves were now the poor after being the rich.

Lorna had no grandparents, they were all dead. They had been very proud of John who had had such a big job in engineering. 'He is the top manager there,' her father would say, swinging his gammy leg along the promenade, the result of a war wound sustained when he was serving on a destroyer in the Mediterranean in the Second World War. 'These black bastards,' he would say, 'they should all be shot.' That was at the beginning when they had sometimes come home on holiday, before independence. She remembered her mother's thin pursed lips, her father's blubbery ones. They had in their time moved from tenement to tenement, flourishing briefly in shop after shop till finally they had to surrender the last one, as if they had reached the last trench of all. They had had so little, and she and John had had so much.

In fact they had got on well with the blacks, they had been respected by them. They had even voluntarily raised their wages. One couldn't say that they had not been fair. And now there was that stupid bishop who acted and thought like a child, when it was them and people like them who had fertilised Rhodesia, made it blossom.

What she missed most was the service: now she had to do everything herself. And what bothered her most was the coldness of the weather. Sometimes it took her all her time to get out of bed, to face that gritty British greyness. My heart will break, she thought, I miss the sun so much. I miss the comradeship. I miss the light. But it was John who had made her come back. 'It is all right for us,' he had pointed out, 'but what will it be like for Lorna? And if we stay we will be too old to move. Now we are not, quite.'

She hung the stockings in front of the fire, listening to the voices of children which came into the room in spite of the closed windows. I am back, she thought, to the place where my parents ended at, before John and I took that leap into the blue, and lived for a while in the fruitful garden. She felt like a Cinderella back in the cinders again after her life with the prince had failed. When she saw Ian Smith speaking on the TV with his strong determined face, and heard his flat Rhodesian voice, it was as if she wanted to cry, because she had been such a traitor as to leave. *O ye of little faith*, she heard, as if it was her mother speaking. In the evening, in summer, the old men walked along the promenade looking out at the sea and the setting sun. If only you had seen our sun, she almost screamed at them. She filled the kettle with water and made coffee for herself.

When I was young, she thought, my mother told me that I must marry well. 'Don't take one of the boys from the tenements,' she had told her, 'they all want to stay where they are.' And so she had married John. In those days the walk along the promenade or among the trees two miles away, had been enough. Holding hands in the café had been a heartbreaking joy. And now, my poor John, you are selling insurance from house to house because there is nothing else for you, under the hostile skies of treacherous Britain.

I can never forgive them that, their treachery. Perhaps we should have gone to America, even to France. Once a Pakistani had come to the door to sell clothes but she had shut it in his face. *Black bastards*, something in her had screamed, black stupid bastard, can we never be free from you? After all we did for you, you turn and spit in our faces. As she drank the coffee she heard her mother saying, *After all I've done for you, you're going abroad*. But she had forgiven herself by saying that wife must cleave to husband, flesh of the one flesh, and if John wanted to go how could she remain behind? She had left her parents in the tenement, their faces inflexible and set. And now she was back in a tenement very like theirs. History had turned on its wheel laughing at her, as if it was all a wooden decorated fair.

The voices of the children outside were faint yet clear. The socks steamed in front of the fire. Where there once had been carpets there was now linoleum. Someone on the radio was singing 'Bridge Over Troubled Water'. She switched it off. Abruptly she left the room and went outside, and standing at the door was dazzled.

'Mummy,' Lorna shouted, as she gathered snow in her hands and brought it over to her like a bouquet. A little Indian girl from one of the other closes gazed across at the two of them from the periphery of the snow.

My God, the whiteness, she thought. The coldness and the whiteness. The dazzle. Her mother was calling to her, as she slid down the long slope, but her father was waiting for her at the bottom.

Lorna placed her white bouquet in her arms, the blossom of winter, harvest of crystal, of diamonds. She stared down stupidly at the snow in her hands, watching it melt in the warmth.

As if the scene had been caught in slow motion she saw Lorna with her arms stopped and fixed, her lips slightly open, her eyes wide and blue.

Her father had brought her chocolate mice, and was handing them to her from his layers of clothes. She held them in her hand, stroking them, from head to tail. Their bodies were brown and elegant and beautiful.

Across the field of snow the little Indian girl, perfect and serious, was gazing across at her.

The snow dazzled her eyes, it was so miraculously white and stainless, the first manna of the year. The desert had suddenly flowered, the greyness had disappeared. She knelt down and touched it with her fingers, as if it were indeed a gift from heaven. Borne to her on the flat windless air, were the voices of other children elsewhere. Some of them were poor and half naked, some of them were rich and warm, and yet their voices were all similar. *Come in to your dinner*, she heard her dead mother saying, and her father winked at her secretively. Lorna and the little Indian girl were talking seriously together. They had both inherited the magic world of the snow. Unexpected, unheralded, it had come. With his insurance books under his arm John trudged through it, arriving at one house, then walking along the road again. His shadow was black on the white snow. Her eyes began to stream with tears as if the light was too strong for them. Through the tears she saw the two little girls talking to each other, consulting each other on some tremendous matter, as if it were a treaty or a manifesto. Her tears flashed in the whiteness, and then it was for a moment as if everything became black and she was dizzily teetering on her heels as she bent down, like a prospector, about to die.

Then the blackness cleared and there was the whiteness in front of her again. She stood up and shouted to Lorna, 'Don't be long now. Your dinner will soon be ready.' Then she went back into the house, leaving them to their grave flowing secrets.

In the Corridor

I see from the paper that Whippy's dead. He died in the Eventide Home, or so it says here. At the age of seventy. His real, full name appears to have been Charles James Macewan, but we called him Whippy, when he was teaching us in school, I mean, and as I look at this bare announcement without pity, without the necessity of flattery, my eyes suddenly flood with tears. She really looked so ugly and splay-footed to a boy of eleven as she walked away that day along the corridor, so ugly, and he . . . Of course he wasn't very handsome himself, though silver-haired then, and I always think of him as old, at least sixty, but comparing my own age with his, as it appears here, I think he must have been only forty-five then. But then people of forty-five look ancient to boys of eleven. Whippy taught me Science and he was called Whippy because he was in the habit of getting into tearing sudden rages and giving people six of the belt, though strangely enough no one disliked him or hated him or anything like that. I don't think he was a good scientist: he belonged to those days when the only equipment in a science room was a bunsen burner and some test tubes and an old sink in the corner. I myself was very good at science (still am) and Whippy used to stare at me in amazement when I would finish a problem he had set in three minutes flat. He would seem so unsure of himself, gazing at me as if I were some prodigy whom he both feared and distrusted. I can still remember that look of puzzlement private to the two of us. And yet I was only eleven and in those days I wore a brown woollen suit.

My story is not long, it consists only of a single moment, but then such moments perhaps reveal a whole life. And what was Whippy's life? Obviously he never married and he ended up in an Eventide Home as the notice of his death, bare and abbreviated, reveals. In those days he was perpetually engaged to a Miss Hewitt who taught in the French Department, an ugly splay-footed woman who seemed even older than he was. I never was taught by her and I never spoke to her in my whole life. All I can remember is the sight of her walking along a long corridor one afternoon in sunlight, so many years ago. And it all comes back to me now and I find myself crying. The human heart, how deep, how frightening it is, how reverberant with footsteps, how bright with almost extinct suns.

There were jokes of course about the two of them, and we all knew about the engagement. It had been a tradition in the school for many years, passed on from pupil to pupil, from class to class. It even occurred to us that his sudden rages were caused by tiffs with his loved one, for they were so quick and so maniacal, dying then to calm zephyrs so that one did not blame him really, but thought of him as one subject to an inexplicable illness. Once during one of them I saw him throw a huge book (perhaps an encyclopaedia) at a girl, missing her by inches, the book hitting the discoloured wall. He was tall and white-haired even then, his face red and pale by turns, fairly well dressed in a navy blue suit and, as a teacher, dedicated though limited.

It happened one particular afternoon. For some reason he had taken a liking to me or perhaps it was that he wanted me on his side. Just as the class was leaving the room he called me and asked me if I would go down town for him to buy some Beecham's Powders. I took the money, thinking to myself how I would tell the other pupils that there was something wrong with old Whippy's stomach, and amazed that he should show his weakness so openly to a boy of eleven. I thought the incident comic but of course I didn't show anything to him and truth to tell he spoke so quietly and so nicely that I was quite happy to go, quite apart from the fact that I would be able to dawdle about a bit downtown. I think he gave me a penny to buy something for myself.

Also in my minute pitiable way I was glad to be going an errand for a teacher.

Anyway I did go down to town and I bought the Beecham's Powders but in fact I didn't buy anything for myself though he had given me the penny. When I returned to the school I went along to the office to find out where he was and I was told that he was along in the staff-room. I walked along to the staff-room (even now I can see that small figure in its brown suit making its way rather fearfully along that stony road) and as I did so I looked along the long corridor and he was standing there looking after Miss Hewitt whose back was to him and to me, and who, squat and splay-footed in her dim suit, was about to disappear round the far end.'

'Sir,' I said as I came up to him, but he didn't appear to hear me. I spoke the word again and this time he turned round. His face was dead white as if he had been hit about the heart. His eyes didn't seem to be properly focussed. Then he seemed to realise who I was and who he was. He seemed to straighten and gather himself together as I looked at him and held out his hand for the Beecham's Powders and the change which I still clutched in my warm sweaty hand. As he did so a ring fell from his hand and on to the stone floor of the corridor. It bounced about, glittering, and rested a good distance away from us. I made as if to pick it up. It didn't occur to me that there was any significance in the ring, I didn't think about it, I didn't connect it with the disappearing Miss Hewitt. The only rings I had ever seen were small Woolworths rings with bright red stones. As I moved to pick it up he said, 'That will be all right, boy, that will be all right.' I ran along to my class, as I wanted to tell them all about the Beecham's Powders.

It is only now as I read this story in the newspaper that I realise what must have happened. She had broken off her engagement to him. I can still see her large, splay-footed body making its way steadily down the corridor to its far end, illuminated by shafts of sunlight coming in through the windows. And I think now, as then, how ugly she was. And that is why I cried there for that moment because she was so ugly and old and he didn't want me to pick up the ring and because he was standing there dazed, seeing ahead of him at that moment the exact announcement, bare and pitiless, that I have just read in this newspaper and whose necessity arose from that ugly splay-footed woman walking away from him down that long corridor with the school windows set at intervals, dusty and old, along one side.

Christine

She found the geriatric ward very interesting and weird. There was fat Mrs Ross whose husband had been dead for ten years and who believed she was going to have a baby.

'I think it will be a boy this time,' she would say to Christine. 'We never had a boy. It was all girls.' Then she would look proudly down at her big belly and say, 'Can you not hear him move.' Her grey hair straggled on the pillow.

There was Mrs Simmons who dressed up every day and stood waiting for the taxi which would take her back to the tenement she had lived in nine years before and which no longer existed.

'Hugh is not usually late. I can't understand it,' she would say, and then, 'I can't find my handbag.'

Outside the window the birds were singing and the trees had put out their first leaves of spring.

'Have you done your homework?' said Miss Leggat, who had been a primary teacher.

'Yes,' said Christine as she tucked in the sheet.

'Well, then,' said Miss Leggat, 'I think you should do your physical jerks. Legs together, legs apart, legs together.' And Christine would do her exercises till Miss Leggat was satisfied.

'I wonder why my bed is wet,' Miss Leggat would say.

'That is because you have wet it yourself,' said Christine.

'Not at all, not at all, that woman must have been in my bed,' and she pointed to the occupant of the next bed who was staring into space.

'Make sure that you do your homework. How else will you get on in the world?'

Christine sang as she moved about the ward.

Miss Campbell called her by the name Helen and thought that she was her daughter.

'When are you going to take me out of here?' she would say.

'It won't be long now,' said Christine.

Miss Leggat talked regularly to her mother who had been dead for twenty years.

'I am sorry,' she would say, 'I'll come in when I've finished playing.'

Her face became dreamy and lost and she would speak to her dolls.

'I don't know my own name,' Christine would say to herself, but she was happy for she liked working with old people. Her own mother had died when she herself was fifteen and she was now eighteen. She had died of cancer. Her father had wept for a whole day and then had gone fishing as he had done in the past. But what was worst of all he had begun to drink heavily.

'God is a bugger,' he would say. 'What else is there to do?'

'Is that not my taxi now?' said Mrs Simmons but it was actually a taxi to take the nurses to the dance.

They left her with no handbag standing beside the door, crying gently.

'If I stay here long I shall go off my head,' said Christine to herself as she emptied a bedpan while the sun poured in through the windows.

'My child is due any day now,' said Mrs Ross. 'He will be a big bouncing boy. I just know it.'

Her daughters never visited her, and she would sing Scottish songs when it came into her head. Sometimes she would whisper a lullaby very low.

'Is this what we are going to come to?' said Christine to herself for she did not want to go home especially as her father was drinking so heavily. She remembered the day her mother had been buried. The young minister had worn a black cloak, and she had seen the sheep nuzzling at the bushes not far from the graveyard. The other fishermen had been there in their black clothes, standing solidly on the earth, after the swaying motion of their boats. The coffin had descended among a hum of bees. A black head had lifted itself from the bushes.

'I will now take your name,' said Miss Leggat opening an imaginary register.

Christine nearly said Helen but caught herself in time.

'Christine,' she said. If only that taxi would come. But then taxis were black as hearses.

'And what are you going to be when you grow up?' said Miss Leggat brightly.

'I shall be a nurse,' said Christine.

'A nurse. That's very good. That's very good indeed. But will you like a hospital?'

Her father stumbled in the door and went straight to the bathroom and vomited. There were scales of fish on his hands.

The sea heaved about her, and through one of the waves she could see her mother's face twisted in pain.

'Helen,' said Miss Campbell, 'I wish you would come in earlier. And what was that I found in your room last night?'

'It was nothing at all,' she nearly screamed. 'And anyway it isn't your business.'

She looked around her, frightened that she might actually have spoken.

'Is there anything wrong?' said Sister Hogg. 'You should go out more. Why don't you go to a dance?'

'I met your mother at a dance,' said her father tearfully, 'She was wearing a yellow dress. We danced the Highland Schottische.'

His vomit was as yellow as the sun and he writhed in her arms as she tried to put him to bed.

The leaves became greener and greener and she saw the sheep through the window of the ward.

Miss Leggat was dying and said, 'Now you make sure that you pass all your examinations. I have done my best for you. Your English is good but your Arithmetic is weak.'

'Please don't leave me,' Christine pleaded in silence. 'I'll do the physical jerks.' And she did them but when she looked at the bed Miss Leggat's eyes were blank, and her mouth had fallen open.

'It was only to be expected,' said Sister Hogg. 'Your colour isn't good.'

Christine thought she was referring to the crayons but didn't say anything.

'If only the taxi would come,' but the taxi never came.

'If only the child would be born,' but the grey haired woman stared proudly at her belly and nothing happened.

The floor of the ward swayed, as if it were the sea, and the sheep looked in at the window.

'Helen,' said Mrs Campbell.

Is she really dead, thought Christine.

'She kept the register beautifully and she was so lonely. She had no one but her pupils all her days.'

She dreamed that the taxi came for Mrs Simmons and that she found her handbag. She dreamed that a child crawled about the floor of the ward and was taught Arithmetic by Miss Leggat. She dreamed that Helen came to see Mrs Campbell.

Sister Hogg kept asking her if she was well.

Miss Leggat sat up in her coffin and marked the register among a dense hum of bees.

When she herself looked in the mirror she thought that her hair was turning grey. The chairs by the side of the beds became branches. There is something I have to do, she thought, but I don't know what it is. The sockets of the old women were as pink as the legs of seagulls; and they hardly ever slept.

At visiting time she sat by the side of Mrs Campbell's bed and told her that she had come to see her. Her name was Helen and she was sorry for having been out every night.

'I am glad you came,' said Mrs Campbell, 'someone is stealing my money.'

Sister Hogg told her to come with her for a while and led her out of the ward.

'I think you should take a holiday,' she said.

'I would do that,' said Christine, 'if it weren't for the sheep. And anyway I have to wait for the baby.'

'What baby?'

'Mrs Ross's baby, of course.' It was odd how pink Sister Hogg's sockets were.

'I see.'

'And Miss Leggat is going to teach him Arithmetic. I shall go on holiday when the taxi comes.'

'What taxi?'

'The hearse,' she said. 'There will be lots of flowers.'

Sister Hogg took her hand in hers and looked deep in her eyes. Her own eyes were frightened to death.

'Come,' she said.

How sunlit the corridor was, and her hand in her mother's hand was warm and trusting.

They walked together to another room in which Miss Leggat, young and beautiful and clad in white was marking a register.

Christine sat down obediently in a chair.

'My name is Helen,' she said, 'and my father drinks all the time.' She added, 'When the taxi comes don't forget to let me know.'

Miss Leggat opened a drawer and a baby came out pink as a seagull's leg. It howled and howled and howled, and all around it the bees hummed and the birds sang.

The Kitten

The first time she saw the kitten it was at the railway line and she was frightened the train would run over it. It was small and entirely black, and it crouched with unblinking eyes staring at her. She knew that there would be a train in fifteen minutes or so and she walked along the railway track towards the kitten, which was still waiting. She pretended not to look at it as she plodded along in her wellingtons. Then quite suddenly she bent and scooped it up in her arms. It dug its claws into her but she didn't release it. She lifted it till it was lying against her breast. She had decided to take it home.

As she was walking through the long wet grass to the house she felt it struggling and told herself, 'The only reason I am taking it is because it may be killed by the train or some other animal.' But she wasn't sure that that was the real reason. If her mother were still alive she wouldn't have wanted a kitten in the house. She disliked cats and dogs, indeed all animals. She herself had once brought a kitten home after being given it by a fellow pupil but her mother had made her give it back that same night. Her mother had died two years ago, after an illness impatiently borne.

When she arrived at the house she opened the back door which led into the kitchen and then shut it quickly behind her. She laid the kitten down and it raced round the chairs as if it were mad. She went to the cupboard and filled a saucer with milk and laid it on the floor. The kitten was crouched in a corner watching her steadily. 'Puss, puss,' she said but it didn't move. It didn't go near the milk. She thought she would leave it in the kitchen and went into the living-room pulling the door shut behind her. She took out the paper and began to read it, all the time thinking about the kitten.

She read a story about a bachelor son who had killed his mother with an axe. When she herself was twenty-six she had tried to run away from home, from her own mother. She had somehow sensed that it was her last chance to do so. As she was making her way to the train with her case her mother who was shouting after her seemed to stagger and fall. She had run back over the autumn leaves, case in hand, thinking that she had killed her. She had helped her into the house, given her some brandy, and revived her. That was her last attempt at escaping.

While she was reading the paper she could hear the kitten scratching against the outside door. After a while it quietened down. She slowly opened the door and saw it lapping the milk. When it heard her it turned and looked at her and then went back to drinking, its eyes slant and inscrutable. She opened the door into the scullery and it ran through behind her into a corner where there was an old jacket. She decided to make tea for herself and put on the kettle. For some time after her mother had died she would put out two cups but now she always remembered only to put out one. She drank her tea slowly and all the time the kitten on the other side of the door was quiet.

Strangely enough, she missed her mother even though it seemed as though she had hated her most of her life. But though she realised that she had no love left for her, her death had almost broken her. She hadn't realised that emptiness was worse than hate. When she used to go for the messages her mother would say, 'What took you so long? I thought something had happened to you.' Now she watched a lot of TV though she didn't particularly care for any of the programmes. After so many years of enforced isolation no one came to see her.

In the morning she left the outer door open when she went for the coal and the kitten ran out, disappearing quickly through the garden under the bird house and into the long grass which led down to the railway line. She didn't know what it lived on. She thought that probably it wouldn't come back. No one much had ever liked her and it wasn't surprising that the kitten didn't either. She sometimes felt that she exuded an odour of complete negativity. 'I think you want to put me into a home,' her mother would say. 'But I won't go.'

In actual fact she had never considered putting her mother into a home. She now thought that the reason she hadn't done so was because she had a sixth sense of what loneliness would mean. She even used her mother to keep away from people and also to avoid tasks which she didn't want to do. She had in fact exploited her mother as much as her mother had exploited her. For instance the minister had wondered whether she would like to play the organ in the church but she had made the excuse that she couldn't leave her mother. In the same manner she had managed to evade serving on committees. Many people admired her for her sacrifice but that didn't mean they liked her.

She wondered what might have happened if she had escaped that day. She had intended to take the train to Glasgow and find a job there, but the odd thing was that afterwards when she replaced her clothes in the wardrobe she found that she hadn't taken a toothbrush or a nightdress. Perhaps she hadn't really meant to go at all. Perhaps she had been waiting for her mother to stop her. She tried to imagine herself serving in a shop in Glasgow. But the thought didn't feel very detailed or real.

That day she had ham and potatoes and tinned pineapples for her dinner and all the time she was wondering if the kitten would come back. Its wild eyes had disturbed her, and yet she was afraid that it would be killed. It belonged to a world that she could hardly envisage, hedgerows, ditches, deep, thick bracken. What things preyed on kittens? Perhaps stoats, weasels, big birds. She saw it eeling through the greenery, stalking birds, mice, voles. She shivered thinking of the darkness of its surroundings, of the secret scurryings, of the broken slummy places among which it might move. Its adventures frightened and yet attracted her.

In the afternoon a letter came addressed to her mother. She stared at it in amazement and after crying a little put it into the waste-paper basket. It was about some furniture or other. She stared out of the window at the people passing along the road, some of them glancing in but not able to see her. There was Cathie and Mary, and Jimmy who worked at the quarry. At night many of the villagers would go to the local hotel for a drink. The kitten definitely wouldn't come back. It had taken one look at her and decided that it didn't like her. Its eyes were too wild and free and too piercing. In a strange sort of way she didn't want it to come back.

She read a book and prepared for early bed. She had switched on the electric blanket and couldn't help but compare her own comfort with the wet spaces through which the kitten might be compelled to wander. Before she went to bed she opened the door which led from the kitchen and looked out but she couldn't see the kitten. There was a moon high in the sky, very bright, like a brilliant barren stone. She snuggled into her bed and was soon asleep. She didn't dream at all.

In the morning she had another look out but the kitten was not to be seen and she determined to forget about it: for all she knew it might now be dead. Nevertheless she put some milk on the saucer. That day she washed her clothes and hung them out on the line to dry. There were still some roses in bloom but most of their petals were lying on the ground.

She took in more coal and filled all her buckets. She hoovered the house and dusted the furniture and the pictures. She stood for a long while gazing at a photograph of her mother who was wearing a white blouse and black skirt: the face was very determined and there was a big brooch at the throat. Her hate for her had disappeaed and she could almost begin to understand her. After all, who wanted to be old, to be a nuisance? Who wasn't frightened of being put in a home?

She herself might end up in a home when she grew old and weak. But that, she hoped, would not be for a few years yet since she was only fifty-four. Her whole life, she realised, had been meaningless and without substance; she might as well not have been born. She had hardly any memories to recall, except ones of childish deprivation.

One night when she had come home from a school dance she had found her mother crouched in a corner of the living-room. 'Whore,' she had shouted. Her father took her into the kitchen and said: 'Your mother is not well. You had better sleep in the spare bedroom.' It had been a full moon that night too.

She stood at the door watching the clothes balloon from the line. She found it a special pleasure to watch them as if they were sails of different colours. But the pegs had them fixed and no matter how much they might have wanted to float all over the countryside they couldn't do so. They flapped and swelled and sometimes on calm days they hung like motionless pictures, flat and rectangular in an airy art gallery. She had given away most of her mother's clothes to that Red Cross woman who had called shortly after her mother's death.

The kitten didn't come that afternoon either. It was odd how even thinking of it gave her something to do, a possible future. But it was as it had always been in the past; the future was in the waiting. No, she would not go in search of it, she was too proud for that, its coming would have to be a voluntary one. They said that, more than dogs, cats chose their owners.

It was they who decided whether to come and stay with you. Maybe if Raymond had been really serious about her he would have come and stayed with herself and her mother. And now he was married to a girl in Glasgow much younger than himself. All her boyfriends had been frightened away by her mother. She could be very dour, strong-willed, and savage in her hates.

She often thought of that day when she had tried to run away. Actually there had been nothing at all wrong with her mother – she had faked what looked on the surface like a heart attack. She could see the train turning the corner when her mother ran out screaming. She should have stayed till her mother was out of the house, at church perhaps, before making her effort to escape. It was odd that she had made the attempt when there was a chance of her mother catching her.

That night she looked out again but there was no sign of the kitten and the moon was still bright and clear. There was the last fragrance of roses in the air. Soon it would be harvest time, with its sharp stubbly forsaken fields.

The next day there was a high wind and she felt that it was lucky that she had brought the washing in. The windows shook in their wooden frames and a fence billowed and swelled. Buzzards were tossed about the sky. The grass swayed to one side in the power of the wind.

I'm frightened, she thought, Lord knows what will happen. She didn't know much about repairing doors or fences and suddenly the house felt vulnerable and helpless. It was about three o'clock in the afternoon that she saw the kitten. It was moving stealthily through the garden, now and again caught by a draught of wind that ruffled its fur. She opened the scullery door even though the wind was rushing through. 'Come in, you stupid beast,' she shouted. She heard the banging of the windows, and the linoleum on the kitchen floor lifted like a blue wave.

And then the kitten was at the door, bedraggled and drenched, for suddenly it had started to rain furiously. She watched it enter and then shut the door behind it against the force of the wind. The kitten went over to the saucer and lapped the milk and then looked up at her. Cautiously she bent and tried to touch, it but it struck out with its needly paw. Its eyes were wild and cold and inhuman.

But she knew that it would return. Whenever it was in trouble it would return. And then gradually it would come more and more often. Eventually it would grow fat and never leave the house at all. It would stop its sudden flurries and rushes and settle down in a basket. It might have memories of past encounters with other animals but these would fade. And in fact it would sense that wild kittens were its enemies.

'I shall call you Safety,' she said in a wheedling voice, that she hardly recognised as her own. It was really very beautiful, so black and so groomed. Its eyes like pieces of jewellery gazed at her.

She was suddenly surprised to find herself crying. What was she crying for? She couldn't understand it. And all the time she was crying the kitten was staring at her unwinkingly. If she touched it it would attack her as if it hated her. It would strike with its needle-sharp claws. She wiped her eyes and got a ball of wool. 'Pretty Safety,' she said, 'pretty Safety.' It watched the swaying ball with disarming intensity, its head held on one side.

The Parade

The night before their son's passing-out parade they stayed in a hotel not far from the air base where the ceremony would take place.

'How's the leg?' she asked. Gerald didn't answer. These days when he did talk it was mostly about money, about the decreasing value of his pension; or was abrupt and ironical when she bought a new hat as every woman had to do now and again.

'If you happened to have a cat you could swing it in here,' she commented as the two of them eased their way into the small hotel bedroom which they had entered at midday after their long train journey. Outside the window she could see the two Dobermann pinschers, long-legged and somehow obscenely naked, which the landlady had mentioned.

Trevor had sent them a photograph of his flight, all sixty of them, sitting with peaked caps like visors, their hands resting in regulation fashion on their knees. After his history of untidy bedrooms and raucous music, he seemed settled happy and proud. Gerald had not looked at the photograph. Her own memory of 1940 was one of young scarved pilots and bright blue skies. At least she had made him put on his best suit for the occasion and he really looked quite smart. She had saved up to buy a new costume for herself: it was made of red velvet.

Saving on taxis they took the bus out to the base and she herself talked for a while to a harassed-looking woman who told her that her son had wanted to leave in the fourth week and only a prolonged phone call from his older brother had made him stay on: 'And now,' she said proudly, 'he is passing out.' It seemed as if she couldn't bring herself to believe it. There was also a man from Dorset who told the two of them that he himself had served, of course, in the Navy, and that he had enjoyed it very much. Leaning over to Gerald, he said, 'My father was a sailor, you know. He was hardly ever at home, and so I decided that I would treat my own sons right.' Gerald didn't answer: Norma thought that as he stood there speechlessly in the cold he seemed to be like someone who had suffered a stroke. She saw him smiling ironically as the Welsh woman gabbled on about the benefits of service life. 'At least you know where they are,' she said in her sing-song voice. 'And they learn discipline, don't they?' Her Welsh husband told the bus driver that they were all there to join up. The driver laughed, but not a great deal; it was possible that he had heard the feeble joke many times before from nervous parents.

When they arrived at the base, they were all ushered into a room where coffee was served, and they were handed a programme by a young pale airman who looked too frightened to speak. He called Norma, 'Ma'am' and Gerald, 'Sir'. She saw through the window a plane lying out on the field, and the flat panorama of the English countryside. They sat at their table drinking their coffee, and not saying very much. She examined carefully the clothes the other women were wearing and concluded that her red velvet costume made her seventh in the league but that her rings came twenty-sixth. Gerald on the other hand came quite high in the ranks she had made in her mind, as he had, naturally, a handsome appearance which seemed to conceal the inexpensiveness of his suit. A grey-haired sergeant came in and told them about the morning's programme. In a short while they would re-enter the bus and be taken to the seats at the edge of the square where the parade would take place. He said, introducing himself, 'I'm the one who's been polishing your boys' boots.' All the parents laughed. It was like being in school again. Gerald was flexing his leg under the table and was, as usual, silent. She thought, not for the first time, that it was a great strain being married to him. She glanced at the programme: everything had been timed to the minute.

After about a quarter of an hour they went into the bus and

were taken to the square. There was in fact a fleet of buses, each painted air force grey. When she got off the bus, she felt the wind cold and bitter, though luckily it wasn't raining. If it had been raining, the parade would have been held in a hangar. 'Oh, look,' she said excitedly to Gerald, 'I can seen them. Do you see them over there? They must be rehearsing.' But Gerald didn't look. They sat beside each other in the front row and she took out her camera. There was a cheer when a young girl, possibly the girl friend of one of the aircraftsmen, crossed the square in a slit skirt which was practically blowing around her carefully coiffured hair. An officer stood on the dais and tested the microphone. 'I am the chap who's been bringing early morning tea to your son,' he said. They all laughed dutifully. A corporal took his place and also tested the microphone. 'One two,' he said. 'Can't you count to three?' the officer shouted. 'Three,' said the corporal, stony-faced. Why, they were all comedians. The officer looked nice and relaxed and young. She thought he might be a flight lieutenant, but she didn't really know. Another man, with a crown at his sleeve, marched extravagantly across the square, as if he were flapping wings and trying to get off the ground. The young officer stood on the wooden dais again, and told them, 'The reviewing officer will arrive in a blue car whose headlights will be on. You are expected to stand. You are also expected to stand when he leaves.' Gerald's face twitched and she turned back to the square again. Maybe the training hadn't been so harsh after all: these officers and NCOs looked quite human. She checked that her camera was ready.

Then she saw them, led by the band, all in grey, arms swinging very high, boots shining, buttons glittering. There were four flights, and they took up their position by their markers making quick scurrying movements as they got into line. An officer with a sword stood in front of them, and they stood easy after being at attention. They were facing her but she couldn't see Trevor at all. At first she thought it was the spectacled one at the extreme right of the front rank, but, no, it wasn't, though he looked very like him.

People were standing up and peering and wondering where their own sons were. She felt part of a group, united by common preoccupations, though she had never seen the other parents in her life before. Now and again Gerald would shiver in the cold. Then the reviewing officer was driven to the dais, the car arriving in an arrogant curve round the perimeter of the square. The driver opened the door for him, and his assistant, whatever rank he was, accompanied his superior to the platform. They both stood there, still and proud. The reviewing officer had a sword dangling at his side. Indeed, all the officers had swords.

The one who had been in charge of things marched briskly up to the reviewing officer, came to attention and said in a loud voice, 'Permission to carry on, SIR.' She couldn't make out what the reviewing officer said but assumed that he had agreed. The flights came to attention and the reviewing officer descended the dais, his assistant discreetly accompanying him, and moved between the ranks, pretty quickly, only stopping to speak to some recruit. As he left a flight behind, it stood easy. The reviewing officer, whose rank she could see from her programme was Group Captain, also apparently had a degree from Cambridge. He moved briskly and competently and with a natural air of authority. Gerald's brother had gone to Cambridge and was now on television in Canada: she didn't like him much. The reviewing officer returned to the dais. She saw that Gerald's knuckles were white.

Then the flights began to march to the music. They were all carrying rifles, with bayonets attached, and they all seemed to have become automatons in weeks. Where are you, Trevor, she thought, frantically searching for him. But all the recruits looked alike, each with his ominous peaked cap, pale, distant, almost aloof, listening to commands from other people who had swords in their hands. It was frightening how tidy and proficient they had become. They presented arms and ordered arms and everyone was supernaturally precise, even Trevor whom she had at last identified. And the proudest moment of all was when two planes (limited perhaps by the Thatcher budget) flew overhead in a sudden roar and then were gone as quickly as they had come. Trevor looked like all the others. She didn't like his tidy unshadowed poise.

After a while the reviewing officer spoke to them. He told them that he and the officers and NCOs were all proud of what they had accomplished: they could all hear from the cheering how proud their parents were of them as well. They had now joined a great family in which every job was important, from cook to pilot. They were a credit to everyone, a future full of possibilities was ahead of them, he himself was proud of them.

Then they marched off, eyes turned towards the reviewing officer. I don't like this, she thought, I don't like this. Seven weeks ago my son was telling me where I could get off, earning money not a fraction of which he gave me, coming in late, leaving lights burning through the night even though he knows that we don't have much money, keeping the volume of his record player high even though he knows his father doesn't like it. And now here he is, entirely transformed, cold, disciplined, remote, in a world of his own which I have never entered and never will.

She turned round as if to say something of this to Gerald and saw that his eyes were slowly filling with tears and she knew that as was the case with herself, they were tears of pride. That was the closest she could get to it. Maybe they were tears dropped for the adventurous baby growing up to the sullen adolescent. Maybe they were an elegy for lost youth, or for a suddenly grasped ideal world where everything moved like clockwork, co-ordinated and accurately ranked. Maybe the tears were for the shades of what she and Gerald had once been; and now she realised that there was much about her husband, especially this, that she had never known. Maybe it was the cold wind that brought the tears out. But, no, she felt them as the salt fruit of shameless pride. And so when she walked round the parade ground with Gerald, instead of taking the bus, she knew that he would welcome Trevor and make a fuss of him as he had used to do, but this time almost as an equal. And her own tears were for that as well, that Trevor should suddenly be as old as Gerald, and also for the fact that the two of them inhabited a world which could be only truly known by experience: and that indeed her own knowledge of what had taken place on that square had only been a partial one, and almost uncomprehending. Trevor in fact was waiting for them when they arrived in the building for lunch: he looked respectful, slightly remote, astonishingly grown up. Gerald ordered two whiskies, for himself and Trevor, and a Cinzano and lemonade for her.

The Yacht

Ralph didn't like it when his father began to sit alone on the balcony of his hotel reading his Greek poetry again, while his mother tanned herself among the rocks. So rather than be with either of them he wandered along the promenade and the streets of the small Yugoslavian town. One morning he saw a man with a prong landing a small, purple squid on the stone, and he studied the fish for a long time, for the man had walked away and left it there as if it was too small for him to bother about.

He spent a whole afternoon watching children playing on swings. One of them was a small but determined-looking girl who swung as high into the air as she could, giving herself stronger and stronger pushes, while the boy tried to emulate her but failed to reach the heights she did, for it seemed as if her ambition was to be lost in the sky up above her. After a while the boy and the girl got off their swings and began to chase each other and fight, throwing little stones and small branches and twigs at each other, while a bare-armed woman watched impassively from a balcony above the street. Later, after the boy had been defeated by the girl, he climbed into a tree with a companion and they began to halloo like Tarzans in their own language which Ralph didn't understand. More children arrived and fought each other and formed a ring around a little boy who had begun to cry and then after being mocked ran away with tears streaming down his face.

Ralph no longer cried. There had been a time when he had cried when his father and mother had quarrelled most bitterly but he didn't cry now. He had formed an armour around himself like the shell of a sea animal. There had been so many of these quarrels between his mother and his father (his mother younger than his father who was a university lecturer). There were things that his mother shouted at his father that he didn't want to hear. Once she had frothed at the mouth with rage and had bitten his father like a beast. Now, every day, she lay in the sun, her blonde hair gleaming, while his father read his Greek poems. Soon she would meet someone, she always did.

Ralph sat down among the rocks further away from the centre of the town than the ones his mother lay among, watching a yacht out in the bay, on the far rim of the horizon a white ghost. He stared at it for a long time. It became confused in his mind with the white page of the Greek poetry book which his father was reading. It seemed different from the other nearer yachts, more remote, less domestic, and he never saw anyone moving about on it, no one tending ropes or sails, it simply stayed there without moving, day after day.

He liked sitting doing nothing. Now and again an old woman in black would pass, a native of the place, and she would gaze past him as if he wasn't there. 'What they must have suffered,' his father had once said to his mother when they had seen one such old woman strolling along the promenade, wrinkled, ancient, as if sprung from another earlier world.

'What do you mean, suffered?' said his mother who was painting her toenails.

'In the war,' his father had said, and his mother had smiled secretly. Ralph preferred his father to his mother. He knew that deep down his mother didn't care for him, and thought only of herself, of her own appearance, was always tending to her body.

Ralph liked looking into the water where everything could be seen clearly and without equivocation. He liked the little coloured umbrellas of the jelly fish, the quick motions of the tiny unnamed fish. He would watch them for hours. Sometimes too he would pick up smooth stones and stroke them.

Once he saw a group of youths – he thought they were German – jumping from the end of the pier into the sea. Then they left the pier and got hold of one of their companions whom they carried struggling towards the end of the pier and threw over. They were laughing and the youth was struggling but after he had come out of the water he walked back to them, smoothing his hair, and pretending that it was all a big joke. But Ralph knew that it wasn't a big joke after all. He realised that the drenched youth was only pretending that it was a joke, that he was trying to get back to his own kind. Ralph had often felt like that in the school he attended, a boarding school. When the youth returned to the group they had forgotten all about him and were listening to their leader who was pointing something out to them on a map.

Ralph didn't like going back to the hotel in the evening and above all he didn't like the dining-room. His mother had taken to talking to two Scandinavian youths who sat at the next table, while his father sat there with a fixed smile on his face. His mother laughed and chattered to the Scandinavians – she could always find something to talk about – and they clearly admired her. She wore a low-cut dress and you could see her breasts. Even when she was asking for the key to the room she would talk for ages to the receptionist who was a German and had corn-coloured hair. Later she and his father would walk in silence to the lift. Then his mother would ask his father if he wanted to come down to the bar but he didn't want to and sometimes she would go down on her own. Ralph would go into his own room and fiddle with the radio. He preferred it when he found some music to which he could listen.

One evening they all went to a classical concert in the local church which felt very cool after the heat outside. A young woman who was very beautiful sang German, Italian, French and English songs, while a pianist, dark-haired and in evening dress, hammered the keyboard with relentless passion. While the woman was singing Ralph's eyes wandered about the church studying the paintings, one of which showed a shrunken Christ bleeding on the cross while a number of people stared up at him. The woman sang *Swing Low Sweet Chariot* with a strange foreign endearing accent. She was very cool and almost remote but the pianist played with furious abandon, expressions of tenderness and agony chasing each other across his face. His father listened intently but his mother left the church at the interval and didn't come back.

His father pretended that he knew she was going to do this but Ralph knew that her departure had been unexpected for his father kept glancing behind him now and again in the middle of the music as if wondering whether she was going to come in. The church was cool and there were a number of Americans there: you could always tell Americans.

An old woman in black entered the church during the performance, curtsied to the altar, waited for a while and then left. It was clear that she did not understand the music. Ralph imagined her walking along the hot cobbled stones. When he and his father arrived back at the hotel his mother wasn't there. Ralph didn't say anything about this nor did he comment when his father poured out some whisky for himself from the bottle he had bought in the duty-free shop on the way over.

Ralph couldn't understand his father. He couldn't understand how he could let his mother insult him as she did. Why didn't he hit her? If a boy had insulted him as his mother insulted his father he would have felt honour bound to try and fight him even if he lost. But his father accepted all the insults and had once said to Ralph, 'You see, I love her.'

Once when the two of them were walking along together his mother had insisted on buying a small blue painting from a street artist whom she took a fancy to.

'It's rubbish,' his father had said. 'It's not much better than a postcard. It's certainly not worth six pounds.' But she had given the street artist, who was young and handsome and impudent, seven pounds and then kissed him dramatically on the cheek. His father had walked away.

Ralph would sit sometimes under a tree in the shade and watch the ants. There were thousands of them and they all rushed about at great speed as if on urgent errands. They would push little twigs ahead of them and their quickness was beyond belief. It was as if you couldn't use the word 'speed' about them, one second they were here and the next there. He would watch them for hours and also the butterflies which swarmed about drunkenly in the warm air. It gave him a great feeling of power to watch the ants, and freedom, to watch the butterflies. He felt that the ants were not conscious of his presence, though perhaps they were: perhaps they sensed him like a huge shadow above them.

Behind all this he could hear the voice of his mother saying, 'But you must admit his hair is beautiful.' His father was almost bald and had hardly tanned at all. He had a thin face which was as white as paper. He pretended not to see his wife sunning herself on the rocks, he pretended not to see the casual way in which she turned on her back when a particularly attractive man passed.

The pages of his book were white in the dazzling day, as white as the sails of the yacht on the far horizon.

Once Ralph saw his mother dancing with a man who had climbed onto the pier from a boat. The man was wearing a pirate cap, he was fat and flabby, and he was singing. His mother danced with him while some of the other men and women also in pirate caps watched and clapped.

Then she suddenly turned and waved to his father who was sitting on the balcony reading. But he did not raise his eyes from his book and did not wave back.

Sometimes Ralph would follow one of the old women dressed in black to the church. He would watch her as she curtsied and bent her head to pray, he would sit quietly at the back of the church and study the painting of the bleeding Christ. Then just as quietly as he had entered he would leave. Even quite late there were swarms of people on the cobbled street, and once four youths shouted after him in a language that he didn't understand. There were two girls with them and they laughed at something the boys said. The boys were older than Ralph, perhaps seventeen: he was fourteen.

As he was coming back to the hotel he saw on the seats outside, under the trees, his mother sitting with the two Scandinavians. They were all laughing and drinking. He knew that his father would be sitting on the balcony reading, exactly like one of those white statues he had seen in the museum.

He had a dream. In the dream he dreamt that he was a girl and that he was on a swing and that he was swinging so high that he eventually disappeared into the sky. A boy was flinging stones up at him but he was so high up that they could not touch him. In the middle of the dream he heard a book being thrown against a wall and his mother's voice shouting, 'You and your f—— books.' His mother while beautiful was also very lively. Everyone in the hotel seemed to like her, even the waiters who hardly smiled at the tourists but laughed and joked among themselves in small secret groups. Once at dinner time while he was sitting in a park he had seen an old woman approaching one of the waitresses with a child and the waitress had kissed it, had swung it over her head, had bought an ice-cream for it, had walked it carefully along a low wall, and taken it to the swings. All this time the old woman sat on a bench knitting. Then after a quarter of an hour or so the waitress had given the child back to the old woman but the child had cried a great deal and while he was doing so the waitress had hurried back to her work in the hotel, not looking back.

All these things Ralph saw because he was on his own. He was used to being on his own even in school. He didn't like Greek but he was good at literature and mathematics. There were boys in the school especially in classes higher than his own who seemed to him to be at least as handsome and godlike as the Scandinavians.

One night he followed a young girl who looked back at him and waved. She was tanned like a gipsy, then quite suddenly she disappeared: one moment she was there and the next she was not to be seen at all. He wondered if she had gone into the church but when he did enter the church there was no one there. He stared up towards the roof and there seemed to be a man there, bent over, reading a book. It was odd how he had not noticed him before.

His father got up that evening from his seat in the dining-room and left his mother talking to the Scandinavians. He had stalked towards the door. Later, from his parents' room, he had heard his mother shouting at his father, 'Bad mannered bastard. Can't I talk to anyone now?'

He didn't hear his father speak at all. Then he had heard the door slam and the sound of his father crying. He had never heard a grown man crying before. It was a terrible sound, it was like cloth tearing. He didn't want to see his father, so he left his room and crept down the stairs. He heard laughter from the bar and saw beneath a television screen, where a man was reading from a newspaper, his mother and the Scandinavians sitting at the one table. As he made his way outside she saw him and the laughter froze, her mouth open in astonishment. But he ran away and as he was running he heard another man saying to another man, 'The *Canberra* has been sunk,' and he knew that this was something to do with the Falklands.

He wandered aimlessly along the street, and glanced at a head set in a wall, its mouth open in stone. You could see many of these heads, ancient and flaking, sometimes ugly, sometimes beautiful. He saw in one of the souvenir shops which was still open an old woman, dressed in black, who seemed to be arguing with a patient shopkeeper about money while two other women looked in laughing.

He walked down to the shore. There were lights in the harbour and people walking up and down the promenade. A boy and a girl strolled past, arm in arm. Outside a hotel a violinist and a pianist were playing to customers seated at tables in the open air. Now and again the pianist would raise his head and smile and then lower his eyes to the keyboard again. Ralph felt the shell shifting slowly and inexorably from his back, and he shivered. He wanted a big stone under which he could crawl but whenever he saw such a stone he also saw a tiny man underneath it reading a book. And towards this man a mermaid was swimming but the man ignored her even though she had green scales and long fair hair.

Ralph didn't want to go back to the hotel at any price. He didn't want to climb the stair and listen to the voices of his father and mother in one of their fierce quarrels. He didn't want to see his mother sitting with the Scandinavians drinking and laughing. He didn't want to see his father reading. He didn't want to go back at all. He wondered why this had never occurred to him before. How could he have been so stupid? It was all quite simple really, he wouldn't go back.

He sat on a bench in the cool of the evening beside a man who had a head as red as a tomato. The man turned towards him and Ralph rose quickly from the bench for he hadn't liked the

expression on the man's face. He walked along the promenade
and it seemed to him that he was tired of the life he was leading.
It seemed to him that he had been in this holiday resort for
centuries and that he didn't like it at all. Nobody had really
asked him whether he had wanted to come here in the first
place.

But most of all he was tired of the quarrels and the rages. He
was so tired that he couldn't tell how tired he was. He was tired
of seeing his father's white face, he was tired of his mother's
laughter. Wherever they went it was always the same, his
mother laughing and talking with other men, his father reading
a book: he was tired of it all. He despised his father and thought
that his mother was a stupid woman. As well as that he didn't
like the food in the hotel. It was giving him stomach ache.

He looked up at the sky and there was the moon with rays
streaming from it like his mother's hair, and there was a chair
formed by stars where his father sat. Then he thought of the
moon as a stone on the end of a sling.

On a sudden impulse he pulled a postcard from his pocket.
On it he wrote, 'Wish you were here', and addressed it to
himself. Then he put it back into his pocket again.

After he had done this he walked away from the town in the
direction of the rocks which were now deserted. The night was
calm and still and warm. Very slowly he peeled off his clothes,
and got into the water. Out there somewhere was the yacht. As
he was removing his clothes he was imagining the yacht: it was
beyond the range of people, their noise and hubbub, and he
knew that if there were people on it it would be ones who had
chosen to stay on the edge of things, at the far horizon. And
perhaps there weren't any people on it at all. He eased himself
into the warm water and began to swim. Slowly the town
distanced itself from him with all its twinkling lights. He was
sure that once from the hotel he could hear his mother's
laughter. But he kept on swimming. He was learning to be a
butterfly but first he had to be an ant.

Record of Work

All during the war with Hitler Mr George Collins, MA, kept his Record of Work. Others might say, It may be that we will not be here next year, it may be that the Nazis will have got us, but Mr Collins didn't seem to listen to them. 'In spite of Hitler the earth turns around the sun and the crops grow,' he would say. 'You wait and see.'

He was an English teacher and had been so for years and years. The pupils quite liked him because when Macbeth killed Duncan in the play he would take out his ruler and stab the desk with it over and over.

He always had chalk on his gown which was holed with mysterious fissures, possibly made by nails which had caught in it. He went to all the school dances and sat patiently by the wall, dressed in what appeared to be his Sunday best. He had however never married.

He wrote meticulously in his Record of Work:

> 3a Parsing
> 2b The Adjective Clause
> 3c Metaphor and Simile

and drew a red line neatly below every entry.

Nobody knew what he did with himself when he was not in school but it was said that he read a lot, and was very learned. To his first year he gave out books by Henty and to his third year the novels of Sir Walter Scott.

'Old Mortality, there's a novel for you,' he would say. His favourite poem was 'Kilmeny' by Hogg.

But the high spot of the year was his murder of the desk with his ruler. On that particular day he would stab and stab with the ruler while the class was in ecstasies.

'In his sleep he was murdered,' he would say. 'A man should not be murdered in his sleep.'

His best recitation was,

> Tomorrow and tomorrow and tomorrow
> creeps in this petty pace from day to day.

'But it's not a petty pace,' he would add. 'Not at all a petty pace.'

Sometimes he would tell his classes stories. 'I remember,' he would say, 'we had a teacher once and he would punch you if you gave the wrong answer. Imagine that. Punch you in the stomach. He was a mathematics teacher. Everyone knew his theorems, I can tell you.' But he himself would never dream of punching anyone in the stomach. As a matter of fact he looked rather frail.

He spent a lot of time on his Record of Work book as if when he died this would be an important elegant memorial to him. His writing was beautiful, his entries orderly with no errors in them, and his register was just as neat.

'A man who keeps his register tidy can't go far wrong,' he would say. When other teachers at the end of the session couldn't bring their additions into harmony with each other, he was openly derisive. He insisted on knowing the full exact name of every pupil. 'After all we must have identification,' he would say. 'We must know who everyone is.'

He was perhaps the only teacher in the school who could distinguish between the Morrison twins who were so alike it was quite frightening. Why, they even wore the same kinds of clothes and combed their hair in exactly the same way.

But he could not be deceived.

Even in the darkest days of the war when it seemed that Hitler's triumph was inevitable he would continue his patient entries. Even during Dunkirk, Stalingrad, Rommel's victories in the desert, he never deviated from this routine.

To the rest of us it was all rather ridiculous. Why, some day his Record of Work would be dust and ashes while the shape of the world would have been changed in the interval.

He never missed a day's school during the war years. He

never joined the Home Guard, or the LDV as it was originally called, saying that he was not a military man, that war was not his forte.

His writing on the blackboard was invariably neat and legible and he was always in his room before his class came in. 'That is very important,' he would say. 'You must show diligence. Otherwise what can you expect of the children?'

One day when he came into the room some children had written his nickname on the blackboard. He asked a few members of the class if they knew who it was but when they could not tell him he smiled. 'That's right,' he said. 'Don't you tell on your friends.' In actual fact the boy who had written his nickname on the blackboard was a newcomer who had been ticked off for not being able to give an example of an Adverbial Clause of Time.

'What I will do,' said Mr Collins, 'is write all your nicknames on the board,' and this he proceeded to do.

When the war ended he was sixty-four years of age and quite frail. Unlike the others he did not celebrate. It was as if he had known all the time that Hitler would be defeated. On the day of his retirement from the school he read some of the entries from his Record of Work book:

3a Adverbial Clause of Reason – Rommel retakes Tobruk
1c Personification – Battle of Britain

and so on. It made an interesting impression on the other teachers who thought he was quite crazy. It was odd to think that grammar could be synchronised with Hitler's advances and retreats.

By that time education in English literature had changed. There was a new emphasis on the imagination, even though spelling declined. 'I'm glad I am leaving,' said Mr Collins. 'I have seen the golden age of teaching. Anything else would be an anticlimax.'

In the Asylum

I see them through the window. There are two of them and they have crewcuts and they are bending down in the cold autumn day, gathering leaves and putting them in a wheelbarrow. They look alien as if they have not quite graduated to humanity. Whenever their faces are turned towards me they look white and blank like loaves.

This is the end of the world: there can be nothing worse, nothing further on. I am frightened that one of these days I shall be where they are, in that other ward of which I have heard so much, in that other room where there is noise, din, bedlam. I don't think I can bear that thought, though I can bear being here, just.

Here in my ward the faces aren't so grossly blank, here at least there is the glimmer of intelligence. And sometimes here too we have discussions: we had one the other day about the soul, about consciousness. It is true that Simmons thinks he is the incarnation of Heydrich and says we should put the canteen staff up against the wall and shoot them because of their bad cooking and their obvious Jewishness. And there is old trembling Mason who endlessly paces his room, counting each step meticulously. And the woman I call Lady Macbeth with the white disordered hair who is always silent, always expressionless.

Then there is Wilson who is writing his history of the world. This is his second time in here, perhaps because there is too much history for him to master, especially as his wife is not interested in it and is liable to put important documents in bins. His house, he tells me, is awash with cuttings from newspapers, books, magazines. He tried to kill himself with aspirins since naturally the doctor won't give him large supplies of sleeping tablets any more.

Then there is young Briggs, noisy, arrogant, negligent, whom the nurses can never get up in the morning. He rolls over on his bed away from the light. He has a record called 'The Mindbenders' and he refuses to take his pills because he maintains they make him impotent.

As for me I believed that my wife was spying on me, that she displaced the pages of my novel, that she tore up the phone book, that she disliked me for my perceptiveness and intelligence. Of course, like the others here, I tried to kill myself. I took a handful of sleeping tablets in a wood on an autumn day. I lay down as if to sleep but I was wakened again. And here I am.

I am rather better than I was. When I came in here first I thought that the nurses and the doctors were all in the pay of my wife: I thought they were hired actors, theatrical people. I admired their professionalism in a remote way. Now I no longer believe that they are fakes. I am sane and soon I shall be allowed out. I am now being permitted to leave the hospital for an hour or so at a time.

Today in the cold autumn weather, as I watch these two men collecting the leaves, I am bothered by an enigma, a question. It is like an itch that I can't get at. I haven't suffered enough. That is what I feel. We sit about so much, sometimes on our beds, sometimes on hard wooden chairs, we drink coffee, we talk. But we are not really alive. I do not feel authentic.

I sometimes have visitors, my brother and his wife often, but they seem so unhelpful. How can they possibly understand what I feel? They talk to me as if I were a child, I who have waves of infernal fire around me. They are so innocent, they tell me that I will be out in another week, they bring me cigarettes and sweets. We talk about gardening, about the restful paintings on the walls. Sometimes I catch them looking at me with an intent seriousness, but most of the time they chat about trivial things. I tell them straight out that I have been mad, but they do not really understand what that means. They have never felt reality bending in front of them like plasticine.

If it is my brother I will say to him, 'How is my wife? How is Diana?'

'Fine,' he will say. 'She will come and see you tomorrow.' But she doesn't come as often as I would wish. Why should she? I would have killed her if I had had the chance. She is frightened of me and with good reason.

And soon I will be out of here and I will see her again, perhaps in a week's time. I think the psychiatrist is pleased with me. I have stopped insulting Diana over the phone. I know that she has done nothing to me, that she has tried to help me. I now know that it must have been myself who tore the phone book in two, with the strength of a maniac. Which is what she told me, which is what the psychiatrist told me as well. Of course I must have done it, only I can't remember.

What I think now is this. I was bored, so my subconscious invented a plot. I built a story of a treacherous wife, of hired nurses, of false doctors, of inauthentic psychiatrists. Soon I shall have to fashion new inventions.

Yesterday when I was walking back to the hospital from the newsagents I stopped and looked at it for the first time. Architecturally it resembles a college or a church with its twin towers flanking the grey entrance. Every day now I pass that other section of the hospital where the worse cases are, as for instance those two who are bending down to pick up the leaves, the loaf-shaped ones and yet I have heard no din from those wards.

In a short while I shall be out of here. And I shall see Diana again. For a moment there one of the men seemed to be staring straight at me as he stood upright with the fork in his hand. It was as if he was looking through perfect blankness, like gazing at an animal perhaps, a cow that had casually raised its head, a forgotten blade of grass in its mouth. I am attracted by that other ward.

The one these two come from, the one which is as blank as an autumn day, the one that I cannot leave without seeing, for that is my destiny. How else can I be a novelist? I have had to come here, I have had to see these two faces, I have had to come to that door beyond which there is unreason, tumult, terror. For how can I leave without seeing it? That would be dishonesty.

The animal faces are raised towards me, they are hungering

for me, they know I am of their kind. I cannot avoid them. I shall have to walk into that room, like an expected guest, where the telephone book has been torn into pieces, where the pages of the unfinished novel have been scattered. And there I shall meet the loaf-headed man who turns his eyes on me and says, 'Who are you?' And he will be placing the leaves in my wheelbarrow, and they are the pages, the leaves, of my torn telephone book, my novel.

The Black Halo

In the middle of the night in her sleep he heard her say, 'Keep away, black halo. You are not going to put out my music. Keep away from me, keep away.' He stared into the darkness.

She had become a Catholic after their marriage because she loved music and colour and they had many quarrels over religion. He belonged to the dour hard church of his fathers. She had also begun to suffer from heart trouble and her nightmares exhausted her. They never kissed when he went off to work because he didn't like to be touched. Nevertheless he worried about her and sometimes phoned home during the day. He was a tax inspector.

'Am I the black halo?' he asked her at breakfast but she didn't answer except to ask what he was referring to.

'No, of course not,' she said after a long time.

He looked round the untidy room and wished to put the rose petals, which had fallen from the vase onto the table, into the bucket. But he refrained by an effort of the will.

By the time he got into the car he was a tax inspector again.

Everyone was deceiving everyone else, he thought, as he sat at his desk. In the old days people paid their taxes because it was the ethical thing to do, and they had some consideration for society. Now I am caught in a wave of deceit, I am like Canute trying to halt the flow of the water. And he felt on his head a phantom crown of paper.

The sherry bottle had been opened, he saw, as he looked into the cupboard. But he couldn't speak to her about it as her heart was bad. When his tea was over he began to work on his papers. She sat reading a woman's magazine and studying diamond rings.

'They get accountants now,' he said. 'Everyone has an account and we can't nail them though they're cheating.' He was the hunter with the sword in a forest of paper sniffing and searching for theft. 'I think,' he considered, 'that I am beginning to lose my sense of smell. And what will happen to me then?'

They had fought over religion but that was long ago. At night he heard her tossing in her sleep, meeting the man with the black halo again. He wondered if she had found someone else and listened for the name, but no name was ever pronounced. Her hand searched blindly for his in the dark. The night seethed with malpractice and secret, deceitful people. 'Are you, too, deceitful?' he asked her in the dark, but she didn't answer.

'My rainbow is going out,' she said.

One day he decided that he had had enough. He wrote out his resignation. After all he was fifty-five now and without children and they had enough to live on. He would tidy the house and look after her. He drove home joyfully through the calm day among the autumn leaves. He was like a father returning to his daughter, for he was older than her.

She lay on the bed, not breathing. He panicked and phoned for the doctor who came and pronounced her dead. The bottle empty of pills lay at her side, the sherry had all been drunk. He stood there in his dark suit while the doctor spoke some words that he couldn't understand. 'I am alone,' he thought. 'And outside in the darkness the thieves are prospering.' That night he took out a blank form and filled it in. Where it said 'Name', he wrote, 'Black Halo'. Where it said 'Income', he wrote, 'I only want justice.' His face fixed as a stone, he sat by the fire. 'My God,' he thought. 'What have I done?'

The cathedral didn't have many mourners for the two of them hardly ever went out and they had few friends. The coffin lay surrounded by four candles. The priest was dressed in purple and there were two boys with bells in red and white gowns. He had come in from a strong wind and there was rain on his face.

> The Lord is my shepherd.
> There is nothing I shall want.
> Fresh and green are the pastures

> where he gives me repose.
> Near restful waters he leads me
> to revive my drooping spirit.

A wooden carving on the wall near him showed Christ carrying his cross. Here there were no thieves, he thought. A hidden organ played. After all, one of the apostles was a tax collector. They are looking at me, he thought, but I shall not cry. It seemed to him that she was whimpering in the church, crying his name. 'Black Halo,' she was saying, 'black halo.' He sat, stiff and unmoving. Once the priest turned his back on him and then faced him with the bread and wine in his hand, and in that sudden flash and turn he thought he saw the black halo, the face.

The incense scattered on the coffin stung his eyes. The pale boys rang their bells. The voice had said,

> I tell you most solemnly
> if you do not eat the flesh of the Son of Man
> and drink his blood
> you will not have life in you.

It seemed to him that he had eaten her flesh and drunk her blood and there was no one in the coffin at all.

I demand justice of these thieves, he said to himself. They have no concern for society, they care only for themselves. But he was confused by the music, the beautiful words and dresses, the incense.

At the end he walked out alone, letting the gale pull at his coat and watching the sea hitting the rocks. He opened the door of his car to enter its dry glass case and was desolated by sobs. He shut the door and covered his face with his hands and the water poured out of his eyes. It was as if the pain was like another being inside him, wrenching him apart. In the east towards the sea he could see the rainbow, arched and colourful, a frail beautiful bridge. He stared at it as if he had not seen a rainbow before. It was not justice, it was mercy, it was a bonus, a concession made by the tax man. Above the waste of sea, raging and white, it curved. 'My love, my love,' he cried, 'how can I sleep tonight without hearing your voice talking to the black halo?' My hunting is over, he thought. I shall have to learn to live on my own. Others can search out the thieves. In the mirror he caught a glimpse of his face. It was set and fixed, a prow cutting the day. The rainbow had gone, the house was tidier than it had ever been. The women's magazines were neatly piled at the bottom of the bookcase. He stood there as if in a flood of water now and again touching his head absently. Then he lay down on the bed fully clothed and slept. In his dreams he saw the priest in his purple robes and behind him the rainbow. It throbbed above the altar.

The Crossing

When she came down the stony path to the shore the boatman was waiting for her. He didn't speak and neither did she at first.

There was a mist over the water and no other boats on the river.

Finally the boatman said, 'What was it like, then?' His cap was low over his forehead and she could't make out his face.

'It was a life,' she said.

'And is that all?'

'I was teaching in a school for thirty years. That is what it was.'

The mist was beginning to rise from the river. And in the distance she could see the long bare outline of the opposite shore.

'Some say one thing, some say another,' said the boatman.

'There wasn't on the whole much to it,' she said. 'It was often the same, day after day.'

'And you never married,' he said.

'No.'

There was a silence and then the boatman said, 'I suppose marriage has its advantages and disadvantages. I always know those who are married and those who are not.'

'How?' she asked, trailing her hand in the water.

'The unmarried ones do what you are doing now. They put their hands in the water.'

As soon as he said these words she drew her hand out of the water and sat again silently watching as the boat moved along, its engine making a clear sound in the morning.

'In the old days we didn't have an engine,' said the boatman, as if he knew what she was thinking.

'I imagine not,' she replied. She was wearing a grey costume and in the dawn it appeared pearly and appropriate. She was as calm and composed as she had always been. In her hand she held a small gift.

'Some ask about the loneliness of it,' said the boatman. 'But you didn't ask. That is another reason why I thought you were unmarried. And also because you have no ring on your finger.'

'I was married to the school,' she said. 'That was my wedding day - the day I started there. And the pupils were my children.'

'I see,' said the boatman. 'I can understand that.' But she still could not see his face. Perhaps he was young, perhaps he was old. But if he had been young he wouldn't have understood what she had been saying.

'Some have gifts with them,' he said. 'Rings, bracelets. Others have nothing. Of these there are few, I mean of those who have nothing. But some there have been.'

'It's possible,' she said. But she could imagine what it would be like to have nothing. They were now more than halfway across the river which was calm and clear though there was a strong current running through it like a muscle.

'You will be quite happy where you are going,' said the boatman. 'I know. You are one of the people who don't expect much.

'Of course.' She had never expected much and she had received what she had expected, except for the gift which she held in her hand. That, she had not foreseen for she had always been strict and severe.

'It won't be long now,' said the boatman. 'Most people ask me about the other side, but you ask me nothing.'

'I take things as they come.'

The boatman puffed smoke from his pipe. The smoke rose like a snake into the sky which was slowly beginning to brighten with a rose of fire.

She could hear quite clearly in her mind the din from the playground, she could see the children, running, playing football, chasing each other, laughing. That ring of stone in which they moved had been her ring. And yet she wasn't regretful, not at all. There comes a time when one must have an end to it, and the end has come. She hadn't been unprepared. In her own way she had been well prepared.

'Well,' said the boatman. 'Another two minutes should see us there.'

'Yes,' she said. The only thing was that she didn't want to wet her shoes but she presumed she wouldn't have to do that. She trusted the boatman as she had trusted the headmaster.

The mist had cleared away and all was serene.

'May I ask,' said the boatman politely, 'what have you in your hand?'

'An apple,' she said. 'A little girl brought it to me on the last day.'

'Is that the gift then?'

'Yes,' she said, 'that is the gift. It is enough.' In the reddening light the apple seemed to redden even more.

'It is what I got. I am content.'

The boat reached the shore and she stepped out of it without wetting her feet. The boatman looked after her for a long time as she strode into the mist of the other land, composed and neat in her grey costume.

The Beautiful Gown

When their father and mother adopted an orphan child, Ben and Robert were pleased at first. The child's name was Joe and he was quiet, respectful and undernourished. Because he owned nothing he was given everything new including shoes, shirts, coats, jackets and a brand new case for school; and this was the beginning of the trouble. For Ben and Robert began to think that their parents loved Joe more than they loved them.

One day Robert, who was twelve, said to his brother Ben, who was ten, 'Joe got a new dressing gown today. It's made of silk. And it's got pictures of animals on it.'

Ben, whose own dressing gown was two years old, didn't say anything but looked at his big brother whom he considered his leader.

Robert continued, 'He gets everything new. Mummy and Daddy say that's because he's got nothing. But now he's got everything.'

Ben waited. His brother always had a plan; he was the one who was always making up new games.

At that moment Joe passed them in his shimmering gown coming from the bathroom. It glittered and seemed as if it were alive, with its golden lions and its striped tigers and its huge elephants. Joe said good morning in his polite way but they didn't answer him.

'We must do something,' said Robert, 'we must do something.' His eyes were angry. Ben didn't like it when Robert became angry, and he remained quiet.

'We must have a plan,' said Robert. He didn't say anything more that day but he brooded. Who was this intruder in their house? They had got on so well with their parents but now Joe was the centre of attention. Their mother even told him longer bedtime stories than she told them. She said that no one had told him stories before and that he was very clever. He listened quietly and absorbed everything. Robert in particular seethed with anger but smiled openly. He thought of Joe as a stranger who wandered about the house in his dressing gown like a king.

One day, Robert said to Ben, 'I know what I'm going to do.'

They were sitting at breakfast one morning when their father, who was a doctor, said, 'I wonder if any of you have seen my cigarette case. I can't seem to find it.' He was very fond of this cigarette case firstly because it was made of silver and secondly because it had been given to him as a present by a grateful patient: in fact he no longer smoked. None of the boys admitted to having seen it. Their father couldn't understand what had happened to it.

They had a maid whose name was Marie; she was eighteen years old and came from France. She was cleaning out the bedrooms when she found the case under Joe's pillow.

'Madame, monsieur,' she said excitedly, 'I have found what monsieur lost.' And she produced the cigarette case and handed it to Dr Fellowes.

'In Joe's room, you say?' he said in a puzzled voice.

'Yes, monsieur, under his peelow.'

Dr Fellowes sent for Joe, who pleaded ignorance.

Finally Dr Fellowes said to him, 'I had thought better of you. Look at what I have done for you and this is the return I get.' For the rest of that day he sat in his study in a sad silence. His wife too turned a cold eye on Joe.

Ben glanced at Robert and realised what had happened. It was Robert who had put the cigarette case in Joe's room.

From that time the doctor and his wife became less friendly to Joe. They sent him to a private school almost as if they wanted to get rid of him. Joe said nothing in his own defence but suffered in silence. He knew, however, who was responsible for his disgrace.

He was in a school different from that of his two foster brothers and was so lonely that he studied very hard, and became the most brilliant student in his class. While he was still in school his foster father died and only his foster mother was left. He often remembered his foster brothers and thought, 'Well, it was natural. It was hard for them not to be envious.' But nevertheless he did feel a slight bitterness.

When their father died and only their mother was left, Robert and Ben, who were now sixteen and fourteen, began to show their real natures, although Robert was the worse of the two and also the leader. When they were home on holiday they would come in late from dances and also ask for large sums of money, and their mother, thinking that she had harmed them by her kindness to Joe, gave them what they wanted. At eighteen and twenty years of age, they began to drink and refused to go to university. They never saw Joe who was still studying as hard as ever; in fact they didn't want to see him.

When their mother died they were left a large sum of money as well as the house, which they sold. They squandered all their money and didn't worry about the future. They bought fast cars and crashed them. They thought their money would last forever. As time passed, their memory of Joe grew dim. They never heard of him and didn't wish to. They lost all their money and were soon very poor, reduced to living in cheap lodgings.

It was a cold winter's night with ice on the street. Ben, now forty, and Robert, thirty-eight, came out of the warm pub. They saw in front of them a jeweller's window which blazed with jewels of all kinds. They stood in front of the window and studied them. Then they looked all around them; there was no one to be seen but themselves.

They had no money at all; the week's dole had been spent.

Robert looked at Ben and Ben looked back at Robert.

It was a most peculiar thing but the jewels in the window reminded Ben at that moment of the glimmering colours of Joe's dressing gown and it came to him as if in a vision that all that had happened to them had begun with that, and he felt resentful towards his big brother Robert. But Robert didn't seem to feel any guilt at all.

Suddenly, while he was still standing in his dream, he saw Robert kicking the jeweller's window, as if he wished to break in amongst the fiery jewellery. A star appeared on the window but the glass didn't break. At that same moment there was the harsh jangling of an alarm bell and a policeman came running towards them across the ice. They stood there as if transfixed and then began to run. They might have got away if it hadn't been for the slipperiness of the ice, for Robert slipped as he was running and Ben waited for him and before he knew where they were they were handcuffed and in a van.

When they were in the police station, the sergeant said to them, 'You can phone a lawyer if you wish.'

Robert replied gruffly, 'We can't afford a lawyer.'

'In that case,' said the sergeant, 'the state can provide you with one. There is a Mr Agnew who is very good, they say. He spends his time helping poor prisoners.'

All the time they were in the cell the brothers didn't speak to each other, except that Robert once said, 'That was bad luck. If it hadn't been for the ice I would have got away.'

The cell they were in was cold and miserable and they recalled more luxurious days. Suddenly a policeman opened the door of the cell and said, 'Mr Agnew to see you.'

At first they didn't recognise him but he recognised them in spite of their ragged appearance. It hadn't occurred to them that their foster brother Joe would become a lawyer. So the three stood there in that miserable cell till finally Joe said, 'Don't you recognise me?'

It was Ben who recognised him first.

'You're Joe, aren't you?' he said quietly.

Robert raised his head and said in a bitter voice, 'Now I suppose you'll get your own back.'

'My own back?' said Joe. 'What do you mean?'

'You know it was me and Ben who framed you, don't you? All those years ago.'

'Yes,' said Joe, 'but it was my own fault too. It was hard for you, I understand. I've thought a lot about that incident.'

Then in a change of tone he said, 'I believe you were trying to break into a jeweller's shop.'

'Yes,' said Robert, and then suddenly, 'It was just me. Ben had nothing to do with it.'

Joe's face became suddenly radiant.

'I see,' he said. And it was only then that he embraced both of them and it was as if they really were brothers.

Robert stared at him in wonderment.

'You mean,' he said, 'that you are going to help us?'

'Yes,' said Joe, 'why do you think I became a poor man's lawyer? Now sit down and let's talk. I feel responsible for you.'

A prisoner, carrying his shaving gear, walked past, wrapped in a grey blanket.

'You see,' said Joe, 'they don't have nice bright dressing gowns in this place. There is nothing to be envious of here.'

'I understand,' said Robert, and it seemed as if for the first time he really understood.

Biblical reference: Genesis chapters 37–45

Do You Believe in Ghosts?

'I'll tell you something,' said Daial to Iain. 'I believe in ghosts.'

It was Hallowe'en night and they were sitting in Daial's house - which was a thatched one - eating apples and cracking nuts which they had got earlier that evening from the people of the village. It was frosty outside and the night was very calm.

'I don't believe in ghosts,' said Iain, munching an apple. 'You've never seen a ghost, have you?'

'No,' said Daial fiercely, 'but I know people who have. My father saw a ghost at the Corner. It was a woman in a white dress.'

'I don't believe it,' said Iain. 'It was more likely a piece of paper.' And he laughed out loud. 'It was more likely a newspaper. It was the local newspaper.'

'I tell you he did,' said Daial. 'And another thing. They say that if you look between the ears of a horse you will see a ghost. I was told that by my granny.'

'Horses' ears,' said Iain laughing, munching his juicy apple. 'Horses' ears.'

Outside it was very very still, the night was, as it were, entranced under the stars.

'Come on then,' said Daial urgently, as if he had been angered by Iain's dismissive comments. 'We can go and see now. It's eleven o'clock and if there are any ghosts you might see them now. I dare you.'

'All right,' said Iain, throwing the remains of the apple into the fire. 'Come on then.'

And the two of them left the house, shutting the door carefully and noiselessly behind them and entering the calm night with its millions of stars. They could feel their shoes creaking among the frost, and there were little panes of ice on the small pools of water on the road. Daial looked very determined, his chin thrust out as if his honour had been attacked. Iain liked Daial fairly well though Daial hardly read any books and was only interested in fishing and football. Now and again as he walked along he looked up at the sky with its vast city of stars and felt almost dizzy because of its immensity.

'That's the Plough there,' said Iain, 'do you see it? Up there.'

'Who told you that?' said Daial.

'I saw a picture of it in a book. It's shaped like a plough.'

'It's not at all,' said Daial. 'It's not shaped like a plough at all. You never saw a plough like that in your life.'

They were gradually leaving the village now, had in fact passed the last house, and Iain in spite of his earlier protestations was getting a little frightened, for he had heard stories of ghosts at the Corner before. There was one about a sailor home from the Merchant Navy who was supposed to have seen a ghost and after he had rejoined his ship he had fallen from a mast to the deck and had died instantly. People in the village mostly believed in ghosts. They believed that some people had the second sight and could see in advance the body of someone who was about to die though at that particular time he might be walking among them, looking perfectly healthy.

Daial and Iain walked on through the ghostly whiteness of the frost and it seemed to them that the night had turned much colder and also more threatening. There was no noise even of flowing water, for all the streams were locked in frost.

'It's here they see the ghosts,' said Daial in a whisper, his voice trembling a little, perhaps partly with the cold. 'If we had a horse we might see one.'

'Yes,' said Iain still trying to joke, though at the same time he also found himself whispering. 'You could ride the horse and look between its ears.'

The whole earth was a frosty globe, creaking and spectral, and the shine from it was eerie and faint.

'Can you hear anything?' said Daial who was keeping close to Iain.

'No,' said Iain. 'I can't hear anything. There's nothing. We should go back.'

'No,' Daial replied, his teeth chattering. 'W–w–e w–w–on't go back. We have to stay for a while.'

'What would you do if you saw a ghost?' said Iain.

'I would run,' said Daial, 'I would run like hell.'

'I don't know what I would do,' said Iain, and his words seemed to echo through the silent night. 'I might drop dead. Or I might . . . ' He suddenly had a terrible thought. Perhaps they were ghosts themselves and the ghost who looked like a ghost to them might be a human being after all. What if a ghost came towards them and then walked through them smiling, and then they suddenly realised that they themselves were ghosts.

'Hey, Daial,' he said, 'what if we are . . . ' And then he stopped, for it seemed to him that Daial had turned all white in the frost, that his head and the rest of his body were white, and his legs and shoes were also a shining white. Daial was coming towards him with his mouth open, and where there had been a head there was only a bony skull, its interstices filled with snow. Daial was walking towards him, his hands outstretched, and they were bony without any skin on them. Daial was his enemy, he was a ghost who wished to destroy him, and that was why he had led him out to the Corner to the territory of the ghosts. Daial was not Daial at all, the real Daial was back in the house, and this was a ghost that had taken over Daial's body in order to entice Iain to the place where he was now. Daial was a devil, a corpse.

And suddenly Iain began to run and Daial was running after him. Iain ran crazily with frantic speed but Daial was close on his heels. He was running after him and his white body was blazing with the frost and it seemed to Iain that he was stretching his bony arms towards him. They raced along the cold white road which was so hard that their shoes left no prints on it, and Iain's heart was beating like a hammer, and then they were in the village among the ordinary lights and now they were at Daial's door.

'What happened?' said Daial panting, leaning against the door, his breath coming in huge gasps.

And Iain knew at that moment that this really was Daial, whatever had happened to the other one, and that this one would think of him as a coward for the rest of his life and tell his pals how Iain had run away. And he was even more frightened than he had been before, till he knew what he had to do.

'I saw it,' he said.

'What?' said Daial, his eyes growing round with excitement.

'I saw it,' said Iain again. 'Didn't you see it?'

'What?' said Daial. 'What did you see?'

'I saw it,' said Iain, 'but maybe you don't believe me.'

'What did you see?' said Daial. 'I believe you.'

'It was a coffin,' said Iain. 'I saw a funeral.'

'A funeral?'

'I saw a funeral,' said Iain, 'and there were people in black hats and black coats. You know?'

Daial nodded eagerly.

'And I saw them carrying a coffin,' said Iain, 'and it was all yellow, and it was coming straight for you. You didn't see it. I know you didn't see it. And I saw the coffin open and I saw the face in the coffin.'

'The face?' said Daial and his eyes were fixed on Iain's face, and Iain could hardly hear what he was saying.

'And do you know whose face it was?'

'No,' said Daial breathlessly. 'Whose face was it? Tell me, tell me.'

'It was your face,' said Iain in a high voice. 'It was your face.'

Daial paled.

'But it's all right,' said Iain. 'I saved you. If the coffin doesn't touch you you're all right. I read that in a book. That's why I ran. I knew that you would run after me. And you did. And I saved you. For the coffin would have touched you if I hadn't run.'

'Are you sure,' said Daial, in a frightened trembling voice. 'Are you sure that I'm saved?'

'Yes,' said Iain. 'I saw the edge of the coffin and it was almost touching the patch on your trousers and then I ran.'

'Gosh,' said Daial, 'that's something. You must have the second sight. It almost touched me. Gosh. Wait till I tell the boys tomorrow. You wait.' And then as if it had just occurred to him he said, 'You believe in ghosts now, don't you?'

'Yes, I believe,' said Iain.

'There you are then,' said Daial. 'Gosh. Are you sure if they don't touch you you're all right?'

'Cross my heart,' said Iain.

At Jorvik Museum

We enter the small chair, we glide along the rails. The faces of the present disappear. We are in a room: it stinks, I hear voices, they are talking Norse. There are leather skins, the face of a dead fox, needles, women knitting, men hunting. This is a rank rank room with the smell of grain, of blood. There are hens, chickens. Two women gossip in a strange dialect.

Who is that in the helmet with the nosepiece protecting him? He is saying, perhaps, We shall stand to the end in the ring, till it fades like the moon, till we are bones among the cans of Coca-Cola, till the workmen emerge out of the dust with shovels, till they beat at our heads.

See, we are bargaining. The city walls protect us. We bring vases, ornaments, we bring the sniff of the future. They cannot protect themselves from that, from everything else but that. The wind is shrieking through the walls, it is changing the fashions; after it has been there there will be no more farriers, no more fletchers, no more guilds.

The children are playing a game that we do not understand. Look, their heads are thorny. The side of one head is shaven, the colours of the other are orange red and blue. They are punching at computers in the dung, with the dead stinking oxen beside them. The dog raises its head, lowers it again: the cat comes in with a rabbit.

What are they saying to each other, these two with the portrait of the Queen beside the television set? The war has ended. There is shouting, there are helmets, there are horses, leather skins, their wireless is beating out a great Norse victory against the English. In their ring of iron they lasted till the end. The women rush out to meet them, they are reading newspapers covered with dirt, dung. They are holding iron coins in their hands. There is a sermon whose words are unintelligible. It blows like the wind.

The boat is covered with skins. There are dead rotting fish on the shore.

Sigurd has died. The men are drinking lager and above them is an advertisement. The words are written in Norse. It is a Norse code. It flickers on and off, banks of lights.

I have brought you this gift, my beloved, it is a deer, it is meat from the butcher's. Sit down and eat it, my beloved, though the worms are dangling at your mouth and the spider's web hangs and quivers. Eat the deer, my beloved, we are safe from the animals, from the shouting hooligans with their flags of red white and blue painted on their bald heads. We are safe from their language. We can hide. Their thorny heads, their shaven heads, are not ours.

Among the new ones we watch the television motor cycles chase each other, charge at bony chariots. The helmet lowers, I have come back from the war. They fought well but we burned their books and ornaments, their saints, their coloured pages and threw them into the sea, we burned their house and smashed their windows. Their trains were attacked with arrows and catapults. But still the trains are bringing new fashions, new luggage.

We cannot avoid them. There is a fresh air coming in here.

It must be the workmen with their shovels. One of them is smoking, spitting on the floor where you are sitting, my beloved.

I have walked among the blossoms. I have seen the litter. I have seen the leather shoes, the fragments of leather left over. I have seen the brooches curled like snakes. I have seen the moon on which men in armour clumsily walk and jump. Bend down, touch the can, I do not understand it, it has writing on it. What is it, a gift from the gods?

You are standing among the women, my beloved. You are wearing leather, a fresh blouse. You are wearing a hat with flowers on it. Your bone needles are in your hand. The dog sniffs at them. Something is attacking us which cannot be defended against by walls. There are people making gaps in the walls, they are standing at the gates, they are holding out new jewellery, stunningly beautiful. We fasten watches on our hands below the iron ringlets, circlets. They have the faces of the gods on them.

You are not dying, my beloved. No one dies. I kneel by your bed in this crowded dungy room. You are reciting words to me that I cannot understand. They are not Norse. Are you feverish? Your face changes, it becomes narrow and then your body changes, it becomes like an arrow pointing in one direction. Your smell, my beloved, is of perfume. The dog has disappeared, where has the cat gone?

Astronomy of night, sound of engines, the owl blinking with a mouse in its claws. The hens rush hither and thither, and there I see the eggs in the straw.

My beloved, you shall not die, not ever. I know it. I shall follow you towards the light where the shovels are, where a man is leaning smiling. Who is he? Does he think he is immortal? I have seen the dead talking on television, I have seen a camera showing blankness; faces slowly coming on the screen; where have they come from, filling the whiteness? We are here. Listen to us. We are all together in the stink, the perfume, the dung.

We talk in the salons with the bone needles in our hands. Our eyes glitter and flash, we are intelligent. The fox stands at the window looking in. So does the wolf. So does the beaver, the badger. And they all stink beyond the tiny coffee cups.

We slide on the rails. You in front of me, why are you wearing a helmet, why are you so joyous? Has a battle been won? You turn towards me. Your nose-piece is long and dark. You are my enemy, you are saying, I shall kill you, kill you, kill you. In the ring that will not die, that will not break, in the circle that will not break, in the circle that is decorated with the face of the god.

You, my beloved, are sitting, sewing. In the sunset that will not fade. I see your body under the skins. It is white and pearl-like. I have wished for you for many years and then suddenly you were there. In the doorway. You are coming towards me. You are removing your blouse, your tights, your legs are clear to me. They have the trace of leather on them, of thongs.

We meet in the darkness. I hear the cries from outside. The thorny-headed ones are shouting, are rioting again. Their hair is like needles, there are holes in their trousers, they are dancing.

The Ship

In her senility she would say to him, 'Who are you? I don't know you. Where did you come from?'

He didn't like this one little bit though their daughter would sometimes find her mother's odd statements amusing. Of course she was a nurse and had worked in geriatric wards: but he wasn't used to this sort of thing. And he didn't like it.

Most of his days he had been a sailor, and had travelled all over the world, Singapore, Sydney, Auckland, you name it, he had been there. And now he was seventy years old. All those years he had been away on voyages she had waited and waited, and he would send her postcards and bring her gifts. His children had grown up without him: he had hardly seen them.

And now she had grown senile.

'I used to live in a house with a name like that,' she would say, pointing at the wooden plaque which read GREENVIEW. He had paid ten pounds for that sign. 'But this isn't the house. I don't know why it's here,' she would say in her sombre almost girlish voice.

Sometimes she would say, 'I used to know Robert Mason. We would go to dances together.' And Robert Mason was his own name. But she would say to her daughter, 'What's that man doing here?'

Those sunny mornings; the ship racing through the sea leaving a white wake behind it. The immense illimitable distances. Those breezes.

He couldn't understand how he couldn't convince her of her errors, but there was no way that he could, since they were now fixed in her mind. He hated the fact that he couldn't get through to her. It was like being a wireless operator who couldn't make sense of the replies to his messages. Her mistakes infuriated him. His anger grew so large that it sank his pity. It was as if she was trying to irritate him. He was a ship in the middle of the sea not knowing where he was, without longitude or latitude. It was all wrong, obscenely wrong.

Sometimes he felt like shaking her. But then she would look at him and say, 'Have you seen Robert Mason? I would like to speak to him.' Good God, he thought, this is terrible, this is awful. Here he was in the middle of the sea without sextant, without communications.

'Don't worry about it too much,' his daughter would say to him. 'She's perfectly happy.'

'How can she be perfectly happy?' he would say. 'How can she be perfectly happy when she doesn't know what is happening.'

Of course she wasn't perfectly happy. She should be dragged out of her dreams into reality where other people lived. How could one be happy unless one was living in the truth, not in a chaotic dream.

He was writing a postcard on the deck of a ship on a fine clear breezy day. 'I miss you,' he wrote. But the truth was that he didn't miss her at all. No, he was perfectly happy sitting in a chair on the deck with the breeze whipping about his bare legs, for he was wearing shorts. The truth was . . . What was the truth? The postcard winged its way home over the blue waters. Did she sense that what he had written was not the truth? Did an odd instinctive sixth sense tell her that?

The sea was all around him, there was not another ship to be seen on the blue sparkling expanse. And he was perfectly happy. At that moment it was a fulfilled perfect day.

One night she said to him, 'I can hear a baby crying. I can hear it in this room. You brute. Why aren't you helping the baby? Robert Mason would help him, but I don't know you.'

'Go to sleep,' he had told her, 'go to sleep at once. Do you know what time it is?' The illuminated clock at the side of the bed told him it was two in the morning. But she didn't want to go to sleep. Not at all. She had to get up in her nightgown to find the baby. That voyage of hers through the dark. How strange it was. How lonely. Later she had come back to bed and had gone to sleep like a child, her hair grey on the pillow.

Like a wave of the sea on a rock.

Oh terrible terrible things happened to people, he hadn't realised how terrible. Not when he was on the ship he hadn't. You could say what you liked but it was with a deep sense of relief that one left land behind with its infections, its insoluble troubles, and sailed away happily into the blue.

And now here she was talking about babies and signs that didn't belong to the house, and not recognising him. He would never survive it. He hated her for her senility. Why had she become like this in their old age which was meant to be sunny and relaxed? Why couldn't she have retained her firm efficient mind? He had been cheated at the end. She was trying to torment him. She knew perfectly well what she was doing. She was pretending all the time, she was deliberately torturing him.

All the time she had been getting his blue postcards she had been growing old. All the time he had been sitting on a chair on the deck writing his letters she had been wrestling with the children, with the cares of the world.

This was actually worse than death, much worse. Death was a clean break, but this went on and on. It would never end.

And he never felt at ease. One day she packed her case and made for the door. 'I am going home,' she said. 'I am going back to my husband.' And he had to wrestle the case out of her hand for she was very strong, though her mind was weak, sending out its maimed flashes as from a defective lighthouse.

'You are not going anywhere,' he said angrily. And she had struggled and then finally given up. It was as if he was keeping her prisoner.

If he didn't watch he would become like her himself, for she wasn't allowing him to sleep. In the middle of the night she would hear voices, her mother for instance calling to her. He couldn't keep this up. He wouldn't survive it. The doctor told him that he would have to find something to take his mind off her, otherwise he would become like her. 'You're not getting any younger,' he said. 'And you say you don't want to put her in a Home.'

No, he wouldn't do that. If he did that she would remain in her forgetful state forever. So he began to make little ships, as his eyesight was still strong. Tiny ships with sails set, and rigging hoisted. He found that his concentration on his ships was helping him and sometimes he completely forgot she was there. Life became almost peaceful for them and she would sometimes touch his ship and say, 'Pretty, pretty,' just like a little girl. She would watch him as he worked, using thin thread for ropes, and her eyes would light up as the ship took shape. He had never been involved in anything in his life so deeply. The tiny ship was so real it looked as if it might set sail.

And now he said to himself, I must try something really difficult. I must try and put my ship in a bottle. I have never tried that before. So he folded the tiny sails and slid the ship in and when it was in he manipulated the threads to raise the masts and sails again. The ship sailed motionlessly inside the bottle.

His wife came over and touched the bottle gently. She was staring at the ship motionlessly carved inside. Tears began to flow from her eyes. 'The poor ship,' she said. 'The poor ship.' He put his hand around her waist. He didn't know whether she was weeping for herself or for him. The ship was like a magnet which had drawn the tears from her eyes.

It wasn't sailing anywhere, he knew. Never again would it see other countries. Never again would it race through the sea. 'It's all right,' he said, patting his wife on the shoulder. 'It's all right. It's quite happy inside the bottle. Perfectly happy.'

That was the moment he accepted he would never be able to speak to her again, that the two of them would travel side by side like ships in the night, without lights, without wireless. And that the truth of their lives was actually what was happening then, at that time, without reservation, without disguise.

In the Silence

The stooks of corn glimmered in the moonlight and boys' voices could be heard as they played hide and seek among them. How calm the night was, how stubbly the field! Iain crouched behind one of the stooks listening, watching for deepening shadows, his face and hands sweaty, his knees trembling with excitement. Then quite suddenly he heard the voices fading away from him, as if the boys had tired of their game and gone home, leaving him undetected. Their voices were like bells in the distance, each answering the other and then falling silent. He was alone.

The moonlight shimmered among the stooks so that they looked like men, or women, who had fallen asleep upright. The silence gathered around him, except that now and again he could hear the bark of a dog and the noise of the sea. He touched the stubble with his finger and felt it sharp and thorny as if it might draw blood. From where he was he could see the lights of the houses but there was no human shape to be seen anywhere. The moon made a white road across the distant sea.

He moved quietly about the field, amazed at the silence. No whisper of wind, no rustle of creature – rat or mouse – moving about. He was a scout on advance patrol, he was a pirate among his strawy treasure chests. If he thrust his hand into one, he might however find not gold but some small nocturnal animal. Very faintly he heard the soft throaty call of an owl. He was on a battlefield among the dead.

He began to count the stooks and made them twelve in all. It was a struggle for him for he was continually distracted by shadows and also not at all good at arithmetic, being only seven years old and more imaginative than mathematical. Twelve stooks set at a certain glimmering distance from each other.

Twelve treasure chests. Twelve men of straw. He counted them again, and again he got twelve so he had been right the first time.

A cat slanted along in front of him, a mouse in its jaws, its eyes cold and green. The mouse's tail was dangling from its mouth like a shoelace. He put out his hand, but the cat quickly ran away from him towards its busy house, carrying its prey. Its green eyes were solid and beautiful like jewels.

He took a handkerchief from his pocket and began to dry his face. In the darkness he couldn't see the handkerchief clearly, it appeared as a vague ghostly shape, and though it had red spots on it he couldn't make them out. This was the quietest he had ever heard the world before. Even the cat had made no noise when it passed him. During the daytime there was always sound, but now even the dog had stopped barking. He could hear no sound of water, not any noise at all. He put his hand out in front of him and could see it only as a faint shape, as if it were separate from the rest of his body.

He looked up at the moon which was quite cold in the sky. He could see the dark spots on it and it seemed to move backwards into the sky as he looked. What an extraordinary calm was everywhere. It was as if he had been left in charge of the night, as if he was the only person alive, as if he must take responsibility for the whole world. No sound of footsteps could be heard from the road that lay between the wall and the houses.

The silence lasted so long that he was afraid to move. He formed his lips as if to speak but he didn't have the courage. It was as if the night didn't want him to speak, were forbidding him to do so, as if it were saying to him, This is my kingdom, you are not to do anything I don't wish you to do. He could no longer hear the noise of the sea, as if it too had been commanded to be quiet. It was like a yellow shield in the distance, flat and made of hammered gold.

For the first time in his life he heard the beating of his own heart. Pitter patter it went, then it picked up power and became stronger, heavier. It was like a big clock in the middle of his chest. Then as quickly as it had started, it settled down again and he held his breath. The laden enchanted night, the strangeness of it. He would not have been surprised to see the stooks beginning to dance, a strawy dance, one which they were too serious to do in the daytime, when everyone was watching. He felt daring as well as frightened, that he should be the only one to stay behind, that he should be the dweller among the stooks. How brave he was and yet how unreal and ghostly he felt. It was as if the boys had left him and gone to another country, pulling the roofs over their heads and putting off the switch beside the bed.

This was the latest he had ever been out, even counting Hallowe'en last year. But tonight he could feel there were no witches, the night was too still for that. It wasn't frightening in that way, not with broomsticks and masked heads, animal faces. Not even Stork would be out as late as this, his two sticks pointed at the boys like guns, as he seemed to fly from the wall which ran alongside the road. No, it wasn't that kind of fear. It was as if he didn't . . . as if he wasn't . . . as if the night had gone right through him, as if he wasn't actually there, in that field, with cold knees and ghostly hands.

He imagined himself staying out there all night and the boys appearing to him in the morning, their faces red with the sun, shouting and screaming, like Red Indians. The sun was on their faces like war paint. They came out of their boxes pushing the lids up, and suddenly there they were among the stubble with their red knees and their red hands.

The stooks weren't all at the same angle to the earth. As he listened in the quietness he seemed to hear them talking in strawy voices, speaking in a sort of sharp, strawy language. They were whispering to each other, deep and rough and sharp. Their language sounded very odd, not at all liquid and running, but like the voice of stones, thorns. The field was alive with their conversation. Perhaps they were discussing the scythe that had cut them down, the boys that played hide and seek among them. They were busy and hissing as if they had to speak as much as possible before the light strengthened around them.

Then they came closer together, and the boys seemed suddenly very far away. The stooks were pressed against each other, composing a thorny spiky wall. He screamed suddenly and stopped, for at the sound the stooks had resumed their original positions. They were like pieces on a board. He began to count them again, his heart beating irregularly. Thirteen, where there had been twelve before. Where had the thirteenth come from?

He couldn't make out which was the alien one, and then counted them again and again. Then he saw it, the thirteenth. It was moving towards him, it had sharp teeth, it had thorny fingers. It was sighing inarticulately like an old woman, or an old man, its sigh was despairing and deep. Far beyond on the road he could sense that the boys were all gathered together, having got out of their boxes. They were sighing, everyone was sighing like the wind. Straw was peeling away from them as if on an invisible gale. And finally they were no longer there, but had returned to their boxes again and pulled the roofs over their heads.

He didn't notice the lights of the house go out as he walked towards the thirteenth stook, laid his head on its breast and fell asleep among the thorns.

The Ladder

Thus it was that one day he stood upright among the roars and cries of mammoths, lions and the rest. His stereoscopic eyes, his new brain, gathered information from the land around him. Standing on two legs was such an achievement that he almost wept with the joy of it. Nor did the small or gigantic animals around him understand what was happening, that his was the empire of the future, but he knew deep within himself, he knew it. On the dim horizon were churches, art galleries, space ships. Beyond the leopards, the bears, the red deer, the reindeer, the wolverines, the musk ox, the arctic fox, the woolly rhinoceros and the arctic ptarmigan they stood out from that blue haze of the early world. What a busy little being he was, such projects in his mind, his hand searching for tools and weapons. Things, beings, beasts, leaped straight out at him and did not stay in their shadowy frieze. Some hunger, thirst, that he did not understand gnawed at him, drove him into the depths of caves. He would climb down an almost vertical abyss and come to a beautiful arcade that led to another shaft round the edge of which he crept on a narrow ledge. And in a very low chamber he would lie on his back and paint a lion on the ceiling that would roar back at him. He would draw a wild determined mammoth, a horse, reindeer. He would create magnificent polychrome paintings in red, black, brown or yellow, holding his lamp close to the wall. He would grind pigment very finely on a stone palette and then fix it with fat. And in the farthest depths of the cave he would paint and draw.

This being, this strange new being.

Sometimes in sunset he would see a ladder of light and in his imagination he would climb it. High, high into the sky which arched himself and his kind – and the others. The others were for his service, he was their master.

Nothing, and again nothing.

Uncle Jim is singing his song again and telling us about Dunkirk. Aunt Jane is inviting us to see her new flat. She has Doulton figures, crystal, a new coffee set of silver.

Night after night the explorer stares at the stars. Into the limitless spaces.

Have you another Cartland, Plaidy? That one was so nice. I enjoyed it so much, it kept the wolf from the door. I do so like a historical novel.

Klonk, take that. What a spiffing day for Bowman of the Lower Fifth. The wind is on his skin. The trees are a glorious tent around him. He can hear nestlings, roars, cries. But not yet see the sea. Not yet set his sail west, not yet hear the humming of the rigging and the cordage.

Nothing, and again nothing. The wind at the door. The tiger sinking into the pit. And himself hammering with a boulder let down on a leather belt. And the scents everywhere. What a world, what a new world. And the clouds coming to visit him.

There she is knitting again. She knits all the time now. Last night they found her naked at midnight. In the village. And someone said, laughing, 'She wasn't much of a picture.' The nurse bends down, arranges the pillow, her fanged mouth gapes.

With his briefcase in his hand he stalks along the road. With his sword at his side he sleeps in the church. At first there was armour everywhere. Our history is an unpeeling of armour to become like eggs.

Do you know this one? This is an Irish one. MacCormick used to sing it. Do you remember MacCormick?

I know she doesn't have a certificate. She thinks she can deceive everybody, but I know for a fact that she wasn't in college.

A bit too left for me, you understand. The children will have to be brought up in their faith, the other faith. They're adamant about that. And their priests, by God if you cross them.

He climbs steadily, he climbs. He speaks.

Hooded he is, his eyes follow you, he stretches his tiny hand out. Pink is the monkey's palm, hanging from the bar, jumping, clutching.

Raphael he is, in the depths of the caves, not far from the icy water, the profile of the horse, the bear springing out at you from the wall. Lord, what a new world.

Nothing, and again nothing. But a lot can be done with these flats even though there is woodworm and damp rot. Have a surveyor in. Let him probe.

Fire burns and the wolverine draws back snarling. But the others knit by the fire, they do not mind the new red beast, glittering with wings, Titian red.

He gnaws at the marrow bone of the mammoth.

Tiptoe he sees the world and beyond that there is another part and then another. There is no end to it. Ledges, steps, ladders, grades, genera. Sometimes he sees one of the tribe sleeping. For days he sleeps, months. He will never wake up. The flesh peels from his bones. And slowly the expression on his face becomes a snarl. The lightning flashes at the tips of the nails, beyond the ——.

Nothing, and again nothing. Coffee, bingo, bridge. What are we going to do about the young ones? They are like wild animals playing their records in caves by themselves.

Let not your heart be troubled. It is Mrs Bett's turn to arrange the flowers. Never have red and white in the one bowl. Unlucky. Anyone could have told her that, but she never asks. Never.

Tiptoe on the earth, the wind nuzzling at his cheeks and hair. And in the calm post-Ice-Age the paintings hang out like washing, in a naked gallery becalmed.

Higher, higher, higher than the dinosaur with its small reptilian head. Higher than anybody, than anything. As high as a cathedral, tumbling into orbit, singing. Deeper than the salmon, the herring, everywhere.

Ivory hairpins, lamps made out of reindeer skulls, whistles made from the bones of deer, ivory chisels, bone discs, decorated pebbles, toilet boxes of ivory. And that body asleep, flaking, with the tiny ring of bone on its finger, so many years ago, so many fresh wounds ago, that dawn, that trembling dawn.

Tommy

He wore new corduroy trousers, two jerseys with Scottish badges on them, new shoes: all these he had been given on his travels. He had a little brown dog which he kept on a lead. He had been trudging all round Britain on a sponsored walk.

He believed that he was a great poet: he believed this because he had nothing else to believe in. His childhood had been one of the most extreme poverty: he had stolen food in order to survive: he had been in prison, and in prison he had begun to write poetry.

He arrived at ten o'clock at night: at first I thought he was a tinker or a Red Indian: he had long black hair and was carrying a blue bag. In the bag we later discovered he had a tape recorder on which he had recorded conversations, monologues, poems. He read us one of his poems. He believed that though he was English he was the reincarnation of Robert Burns. People, he said, called him the Rabbie Burns of England.

We listened to his poem. One of the verses went as follows:

> When Burns arrives in the Highlands
> make sure you look after your strays
> for Burns loved always the lassies
> and knew them and their ways.

That is my best poem, he told us, taking a coffee. (He loved coffee and drank a great deal of it.) I met some Americans on the Mull boat and they took a copy of my poem. They gave me money for a pint. Mull is Paradise. You could write a lot of poems on Mull. I could live on Mull, only I don't want to be tied down.

The little brown dog which was called Maggie lay slavishly at his feet.

He said, I don't know why the Scots have taken to me. See this jersey. It's got SCOTLAND written on it. The Scots look like their own, not like the English. They have taken me to their hearts. Only I went to this hotel in the village here and they told me they had no rooms which was funny because the manager of another hotel in Connel phoned up to tell them to keep a room for me.

You and your wife are very kind. Do you think it's because I'm such a good poet? I look on you as your son. Maybe you should adopt me.

(And he laughed. His laugh was easy and unaffected and in a way innocent. His teeth shone white in his tanned face.)

When I die, he said, I shall have a statue in Scotland like Rabbie Burns had. That's what the Scots think about me. All the way round Britain I've been interviewed by the press, and I've been on radio, and TV. I was on Granada television and Grampian and Yorkshire. Only they ask you such stupid questions, like what I'm doing walking. They could have seen that in the press.

I sent a letter to Maggie Thatcher – she's not as pretty as my Maggie here – saying that Scotland should be given its independence. She answered me very politely and wished me good luck in America. I'm going to America in the autumn to raise money. There's a man going to meet me at the airport. I'm world-famous, did you know that?

I read that poem you wrote on the exiles. It's the words, I think, I think I feel like that too. I've got two kids, a daughter and a son. My daughter has a child, though she's not married. Still, there's this Scotsman who's got an eye on her. I wouldn't wonder if he was a millionaire in a few years. He sells things, you know, articles. I phoned to the woman next door to ask about my kids since we don't have a phone but she wasn't in so I didn't phone again: I forgot. When I'm home my kids tell me, isn't it time you were away again, dad? That's the way they are, always joking.

(He smoked incessantly and ate little: but drank much coffee. The dog chewed at its lead. We gave it some cat food which it ate ravenously. At one time our cat came into the room, stared at the dog with its hair standing on end, and then went into our bedroom where it sleeps on the bed. The tiny brown dog whimpered.)

What's that mountain called? (said Tommy, looking out the kitchen window.) I'll call it Tommy's mountain. That's what I'll call it. Imagine if I went up there with a brush and whitewash and wrote my name on it.

I don't like aristocrats much though I met one or two. I'm going to meet the Duke of Sutherland. Aristocrats don't do much for the country. I can tell an aristocrat in two minutes. It's the way they speak.

Now you're a poet, Iain. Do you think I'll be a poet too? Tell me the truth now. Do you think it sounds too confident? Maybe people don't like it if you sound too confident. There's a book in these tapes. Maybe you could edit them for me. There's a great book in them. I'll call it *The Thoughts of Tommy*.

Now what would you say if someone asked you what I was like? Fascinating, wouldn't you say? Wouldn't you say I was a fascinating man? He's seen the world, that one, wouldn't you say?

Glasgow people I don't like. You don't need to be foul mouthed. It doesn't cost anything to have good manners. They don't have a worse life than me and I'm good-mannered.

But it's really strange how the Scots took to me. See, I didn't say Scotch. I must be like one of them, they must think of me as one of their own. At first they didn't like me but when they read about my interviews they knew I was internationally famous. See what I mean?

Actually I feel quite cold in the morning till the coffee warms me up. I collapsed in Wales, you know. The doctor told me to rest for a month but I was on the road next day.

The thing is I get drenched a lot, and once I was walking through a snowstorm. Listen, you can hear it on the tape. That's the sound of the wind there. I speak to Maggie on the tape, and I say, Maggie, I wish this snow would stop. Sometimes I shout out, snow, snow go away. And sometimes it does. Seagulls, you know, are the spirits of the dead, that's well known. But it's lucky to see one. I saw one last night on my way to your house so this is going to be my lucky day.

When I went to prison my wife left me. That was the worst. That's why I wonder whether I can manage. I'll phone you tonight when I get to the Edinburgh Festival. I'm going to be on the Edinburgh Festival. I'm going to see the Director when I get there. He told me to call in. I haven't heard from him lately, being on my travels, you understand.

Yes, she left me when I went to prison. She stays with a dosser now. She came back to me for a while but when I went on my travels she left me. I have a lovely grandchild but she doesn't come to see him. People are selfish, you know.

(He took off his socks showed us one of his toes which was bruised and blue.)

That slows me down. I hope it's not gangrene. But I don't think it is. I have faith in God. At the beginning I lost my faith but then it came back again. I believe in Heaven and Hell. I've been through hell and I don't want it to come back again.

I really don't know why the Scots have taken to me. When I go to America I'll wear a kilt, that's how much I like the Scots. It's my poetry, you see the Scots appreciate poets. That's the thing about a poet, he's got to travel, he can't stay around all the time, he's got to see the world. See, I sometimes pay for my keep with a poem.

I met this woman in Inverness, and she wanted me to settle down with her and her two kids. She stays in a caravan, two lovely kids she's got. See that dog lead, she gave me that, it's got their names on it. From Anne and Christopher and Helen, that's their names. But I'm going to America, I can't settle down. I don't want to let anyone down.

(We gave him some Hawaiian shirts which I had bought in Australia but wouldn't subsequently wear and he danced in front of the mirror with one of them on.)

Lovely they are. I think Tommy will be a Hollywood star. When I get to America I'll go to Hollywood, my Highland poems and I'm sure they'll give me something to do. My Highland poems go down well with everybody. They've my masterpieces. You see, Burns was one for the ladies, excuse me, Mrs Iain. The strays in my poem are the ladies. That poem was put in a newspaper. The editor told me, I'll put that in my newspaper, I was in his office at the time, but I haven't seen a copy. He said he would post it to my home address.

Iain, you've got plenty of time, you could edit my tapes. No, you wouldn't lose them. I haven't got much time myself, you see. Do you want to hear what I put on the tape last night when you went to bed?

Iain and his wife have gone to bed. It's twelve fifteen. I feel very tired and I want to lay down my pen. Good night, world.

That's what I put on the tape. I don't sleep very well. And I don't eat much. One meal a day, that's what I have. Maggie gets scraps. But she's lovely, isn't she? Maggie and I are great friends, aren't we, Maggie? I carried her all the way. You look at her paws, you'll see there's nothing wrong with them. That's because I carried her.

Prison was terrible. It was the lack of freedom, you see. But I've won through, haven't I? I've been very lucky. God has been on Tommy's side. I believe in God now though at one time I didn't. I used to steal, you know, to get food. I used to be a real rascal.

Orkney now I didn't like, but Mull I did. Mull is a paradise, I swear it's a paradise. What's that place, Gervaig, sorry, Dervaig, that's beautiful. I met this girl in a bar there and she signed one of my poems. With love to Rabbie Burns, it says. She's a student, lovely she is. But I'll tell you something, when I ask women if they can remember their first kiss, they can't remember.

You could come with me to America, Mrs Iain. Iain would come as a chauffeur. What do you think of that, Iain?

(He had an indescribable charm which flashed and lit up his whole face when he smiled. His face looked like the face of a Red Indian seen on a totem pole.)

Feel the weight of my bag? I washed my socks, you see, and they're still drying, that's why it's so heavy. I walked twelve thousand miles and I raised twelve thousand pounds for this boy who has to be sent to America for an operation. People have been so kind to me, you wouldn't believe it. I have never been attacked or anything. But the Scots . . . they look after their own. They should have home rule. I wrote to Mrs

Thatcher about it, telling her to leave Ireland to the Irish. There should be peace in the world. Some of the Irish are nice but they don't like the English. When I was reading my poems do you think I should have put on a Scottish accent? I thought of it but then I thought it wouldn't be good-mannered. The Scots have been good to me and bought my poems. I'm internationally famous, you see.

Now, Iain, you've got everything you want. You always smile, don't you? A lovely wife and a nice house. You're contented. Doesn't he smile all the time, Mrs Iain?

Me, I've to travel but that's the way I am. I am a poet, you see, and poets have to keep walking. They're exiles, as you wrote in that poem, Iain. I liked the poem. It was the words, I think. Isn't it the words that make the poem, in your opinion, Iain? I would say it's the words that make the poem. I don't have education but I understand about poetry. It's your feelings. Sometimes poems come to me and I write dozens of them. All them feelings, you understand.

Do you think I could have another cup of coffee? It looks dry today but you can't tell, can you? I'm making for Edinburgh. You'll see me being interviewed on TV, you watch out for me, and you can say to your friends, That's my mate, Tommy there. I'm famous you see, they'll put up a statue to me when I die. In Scotland, that's where I would like it to be.

He was a great one for the lassies, Rabbie Burns, excuse me, Mrs Iain. This woman in Newcastle wanted me to stay with her but I said I couldn't. The poet has to be on his own. Solitude, that's what the poets want, Iain, excuse me, Mrs Iain.

I talk to my dog when I'm walking. There's no one else to talk to. A poet is a philosopher. And I talk philosophy to Maggie here. I carry her, you see. I don't let her walk.

(He adjusted his blue bag and put his tape recorder and his tapes in it, and the two pairs of socks and the two shirts we had given him. The shirts had a wild romantic look.)

Have to be going now, he said.

He turned at the door and kissed my wife. I'm not going to kiss you, Iain. I'll phone when I get to Edinburgh. I won't let you down.

But before I go I'll just visit my friend in the tea shop. She would never forgive me if I went past without calling.

(It was a dry day but there were black rainclouds piling up in the east.)

I never ask for lifts, he said. I always walk. It wouldn't be right to ask for lifts. It would be cheating.

The Whale's Way

His special period was Old English: and it looked as if he would be made redundant in the next round of cuts. 'Death by a thousand cuts,' was the macabre joke at the university.

Celia of course spoke of his redundancy as if it were his fault. 'You were never a good lecturer anyway,' she would say. 'You mumbled. No one could understand what you were talking about.'

Actually many years ago she had taken his class. And now the Head of Department was a frighteningly young man who had been born in South Africa.

'Vernon, it's possible you might be thinking of ... ' the young man had said over coffee in the Staff Club. 'You know how things are.'

'You should fight,' Celia would say. 'What are you thinking of doing with yourself?'

She buttoned up her coat and went to meet her two friends, who were lecturers' wives.

'Though I don't know why I do it. They'll be laughing at me.'

Vernon had the terrible idea that she would leave him, she had a hard pitiless mind though she had done nothing with it. She was also considerably younger than him: and they had no children.

He was feeling more and more his own isolation both at home and at the university, where no one casually knocked at the door to discuss his subject with him, as they had done in the past. The other thing was that he was not published: he was too scrupulous.

'You used to stare at the ceiling when you lectured,' Celia would say in friendlier days. 'All that stuff about Beowulf. But you had a sort of passion. I give you that. That's probably why I married you.'

She herself was English and belonged to a talented family: two of her own brothers were lecturers: he had never liked either of them, he had felt inferior in their company. They were glib entrepreneurs. Also they had a lot of in-jokes which he didn't understand.

He stared at the window through the falling snow, after Celia had left. He imagined it falling over the North Sea, random, complex, desolate.

He didn't understand why he should be made redundant. Some of the people in the Department travelled abroad, to America and even to the Far East, in search of students. Naturally he hadn't been asked to go. It was all a business now. 'You could have taken me if you had been asked,' Celia would say. Their quarrels were now very frequent. She screamed at him like a seagull over a waste of waves. The whale's way. He was like a stranded whale on a beach, that was being beaten to death.

Sometimes he would look out of the window of his university room at the quadrangle. He would watch the leaves blowing in desolate rings and circles, and the students strolling through them, long-haired, in jeans. Circular autumn: the circular seasons and the circular students. It was a pagan godless world. Did they know he was being made redundant?

Redundant. What a word. As if it was being withdrawn from circulation like a flawed coin: leaving a space where he had been.

What was he going to do about money? Celia would say relentlessly. My pension will be made up, he had answered. After all, he was fifty-five (Celia was forty-two). He wondered sometimes if she had been seeing other men when he was working at the university: there had been periods of jealousy but he had never found any evidence. At sherry parties she was always bright and witty: he had been proud of her for he himself had no small talk.

The desolate world he had studied, of battles, fights, exile, wanderings, had there been redundancy there? Of course there had been. Poets wrote of deserted halls, of festivities which had suddenly ceased, of silent harps. And that was how he felt. Abandoned. Stricken.

It had been a cosy would which he had inhabited in the university while it lasted. He loved the students, and they realised it, though he had never been able to communicate with them outside his subject. And of course they weren't all that fond of the subject anyway, they had considered it a pedantic compulsion which was rather unfair. The language stood up in front of them like a field of thorns. But sometimes on gifted days he felt he had given them a hint of its resonance, of its concept of endurance. Endure, endure, if nothing can be changed. Endure the violence of battle. Stand there till you are cut down. Once he had said (he thought wittily) to them, it prepares you for the Thatcherite world.

He knew Celia would leave him. She was the child of a more clear-headed world than his own. And anyway she wouldn't be able to take her wounded husband to see the family. She had put up with him long enough. He knew she could be merciless, and loved status: as time passed she would become even more bitter because of her desperation. She would have to make the leap soon. Perhaps without his knowing it she was making the leap even now.

The snow was very thick, its complex flakes drifting hypnotically before his eyes. He thought he should switch on the second bar of the electric fire but decided against it. The bar that was on looked red and raw like a newly opened wound.

As a matter of fact there had been a number of suicides already. People had settled into a nest and had been asked to leave it. It was too hard for them to start again, it was impossible.

He and Celia slept in different rooms now. He didn't get to sleep till he had read for a long while. Had he been betrayed by his subject? Should he have read something else, explored some other field? But sometimes he was comforted by these wanderers, seafarers, exiles.

Endure, endure, endure to the end. The monster is searching for you in your lighted house. The mouth and claws are seeking for weakness in your walls. The bodies dripping blood are lying in the snow. Night falls and you are waiting for the monster. He is heaving his malicious body along, he has come out of the depths: he is crusted with seaweed. He will drag you down to the bottom of the sea where you must fight for your life.

And what, my friend, will you do then? Will you put up your pension like a shield?

Power seeps away from you: and respect. You will be always on the edge of things, listening. No one will pay any attention to you: your words aren't backed by even a tiny measure of power. If you have a lot of power you can afford clichés. If you haven't you must be witty.

He knew that Celia would leave him. She was like the bird that would set off in spring over the waste of waters. It was not her style to stay with the wounded. She was not one for the long haul of endurance. Already he could sense the inattention in her, as if she was feeling the stirring of her last spring. She must launch herself out soon, or die. It was quite natural really.

If he had the energy he would launch out and leave his bereaved furniture as well. But he didn't have the energy. The university had been his lord: without his lord he was doomed, disorientated. Without that steady walk to his room every morning. And the new lord obviously had no time for him. The new lord was brisk and competent, an entrepreneur, salesman. The new lord had the indefinable quality of hope. He himself had lived too long in the castle, listening to the seductive harp music.

In a short time she would leave him, she would walk into the snow with her case (though before that she would have found someone to replace him). His philosophy of endurance had been overtaken by events. There were stirrings around him, wings were being tested. The philosophy of endurance did not itself endure.

A new world was breaking out around him, of salesmanship, of opportunism. Birds were flying everywhere with their beaks, greedy exotic birds, seeking for food with opportunistic instinct. His nest had been raided by the cuckoo, the bird of spring, the source of whose voice was invisible.

It was a world in which Celia might thrive.

He looked out at the snow. Maybe he should draw the curtains.

No, he told himself with a sudden burst of energy. I must not do that, I must watch, I must not hide. I shall watch it out to the end. I owe myself that. I owe myself a seat in the theatre of nature, however painful.

And when she leaves me I must endure that too.

It is the least that my special subject can give me.

The Dawn

I imagine this Israeli soldier in his olive-green uniform standing by himself on the Golan Heights. The battle has just finished. With half a dozen tanks the positions were held till the reserves were called up. These included David, Saul, Abraham and many other great Jews, for history is in the present as well as in the past. This Israeli soldier forms in front of his own eyes the history of his people, Joseph and his coloured coat, Abraham, Isaac, Moses and the general who actually entered the Promised Land. It was Joshua who aligned the guns and used the field glasses. The Syrians were in fact Philistines, Germans, Assyrians.

It is morning. The land is silent, the dew is falling gently on the grass. He can almost hear it falling. There is a spectral quality about the morning light. The tanks lie in the mist like stranded beasts.

God was with them again, history was with them again. God was in the concentration camps too. At one time he demanded sacrifices, now he demands morality, discipline. It is better to be ethical than to offer sacrifices in smoke and fire. God followed them however in symbolic fire and cloud. The concentration camps had meaning, even the children's shoes lying on top of each other in the Holocaust Museum had meaning.

I fought for my country, for the True Land, thought the Israeli soldier. I am proud of what I have done. This is my predestined country. I have not let my people down, he thought in the spectral light. God is with us, who then can be against us? Even the long years in Babylon had meaning. The world blazes with the presence of God.

But the spectral light troubled him and the bodies of the enemy troubled him, especially of one of them who was young, and at whose breast a rose of blood faded. His face had a severe purity. It was like a face he had once seen in a painting.

The Israeli soldier turned away. The tanks were spectral in the light. The army had held out till help came. Everyone was involved in the common battle, with the historically dead and the living. He had seen Joshua waving them on. His face had flashed among the maps. They were invincible: even the Romans had learnt that when the Jews had killed each other at Masada rather than surrender.

His eyes returned to the Syrian whose proud dignified face troubled him. The boy was about his own age. It was as if he was looking at himself. Consider how free of ideological ardours a body is in the spectral light of dawn.

A thought struck him thunderously. If everything that happened was God, then God was the same as history. If the concentration camps and victories were the same in God's sight, then God was only another name for history. If one praised the concentration camps, the exiles, then one was only praising history.

He stood there shivering in the gathering light. God ... history. Then there was no need for God at all. He put his hands to his head. Where had the evil thought come from? Was it the work of the Devil? No, the light wasn't getting stronger. The mist was was still swirling about the ground. And yet he could see a red sun through the mist, a raw red sun, the temporal face of God. If all events were important or unimportant God was only another name for Time, for History.

He shook in the suddenly cold morning.

We have been betrayed, he thought. The concentration camps happened. So did this victory. If we had lost, the event would still have been praised: it would still have been God's holy work. History and defeat are the same in the ideological enigma that has always been propounded. Joy and sorrow are the same. If this victory is equal to defeat what follows? God therefore is archaic, a superfluous quantity.

The young dead swart face stared up at him. It was a flower like the flowers that surrounded it. If we had not committed suicide at Masada, if instead we had surrendered, that too would have been considered God's will.

The electronic fence surrounds us. If the nose of a dog touches it, we know of it. The mines around our feet flower. Joseph lived in Egypt, became an Egyptian and saved his brothers. His dazzling robe was bright and terrible. It glowed with an infernal duplicity.

There they were together, the Israeli and the Palestinian soldiers. In death they did not seem so different. They seemed pure and inviolable. They were lying in all sorts of positions, some had one arm, some had one leg, some had torn breasts. There was no ideology here, only silence.

He looked down as if he was examining the pages of some holy book. But these pages yielded nothing. Questions and answers, they were all the same. The bodies did not suffer, they simply were.

The sun was reddening and reddening. It was no longer God's head. It was simply the sun. It was not spiritual power, it was a combination of heat and gases. The land was not symbolic at all. It was simply grass and stone and flowers, tanks and dead bodies. It was history, event, it had no authority.

He passed his hand over his eyes. It was almost as if he was about to fall down, so dizzy he felt. He sat among the bodies and watched them. But they remained inflexibly as they were. The sun was solid in the sky and he felt heat on his shoulders. Time was itself and history. Ideology did not know of these shadows and these guns. He put his hand out and touched the face of the Syrian soldier. It was not as cold as he had thought it would be. Changed forever, he sat among the dead bodies, each different from each other, the more minutely he examined them. The mist had moved away from them and showed them exactly as they were, unique, dignified and devastatingly individual.

The Red Coffin

Sometimes she believed that her son was simply lying, at other times she was not so sure. He didn't look like a liar, there was nothing furtive about him when he was telling his stories, but he did seem to dream a great deal. It was as if he wasn't quite of the common earth. Perhaps that was why he was called the Lark by the other boys; they had seized on this unworldliness and his flights of fancy. His latest story however was rather odd. He had come in and asked her casually whether there had been a funeral that day.

'No', she said, though her own dress looked funereal enough.

'That's funny,' he said.

'Why should it be funny?' she asked. Her hands were white with the flour she had been using for baking.

'Nothing,' he said.

'There is,' she said, 'or you wouldn't have asked.' Was this another lie, another flight? These lies, if they were lies, worried her for she had been brought up to tell the direct truth.

Sometimes however he didn't want to tell her and she had to force what she thought was the truth out of him. Already it seemed as if he regretted his question. But she wouldn't rest.

'Well, what is it then? Why do you think there might have been a funeral?' She would get to the bottom of this, she wouldn't leave it alone.

'It was just . . . ' he said,

'Just what?'

'I thought I saw . . . what looked like a funeral. Only it couldn't have been a funeral.'

'Why not?'

'They weren't wearing black.'

'Who?'

'The people.'

'What people?'

'The people carrying the . . . '

'Coffin, you mean.'

There was a pause.

'Do they always wear black, mother?'

'Of course they always wear black,' she said. 'What would you expect them to wear?'

'Yes, only they . . . '

'Only they what?'

'They were wearing sort of tunics.'

'Tunics?'

'Yes, like . . . You see them in books. They were red and green. And they were wearing pointed hats. Yellow.'

'What are you talking about?'

'That's what they were wearing,' he insisted stubbornly.

'Who?'

'The people at the funeral. And the . . . coffin was red.'

'What on earth? Where did you see this?'

'At the brae. They were close as . . . just next to me. They never looked.'

'It was your imagination. Who ever heard of a red coffin? And people wearing pointed hats at funerals. It's all these books you read. You must have seen it in a book.'

'They were just next to me. I knew one of them.'

'Who?'

'I knew Calum Mor. And I think it was Angusan.'

'What a liar you are,' she said.

'I'm not, I'm not,' he screamed.

'Or you dreamed it then. Perhaps you fell asleep and dreamed it.'

'I didn't dream it.'

But she was relentless.

'Well, then it couldn't have been a funeral. It must have been something else. Maybe you saw a circus.' And she laughed.

'There was a coffin,' he said. 'And it was red. And they were all wearing these clothes.'

'A red coffin,' she said. 'Who ever heard of a red coffin?'

'I saw it,' he said. 'I did see it.'

She looked deep into his eyes which were candid and clear. Something strange stirred within her. Something uncomfortable, eerie. Her own child appeared strange to her. Perhaps he had the second sight. But even if he had, who had ever heard of a red coffin?

She looked down at her hands which were white with flour. This puzzling boy who always seemed to be dreaming.

She tried to imagine a red coffin and couldn't.

'There was something else,' he said.

'What was that?' she said absentmindedly.

'There was a picture on the coffin.'

What was this? A Catholic funeral. Was that what he had seen?

'Of the man in the coffin, maybe. He was wearing the same kind of clothes as the others. He was winking at me. He looked like . . .'

'Like who?'

'Like Calum Macrae.'

'It couldn't be Calum Macrae.' Calum Macrae was an elder of the church. He would never wink at anyone, never. He was a big heavy man and looked solemn and important . . . 'No, it couldn't have been Calum Macrae.'

This was really the height of nonsense. Why should she be listening to this?

'Hadn't you better go and bring in some peats,' she said.

'Right,' he said. He was always very obedient. After a while he came in with the pail and stood in the door again, the sun behind him. And suddenly she saw it, that extraordinary picture. He was wearing a tunic, red and blue, perpendicular colours. And on his head was a pointed hat. And he was laughing hilariously. She made as if to walk towards him in her black dress but he kept moving on and she followed him out into the sunlight. There he was, a good distance from her, and he was waving to her and she was following him. It was so strange, she seemed to be dancing, and he was dancing as well. And there were flowers all round them, red and white and yellow. How extraordinary.

And in his hand he was carrying a little red box, a beautiful red box like a jewellery box which she had once seen and never had.

And the sun poured down reflecting back from the box while he danced away with it. And she felt so happy, never, never had she felt so happy.

And when she looked down at her dress, it was no longer black but green. And his eyes were candid like water. And in them she saw a picture of herself. And the two of them danced onwards together.

The Bridge

My wife and I met them in Israel. They were considerably younger than us and newly married. They came from Devon and they had a farm which they often talked about. For some reason they took a fancy to us, and were with us a fair amount of the time, sometimes on coach trips, sometimes at dinner in the evenings. They were called Mark and Elaine.

I didn't like Israel as much as I had expected I would. I read the *Jerusalem Post* regularly, and was disturbed by some of the stories I found there, though the paper itself was liberal enough. There were accounts of the beatings of Palestinians, and pictures of Israeli soldiers who looked like Nazis.

Certainly it was interesting to see Bethlehem, Nazareth, the Garden of Gethsemane, and they reminded me of the security of my childhood: but at the same time seemed physically tatty, and without romance. Also we were often followed, especially in Jerusalem, by Arab schoolchildren who tried to sell us postcards: the schools were in fact shut by official order.

Though this was the first time Mark and Elaine were abroad they were brighter than us with regard to money. Mark had a gift for finding out the best time for exchanging sterling and was, I thought, rather mean. Sometimes we had coffee in a foursome during the day or at night, and he would pull his purse out very carefully and count out the money: he never gave a tip. He was also very careful about buying for us exactly what we had bought for him on a previous occasion. On the other hand he bought his wife fairly expensive rings which she flourished expansively. They walked hand in hand. They were both tall and looked very handsome.

One day the coach took us to the Golan Heights. There were red flowers growing there, and some abandoned tanks were lying in a glade. The guide, who was a Jew originally from Iraq, told us that a few tanks had held off the attacks till the reservists had been called up. 'They can be called up very quickly,' he said. It was very peaceful, looking across the valley to the other side but there were notices about unexploded mines.

Often we met young boys and girls on the buses. They hitched rides from place to place in their olive-green uniforms. They were of the age of schoolboys and schoolgirls. One morning on a bus I heard a girl listening to a pop song on a radio that she carried with her. It seemed very poignant and sad.

I used to talk quite a lot about articles I had read in the *Jerusalem Post*, which was my Bible because it was the only paper written in English. But neither Mark nor Elaine read much, not even the fat blockbusters that passengers on the coach sometimes carried with them. They told us a great deal about their farm, and what hard work it was. Then there was also a lot of paper work, including VAT. They were very fond of each other, and, as I have said, often walked hand in hand. He was very handsome: she was pretty enough in a healthy sort of way.

We were told by the guide a great deal about the history of Israel, about the Assyrians, about the Crusaders, about the Philistines. I especially remember a beautiful little simple Catholic church above Jerusalem. Then in Jerusalem we were shown the Via Dolorosa. At intervals along the route, young Jewish soldiers with guns were posted. 'Here is where Christ's hand rested,' said the guide, pointing to the wall. He himself had emigrated to Israel from Iraq. 'They took everything from us, even our clothes,' he said; 'for years we lived in a tent.' He had served in the paratroopers and was still liable for call-up.

We saw Masada, which was very impressive. Here the Jews had committed suicide *en masse* rather than surrender to the Romans. At one time the Israeli soldiers had been initiated into the army at a ceremony held at Masada, but that had been discontinued because of its passive associations. Thoughts of suicide were not useful against the Arabs.

I found it difficult to talk to the young couple about farming since I didn't know much about it. My wife, however, who had been brought up on a farm, chattered away about sheep, cattle, and hay. For myself I was more interested in the information I was getting from the *Jerusalem Post*. For instance, an American rabbi had said that the reason for the stone-throwing which had started was that the cinemas at Tel Aviv had been opened on a Saturday night.

We often saw Orthodox Jews wearing black hats, and beards. They sometimes read books while they were walking along the street. Also we saw many of them chanting at the Wailing Wall, where the men were separated from the women. My wife wrote a message and left it in the Wall as if it were a secret assignation. There was one comic touch: some of the Orthodox Jews covered their hats with polythene if it was raining, as the hats were very expensive.

I read diligently in the *Jerusalem Post*. Apparently in the past there has been stone-throwing against Jews. This was in mediaeval times and when they were living in Arab countries. But though Jews complained nothing was done about it. It was considered a reasonable sport.

My wife often used to wonder why Mark and Elaine had picked us for friends since they were so much younger. Did we look cosmopolitan, seasoned travellers, or did they simply like us? Sometimes Elaine talked to my wife as if she were talking to her mother. I found it hard to talk to Mark when the women were in the shops. He often spoke about money, I noticed, and was very exact with it. I sometimes thought that it was he who looked like the seasoned traveller, since he was always totally at ease and was excellent with maps.

The two of them didn't take so many coach trips as we did. Often they went away on their own, and we only met them in the evening.

They didn't go to the Holocaust Museum with us the day we went there. The place was very quiet apart from some French schoolchildren who scampered about. My wife hissed at them to be quiet, but they only grinned insolently. There were piles of children's shoes on the floor: these had been worn by victims of the Holocaust. There were many photographs, and a film that ran all the time.

There was also a room which was in complete darkness apart from thousands of candles reflected from a range of mirrors, so that it seemed that we were under a sky of stars. A voice repeated over and over again the names of the children who had been killed. The Jews had suffered terribly, but were now in turn inflicting terror themselves.

We met a woman who had come to Israel from South Africa. She opposed the Jewish attitude to the Palestinians, though she was a Jew herself. She said that mothers everywhere were against the continued war. She herself had driven her son in her own car to the front, not during the Seven Days War but the one after it.

We were in Israel on Independence Day. Jewish planes, streaming blue and white lines of smoke behind them, formed the Jewish flag. It was very impressive and colourful but also rather aggressive.

The coach took us to a kibbutz where we were to stay for two nights. Immediately we arrived, Mark and Elaine found that there were cattle there, and they left us in order to find out about the price of milk, etc.

The kibbutz itself had been raised out of a malarial swamp. Everyone had to work, and the place looked prosperous. It even had a beautiful theatre which the kibbutzers had built themselves. I ordered coffee from an oldish waiter, and when I offered him a tip he wouldn't accept it. I found out that he had been a lieutenant-colonel on Eisenhower's staff.

The kibbutzers, we were told by the guide, had their own problems. Sometimes when the young ones who had been reared in a kibbutz were called up on national service they entered an enviable world which they had not known of, and they left the kibbutz forever. Also some Jews had accepted compensation money from the Germans while others hadn't, and so there was financial inequality. Thus some could afford to take holidays while others couldn't. This introduced envy into the kibbutz.

Mark and Elaine were pleased with the cattle they had seen and full of praise. Mark had brought a notebook with him and had jotted down numbers of cattle, type of feeding stuff, etc.

They had been given a tour of the farm with which they had been very happy.

One night they had told us that they recently had been in a place in England, it might have been Dorset, and they had come to a little bridge. There was a notice on the bridge that according to legend a couple who walked across the bridge hand in hand would be together forever. They smiled tenderly as they told us the story. In fact they had been on a coach trip at the time, and the passengers on the coach had clapped as the two of them volunteered to walk across the bridge. I thought it was a touching little story and I could imagine the scene; on the other hand I am not superstitious. 'How lovely,' said my wife.

My wife and I had been to Devon once. One day quite by accident we arrived at a house which was said to be haunted, and which had been turned into a restaurant. The owner of the restaurant, who made full use of the legend for commercial purposes, told us that many years before, there used to be criminals who used lanterns to direct ships onto the rocks. One man had done this only to find that one of the passengers on the wrecked ship had been his own daughter coming home from America. He had locked the body up in a room in his house. Many years afterwards the farmer who now owned the house noticed a mark on the wall which suggested the existence of an extra room. He knocked the wall down and found a skeleton there. An American tourist had said that she had seen the ghost of the young girl in broad daylight, and so had been born the legend of the Haunted House. So romance and death fed money and tourism.

We told Mark and Elaine the story, which they hadn't heard before. Suddenly there was a chill in the day as I imagined the father bending down to tear the jewellery from a woman's neck and finding that it was his own daughter.

'Should you like a coffee?' I said. I saw Mark fumbling with his purse. I thought of the Samaritan Inn which had been built at the presumed point where the Good Samaritan had helped his enemy. And indeed in Israel much of the biblical story had been converted into money.

Nevertheless I couldn't love Israel. There was too much

evidence of Arab poverty. The dead bodies of Palestinian children were mixed up in my mind with the dead bodies of Jewish children. The mound of worn shoes climbed higher and higher.

On the last night of the tour we exchanged addresses. Mark and Elaine said they would write and my wife and I said we would do the same. And in fact we did do that for a while.

Today, this morning in fact, my wife received a letter from Elaine saying that she and Mark had split up. She said little, but reading between the lines we gathered that he had met a richer woman who was able to invest money in his farm.

We looked at each other for a long time, thinking of the young radiant couple who had walked hand in hand across the bridge.

Finally my wife said, 'At least they didn't have children. It would have been much worse if they had children.'

The Tool Chest

When Donald came from the island to visit us, he was at first very depressed, as he had had a hard lonely winter. We used to hear him praying in the middle of the night, groaning and sighing and saying, 'God have pity on me.' He would sit for hours without speaking, or go to his room and read the Bible. We found his silences oppressive. We tried to take him out on visits: at first he would say he was coming with us and then he would change his mind at the last minute.

He wore a black hat and a big black jacket, though the weather was sultry and close. His face was fixed and pale and strained, and he would often press his hand to his eyes as if he were suffering from a headache. His arm too was swollen with some mysterious ailment.

One morning he decided to go down to the shed which we have in the field below the house. There are actually two sheds, one a proper bought shed which was taken home from a firm and assembled, and a large black byre which has almost been flattened by the wind, the door hanging open. The windows of both buildings have been smashed by young local boys who cross the field in the evening to play football in a neighbouring park. He was suddenly quite happy searching in the shed, for it was full of boxes containing tools of all kinds.

He said, 'You don't have a tool chest in the house, I've noticed. How don't you have one: Every house should have a tool chest.' And he looked at me accusingly. Of course I never used tools much myself, preferring to pay tradesmen for any jobs that had to be done. In any case I was what they call handless. He muttered again to himself, as if he couldn't imagine how anyone could exist without having a tool chest.

Sometimes when I saw him walking about near the house, I

thought he was going to fall down. He was of course eighty-five years old, and ever since the death of his wife he hadn't been well, catching colds every winter, as his house which stood on a headland near the sea was draughty and damp. Often he would say, 'The body is weak, but the mind is still clear.'

So he decided that he would build us a tool chest. He found some old pieces of wood, a hammer, a rusty-toothed saw, and a chisel, and he carried them up through the long wet grass of the field, past the little snarling dogs which belonged to our neighbour and which barked at him incessantly. Most of the time his chest was sizzling as if he had asthma.

He took his booty down to the back of the house and began to build the tool chest. Suddenly his life appeared to take on point and meaning, though he was still puffing and panting, and it occurred to me that he felt that he ought to be paying us for his holiday and that this was his method of doing so.

Anyway, the tool chest became the centre of the day for us. I had to discontinue my own work and help him with the sawing while he directed operations.

'Not like that,' he would say to me irritably. 'You have to cut with a steady movement.'

The work was hard and I found the sawing difficult, especially as the saw was quite old and rusty. Meanwhile Donald held down the plank of wood while I sawed. He was of course often complaining that the tools were inadequate. 'I need a spirit level,' he would say, 'and you don't have a plane either.'

The sawing took rather a long time, as we were often interrupted by showers of rain. We were in fact worried that he would catch a cold, and would bring him in at the first drops. If the rain lasted a long time he would continue with a book about Martin Luther which he was reading. At times his lips were blue and we thought he was going to have a heart attack, and we would tell him that he should stop work for the day. But he was very stubborn and he would answer, 'I don't like to leave a job unfinished. It preys on my mind.' But I would say to him, 'You have another fortnight of your holiday left,' and he would reply sharply, 'You never know the day or the hour.'

Actually, I was at first irritated that I couldn't carry on with my own writing, but he didn't think that my work was of any importance. In his eyes the tool chest was a much superior project. When I stayed in my work room he would come looking for a pencil, and so I had to go out to the tool chest again. I spent hours screwing nails into wood for him. He was a perfectionist: often he had to remove a piece of wood because it wasn't exactly in the right place: and all the time his chest was puffing like an engine and his face was pale and gaunt.

If we had bought a tool chest we wouldn't have had all this hassle, I told my wife. We could even have had bright new wood, instead of these warped planks. For the wood he was using was of inferior quality, and as he didn't have proper tools he had to be content with approximate measurements, which enraged him. In fact the tool chest was rather ramshackle, as it consisted of different kinds of wood, some of which had been painted and some not. The top was an old sheet of iron which he hammered flat. All in all it wasn't a beautiful artefact, though as good as his materials would permit.

However, he was no longer depressed, and indeed in the evening he would talk about the day's work and about the work which, if God permitted, might be done on the following day. He was very knacky and skilful with his hands, there was no doubt about that. But if we praised the tool chest he would say, 'No, it's a poor thing. I'm not happy with it, but what can you do if you don't have the tools. If it had been twenty years ago . . . ' And he would sigh heavily.

Tools were real, I thought, wood was real, and while all the real things existed I was working on my stories in my quiet room. At the side of the fence where we worked at the back of the house, the ferns climbed, a tall dense green jungle. He was trying to make a sliding panel from a piece of wood that had been painted green.

So it had been with early man when he discovered tools. He had differentiated himself from the insatiable greenery round him, he had separated himself from the grass, he had stood isolated and upright in the world. By the sweat of his brow he had earned his bread.

He adopted a teasing attitude to me. He would call me Charlie. 'Oh Charlie did a good job today with the screwdriver,' he would say to my wife. 'He'll make an apprentice yet.' And he would laugh, for he knew that I wasn't an adept worker with tools.

The tool chest had become the centre of our lives; it was necessary that he finish it before he returned to his draughty room and the attention of caring neighbours on the island.

'There is an old woman beside me,' he told us, 'and she won't have a home help. She plants the potatoes every year, and she's eighty-eight. But there's another one who reads romances all the time and smokes like a chimney.'

Though his health seemed to be improving during the day, at night I could hear him coughing and spluttering and praying very loudly. It sounded strange to hear that intense voice calling on God at four in the morning.

He will die here, we worried, making this tool chest, and we felt guilty about it. What does he feel that he owes us? But then I thought, if he does die it would be better for him to do so while working. At first certainly I had tried to keep him in the house, but later as time passed, I saw that the freedom of building the tool chest was necessary to him. After all, didn't I have the urge of creativity myself, though in my case it was the compulsion to create stories, and in his to work with tools.

Sometimes he would stay out when it was raining, in spite of our protests. 'No, it's only a few drops,' he would say, and put on his black hat so that against the background of ferns and leaves he looked like a minister in an orchard.

I disregarded my writing and stayed out with him. I watched him and learned a lot. For instance, before putting a screw in the wood he would hammer a nail in first to make a hole. Actually he didn't have the strength to put the screw in himself and relied on me to do that.

In the evenings, as time went on, he would relax and talk to us. He would say, 'The worst job I have at home is the dishes.

'The morning I left to come down here, I thought I would not able to rise from my bed. I managed it however, and a man on the boat took my case up the gangway for me. But I've got good neighbours, I really have. On my right there's a young couple who are very kind to me, and then in front of me there's an older couple, and they paid my electricity bill for me when I was out here on holiday last time. I leave them the key, you see. And then further up the street there's a retired nurse who takes me to church every Sunday in her car.

'The only problem I have is that I don't want to eat anything I cook myself. All last winter I could only eat jellies because my stomach was bad.

'But there's one thing sure, this holiday has done me the world of good. I feel better in every way, and Donalda's cooking is first rate.'

One day I went to the back of the house to call him in for his dinner. He was bending over the tool chest, which was almost finished. He was puffing and panting and taking deep breaths.

I saw the open shelves of the box and it seemed to me for a moment as if it was the box he would shortly inhabit. I imagined his face rigid and stern as he lay in that box, his nose pointing towards the saw-toothed mountains of the west.

Suddenly he heard my footsteps and straightened up. He made a conscious effort to keep from coughing. He took the hammer again in his hand.

And just as suddenly the box seemed to put on a green foliage. Flowers both red and white rose from it. And he stood in the middle of the foliage, old and upright, the hammer blunt and solid in his hand, though it looked rusty enough in the bright sparkling and eternally young light.

Murdo at the BBC

When Murdo was invited to a Glasgow studio at the BBC to talk about his new book *The Thoughts of Murdo*, he spoke for a while about literary matters such as his train journey, what he had for breakfast, and his expenses.

That done he launched into praising his book which he said was modelled on *The Thoughts of Chairman Mao*, Mao being, he understood, the Chinese equivalent of Murdo.

He suggested very strongly that if the listener was of the ilk which hadn't smiled for a long time e.g. a Celtic supporter, he should buy the book and, addressing his listeners directly, he continued, you will find here anarchic ideas, revolutionary concepts, animadversions on the laughable nature of reality in which we are all enmired. If, he went on, you are moved to laughter by the signing of the Magna Carta or the Monroe Doctrine, or the Scottish International Football Team, you will find here much to amuse: if you think that MacGonagall was a great creative genius; if you enjoy the catastrophes that happen to other people, then you will enjoy this book. If you like similes such as, e.g., as hectic as a cucumber, as foreign as an eel, or as brave as a traffic warden, you will find such plays on words here. Indeed the pun is part of its essence such that you may hear a pun drop or indeed a pan drop. Other topics adumbrated are *Neighbours* and *Take the High Road*.

Moreover, he continued, humour breaks down all boundaries except those between Lewis and Harris. It raises a smile in toilets and in supermarkets, it joins us all together by elasticated bands, it breaks down dogmas (such as e.g. love me, love my dogma), it recognises the futility of all effort, reconstitutes well-known poems into new language such as 'When I consider what my wife has spent', by Milton, it creates new denouements for books, and so on. All these you will find in this valuable though not priceless volume.

It has been said of me that I am the greatest humorist since Ecclesiastes or Job. While not disputing that for a moment, let me add that in buying this book you will be joining a certain class of people as ignorant as yourselves, uninterested in such serious topics as litter, and able to lie in bed for a long period of time without moving. Your vacant gaze will be fully reflected in this book, as also your anthropoid opinions. Verbs, adverbs and nouns will turn somersaults, and you will see the triviality of all that passes for power and progress e.g. Visa Cards, the Westminster Confession etc.

If you are of that ilk which yearns for meaninglessness, I am your instant guru. I sign no agreements without laughter, I am an enemy of the working breakfast. A book such as mine will give you arguments for maintaining a prudent lethargy, and for avoiding tax; it will sustain you in your night of deepest laziness; and will remind you of famous figures which include Mephistopheles and Mrs Robb, 3 Kafka Rd, East Kilbride.

If you wish for history, you will not find it here, you will not be burdened by anthropology, genealogies or any formal logic. The Chaos Theory will not be examined even with a broad brush, nor will there be much reference to thermodynamics. Dante however gets a brief mention. Cultural influences on the whole will be avoided and there are no quotations from St John of the Cross. Some reference however is made to herring and to those golden days when you could buy a tenement for sixpence. Clichés as far as they are understood will not be used and neither will metonymy, synecdoche, personification etc. Wittgenstein along with Partick Thistle will be relegated, and so will remarks of football managers such that 'If you do not score goals you will never win a match.'

If you are looking for passion you will have to look elsewhere. Enthusiasm is avoided as is any form of élan or hope. Optimism is evaded and no one learns by experience. It has taken the writer many years to arrive at this position, having endured friendly fire etc. and he is now as happy as a red herring in May.

He no longer believes that the British working man will ever come to repair any form of machinery. He eschews the illusion of efficiency. He believes that the class system will remain unchanged, and that television will not be better than it is today. British Rail will fail and MacBraynes will be as grass. Asses will be coveted and adultery will rear its ugly head. The Royal Family will perish in the Bog of the Tabloid, and the Queen will reign forever, though otherwise the weather will not be too bad. Middle-of-the-road politics will be run over by speedsters, and sanity will no longer be accepted as an alibi.

In conclusion buy this book, as it will not be published again in a hurry, unless there is a great demand for animadversions on hopelessness.

And finally God bless you all, though the probability is that he will not.

The Wind

It was an autumn of high winds, and the house that he had taken for three weeks was perched on a headland facing the sea. The area was more desolate than he had imagined it would be. There were the straggling houses of the village about half a mile away; and a little shop which sold miscellaneous stuff, and was also a post office.

His father had always told him of the close community that existed in the village, but it was hard to visualise it. During the day the village looked quiet and almost dead: the few children were back in school. 'Songs and dances,' his father would say, 'what we called ceilidhs': and his face would shine with the memories of them. Of course, the place would look better in fine weather: perhaps he should have come in June or July.

Naturally, the villagers knew he was here, and who he was. But his father's generation was dead, and the middle-aged people like himself were not hospitable in the old way. Some of the houses were surprisingly fine, indeed impressive; there were of course no thatched houses left, not even their ruins. The fields here and there held wrecks of abandoned cars.

Why had he come here in the first place from South Africa? Sheila naturally wouldn't come.

'You can go,' she had said, 'but I don't see any need for all this pseudo-nostalgia.' One certainly couldn't call her sentimental. She hadn't, for instance, gone home when her father and mother had died, with a short interval between them, in Dunoon. She had always travelled light.

Yet he had always wanted to see this world that his father had told him about. It had sounded like a sort of paradise, carefree and generous.

The people cared for each other, helped each other, his

father would say. Yet in the post office he had heard them complain of 'white settlers', and he had gathered that there was a Dutch family in the village as well as English ones. 'They come here, and drive the price of property up, and the young people can't afford to buy a house.'

He had gone to see the croft on which his father had grown up. ('Plenty of milk and crowdie.') But there was no sign of the original home, and a large new house had been built in its place.

No one had invited him to visit. He had been able to rent the house he was in for three weeks while the owners were on holiday: they did Bed & Breakfast in the summer, and autumn was the time when they took their break. They had in fact gone to Malta.

It was a nice house with all the modern conveniences that he had in his own home in Johannesburg, except of course that there was no swimming pool. But then who would use a swimming pool in weather like this? In fact, he felt cold a good deal of the time: and he missed the colour of the jaracanda trees. There were no trees here at all, and little colour. The wind swept over desolate bleak moorlands, and the sea looked sullen and strong.

He read most nights or watched television. Certainly he rested, though in fact he didn't need much rest. He had his own accountancy business, and it was successful enough. Whatever stress he felt was not because of the business but because of what was happening in the country generally. There had been a large number of murders in Johannesburg.

Though his father had been briskly kind to the blacks, he had a profound contempt for them. To him they were stupid, careless, childlike and dilatory. Sometimes he would say that there had been people like that in the village where he had grown up on the island. That was why he had joined the police in Glasgow, and later emigrated to South Africa where he had been manager of a diamond mine.

Angus himself didn't think like his father: he was much more confused, far less definite in his opinions. He sensed danger and potential chaos: an office not far from his own had been blown up in the middle of the day: buses too had been blown up. The biblical certainties that his father had recognised in South Africa were not so strong among his own generation.

We made this country, his father would say, though he had in fact been an incomer. Still, South Africa was different from Rhodesia, it didn't have so many fly-by-nights who fled when the going got rough.

What troubled him here was the incessant wind. It had a curious keening sound almost as if it spoke of all the exiles who had left the island. He found it piercing and melancholy, especially when he was sitting at night trying to relax with a book. He had never heard this kind of wind before. It bothered him for some reason that he couldn't understand.

He had time to think a great deal in this strange and almost alien environment. He thought of his father setting off on the boat to Glasgow. He thought of Sheila handing round drinks to their friends on a fine evening when the sun was setting. Sheila wouldn't have his father to stay with them when he had his stroke. He must go to a home instead.

'Can you imagine me lifting him?' she had said contemptuously. 'I have more to do with my time,' though in fact she hadn't, since she hadn't worked since their wedding. She had been a secretary in a law firm. Angus had felt guilty about his father, who had for some unaccountable reason reverted to speaking in Gaelic after his stroke: he himself had no Gaelic.

Yet it was probably true that Sheila wouldn't have been able to cope: it wasn't so much that, it was the decisive manner in which she had spoken, like his own father almost. There was no hesitation: and in fact she hadn't visited him much in the Home.

'I don't understand that weird language,' she would say. And that was it, the language thereupon dismissed as having no use and no meaning.

She had a firm belief that there would be no fundamental changes in South Africa. She would remain mistress of her servants: the regime would last her lifetime and perhaps for ever.

Yet he himself knew perfectly well, as an accountant, that this wasn't right. Businesses weren't doing well: and even the business community had begun to talk of the harmfulness of apartheid. The blacks had begun to use economic weapons against their masters: boycotts of shops, strikes. The day he had been to Stornoway, a little while after the loss of £23 million in the débàcle of BCCI, he had felt a certain familiarity in the scene. The people looked stunned, disbelieving, angry. The outside world had struck at them savagely. They could no longer be protected by seas and tradition. And anyway what was their council doing dealing with a bank that was connected with drugs? Even their religious feelings had been shaken. Also, roads and schools could not be built now. There would be more poverty, more constriction. Just as in South Africa when the sanctions had been initiated. No one was isolated now: it was all a vast web: if you tugged one part of it the whole structure would vibrate. A minister had preached that it was the will of God. Such complexity, along with such naïvité!

He didn't think much of Stornoway itself. It was a grey little fishing town and yet for his own father it had been a metropolis. He would say to him, 'We used to visit Stornoway once a year when I was young. I remember the smell of apples, and the ice-cream.'

Here the people didn't seem to care whether he was a South African or not, unlike London where a bearded fellow had suddenly, hearing his accent, lashed out at him verbally. 'What about your police?' he had shouted, 'Fascists, the lot of them. What about the black suicides in jail? Butchers, Nazis, bloody sadists.' And all the while he himself had remained calm, though shaken by the depth of the man's hatred. A bearded, literary-looking man suddenly raging at him in a bookstall.

From what he could gather, there was a lot of sympathy on the island for the white South African. Bible-thumping Protestants together?

It was the wind however that troubled him. Sometimes at night he couldn't sleep because of its high wailing sound. It was almost like the cry of an abandoned child: it seemed to have a human quality. It spoke of an infinite pain, of a tremendous heartbreaking loss. And there was no community here that he could see. Perhaps there had been in his father's time. Perhaps it had something to do with the thatched houses that his father had talked about.

He rose from his chair. It was dark outside and the sea was a deep black apart from the light cast by a moon careering among the clouds as if out of control. Now and again the windows of the house would shake. It seemed to him that he could see his father's white disordered face after the stroke. Of course he had led a very hard, diligent life: he had also been a strict disciplinarian.

'Why can't you make up your mind?' Sheila would shout at him. 'Why can't you be more like your father?' But how could he be like his father? He was not, for instance, religious. But there was an absence that he had become more and more aware of, and that was why perhaps he had come to the island. If only that bloody whining wind would stop!

His health was good and so was Sheila's, and so was Rosemary's. Rosemary was doing well as a teacher in a Pietermaritzburg school: a private school, in leafy surroundings, where she had once been a pupil.

He had bought a copy of the local paper. On the letter page a correspondent had gone on at great length about Sunday Observance: while another gave a religious reason for the financial collapse. There was an elaborate scenario, on a news page, about whether litter should be removed from the streets on Sunday even in the face of a mandatory law. In a curious way it reminded him of South African fundamentalism. Draw back into the laager while the wind howls around you! Hope that the storm will pass!

He remembered a story his father had told him. He had once been home on holiday in the island and he had bought a van for a nephew of his, so that he could sell fish. Earning a lot of money for the first time in his life, the nephew had taken to drink and had smashed up the van. Then he had run away from home, taken a job on the mainland and married his landlady, who was much older than him.

A kaffir, Angus's father had called him, nothing but a kaffir.

Of course the boy's mother had been angry and had blamed him for the disaster. But it wasn't his fault: he had only been trying to help. 'I also bought her a washing machine,' his father said, 'but she never used it; she would rather gossip with her neighbour at the washing line.'

On his own on the island, Angus thought about a lot of things. About Sheila, for instance, and her extremely rightist views and her mishandling of the servants. Even his father had complained about her tactlessness. There were some things she was incapable of learning. It was a question of knowing from the inside what to do, what not to do. There was no reason why one shouldn't be kind to one's servants, his father would say. But she had always been brusque and contemptuous. And in argument she was the same, ignorant and aggressive, uninterested in finding common ground. Nevertheless she was still beautiful – when he had first met her, astonishingly so: blonde and tall and high-boned, long-legged and blue-eyed, a secretary such as one might see in a television advertisement.

'There are certain ways of doing things,' his father would mutter angrily. He didn't seem to know how to deal with Sheila's beauty, and her essentially cruel and crude beliefs.

Still, there was no question but that the blacks could at times be irritating. He himself had offered a rise in wages to one of the servants, and the servant had immediately left on the grounds that he had been cheated, that he should have had the money from the beginning. What could you make of such economic thinking?

Really, what was he doing here? He paced restlessly about the living-room. In a bookcase there were volumes by Alasdair Maclean, Jack Higgins, Frederick Forsyth. There were no Gaelic books that he could see, except for a rather old Bible with a black cover. It wasn't actually all that different from a house in South Africa with its big round globe in which there were bottles of vodka, gin and whisky. On the walls and sideboards there were many photographs, mostly of young children.

'When we were children,' his father would say, 'we would fish for eels in the rivers and pick blaeberries on the moors.'

That bloody whining wind! He was beginning to feel that it was a constant unavoidable universal noise. He couldn't explain what he felt about it; it was like a ghostly permanent dirge that never stopped, as if it were composed of many voices in concert. A wind at the end of the world, among these ancient stones. It seemed to be saying to him, What are you doing here? You are a stranger, you are an interruption to this wind of death.

He made himself a cup of coffee and sat staring into the electric fire. 'They sit and stare into the fire,' his father had said. 'They say they have all kinds of sicknesses and diseases, but it's all laziness. They need a good shake.' And his face would redden with rage and high blood pressure. 'Our history, they say, what can we do? And they whine and whine. I bought a set of false teeth for my sister Chrissie but she wouldn't wear them.'

Here I am on the edge of things, he thought, as if I was at the Cape; this house shaky and shivering, and the sea below the headland black as tar, heaving and swelling, and monotonously stormy.

White houses these are known as, he thought, as distinct from black houses; that was what his father had told him. The black houses were the thatched ones: and in them the fire was in the middle of the floor, and it was in them also that the ceilidhs took place.

When people moved into the white houses, it was different, his father had said. Somehow the fire in the middle of the floor made a difference.

That woman in South Africa in a rural area who had found her husband's head hung in a tree like a strange fruit!

The wind was rising to a shriek, as if it were demented. He couldn't take much more of this. Maybe it hadn't been a good idea, after all, coming here. My father romanticised the place because it was connected with a relatively carefree childhood. But that was long before they had lost their £23 million, before the intricate outside world had impinged on them, whether they liked it or not. Bloody fools, he thought sourly, from his knowledge of accountancy, putting all their money in one bank like that. Bloody idiots. But South Africa could not insulate itself from the wide world either. The famous treks had probably been sentimentalised too. The Bible-wielding patriarchs would crack as the sea eventually breaks rocks.

And people would hear that whine, they would no longer be able to shut it out. It would shake orange trees, jaracarandas. It would blow and blow, and the voices of the dead would be heard in it: the voices of the dying and the living. Even Sheila would eventually hear it, among her cosmetics and her vodkas and gins. Infinite eternal whining wind!

'My mother and father died on the island when I had just come to South Africa,' his father told him. 'I couldn't afford to go home at that time.' And later Sheila wouldn't go home to her father's funeral. She had despised him. He had never made anything of himself, and he boasted to the neighbours that she was married to a very rich man. 'She's never had to work since she got married,' he would say, leaning on his stick. He was always whining about what the world had done to him. During the war he had been wounded in both legs. She couldn't forgive him his bad luck: he had wanted to visit them but she wouldn't have it.

He looked at a picture hanging on a wall of the living-room. It showed a woman carrying peats in a creel: she was knitting as she walked along.

No, he couldn't stay here. He would pay for the full three weeks, but he would leave the island as soon as possible. If he couldn't get a plane he would stay in London, among people.

All night the wind continued, and he could hardly sleep. Sometimes he thought it was a voice trying to speak to him in Gaelic: perhaps his father after his stroke. Sometimes he thought it came from inside himself and that would be the worst of all; that would be madness.

The following day he locked everything carefully behind him and abandoned the white house. The sea was still turbulent and black. The houses crouched against the rocky ground like seashells. As he drove away from the village in the blue car he had hired in Stornoway, he said, 'Goodbye, Father.' And, whistling, to keep out that whine, he headed towards the town from which he would get the boat that would take him to the mainland and on the first stage of his homeward journey.

The Blue Vase

When the woman asked for the vase, I remembered the two vases that had been stolen from the wall of our house. It had happened about a month before in the middle of the night. The vases were made of stone, and lion-shaped, and had been cemented to the wall. The thieves, whoever they were, had obviously had a van, and then had somehow cut the vases from the cement and taken them away. Lord knew where they were now. They had belonged to my wife's people originally and had been on the wall for years and years. She had been shocked when she had discovered the loss two days after it had happened, because in fact she had been so used to their being on the wall that she hadn't at first noticed their disappearance.

This came back to me when I was at the funeral of my poor brother, who had died on the island. He had lived alone and wouldn't come to visit us because he had looked after our mother, and I hadn't. Neither my wife nor myself had liked my mother and so we never visited her, nor had we attended her funeral. My brother hadn't communicated with me since. However, when he died, we returned to the island, for, in spite of everything, he had made me his heir.

He had never married, and there was a fair amount of money, some of which he had left to the church. In his later years it appeared that he had been a constant church-goer, though I remembered that in his youth he had been aesthetic and free-thinking.

I didn't like going back to the island and neither did my wife. It was bare and treeless and when the weather was bad it looked like the end of the world. However, the funeral took place on a day in June, and the sea was blue and sparkling. When we arrived my brother was already dead and his body was coffined in the house (on the island they don't put the body in the church overnight). This had been arranged by a cousin of ours whom I had not seen for a long time and who in fact had phoned to tell us that my brother had died. This cousin had often visited him and had a key.

When we arrived at the house she was already there and had put on a fire, though it was June. She was a large plump woman, and when she talked of Norman her eyes brimmed with tears. Now and again she would look at Sheila's costume as if she was saying to herself, Imagine coming to a funeral in a blue costume.

'I suppose you would like to see him,' she said, opening the lid of the coffin, and we looked down at my brother's calm, distant face.

'What happens here with regard to funerals?' I asked.

'People will come along later and there will be prayers and psalms,' she said. 'And you'd better get in touch with the grave-digger. I've got his number. I thought the funeral might take place tomorrow. Is that all right?'

'Yes, of course,' I said. 'You'll know the procedure here.' While I was dialling the grave-digger Sheila said, 'The under-taker arranges all that, where we are.'

'Not here,' said my cousin. 'Here, the two people, the under-taker and the grave-digger, have to be contacted separately.'

When the grave-digger answered I could hardly hear him, as if his voice was coming from the depths of the earth. However, he agreed to carry out the digging and I think he made a ponderous note of the date.

'I believe my brother was very religious latterly,' I said.

'Yes,' said my cousin, 'he was a strong follower, ever since his mother died. Oh, by the way, I got some groceries for you.'

I reached for my cheque book but she said, 'No, I wouldn't dream of taking money. It's only for yourselves that I bought them. The visitors won't take any food. There will be a lot of them.'

'Where are they going to sit?' said Sheila.

'Oh, my husband's arranging for chairs to be brought in. He will be along shortly. He will have help. Now I must run along and make the family's tea. I will be back.'

When she had gone, Sheila and I looked round the room. There was not much there of any value. There was however a really beautiful blue vase on the mantelpiece.

'He must have decided that he didn't want any material things,' said Sheila. The tears suddenly brimmed her eyes.

I thought of him. After all, we had been young together and had, as they say, 'paidlt in the burn'. My mother had always preferred him to me and hadn't wanted him to marry. I however had left for the mainland and was now a chartered accountant.

Sheila went into the kitchen and looked around. She opened the fridge and found milk and butter there as well as some cheese. In a cupboard she found tea-bags, bread, marmalade and jam.

'We don't need much,' I said, 'as we shall be leaving after the funeral.' I had decided that we would return to the island later and arrange for the sale of the house. However, I hoped to see the lawyer before we left.

I went upstairs and saw a number of photographs of my mother and, surprisingly, one of myself when I was about nineteen. I looked young, happy and hopeful. I glanced out through the window towards the sea which sparkled in the sunlight.

'It'll be heavy going,' said Sheila, 'all these religious people coming.'

She had removed her blue costume and was rummaging in our case for a darkish skirt and blouse.

'You'll have to wear a hat,' I said. 'I imagine it will be like a church service.'

She didn't say anything, but I knew that she didn't like the religion on the island and wasn't used to it. Her own religion was sunnier.

'We might come and stay here,' I said jokingly.

At that moment I heard a knock on the door. My cousin's husband, whom I vaguely remembered, and another man, were bringing chairs in from a van.

I shook hands with them and helped place chairs in various rooms. 'Where did you get them?' I asked.

'They're from the Sunday school,' said my cousin's husband, whose name I didn't know. He was a smallish man and he was wearing dungarees. His companion, who was taller, said nothing at all except that when I asked politely if there was any fresh news on the island he replied, 'No, only the good news of the gospel.' After that he remained silent.

'I'm sorry,' I said to my cousin's husband, 'I can't even offer you a dram.'

'Oh, that's all right,' he said. The tall gaunt man stared at me as if I had laughed out loud in church.

When they had gone Sheila and I began to rearrange the chairs in silence.

While I was doing so, I was thinking of my brother and his life. Had it really been my fault that I hadn't liked my mother any more than my wife had? She had been a very domineering woman who had certainly dominated my brother. He had tried to marry two or three times but each time she had taken to her bed, and also objected to the girls on various grounds, such as that one of them smoked and another one didn't attend church, and so on.

'What a lonely life he must have led,' I said, looking round the room. On a table near the window there were four Bibles and a radio.

'He would have died peacefully,' said my wife. 'He would have faith.'

The doctor had told me that it was cancer of the stomach. Norman had been very bitter towards me and it was only his regard for family that had caused him to make me his heir.

A picture flashed into my mind. The two of us were standing on the bank of a river. 'Dare you to jump to the other side,' I said. But he wouldn't jump, though I did. In his youth he was very nervous and imaginative. Perhaps that was why he had become so religious, as if he was looking for a protective armour. I wandered about the room as if seeking evidence of what his later years had been like. I found a black hat hanging on a nail in the lobby and a number of coats in the wardrobe. In his bedroom there was a small library of spiritual books.

'What happened to the picture I gave him?' said Sheila. This was a picture which she had herself painted of the area in which we lived. It was not to be seen anywhere.

I left the house and went outside. There was still some coal in the bin, and the grass was long and uncut.

When I returned to the house, I shouted to my wife, 'It was good of my cousin to bring groceries.' However, Sheila wasn't in the kitchen or in the living-room. She was upstairs and when I went up she was sitting on the bed crying.

'Are you all right?' I said.

'Yes, I'm all right. You go down.'

I left her and descended the stairs. Had it been my fault that my brother had broken with me, I thought. Had I been too honest, too inflexible, in refusing to attend my mother's funeral? To tell the truth, I think she ruined Norman, but no one could have told her that. He seemed bound to her by indissoluble ties. I think the main reason for that was that when he was young he had suffered from bronchitis and he had been off school a great deal. The other boys hadn't liked him very much and I had often fought them to protect him.

When Sheila came downstairs, I said, 'We have got out of the habit of expressing simple feelings.'

'What do you mean?' she said.

'Just that. We can't express our feelings, though I suppose women can do so more than men.'

'He was very lonely,' she said. 'I feel sorry for him. Look at this house. It feels cold and without character. Why all these Bibles too? Why four of them?'

'Maybe he wanted to check their authenticity,' I said jokingly.

But what she had said was true. There was a bareness about the house in spite of the fire. On one of the walls there was a patch of damp like a section of a map.

'And another thing,' she said, 'there don't seem to be any ordinary books, or any newspapers for that matter.'

'I'd noticed that,' I said, 'and yet when he was young he read far more than I did. Novels, history, poetry, and adventure stories.'

'And yet he never left the island apart from the period of his teacher training.'

'That's true,' I said. 'He couldn't go to the war because of his weak chest.'

I imagined him coming home to this bare house after his mother died. She must have been a presence there for him. In the photographs I had seen she sat calm and tranquil like a Buddha, her hands in her lap, staring peacefully at the camera.

His coffin lay in the room and his face was cold and still. Tomorrow he would be buried in the churchyard that stood beside the sea, and the flowers would grow through his bones. Time had passed and this was not the boy I had once known. Sometimes I think there is a disjunction in our lives, and the older man is not a continuation of the boy at all.

I think I became a chartered accountant because I didn't wish to be involved in the history of the island. I wanted something material, and not at all spiritual. But at times I wondered if my job had made me unfeeling. My wife had more feeling for Norman than I had.

'I'm sure they'll be coming shortly,' said Sheila, glancing at the clock.

'I'm sure. I should have asked my cousin when they would be here.'

The room with its chairs was like a room in a church.

'I think we had better move some of these chairs,' I said. 'Some of them are too near the fire. The knees of the people will be burnt.' And I laughed.

'It was a terrible religion,' said my wife. 'I wonder if he was frightened.'

'Of the cancer?'

'No, I mean of hell.'

'It's possible,' I said. I suddenly remembered Norman as young, his hair light brown, his eyes bright and argumentative. Because I had failed him he had been impelled towards the church. And yet the truth of feeling was important. Why should I have pretended to like my mother when I hadn't in fact done so? When we were young she would prevent us from playing football whenever she could. Not that Norman had played much, but playing might have improved his chest. On the other hand she held him in subjection so long as he was ill.

On the way over on the boat I had heard an English voice saying, 'Soon we will be home in Bayble.' I found this disconcerting since I thought of the island as my home, even though I hadn't been there for years. I suddenly realised however that I was a stranger there.

'I'd like to phone Gerald,' said Sheila.

Gerald was our son and was studying in art college in Edinburgh. He didn't like me being a chartered accountant and he would go on about children in Ethiopia, and want us to send money. I used to say, 'There is no guarantee that this will ever reach the right people.' Gerald was very emotional, untidy, and kind-hearted. I couldn't stand his untidiness since I myself am obsessively neat. I also found it very hard to talk to him. There would be long silences between us and for the life of me I couldn't think of anything to say. I couldn't understand his paintings, they were impenetrably abstract.

'You'd better get yourself a teacher's certificate,' I would say to him. 'If you don't succeed as an artist you will always have teaching to fall back on.' But he wouldn't become a teacher, as all teachers in his judgement were middle-class. He hated us for being middle-class. At one time he had been rebellious.

Once we had some friends in the house, and a woman had said, while were having drinks, 'I suppose Gerald here will have Coca-Cola.'

'Not at all,' he had said, 'Coca-Cola makes me fart.'

Sheila had hidden her laughter, but I was really angry. In short, I don't get on well with Gerald and I am sure he despises me.

Sheila turned away from the phone. 'I can't get hold of him. He must be out.'

'I'm not surprised,' I said.

Suddenly she burst out, 'Why did you say that? You didn't have to say that. I come all the way up here, but you don't want to make any concessions, do you? I *like* his paintings.'

I kept silent. I didn't want us to quarrel before these people came. I have, I think, much greater self-control than Sheila: it is only very rarely that I lose my temper.

The posters on the walls of Gerald's room are highly political. 'What's this one about Nicaragua?' I once asked him.

'What do you mean, what's this one about Nicaragua?'

'I just don't understand what you have to do with Nicaragua,' I said.

'Really?'

And when he's at home he plays his music very loudly. I have often told him to turn the volume down but as soon as I leave his room he turns the volume up again. Also he has to help me with the video and he makes sarcastic comments about my intelligence.

I wonder how Norman and he would have got on: he did at one time talk about him and suggest that he might take a croft on the island. I discouraged that.

'I should have taken these curtains down and replaced them,' Sheila said.

'Why?'

'Well, these people may be talking about them. They don't look very clean.'

'It's fine,' I said, 'the house is fine and tidy.'

'It's tidy enough,' she agreed. 'I can't understand why he didn't buy some decent furniture.'

'Perhaps he gave most of his money to the church.'

'That's possible,' she said seriously.

At least not to Nicaragua, I thought. If it was to the woman next door that would make sense, but why Nicaragua?

And in any case Gerald never had any money. He had left a good job in a supermarket because it sold South African oranges.

'Look,' I told him, 'in my youth we couldn't pick and choose like that.' I myself had once worked on a fishing boat. I remembered that Norman never took a job: he had spent his time studying. I supposed he had been a good teacher, though I had never met anyone who had been taught by him. If he had brought his religion into the classroom he would have been a conservative unimaginative one. Then again, since he hadn't any children himself, how could he understand children.

In the early days, for instance, he would never play with Gerald, or lift him up in his arms. He obviously felt uncomfortable with him, while Gerald stared at him, his thumb in his mouth.

'Here they come,' said my wife, and we saw the first visitors at the gate. I went to the door and shook hands with them and looked suitably grave. They seemed sad and said very little. They were in fact two women, and when they came into the house they sat down on chairs in the bedroom facing the sea. They wore coats even though the evening was warm. They also wore hats.

My wife glanced at me, raising her eyebrows. She had offered them tea but they refused. They sat perfectly still on their chairs like polite children.

After their arrival more and more people started to come. I shook hands with all of them. My cousin also came and told me that I should keep the front seats for the elders. However, one doddering old woman took one of them and I didn't have the heart to move her.

The rooms became very crowded. There were even people sitting on the beds of the upstairs bedrooms. They talked quietly among each other.

The sturdy-looking elders introduced themselves, and one of them said, 'Would you like the service in English or in Gaelic?'

'English,' I said.

Suddenly Sheila said, 'Could we have it in both English and Gaelic?'

'Whatever you want.' said the elder.

He seemed pleased with the decision and visibly brightened.

'I think he would have preferred that himself, if I may say so,' he said.

We all sat down.

Many people stood up and prayed. I needn't describe what they said since it was the usual thing. Then they began to sing the beautiful Gaelic psalms whose music rose and fell like the sea. I hadn't realised how moving and aesthetically satisfying they were.

When it was all over Sheila said to me, 'Do you know that one of the elders winked at me?'

'He was probably trying to put you at your ease,' I said.

The service had lasted about an hour and finished about nine o'clock. Then they all left and we were alone again.

'We will leave the chairs here till tomorrow,' my cousin had said. 'There will be another service before the funeral.' The house was quiet after the visitors had gone. I could hear the clock ticking.

'They all look very strong physically,' my wife suddenly said. 'I mean the elders.'

'Yes,' I said absently.

I wondered why my brother himself hadn't become an elder. Perhaps he hadn't felt holy enough: he had always been a bit hesitant about his own abilities.

I remembered one night when I had come home late from town and he was lying in his bed wheezing because of his bronchitis. I had brought him a chocolate. I gave him some squares of it as I got into bed.

'Did you enjoy yourself?' he asked.

'Yes,' I said, but I didn't tell him about red-haired Peggy whom I had kissed after the dance was over.

'My mother is very angry that you were so late,' he told me.
'I know.'

He wheezed heavily during the night and I was kept awake for a while, for we slept in the same bed. In the morning I would have to face my mother, and she would say to me, 'after all I've done for you, you keep defying me.'

When Sheila and I were in bed together I could hear the sound of the sea, and I could see the moonlight on the walls.

'Look,' I said, 'he even left the electric flex bare. A lot will have to be done to the house.'

'I suppose,' she said, 'he would have slept in the bedroom downstairs.'

Directly in front of me was a photograph of our mother. In my mind the music of the psalms rose and fell. Below us the coffin rested. His face had become stern as my mother's had been, purified of emotion, severe and in a strange way beautiful.

We slept well and did not get up till nine in the morning. I could hear the cries of the seagulls all around the house and felt suddenly at home.

When we were having breakfast, I looked at the blue vase. It was plain and very clear with a sea-blue glaze. I thought it was very beautiful.

'Don't you think it's lovely?' I said to Sheila.

'What is?'

'The vase,' I said, 'the vase on the mantelpiece.'

She studied it for a while. 'Yes,' she said, 'I suppose it is. It's the most beautiful thing in the house.'

'We won't have time to go down town,' I said.

'Did you wish to go?'

'Oh, just to see it again. I remember it from my youth as being very pretty. There were trees round the castle.'

'It is very pretty here too,' said Sheila.

And indeed it was. It was going to be a fine day, though still rather hazy. I saw a white ship sailing into the bay. It looked foreign.

Pictures floated into my head. Norman and I were at the pier climbing seaweed-entangled steps. He was trembling beside me, looking out at the brine where the almost transparent jelly fish floated.

Abstractedly I arranged the chairs.

There was a knock on the door and my cousin came in.

'I thought I'd see if you were all right,' she said.

'We're fine,' I said.

'One thing I forgot to mention,' she said, 'you as next of kin have to walk at the head of the coffin. The coffin is carried for about a hundred yards to the hearse. You don't have to carry it though.'

'Do they still carry the coffin?' I said.

'Here they do. My husband arranged the cord holders,' she said. 'You will be one of them yourself. But that will be arranged at the graveside. Is that all right?'

'That will be fine,' said Sheila, 'and thanks for all your help. We want to do what's right.'

My cousin looked harassed, as if she had too much on her mind.

'You visited him a lot?' I asked her.

'Yes.'

'What was he like?'

'He was very happy since he was converted. He went to church regularly. It was his life.'

There was something about a vase that returned to me. It was a poem I had once read in school and which Norman had been very fond of. I don't remember much poetry but that poem stayed with me. It told of a vase which had pictures on it: I think one of the pictures had to do with a sacrifice. The details were very vague in my mind but I remember that Norman liked it. When he liked a poem he would go about the house reciting verses and lines from it for days. I recalled his thin animated face as if it belonged to a different world, a different person even.

'That's it then,' said my cousin. 'There will be a service before the funeral. The minister himself will be there.'

She referred to the minister as if he were some god.

'Thank you,' I said, 'for everything, and for the food.' I saw her to the door. Her harassed face looked back at me.

'He was a good man,' she said, 'a good man.'

The service brought a large number of people as before. I noticed a little old woman in the corner near the fire who was weeping uncontrollably.

'Who is that?' I whispered to my cousin.

'She is an old relative of your own. On your father's side.'

It was amazing how little I knew of my relatives: but then I hadn't wanted to be involved in genealogy or history. The woman was weeping bitterly and I saw Sheila trying to comfort her.

When the service was over the coffin was carried out of the house into the bright sunshine. The women remained behind: only the men went to the cemetery.

I walked behind the coffin, at the head. Because of the weight of it the men had an intricate way of changing places, and then moving out from under the burden. I saw an eighty-year-old man bent under its considerable weight.

When we arrived at the cemetery in the hearse, the coffin was taken up some steps. We all gathered round to listen to a short service. There was a slight breeze blowing from the sea as we took the cords in our hands and lowered the coffin slowly into the ground.

This is my brother, I thought, this is the last I will ever see of him. I found myself weeping as I looked down at the coffin, and then I wiped my eyes shamefacedly.

He who had been a vivid excited young man had declined into a religious hermit. I could hardly bear the thought.

Again, however, when I looked out at the sea, the image of the vase, tall and slender and plain, rose up in front of me. What is happening to me, I thought. I am a chartered accountant, that is all I am. This that I see around me is all there is.

There came into my mind the picture of an old farmer who was very rich and who had tried to persuade me to declare only a fraction of his true earnings. He was a fat red-faced gross man.

'You can arrange this,' he kept saying to me.

'No,' I said, 'I can't. You don't seem to understand. I am not here to cheat the tax man.'

'Why not?' he said innocently, leaning back, his legs spread.

'Because,' I said, 'that is not my job. My job is to tell you what you can legally claim. We must work within the rules.'

The farmer's face suddenly became swollen and enraged.

'I bet you cheat the tax man yourself,' he shouted, the veins on his neck standing out. 'You're no use to me.'

And that was how I lost another customer.

My son of course despised me for being a chartered accountant. He despised the fairly prosperous life I offered him. Maybe he would prefer living among the starving peasants in Nicaragua.

Standing at the graveside I felt very confused.

I had never been pierced by such pure pain as I felt then.

When the funeral was over a small man came over to me hesitantly.

'My name is Duncan Macleod,' he said. 'I was in the same class as you at school. Do you remember me?'

'I can't say that I do,' I said pleasantly.

'We sat in the same seat,' he said. 'Do you remember Miss Gracie?'

'Vaguely,' I said.

'She taught French,' he said. 'Anyway, I thought I'd introduce myself.'

'That was very nice of you,' I said.

And then suddenly I did remember Miss Gracie.

'Was Miss Gracie a thin grey-haired woman?' I said.

'Yes, that's her.'

For some reason I had hated French in school, but I loved mathematics and its indisputable naked logic. In French we concentrated eternally on grammar, and the thin grey-haired woman became the emblem for boredom. I don't think she had been married. I couldn't remember the boy who had turned into this small stout man.

'How are you doing now?' I said.

'I'm a headmaster,' he said. 'As a matter of fact I took the afternoon off to come to your brother's funeral. We used to exchange books and he would show me some of his poems. He loved spy stories. He was off school a lot as I remember.'

'Yes,' I said. This person in the coffin had been off school a lot. I remembered the two of us putting on our bags as we left for school. The smell of the leather returned to me agonisingly fresh. It was so clear and distinct that I nearly fainted with the unutterable pathos of it. I felt naked and vulnerable in the sea air.

'Glad to have met you,' the small stout man said.

When I returned to the house, Sheila was there alone.

'Listen,' she said eagerly, 'do you remember that woman who was weeping all the time? Someone said she was a relative of yours.'

'Yes,' I said, 'what about her?'

'Well, immediately the coffin left the house she asked for the blue vase. She said she would like a memento of your brother. One moment she was weeping, the next she wanted the blue vase.'

'Did you give it to her?' I said.

'Yes, of course. We have no use for it.'

'You shouldn't have done that,' I shouted. 'I wanted that blue vase myself as a memento. You had no right to give it to her.'

'What?'

'It was important to me, that blue vase,' I shouted. 'Do you know that I met a friend of my brother's at the funeral. He said that I had sat in the same seat as him at school. How can that have happened? How did I not know about it?'

'I don't understand,' said Sheila. 'I don't know what you're talking about.'

'And then our vases were stolen from the wall. I liked that blue vase.'

'But it wasn't worth anything.'

'I don't care. It wasn't because of its value that I wanted it. It was blue and it was lovely,' I shouted, and I almost broke down in tears. There was my son who wanted to be in Nicaragua and there was my school-friend whom I couldn't remember, and my cousin who had brought us the groceries free. And above all, there was the blue vase.

'I've a good mind to go and take it from her,' I shouted. 'She has no right to it.'

'Oh, shut up,' said Sheila. 'I don't understand any of this.'

'Can you not see that it's very important,' I screamed. 'It's to do with everything. My son is an artist, and he doesn't speak to me. I've tried my best but I neglected my brother, and he died here, and he was a religious hermit.'

'But what has all this to do with the blue vase?' Sheila said.

'It has,' I said. 'We were standing at the graveside and this man said that he and my brother had exchanged books and that Norman was off school a lot. And there he was in his grave. I find that strange.'

'I think you're going off your head,' said Sheila. 'All this may be true, but what has it to do with the vase?'

And yet it had something to do with it. I was sure of that. The thieves had come and stolen the pair outside the house in the middle of the night. They were strangers, and I had felt vulnerable for the first time in my life.

And now Sheila was asking me what the blue vase had to do with anything.

Of course it was all connected: the sea, the death of my brother, my cousin, the thieves, the farmer, my school-friend whom I hadn't recognised. My school-friend had sat in the same wooden desk as me a long time ago in another life. Norman and I were setting off for school, our leather bags over our shoulders, and the birds were singing, and my mother was watching him protectively as she had always done so that he would die alone and friendless.

'Can't you see,' I said, 'that the blue vase is very important?'

'Well, I'm sorry,' said Sheila distantly, 'I didn't realise it meant so much to you.'

'It meant everything to me,' I shouted. 'Everything. Can't you understand?'

And I suddenly began to weep and I couldn't stop, and Sheila was looking at me in amazement. She put her arms around me and cradled my head on her breast as if I were a child again.

'It's all right,' she said, 'it's all right.' But it wasn't all right. I could see Gerald's face as he looked at me mockingly, hatingly, from a ring of starving children. He was holding out an empty plate. The sky above was mercilessly blue.

When I had stopped weeping I was suddenly quite calm.

'I'm sorry,' I said.

'I'm glad you broke down,' said Sheila. But she was staring at me as if she hadn't known me before.

'It's just the responsibility for everything,' I said. 'I should have written to my brother. I should have been less proud.'

And all the time the blue vase revolved in front of me, distant, uninvolved with history or genealogy.

And my brother's face was buried in my mother's breast like a child's in Nicaragua. Gerald's starved face was gazing at me as well.

And the sky opened in front of me, and there was a strong perfume of flowers as the two of us ran along a dusty March road towards the school with its carved wooden desks.

The Open University

When Hugh opened the big brown envelope which had fallen on to the mat below the letter-box, he saw that he had been accepted for the Open University. He knew it was a mistake but said to himself after a while, 'Why shouldn't I do it? After all, I am not stupid.' And immediately the world around him which was the world of the village became more real to him, and his life more purposeful. He studied the papers for a while and decided that he would do the Foundation Course.

He never found out exactly how the mistake had occurred, but knew that there was another Hugh MacCallum in the village next to his own and it occurred to him that this was how the error had been made.

Hugh was sixty-five years old and very good at genealogies, derivations of names of places, and the meanings of old words. He had left school at the age of thirteen and had later served in the Merchant Navy: he had seen Australia, New Zealand, and South Africa, among many other countries. Why shouldn't he do the Open University? He was no fool, and after all he might have letters after his name, and that would put a spoke in Alastair's wheel. Alastair thought that Mary Maclachlan was the best Gold Medallist there had ever been, though she was so drunk that she had to be supported on to the stage, but Hugh knew better. Hugh knew that the best medallist who had ever been was Anna MacDougall, who had died with cancer of the throat. But you couldn't tell Alastair anything.

Hugh was a bachelor and so was Alastair. Hugh's mother had died when he was forty-eight years old, and now he lived alone. Alastair too lived alone after his sister had died. Once when she was on the train to Yarmouth to the fishing she had pulled the communication cord out of curiosity, and it was only when the other two girls who were with her had pointed to their foreheads that the little man with the moustache, who had run along to the carriage with a notebook, had been placated.

Hugh decided that he would do the Open University. After all, he had a television set and a radio and plenty of time on his hands.

When he told Alastair about it, Alastair was very angry. He knew at once that this represented a threat to their relationship, and said so. 'Anyway,' he said, his moustache bristling, 'what do you want to go to the university for at your age?'

'I am not going to the university,' said Hugh. 'You do this at home. There are what are called assignments.'

'Assignments? What's that?'

'Compositions,' said Hugh, whose left eye blinked compulsively. He also had a habit of twisting his neck around inside his collar when he was nervous or embarrassed.

'And what will you get at the end of it?'

'I will get a degree,' said Hugh. Already he seemed to be moving away from Alastair and from the village, which was in any case dying. There were hardly any children left, and the buses which had once taken them to school were lying rusting in the fields.

'I see what you are at,' said Alastair.

Hugh didn't say anything to this: he knew that Alastair was angry and that this was his method of getting his own back on him. Maybe, he thought, we shall never discuss genealogies again, and the idea bothered him, for these discussions which had gone on endlessly and inconclusively had passed the time for both of them.

'Think of it, Alastair, we shall soon be dead and I might as well spend my time studying. Don't you want to do it yourself?'

'Not at all,' said Alastair bristling. 'Not at all.'

They were silent for a long while and then Alastair excused himself and went home. It seemed to Hugh that he was saying goodbye to him forever and he didn't like the feeling. He considered that he was doing something very striking and original by studying for the Open University and maybe cutting himself off from the village. But on the other hand why shouldn't he do it? There was nothing wrong with the quality of his mind. He stared out at the sea which he could see through the window. Its horizon stretched into the distance, blue and infinite.

A strange thing happened to Hugh after a while. He was seeing the people of the village as not really people at all. At first he was puzzled about this but then he realised that it must be something to do with the Open University. Also he seemed to be losing his sense of smell, and one day he ate rancid butter without realising it till a long time afterwards. As well as that, he thought that the mountains that he could see from his bedroom were growing smaller. In the old days he would admire the sunset flaring over the hills, but he no longer did so. It was as if the village was becoming a toy to him and in its place there was building up inside his head another place larger than the village which was inhabited by philosophies, paintings, novels, great cities, open seas. It was as if he had renewed his youth and saw the oceans sparkling as they had been then. Dang it, he thought, this is a fine big world I've got myself into. This is a big sky that I'm seeing.

When he looked at Alastair pottering around his house, he saw him as a little fellow with a blue jersey and a moustache. Alastair, he knew, had a history of high blood pressure in his family: this was because they were all abrupt and irascible. Of course his father had been a bard, like Alastair himself, but what were their poems compared to the ones he was reading now. Childish, that was what they were.

The bees hummed about the moor and when he put his feet down in the spongy moss it was not as it had been. The birds seemed different and so was the sea, and so was the cow which he saw staring at him one day, a long blade of fresh green grass in its mouth.

He heard in a roundabout way that the schoolmistress, Miss Gibson, didn't approve of what he was doing. The old sour bitch, he thought, she only has her Primary Teacher's Certificate, she doesn't even have a university degree. He had actually been going to consult her about his English, for his greatest difficulty was not in understanding the material but in setting down his answers in correct sentences. Old bitch, he thought, I won't go and see her; if he ever met her he would casually mention the Renaissance and discover what she knew about it. In any case she was rather mad and would scream at the children and throw chalk at them. Nevertheless, he had great difficulty with his sentence structure and would spend hour after hour struggling to compose a version of his answer that would satisfy an examiner. His light could be seen burning at two o'clock in the morning.

But he could feel a coldness all around him. Who was he to do the Open University? Even when he went to the Post Office to send away his completed assignments, Seordag would hardly speak to him.

'Special delivery,' he would say, and she would look contemptuously at the address. She would purse her lips but would not give him the satisfaction of asking what was in the envelope.

He also missed the human presence of Alastair.

He often felt now that he was entirely alone, and at nights he would hear the wind moaning in the chimney. Once he had looked at an egg from which a chick was emerging. The shell shook and broke under the vehement restless assault of life and then the chick, bare and skinny, could be seen pushing and struggling. The crown of the shell fell off, the chick pushed, and sometimes it was entangled with the shell and sometimes it seemed to be clear of it. But it thrust and thrust with determined impatience and finally it was out in the open air, an explorer, a small, thin, skinny adventurer that had shed its armour.

He had his first assignment back. It was only a D, but still a bare pass. Dang it, he thought. I must do better than this.

But while he was reading about Constable and studying his paintings he soon forgot the village. How much richer the land in Constable's paintings was, that river smooth and wide, those lush cornfields, and in the background an old mill. He raised his head from his book and wondered why no one had ever painted the village. Think of all those subtle lights that were everywhere, the pearly grey light that you sometimes saw over the sea. No one had ever painted the people who had left on the boats for Canada and Australia and New Zealand, no one had painted the roofless, once-thatched, houses that were to be found all over the village. No one had painted the disused ruined buses which had once carried children to school but which now lay rusting on their sides among the buttercups and the daisies: or even the blue hills which ringed the village and turned purple in the vague evenings.

He scratched the back of his neck as he thought of these things. Then after a while he left his books and went outside and saw Alastair carrying vegetables into the house from his little wind-blown garden. He went over to him and at first Alastair pretended not to know that he was there. His face was red with the effort of bending down. Finally, he couldn't ignore Hugh any longer and stood in front of him with a turnip and a clump of dirty roots dangling from his hand.

'It's a fine day,' said Hugh.

'It's cold enough,' said Alastair.

'Are the turnips good this year?'

'They're not bad. They're not too wet.'

The breeze stirred Alastair's jersey and he seemed somehow to have shrunken. Hugh felt a little panic quivering in his chest, a tiny mouse of fear. At his age he should be thinking about death, attending the church, reading religious books, and not studying the Renaissance, but he didn't feel like confining himself to spirituality. Constable irradiated his mind.

'Have you been composing any poems?' he asked Alastair.

'I have that,' said Alastair, but he didn't want to let Hugh see them.

'What are they about?' said Hugh.

'Oh, there's one about ... but you won't like it, it's in Gaelic,' said Alastair spitefully.

'But why shouldn't I want to see it?' said Hugh. 'I can read Gaelic as well as you.'

Alastair however was stubbornly silent, and then he said grudgingly, 'It's about the sea.'

Alastair couldn't feel himself settled now in Hugh's company.

He felt that Hugh was superior to him, that he knew things that he himself didn't; he felt that Hugh had deserted him, was trying to be better than him. What did his poetry matter? In the old days he would have shown his poem to Hugh and listened to his criticisms of it, but now he didn't want to in case Hugh mocked him. No, he wouldn't show Hugh his poem. After all, Hugh had kept his television on when he was visiting him. He had told him that the programme was in connection with an assignment he was doing, but there was nothing more inhospitable than leaving your television on in front of a visitor. Also he missed his conversations about genealogies. And damn him if he would show him his poem.

What is his poem to me anyway, thought Hugh. It's very thin poor stuff. How could one expect good poetry or bardachd from Alastair who had hardly ever left the village in his life. Look at his stringy neck, his jersey, his dungarees. It seemed to him that he had had a poor opinion of Alastair for a long time, but had refused to admit it to himself. Now he was admitting it.

'If you don't want to show it to me,' he said, 'I don't want to see it.'

'That's that then,' said Alastair. 'I'd better be putting the dinner on.' And he went back into the house. As Hugh was returning to his own house, he saw little Colin coming towards him. Colin was the son of a fisherman called Angus Macleod, and his mother was the daughter of Iain MacFarlane from another part of the island.

Colin was wearing a black magician's robe.

'And how are you today, Colin?' Hugh asked him.

Colin stood and looked at him, not speaking, very shy. Finally he said in a burst of words, 'I've got a magic kit.'

'I can see that,' said Hugh, 'and what tricks can you do?'

'I've got a magic coin,' said Colin, in another burst of words. 'Abacadabra,' he shouted, jumping up and down. 'You have to say abacadabra,' he said seriously. 'What hand have I got my coin in?'

'I don't know,' said Hugh, 'I'm not sure that I know that.'

'It's this one, it's this one,' Colin shouted, and held his hand out, showing the coin. Then he was dashing away, shouting, the triumphant magician.

Hugh stood staring after him. At one time he himself must have been like Colin, but he couldn't remember. He could remember very little of his early childhood except that on his first day in school a small woman with grey hair had told him to use some plasticine, which he did. He couldn't even remember how he had learned English, but he must have done so. In the distance he could see Colin jumping up and down spreading out his black wings. How small this village had become, how strange, he felt; maybe it would have been better for him if he had never left the village in the first place.

The village drowsed in time. The houses seemed sunk, each in its own hollow. At night their television sets told the villagers of other countries, of violence, of foreign streets. Why, they had even stopped cutting peat and were now burning coal, though it was very dear: one or two of the houses were all-electric. In winter there was snow and rain. In autumn one felt the nostalgia of the past; the sea was both shield and stimulus and unimaginable depth, a ring around the village, a blue salty ring. There was an air of despair and weariness everywhere. Alastair himself felt the change in his bones and wished that his sister were still alive so that he could torment her. At least Hugh had his Open University. Tears of rage and self-pity filled his eyes.

Alastair worked away at his poem, which was called the 'Song of the Open University.'

> Bha fear againn anns a' bhaile
> a bha aosd is pròiseil,
> smaoinich esan air an oilthigh,
> chuireadh e air dòigh e.
>
> Nach robh esan cheart cho math ri
> fear sam bith na b'òige,
> oir 'na mo bheachd'sa 's na mo bharail
> chan eil an t-àit' s gu leòr dhomh.'

> We had a man in the village
> who was old and proud.
> He thought of the university
> and how he would put it right.
> Wasn't he as good as anyone
> who was even younger
> for, 'In my opinion and judgment
> this place is not good enough for me.'

Alastair walked up and down his room, listening to the rhymes. He always composed his poem aloud, not on paper, and some time soon he would recite it to some of the villagers. He should be able to make a good poem, for all his ancestors had been fine bards, and many of his poems were already well known, especially the one about the original coming of the electricity to the village. In fact one or two of them had been sung on the wireless and he had strutted about like a peacock after that. But there were a few verses to be added yet.

Imagine the Renaissance, thought Hugh, as he sat down at his oil-clothed table. The sea that stretched outwards into unimaginable distances, the paintings, the cathedrals. The village seemed to be inhabited by Virgin Marys with their holy children. Its colours were marvellous blues and velvet reds and indigos.

Then he read about the Claude glass in the eighteenth century which was designed to convert an ordinary landscape into a formal picture. Imagine that, he thought. Imagine the sky above Constable, so huge, so vast.

Imagine the crazy cornfields of Van Gogh which seemed to echo his thin shrunken whiskers.

All through the night Hugh worked.

And Alastair continued with his poem.

> Dh' fhàg e chompanaich a' gearain,
> shuidh e aig a leabhrain
> or b'e iadsan a chuid arain;
> cha robh fiù di-domhnaich

nach robh e ann an solus an dealain
a' sgrìobhadh is a' sgròbadh,
mar chat a tha air tòir air ealain
le peann an àite spògan.

He left his companions to complain,
he sat at his booklets
for they were now his bread.
There wasn't even a Sunday
that he wasn't in the light of the electricity
writing and scraping
like a cat that is in search of science
with a pen instead of claws

Hugh's father had been in fact the very first person to have a car in the village. It was more a van than a car, for in those days he had a butcher's shop, and he travelled through all the villages selling meat. He had been a good businessman, and his shop was a successful one till one night his car had been hit by a bus, and he had been killed outright. Hugh and his mother were left alone, the shop had to be sold, and the memory of the first van faded. However, in his lonely nights, Hugh thought, My father was a clever man, everyone said that, and I must have inherited his cleverness. It's not everyone who would be doing what I am doing at my age. This thought sustained him, as he read and worked under the light of the electric bulb.

In the village there was an incomer called Stella Simpson who kept pigs. She had tried to learn Gaelic, but Alastair made fun of it.

'Do you know,' he had once said to Hugh, 'that woman said to me "Is latha math ann" instead of "Tha latha math ann".'

In spite of that, however, she continued to learn Gaelic.

The villagers didn't like her pigs. They were like big pink submarines in a sea of mud. They were alien beings; in any case, pigs would eat anything, even each other.

Stella slopped about in yellow wellingtons and tried to learn how to cook oatcakes and scones. But these were not successful. When she went to the Post Office, which was also the local shop, she often wore a long red coat and black glasses. No one could make out what her age was, but it was considered that she must be about fifty. Her face was often dead white like a vampire's and at other times well-rouged.

She was, however, from England: everyone knew that, though no one had discovered anything about her background. When she had arrived first she had asked for buttock steak at the butcher's van instead of rump steak.

In the summertime she sat on the headland, painting the sea. 'I told her once,' said Alastair gleefully, 'that there was a man who went out fishing one night and a storm blew up, and he had to shelter in a cave which was full of rats. "How did he survive?" she asked me. "Well," I said, "he fed them on fish till the morning came and he escaped." '

One morning Hugh was passing her house, looking askance at the pigs which wallowed in the sea of mud, pink and obscene and naked, when she came out in her yellow wellingtons, carrying a bucket.

'I hear you're doing the Open University,' she said to Hugh.

'I am that,' said Hugh.

'That's good,' she said. 'I might be able to help you. I have paintings. And I have some records. I believe you have to study music as well.'

The pigs attacked the bucket. Her scarf blew in the wind.

'Yes, I have to do music,' said Hugh. 'That's the worst part of it. You see, I never learned about music.'

What am I doing talking to this woman, he asked himself. In the old days I wouldn't have. If the villagers see me talking to her they'll think I'm courting her. On the other hand, he was beginning to feel lonely, to miss the company of Alastair who had become inflexible and distant, especially since the night he had seen pictures of the Virgin Mary in a book Hugh had.

'So you're becoming a Catholic now,' he said contemptuously to Hugh.

'Not at all, I'm studying,' said Hugh. But Alastair went away, snorting incredulously.

'I shall come over and bring you some records. Have you a record player?' Stella asked.

'No.'

'In that case I shall bring my record player as well.'

What an odd-looking woman, thought Hugh. She tries to be like one of us, but she isn't really. She cannot disguise the fact that she is an alien. Even her red coat flung a strange radiance on the landscape. And as for her pigs, who ever saw pigs in a village? With their horrible snouts and their vivid fleshy nakedness.

By talking to this woman, by allowing her to come to his house with her records, he felt that he had crossed another frontier which was taking him further and further away from Alastair. And yet at the same time the logic was inevitable. It was true that he didn't know about classical music, and this woman might teach him or at least give him an insight into it. His work was not enough, knowledge was also essential.

When Stella arrived at his house under cover of darkness, she was carrying a torch, a record player, and some records. Hugh ushered her into the living-room where a bright fire was burning. He had put away the dishes, and the room was tidy and warm.

'What a nice little place you have,' said Stella, putting down her burden. She took off her coat without asking Hugh to help her. She looked much prettier, her face composed and relaxed, with a certain amount of colour in it. She was wearing a yellow blouse and skirt.

Well, well, said Hugh to himself, well, well. How women can change.

'Your mother's dead?' said Stella, looking at him keenly.

'Yes, I'm on my own here,' said Hugh. 'She died some years ago.'

'I see you have a picture of her on the wall,' said Stella. 'It is her, isn't it?'

'Yes,' said Hugh.

'A strong-looking woman,' said Stella. And indeed his mother did look formidable in her white blouse staring at the camera and not smiling at all.

'I have brought you some Mozart,' said Stella. 'I presume you have a plug?'

'Oh, yes, I have that,' said Hugh awkwardly. Electrical things were not what he was best at. But this woman seemed to have no trouble with them.

The room, which at times appeared austere and cold, had become humanised. He wondered what his mother would have thought of this woman. 'Not for you, Hugh,' she would have said. 'You don't know anything about her. And she might even smoke.'

And sure enough, before sitting down, she did ask for an ashtray, which she laid on the table beside her. It was one which Hugh had brought home from Australia and which showed Sydney Opera House.

Hugh sat down beside the fire and smoked his pipe, first asking permission.

'My late husband smoked,' said Stella, 'when he was well. He was ill for a long time,' she added. 'Mental trouble. He became very bitter in argument. I find this place very good for me. I needed the rest. He was a very clever scientist and therefore very ingenious at devising torments for me.'

'Oh,' said Hugh.

'You don't want to know about that,' she said, stubbing out her first cigarette. 'And now we will listen to Mozart.'

That night she told him a great deal about classical music and especially about Mozart, whom she idolised. She and her husband, before he became ill, had often gone to concerts in Bath, where in fact she came from. Music was later the only thing that could soothe her husband's savage breast.

As they listened to the music, she would ask him questions.

Why had he wanted to do the Open University? Did he do a lot of studying? When had he left school? Had he read a lot?

Of course, he told her, he had always been reading even when he was in the Merchant Navy. He had read Conrad, Stevenson, Melville. She seemed surprised at this.

'Is that right,' she said, staring at him, her cigarette in a long holder. It was as if she was seeing a strange specimen in the village, as alien to her as pigs were to him.

'Mozart is pure intuitive genius,' she told him. 'Better even than Beethoven.' He listened, and as he did so he seemed to hear what she was talking about, but shortly afterwards he was lost again. He had had no training in that kind of music, no previous understanding of it.

'I see I shall have to teach you a great deal,' she said. 'And now perhaps you could give me a cup of tea.'

The request astonished him, and at first he thought her bad-mannered, but then realised that her blunt demand was quite natural for her. In fact, when he showed her the kitchen, she made the tea herself.

'Have you any biscuits or anything?' she asked him.

'I think so,' he said. He found some digestives, and they ate and drank together in front of the bright fire.

He became aware of the steady ticking of the old grandfather clock which he had inherited. He couldn't understand how this woman was here at all, nor why he was entertaining her, nor why he was listening to classical music. It was like a dream.

'I'll tell you why I came to live in this village,' she told him. 'My husband and I were on holiday here years ago. He was interested in bird-watching, you see. And we enjoyed our visit so much that I decided that I would come and stay. Of course the village was healthier then than it is now. I know what people are saying about me. They think I'm odd and that my oatcakes are appalling, which they are. And so is my Gaelic. But these things don't matter.'

She stubbed out her fifth cigarette. Hugh blew leisurely rings from his pipe.

'It's very courageous of you to do the Open University. Very courageous. And in any case if you don't pass you will have learned a great deal.'

Not pass, thought Hugh, and his face reddened. Of course I'll pass. No question about it. I once climbed the crow's nest even though I was trembling with fear. And I'll pass this too.

'What I'll do is leave the record player and the records here,' she told him. 'There's no point in taking them back. At the moment you know nothing about classical music, it's quite obvious.' Her honesty disconcerted Hugh. He wasn't used to it. One was never as direct as this in the islands. And, by gosh, she was a fine-looking woman too if only she would stop keeping pigs and wearing yellow wellingstons.

It was midnight before she left, and the darkness was absolute.

'I'll be all right,' she told Hugh, 'I have my torch. You listen to your Mozart, if you wish to.' And in fact Hugh did this, till one in the morning. At that time he went outside. The sky was ablaze with stars, and he even saw some shooting stars, which astonished him. The music seemed strange in the house and he couldn't make out whether his mother was frowning more than usual or not.

Every evening after this she would visit him, and sometimes she would even come over in the morning. He found himself waiting expectantly for her, and if for some reason she didn't come he felt disappointed and empty. Now and again he would visit his mother's bedroom and stare down at the hairpins and meagre jewellery she had left behind her. Stella would hoover the house for him, clean the dishes, say to him,

'I'm not sure that you should keep that dresser. It looks to me as if it has woodworm. You should get rid of it.'

I can't believe it, thought Hugh. Here I am doing the Open University and also meeting this Englishwoman every day. It's all very odd.

He began to wear a tie, which he hadn't done before unless he was going out somewhere. Stella too began to dress in softer colours. Pinks and yellows were her best colours, blue didn't suit her.

She would tell him about her husband. 'He was a chemist, as I told you. But he would have long periods of depression in which he became very cruel. He would hide my things around the house and pretend I had forgotten where they were. No wonder I nearly went mad.'

She smoked heavily; the tips of her fingers were stained with nicotine. She was a compulsive walker about the house. Now and again she would rearrange a picture.

'That is awful,' she would say, 'really awful. I don't know who painted it, but it's dreadful. I could bring you some pictures, not of course ones I painted myself.' But Hugh insisted on some of them as well. One day she put up new curtains for him which she had found lying in a chest. 'Your mother has a lot of things,' she said. 'But I don't think you changed the curtains since she died.'

She told him about art as well. Vermeer was her favourite painter. 'His pictures are full of love,' she said. 'Love and light.' He found that he was understanding art and music much better than he had done before, since they were in fact part of Stella's life. His marks improved. He even earned a B. 'Why, that's splendid,' she said, 'splendid.'

It was as if he was Columbus discovering a new world.

Alastair wasn't speaking to him at all, though now and again he would see him staring across from his garden, in the cold wind which had grown between them.

Alastair has nothing, he thought, and I have everything.

'You must, however,' said Stella, 'not neglect your own culture. After all, think of that lovely psalm-singing. I have heard it and it's truly beautiful. Eerie and beautiful. Like the sound of the sea.'

And he began to teach her Gaelic in return for her teaching him about music and art.

She was as apt a pupil as he was himself. One day she made oatcakes for him and he said they were very good, which they were, though he told her that not many people in the island ate oatcakes now. She even made a lovely dumpling.

'This is my mother's ring,' he told her one day.

'It's beautiful,' she said.

'You keep it,' he said. The ring had been removed from his mother's finger before she had been put in the coffin. He didn't know why he had agreed when the undertaker had suggested it, but he had.

'You keep it,' she said. And she kissed him.

It was then that he realised that he would ask her to marry him. Life was very full and precious. There was Stella and there was Hume and Vermeer and Charlotte Brontë. Images swam about the village from other countries, marvellously unique and costly and beautiful.

Stella's footsteps could be heard on the flagstones before she came to the door. Their heads were bent over books; she was learning while he played Gaelic music to her; she played Bach and Liszt. The house was a hive of industry, much more so than in his mother's day. He would find her shawl slung carelessly over a chair and touch it gently. Death is very far away, he thought, death is distant. Why should I think of it, though many others on the island do. Also it turned out that she had a lovely voice and could sing Gaelic songs with feeling.

Alastair continued with his poem about the Open University. He added new verses. The third verse was as follows:

> O gach feasgar agus madainn
> bha mo liadh ag éisdeachd
> ri ceòl anabarrach á Sasunn.
> abair thusa céilidh.
> An àite Gàidhlig anns an fhasan
> bha Eadailtich ag éigheachd
> am measg na soithichean 's na praisean
> coltach ri na béisdean.

> Every evening and morning
> my good fellow was listening
> to strange music from England.
> What a ceilidh that was.
> Instead of Gaelic in the fashion
> Italians were shrieking
> among the dishes and the pots
> just like the beasts themselves.

His dislike of Hugh was now settled, for not only did he have the Open University but he also had a handsome woman who did not spend so much time with her pigs as she had done. Everyone commented on her sudden radiance, on her dress sense: of course she made most of her own clothes. Stella had emerged like a strange flower from the common earth of the village. Alastair seethed and seethed. Why, she would even smile at him and speak in Gaelic. How cunning Hugh was! Of course his father had been like that before him. He had clearly worked all this out with long-term intelligence. He must have seen in Stella what no one else had seen. Of course his father had had the first car in the village. Now he was proud as a peacock and doing well with his Open University too.

Stella insisted that Hugh go to the ceilidh in the village hall. Hugh didn't want to go, for he sensed that there would be something about himself on the programme. Furthermore, he didn't see many of the villagers now; they had become very distant. It was a tradition too in the village that any new event was celebrated, usually in a comic song. And certainly the Open University was an unusual and significant event.

Hugh listened to the songs and then saw Alastair stand up. Without looking in his direction Alastair began to recite his poem, which had become enormously long. The audience rocked with laughter. Hugh too smiled, determined not to appear ungracious or bad-tempered. Certainly there were hits against himself in the poem, the rhymes were better than ever, sharpened by Alastair's venom. Stella asked him what the poem was about and he told her. She too smiled and laughed at the parts which she understood. Alastair did not look at them at all. He was proud and confident. This was one of the best things he had done. There was prolonged and delighted applause when he had finished. Hugh made a point of congratulating him at the interval when everyone was eating cakes and drinking tea.

'That was a good poem,' he said, 'but you should have showed it to me first. There were one or two things I would have changed.'

'What?' said Alastair, taken by surprise.

'Just one or two,' said Hugh. 'You'll have to come to the house and I'll discuss them with you. This is Stella, by the way.' Stella shook hands with him gravely. 'I liked what I understood,' she said. Others came round and began to talk to them, as if now that the poem was over normal relations could be resumed. It was as if a balance which had been disturbed was now restored. And this was even more the case when Stella sang a Gaelic song which was received perhaps with greater acclamation than it deserved.

After a while Hugh saw Stella and Alastair deep in conversation. He was saying to her, 'Your pronunciation was not right in places. I'll have to explain to you.'

When the ceilidh was over, Stella and Hugh went out into the night engraved with stars. Around them was music and also the skies of Constable and Van Gogh. What a vast world this was.

'I think we should get married soon,' said Hugh.

'Of course,' said Stella.

They walked on in silence in a village that had become huge.

'I think that Alastair will visit us,' said Hugh shortly. 'He will make fun of your Gaelic.'

'That's all right,' she said.

'And we'll have to put away our pictures of the Virgin Mary. He thinks I'm a Catholic.'

'Poor Alastair,' she said. Poor Alastair, indeed, thought Hugh.

Maybe, he thought, I am cleverer than I thought I was. Maybe I did work out in advance everything that has happened without realising it. He looked up at the intricate forest of stars. Never had they seemed so bright, so challenging, so interesting.

The Boy and the Rowan Tree

Every day I look at the rowan tree. It brings me such joy with its clusters of red berries, and sometimes a blackbird among them or flitting from branch to branch.

The other day, however, there was heavy rain, and a boy came to the door with some trifles or other that he was trying to sell. He was handicapped in speech and we found it very hard to make out what he was saying. The rain streamed down his forehead and down his jacket and trousers.

At first we nearly shut the door in his face. We did not wish to be involved with him, he was so piteous. Someone some-where out beyond the rain was making a gross appeal to our compassion. However, we did invite him in and sat him down in a chair. He was shivering, and we made him take off his jacket. We thought for a bit and then gave him a dry shirt instead of a wet one. Also eventually a jersey which we no longer needed.

What a piteous site he presented. He had been dropped off by a man in a van and was trying to sell his pathetic trifles – brushes etc. – in the village. Probably most of the villages had shut the door in his face. The bare world confronted him with its rain and wind. We could hardly make out his words but it seemed that he was from Nottingham. There were three other lads with him in the van, though we didn't know whether they were also handicapped. They were to wait at the side of the road to be picked up by their driver and boss. The boy told us that he got a D in geography in his examinations. He had recently left school. He had, we gathered, some brothers and sisters. His boss had told him and his companions that they were making more money than he was. He had some damp pound notes in his pockets which he showed us.

The boss of course was driving about in the comparative comfort of his van. Through the window as I was talking to the boy, I could see rain pouring from the leaves of the swaying rowan tree.

The pathetic things he was supposed to sell – brushes, recycled envelopes, dusters. He didn't even have the exotic glamour of the gypsy or the tinker. I imagined him in the midst of a seething family – the father perhaps unemployed. It was difficult to envisage much in such a hopeless drench of rain.

Let me be quite honest and plain about this. The boy caused me concern yet I was trying to justify the workings of the universe. That was why I summoned up the image of the rowan tree, with its red berries. The boy was dripping as was the rowan tree. In the end however, poetic imagery may fail.

The boy talked with great effort as if he had a stone in his mouth. He thanked us profusely for the shirt and the jersey. He asked us if we had ever been to Nottingham. We hadn't been through, though we had visited Manchester, Birmingham, Stratford-upon-Avon. But not Nottingham. Though of course we had heard of it. Robin Hood etc. In the green multi-leaved forest.

All of this I may add is true. Every word of it. And while the boy was sitting in the house he was worried that he hadn't made enough money and that his boss would shout at him. And I thought of Nottingham again. Robin Hood robbed the rich to give to the poor. And this boy walked with his bag through the pouring rain.

Naturally that is what literature is about, to put on the boy a suit of good dry clothes. The shirt belonged to my stepson. And the jersey as well. He was now in the Air Force and at one time, curiously enough, he was stationed near Nottingham in Robin Hood country. We had been at his passing-out parade where he had looked extremely smart: before he had looked quite scruffy – and we had stayed in a hotel in a small town in that area. We had looked out of the window, and there tied to posts, were two fierce-looking Dobermanns. I've remembered the name of the town. It was called Newark.

Shall I lead you away with a mention of Robin Hood country

so that you won't see the boy among the green leaves. Shall I bring to your mind stories of your schooldays about Friar Tuck, Maid Marian, etc.: and the warm companionship of those days, even in the dripping wood. If of course there was warm companionship. We tend to romanticise these antique adventures. But I suppose in some sense Robin Hood was victorious, we remember his name, but not that of the sheriff. He is victorious in our imagination.

But the boy is not in our imagination. He is here shivering by the fire, hair dripping. He is quite a tall boy and he is clinging to his bag of rubbishy brushes, heavily overpriced incidentally. For instance, a yellow duster costs a pound. Where shall I get warmth from? I mean for my imagination. In a short while the boy will have to leave. And go out into the pouring rain again.

We have given him some tea and some fig biscuits. It is the case that he has probably been luckier than the others, though one cannot be quite sure of that. He picks at the jersey with pride. It is yellow and quite thick.

I don't see the blackbird about the rowan tree today. It may be that blackbirds shelter somewhere when there is heavy rain. Yet the rowan tree does appear beautiful with its wide presence of berries. How can one tell the dancer from the dance as one poet wrote.

What sort of man is this boy's boss? I think that he has a moustache. I imagine him in the dry van seeing his workers off into the rain. He is supposed to collect them at the side of the road. Will some of them arrive in time or will they forget? But of course, he can't drive into England without them. This boy doesn't seem to know the value of money. That is what their boss is counting on among other things. It is all so sad.

And yet, when I look at the rowan tree I do not feel sad. It is so brave with its red berries. It is so naturally beautiful. I cannot tell you how much I love the rowan tree.

We tell the boy that he should stand in our doorway rather than out at the side of the road. The van is already overdue according to the boy but he is confident that it will come. It is a white van, he tells us. There goes a white van at this moment but it is not his white van. Even in the shelter of the doorway there is rain blowing in.

What did they do in the green wood on such a day of relentless rain? It must have been difficult to keep themselves dry, they too must have shivered, and yet Robin Hood surmounted all that. He is present on sunny glades. He appears in a guise of green leaves, sun and shadow, and a feather in his cap. Always jaunty. Merry, merry Robin.

We stand in the doorway looking for a white van, the correct white van. Surely his boss wouldn't have set off without him. No, no, he hasn't the boy says. The boss will come.

And then quite suddenly I say to myself, I wish he would leave. I feel cold standing in the doorway and the rain is driving in on me. I don't like this at all. Then, this boy really isn't very interesting, he can't articulate correctly. I imagine the rain as going on forever.

My rowan tree, I cry to myself despairingly. And it does not fail me. It flares outwards with such abandon, almost wastefully. All the time the boy is muttering angrily to himself, 'Why is the driver late? He obviously doesn't care.' The boy however seems to know the time. In front of us, on the other side of the road, the sheep are cowering hopelessly in the rain.

My rowan tree with red berries is brave. It protects houses from witches, from evil. And there is the girl who always walks past exercising her two black shiny dogs, who always seem to be leading her rather than she leading them.

Still the white van has not appeared. The driver is now twenty minutes late.

The boy turns to say to me, maybe he has stopped in the village. I make out his words with difficulty. Maybe he should walk to the village, he says. I remain silent though I think I should advise that he shouldn't go to the village in this rain. He picks up his bag and sets off. I feel quite relieved. Suddenly I think of a tinker who had once come to our cottage door in my island home in the north west. My mother gave her a jersey belonging to my younger brother. It happened that the tinker woman's son was in the same class in the village school, and when my brother saw the boy wearing his jersey he began to fight with him. This happened a long time ago when my brother was perhaps eight years old. He is now in Australia and we haven't heard from him for years. He has been an unsuccessful exile: he is not even married.

The boy headed off into the still heavy rain, an arrowfall of rain. He would surely find the white van eventually. I should really wait and take its number and report its driver for exploiting young handicapped people. But then who would I write to or phone. But did I want to wait till the white van passed. And maybe it wouldn't be the correct white van after all.

I turned to my rowan tree again, proud and beautiful with its natural grace and blood red berries. The rain was pouring down among the leaves. What do we do at certain times but search for the beautiful. Is that not the case. One does what one can. And the works of nature are often so lovely. So random and lovely.

I think the boy will find the driver of the white van. He will be taken down to Nottingham: the driver wouldn't leave him here, I'm pretty sure of that. And very soon the blackbird will return to the rowan tree. And then the story will be complete.

At the Stones

She watched him as he bent down in the windy grass to study one of the stones. She felt cold but he didn't seem to be cold at all.

If you're looking for writing, she said, there won't be any.

I wasn't looking for writing, he said.

These stones, she thought, must be sunk deep in the ground. It was inconceivable how they had been transported.

It was Ronald's idea to visit this island to have a look at the Callanish stones. Of course the islanders had a Norse background and Ronald had studied Norse.

He had studied Norse, as well as Old English and Middle English which comprised his 'field'.

She looked wryly at the grass in front of her – her field.

As a matter of fact she rather liked the island, being used from her days in Wales to a rural community; indeed she remembered their days in Wales with untrammelled affection. If only they had remained there . . .

The brochure which told her about the stones shook in her hand.

They are not connected with the Druids according to this, she said.

No, they go back much further than that. Much much further than that.

In her mind she had a picture of robed Druids holding their hands up to the rising sun, though she couldn't think where she had come by it. The rising sun, the Druids, sacrifice.

Much further than that, he repeated, thousands of years. There were Druids in Colomba's time and that's only thirteen hundred years ago.

His round red-cheeked face glowed in the cold day. Often he looked quite cherubic.

It is all to do with the position of the stones, he said, and the moon rising at midsummer. At least I read that somewhere.

A boy and a girl with rucksacks were sitting in the hollow at the centre of the stones. They were eating sandwiches and drinking tea or coffee from a flask. She took shelter by the side of one of the tall bare stones.

They had remained five years in Wales when Ronald had started his career. They were the happiest years of her life, she was sure. Neither the town nor the university was large and she knew a fair number of people and not only the ones connected with the university. And, of course, Ronald could speak Welsh after a fashion. She had tried to learn the language but failed.

There was a constellation of certain languages that Ronald knew, old Norse, Old and Middle English and old Welsh. And now he was having a look at Gaelic.

The names of villages ending in 'bost' are all Norse, he told her. There's Garrabost, Shawbost, Melbost, etc.

Sometimes she hated him; he was like a little doll, twinkling and well-meaning.

There is some theory about the shape of the hills over there, he said. Taken together they have the form of a recumbent woman. Can you see it?

At first she didn't and then she did.

That would be their goddess, he said. Imagine in midsummer the moon rising there. They would have worshipped a goddess, an Earth Mother.

Then they had left Wales for Cambridge. Cambridge was a much more complicated place. She had found it cold, over-intellectual though Ronald avoided as many functions as he could; he had little small talk and wasn't witty.

The students too were different from the Welsh ones. They were more 'superior', more sophisticated, very bright.

The Welsh ones didn't stretch me so much, said Ronald. They didn't question much. And at seminars and tutorials they were less talkative.

And so he had to work much harder, wrote new lectures. Wales had made him lazy, he said.

The two young people sitting in the hollow looked like

students, perhaps foreign ones, from Germany or France. She couldn't actually make out their language.

She had disliked Cambridge intensely, to put it mildly. There was a sort of formality and impersonality that threatened her. And Ronald didn't have time to talk to her. He was studying and writing harder than ever.

The calibre of student is much higher here, he said. And I have to keep up.

But I thought you knew your work already.

Yes, but you don't know what some of the students will unearth. They are more . . . unexpected.

And so he tried to insure against the unexpected.

And it was then that she began . . . expecting.

When she told him, he had taken it absent-mindedly as if it was nothing to do with him at all. It seemed he was so busy that he did not exist in the present. She herself had done some Anglo-Saxon when she had attended Aberdeen University; it was there that they had met.

She remembered certain poems about wanderers and sea-farers whose philosophy was to 'endure'. To endure loss and masters, unemployment. To endure storms, blizzards, turbulent seas.

He was taking photographs now.

How would he cope, she wondered, if something happened to her. He was buoyed up by her, his existence hung from hers, he was a little twinkling satellite of hers. He couldn't cook, or fix a plug. There were many quite simple things that he couldn't do. But all this was permissible in him because he was a professor. It was as if people equated brilliance with academe and forgave professors who couldn't change a lightbulb. How many Anglo-Saxon professors would it take to change a light-bulb? She smiled wryly.

The child was much more to her than it was to him. Now she had a reason to look after herself. Now she had a future. She felt happy, at times elated. For the life of her she couldn't imagine him as a father. And neither, she was sure, could he. She couldn't imagine him playing with a child, be it son or daughter. If the child spoke Middle English that might be different.

She looked at the configuration of the hills again. They did in fact look like a recumbent woman and she imagined a mild midsummer moon above them, a moon that would in autumn appear red.

The two young people stood up, put their rucksacks on, and walked towards the exit.

She had imagined the child in her womb as a tiny helmeted Anglo-Saxon. Her great trouble was that neither Ronald nor she had made any friends in Cambridge. She thought that Ron was boring, and she knew that in this environment she herself was boring. She was intimidated. But perhaps the child would not be boring, it might spring fully-armed from this hard bright Cambridge world. This world of quiet streets, bicycles, second-hand bookshops. Oh Cambridge so lovely in summer . . . but no place for a child.

Those big blank stones in front of her. Surely there should be writing on them. But then again they had been planted here before writing was invented. When people communicated in grunts perhaps as Ronald absent-mindedly did. Though he spoke more to her since his retirement. But he really was quite useless in the house, quite, quite useless . . .

Quite, quite useless.

Could you come in here, please, he shouted to her from his study. The four walls were lined with books, and some were piled on the floor.

There's a book I want to get from the top shelf, he said, and told her the title. I haven't used it for a while but I believe it's there. I tried to stand on the step ladder but I felt dizzy.

He left her everything to do; he had surrendered the motions of his outward life to her. It was true that he sometimes felt dizzy, perhaps because of his intense study. Or perhaps he had only said that he felt dizzy. No, that was unfair; it would be wrong for an Anglo-Saxon scholar to tell a lie. On the other hand, he often evaded the 'shield wall'.

She should have tidied away the books on the floor, she should have been more careful where she had placed the ladders, he should have held the ladder more tightly . . . In her fall she knew immediately that the child had gone. As she tumbled on the books, as she lay recumbent among them, she knew that it was somehow fitting that she should find herself among books. In the blood. Later he looked at her, white-faced.

I'm sorry, he bumbled.

Sorry, sorry, sorry. She opened her eyes and then closed them. Her small helmeted Anglo-Saxon had gone. Yes, there was perhaps satisfaction to be discovered behind the sorrow. Who knew the intricacies of the human mind?

Now she saw him wearing his university gown and holding his knife up as he slit the child's throat while the red sun rose over the horizon. University gown, doctor's gown.

He walked to the car and waited helplessly for her to unlock the door. Her child, her only child, her twinkly-faced child, the one who endured to the end. The fresh-faced one who fussed about the stones on which nothing was written, whose origin was unintelligible, inconceivable, in the field, in the windy grassy field.

The Game

We were playing football with a fishing cork, Daial and myself, on a full-sized football pitch. We were both wearing shirts; mine was green, his was blue. He looked very thin. Of course, he had been ill and some said it was TB: everyone was frightened of TB.

What a beautiful summer's day it was. No smoke rose from the chimneys for no fires were required. We played in silence for the pitch was a big one, and very demanding. Also the cork screwed sideways when you hit it with your shoe. Normally in summer we didn't wear shoes but we couldn't play 'football' without them.

Neither of us was winning: in fact, no goals at all had been scored. This was our favourite pastime and we had many heroes among the adult footballers, including Stoodie and Hoddan. One was a centre-forward, the other a centre-half: both strongly-built and adventurous. Maybe some day we would play for the district too.

A good distance away from the pitch, Strang passed with his dog. He didn't notice us: he always strode forward in a great hurry. Tall and red-faced, he was one of the healthiest among us and we couldn't work out why he wasn't in the war. We liked his collie dog Patch very much.

I must be getting better, I thought, I'm not sweating as much as usual. Daial wasn't sweating so much either. It was wonderful to be out in the fresh air: as we ran we felt it streaming around our necks. I dribbled past Daial but lost the cork at the corner flag. We were really very poor; we used to have a proper ball but since it burst, we couldn't afford another one. Indeed, I don't know who was the poorer, Daial or myself. Though our poverty didn't usually bother us, except when we couldn't afford a ball.

The cork was of course one that would normally be found attached to a fishing net. When he grew up Daial was going to be a fisherman: I didn't want to be one. I was more ambitious, I wanted to go to university or college though it was hard to see how I could afford to do that unless I won a bursary.

At half-time we lay on our backs gazing up at the white clouds. I was quire tired though pleasantly so. I nibbled a blade of grass at the side of the pitch. In the distance I could hear Strang shouting to his dog; also I could see Maggie hanging out her washing: her legs were very red and fat. I wondered what Janet would be doing. Once, playing draughts with her father and she sitting between us, I placed my hand on her thigh under the table: she didn't move a muscle. What an extraordinary sensation that was.

We rose to our feet at the end of ten minutes or what we thought was ten minutes for neither of us had a watch. Some day I might have a watch but not yet. Janet had a thin gold watch which her father had given her but he owned the village shop. I thought I heard my mother's voice calling me but that must have been an error for I didn't see her about the house. She didn't like me playing football in case I became ill again. I was often ill with bronchitis: TB however was more dangerous and my father had died of it. He used to give me rides on his shoulders and at one time he would smoke a pipe. He was also less strict than my mother.

As I dribbled past Daial I was looking straight at the sea and what seemed to be a becalmed ship. All day, though often we were not aware of it, there was the sound of the sea. Indeed, one of my favourite Gaelic poems was entitled in English, 'The High Swelling of the Sea'. It was about an exile who wanted to be buried beside the sea; it was a sad, beautiful song.

Looking at the sea I had forgotten about the cork and now Daial was in a good position to score. A few months ago we had gathered scrap iron for the War Effort. We had found an old wreck of a car which we were pretending to drive; there were hardly any cars in the village.

Daial screwed the cork past the post so it was still nil-nil. Since this was wartime, we could see many ships passing and wondered whether any of the village boys was on any of them. Daial had two brothers in the navy: I had one. The last we heard from him he was in New York. The money he sent my mother arrived late, and this caused us problems, for we were absolutely dependent on it. I couldn't imagine New York at all: our only town, Stornoway, was large enough for me. Whenever I thought of Stornoway I felt the intensely cold ice-cream on my teeth, or I smelt apples. Red apples nesting among straw; though I hadn't seen many recently. I hadn't seen many oranges either, or sweets. Once I had eaten whale meat but didn't like it.

I could hear the barking of a dog: Strang must be coming back. And what was very strange, he was crossing the pitch. I shouted at him because he was coming between me and the 'ball'. His face looked very red and healthy and smooth-shaven. He didn't see me at all nor did he see the 'ball' though it was at his feet. He strode forward relentlessly towards the smokeless village.

Publication Acknowledgements

from *The Hermit and other stories* (1977),
first published by Victor Gollancz Ltd, London:

The Hermit; The Impulse; Timoshenko; The Spy; The
Brothers; The Incident; Listen to the Voice; The Exorcism;
Macbeth; Leaving the Cherries

from *Murdo and other stories* (1981),
first published by Victor Gollancz Ltd, London:

In the Castle; The Missionary; At the Fair; The Listeners;
Mr Heine; The Visit.

from *Mr Trill in Hades* (1984),
first published by Victor Gollancz Ltd, London

What to do About Ralph?; The Ring; Greater Love; The
Snowballs; The Play; In the School; Mr Trill in Hades.

from *Selected Stories* (1990),
first published by Carcarnet Press Ltd, Manchester:

By their Fruits; Mac an t-Sronaich; I Do Not Wish to Leave;
The Ghost; The True Story of Sir Hector Macdonald;
Chagall's Return; Napoleon and I; Christmas Day; The Arena;
The Tour; The Travelling Poet; The Scream; The Old
Woman, the Baby and Terry; On the Train; The Survivor; The
Dead Man and the Children; A Night with Kant; The Maze

Uncollected Stories

On the Island first published in *The Scotsman*, July 1978;The
Button first published in *Helix* 2, August 1978; A September
Day first published in *North* 7, March/April 1979 The Snow
first published in *New Edinburgh Review*, May 1979; In the

Corridor first published in *Words* 5 1979/80; Christine *Words* 9, 1980/81; The Kitten first published in *The Scotsman* July 1982; The Parade first published in *New Edinburgh Review*, Autumn 1982; The Yacht first published in *New Edinburgh Review*, Autumn 1983; Record of Work first published in *Stand* 25, no. 3, Summer 1984; In the Asylum first published in Chapman 42, 1985; The Black Halo and The Crossing first published in *Chapman* 42, 1985; The Beautiful Gown first published in *Tales to Tell*, Edinburgh, 1986; Do You Believe in Ghosts? first published in *The Wild Ride and Other Scottish Stories*, Harmondsworth, 1986; At Jorvik Museum first published in *PN Review* 55, 1987; The Ship first published in *Chapman* 54, 1988; In the Silence first published in *Chapman* 54, 1988; The Ladder first published in *Chapman* 54, 1988; Tommy first published in *Cencrastus*, Winter 1989; The Whale's Way first published in *Cencrastus*, Winter 1989; The Dawn first published in *Cencrastus*, Winter 1989; The Bridge first published in *New Writing Scotland 10: Pig Squealing* A.S.L.S., Autumn 1992;The Tool Chest, and The Wind first published in *Chapman* 73, 1993; The Boy and the Rowan Tree first published on the Internet in 1996; At the Stones first published in *New Writing Scotland 14: Full Strength Angels*, A.S.L.S., Autumn 1996; The Game first published in *New Writing Scotland 15: Some Sort of Embrace*, A.S.L.S., Autumn 1997.